PRAISE FOR TERRY GOODKIND

"Mr. Goodkind's compelling prose weaves a magic spell over readers." —*Romantic Times BOOKreviews*

"Makes an indelible impact." —*Publishers Weekly*

"Outstanding . . . Characters who actually behave like adults. Highly recommended."
—*The San Diego Union-Tribune*

"Few writers have Goodkind's power of creation . . . a phenomenal piece of imaginative writing, exhaustive in its scope and riveting in its detail." —*Publishing News*

"Goodkind's greatest triumph: the ability to introduce immediately identifiable characters. His heroes, like us, are not perfect. Instead, each is flawed in ways that strengthen rather than weaken their impact. You'll find no two-dimensional oafs here. In fact, at times you'll think you're looking at your own reflection." —*SFX*

Tor Books by Terry Goodkind

THE SWORD OF TRUTH

Wizard's
First
Rule

TERRY GOODKIND

TOR®

A TOM DOHERTY ASSOCIATES BOOK
NEW YORK

This is a work of fiction. All the characters and events portrayed in this book are either products of the author's imagination or are used fictitiously.

WIZARD'S FIRST RULE

Copyright © 1994 by Terry Goodkind

All rights reserved.

Edited by James Frenkel
Cover art by Doug Beekman
Maps by Terry Goodkind

A Tor Book
Published by Tom Doherty Associates, LLC
175 Fifth Avenue
New York, NY 10010

www.tor-forge.com

Tor® is a registered trademark of Tom Doherty Associates, LLC.

ISBN-13: 978-0-7653-6264-3
ISBN-10: 0-7653-6264-3
Library of Congress Catalog Card Number: 93-43241

First Edition: September 1994
First International Mass Market Edition: February 1995
First U.S. Mass Market Edition: September 1995
Second U.S. Mass Market Edition: September 2008

Printed in the United States of America

10 9 8 7 6 5 4 3 2 1

For Jeri

ACKNOWLEDGMENTS

I would like to thank some special people:

My father, Leo, for never once telling me to read, but instead reading himself, and thus infecting me with curiosity.

My good friends, Rachel Kahlandt and Gloria Avner, for taking on the task of reading the raw manuscript and offering valuable insights, and for their steadfast belief in me when I needed it most.

My agent, Russell Galen, for having the guts to be the first to pick up the sword, and for making my dreams reality.

My editor, James Frenkel, not only for his exceptional editorial talent, guidance, and help in making improvements in this book, but also for his boundless good humor and patience as he has taught me to be a better author along the way.

The good people at Tor, one and all, for their enthusiasm and hard work.

And two very special people, Richard and Kahlan, for choosing me to tell their story. Their tears and triumphs have touched my heart. I will never be the same again.

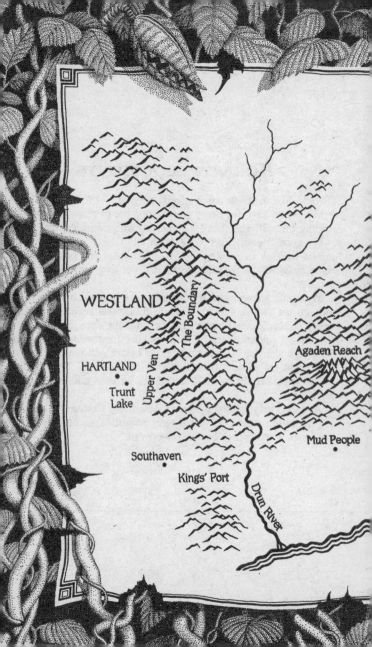

WESTLAND

The Boundary

Upper Ven

HARTLAND
•
Trunt
Lake
•

Agaden Reach

Mud People
•

Southaven
•
Kings' Port
•

Drun River

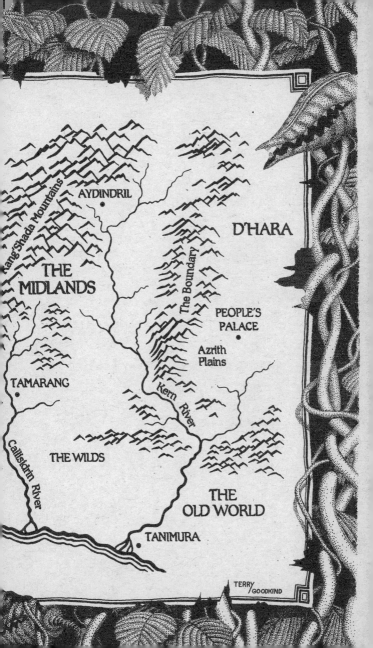

RANG'SHADA MOUNTAINS

AYDINDRIL

D'HARA

THE
MIDLANDS

THE BOUNDARY

PEOPLE'S
PALACE

Azrith
Plains

TAMARANG

Kern River

THE WILDS

Callisidrin River

THE
OLD WORLD

TANIMURA

TERRY
GOODKIND

Wizard's
First
Rule

CHAPTER 1

IT WAS AN ODD-LOOKING vine. Dusky variegated leaves hunkered against a stem that wound in a stranglehold around the smooth trunk of a balsam fir. Sap drooled down the wounded bark, and dry limbs slumped, making it look as if the tree were trying to voice a moan into the cool, damp morning air. Pods stuck out from the vine here and there along its length, almost seeming to look warily about for witnesses.

It was the smell that first had caught his attention, a smell like the decomposition of something that had been wholly unsavory even in life. Richard combed his fingers through his thick hair as his mind lifted out of the fog of despair, coming into focus upon seeing the vine. He scanned for others, but saw none. Everything else looked normal. The maples of the upper Ven Forest were already tinged with crimson, proudly showing off their new mantle in the light breeze. With nights getting colder, it wouldn't be long before their cousins down in the Hartland Woods joined them. The oaks, being the last to surrender to the season, still stoically wore their dark green coats.

Having spent most of his life in the woods, Richard knew all the plants—if not by name, by sight. From when Richard was very small, his friend Zedd had taken him along, hunting for special herbs. He had shown Richard which ones to look for, where they grew and why, and put names to everything they saw. Many times they just talked, the old man always treating him as an equal, asking as much as he answered. Zedd had sparked Richard's hunger to learn, to know.

This vine, though, he had seen only once before, and not in the woods. He had found a sprig of it at his father's house, in the blue clay jar Richard had made when he was a boy. His father had been a trader and had traveled often, looking for the chance exotic or rare item. People of means had often sought him out, interested in what he might have turned up. It seemed to be the looking, more than the finding, that he had liked, as he had always been happy to part with his latest discovery so he could be off after the next.

From a young age, Richard had liked to spend time with Zedd while his father was away. Richard's brother, Michael, was a few years older, and having no interest in the woods, or in Zedd's rambling lectures, preferred to spend his time with people of means. About five years before, Richard had moved away to live on his own, but he often stopped by his father's home, unlike Michael, who was always busy and rarely had time to visit. Whenever his father went away, he would leave Richard a message in the blue jar telling him the latest news, some gossip, or of some sight he had seen.

On the day three weeks before when Michael had come to tell him their father had been murdered, Richard had gone to his father's house, despite his brother's insistence that there was no reason to go, nothing he could do. Richard had long since passed the age when he did as his brother said. Wanting to spare him, the people there didn't let him see the body. But still, he saw the big, sickening splashes and puddles of blood, brown and dry across the plank floor. When Richard came close, voices fell silent, except to offer sympathy, which only deepened the riving pain. Yet he had heard them talking, in hushed tones, of the stories and the wild rumors of things come out of the boundary.

Of magic.

Richard was shocked at the way his father's small home had

2

been torn apart, as if a storm had been turned loose inside. Only a few things were left untouched. The blue message jar still sat on the shelf, and inside he found the sprig of vine. It was still in his pocket now. What his father meant him to know from it, he couldn't guess.

Grief and depression overwhelmed him, and even though he still had his brother, he felt abandoned. That he was grown into manhood offered him no sanctuary from the forlorn feeling of being orphaned and alone in the world, a feeling he had known before, when his mother died while he was still young. Even though his father had often been away, sometimes for weeks, Richard had always known he was somewhere, and would be back. Now he would never be back.

Michael wouldn't let him have anything to do with the search for the killer. He said he had the best trackers in the army looking and he wanted Richard to stay out of it, for his own good. So Richard simply didn't show the vine to Michael, and went off alone every day, searching for it. For three weeks he walked the trails of the Hartland Woods, every trail, even the ones few others knew of, but he never saw it.

Finally, against his better judgment, he gave in to the whispers in his mind, and went to the upper Ven Forest, close to the boundary. The whispers haunted him with the feeling that he somehow knew something of why his father had been murdered. They teased him, tantalized him with thoughts just out of reach, and laughed at him for not seeing it. Richard lectured himself that it was his grief playing tricks, not something real.

He had thought that when he found the vine it would give him some sort of answer. Now that he had, he didn't know what to think. The whispers had stopped teasing him, but now they brooded. He knew it was just his own mind thinking, and he told himself to stop trying to give the whispers a life of their own. Zedd had taught him better than that.

Richard looked up at the big fir tree in its agony of death. He thought again of his father's death. The vine had been there. Now the vine was killing this tree; it couldn't be anything good. Though he couldn't do anything for his father, he didn't have to let the vine preside over another death. Gripping it firmly, he pulled, and with powerful muscles ripped the sinewy tendrils away from the tree.

That's when the vine bit him.

One of the pods struck out and hit the back of his left hand, causing him to jump back in pain and surprise. Inspecting the small wound, he found something like a thorn embedded in the meat of the gash. The matter was decided. The vine was trouble. He reached for his knife to dig out the thorn, but the knife wasn't there. At first surprised, he realized why and reprimanded himself for allowing his depression to cause him to forget something as basic as taking his knife with him into the woods. Using his fingernails, he tried to pull out the thorn. To his rising concern, the thorn, as if alive, wriggled itself in deeper. He dragged his thumbnail across the wound, trying to snag the thorn out. The more he dug, the deeper it went. A hot wave of nausea swept through him as he tore at the wound, making it bigger, so he stopped. The thorn had disappeared into the oozing blood.

Looking about, Richard spotted the purplish red autumn leaves of a small nannyberry tree, laden with its crop of dark blue berries. Beneath the tree, nestled in the crook of a root, he found what he sought: an aum plant. Relieved, he carefully snapped off the tender stem near its base, and gently squeezed the sticky, clear liquid onto the bite. He smiled as he mentally thanked old Zedd for teaching him how the aum plant made wounds heal faster. The soft fuzzy leaves always made Richard think of Zedd. The juice of the aum numbed the sting, but not his worry over being unable to remove the thorn. He could feel it wriggling still deeper into his flesh.

Richard squatted down and poked a hole in the ground with his finger, placed the aum in it, and fixed moss about the stem so it might regrow itself.

The sounds of the forest fell dead still. Richard looked up, flinching as a dark shadow swept over the ground, leaping across limbs and leaves. There was a rushing, whistling sound in the air overhead. The size of the shadow was frightening. Birds burst from cover in the trees, giving alarm calls as they scattered in all directions. Richard peered up, searching through the gaps in the canopy of green and gold, trying to see the shadow's source. For an instant, he saw something big. Big, and red. He couldn't

4

imagine what it could be, but the memory of the rumors and stories of things coming out of the boundary flooded back into his mind, making him go cold to the bone.

The vine was trouble, he thought again; this thing in the sky could be no less. He remembered what people always said, "Trouble sires three children," and knew immediately that he didn't want to meet the third child.

Discounting his fears, he started running. Just idle talk of superstitious people, he told himself. He tried to think of what could be that big, that big and red. It was impossible; there was nothing that flew that was that large. Maybe it was a cloud, or a trick of the light. But he couldn't fool himself: it was no cloud.

Looking up as he ran, trying for another glimpse, he headed for the path that skirted the hillside. Richard knew that the ground dropped off sharply on the other side of the trail, and he would be able to get an unobstructed view of the sky. Tree branches wet with rain from the night before slapped at his face as he ran through the forest, jumping fallen trees and small rocky streams. Brush snatched at his pant legs. Dappled swatches of sunlight teased him to look up but denied him the view he needed. His breath was fast, ragged, sweat ran cold against his face, and he could feel his heart pounding as he ran carelessly down the hillside. At last he stumbled out of the trees onto the path, almost falling.

Searching the sky, he spotted the thing, far away and too small for him to tell what it was, but he thought it had wings. He squinted against the blue brightness of the sky, shielded his eyes with his hand, trying to see for sure if there were wings moving. It slipped behind a hill and was gone. He hadn't even been able to tell if it really was red.

Winded, Richard slumped down on a granite boulder at the side of the trail, absently snapping off dead twigs from a sapling beside him while he stared down at Trunt Lake below. Maybe he should go tell Michael what had happened, tell him about the vine and the red thing in the sky. He knew Michael would laugh at the last part. He had laughed at the same stories himself.

No, Michael would only be angry with him for being up near the boundary, and for going against his orders to stay out of the search for the murderer. He knew his brother cared about him or he wouldn't always be nagging him. Now that he was grown, he could laugh off his brother's constant instructions, though he still had to endure the looks of displeasure.

Richard snapped off another twig and in frustration threw it at a flat rock. He decided he shouldn't feel singled out. After all, Michael was always telling everyone what to do, even their father.

He pushed aside his harsh judgments of his brother; today was a big day for Michael. Today he was accepting the position of First Councilor. He would be in charge of everything now, not just the town of Hartland anymore, but all the towns and villages of Westland, even the country people. Responsible for everything and everyone. Michael deserved Richard's support, he needed it; Michael had lost a father, too.

That afternoon there was to be a ceremony and big celebration at Michael's house. Important people were going to be there, come from the farthest reaches of Westland. Richard was supposed to be there, too. At least there would be plenty of good food. He realized he was famished.

While he sat and thought, he scanned the opposite side of Trunt Lake, far below. From this height the clear water revealed alternating patches of rocky bottom and green weed around the deep holes. At the edge of the water, Hawkers Trail knitted in and out of the trees, in some places open to view, in some places hidden. Richard had been on that part of the trail many times. In the spring it was wet and soggy down by the lake, but this late in the year it would be dry. In areas farther north and south, as the trail wound its way through the high Ven Forests, it passed uncomfortably close to the boundary. Because of that, most travelers avoided it, choosing instead the trails of the Hartland Woods. Richard was a woods guide, and led travelers safely through the Hartland forests. Most were traveling dignitaries wanting the prestige of a local guide more than they wanted direction.

His eyes locked on something. There was movement. Unsure what it had been, he stared hard at the spot on the far side of the lake. When he saw it again, on the path, where it passed behind a thin veil of trees, there was no doubt; it was a person. Maybe it was his friend Chase. Who else but a boundary warden would be wandering around up here?

He hopped down off the rock, tossing the twigs aside, and took a few steps forward. The figure followed the path into the open, at the edge of the lake. It wasn't Chase; it was a woman, a woman in a dress. What woman would be walking around this far out in the Ven Forest, in a dress? Richard watched her making her way along the lakeshore, disappearing and reappearing with the path. She didn't seem to be in a hurry, but she wasn't strolling slowly either. Rather, she moved at the measured pace of an experienced traveler. That made sense; no one lived anywhere near Trunt Lake.

Other movement snatched his attention. Richard's eyes searched the shade and shadows. Behind her, there were others. Three, no, four men, in hooded forest cloaks, following her, but hanging back some distance. They moved with stealth, from tree to rock to tree. Looking. Waiting. Moving. Richard straightened, his eyes wide, his attention riveted.

They were stalking her.

He knew immediately: this was the third child of trouble.

CHAPTER 2

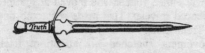

AT FIRST, RICHARD STOOD frozen, not knowing what to do. He couldn't be sure the four men really were stalking the woman, at least not until it was too late. What business was it of his anyway? And besides, he didn't even have his knife with him. What chance did one man with no weapon have against four? He watched the woman making her way along the path. He watched the men follow.

What chance did the woman have?

He crouched, muscles tight and hard. His heart raced as he tried to think of what he could do. The morning sun was hot on his face, his breathing was shallow. Richard knew there was a small cutoff from Hawkers Trail somewhere ahead of the woman. Hurriedly, he tried to remember exactly where. The main fork to her left continued around the lake and up the hill to his left, to where he stood and watched. If she stayed on the main trail he could wait for her, then tell her about the men. Then what? Besides, that was too long. The men would be on her before then. An idea began to take shape. He sprang up and started running down the trail.

If he could reach her before the men caught her, and before the cutoff, he could take her up the right fork. That trail led up out of the trees onto open ledges, away from the boundary, and toward the town of Hartland, toward help. If they were quick, he could hide their tracks. The men wouldn't know that the two of them had taken the side trail. They would think she was still on the main trail, at least for a while, long enough to fool them and lead her to safety.

Still winded from the earlier run, Richard panted in labored breaths, running down the trail as fast as he could go. The path had quickly turned back in to the trees, so at least he didn't have to worry about the men being able to see him. Shafts of sunlight flashed by as he raced along. Old pine trees lined the path, leaving a soft mat of needles to cushion his footfalls.

After a time, driving himself headlong down the path, he started looking for the side trail. He couldn't be sure how far he had gone; the forest offered no view for a fix, and he didn't remember exactly where the cutoff was. It was small and would be easy to miss. With every bend bringing new hope that this would be the place he found the cutoff, he pushed himself on. He tried to think of what he would say to the woman when he finally reached her. His mind raced as fast as his legs. She might think he was with her pursuers, or be frightened by him, or not believe him. He wouldn't have much time to convince her to go with him, that he wanted to help.

Coming over the top of a small rise, he looked anew for the fork, but didn't see it and kept running. Now his breath came in ragged gasps. He knew that if he didn't reach the split before she did, they would be trapped, and their only options would be to outrun the men, or to fight. He was too winded for either. That thought drove him on harder. Sweat ran down his back, making his shirt stick to his skin. The coolness of the morning had turned to choking heat, though he knew it was only his exertion that made it seem that way. The forest passed in a blur to each side as he ran.

Just before a sharp bend to the right, he came at last to the cutoff, almost missing it. He made a quick search for tracks to see if she had been there and taken the small path. There were none. Relief washed over him. He dropped to his knees and sat back

9

on his heels in exhaustion, trying to catch his breath. The first part had worked. He had beaten her here. Now he had to make her believe him before it was too late.

Holding his right hand over a painful stitch in his side and still trying to catch his breath, he started to worry that he was going to look silly. What if it was just a girl and her brothers playing a game? He would be the fool. Everyone but him would have a good laugh.

He looked down at the bite on the back of his hand. It was red and throbbed painfully. He remembered the thing in the sky. He thought about the way she had been walking, with a sense of purpose, not like a child at play. It was a woman, not a girl. He remembered the cold fear he had felt when he saw the four men. Four men warily shadowing a woman: the third strange thing to happen this morning. The third child of trouble. No—he shook his head—this was no game, he knew what he had seen. It was no game. They were stalking her.

Richard came partway to his feet. Waves of heat rolled from his body. Bent over at the waist with his hands braced on his knees, he took a few deep breaths before straightening to his full height.

His eyes fell on the young woman as she came around the bend in front of him. His breath caught for an instant. Her brown hair was full, lush, and long, complementing the contours of her body. She was tall, almost as tall as he, and about the same age. The dress she wore was like none he had ever seen: almost white, cut square at the neck, interrupted only by a small, tan leather waist pouch. The weave of the fabric was fine and smooth, almost glistening, and bore none of the lace or frills he was used to seeing, no prints or colors to distract from the way it caressed her form. The dress was elegant in its simplicity. She halted, and long graceful folds regally trailing her gathered about her legs.

Richard approached and stopped three strides away so as not to appear a threat. She stood straight and still, her arms at her side. Her eyebrows had the graceful arch of a raptor's wings in flight. Her green eyes came unafraid to his. The connection was so intense that it threatened to drain his sense of self. He felt that he had always known her, that she had always been a part of him, that her needs were his needs. She held him with her gaze as surely as a grip of iron would, searching his eyes as if searching his soul, seeking an answer to something. I am here to help you, he said in his mind. He meant it more than any thought he had ever had.

The intensity of her gaze relaxed, loosening its hold on him. In her eyes he saw something that attracted him more than anything else. Intelligence. He saw it flaring there, burning in her, and through it all he felt an overriding sense of her integrity. Richard felt safe.

A warning flashed in his mind, making him remember why he was there, that time was dear.

"I was up there"—he pointed toward the hill he had been on— "and I saw you." She looked where he pointed. He looked, too, and realized he was pointing to a tangle of tree limbs. They couldn't see the hill, because the trees blocked the view. He dropped his arm dumbly, trying to ignore the miscue. Her eyes returned to his, waiting.

Richard started over, keeping his voice low. "I was up there on a hill, above the lake. I saw you walking on the path by the shore. There are some men following you."

She betrayed no emotion, but continued to hold his gaze. "How many?"

He thought her question strange, but answered it. "Four."

The color drained from her face.

She turned her head, surveying the woods behind her, scanning the shadows briefly, then looked back to him once more, her green eyes searching his.

"Do you choose to help me?" Except for her color, her exquisite features gave no hint as to her emotions.

Before his mind could form a thought, he heard himself say, "Yes."

Her countenance softened. "What would you have us do?"

"There's a small trail that turns off here. If we take it, and they stay on this one, we can be away."

"And if they don't? If they follow our trail?"

"I'll hide our tracks." He was shaking his head, trying to reassure her. "They won't follow. Look, there's no time. . . ."

"If they do?" she cut him off. "Then what is your plan?"

11

He studied her face a moment. "Are they very dangerous?"

She stiffened. "Very."

The way she spoke the word made him have to force himself to breathe again. For an instant, he saw a look of blind terror pass across her eyes.

Richard ran his fingers through his hair. "Well, the small trail is narrow and sheer. They won't be able to surround us."

"Do you have a weapon?"

He answered by shaking his head no, too angry with himself for forgetting his knife to voice it out loud.

She nodded. "Let's be quick then."

They didn't talk once the decision had been made, not wanting to give away their location. Richard hurriedly concealed their tracks and motioned her to go first so he would be between her and the men. She didn't hesitate. The folds of her dress flowed behind as she moved quickly at his direction. The lush, young evergreens of the Ven pressed tight at their sides, making the path a narrow, dark, green, walled route cut through the brush and branches. They could see nothing around them. Richard checked behind as they went, though he couldn't see far. At least what he could see was clear. She went swiftly without any encouragement from him.

After a time, the ground started rising and becoming rockier, and the trees thinned, offering a more open view. The trail twisted along deeply shaded cuts in the terrain and across leaf-strewn ravines. Dry leaves scattered at their passing. Pines and spruce gave way to hardwood trees, mostly white birch, and as the limbs swayed overhead, little patches of sunlight danced on the forest floor. The birches' white trunks with black spots made it look as if hundreds of eyes were watching the two pass. Other than the raucous racket of some ravens, it was a very quiet, peaceful place.

At the base of a granite wall that the path followed, he motioned to her, putting a finger over his lips, letting her know they had to step carefully to avoid making sounds that would echo their location. Whenever a raven cawed he could hear it reverberate through the hills. Richard knew this place; the shape of the rock wall could carry a sound for miles. He pointed to the moss-covered round rocks littering the flat forest floor. He showed her that he meant for the two of them to step on the rocks to avoid snapping sticks hidden under the leaf litter. He moved some leaves to show her sticks hidden there and pretended to break them, then cupped his hand to his ear. She nodded her understanding, lifted her skirts with one hand, and began to step up on the rocks. He touched her arm to make her look back again and mimed slipping and falling, to let her know she had to be careful because the moss was slippery. She smiled and nodded again before hurrying on. Her smile was unexpected, and it warmed him, softening the edge of his fear. Richard allowed himself a small dose of confidence about their escape as he stepped from one mossy rock to another.

As the path climbed steadily upward, the trees thinned more. The rock taking over from the soil offered trees infrequent opportunity to put down roots. Soon the only trees grew in crevices and were gnarled, twisted, and small, wanting to offer no purchase to the wind that could pull them from their meager anchoring.

They slipped quietly out of the trees and onto the ledges. The path wasn't always clearly marked, and there were many false trails. She often had to turn to him, and he directed her by pointing, or with a nod of his head. Richard wondered what her name was, but his fear of the four men kept him from talking. Even though the trail was steep and hard, he didn't have to slow on her account. She was a strong climber, and quick. He saw that she wore good boots of soft leather: the kind of boots worn by one used to traveling.

It had been well over an hour since they had come out of the trees, climbing steadily upward, into the sun. They were heading east on the ledges before the trail cut back to the west later. The men, if they had followed, would have to look into the sun to see them. Richard kept them crouched as low as possible and checked over his shoulder often as they climbed, scanning for any sign of the men. When he had seen them by Trunt Lake they were staying well hidden, but it was too open out here for them to hide. He saw nothing, and started to feel better. They weren't being followed; the men were nowhere to be seen, and were probably miles down Hawkers Trail by now. The farther from the boundary and the closer to town they got, the better he felt. His plan had worked.

Seeing no sign that they were being followed, Richard wished they could stop for a rest, as his hand was throbbing, but she gave no sign that she needed or wanted a break. She kept pushing on as if the men were right on their heels. Richard remembered the look on her face when he had asked if they were dangerous, and quickly rejected any thought of stopping.

As morning wore on, the day became warm for this late in the year. The sky was a bright, clear blue, with only a few white, wispy clouds drifting by. One of the clouds had taken on the undulating form of a snake, with its head down and tail up. Because it was so unusual, Richard remembered seeing the same cloud earlier in the day—or was it yesterday? He would have to remember to mention it to Zedd the next time he saw him. Zedd was a cloud reader, and if Richard failed to report his sighting he would have to endure an hour-long lecture on the significance of clouds. Zedd was probably watching it this very moment, fretting over whether or not Richard was paying attention.

The path took them to the south face of small Blunt Mountain, where it crossed a sheer cliff face for which the mountain was named. Crossing the cliff near midheight, the trail offered a panoramic view of the southern Ven Forest and, to their left, in cloud and mist, almost hidden behind the cliff wall, the high, rugged peaks belonging to the boundary. Richard saw brown, dying trees standing out against the carpet of green. Up closer to the boundary the dead trees were thick. It was the vine, he realized.

The two of them advanced quickly across the cliff trail. They were so clearly in the open, with no chance to hide, that anyone could spot them easily, but across the cliff the trail would begin to head down into the Hartland Woods and then into town. Even if the men did figure out their mistake and follow, Richard and the woman had a safe lead.

As it neared the far side of the cliff face, the path started to broaden from its treacherous, narrow width to a space wide

14

enough for two to walk side by side. Richard trailed his right hand along the rock wall for reassurance while looking over the side to the boulder fields several hundred feet below. He turned and checked behind. Still clear.

As he turned back, she froze in midstride, the folds of her dress swirling around her legs.

In the trail ahead, that only a moment earlier had been empty, stood two of the men. Richard was bigger than most men; these men were much bigger than him. Their dark green hooded cloaks shaded their faces but couldn't conceal their heavily muscled bulk. Richard's mind raced, trying to conceive of how the men could have gotten ahead of them.

Richard and the woman spun, prepared to run. From the rock above, two ropes dropped down. The other two men plummeted to the path, landing on their feet with heavy thuds, blocking any retreat. They were as big as the first two. Buckles and leather straps beneath their cloaks held an arsenal of weapons that glinted in the sunlight.

Richard wheeled back to the first two. They calmly pushed their hoods back. Each had thick blond hair and a thick neck; their faces were rugged, handsome.

"You may pass, boy. Our business is with the girl." The man's voice was deep, almost friendly. Nonetheless, the threat was as sharp as a blade. He removed his leather gloves and tucked them in his belt as he spoke, not bothering to look at Richard. He obviously didn't consider Richard an obstacle. He appeared to be the one in charge, as the other three waited silently while he spoke.

Richard had never been in a situation like this before. He never allowed himself to lose his temper, and could usually turn scowls to smiles with his easy manner. If talk didn't work, he was quick enough and strong enough to stop threats before anyone was hurt, and if need be he would simply walk away. He knew these men weren't interested in talking, and they clearly weren't afraid of him. He wished he could walk away now.

Richard glanced to her green eyes and saw the visage of a proud woman beseeching his help.

He leaned closer, and kept his voice low, but firm. "I won't leave you."

15

Relief washed over her face.

She gave a slight nod as she settled her hand lightly on his forearm. "Keep between them, don't let them all come at me at once," she whispered. "And be sure you aren't touching me when they come." Her hand tightened on his arm and her eyes held his, waiting for confirmation that he understood her instructions. He nodded his agreement. "May the good spirits be with us," she said. She let her hands drop to her sides, turning to the two behind them, her face dead calm, devoid of emotion.

"Be on your way, boy." The leader's voice was harder. His fierce blue eyes glared. He gritted his teeth. "Last time offered."

Richard swallowed hard.

He tried to sound sure of himself. "We will both be passing." He heart felt as if it were coming up into his throat.

"Not this day," the leader said with finality. He pulled free a wicked-looking curved knife.

The man to his side pulled a short sword clear of the scabbard strapped across his back. With a depraved grin, he drew it across the inside of his muscled forearm, staining the blade red. From behind, Richard could hear the ring of steel being drawn. He was paralyzed with fear. This was all happening too fast. They had no chance. None.

For a brief moment no one moved. Richard flinched when the four gave the howling battle cries of men prepared to die in mortal combat. They charged in a frightening rush. The one with the short sword swung it high, coming at Richard. He could hear one of the men behind him grab the woman as the man with the sword raced toward him.

And then, just before the man reached him, there was a hard impact to the air, like a clap of thunder with no sound. The violence of it made every joint in his body cry out in sharp pain. Dust lifted around them, spreading outward in a ring.

The man with the sword felt the pain of it, too, and for an instant his attention was diverted past Richard, to the woman. As he came crashing forward, Richard fell back against the wall and with both feet hit the man square in the chest as hard as he could. It knocked him clear of the path, into midair. The man's

16

eyes went wide in surprise as he dropped backward to the rocks below, the sword still held over his head in both hands.

To Richard's shock, he saw one of the other two men from behind him falling through space, too, his chest ripped and bloody. Before Richard could give it a thought, the leader with the curved knife charged past, intent on the woman. He hammered the heel of his free hand into the center of Richard's chest. The jolt knocked the wind out of him and flung him hard against the wall, smacking his head against the rock. As he fought to remain conscious, his only thought was that he had to stop the man from getting to her.

Summoning strength he didn't know he had, Richard snatched the leader by his husky wrist and spun him around. The knife came around in an arc toward him. The blade flashed in the sunlight. There was a savage hunger in the man's blue eyes. Richard had never been so afraid in his life.

In that instant he knew he was about to die.

Seemingly from out of nowhere, the last man, with a short sword covered in gore, smashed into the leader, driving his sword through the other's gut, slamming the wind out of him. The collision was so fierce it carried both over the side of the cliff. All the way down the last man howled in a cry of rage that ended only when they met the boulders below.

Richard stood stunned, staring over the edge. Reluctantly he turned to the woman, afraid to look, terrified he would see her gashed open and lifeless. Instead, she was sitting on the ground, leaning against the cliff wall, looking drained but unhurt. Her face had a faraway look. It was all over so fast he couldn't understand what had happened or how. Richard and the woman were alone in the sudden silence.

He slumped down beside her on rock warm from the sun. He had a powerful headache from having his head whacked on the wall. Richard could see she was all right, so he didn't ask. He felt too overwhelmed to talk and could sense the same in her. She noticed blood on the back of her hand and wiped it off on the wall, adding it to the red splatters already there. Richard thought he might throw up.

He couldn't believe they were alive. It didn't seem possible. What was the thunder without sound? And the pain he felt when

17

it had happened? He had never felt anything like it before. He shuddered recalling it. Whatever it was, she had something to do with it, and it had saved his life. Something unearthly had occurred, and he wasn't at all sure he wanted to know what it was.

She leaned her head back against the rock, rolling it to the side, toward him. "I don't even know your name. I wanted to ask before, but I was afraid to talk." She vaguely indicated the drop-off. "I was so frightened of them. . . . I didn't want them to find us."

He thought maybe she was about to cry and looked over at her. She wasn't, but he felt that he might. He nodded his understanding of what she said about the men.

"My name is Richard Cypher."

Her green eyes studied his as he looked at her. The light breeze carried wisps of hair across her face.

She smiled. "There are not many who would have stood with me." He found her voice as attractive as the rest of her. It matched the spark of intelligence in her eyes. It almost took his breath away. "You are a very rare person, Richard Cypher."

To his intense displeasure Richard felt his face flush. She looked away, pulling the strands of hair off her face, and pretended not to notice his blushing.

"I am . . ." She sounded as if she was going to say something she then thought better of. She turned back to him. "I am Kahlan. My family name is Amnell."

He looked into her eyes a long moment. "You too are a very rare person, Kahlan Amnell. There are not many who would have stood as you did."

She did not blush, but smiled again. It was an odd sort of smile, a special smile, not showing any teeth. Her lips were pressed together, as one would do when taking another into one's confidence. Her eyes sparkled. It was a smile of sharing.

Richard reached behind, felt the painful lump on the back of his head, and checked his fingers for blood. There was none, though he thought that by all rights there should have been. He looked back at her, again wondering what had happened, wondering what she had done, and how she had done it. There was that thunder with no sound, and he had knocked one of the men off the cliff; one of the two behind him had killed the other instead of her, and then killed the leader and himself.

"Well, Kahlan, my friend, can you tell me how it is that we are alive and those four men are not?"

She looked at him in surprise. "Do you mean that?"

"Mean what?"

She hesitated. " 'Friend.' "

Richard shrugged. "Sure. You just said I stood with you. That's the kind of thing a friend does, isn't it?" He gave her a smile.

Kahlan turned away. "I don't know." She fingered the sleeve of her dress as she looked down. "I have never had a friend before. Except maybe my sister. . . ."

He felt the pain in her voice. "Well, you have one now," he said in his most cheerful tone. "After all, we just went through something pretty frightening together. We helped each other, and we survived."

She simply nodded. Richard looked out over the Ven, the forests where he was so at home. Sunlight made the green of the trees vibrant, lush. His eyes were drawn to the left, to spots of brown, the dead and dying trees that stood out among their healthy neighbors. Until that morning, when he found the vine and it bit him, he had had no idea that the vine was up by the boundary, spreading through the woods. He rarely went up into the Ven, that close to the boundary. Other people wouldn't go within miles of it. Others went closer, if they traveled on Hawkers Trail, or to hunt, but none went too close. The boundary was death. It was said that to go into the boundary was not only to die but to forfeit your soul. The boundary wardens made sure people stayed away.

He gave her a sideways glance. "So what about the other part? The part about us being alive. How did that happen?"

Kahlan didn't meet his gaze. "I think the good spirits protected us."

Richard didn't believe a word of it. But as much as he wanted to know the answers, it was against his nature to force someone to tell something she didn't want to. His father had raised him to respect another person's right to keep his own secrets. In her own time she would tell him her secrets, if she wanted to, but he would not try to force her.

Everyone had secrets; he certainly had his own. In fact, with his father's murder and with today's events he felt those secrets stirring unpleasantly in the back of his mind.

"Kahlan," he said, trying to make his voice sound reassuring, "being a friend means you don't have to tell me anything you don't want to, and I'll still be your friend."

She didn't look at him, but nodded her agreement.

Richard got to his feet. His head hurt, his hand hurt, and now he realized his chest hurt where the man had hit him. To top it off he remembered he was hungry. Michael! He had forgotten about his brother's party. He looked at the sun and knew he was going to be late. He hoped he wouldn't miss Michael's speech. He would take Kahlan, tell Michael about the men, and get some protection for her.

He held out his hand to help her up. She stared at it in surprise. He continued to hold it out for her. She gazed up into his eyes, and took the hand.

Richard smiled. "Never had a friend give you a hand up before?"

She averted her eyes. "No."

Richard could tell she felt uncomfortable, so he changed the subject.

"When's the last time you had something to eat?"

"Two days ago," she said without emotion.

His eyebrows went up. "Then you must be even more hungry than I am. I'll take you to my brother." He peered over the edge of the cliff. "We'll have to tell him about the bodies. He'll know what to do." He turned again to her. "Kahlan, do you know who those men were?"

Her green eyes turned hard. "They are called a quad. They are, well, they are like assassins. They are sent to kill . . ." She caught herself again. "They kill people." Her face regained the calm countenance it had when he first saw her. "I think that maybe the fewer people who know about me, the safer I will be."

Richard was startled; he had never heard of anything like this. He ran his fingers through his hair, trying to think. Dark, shadowy thoughts started to swirl again. For some reason, he was terrified of what she might say, but had to ask.

He looked hard into her eyes, expecting the truth this time. "Kahlan, where did the quad come from?"

She studied his face a moment. "They must have tracked me out of the Midlands, and through the boundary."

Richard's skin went cold, and prickles bumped up along his arms in a wave that rolled up to the back of his neck, making the fine hairs there stand stiffly out. An anger deep within him awakened and his secrets stirred.

She had to be lying. No one could cross the boundary.

No one.

No one could go into or come out of the Midlands. The boundary had sealed it away since before he was born.

The Midlands was a land of magic.

CHAPTER 3

MICHAEL'S HOUSE WAS A massive structure of white stone, set back quite a distance from the road. Slate roofs in a variety of angles and rakes came together in complicated junctures topped with a leaded-glass peak that let light into the central hall. The walkway to the house was shaded from the bright afternoon sun by towering white oaks as it passed through sweeping stretches of lawn before coming to formal gardens laid in symmetrical patterns to each side. The gardens were in full bloom. Since it was so late in the year, Richard knew the flowers had to have been raised in greenhouses just for the occasion.

People in fine clothes strolled the lawns and gardens, making Richard feel suddenly out of place. He knew he must look a mess in his dirty, sweat-stained forest garb, but he hadn't wanted to waste the time going out of his way to his house to get cleaned up. Besides, he was in a dark mood and didn't much care how he looked. He had more important things on his mind.

Kahlan, on the other hand, didn't look so out of place. The unusual but striking dress she wore belied the fact that she, too, had just walked out of the woods. Considering how much blood there had been up on Blunt Cliff, he was surprised that she didn't have any on her. She had somehow managed to stay clear while the men killed each other.

When she had seen how upset he had become when she had told him she had come through the boundary from the Midlands, she had fallen silent on the subject. Richard needed time to think about it, and hadn't pressed. Instead she asked him about Westland, what the people were like and where he lived. He told her about his house in the woods, how he liked living away from town, and that he was a guide for travelers through the Hartland Woods on their way to or from the town itself.

"Does your house have a fireplace?" she had asked.

"It does."

"Do you use it?"

"Yes, I cook on it all the time," he had told her. "Why?"

She had merely shrugged as she looked off to the countryside. "I just miss sitting in front of a fire, that's all."

As unsettling as the day's events had been, on top of his grief, it felt good to have someone to talk to, even if she did dance around her secrets.

"Invitation, sir?" someone called in a deep voice from the shade beside the entry.

Invitation? Richard spun around to see who had addressed him and was met by a mischievous grin. Richard broke into a grin of his own. It was his friend Chase. He clasped hands with the boundary warden in a warm greeting.

Chase was a big man, clean-shaven, with a head of light brown hair that showed no sign of receding but instead gave way to age by going gray at the sides. Heavy brows shaded intense brown eyes that stole slowly about, even as he talked, and saw everything. This habit often gave people the impression—a seriously mistaken impression—that he wasn't paying attention. Despite his size, Chase was, Richard knew, frighteningly quick when there was need. Chase wore a brace of knives to one side of his belt, and a six-bladed battle mace to the other. The hilt of a short sword stood above his right shoulder, and a crossbow with a full complement of barbed, steel-tipped bolts hung from a leather strap on his left.

Richard lifted an eyebrow. "Looks like you plan on getting your share of the food."

The grin left Chase's face. "Not here as a guest." His gaze settled on Kahlan.

Richard felt the awkwardness. He took Kahlan's arm and drew her forward. She came easily, unafraid.

"Chase, this is my friend, Kahlan." He gave her a smile. "This is Dell Brandstone. Everyone calls him Chase. He's an old friend of mine. We're safe with him." He turned back to Chase. "You can trust her, too."

She looked at the big man and gave him a smile and nod of acknowledgment.

Chase nodded once to her, the matter settled, Richard's word being all the reassurance he needed. His eyes scanned the crowd, lingering on various people, checking their interest in the three of them. He pulled them both away from the sunlit openness of the steps and into the shade off to the side.

"Your brother called in all the boundary wardens." He paused, taking another look around. "To be his personal guards."

"What! That doesn't make any sense!" Richard was incredulous. "He has the Home Guard, and the army. What does he need a few boundary wardens for?"

Chase rested his left hand on one of the knife handles. "What, indeed." His face gave no hint of emotion. It rarely did. "Could be he just wants us around for effect. People are afraid of the wardens. You've been away to the woods since your father was killed, not that I'm saying I wouldn't do the same if I were you. All I'm saying is you haven't been around. Strange things have been going on, Richard. People coming and going in the night. Michael calls them 'concerned citizens.' He's been talking some nonsense about plots against the government. He has the wardens all over the grounds."

Richard looked around, but didn't see any. He knew that didn't mean anything. If a boundary warden didn't want to be seen, he could be standing on your foot and you wouldn't be able to find him.

Chase drummed his fingers on a knife handle as he watched Richard's eyes scan about. "My boys are out there, take my word."

"Well, how do you know Michael isn't right, what with the father of the new First Councilor being murdered and all?"

Chase gave his finest look of disgust. "I know every little slime in Westland. There's no plot. Might be a bit of fun to be had if there were, but I think I'm just part of the decoration. Michael said I should 'stay visible.'" His expression sharpened. "And about your father's murder, well, George Cypher and I go way back, way back to before when you were born, back to before the boundary. He was a good man. I was proud to call him friend." Anger heated in his eyes. "I've twisted a few fingers." He shifted his weight, taking another look around before bringing his fierce expression back to Richard. "Twisted hard. Hard enough to cause their owners to spit out their own mother's name if it had been the right one. No one knows a thing, and believe me, if they did they would have been happy to have shortened our conversation. First time I've ever chased anyone and not been able to get even a whiff." He folded his arms, and his grin came back as he eyed Richard up and down. "Speaking of slime, what have you been about? You look like one of my customers."

Richard glanced to Kahlan, and then back to Chase. "We were up in the high Ven." Richard lowered his voice. "We were attacked by four men."

Chase raised an eyebrow. "Anyone I would know?"

Richard shook his head.

Chase frowned. "So where did these four fellows go after they jumped you?"

"You know the trail across Blunt Cliff?"

"Of course."

"They're on the rocks at the bottom. We're going to have to have a talk."

Chase unfolded his arms and stared at the two of them. "I'll have a look." His eyebrows knitted together. "How'd you manage it?"

Richard exchanged a quick glance with Kahlan and looked back to the boundary warden. "I think the good spirits protected us."

Chase shot them each a suspicious glare. "That so? Well, better not to tell Michael about this right now. I don't think he be-

25

lieves in good spirits." He studied both their faces. "And if you think there's a need, you two come stay at my place. You'll be safe enough there."

Richard thought about all of Chase's children and knew he didn't want to endanger them, but he didn't want to argue the point either, so he just nodded.

"We better get in there. Michael is sure to be missing me."

"One more thing," Chase said. "Zedd wants to see you. He's in a big fret about something. Says it's real important."

Richard looked up over his shoulder and saw the same strange snakelike cloud. "I think I need to see him, too." He turned and started to leave.

"Richard," Chase said with a look that would have withered anyone else, "tell me what were you doing in the high Ven."

Richard didn't shy away. "Same as you. Trying to get a whiff."

Chase's hard face softened, and a hint of his smile came back. "Get one?"

Richard nodded as he held up his red, sore left hand. "And it bites."

The two turned and melted into the crowd entering the house, moving through the entry, across white marble floors, to the elegant central meeting hall. Marble walls and columns glowed with a cold eerie cast where the sunlight streaming in from above touched them. Richard had always preferred the warmth of wood, but Michael had maintained that anyone could go out and make what they wanted from wood, but if you wanted marble, you had to hire a lot of people who lived in wood houses to do the work for you. Richard remembered a time before their mother died, when he and Michael played in the dirt, building houses and forts with sticks. Michael had helped him then. He wanted so much for Michael to help him now.

People Richard recognized greeted him, getting only a wooden smile or quick handshake. Since Kahlan was from a strange land, Richard was a little surprised to see how comfortable she was around all the important people. It had already occurred to him that she, too, must be someone important. Gangs of assassins didn't hunt down unimportant people.

Richard found it difficult to smile at everyone. If the rumors about things coming out of the boundary were true, then all of Westland was in-danger. Country people in the outlying areas of the Hartland were already terrified to go out at night and had recounted stories to him of people being found partly eaten. He had told them it was just that they had died of some natural cause, and wild animals had found the bodies. Happened all the time. They said it was beasts from the sky. He had passed it off as superstitious nonsense.

Until now.

Even with all the people around, Richard felt overwhelmingly lonely. He was confused and didn't know what to do about it. He didn't know who to turn to. Kahlan was the only one who made him feel better, but at the same time she frightened him. The encounter on the cliff frightened him. He wanted to take her and leave.

Zedd might know what to do. He used to live in the Midlands before the boundary, though he would never talk about it. And then there was the unsettling feeling he had that all of this had something to do with his father's death, and his father's death had something to do with his own secrets, the secrets his father had placed upon him and him alone.

Kahlan laid a hand on his arm. "Richard, I'm sorry. I didn't know . . . about your father. I'm sorry."

With the frightening events of the day he had almost forgotten about it until Chase had brought it up. Almost. He gave a little shrug. "Thanks." He waited a moment as a woman in a blue silk dress with ruffles of white lace at the neck, cuffs, and down the front walked past. He looked down at the floor as she moved by so he wouldn't have to return her smile if she gave him one. "It was three weeks ago." He told Kahlan a little of what had happened. She listened sympathetically.

"I'm sorry, Richard. Perhaps you would rather be alone."

He forced himself to smile. "No, it's all right. I've been alone enough. It helps to have a friend to talk to."

She gave him a small smile and a nod, and they moved on through the crowd. Richard wondered where Michael was. It seemed odd that he wasn't out yet.

Even though he had lost his appetite, he knew Kahlan hadn't eaten in two days. With all the tempting food around, he decided she must have remarkable self-control. The delicious smells were starting to change his mind about his appetite.

He leaned closer to her. "Hungry?"

"Very."

He guided her over to a long table with food piled in tiers. There were large steaming platters of sausages and meats, boiled potatoes, dried fish of several kinds, grilled fish, chicken, turkey, mounds of raw vegetables sliced into strips, big tureens of cabbage and sausage soup, onion soup, and spice soup, platters of breads, cheeses, fruits, pies, and cakes, and casks of wine and ale. Servants were constantly coming and going to keep the platters full.

Kahlan scrutinized them. "Some of the serving girls have long hair. That is allowed?"

Richard looked around, a little bewildered. "Yes. Anyone can have any kind of hair they want. Look." He held his arm close to his chest and pointed as he leaned toward her. "Those women over there are councilors, some have short hair, some have long. Whatever they want." He looked at her out of the corner of his eye. "Do people tell you to cut your hair?"

She lifted an eyebrow to him. "No. No one has ever asked me to cut my hair. It is simply that where I come from, the length of a woman's hair has a certain social significance."

"Does that mean that you are someone of considerable standing?" He took the edge off the question with a playful smile. "Seeing as how you have such long, beautiful hair, I mean."

She gave him back a small smile, devoid of joy. "Some think so. I could only expect that after this morning, the thought had entered your mind. We all can be only what we are, nothing more, or less."

"Well, if I ask anything a friend shouldn't, just kick me."

Her smile brightened into the same tight-lipped one she had given him before. The smile of sharing. It made him grin.

He turned to the food and found one of his favorites, small ribs with a spice sauce, put a few on a small white plate, and handed it to her.

"Try these first. They're my most treasured."

Kahlan held the dish at arm's length, eyeing it suspiciously. "What creature's meat is this?"

"It's pork," he said, a little surprised. "You know, from a pig. Try it, it's the best thing here, I promise."

She relaxed, brought the plate close, and ate the meat. He ate a half dozen himself, savoring every bite.

He put some sausages on their plates. "Here, have some of these, too."

Her suspicion flared anew. "What are they made of?"

"Pork and beef, some spices, I don't know what kinds. Why? There are some kinds of things you don't eat?"

"Some kinds," she said noncommittally before eating a sausage. "May I have some spice soup, please?"

He ladled the soup into a fine white bowl with a gold rim and traded it for her plate. She took the bowl in both hands and tried it.

A smile came to her face. "It's good, just like I make. I don't think our two homelands are as different as you fear."

As she drank the remainder of the soup, Richard, feeling better about what she said, picked up a thick slice of bread, put strips of chicken meat on it, and, when she finished the soup, exchanged the bread for her bowl. She took the bread with chicken and started moving to the side of the room while she ate. He set the soup bowl down and followed behind, shaking an occasional hand. Their owners cast a critical eye at the way he was dressed. When she reached a deserted spot near a column, she turned to face him.

"Please get me a piece of cheese?"

"Sure. What kind?"

She scanned the throng. "Any kind."

Richard worked his way back through the crowd to the food table and picked up two pieces of cheese, eating one along his way back to Kahlan. She took the cheese when he handed it to her, but instead of eating it, she let her arm slip to her side, and let the cheese fall to the floor, as if she had forgotten she was holding it.

"Wrong kind?"

Her tone was distant. "I hate cheese." She was staring past him to a spot across the room.

Richard frowned. "Then why did you ask for it?" There was a hint of irritation in his voice.

"Keep looking at me," she said, her eyes returning to his. "There are two men behind you, across the room. They have been watching us. I wanted to know if it was me or you they were watching. When I sent you for the food they watched you go and come back. They paid no attention to me. It is you they are watching."

Richard put his hands on her shoulders and turned her to see for himself. He scanned over the heads of the crowd, to the far side of the room. "They're just two of Michael's aides. They know me. They're probably wondering where I've been and why I look such a mess." He looked into her eyes and spoke softly so that no one would hear. "It's all right, Kahlan, relax. Those men from this morning are dead. You're safe now."

She shook her head. "More will follow. I should not be with you. I do not want to endanger your life any more than I already have. You are my friend."

"There is no way another quad could track you now, not once you have come here, to Hartland. It's impossible." He knew enough about tracking to feel confident that he was telling her the truth.

Kahlan hooked a finger in the neck of his shirt and drew his face close. There was a flash of angry intolerance in her green eyes.

Her voice came in a slow, harsh whisper. "When I left my homeland, five wizards cast spells over my tracks so none could know where I went, or follow, and then they killed themselves so they could not be made to talk!" Her teeth were gritted in anger, and her eyes were wet. She was starting to tremble.

Wizards! Richard went rigid. At last, he let out his breath and took her hand gently from his shirt, holding it in both of his, his voice barely audible over the din. "I'm sorry."

"Richard, I am scared to death!" She was trembling more now. "If you hadn't been there today, you don't know what would have happened to me. The dying would have been the best of it. You don't know about those men." She shook uncontrollably, giving herself over to her fear.

He felt goose bumps on his arms. He eased her back behind the column where they couldn't be observed. "I'm sorry, Kahlan. I don't know what any of this is about. You know at least some

30

of it, but I'm in the dark. I'm scared, too. Today on the cliff . . .
I've never been that afraid. And I didn't really do much of anything that would have saved us." Seeing her need was giving him
the courage to reassure her.

"What you did," she said, struggling to get the words out,
"was enough to make a difference. It was enough to save us. No
matter how little you think it was, it was enough. If you hadn't
helped me . . . I don't want my being here to bring you to harm."

He squeezed her hand tighter. "It won't. I have a friend, Zedd.
He may be able to tell us what we can do to keep you safe. He's
a little strange, but he's the smartest man I know. If there's anyone who would know what to do, it's Zedd. If you can be
tracked anywhere, then there is no place for you to run; they will
find you. Let me take you to Zedd. As soon as Michael gives his
speech we will go to my house. You can sit in front of the fire,
and in the morning I'll take you to Zedd." He smiled, and
pointed with his chin to a window near them. "Look over there."

She turned to see Chase outside a tall, round-topped window.
The boundary warden glanced back over his shoulder and gave
her a wink and a heartening grin before resuming his scan of the
area.

"To Chase, a quad would be just a bit of fun. While he was
taking care of them, he'd be telling you a story about some real
trouble. He's been watching out for you since we told him of the
men."

That brought a small smile, but it quickly faded.

"There is more to it. I thought I was going to be safe by coming to Westland. I should have been. Richard, I came across the
boundary only with the help of magic." She was still shaking but
starting to regain control of herself, taking strength from him. "I
do not know how those men came across. They should not have
been able to. They should not have even known I left the Midlands. Somehow, the rules have changed."

"We'll deal with that tomorrow. For now, you are safe. Besides, it would take another quad days to get here, wouldn't it?
That will give us time to make plans."

She gave a nod. "Thank you, Richard Cypher. My friend. But
know that if I bring danger to you, I will leave before it can

harm you." She took her hand back and wiped the bottom lids of her eyes. "I am still hungry. Could we have more?"

Richard smiled. "Sure, what would you like?"

"Some more of your little treasures?"

They went back to the food and ate while they waited for Michael. Richard felt better, not about the things she told him, but because at least he knew a little more, and because he had made her feel safe. Somehow he would find the answer to her problem, and he would know what was going on with the boundary. As much as he feared the answers, he would know them.

Whispers rippled through the crowd as heads turned to the far side of the room. It was Michael. Richard took Kahlan's hand and moved to the side of the room, closer to his brother, so they could watch.

As Michael stepped up onto a platform, Richard realized why it had taken him so long to come out. He had been waiting for the sunlight to fall on that spot, so he could stand in the light and be lit in its glory for all to see.

Not only was he shorter than Richard, but heavier and softer. Sunlight lit his mop of unruly hair. His upper lip proudly displayed a mustache. He wore baggy white trousers, and his white tunic with bloused sleeves was cinched at the waist by a gold belt. Standing there in the sunlight, Michael positively gleamed, casting the same cold, eerie glow the marble did when struck by the sun. He stood out in stark relief against the shadowed background.

Richard held up his hand to catch his attention. Michael saw the hand and smiled at his brother, holding his eyes for a moment as he began speaking, before shifting his gaze to the crowd.

"Ladies and gentlemen, today I accepted the position of First Councilor of Westland." A roar went up from the room. Michael listened without moving, then thrust his arms suddenly into the air, calling for silence. He waited until every last cough died out. "The councilors from all of Westland selected me to lead us in these times of challenge because I have the courage and vision to take us into a new era. Too long we have lived looking to the past and not to the future! Too long we have chased old ghosts and been blind to new callings! Too long we have listened to

32

those who would seek to drag us into war and ignored those who would guide us on a path to peace!"

The crowd went wild. Richard was dumbfounded. What was Michael talking about? What war? There was no one to have a war with!

Michael held up his hands again and, not waiting for quiet this time, went on. "I will not stand by while the Westland is put into peril by these traitors!" His face was red and angry. The crowd roared again, this time with fists jabbing the air. They chanted Michael's name. Richard and Kahlan looked at each other.

"Concerned citizens have come forward to identify these cowards, these traitors. At this very moment, as we join our hearts here today in a common goal, the boundary wardens protect us while the army is rounding up these conspirators who plot against the government. They are not the common criminals you might think, but respected men in high authority!"

Murmurs swept across the assembly. Richard was stunned. Could it be true? A conspiracy? His brother hadn't gotten where he was by not knowing what was going on. Men in high authority. That would certainly explain why Chase didn't know anything about it.

Michael stood in the shaft of sunlight, waiting for the whispering to die down. When he began again his voice was low and warm.

"But that is past history. Today we look to our new course. One reason I was chosen as First Councilor is because being a Hartlander, I have lived my life in the shadow of the boundary, a shadow that has shaded all our lives. But that is looking to the past. The light of a new day always chases the shadows of the night away, and shows us that the shape of our fears is only the ghost of our own minds.

"We must look forward to a day when the boundary will no longer be there, for nothing lasts forever, does it? And when that day comes we must be ready to extend a hand of friendship and not a sword, as some would have us do. That only leads to the futility of war and needless dying.

"Should we be wasting our resources, preparing to do battle with a people we have been long separated from, a people who were the ancestors to many of us here? Should we be ready to do violence to our brothers and sisters simply because we don't know them? What a waste! Our resources should be spent eliminating the real suffering around us. When the time comes, maybe not in our lifetime, but it will come, we should be ready to welcome our long-separated brothers and sisters. We must not join only the two lands, but all three! For someday, just as the boundary between Westland and the Midlands will fade away, so too will the second boundary between the Midlands and D'Hara, and all three lands shall be one! We can look to a day when we can share the joy of reunion, if we have the heart! And that joy will spread from here, today, in Hartland!

"This is why I have moved to stop those who would plunge us into war with our brothers and sisters merely because someday the boundaries will fade away. This does not mean we don't need the army, for we can never know what real threats lie in our path to peace, but we know there is no need to invent them!"

Michael swept his hand out over the crowd. "We in this room are the future. It is your responsibility as councilors of Westland to carry the word throughout the country! Take our message of peace to the good people. They will see the truth in your hearts. Please help me. I want our children and our grandchildren to be the beneficiaries of what we lay down here today. I want us to set a course for peace to carry us into the future, so when the time comes, future generations will benefit and thank us."

Michael stood with his head bowed and both his fists held tightly to his chest. The sunlight glowed about him. The audience was so moved that they stood in absolute silence. Richard saw men in tears, and women weeping openly. All eyes were on Michael, who stood still as stone.

Richard was stunned. He had never heard his brother speak with such conviction or eloquence. It all seemed to make such sense. After all, here he stood with a woman from across the boundary, from the Midlands, and she was already his friend.

But then, four others had tried to kill him. No, not exactly, he thought; they wanted to kill her; he was just in the way. They had offered to let him go, and it was his decision to stand and fight. He had always been fearful of those from across the boundary, but now he was friends with one, just as Michael said.

He was starting to see his bother in a new light. People had

34

been moved by Michael's words in a way Richard had never witnessed. Michael was pleading for peace and friendship with other peoples. What could be wrong with that?

Why did he feel so uneasy?

"And now, to the other part," Michael continued, "to the real suffering around us. While we have worried about the boundaries that have not harmed a single one of us, many of our families, friends, and neighbors have suffered, and died. Tragic and needless deaths, in accidents with fire. Yes, that is what I said. Fire."

People mumbled in confusion. Michael was starting to lose his bond with the crowd. He seemed to expect it; he looked from face to face, letting the confusion build, and then dramatically he thrust his hand out, his finger pointing.

At Richard.

"There!" he screamed. Everyone turned as one. Hundreds of eyes looked at Richard. "There stands my beloved brother!" Richard tried to shrink. "My beloved brother who shares with me"—he pounded a fist to his chest—"the tragedy of losing our own mother to fire! Fire took our mother from us when we were young, and left us to grow up alone, without her love and care, without her guidance. It was not some imagined enemy from across a boundary that took her, but an enemy of fire! She couldn't be there to comfort us when we hurt, when we cried in the night. And the thing that wounds the most is that it didn't have to be."

Tears, glistening in the sunlight, ran down Michael's cheeks. "I am sorry, friends, please forgive me." He wiped the tears with a handkerchief he had handy. "It's just that only this morning I heard of another fire that took a fine young mother and father, and left their daughter an orphan. It brought my own pain back to me and I couldn't remain silent." Everyone was now solidly back with him. Their tears flowed freely. A woman put her arm around Richard's shoulder as he stood numb. She whispered how sorry she was.

"I wonder how many of you have shared the pain my brother and I live with every day. Please, those of you who have a loved one, or a friend, who has been hurt, or even killed, by fire, please, hold up your hands." Quite a few hands went up, and there was wailing from some in the crowd.

"There, my friends," he said hoarsely, spreading his arms wide, "there is the suffering among us. We need look no further than this room."

Richard tried to swallow the lump in his throat as the memory of that horror came back to him. A man who had imagined their father had cheated him lost his temper and knocked a lamp off the table as Richard and his brother slept in the back bedroom. While the man dragged his father outside, beating him, his mother pulled Richard and his brother from the burning house, then ran back inside to save something, they never knew what, and was burned alive. Her screams brought the man to his senses, and he and their father tried to save her, but couldn't. Filled with guilt and revulsion at what he had caused, the man ran off crying and yelling that he was sorry.

That, his father had told them a thousand times, was the result of a man losing his temper. Michael shrugged it off; Richard took it to heart. It had instilled in him a dread of his own anger, and whenever it threatened to come out, he choked it off.

Michael was wrong. Fire had not killed their mother; anger had.

Arms hanging limply at his side, head bowed, Michael spoke softly again. "What can we do about the danger to our families from fire?" He shook his head sadly. "I do not know, my friends.

"But, I am forming a commission on the problem, and I urge any concerned citizen to come forward with suggestions. My door always stands open. Together we can do something. Together we will do something.

"And now my friends, please excuse me, and allow me to go comfort my brother, as I am afraid bringing out our personal tragedy was a surprise to him, and I must ask his forgiveness."

He hopped down off the stand, the crowd parting to let him through. A few hands reached out to touch him as he passed. He ignored them.

Richard stood and glared as his brother strode to him. The crowd moved away. Only Kahlan stayed at his side, her fingers lightly touching his arm. People went back to the food and began talking excitedly among themselves, about themselves, and forgot him. Richard stood tall and choked off his anger.

Sm.ling, Michael slapped Richard on the shoulder. "Great speech!" he congratulated himself. "What did you think?"

Richard looked down at the patterns on the marble floor. "Why did you bring her death into it? Why did you have to tell everyone about it? Why did you use her like that?"

Michael put an arm around Richard's shoulder. "I know it hurts, and I am sorry, but it's for a greater good. Did you see the tears in their eyes? The things I've started are going to take us all to a better life, and help Westland grow to prominence. I believe what I said; we have to look to the challenge of the future with excitement, not fear."

"And what did you mean about the boundaries?"

"Things are changing, Richard. I have to stay ahead of them." The smile was gone. "That's all I meant. The boundaries won't last forever. I don't think they were ever meant to. We all have to be ready to face up to that."

Richard changed the subject. "What have you found out about Father's murder? Have the trackers picked up anything?"

Michael took his arm back. "Grow up, Richard. George was an old fool. He was always picking up things that didn't belong to him. He probably got caught with something that belonged to the wrong person. A person with a bad temper, and a big knife."

"That's not true! And you know it!" Richard hated the way Michael called their father "George." "He never stole anything in his life!"

"Just because the person you take it from is long dead, that doesn't mean you have any right to it. Someone else obviously wanted it back."

"How do you know all this?" Richard demanded. "What have you found out?"

"Nothing! It's common sense. The house was torn apart! Someone was looking for something. They didn't find it, George wouldn't tell them where it was, they killed him. That's all there is to it. The trackers said there were no tracks. We'll probably never know who did it." Michael glared. "You had better learn to live with that fact."

Richard let out a deep breath. It made sense; someone was looking for something. He shouldn't be angry with Michael because he couldn't find out who. Michael had tried. Richard wondered how there could be no tracks.

"I'm sorry. Maybe you're right, Michael." Another thought struck him. "So, it didn't have anything to do with this conspiracy? It wasn't those men trying to get to you?"

Michael waved his hand. "No, no, no. It had nothing to do with that. That problem has been taken care of. Don't worry about me, I'm safe, everything is all right."

Richard nodded. Michael's face turned to a look of annoyance. "So, little brother, how come you're such a mess? Couldn't you at least clean yourself up? It's not like you didn't have notice. You have known about this party for weeks."

Before he could answer, Kahlan spoke up. Richard had forgotten she was still standing next to him.

"Please forgive your brother, it was not his fault. He came to guide me into Hartland and I was late in coming. I pray he is not dishonored in your eyes because of me."

Michael's eyes glided down the length of her before returning to her face. "And you are?"

Her back stiffened as she stood tall. "I am Kahlan Amnell."

Michael gave a slight smile and a small bow of his head. "So, you are not my brother's escort, as I thought. And where have you traveled from?"

"It is a small place, far away. I am sure you would not know of it."

Michael didn't challenge the answer, but turned to his brother instead. "You will stay the night?"

"No. I have to go see Zedd. He's been looking for me."

Michael's smile melted. "You should find better friends. No good can come of spending your time with that contrary old man." He turned back to Kahlan. "You, my dear, will be my guest tonight."

"I have other arrangements," she said warily.

Michael reached around her with both arms, cupped both hands to her bottom and pulled the lower half of her body hard against him. His leg pressed between her thighs.

"Change them." His smile was as cold as a winter night.

"Remove. Your. Hands." Her voice was hard and dangerous. Each stared into the other's eyes.

38

Richard was dumbfounded. He couldn't believe what his brother was doing. "Michael! Stop it!"

They both ignored him and continued to confront one another, faces close, eyes locked together. Richard stood next to them, feeling helpless. He could sense that both wanted him to stay out of it. His body tensed, muscles hard, ready to disregard the feeling.

"You feel good," Michael whispered. "I think I could fall in love with you."

Kahlan's breathing was slow and restrained. "You do not know the half of it." Her voice was even and controlled. "Now, remove your hands."

When he did not, she slowly placed the fingernail of her first finger on his chest, just below the hollow at the base of his neck. As they glared at each other, she slowly, ever so slowly, began to drag her nail downward, ripping his flesh open. Blood ran down skin in rivulets. For a brief moment, Michael didn't move, but then his eyes could not disguise the pain. He flung open his arms and staggered back a step.

Without looking back, Kahlan stormed out of the house.

Richard gave his brother an angry glare he could not suppress, and followed her out.

CHAPTER 4

RICHARD RAN DOWN THE walkway to catch up with her. Kahlan's dress and long hair flowed behind as she marched along in the late-afternoon sunlight. When she reached a tree, she stopped and waited. For the second time that day, she wiped blood off her hand.

As he touched her shoulder, she turned, her calm face showing no emotion.

"Kahlan, I'm sorry. . . ."

She cut him off. "Do not apologize. What your brother did, he was not doing to me, he was doing to you."

"To me? What do you mean?"

"Your brother is jealous of you." Her face softened. "He is not stupid, Richard. He knew I was with you and he was jealous."

Richard took her arm and started walking down the road, away from Michael's house. He was furious with Michael, and at the same time he was ashamed of his anger. He felt as if he were letting his father down.

"That's no excuse. He's First Councilor; he has all anyone could want. I'm sorry I didn't put a stop to it."

"I did not want you to. It was for me to do. What he wants is whatever you have. If you had stopped him, having me would be a contest he would have to win. This way he has no more interest in me. Besides, what he did to you, about your mother, was worse. Would you have wanted me to have stepped in on your behalf?"

Richard put his eyes back to the road. He choked off his anger. "No, that was not for you to do."

As they walked, the houses became smaller, closer together, but remained clean and well kept. Some of their owners were out taking advantage of the good weather to make repairs before winter. The air was clean and crisp, and Richard knew by the dryness of it that it would be a cold night; the right kind of night for a fire of birch logs, fragrant but not too hot. The white-fenced yards gave way to larger garden plots in front of small cottages set farther back from the road. As he walked, Richard plucked an oak leaf from a branch hanging close to the road.

"You seem to know a lot about people. You're very perceptive, I mean about why they do what they do."

She shrugged. "I guess."

He tore little pieces off the leaf. "Is that why they hunt you?"

She looked over as they walked, and when his eyes came to her, she answered. "They hunt me because they fear truth. One reason I trust you is because you do not."

He smiled at the compliment. He liked the answer, even though he wasn't sure what it meant. "You aren't about to kick me, are you?"

A grin came to her face. "You are getting close." She thought a moment, the smile fading, and went on. "I am sorry, Richard, but for now you must trust me. The more I tell you, the greater the danger, to both of us. Still friends?"

"Still friends." He threw the skeleton of the leaf away. "But someday you will tell me all of it?"

She nodded. "If I can, I promise I will."

"Good," he said cheerfully. "After all, I am a 'seeker of truth.' "

Kahlan jerked to a halt, grabbed his shirtsleeve, and spun him to face her wide eyes.

"Why did you say that?" she demanded.

41

"What? You mean 'seeker of truth'? That's what Zedd calls me. Ever since I was little. He says I always insist on knowing the truth of things, so he calls me 'seeker of truth.'" He was surprised by her agitation. His eyes narrowed. "Why?"

She started walking again. "Never mind."

Somehow, he seemed to have broached a sensitive subject. His need to know the answers started to shoulder its way around in his mind. They hunted her because they feared truth, he thought, and she became upset when he said he was a "seeker of truth." Maybe she had become upset, he decided, because it made her fear for him, too.

"Can you at least tell me who 'they' are? Those who hunt you?"

She continued to watch the road as she walked next to him. He didn't know if she was going to answer him, but at last she did.

"They are the followers of a very wicked man. His name is Darken Rahl. Please do not ask me any more for now; I do not wish to think of him."

Darken Rahl. So, now he knew the name.

The late-afternoon sun was behind the hills of the Hartland Woods, allowing the air to cool as they passed through gently rolling hills of hardwood forest. They didn't talk. He didn't care to talk anyway, as his hand was hurting and he was feeling a little dizzy. A bath and a warm bed were what he wanted. Better to give her the bed, he thought; he would sleep in his favorite chair, the one with the squeak. That sounded good, too; it had been a long day and he ached.

By a stand of birch he turned her up the small trail that would lead past his house. He watched her walking in front of him on the narrow path, picking spiderwebs off her face and arms as she broke the strands strung across their way.

Richard was eager to get home. Along with his knife and the other things he had forgotten to take along, there was something else he had to have, a very important thing his father had given him.

His father had made him the guardian of a secret, made him the keeper of a secret book, and had given Richard something to keep always, as proof to the true owner of the book, that it was not stolen, but rescued for safekeeping. It was a triangular-shaped tooth, three fingers wide. Richard had strung a leather thong to it so he could wear it around his neck, but like his knife and backpack he had stupidly left the house without it. He was impatient to have it back around his neck; without it, he couldn't prove his father wasn't a thief.

Higher up, after an open area of bare rock, the maples, oaks, and birches began to give way to spruce. The forest floor lost its green for a quiet, brown mat of needles. As they walked along, an uneasy feeling began to itch at him. He gently took Kahlan's sleeve between his thumb and forefinger, pulling her back.

"Let me go first," he said quietly. She looked at him and obeyed without question. For the next half hour he slowed the pace, studying the ground and inspecting every branch close to the trail. Richard stopped at the base of the last ridge before his house and squatted them down beside a patch of ferns.

"What's wrong?" she asked.

He shook his head. "Maybe nothing," he whispered, "but someone has been up the trail this afternoon." He picked up a flattened pinecone, looking at it for a short time before tossing it away.

"How do you know?"

"Spiderwebs." He looked up the hill. "There aren't any spiderwebs across the trail. Someone has been up the trail and broken them. The spiders haven't had time to string more, so there aren't any."

"Does anyone else live up this trail?"

"No. It could be just a traveler, passing through. But this trail isn't used much."

Kahlan frowned, perplexed. "When I was walking in front, there were spiderwebs all over. I was picking them off my face every ten steps."

"That's what I'm talking about," he whispered. "No one had

been up that part of the trail all day, but since the open place we came through, there haven't been any more."

"How could that be?"

He shook his head. "I don't know. Either someone came out of the woods back by the clearing, and then went up the trail, a very hard way to travel"—he looked her in the eyes—"or they dropped in out of the sky. My house is over this hill. Let's keep our eyes sharp."

Richard carefully led the two of them up the rise, both scanning the woods as they went. He wanted to run in the other direction, take them away from there, but he couldn't. He wasn't running away without the tooth his father had given him for safe-keeping.

At the top of the rise they crouched behind a big pine and looked down on his house. Windows were broken, and the door, which he always locked, stood open. His possessions were scattered about on the ground.

Richard stood. "It's been ransacked, just like my father's house."

She grabbed a fistful of his shirt and hauled him back down.

"Richard!" she whispered angrily. "Your father may have come home just like this. Maybe he went in just like you are about to do, and they were waiting for him."

She was right, of course. He ran his fingers through his hair, thinking. He looked back toward the house. Its back sat hard up against the woods with its door facing the clearing. Since it was the only door, anyone inside would expect him to come running in that way. That's where they would wait, if they were inside.

"All right," he whispered back, "but there's something inside I have to get. I'm not leaving without it. We can sneak around the back, I'll get it, and then we will be away from here."

Richard would have preferred not to take her, but he didn't want to leave her waiting on the trail, alone. They made their way through the woods, through the tangle of brush, skirting the house, giving it a wide berth. When he reached the place where he would have to approach the back of the house, he motioned her to wait. She didn't like the idea, but he would take no argument. If there was anyone in there, he didn't want them getting her as well.

44

Leaving Kahlan under a spruce tree, Richard started cautiously toward the house, following a serpentine route to stay on the areas of soft needles instead of treading on dry leaves. When he finally saw the back bedroom window, he stood frozen, listening. He heard no sound. Carefully, his heart pounding, he took slow crouched steps. There was movement at his feet. A snake wriggled past his foot. He waited for it to pass.

At the weathered back of his house, he gently put his hand on the bare wooden frame of the window and raised his head high enough to look inside. Most of the glass was broken out, and he could see that his bedroom was a mess. The bedding was slashed open. Prized books were torn apart and their pages strewn about the floor. To the far side of the room the door to the front room was opened partway, but not enough to see beyond. Without a wedge under it, that was the spot the door always swung to on its own.

Slowly, he put his head in the window and looked down at his bed. Below the window was the bottom bedpost, and hanging from it were his pack and the leather thong with the tooth, right where he had left them. He brought his arm up and started to reach through the window.

There was a squeak from the front room, a squeak he knew well. He went cold with fright. It was the squeak his chair made. He had never fixed the squeak because it seemed a part of the chair's personality, and he couldn't bring himself to alter it. Soundlessly, he dropped back down. There could be no doubt: someone was in the front room, sitting in his chair, waiting for him.

Something caught his eye, making him look to the right. A squirrel sat on a rotting stump watching him. Please, he thought desperately to himself, please don't start chattering at me to leave your territory. The squirrel watched him for a long moment, then jumped off the stump to a tree, scurried up, and was gone.

Richard let out his breath, and raised himself back up to look in the window again. The door still stood as it had before. Quickly he reached inside and carefully lifted the pack and leather thong with the tooth off the bedpost, listening wide-eyed all the time for the slightest sound from beyond the door. His knife was on a small table on the other side of the bed. There was no chance of retrieving it. He lifted the pack through the window, being careful not to let it bump against any of the remaining shards of broken glass.

With his booty in hand, Richard moved quickly but silently back the way he had come, resisting a strong urge to break into a run. He looked over his shoulder as he went to be sure no one followed. He put his head through the loop of leather and tucked the tooth into his shirt. He never let anyone see the tooth; it was only for the keeper of the secret book to see.

Kahlan waited where he had left her. When she saw him, she sprang to her feet. He crossed his lips with his finger to let her know to keep silent. Slinging the pack over his left shoulder, he put his other hand gently on her back to move her along. Not wanting to go back the way they had come, he guided her through the woods to where the trail continued above his house. Spiderwebs strung across the trail glistened in the last rays of the setting sun and they both breathed out in relief. This trail was longer and much more arduous, but it led where he was going. To Zedd.

The old man's house was too far to reach before dark and the trail was too treacherous to travel at night, but he wanted to put as much distance as he could between them and whomever waited back at his house. While there was light, they would keep moving.

Coldly, he wondered if whoever was in his house could be the same person who had murdered his father. His house was torn up just like his father's had been. Could they have been waiting for him as they had waited for his father? Could it be the same person? Richard wished he could have confronted him, or at least seen who it was, but something inside him had strongly warned him to get away.

He gave himself a mental shake. He was letting his imagination have too free a rein. Of course something inside had warned him of danger, warned him to get away. He had already gotten away with his life when he shouldn't have once this day. It was foolish to trust in luck once; twice was arrogance of the worst kind. It was best to walk away.

Still, he wished he could have seen who it was, been sure

there was no connection. Why would someone tear his house apart, as his father's had been torn apart? What if it was the same person? He wanted to know who had killed his father. He burned to know.

Even though he had not been allowed to see his father's body at his house, he had wanted to know how he was killed. Chase had told him, very gently, but he had told him. His father's belly had been cut open and his guts had been spread out all over the floor. How could anyone do that? Why would anyone do that? It made him sick and light-headed to think of it again. Richard swallowed back the lump in his throat.

"Well?" Her voice jolted him out of his thoughts.

"What? Well, what?"

"Well, did you get whatever it was you went to get?"

"Yes."

"So what was it?"

"What was it? It was my backpack. I had to get my backpack."

She turned to face him with both hands on her hips and a scowl on her face. "Richard Cypher, you expect me to believe you risked your life to get your backpack?"

"Kahlan, you are coming close to getting kicked." He couldn't manage a smile.

Her head was cocked to the side, and she continued to give him a sideways look, but his remark had taken the fire out of her. "Fair enough, my friend," she said gently, "fair enough."

He could tell Kahlan was a person who was used to getting answers when she asked a question.

As the light faded and colors muted into grayness, Richard started thinking of places to spend the night. He knew of several wayward pines along the way that he had used on many occasions. There was one at the edge of a clearing, just off the trail ahead. He could see the tall tree standing out against the fading pinks of the sky, standing above all the other trees. He led Kahlan off the trail toward it.

The tooth hanging around his neck nagged at him. His secrets nagged at him. He wished his father had never made him the keeper of the secret book. A thought that had occurred to him back at his house, but he had ignored, forced itself to the front of his mind. The books at his house looked like they had been torn apart in a rage. Maybe because none was the right book. What if it was the secret book they were looking for? But that was impossible; no one but the true owner even knew of the book.

And his father . . . and himself . . . and the thing the tooth came from. The thought was too farfetched to consider, so he decided he wouldn't. He tried very hard not to.

Fear, from what had happened on Blunt Cliff and from what had been waiting for him at his house, seemed to have sapped his strength. His feet felt almost too heavy to lift as he trudged across the mossy ground. Just before he went through the brush into the clearing he stopped to swat a fly that was biting his neck.

Kahlan grabbed his wrist in midswat.

Her other hand clamped over his mouth.

He went rigid.

Looking into his eyes, she shook her head, then released his wrist, putting the hand behind his head while continuing to keep her other hand over his mouth. By the expression on her face he knew she was terrified he would make a sound. She slowly lowered him to the ground, and by his cooperation he let her know he would obey.

Her eyes held him as hard as her hands. Continuing to watch his eyes, she put her face so close to his he could feel the warmth of her breath on his cheek.

"Listen to me." Her whisper was so low he had to concentrate to hear her. "Do exactly as I say." The expression on her face made him afraid to blink. "Do not move. No matter what happens do not move. Or we are dead." She waited. He gave a small nod. "Let the flies bite. Or we are dead." She waited again. He gave another small nod.

With a flick of her eyes she indicated for him to look across the clearing. He slowly moved his head just a little so he could

48

see. There was nothing. She kept her hand over his mouth. He heard a few grunts, like those of a wild boar.

Then he saw it.

He flinched involuntarily. She clamped her hand harder against his mouth.

From across the clearing, fading evening light reflected in two glowing green eyes as their gaze swept in his direction. It stood on two feet, like a man, and was about a head taller than him. He guessed it weighed three times as much. Flies bit his neck, but he tried to ignore them.

He looked back to her eyes. She had not looked at the beast; she knew what waited across the clearing. Instead she continued to watch him, waiting to see if he would react in a way that would betray them. He nodded again to reassure her. Only then did she remove her hand from his mouth and put it over his wrist, holding it to the ground. Trickles of blood ran across her neck as she lay motionless on the soft moss, letting the flies bite. He could feel each sharp sting as they bit his neck. Grunts came short and low, and both turned their heads slightly to see.

With astonishing speed, it charged into the center of the clearing, moving in a shuffling, sideways motion. It grunted as it came. Glowing green eyes searched, while its long tail slowly swished the air. The beast cocked its head to the side and pricked its short, rounded ears ahead, listening. Fur covered the great body everywhere except its chest and stomach, which were covered with a smooth, glossy, pinkish skin that rippled with corded muscles underneath. Flies buzzed around something smeared over the taut skin. Throwing back its head, the beast opened its mouth, hissing into the cold night air. Richard could see the hot breath turning to vapor between teeth as big as his fingers.

To keep from shrieking in terror, Richard concentrated on the pain of the biting flies. They could not sneak away, or run; the thing was that close and, he knew, that fast.

A scream erupted from the ground right in front of them, making Richard flinch. Instantly the beast charged toward the two of them in a sideways run. Kahlan's fingers dug into his wrist, but otherwise she didn't move. Richard was paralyzed as he saw it pounce.

A rabbit, its ears covered with flies, bolted right in front of them, screaming again, and was swept up and torn in half in a blink. The front half went down in one swallow. The beast stood right over them and tore at the insides of the rabbit, taking some of the gore and smearing it on its pink-skinned chest and stomach. The flies, even the ones biting Richard's and Kahlan's necks, returned to the creature to feast. The rest of the rabbit was taken by each hind leg, ripped in half, and eaten.

When done, the beast cocked its head again, listening. The two of them were right underneath it, both holding their breath. Richard wanted to scream.

Large wings spread from its back. Against the failing light, Richard could see the veins pulsing through the thin membranes that were its wings. The beast took one last look around and skittered sideways across the clearing. It straightened, hopped twice, and flew off, disappearing in the direction of the boundary. The flies were gone with it.

Both flopped onto their backs, breathing fast, exhausted by the level of fright. Richard thought of the country people who had told him of things from the sky that ate people. He hadn't believed them. He believed them now.

Something in his pack was poking him in the back, and when he could stand it no longer, he rolled onto his side, propping himself up on one elbow. He was drenched in sweat, and it now felt like ice in the cold evening air. Kahlan still lay on her back with her eyes closed, breathing rapidly. A few strands of her hair stuck to her face, but most of it flowed out over the ground. Sweat covered her, too; around her neck it was tinted red. He felt an overwhelming sense of sadness for her, for the terrors in her life. He wished she didn't have to face the monsters she seemed to know all too well.

"Kahlan, what was that thing?"

She sat up, taking a deep breath as she looked down at him. Her hand came up and hooked some of her hair behind her ear; the rest fell forward over her shoulders.

"It was a long-tailed gar."

Reaching out, she picked up one of the biting flies by its wings. Somehow it must have gotten caught in a fold of his shirt and was smashed when he flopped onto his back.

"This is a blood fly. Gars use them to hunt. The flies flush out

50

the quarry, the gar grabs it. They smear some on themselves, for the flies. We are very lucky." She held the blood fly right in front of his nose to make her point. "Long-tailed gars are stupid. If it had been a short-tailed gar, we would be dead right now. Short-tails gars are bigger, and a lot smarter." She paused to make sure she had his full attention. "They count their flies."

He was frightened, exhausted, confused, and in pain. He wanted this nightmare to end. With a moan of frustration he sagged back down onto his back, not caring anymore about whatever it was that was poking him.

"Kahlan, I'm your friend. After those men attacked us, and you didn't want to tell me more about what is going on, I didn't press you." His eyes were closed. He couldn't bear the scrutiny of her eyes. "Now someone is after me, too. For all I know, it could be the same person who murdered my father. It's not just you anymore; I can't go home either. I think I have a right to know at least some of what's going on. I'm your friend, not your enemy.

"Once, when I was little, I got a fever and almost died. Zedd found a root that saved me. Until today, that was the only time I've ever been close to death. Today I was close three times. What do I . . ."

Her fingertips touched his lips to silence him.

"You're right. I will answer your questions. Except about me. For now, I cannot."

He sat up and looked at her. She was starting to shake with cold. Shrugging the straps of the pack off his shoulders, he pulled a blanket out and wrapped it around her.

"You promised me a fire," she said as she shivered. "Is it a promise you intend to keep?"

He couldn't help but to laugh as he got to his feet. "Sure. There's a wayward pine right over there on the other side of the clearing. Or if you want there are others up the trail a little way."

She looked up and give him a worried frown.

"Right," he smiled, "we'll find another wayward pine up the trail."

"What is a wayward pine?" she asked.

CHAPTER 5

RICHARD HELD BACK THE boughs of the tree. "This is a wayward pine," he announced. "Friend to any traveler."

It was dark inside. Kahlan held the boughs aside so he could see by the moonlight to strike steel to flint and start a fire. Clouds scudded across the moon, and they could see their breath in the cold air. Richard had stayed here before on trips to and from Zedd's, and had made a small fire pit of stones. There was dry wood and to the far side a stack of dry grass he had used for bedding. Since he didn't have his knife he was thankful he had left a supply of tinder. The fire was quickly started, filling the interior of the tree's skirt with flickering light.

Richard was not quite able to stand under the branches where they began growing out from the trunk. The branches were bare near the trunk, with needles on the ends, leaving a hollow interior. The lower branches dipped all the way to the ground. The tree was fire-resistant, as long as one was careful. The smoke from the small fire curled up the center, near the trunk. The needles grew so thick that even in a good rain it remained dry inside. Richard had waited out many a rain in a wayward pine. He always enjoyed staying in the small but cozy shelters as he traveled the Hartland.

Now he was especially glad for its concealing shelter. Before their encounter with the long-tailed gar, there had been plants and animals in the forest he had strong respect for, but there had been nothing in the woods he feared.

Kahlan sat herself down cross-legged in front of the fire. She was still shivering and kept the blanket over her head formed into a hood, and held tightly up around her chin.

"I never heard of wayward pines before. I am not used to staying in the woods when I travel, but they look like a wonderful place to sleep." She looked even more tired than he.

"When was the last time you slept?"

"Two days ago, I think. It has all become a blur."

Richard was surprised she could keep her eyes open. When they were running from the quad, he had barely been able to keep up with her. It was her fear that pushed her on, he knew.

"Why so long?"

"It would be very unwise," she said, "to go to sleep in the boundary." Kahlan watched the fire, spellbound in its warm embrace, the light from it fluttering on her face. She loosened the blanket from around her chin and let it hang so she could put her hands out to warm them closer to the fire.

A chill ran through him when he wondered what was in the boundary, and what would happen if you went to sleep there.

"Hungry?"

She nodded her head.

Richard dug around in his pack, retrieving a pot, and went outside to fill it in a pool of water at a small brook they had passed a short distance back. Sounds of the night filled air so cold it felt as if it might break if he wasn't careful. Once again he cursed himself for leaving home without his forest cloak, among other things. The memory of what had been waiting for him at his house made him shiver all the more.

Every bug that looped past made him recoil in fear it was a blood fly, and several times he froze in midstep, only to exhale in relief when he saw it was only a snowy tree cricket, or a moth, or a lacewing. Shadows melted and materialized as clouds passed in front of the moon. He didn't want to, but he looked up anyway. Stars winked off and back on as soft, gauzelike clouds moved silently across the sky. All except one, which did not move.

Cold to the bone, he came back in and put the pot of water on the fire, balancing it on three stones. Richard started to sit across from her, but then changed his mind and sat next to her, telling himself it was because he was so cold. When she heard his teeth chattering, she put half the blanket around his shoulders, letting her half slip from her head down to her shoulders as well. The blanket, heated by her body, felt good around him, and he sat quietly letting the warmth soak in.

"I've never seen anything like a gar. The Midlands must be a dreadful place."

"There are many dangers in the Midlands." A wistful smile came over her face. "There are also many fantastic and magical things. It is a beautiful, wondrous place. But the gar are not from the Midlands. They are from D'Hara."

He stared in astonishment. "D'Hara! From across the second boundary?"

D'Hara. Until his brother's speech today he had never heard the name spoken in anything other than the cautious whispers of older people. Or in a curse. Kahlan continued to watch the fire.

"Richard—" She paused as if afraid to tell him the rest. "—there is no longer a second boundary. The boundary between the Midlands and D'Hara is down. Since the spring."

That shock made him feel as if the shadowy D'Hara had just taken a frightening, giant leap closer. He struggled to make sense of the things he was learning.

"Maybe my brother is more of a prophet than he knows."

"Maybe," she said noncommittally.

"Although it would be hard to make a living as a prophet by predicting events that had already taken place." He gave her a sidelong glance.

Kahlan smiled as she idly twisted a strand of hair. "When I first saw you, my thought was that you were no fool." Firelight sparkled in her green eyes. "Thank you for not proving me wrong."

"Michael is in a position to have knowledge others don't.

54

Maybe he's trying to prepare the people, get them used to the idea, so when they find out, they won't panic."

Michael often said that information was the coin of power, and that it was not a coin to be spent frivolously. After he had become a councilor, he encouraged people to bring their information to him first. Even a farmer with a tale received an ear, and if the tale proved true, a favor.

The water was starting to boil. Richard leaned over, hooked his finger through a strap and pulled his pack to him, then rearranged the blanket. Rummaging around, he located the pouch of dried vegetables and poured some into the pot. From his pocket he pulled a napkin that held four fat sausages, which he broke up and tossed into the soup pot.

Kahlan looked surprised: "Where did those come from? Did you snatch those from your brother's party?" Her voice carried a tone of disapproval.

"A good woodsman," he said, licking his fingers and looking up at her, "always plans ahead and tries to know where his next meal will come from."

"He will not think much of your manners."

"I do not think much of his." He knew he would get no argument from her on that point. "Kahlan, I won't justify the way he acted. Ever since our mother died he's been a hard person to be close to. But I know he cares about people. You have to, if you want to be a good councilor. It must be a lot of pressure. I certainly wouldn't want the responsibility. But that's all he ever wanted: to be someone important. And now that he's First Councilor, he has what he's always wanted. He should be satisfied, but he seems even less tolerant. He's always busy, and always snapping orders. He is always in a bad mood lately. Maybe when he got what he wanted, it wasn't what he thought it would be. I wish he could be more like he used to be."

She grinned. "At least you had the good sense to pick the best of the sausages."

That eased the tension. They both laughed.

"Kahlan, I don't understand, about the boundary, I mean. I don't even know what the boundary is, except it's meant to keep the lands separated so there will be peace. And of course everyone knows that whoever goes into the boundary will not come out alive. Chase and the boundary wardens patrol to make sure people stay away for their own good."

"Young people here are not taught the histories of the three lands?"

"No. I always thought it odd myself, because I wanted to know, but no one would ever tell me much. People think I'm strange because I want to know, and I ask questions. Older people seem suspicious when I ask, and tell me it was too long ago to remember, or give some other excuse.

"Both my father and Zedd told me they used to live in the Midlands before the boundary. Before it went up, they came to Westland. They met here before I was born. They said that back before the boundaries was a terrible time, and that there was a lot of fighting. They both told me there was nothing I needed to know except it was a dreadful time best forgotten. Zedd always seemed the most bitter about it."

Kahlan snapped a piece off a dry stick and tossed it into the fire, where it flamed into a bright ember.

"Well, it is a long story. If you want I will tell you some of it." When she turned to him, he nodded for her to go on.

"Long ago, back in the time before our parents were born, D'Hara was just a confederation of kingdoms, as was the Midlands. The most ruthless of the D'Haran rulers was Panis Rahl. He was avaricious. From the first day of his reign, he started swallowing up all of D'Hara for himself, one kingdom after another, many times before the ink was dry on a peace treaty. In the end, he held sway over all of D'Hara, but instead of satisfying him, it only whetted his appetite, and he soon turned his attention to the lands that are now the Midlands. The Midlands is a loose confederation of free lands; free, at least, to rule as they see fit, and only so long as they live in peace with one another.

"By the time Rahl had conquered all of D'Hara, the people of the Midlands had seen what he was about, and were not to be taken so easily. They knew that signing a peace treaty with him was as good as signing an invitation to invasion. Instead, they chose to remain free, and joined together, through the council of the Midlands, in a common defense. Many of the free lands held no favor with each other, but they knew that if they did not fight together, they would die separately, one at a time.

56

"Panis Rahl threw the might of D'Hara against them. War raged for many years."

Kahlan broke off another piece of the stick and fed it to the fire. "As his legions were finally slowed and then halted, Rahl turned to magic. There is magic in D'Hara, too, not just in the Midlands. Back then there was magic everywhere. There were no separate lands, no boundaries. Anyway, Panis Rahl was ruthless in his use of magic against the free people. He was terribly brutal."

"What kind of magic? What did he do?"

"Some was trickery, sickness, fevers, but the worst of it was the shadow people."

Richard frowned. "Shadow people? What were they?"

"Shadows in the air. Shadow people had no solid form, no precise shape, they were not even alive as we know it, but beings created out of magic." She held out her hand, gliding it across in front of them. "They would come floating across a field or through a wood. Weapons had no effect on them. Swords and arrows went through them as if they were nothing more than smoke. You couldn't hide; shadow people could see you anywhere. One would drift right up to a person and touch him. The touch caused the person's whole body to blister and swell and finally split open. No one touched by a shadow person ever survived. Whole battalions were found killed to a man."

She pulled her hand back inside the blanket. "When Panis Rahl started using the magic in that way, a great and honorable wizard joined the side of the Midlands cause."

"What was his name, this great and honorable wizard?"

"That is part of the story. Have patience until I get to it."

Richard stirred some spices into the soup, listening intently while she resumed her story.

"Many thousands had already died in battle, but the magic killed many more. It was a dark time, after all those years of struggle, to have so many taken by the magic Rahl called forth. But with the help of the great wizard holding Panis Rahl's magic in check, his legions were driven back into D'Hara."

Richard added a stick of birch to the fire. "How did this great and honorable wizard stop the shadow people?"

"He conjured up battle horns for the armies. When the shadow

57

people came, our men blew the horns and magic swept the shadow people away like smoke in the wind. It turned the course of battle to our side.

"The wars had been devastating, but it was concluded that going into D'Hara to destroy Rahl and his forces would be too costly. Yet something had to be done to keep Panis Rahl from trying again, as they knew he would, and many were more frightened of the magic than of the hordes from D'Hara, and they wanted to have nothing to do with it ever again. They wanted a place to live where there would be no magic. Westland was set aside for those people. So it was that there came to be three lands. The boundaries were created with the help of magic . . . but they themselves are not magic."

Richard watched as she looked away. "So what are they?"

Even though her head was turned, he could see her eyes close for a moment. She took the spoon from him and tasted the soup, which he knew wasn't ready yet, then turned to him, as if asking if he really wanted to know. Richard waited.

Kahlan stared into the fire. "The boundaries are part of the underworld: the dominion of the dead. They were conjured into our world by magic, to separate the three lands. They are like a curtain drawn across our world. A rift in the world of the living."

"You mean that going into the boundary is, what, like falling through a crack into another world? Into the underworld?"

She shook her head. "No. Our world is still here. The underworld is there in the same place at the same time. It is about a two-day walk across the land where the boundary, the underworld, lies. But while you are walking the land where the boundary is, you are also walking through the underworld. It is a wasteland. Any life that touches the underworld, or is touched by it, is touching death. That is why no one can cross the boundary. If you enter it, you enter the land of the dead. No one can return from the dead."

"Then how did you?"

She swallowed as she watched the fire. "With magic. The boundary was brought here with magic, so the wizards reasoned they could get me safely through with the aid and protection of magic. It was frightfully difficult for them to cast the spells. They were dealing in things they didn't fully understand, dangerous things, and they weren't the ones who conjured the boundary into this world, so they weren't sure it would work. None of us knew what to expect." Her voice was weak, distant. "Even though I came through, I fear I will never be able to entirely leave it."

Richard sat spellbound. He was horrified to think that she had faced that, that she had gone through a part of the underworld, the world of the dead, even with the aid of magic. It was unimaginable. Her frightened eyes came to his, eyes that had seen things no one else had ever seen.

"Tell me what you saw there," he whispered.

Her skin was ashen as she looked back into the fire. A birch twig popped, making her flinch. Her lower lip began to quiver, and her eyes filled with tears that reflected the flickering flames, but she was not seeing the fire.

"At first," she said in a distant tone, "it was like walking into the sheets of cold fire you see at night in the northern sky." Her chest began heaving. "Inside, it is beyond darkness." Her eyes were wide, wet. A small moan escaped with her breath. "There is ... someone ... with me."

She turned to him, confused, seeming not to know where she was. It panicked him to see the pain in her eyes—pain he brought there with his question. She put her hand over her mouth as tears rolled down her cheeks. Her eyes closed as she gave a low, mournful cry. Bumps ran up Richard's arms.

"My ... mother," she sobbed, "I haven't seen her in so many years ... and ... my dead sister ... Dennee.... I'm so alone ... and afraid...." As she cried, she started gasping for air.

Somehow, he was losing her to the powerful specters of what she had seen in the underworld, as if they were pulling her back to drown her. Frantic, Richard put his hands on her shoulders and twisted her to face him.

"Kahlan, look at me! Look at me!"

"Dennee ..." she gasped, her chest heaving as she tried to break free of him.

"Kahlan!"

"I'm so alone ... and afraid...."

"Kahlan! I'm here with you! Look at me!"

She continued to cry convulsively, choking for air. Her eyes opened, but they didn't focus on him; they were looking into another place.

"You're not alone, I'm here with you! I won't leave you!"

"I'm so alone," she wailed.

He shook her, trying to make her listen. Her skin was white and dead cold. She struggled to breathe. "I'm right here. You're not alone!" Desperate, he shook her again, but it wasn't helping. He was losing her.

Struggling to control his rising panic, Richard did the only thing he could think of. When he had been confronted with fear in the past, he had learned to control it. There was strength in control. He did that now. Maybe he could give her some of his strength. Closing his eyes, he shut his fear away, blocked off the panic, and sought the calm within himself. He let his mind focus on the strength within himself. In the quiet of his mind, he blocked off his fears and confusion, and centered his thoughts on the strength of that peace. He would not let the underworld have her.

He spoke her name in a calm voice. "Let me help you. You are not alone. I am here with you. Let me help you. Take my strength."

His hands gripped her shoulders. He could feel her shaking as she cried in choking sobs and struggled to breathe. He visualized sending her his strength, through his hands, through his contact with her. He visualized that contact extending to her mind, lending her all of his strength and drawing her back, away from the blackness. He would be the spark of light and life in that blackness that would lead her back to this world, to him.

"Kahlan, I am here. I won't leave you. You are not alone. I am your friend. Trust in me." He gently squeezed her shoulders. "Come back to me. Please."

He pictured the white-hot light in his mind, hoping it would help her. Please, dear spirits, he prayed, let her see it. Let it help her. Let her use my strength.

"Richard?" She called out the name as if searching for him.

He squeezed her shoulders again. "I'm here. I won't leave you. Come back to me."

She started breathing again. Her eyes focused on his face. Relief flooded her features when she recognized him, and she began to cry in what seemed a more normal way. She collapsed against him and held him as she would a rock in a river. He held her to him and let her cry on his shoulder while he told her it was all right. He was so afraid he had lost her to the underworld that he didn't want to let go of her either.

Reaching down, he got a hold of the blanket and pulled it back up around her, wrapping her with it as best he could. Warmth was returning to her body again, another sign that she was safe now, but he was disturbed by how quickly the underworld had pulled her back. He didn't think that was supposed to happen. She hadn't been there long, and exactly how he had gotten her back, he didn't know, but he knew it had been none too soon.

The fire lent a soft red cast to the inside of the wayward pine, and in the silence it seemed a secure haven again. An illusion, he knew. He held her and stroked her hair and rocked her gently for a long time. Something in the way she clung to him made him realize that no one had held her and comforted her for a very long time.

He didn't know anything about wizards, or magic, but no one would send Kahlan through the boundary, through the underworld, without a powerful reason. He wondered what could be that important.

Pushing herself off his shoulder, she sat up, embarrassed. "I'm sorry. I should not have touched you in that manner. I was . . ."

"It's all right, Kahlan. It is the first responsibility of a friend to provide a shoulder to cry on."

She nodded but didn't raise her head. Richard felt her eyes on him as he took the soup off the fire to let it cool a little. He put another piece of wood into the flames, sending sparks swirling up with the smoke.

"How do you do that?" she asked in a soft voice.

"Do what?"

"How do you ask questions that fill my mind with pictures and make me answer, even when I have no intention to?"

He shrugged, a little self-conscious. "Zedd asks me that too. I guess it's just something I was born with. Sometimes I think it's a curse." He turned from the fire to face her again. "I'm sorry, Kahlan, for asking you what you saw there. It was a thoughtless thing to do. Sometimes my common sense doesn't keep up with

61

my curiosity. I'm sorry I brought you pain. You being pulled back into the underworld, though, that shouldn't have happened, should it?"

"No, it shouldn't. It was almost as if when I thought back to what I had seen, someone was waiting to pull me back. I fear if you hadn't been here, I might have been lost there. In the darkness, I saw a light. Something you did brought me back."

Richard picked up the spoon while he thought. "Maybe just that you weren't alone."

Kahlan gave a weak shrug. "Maybe."

"I only have one spoon. We can share it." He took a spoonful of soup and blew on it before tasting it. "Not my best work, but it's better than a poke in the eye with a sharp stick." That had the desired effect: she smiled. He gave her the spoon.

"If I'm to help you to stay ahead of the next quad, to stay alive, I need answers. And I don't think we have much time."

She nodded. "I understand. It's all right."

He let her eat some soup before he went on. "So what happened after the boundaries went up? What about the great wizard?"

Before handing him the spoon she took a piece of sausage. "One more thing happened before they went up. While the great wizard was holding the magic at bay, Panis Rahl took a final revenge. He sent a quad out of D'Hara. . . . They killed the wizard's wife, and his daughter."

Richard stared at her. "What did the wizard do to Rahl?"

"He held Rahl's magic back and held him in D'Hara until just as the boundary was going up. At that very moment he sent a ball of wizard's fire through it, letting it touch death, to give it the power of both worlds. Then the boundaries were there."

Richard had never heard of wizard's fire, but he didn't think it required an explanation. "So what happened to Panis Rahl?"

"Well, the boundaries were there, so no one can say for sure, but I don't think anyone would have traded their lot for that of Panis Rahl."

Richard gave her the spoon, and she ate some more while he tried to imagine the righteous wrath of a wizard. After a few bites she gave back the spoon and continued.

"At first everything was fine, but then the council of the Midlands started taking actions the great wizard said were corrupt. Something to do with the magic. He found out the council had reneged on agreements about how the power of magic was to be controlled. He told them that their greed and the things they were doing would lead to worse horrors than those put down in the wars. They thought they knew better than he how the magic should be managed. They made a political appointment of a very important position that was a wizard's and a wizard's alone to fill. He was furious, he told them the position was one for which only a wizard could find the right person, and the appointment only a wizard's to make. The great wizard had trained other wizards, but in their greed, these others sided with the council. He was enraged. He said his wife and daughter had died for nothing. As punishment, the great wizard told them he would do the worst thing possible to them; he would leave them to suffer the consequences of their actions."

Richard smiled. That sounded like something Zedd would say.

"He said that if they knew so well how things were to be done, they did not need him. He refused to help them further, and vanished. But as he left, he cast a wizard's web . . ."

"What's that, a wizard's web?"

"It is a spell a wizard casts. As he left, he cast a wizard's web over everyone, making them forget his name, even what he looked like. So that is why no one knows what his name is or who he is."

Kahlan tossed a stick in the fire, staring off into her thoughts. He went back to eating soup while he waited for her go on with the story. After a few minutes, she did.

"At the beginning of last winter, the movement started."

He backed the spoonful of soup away from his mouth as he looked up. "What movement?"

"The Darken Rahl movement. It seemed to spring up out of nowhere. All of a sudden crowds of people in the bigger cities were chanting his name, calling him 'Father Rahl,' calling him the greatest man of peace that ever lived. The strange thing is, he is the son of Panis Rahl, from D'Hara, on the other side of the boundary, so how did anyone even know anything about him?" She paused, allowing him to ponder the significance of this.

"Anyway, then the gars started coming over the boundary.

They killed a lot of people before everyone learned to stay inside at night."

"But how did they get across the boundary?"

"It was weakening, only no one knew it. As it weakened, it faded from the top first, so the gars could fly over. In the spring it faded completely away. Then the People's Peace Army, Darken Rahl's army, marched right into the bigger cities. Instead of fighting him, crowds of Midlanders threw flowers at them wherever they went. People who didn't throw flowers were hung."

Richard stared wide-eyed. "The army killed them?"

She looked at him hard. "No. The flower throwers did. Said they were a threat to peace, so they killed them. The People's Peace Army never had to lift a finger. The movement said that proved Darken Rahl only wanted peace, since his army didn't kill the dissenters. After a time, the army stepped in and stopped the killing. Instead, the dissenters were sent to the schools of enlightenment to learn about the greatness of Father Rahl, about what a man of peace he is."

"And did they learn at these schools of enlightenment how great Darken Rahl is?"

"No one is as fanatical as a convert. Most just sit around all day, chanting his name."

"So the Midlands didn't fight back?"

"Darken Rahl went before the council and asked them to join him in an alliance of peace. Those who did were held up as champions of harmony. Those who did not were held up as traitors, and publicly executed on the spot by Darken Rahl himself."

"How did . . ."

She held up her hand and closed her eyes. "Darken Rahl has a curved knife he keeps at his belt. He takes great pleasure in using it. Please, Richard, do not ask me to tell you what he did to those men. My stomach cannot bear its recounting."

"I was going to ask how the wizards reacted to all this."

"Oh. Well, it started to open their eyes.

"Rahl then outlawed the use of all magic and declared anyone using it an insurrectionist. You must understand that in the Midlands magic is a part of many people, many creatures. It would be like saying you are a criminal for having two arms and two legs, and must have them cut them off. Then he outlawed fire."

His eyes came up from the soup. "Fire? Why?"

"Darken Rahl does not explain his orders. But wizards use fire. Even so he does not fear wizards. He has more power than his father ever did, more than any wizard. His followers give all kinds of reasons, the main one being that it was used against Darken Rahl's father, so fire is a sign of disrespect to the house of Rahl."

"That's why you wanted to sit in front of a fire."

She nodded. "To have a fire in the wrong place in the Midlands, without the approval of Darken Rahl or his followers, is to invite death." She pushed at the dirt with a stick. "Maybe in Westland, too. Your brother seems close to outlawing fire. Maybe . . ."

He cut her off. "Our mother was burned to death in a fire." His tone was a hot warning. "That's why Michael is concerned about fire. That's the only reason. And he never said anything about outlawing it, only that he wanted to do something so others wouldn't be hurt like she was. There's nothing wrong with wanting people not to be hurt."

She looked up at him from under her eyebrows. "He didn't seem to care about hurting you."

Richard let his anger die as he took a deep breath. "I know it seemed that way, but you don't understand him. That's just his way. I know it isn't his intention to hurt me." Richard pulled his knees up and folded his arms across them. "After our mother died, Michael spent more and more time with his friends. He would make friends with anyone he thought was important. Some of them were pompous and arrogant. Father didn't like some of Michael's friends, and told him so. They would argue about it.

"One time Father came home with a vase that had these little figures sculpted around the top, like they were dancing on the rim. He was proud of it. He said it was old, and he thought he could get a gold piece for it. Michael said he could get more. They argued, and finally Father let Michael take the vase to sell. Michael came back and threw four gold pieces on the table. My father just stared at them for the longest time. Then he said, in a real quiet voice, that the vase wasn't worth four gold pieces, and wanted to know what Michael had told the people. Michael said he told them what they wanted to hear. Father reached out to pick up the four coins, and Michael slapped his hand over them. He picked up three and said only one was for my father, because one was all he expected to get. Then he said, 'That is the value of my friends, George.'

"That was the first time Michael called him 'George.' My father never let him sell anything for him again.

"But do you know what Michael did with the money? The next time my father left on a trip, he paid off most of the family debts. He didn't even buy anything for himself.

"Sometimes Michael is crude in the way he does things, like today when he told everyone about our mother, and pointed at me, but I know . . . I know that he has everyone's best interests at heart. He doesn't want anyone hurt by fire. That's all, he just doesn't want anyone to go through what we did. He is only trying to do what is best for everyone."

Kahlan didn't look up. She pushed at the dirt a moment more and then tossed the stick in the fire. "I'm sorry, Richard. I shouldn't be so suspicious. I know how much it hurts to lose your mother. I'm sure you're right." Finally, she looked up. "Forgive me?"

Richard smiled and gave her a nod. "Of course. I guess if I had been through all you have, I would be quick to think the worst, too. I'm sorry I jumped on you. If you will forgive my tone, I'll let you finish the soup."

She nodded her agreement with a smile as he handed her the last of the soup.

He wanted to hear the rest of her story, but he waited and watched her eat for a while before he asked, "So have the D'Haran forces conquered all of the Midlands?"

"The Midlands is a big place; the People's Peace Army occupies only a few of the larger cities. People in many areas ignore the alliance. Rahl does not really care. He considers it a petty problem. His attention has been diverted to something else. The wizards found out his real goal was the magic the great wizard had warned the council about, the magic they had mishandled for their own avarice. With the magic Darken Rahl seeks, he will be master of all, without having to fight anyone.

"Five of the wizards realized they had been wrong, that the great wizard was right after all. The sought to gain redemption in his eyes, and save the Midlands, and Westland, from what will happen if Darken Rahl gains the magic he seeks. So they searched for the great wizard, but Rahl hunts him also."

"You said five wizards. How many are there?"

"There were seven: the great wizard and his six students. The old one has vanished; one of the others sold his services to a queen, a very dishonorable thing for a wizard to do." She paused, considering that a moment. "And as I told you before, the five others are dead. Before they died they had the whole of the Midlands searched, but the great one was not to be found. He is not in the Midlands."

"So they believed him to be in Westland?"

Kahlan dropped the spoon in the empty pot. "Yes. He is here."

"And they thought this great wizard could stop Darken Rahl, even though they could not?" Something was wrong with this story, and Richard wasn't sure he wanted to know what was coming next.

"No," she said after a pause, "he does not have the power to go against Darken Rahl either. What they wanted, what we need to save and keep us all from what will be, is for the great wizard to make the appointment only he can make."

By the care with which she was choosing her words, he knew she was dancing around secrets he was not to ask about, so he didn't, and instead asked, "Why didn't they come after him themselves, and ask him to do it?"

"Because they feared he would say no, and they did not have the power to force him."

"Five wizards did not have the power of this one?"

She shook her head with a sad smile. "They were his students, ones who wanted to be wizards. They were not born wizards, born with the gift. The great one was born to a father who was a wizard and a mother who was a sorceress. It is in his blood, not just his head. They could never be the wizard he is. They simply did not have the power to make him do what they wanted." She fell silent.

"And . . ." He didn't say anything else. With his silence he let her know his next question, and that he would have the answer to it.

At last, she gave him the answer in a soft whisper.

"And so they sent me, because I do."

The fire crackled and hissed. He could feel the tension in her, and he knew she had gone as far with that answer as she would on the subject, so he remained still to let her feel safe. Without looking over, he put his hand on her forearm, and she put her other hand over his.

"How are you to know this wizard?"

"I only know I must find him, and soon, or we are all lost."

Richard thought in silence. "Zedd will help us," he said at last. "He's a cloud reader. Finding lost people is what a cloud reader does."

Kahlan gave him a suspicious look. "That sounds like magic. There is not supposed to be any magic in Westland."

"He says it's not; that anyone can learn. He's always trying to teach me. He mocks me whenever I say it looks like it will rain. His eyes get real big and he says, 'Magic! You must have magic, my boy, to read the clouds and know the future so.' "

Kahlan laughed. It was a good sound to hear. He didn't want to press her further even though the weave of her story had many loose threads; there was much she wasn't telling him. At least he knew more than he did before. The important thing was to find the wizard and then get away; another quad would be coming for her. They would have to go west while the wizard did whatever it was he had to do.

She opened her waist pouch and pulled something out. Untying a string, she laid back the folds of a waxed cloth that held a tan substance. Dipping her finger in it, she turned to him. "This will help the fly bites heal. Turn your head."

The ointment soothed the sting. He recognized the fragrances of some of the plants and herbs it was made from. Zedd had taught him to make a similar ointment, but with aum, that would take pain from flesh wounds. When finished with him, she put some on herself. He held out his sore red hand.

"Here, put some on this, too."

"Richard! What have you done?"

"I was stuck by a thorn, this morning."

She dabbed the ointment carefully on his wound. "I have never seen a thorn do this."

"It was a big thorn. I'm sure I'll be better by morning."

The ointment didn't help the pain as much as he had hoped, but he told her that it did, not wanting to worry her. His hand was nothing compared to the things she had to worry about. He watched as she retied the string around the little package and replaced it in her waist pouch. Her forehead was creased in thought.

"Richard, are you afraid of magic?"

He thought carefully before answering. "I was always fascinated by it; it sounded exciting. But now I know there is magic to fear. But I would guess it's like people: some you stay clear of and some you are fortunate to know."

Kahlan smiled, apparently satisfied with his answer. "Richard, before I can sleep, there is something I must tend to. It is a creature of magic. If you would not be afraid, I will let you see it. The opportunity is a rare one. Few have ever seen it, and few ever will. But you must promise me you will leave and take a walk when I ask, and not ask me any more questions when you return. I am very tired and must sleep."

Richard smiled at the honor. "Promise."

Opening her waist pouch once more, Kahlan withdrew a small round bottle with a stopper. Blue and silver lines spiraled around the fat part. There was light inside.

Her green eyes came to his. "The creature is a night wisp. Her name is Shar. A night wisp cannot be seen in the day, only at night. Shar is part of the magic that helped me cross the boundary; she was my guide. Without her, I would have been lost."

Kahlan's eyes filled with tears, but her voice remained steady and calm. "Tonight, she dies. She can live no longer away from her home place and the others of her kind, and she does not have the strength to cross the boundary again. Shar has sacrificed her life to help me because if Darken Rahl succeeds, all her kind, among others, will perish."

Pulling the stopper free, Kahlan placed the little bottle in the flat of her palm and held it out between them.

A tiny flare of light lifted clear of the bottle, floating up into the cool, dim air of the wayward pine, giving everything a silvery cast. The light softened as the wisp came to a stop in the air between them, hovering. Richard was astonished. His mouth hung open as he watched, transfixed.

"Good evening, Richard Cypher," it said in a tiny little voice.

"Good evening to you, Shar." His own voice was not much more than a whisper.

"Thank you for helping Kahlan today. In so doing you are also helping my kind. If you ever need the help of the night wisps, say my name and they will help you, for no enemy may know it."

"Thank you, Shar, but the Midlands are the last place I would want to go. I'll help Kahlan find the wizard, but then I must take us west and get us safely away from those who would kill us."

The night wisp seemed to turn in the air for a time, considering. The silvery light felt warm and safe on his face.

"If that is what you wish, then you must do so," Shar said. Richard felt relieved. The tiny point of light spun in the air before them again.

Shar spun to a stop. "But know this; Darken Rahl hunts you both. He will not rest. He will not stop. If you run, he will find you. There is no doubt of that. You have no defense against him. He will kill you both. Soon."

Richard's mouth was so dry he could hardly swallow. At least the gar would have been quick, he thought, and then it would be over. "Shar, isn't there a way for us to escape?"

The light spun again, making flashes on his face and the branches of the wayward pine.

Shar stopped again. "If your back is to him, your eyes will not be. He will get you. He enjoys it."

Richard stared. "But . . . is there nothing we can do?"

The tiny point of light spun again, coming closer to him this time before stopping. "Better question, Richard Cypher. The answer you want is within yourself. You must seek it. You must seek it or he will kill you both. Soon."

"How soon?" His voice turned harder; he couldn't help himself. The light backed away a little as it spun. He would not let this opportunity pass without finding out at least something he could hold on to.

The night wisp stopped. "The first day of winter, Richard Cypher. When the sun is in the sky. If Darken Rahl does not kill you before then, and if he is not stopped, then on the first day of winter when the sun is in the sky, my kind will all die. You both will die. He will enjoy it."

Richard tried to decide the best way to question a spinning point of light. "Shar, Kahlan is trying to save the others of your kind. I am trying to help her. You are giving your life to help her. If we fail, everyone dies, you just said so. Please, is there anything you can tell me to help us against Darken Rahl?"

The light spun and went in a little circle around the inside of the wayward pine, bringing light to the areas it went near. It stopped again in front of him.

"Already told you the answer. It is in you. Seek it or die. Sorry, Richard Cypher. Want to help. Don't know the answer. Just that it is in you. Sorry sorry."

Richard nodded, running his fingers through his hair. He didn't know who was more frustrated, Shar or himself. Glancing over, he saw Kahlan sitting calmly, watching the night wisp. Shar spun and waited.

"All right, can you tell me why he's trying to kill me? Is it because I help Kahlan, or is there another reason?"

Shar came close. "Other reasons? Secrets?"

"What!" Richard jumped to his feet. The night wisp followed him up.

"Don't know why. Sorry. Just that he will."

"What's the wizard's name?"

"Good question, Richard Cypher. Sorry. Don't know."

Richard sat back down and put his face in his hands. Shar spun, throwing off shafts of light, and flew in slow circles around his head. Somehow he knew she was trying to comfort him, and that she was near her end. She was dying, and she was trying to comfort him. He tried to swallow back the lump in his throat, so he could talk.

"Shar, thank you for helping Kahlan. My life, as short as it seems it will be, has already been made longer because she saved me from doing something foolish today. My life is also better for knowing her. Thank you for helping bring my friend safely through the boundary." His vision turned watery.

The night wisp floated to him and touched against his forehead. Her voice seemed to be as much in his head as in his ears.

"I am sorry, Richard Cypher. I do not know the answers that would save you. If I did, please believe I would give them eagerly. But I know the good in you. I believe in you. I do know that you have within you what you must to succeed. There will be times when you doubt yourself. Do not give up. Remember then that I believe in you, that I know you can accomplish what you must. You are a rare person, Richard Cypher. Believe in yourself. And protect Kahlan."

He realized his eyes were closed. Tears were running down freely, and the lump in his throat kept catching his breath.

"There are no gars about. Please let me be alone with Kahlan now. My time comes."

Richard nodded. "Good-bye, Shar. It has been my deep honor to have known you."

He left without looking at either of them.

After he was gone, the night wisp floated to Kahlan and addressed her properly.

"Mother Confessor, my time passes soon. Why have you not told him what you are?"

Kahlan's shoulders were slumped, and her hands nested in her lap as she stared into the fire. "Shar, I cannot, not yet."

"Confessor Kahlan, that is not fair. Richard Cypher is your friend."

Tears began rolling down her face. "Don't you see? That is why I cannot tell him. If I tell him, he will no longer be my friend, will no longer care for me. You cannot know what it is like to be a Confessor, to have everyone fear you. He looks into my eyes, Shar. Not many have ever dared that. No one could ever look into me the way he does. His eyes make me feel safe. He makes my heart smile."

"Others might tell him before you do, Confessor Kahlan. That would be worse."

She looked up at the night wisp, her eyes wet. "I will tell him before that happens."

"You play a dangerous game, Confessor Kahlan," Shar warned. "He could fall in love with you first. Then your telling would hurt him unforgivably."

"I won't let that happen."

"You will choose him?"

"No!"

The night wisp spun back at the sound of Kahlan's shriek, then slowly came back by her face. "Confessor Kahlan, you are the last of your kind. Darken Rahl has killed all the others. Even your sister, Dennee. You are the Mother Confessor. You must choose a mate."

"I could not do that to someone I cared for. No Confessor would," she sobbed.

"Sorry, Mother Confessor. It is for you to choose."

Kahlan pulled her legs up, wrapped her arms around them, and rested her forehead against her knees. Her shoulders heaved as she cried, her thick hair cascading down to encircle her. Shar flew slowly around her head, throwing off shafts of silvery light, comforting her companion. She continued to circle until Kahlan's weeping slowed and finally stopped. When it did, Shar returned to hover in front of her.

"Hard to be Mother Confessor. Sorry."

"Hard," Kahlan agreed.

"Much on your shoulders."

"Much," Kahlan agreed again.

The night wisp landed lightly on the woman's shoulder and rested there quietly while Kahlan watched the fire glow with small slow flames. After a time the night wisp rose from her shoulder and floated to a spot in the air in front of her.

"Wish to stay with you more. Good times. Wish to stay with Richard Cypher. Asks good questions. But I cannot hold on longer. Sorry. I die."

"You have my word, Shar, that I will give my own life, if necessary, to stop Darken Rahl. To save your kind and the others."

"I believe in you, Confessor Kahlan. Help Richard." Shar came closer. "Please. Before I die. Touch me?"

Kahlan pushed herself away from the wisp until her back was against the trunk of the tree. "No ... please ... no," she implored, shaking her head. "Don't ask me to do that." Her eyes filled with tears again. She put her trembling fingers to her lips, trying to hold back the crying.

Shar came forward. "Please, Mother Confessor. I feel such pain of aloneness away from the others. I will never share their company again. It hurts so. I pass now. Please. Use your power. Touch me and let me drink in the sweet agony. Let me die with the taste of love. I have forfeited my life to help you. I have asked nothing else of you. Please?"

Shar's light was growing dimmer, fainter. Kahlan, crying, held her left hand over her mouth. At last, she reached out with her right hand, until her trembling fingers touched the wisp.

All about there was thunder but no sound. The violent impact to the air jolted the wayward pine, causing a rain of dead needles, some flaring when they touched the fire. Shar's dim silvery color changed to a pink glow, growing in intensity.

Shar's voice was faint. "Thank you, Kahlan. Good-bye, my love."

The spark of light and life faded and was gone.

After the thunder without sound, Richard waited for a time before he returned to her. Kahlan sat with her arms around her legs and her chin resting on her knees as she stared into the fire.

"Shar?" he asked.

"She is gone," came the answer in a distant voice.

He nodded and, taking her arm, led her to the mat of dry grass and laid her down. She went without resistance or comment. He put the blanket over her and piled on some of the dry grass to help keep her warm through the night, then burrowed himself into it next to her. Kahlan turned on her side, away from him, and pushed her shoulders back against him the way a child would put its back to a parent when peril approached. He sensed it, too. Something was coming for them. Something deadly.

Already, she was asleep. He knew he should feel cold, but he didn't. His hand throbbed. He felt warm. Richard lay there, thinking about the thunder without sound. He wondered what she would do to make the great wizard do what she wanted. The idea frightened him. Before he could worry more he, too, was asleep.

CHAPTER 6

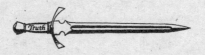

BY NOON THE NEXT day, Richard knew the bite of the vine was bringing on a fever. He had no appetite. At times he was unbearably hot, sweat making his clothes stick to his skin; then he would shiver with chills. His head pounded in a way that made him sick to his stomach. There was nothing he could do about it, except seek Zedd's help, and since they were nearly there he decided not to tell Kahlan. Dreams had troubled his sleep, whether from the fever or the things he had learned, he didn't know. What Shar had told him was the most disturbing: seek the answer or die.

The sky was thinly overcast, the cold gray light foretelling the coming of winter. Trees grown large and close held back the breeze and its chill, making the trail a quiet sanctuary filled with the aromatic fragrance of balsam fir: a refuge from winter's breath above.

Crossing a small brook near a beaver pond, they came upon a patch of late wildflowers, their yellow and pale blue blossoms blanketing the ground in a sparsely wooded hollow. Kahlan stopped to pick some. Finding a scoop-shaped piece of dead wood, she started arranging the flowers within the hollow of the wood. Richard thought she must be hungry. He found an apple tree he knew to be nearby and filled his pack half full while she bent to her task. It was always a good idea to bring food when going to see Zedd.

Richard finished before Kahlan, and waited, leaning against a log, wondering what she was doing. When she was satisfied with the arrangement, she lifted the hem of her dress and knelt beside the pond, floating the wood out onto the water. She sat back on her boots with her hands folded in her lap, watching for a time as the small raft of flowers drifted out onto the quiet water. When she turned and saw him leaning against the log, she stood and joined him.

"An offering to the spirits of our two mothers," she explained. "To ask their protection and help in finding the wizard." Kahlan looked to his face, and concern came over her features. "Richard, what's wrong?"

He held out an apple. "Nothing. Here, eat this."

She slapped his hand away and in a blink had him by the throat with her other hand. Anger flared in her green eyes. "Why would you do this?" she demanded.

Shock raced through his mind. He went rigid. Something told him not to move. "Don't you like apples? I'm sorry, I'll find you something else to eat."

The fury in her eyes faltered, changing to doubt. "What did you call them?"

"Apples," he said, still not moving. "Don't you know what apples are? They're good to eat, I promise. What did you think they were?"

Her hand loosened its grip a little. "You eat these . . . apples?"

Richard kept himself still. "Yes. All the time."

Embarrassment replaced her anger. She released his throat and put her fingers over her mouth. Her eyes were wide. "Richard, I'm so sorry. I didn't know you could eat these things. In the Midlands, any red fruit is deadly poison. I thought you meant to poison me."

Richard laughed as the tension went out in a rush. Kahlan laughed, too, while protesting that it wasn't funny. He took a bite

77

to show her, then offered her another. This time she took it, but looked at it long and hard before taking a bite.

"Umm, these things are good to eat." Kahlan's brow wrinkled. She put her hand on his forehead. "I thought there was something wrong. You are burning with fever."

"I know, but there's nothing we can do until we get to Zedd's. We're almost there."

Zedd's squat house came into sight a short distance farther up the trail. A single plank from the sod-covered roof served as a ramp for his old cat, who was better at getting up than down. White lace curtains hung on the inside of the windows, flower boxes on the outside. The flowers had dried and wilted with the passing of the season. The log walls were dull gray with age, but a bright blue door greeted visitors. Other than the door, the whole place gave the appearance of hunkering into the grasses surrounding it, of trying to go unnoticed. The house wasn't large, but it did have a porch running the length of the front.

Zedd's "reason" chair was empty. The reason chair was where Zedd sat and thought until he figured out the reason for whatever it was that had snagged his curiosity. He had once sat in the chair for three days straight, trying to figure out why people were always arguing over how many stars there were. He himself didn't care. He thought the question trivial, and he only wondered why people spent so much time debating the subject. At last he stood and pronounced that it was because anyone could express his profound conviction on the subject without fear of being proven wrong, as it was impossible to know the answer. Such fools simply didn't have to worry about contradiction when proclaiming expertise. Having settled the matter, Zedd then went in the house and ate in earnest for three solid hours.

Richard called out but received no answer. He smiled at Kahlan. "I bet I know where he is. Out back on his cloud rock, studying the latest batch of clouds."

"Cloud rock?" Kahlan asked.

"It's his favorite place to stand and watch clouds. Don't ask me why. Ever since I've known him, whenever he sees an interesting cloud, he runs out back to watch it while standing on that rock." Richard had grown up with the rock, and didn't think the behavior peculiar; it was just part of the old man.

The two of them walked through the tall, wild grasses that surrounded the house and up a rise to the top of a small barren hill, where the cloud rock sat. Zedd was standing on the flat cloud rock with his arched back to them, his spindly arms outstretched and his wavy white hair hanging away from his head as it tilted back in scrutiny.

Zedd was stark naked.

Richard rolled his eyes; Kahlan averted hers. Pale leathery skin draped loosely over a collection of bony projections made him look as frail as a dry stick. Richard knew him to be anything but frail, though. His bottom lacked any padding whatsoever, leaving the skin there to droop.

One scrawny finger rose, pointing skyward. "I knew you were coming, Richard." His voice was as thin as the rest of him.

The plain, unadorned robes that were his only clothes lay in a heap behind him. Richard bent and picked them up while Kahlan, smiling, turned around to avoid any further embarrassment. "Zedd, we have company. Put on your clothes."

"Do you know how I knew you were coming?" Still he did not move or turn.

"I would say it has something to do with a cloud that has been following me for the last few days. Here, let me help get this on you."

Zedd spun around, arms flailing in excitement. "Days! Bags! Richard, that cloud has been following you for three weeks! Ever since your father was killed! I haven't seen you since George's death. Where have you been? I've been looking all over for you. I can find a lost bug in a barn easier than I can find you when you get it in your head not to be found!"

"I've been busy. Hold your arms up so I can help you put this on." Richard shoved the robes over Zedd's outstretched arms and helped pull the folds down the bony body while the old man shrugged his way into the outfit.

"Busy! Too busy to look up once in a while? Bags, Richard, do you know where that cloud is from?" Zedd's eyes were wide with concern as his forehead wrinkled above his raised brow.

"Don't curse," Richard said. "And I would say the cloud is from D'Hara."

79

Zedd's arms shot back into the air. "D'Hara! Yes! Very good, my boy! Tell me, what gave it away for you. Was it the texture? The density?" Zedd was becoming ever more excited as he wiggled around in his robe, dissatisfied with the way it twisted.

"Neither. It's an assumption I make based on independent information. Zedd, as I said before, we have company."

"Yes, yes, I heard you the first time." He waved the matter away with his hand. "Independent information, you say." He drew his forefinger and thumb down his smooth jaw. His hazel eyes lit up. "That's very good too. Very good, indeed! Did this information also tell you this is bad business? Well, yes, of course it did," he said, in answer to his own question. "Why are you sweating?" He put his twiglike fingers to Richard's forehead. "You have a fever," he pronounced. "Did you bring me anything to eat?"

Richard already had an apple at hand; he knew Zedd would be hungry. Zedd was always hungry. The old man bit into the apple with a vengeance.

"Zedd, please listen to me. I'm in trouble, and I need your help."

Zedd put his scrawny fingers on the top of Richard's head while he chewed, and with his thumb, lifted an eyelid. Leaning forward, he thrust his sharply featured face close to Richard's and peered into his eye, then repeated the procedure on the other eye. "I always listen to you, Richard." He lifted Richard's arm by the wrist, feeling his pulse. "And I agree, you are in trouble. In three hours, maybe four, no more, you will be unconscious."

Richard was taken aback; Kahlan looked worried, too. Zedd knew about fevers, among other things, and did not make precise pronouncements like this that ever proved in error. Richard's legs had felt weak since he awoke with chills, and he knew he was getting worse. "Can you do anything to help?"

"Probably, but it depends on what caused it. Now, stop being rude and introduce me to your girlfriend."

"Zedd, this is my *friend*, Kahlan Amnell. . . ."

The old man peered closely into his eyes. "Oh, was I wrong? She is not a girl then?" Zedd cackled. He smiled over the trick as he shuffled to Kahlan, bowed dramatically at the waist, lifted her hand only a little, kissed it lightly, and said, "Zeddicus Zu'l Zorander, humbly at your whim, my dear young lady." He straightened himself up to have a look at her face. When their eyes met, his smile evaporated and his eyes went wide. His keen features transformed to anger. He released her hand as if he had discovered himself holding a poisonous snake. Zedd spun to Richard.

"What are you doing with this creature!"

Kahlan was calm and impassive. Richard was aghast. "Zedd . . ."

"Has she touched you?"

"Well, I . . ." Richard was trying to remember the times she had touched him, when Zedd cut him off again.

"No, of course not. I can see she hasn't. Richard, do you know what she is?" He turned to her. "She's a . . ."

Kahlan gave Zedd a look of such cold danger that it froze him in place.

Richard kept his voice calm, but firm. "I know exactly what she is: she is my friend. A friend who yesterday saved me from getting killed as my father was, and again saved me from being killed by some beast called a gar." Kahlan's expression relaxed. The old man stared at her a little longer before turning to Richard. "Zedd, Kahlan is my friend. We are both in a lot of trouble and need to help each other."

Zedd stood in silence, searching Richard's eyes. He nodded. "Trouble indeed."

"Zedd, we need your help. Please?" Kahlan came and stood next to him. "We don't have much time." Zedd didn't look inclined to be any part of it, but Richard went on anyway, watching Zedd's eyes. "Yesterday, after I found her, she was attacked by a quad. Another will come soon." He saw what he was looking for; a quick flash of hatred, softening into empathy.

Zedd looked to Kahlan as if seeing her for the first time. They faced each other for a long while. At the mention of the quad the look on Kahlan's face became one of torment. Zedd came forward and put his spindly arms around her protectively, holding her head to his shoulder. She reached around and embraced him gratefully, burying her face in his robes to conceal her tears. "It's all right, dear one, you are safe here," he said softly. "Let's go down to the house and you can tell me of this trouble, and then we must tend to Richard's fever." She nodded against his shoulder.

Kahlan parted from him. "Zeddicus Zu'l Zorander. I have never heard such a name."

He smiled proudly, his thin lips pushing back his cheeks into deep wrinkles. "I'm sure you haven't, dear one, I'm sure you haven't. By the way, can you cook?" He put his arm around her shoulder, holding her tight as he started walking her down the hill. "I'm hungry and haven't had a suitably cooked meal in years." He glanced back. "Come along, Richard, while you still can."

"If you help Richard's fever, I will make you a big pot of spice soup," she offered.

"Spice soup!" Zedd swooned. "I haven't had a proper spice soup in years. Richard is lousy at making it."

Richard trudged behind, the emotional strain having taken much of his remaining strength. The casual way Zedd was handling the fever scared him. He knew this was his old friend's way of trying not to frighten him about the seriousness of the matter. He could feel his pulse in his sore hand.

Since Zedd was from the Midlands, Richard had thought he could gain his compassion with the mention of the quad. Richard was relieved, if somewhat surprised, at how the two of them were suddenly so amiable. He reached up as he walked, touching the tooth for reassurance.

He was, however, quite disturbed by what he now knew.

Near a back corner of the house sat a table where Zedd liked to take his meals in good weather. It afforded him the opportunity to keep an eye to the clouds while he ate. Zedd sat them down together on a bench while he went inside and brought out carrots, berries, cheese, and apple juice, putting them on the wooden tabletop worn smooth with years of use, then sat himself on the bench opposite them. He gave Richard a mug of something brown and thick that smelled of almonds and told him to drink it slowly.

His eyes came to Richard. "Tell me of the trouble."

Richard related how he was bitten by a vine, and told Zedd about seeing the thing in the sky, seeing Kahlan at Trunt Lake, and being followed by the four men. He told the whole story with every detail he could remember. He knew Zedd liked to have every detail, no matter how unimportant. Occasionally Richard stopped to take a sip from the mug. Kahlan ate some carrots and berries, and drank the apple juice, but she pushed away the plate with the cheese. She nodded or offered help when he couldn't remember a particular point. The only thing he left out was the story Kahlan had told him of the history of the three lands and about Darken Rahl taking over the Midlands. He thought it better that she tell it in her own words. At the end, Zedd made him go back to the beginning, wanting to know what Richard had been doing in the high Ven in the first place.

"When I went to my father's house after the murder, I looked in the message jar. It was about the only thing not broken. Inside was a piece of vine. For the last three weeks, I've been looking for the vine, trying to find out what my father's last message meant. And when I found it, well, that's the thing that bit me." He was glad to be finished; his tongue felt thick.

Zedd bit off a chunk of carrot while thinking. "What did the vine look like?"

"It was . . . Wait, I still have it in my pocket." He took out the sprig and plunked it down on the table.

"Bags!" Zedd whispered. "That's a snake vine!"

Richard felt a shock of icy cold sweep through him. He knew the name from the secret book. He hoped against hope it did not mean what he feared it did.

Zedd sat back. "Well, the good part is now I know the root to use to cure the fever. The bad part is I have to find it." Zedd asked Kahlan to tell her part but to make it short, as there were things he must do and not much time. Richard thought about the story she had told in the wayward pine the night before, and wondered how she could possibly make it shorter.

"Darken Rahl, son of Panis Rahl, has put the three boxes of Orden in play," Kahlan said simply. "I have come in search of the great wizard."

Richard was thunderstruck.

From the secret book, the Book of Counted Shadows, the book his father had had him commit to memory before they destroyed it, the line jumped into his mind: *And when the three boxes of Orden are put into play, the snake vine shall grow.* Richard's worst nightmares—everyone's worst nightmares—were coming to pass.

CHAPTER 7

PAIN AND DIZZINESS FROM the fever made Richard only dimly aware that his head had sunk to the table. He groaned while his mind spun with the implications of what Kahlan had told Zedd; of the prophecy of the secret Book of Counted Shadows come to life. Then Zedd was at his side, lifting him, telling Kahlan to help get him into the house. As he walked with their help, the ground slipped this way and that, making it difficult to catch it with his feet. Then they were laying him down on a bed, covering him up. He knew they were talking, but he couldn't make sense of the words, which slurred in his mind.

Darkness sucked his mind in; then there was light. He seemed to float back up, only to spiral down again. He wondered who he was and what was happening. Time passed as the room spun and rolled and tilted. He gripped the bed to keep from being flung off. Sometimes he knew where he was, and tried desperately to hold on to what he knew . . . only to slip away again into blackness.

He became aware again, realizing that time had passed, though he didn't have any idea how much. Was it dark? Maybe it was just that the curtains were pulled. Someone, he realized, was putting a cool, wet cloth on his forehead. His mother smoothed back his hair. Her touch felt comforting, soothing. He could almost make out her face. She was so good, she always took such good care of him.

Until she died. He wanted to cry. She was dead. Still, she smoothed his hair. That couldn't be; it had to be someone else. But who? Then he remembered. It was Kahlan. He spoke her name.

Kahlan was smoothing his hair. "I am here."

It came back to him, rushing back in a torrent: the murder of his father, the vine that bit him, Kahlan, the four men on the cliff, his brother's speech; someone waiting for him at his house, the gar, the night wisp telling him to seek the answer or die; what Kahlan said, that the three boxes of Orden were in play; and his secret, the Book of Counted Shadows. . . .

He remembered how his father had taken him to the secret place in the woods, and had told him how he had saved the Book of Counted Shadows from the peril it was in from the beast that guarded it until its master could come. How he had brought it with him to Westland to keep it from those covetous hands, hands that the keeper of the book didn't know threatened. His father had told him how there was danger as long as the book existed, but he couldn't destroy the knowledge in it; he had no right. It belonged to the keeper of the book, and it must be kept safe until it could be returned. The only way to do that was to commit the book to memory, and then burn it. Only in that way could the knowledge be preserved, but not stolen, as it otherwise surely would be.

His father chose Richard. That it was to be Richard and not Michael was for reasons of his own. No one could know of the book, not even Michael; only the keeper of the book, no one else, only the keeper. He said Richard might never find the keeper, and in that case he was to pass the book on to his child, and then that child to his own, and so on, for as long as was necessary. His father couldn't tell him who the keeper of the book was, as he didn't know. Richard asked how he was to know the keeper, but his father said only that he would have to find the answer himself, and not to tell anyone, ever, except the keeper. His father told Richard he was not to tell his own brother, or even his best friend, Zedd.

Richard swore on his life.

His father had never once looked in the book, only Richard. Day after day, week after week, with breaks only when he traveled, his father took him to the secret place deep in the woods, where he sat and watched Richard reading the book, over and over. Michael was usually off with his friends, and had no interest in going into the woods even if he was at home, and it wasn't uncommon for Richard not to visit Zedd when his father was home, so neither had reason to know of the frequent trips to the woods.

Richard would write down what he memorized and check it against the book. Each time, his father burned the papers and had him do it again. His father apologized every day for the burden he was placing on Richard. He asked for forgiveness from his son at the end of every day in the woods.

Richard never resented having to learn the book; he considered it an honor to be entrusted by his father. He wrote the book from beginning to end a hundred times without error before he satisfied himself that he could never forget a single word. He knew by reading it that any word left out would spell disaster.

When he assured his father that it was committed to memory, they put the book back in the hiding place in the rocks and left it for three years. After that time, when Richard was beyond his middle teens, they returned one fall day and his father said if Richard could write the whole book, without a single mistake, they could both be satisfied it was learned perfectly and they would burn the book. Richard wrote without hesitation from beginning to end. It was perfect.

Together they built a fire, stacking on more than enough wood, until the heat drove them back. His father handed him the book, and told him that if he was sure, to throw the book into the fire. Richard held the Book of Counted Shadows in the crook of his arm, running his fingers over the leather cover. He held his father's trust in his arms, held the trust of everyone in his arms, and he felt the weight of the burden. He gave the book to the fire. In that moment, he was no longer a child.

The flames swirled around the book, embracing, caressing,

consuming. Colors and forms spiraled up, and a roaring cry came forth. Strange beams of light shot skyward. Wind made their cloaks flap as the fire sucked leaves and twigs into itself, adding to the flames and heat. Phantoms appeared, spreading their arms as if being fed by the blaze, their voices racing away on the wind. The two of them stood as if turned to stone, unable to move, unable even to turn away from the sight. Searing heat turned to wind as cold as the deepest winter night, sending chills up their spines, taking their breath from them. Then the cold was gone and the fire turned to a white light that consumed everything in its brightness, as if they were standing in the sun. Just as suddenly, it was gone. In its place, silence. The fire was out. Wisps of smoke rose slowly from the blackened wood into the autumn air. The book was gone.

Richard knew what he had seen; he had seen magic.

Richard felt a hand resting on his shoulder and opened his eyes. It was Kahlan. In the firelight coming through the doorway he could see she was sitting in a chair pulled close to his bed. Zedd's big old coon cat was curled up sleeping in her lap.

"Where's Zedd?" he asked, sleepy-eyed.

"He has gone to find the root you need." Her voice was soft and calming. "It has been dark for hours now, but he said not to be concerned if it took him time to find the root. He said that you would go in and out of sleep but would be safe until he returned. He said the drink he gave you before would keep you safe until he is back."

Richard realized, for the first time, that she was the most beautiful woman he had ever seen. Her hair was tumbled down around her face and shoulders, and he wanted very much to touch it, but didn't. It was enough to feel her hand on his shoulder, to know she was there and that he was not alone.

"How do you feel?" Her voice was so soft, so gentle, that he couldn't imagine why Zedd had been afraid of her.

"I would rather fight another quad than another snake vine."

She smiled her special smile, her private smile of sharing

something with him, as she wiped his brow with the cloth. He reached up and grabbed her wrist. She stopped and looked into his eyes.

"Kahlan, Zedd is my friend of many years. He is like a second father to me. Promise me you won't do anything to hurt him. I could not bear it."

She looked at him reassuringly. "I like him, too. Very much. He is a good man, just as you said. I have no desire to hurt him. Only to seek his help in finding the wizard."

He gripped her wrist tighter. "Promise me."

"Richard, everything will be fine. He will help us."

He remembered her fingers on his throat and the look in her eyes when she thought he was trying to poison her with an apple. "Promise me."

"I have already made promises, to others, some of whom have given their lives. I have responsibilities to the lives of others. Many others."

"Promise me."

She put her other hand on the side of his face. "I am sorry, Richard, I cannot."

He released her wrist, turned, and closed his eyes as she took her hand from his face. He thought about the book, all that it meant, and realized he was making a selfish request. Would he trick her to save Zedd, only to have him die with them? Would he doom all the others to death or slavery just to see his friend live a couple more months? Could he condemn her to death, too, for nothing? He felt ashamed at his own stupidity. He had no right to ask her to make such a promise. It would be wrong for her to do so. He was glad she had not lied to him. But he knew that just because Zedd had asked about the trouble they were in did not mean he would help with anything to do from across the boundary.

"Kahlan, this fever is making me foolish. Please forgive me. I have never met another with your courage. I know you are trying to save us all. Zedd will help us; I will see to it. Promise me only that you will wait until I am better. Give me the chance to convince him."

She squeezed her hand on his shoulder. "That is a promise I

can make. I know you care about your friend; I would despair if you didn't. That does not make you foolish. Rest now."

He tried not to close his eyes, since when he did, everything started spinning uncontrollably. But talking had sapped his strength, and soon the blackness pulled him back in. His thoughts were once again sucked into the void. Sometimes he came partway back and wandered in troubled dreams; sometimes he wandered in places empty even of illusion.

The cat came awake, his ears perking up. Richard slept on. Sounds that only the cat could hear made him jump off Kahlan's lap, trot to the door, and sit on his haunches, waiting. Kahlan waited, too, and since the cat didn't raise his fur, she stayed by Richard. A thin voice came from outside.

"Cat? Cat! Where have you gotten to? Well, you can just stay out here then." The door squeaked open. "There you are." The cat ran out the doorway. "Suit yourself," Zedd called after him. "How is Richard?" he called to her.

When he came into the room, Kahlan answered from the chair. "He came awake several times, but he is sleeping now. Did you find the root you need?"

"I wouldn't be here otherwise. Did he have anything to say when he was awake?"

Kahlan smiled up at the old man. "Just that he was worried about you."

He turned and went back into the front room, grumbling. "Not without good reason."

Sitting at the table, he peeled the roots, cut them into thin wafers, put the wafers into a pot with some water, and then hung the pot on the crane over the fire. He threw the peels and then two sticks of wood into the fire before going to the cupboard and pulling down a number of different-sized jars. Without hesitation he selected first one jar, then another, pouring different-colored powders into a black stone mortar. With a white pestle, he ground the reds, blues, yellows, browns, and greens together until it was all the color of dry mud. After licking the end of his finger, he dipped it in the mortar to collect a sample. He put the finger to his tongue for a taste and lifted an eyebrow while he smacked his lips and pondered. At last he smiled and nodded in satisfaction. He poured the powder into the pot, blending it in with a spoon from a hook at the side of the fireplace. He stirred slowly while watching the concoction bubble. For nearly two hours he stirred and watched. When at last he determined that the work was done, he plunked the pot on the table to cool.

Zedd collected a bowl and cloth and after a while called to Kahlan to come help him. She came quickly to his side and he instructed her how to hold the cloth over the bowl while he poured the mixture through.

He spun his finger around in the air. "Now twist the cloth around and around to squeeze the liquid out. When it's all out, throw the cloth and its contents in the fire." She looked at him, puzzled. Zedd lifted an eyebrow. "The part left in there is poison. Richard should be awake any time now; then we give him the liquid in the bowl. You keep squeezing. I will check on him."

Zedd went into the bedroom, bent over Richard, and found him to be deeply unconscious. He turned and saw that Kahlan's back was to him as she worked at her task. He bent over, placing a middle finger to Richard's forehead. Richard's eyes snapped open.

"Dear one," Zedd called into the other room, "we are in luck. He has just come awake. Bring the bowl."

Richard blinked. "Zedd? Are you all right? Is everything all right?"

"Yes, yes, everything is fine."

Kahlan came in holding the bowl carefully, trying not to spill any. Zedd helped Richard sit up so he could drink. When he finished, Zedd helped him to lie back down.

"That will make you sleep, and break the fever. The next time you awake, you will be well, you have my word, so worry no more as you rest."

"Thank you, Zedd. . . ." Richard was asleep before he could say more.

Zedd left and then returned with a tin plate, insisting that Kahlan take the chair. "The thorn will not be able to stand the root," he explained. "It will have to leave his body." He put the plate under Richard's hand and sat down on the edge of the bed to wait. They both listened to Richard's deep breathing and the crackling of the fire from the other room; otherwise the house was still. It was Zedd who broke the silence first.

"It is dangerous for a Confessor to travel alone, dear one. Where is your wizard?"

She looked up at him with tired eyes. "My wizard sold his services to a queen."

Zedd gave a disapproving scowl. "He abandoned his responsibilities to the Confessors? What is his name?"

"Giller."

"Giller." He repeated the name with a sour expression, then leaned toward her a bit. "So why did another not come with you?"

She gave him a hard look. "Because they are all dead, at their own hands. Before they died, they all gathered and cast a web to see me safely through the boundary, with the guidance of a night wisp." Zedd stood at this news. Sadness and concern etched his face as he rubbed his chin. "You knew the wizards?" she asked.

"Yes, yes. I lived in the Midlands a long time."

"And the great one? You know him also?"

Zedd smiled, rearranged his robes, and seated himself again. "You are persistent, dear one. Yes, I knew the old wizard, once. But even if you could find him, I don't think he would have anything to do with this business. He would not be inclined to help the Midlands."

Kahlan leaned forward, taking his hands in hers. Her voice was soft but intense.

"Zedd, there are many people who disapprove of the High Council of the Midlands and its greed. They wish it were not so, but they are just common people who have no say. They only wish to live their lives in peace. Darken Rahl has taken the food that was stored for the coming winter and given it to the army. They waste it, or let it rot, or sell it back to the people they stole it from. Already there is hunger; this winter there will be death. Fire has been outlawed. People are cold.

"Rahl says it is all the great wizard's fault, for not coming forward to be put on trial as an enemy of the people. He says the wizard has brought this on them, that he is to blame. He doesn't explain how this could be, but many believe it anyway. Many believe everything Rahl says, even though what they see with their own eyes should be enough to tell them otherwise.

"The wizards were under constant threat, and forbidden by edict from using magic. They knew that sooner or later they would be used against the people. They may have made mistakes in the past, and disappointed their teacher, but the most important thing they were taught was to be protectors of the people and in no way to bring them harm. As their most loving act for the people, they gave their lives to stop Darken Rahl. I think their teacher would have been proud.

"But this is not about just the Midlands. The boundary between D'Hara and the Midlands is down, the boundary between the Midlands and Westland is failing, and soon it too will be down. The people of Westland will be taken by the very thing they fear most: magic. Terrible, frightening magic like none they have ever imagined."

Zedd showed no emotion, offered no objection or opinion, only listened. He continued to allow her to hold his hands.

"All I have said, the great wizard could have an argument for, but the fact that Darken Rahl has put the three boxes of Orden into play is something altogether different. If he succeeds, then on the first day of winter it will be too late for anyone. That includes the wizard. Rahl already searches for him; it is personal vengeance he seeks. Many have died because they could not offer his name. When Rahl opens the correct box, though, he will have unchallenged power over all things living, and then the wizard will be his. He can hide in Westland all he wants, but come the first day of winter, his hiding is over. Darken Rahl will have him."

There was bitterness in her expression. "Zedd, Darken Rahl has used quads to kill all the other Confessors. I found my sister after they were finished with her. She died in my arms. With all the others dead, that leaves only me. The wizards knew their teacher did not want to help, so they sent me as the last hope. If he is too foolish to see that in helping me, he helps himself, then I must use my power against him, to make him help."

Zedd raised an eyebrow. "And what is one dried-up old wizard to do against the power of this Darken Rahl?" He was now holding her hands in his.

"He must appoint a Seeker."

"What!" Zedd jumped to his feet. "Dear one, you don't know what you are talking about."

Confused, Kahlan leaned back a little. "What do you mean?"

"Seekers appoint themselves. The wizard just sort of recognizes what has happened, and makes it official."

"I don't understand. I thought the wizard picked the person, the right person."

Zedd sat back down, rubbing his chin. "Well, that's true in a sense, but backwards. A true Seeker, one who can make a difference, must show himself to be a Seeker. The wizard doesn't point to someone and say, 'Here is the Sword of Truth, you will be the Seeker.' He doesn't really have a choice in the matter. It isn't something you can train someone for. One should simply be a Seeker and show himself to be so by his actions. A wizard must watch a person for years to be sure. A Seeker doesn't have to be the smartest person, but he has to be the right person; he has to have the right qualities within himself. A true Seeker is a rare person.

"The Seeker is a balance point of power. The council made the appointment a political bone to be thrown to one of the sniveling dogs at their feet. It was a sought-after post because of the power a Seeker wields. But the council didn't understand: it wasn't the post that brought the power to the person, it was the person that brought the power to the post."

He edged closer to her. "Kahlan, you were born after the council took this power upon itself, so you may have been a Seeker when you were young, but in those days they were pretend Seekers; you have never seen the real thing." His eyes got round in the telling, his voice low and full of passion. "I have seen a true Seeker make a king quake in his boots with the asking of a single question. When a real Seeker draws the Sword of Truth . . ." He held his hands up and rolled his eyes in delight. "Righteous anger can be an extraordinary thing to behold." Kahlan smiled at his excitement. "It can make the good tremble with joy, and the wicked shiver in fear." The smile left his face. "But people rarely believe the truth when they see it and less so

94

when they don't want to, and that makes the position of Seeker a dangerous one. He is an obstacle to those who would subvert power. He draws lightning from many sides. Most often he stands alone, and frequently not long."

"I know the feeling well," she said, with only the hint of a smile.

Zedd leaned closer. "Against Darken Rahl, I doubt even a true Seeker would last long. And then what?"

She took up his hands again. "Zedd, we must try. It is our only chance. If we don't take it, we have none."

He sat up, pulling away from her. "Any person the wizard picks would not know the Midlands. He would have no chance there. It would be a sentence of quick death."

"That is the other reason I was sent. To be his guide, and stand with him, to offer my life if need be, to help protect him. Confessors spend their life traveling the lands. I have been almost everywhere in the Midlands. A Confessor is trained from birth in languages. She has to be, because she never knows where she will be called. I speak every major language, and most of the minor ones. And as far as drawing lightning, a Confessor draws her fair share. If we were easy to kill, Rahl would not need to send quads to get the job done. And many of them have died in the doing. I can help protect the Seeker; if need be, with my own life."

"What you propose not only would put someone's life at terrible risk, as Seeker, dear one, but yours also."

She raised an eyebrow. "I am hunted now. If you have a better way, put words to it."

Before Zedd could answer, Richard moaned. The old man looked over at him and then rose. "It is time."

Kahlan stood up next to him as he lifted Richard's arm by the wrist, holding the wounded hand over the tin plate. Blood dripped onto the plate with soft, hollow sounds. The thorn fell out with a small, wet splash. Kahlan reached for it.

Zedd grabbed her wrist. "Don't do that, dear one. Now that it has been expelled from its host, it will be anxious to have a new one. Watch."

She took her hand back as he put his bony finger on the plate several inches from the thorn. It wiggled its way toward the finger, leaving a thin trail of blood. He took his finger away and handed her the plate. "Hold it from underneath, and take it to the hearth. Put it on the fire, facedown, and leave it there."

While she did as Zedd requested, he cleaned the wound and applied a salve. When Kahlan returned, he held Richard's hand while she wrapped it. Zedd watched her hands as she worked.

"Why have you not told him what you are, that you are a Confessor?" There was a hard edge to his voice.

Hers came back in kind. "Because of the way you reacted when you recognized me as a Confessor." She paused, and the harshness left her voice. "Somehow we have become friends. I am inexperienced in that, but I am very experienced at being a Confessor. I have seen reactions like yours all my life. When I leave with the Seeker, I will tell him. Until then, I would very much like to have his friendship. Is that too much to ask, to be allowed the simple human pleasure of a friend? The friendship will end soon enough, when I tell him."

When she finished, Zedd put a finger under her chin, raising her face to his gentle smile. "When I first saw you, I reacted foolishly. Mostly to the surprise of seeing a Confessor. I had not expected ever to see one again. I quit the Midlands to be free of the magic. You were an intrusion into my solitude. I apologize for my reaction and for making you feel unwelcome. I hope I have made it up to you. I am one who has respect for the Confessors, perhaps more than you will ever know. You are a good woman, and you are welcome in my house."

Kahlan looked into his eyes a long moment. "Thank you, Zeddicus Zu'l Zorander."

Zedd's expression turned more dangerous than hers had when they had first met. She stood frozen with his finger still under her chin, afraid to move, her eyes wide.

"Know this, though, Mother Confessor." His voice was only one step above a whisper, and deadly. "This boy has been my friend a good long time. If you touch him with your power, or if you choose him, you will answer to me. And you would not like that. Do you understand?"

She swallowed hard and managed to give a weak nod. "Yes."

"Good." The danger left his face, leaving calm again in its

place. He removed his finger from under her chin, and began to turn to Richard.

Kahlan let her breath out and, not willing to be intimidated, grabbed his arm, turning him back to her. "Zedd, I would not do that to him, not because of what you said, but because I care for him. I want you to understand that."

They faced off a long while, each measuring the other. Zedd's impish smile returned, as disarming as ever.

"If offered a choice, dear one, that is the way I would prefer it."

She relaxed, satisfied at having made her point, and gave him a quick hug that was returned earnestly.

"There is one thing you have left unspoken. You have not asked for my help in finding the wizard."

"No, and for now I won't. Richard fears what I would do if you were to say no. I promised I would not ask until he has a chance to ask you first. I gave him my word."

Zedd put a bony finger to his chin. "How interesting." He laid his hand on her shoulder conspiratorially, and changed the subject. "You know, dear one, you might make a good Seeker yourself."

"Me? A woman can be Seeker?"

He lifted an eyebrow. "Of course. Some of the best Seekers have been women."

"I already have an impossible job." She frowned. "I don't need two."

Zedd chuckled, his eyes sparkling. "Perhaps you are right. Now, it's very late, dear one. Go to my bed in the next room and get yourself some needed sleep. I will sit with Richard."

"No!" She shook her head and plopped down in the chair. "I don't want to leave him for now."

Zedd shrugged. "As you wish." He walked behind her and patted her shoulder reassuringly. "As you wish." He gently reached up and put a middle finger to each of her temples, rubbing in little circles. She moaned softly as her eyes closed. "Sleep, dear one," he whispered, "sleep." She folded her arms down onto the edge of the bed, and her head sank onto her arms. She was deeply asleep. After he put a blanket over her, Zedd went to the front room and pulled open the door, looking out into the night.

"Cat! Come here, I want you." The cat came running in and rubbed himself against Zedd's legs, swishing his tail up. Zedd bent down and scratched him behind the ears. "Go in and sleep on the young woman's lap. Keep her warm." The cat padded off to the bedroom as the old man stepped out into the cold night air.

The wind whipped Zedd's robes as he walked the narrow path through the tall grass. The clouds were thin, illuminated by the moon, which gave enough light to see by, even though he didn't need it; he had walked the same route thousands of times.

"Nothing is ever easy," he muttered as he went.

Near a stand of trees he stopped, listening. Slowly, he turned about, peering into the shadows, watching the branches bend and sway in the breeze, testing the air with his nose. He searched for an alien movement.

A fly bit his neck. He swatted it angrily, picked the offender off his neck, and glared at it. "Blood fly. Bags. I thought as much," he complained.

From the brush near by, something came toward him in a terrible rush. Wings and fur and teeth came charging. Hands on his hips, Zedd waited. Just before it was on him, he held up his hand, bringing the short-tailed gar to a lurching halt. It was half again as tall as he, full grown, and twice as fierce as a long-tailed gar. The beast growled and blinked, its great muscles flexing as it fought against the force that kept it from reaching out and grabbing the old man. It was furious that it had not yet killed him.

Zedd reached up and with a crooked finger beckoned it to lean closer. The gar, panting in rage, bent toward him. Zedd jammed his finger hard under its chin.

"What is your name?" he hissed. The beast grunted twice and made a sound from deep in its throat. Zedd gave a nod. "I will remember it. Tell me, do you wish to live, or to die?" The gar struggled to back away, but was unable to. "Good. Then you will do exactly as I say. Somewhere between here and D'Hara, a quad comes this way. Hunt them and kill them. When you have done so, go back to D'Hara, to where you came from. Do these things and I will let you live, but I will remember your name, and if you fail to kill the quad, or ever come back after your task is done, I will kill you and feed you to your flies. Do you agree to my terms?" The gar grunted an acknowledgment. "Good. Then be gone." Zedd removed his finger from under the gar's chin.

Scrambling to get away, the beast flapped its wings frantically, beating down the grass as it stumbled along. At last the gar was airborne. Zedd watched it as it circled, searching for the quad. As the hunt moved steadily east, the circles seemed to get smaller until the old man could no longer see the beast. Only then did he continue on to the top of the hill.

Standing next to his cloud rock, Zedd pointed down at it and began turning his bony finger in a circle as if stirring a stew. The massive rock grated against the ground as it tried to revolve with the movement of Zedd's finger. The rock shuddered, trying to rotate its own weight. Popping and snapping, it fractured, sending hairline cracks shooting across its surface. Its trembling bulk struggled against the force being applied. The granular structure of the stone began to soften. Unable to maintain its state any longer, the texture of the rock liquefied enough to allow its mass to rotate with the movement of the finger above it. Gradually the speed of Zedd's stirring increased until light erupted from the rotating liquid rock.

The light built in intensity with the speed of Zedd's hand. As colors and sparkles of light spun, shadows and forms came into the center of the light and vanished as the fog of brightness increased. Light threatened to ignite the air about him. A dull roar, like the sound of wind rushing through a fissure, came forth. The smells of autumn changed to winter clarity, then spring's new plowed ground, summer's flowers, and back to autumn again. Clean, pure illumination chased the colors and sparkles away.

The rock abruptly solidified and Zedd stepped atop it, into the light. The brightness faded to a faint glow that swirled like smoke. Before him stood two apparitions, mere shadows of form. Where sharpness should have been, their shapes softened like a dim memory, yet they were still recognizable, and the sight of them brought a quickness to Zedd's heart.

His mother's voice came hollow and distant. "What troubles you, son? Why have you called us after so many years?" Her arms stretched out to him.

Zedd's arms reached out, but could not touch her. "I am troubled by what the Mother Confessor tells me."

"She speaks the truth."

He closed his eyes and nodded as his arms lowered with hers. "It's true, then, all my students, save Giller, are dead."

"You are the only one left to protect the Mother Confessor." She drifted closer. "You must appoint the Seeker."

"The High Council sowed these seeds," he protested, frowning. "Now you want me to help? They turned my advice away. Let them live and die by their own greed."

Zedd's father floated closer. "My son, why were you angry with your students?"

Zedd scowled. "Because they put themselves before their duty to help their people."

"I see. And how is this different from what you do now?" The echo of his voice hung in the air.

Zedd's fists tightened. "My help was offered, but turned away."

"And when has it not been so, that there would be those who were blind, or foolish, or greedy? Would you let them have their way over you so easily? Would you let them so simply prevent you from helping those who would be helped? Your abandonment of the people may have a reason that seems just to you, unlike the actions of your students, but the results are the same. In the end they saw their mistake, and did the right things, the things you taught them. Learn from your students, son."

"Zeddicus," his mother said, "would you let Richard die too, and all the other innocents? Appoint the Seeker."

"He's too young."

She shook her head with a gentle smile. "He will not get the chance to grow older."

"He has not passed my final test."

"Darken Rahl hunts Richard. The cloud that shadows him was sent by Rahl to track him. The snake vine was put in the jar by

Darken Rahl, in the expectation that Richard would search for it, and it would bite him. The snake vine wasn't meant to kill; Rahl sought to have him put to sleep by the fever until he could come for him." Her form drifted closer, her voice becoming more loving. "You know in your heart you have been watching him, hoping he would show himself to be the one."

"To what avail?" Zedd closed his eyes, his chin sinking to his chest. "Darken Rahl has the three boxes of Orden."

"No," his father said, "he has only two. He still seeks the third."

Zedd's eyes snapped open, his head jerked up. "What! He doesn't have them all?"

"No," his mother said, "but he soon will."

"And the book? Surely he must have the Book of Counted Shadows?"

"No. He searches for it."

Zedd put a finger to his chin, thinking. "Then there's a chance," he whispered. "What sort of fool would put the boxes of Orden in play before he had all three, and the book?"

His mother's features sharpened into a look of ice. "A very dangerous one. He travels the underworld." Zedd stiffened, and his breath caught in his throat. His mother's eyes seemed to pierce him. "That is how he was able to cross the boundary and recover the first box: by traveling the underworld. That is how he was able to begin the undoing of the boundary: from within the underworld. He commands some in it, more with his every coming. If you choose to help, be warned: do not go through the boundary, or send the Seeker through. Rahl expects it. If you enter, he will have you. The Mother Confessor came through only because he did not expect it. He will not make the same mistake again."

"But then how am I to get us to the Midlands? I can't help if I can't get to the Midlands." Zedd's voice was tense with frustration.

"We're sorry, but we don't know. We believe there must be a way, but it is not known to us. That is why you must appoint the Seeker. If he is the right one, he will find a way." Their forms began to shimmer, to fade.

"Wait! I must have the answers to my questions! Please, don't leave me!"

"We're sorry, it is not our choice, we are called back behind the veil."

"Why is Rahl after Richard? Please help me."

His father's voice was weak and distant. "We don't know. You must search for the answers yourself. We have trained you well. You are more talented than we ever were. Use what you were taught and what you feel. We love you, son. Until this is settled, one way or the other, we cannot come to you again. With Orden in play, coming again could tear the veil."

His mother kissed her hand and held it out to him as he did the same in return, and then they were gone.

Zeddicus Zu'l Zorander, the great and honorable wizard, stood alone on the wizard's rock his father had given him, and stared out into the night, thinking wizard's thoughts.

"Nothing is ever easy," he whispered.

CHAPTER 8

RICHARD CAME AWAKE WITH a start. Warm midday light filled the room, and the wonderful, tangy aroma of spice soup filled his lungs. He was in his room at Zedd's house. He looked up at the familiar knots in the wood walls, and the faces he always made them into in his mind stared back. The door to the front room stood shut. A chair waited next to the bed, empty. He sat up, pushing the covers down, and saw that he still wore his dirty clothes. He felt for the tooth under his shirt and sighed in relief when he found it still there, safe. A short stick held the window open a few inches, letting in fresh air and the sound of Kahlan's laughter. Zedd must be telling stories, he thought. Richard looked at his left hand. It was wrapped but no longer sore when he flexed his fingers. His head didn't hurt anymore, either. In fact, he felt wonderful. Hungry, but wonderful. He amended that to dirty, in filthy clothes, and hungry, but wonderful.

A tub of bathwater, soap, and clean towels sat in the center of the small room. A clean outfit of his forest garb was folded and stacked neatly on the chair. The bathwater looked deliciously inviting. He dipped his hand in and found the water warm. Zedd must have known when he would wake. Knowing Zedd as well as he did, that didn't surprise him.

Richard undressed and slipped into the welcoming water. The soap smelled almost as good to him as the soup. He liked to stay in the tub for a good long soak, but he felt too wide awake for soaking, and was eager to be outside with the other two. Unwrapping the hand, he was surprised to find how much it had healed overnight.

When he came out, Kahlan and Zedd were sitting at the table waiting for him. Kahlan's dress was freshly washed, he noticed, and she looked bathed, too. Her hair was clean and glistened in the sunlight. Green eyes sparkled up at him. A big bowl of soup waited for him next to her at the table, along with cheese and fresh bread.

"I wouldn't have expected to have slept until noon," he said, swinging his leg over the bench. They both laughed. Richard eyed them suspiciously.

Kahlan straightened her face. "This is the second noon you have slept to, Richard."

"Yes," Zedd added, "you slept right through the first. How do you feel? How is your hand?"

"I'm fine. Thank you, Zedd, for helping me. Thank you both." He opened and closed his fingers to show them the improvement. "The hand feels much better, except it itches."

"My mother always said that if it itched, that meant it was getting better."

Richard grinned at her. "Mine too." He fished a piece of potato and a mushroom into his spoon and tasted it. "It's as good as mine," he said to her earnestly.

She sat crosswise on the bench, facing toward him, her elbow resting on the table with the side of her jaw nestled in the heel of her hand. She gave him a knowing smile. "Zedd tells it differently."

Richard cast a reproachful eye at Zedd, who looked up at the sky in an exaggerated manner. "Does he now? I will have to remind him of that the next time he is begging me to make it for him."

"Frankly," she said in a low voice, but not low enough that

104

Zedd couldn't hear, "from what I've seen, I think he would eat dirt if someone else dished it up for him."

Richard laughed. "I see you've gotten to know him well."

"I tell you, Richard," the old man said, pointing a bony finger, not about to let them get the best of him, "she could make dirt taste good. You would do well to take lessons from her."

Richard broke off a piece of bread and dunked it in the soup. He knew the joking was a release for the tension he sensed, a way to pass the time while they both waited for him to finish. Kahlan had given Richard her word that she would wait for him to ask Zedd's help; it was apparent that she had kept her word. And Zedd's way was to play ignorant and innocent, and wait for you to ask something first so he could better judge what you already knew. This day, Richard could not allow any of his games. This day, things were different.

"There is one thing I don't trust about her, though." Zedd's tone was dark, menacing.

Richard froze in mid-chew. He swallowed and waited, not daring to look at either of them, while the other paused.

"She doesn't like cheese! I don't think I could ever trust anyone who doesn't like cheese. It's not natural."

Richard relaxed. Zedd was just twiddling with his mind, as he always called it. His old friend seemed to have a knack for catching him off guard, and he delighted in it. Richard stole a glance at Zedd to see him sitting there with an innocent smile on his face. Richard smiled, too, in spite of himself. While he relished the bowl of soup, Zedd nibbled on a piece of cheese to make his point. Kahlan nibbled on a piece of bread to make hers. The bread tasted delicious. Kahlan was pleased when he pointed it out.

As Richard neared the end of his meal he decided it was time to change the tone of things back to business. "The next quad? Has there been any sign?"

"No. I was worried, but Zedd did a cloud reading for me and said it appeared they must have run into trouble of some kind, since they were nowhere to be found."

He gave Zedd a sideways glance. "Is that true?"

"True as toasted toads." Zedd had used the expression since Richard was young, to win him over with humor and let him know he could always trust the old man to be truthful with him above all else. Richard wondered what sort of trouble a quad could "run into."

For better or worse, he had succeeded in changing the mood at the table. He felt Kahlan's impatience for him to get on with it, and he sensed impatience in Zedd, too. Kahlan turned back to the table and put both hands in her lap, waiting. Richard feared that if he didn't handle things properly, she would do whatever it was she was here to do, and he would have no control over it.

Richard finished his meal and pushed the bowl away with his thumbs, at the same time meeting Zedd's eyes. His friend's humor was gone, but otherwise he showed nothing of what he was thinking. He simply waited. It was Richard's turn now, and once he began there could be no going back.

"Zedd, my friend, we need your help to stop Darken Rahl."

"I know. You want me to find the wizard for you."

"No, that won't be necessary. I have already found him." Richard felt Kahlan's questioning eyes on him, but he continued to fix his gaze on Zedd. "You are the great wizard."

Kahlan began to rise from the bench. Without taking his eyes from Zedd, Richard reached under the table and clutched her forearm, forcing her to sit back down. Still Zedd showed no emotion. His voice came even and soft.

"And what makes you think this, Richard?"

Richard took a deep breath, letting it out slowly as he put his hands on the table, intertwining his fingers. He watched his hands as he spoke. "When Kahlan first told me about the history of the three lands, she said the council had taken actions that made the death of the wizard's wife and daughter at the hands of a quad stand for nothing, and as punishment the wizard did the worst thing possible to them: he left them to suffer the consequences of their own actions.

"That sounded like the very thing you would do, but I couldn't be sure then; I had to find a way to know. When you first saw Kahlan, and were angry that she had come here from the Midlands, I told you she had been attacked by a quad. I watched your eyes. They told me I was right. Only someone who had suffered a loss like yours would have had that look in his eyes. And, you changed your attitude toward her after I told you.

106

Completely. Only someone who had known the terror personally would have that kind of empathy. But still I didn't trust my instinct. I waited."

He looked up at Zedd and held the other's gaze while he spoke. "Your biggest mistake was when you told Kahlan she was safe here. You would not lie, especially about something like that. And you know what a quad is. How could an old man make it safe here, against a quad, without magic? He couldn't, but one old wizard could. The next quad is nowhere to be found, you said so yourself; they ran into some trouble. I think they ran into some wizard trouble. You were as good as your word. You always are."

Richard's voice turned gentler. "I have always known, in a thousand little ways, that you were more than you claimed to be, that you were a special person. I have always been honored to have you as my friend. And I know that as my friend, you would do anything, anything you must, to help me if my life were in danger, just as I would do anything for you. I trust you with my life, and it is now in your hands." Richard hated closing the trap in this fashion, but all their lives were at risk. There could be no games.

Zedd put his hands on the table and leaned forward. "I have never before been this proud of you, Richard." His eyes told that he meant it. "You got it all right." He stood and came around the table. When Richard stood, they hugged. "I have also never been this sad for you." Zedd held Richard in a tight embrace for a moment longer. "Sit. I will be right back. I have something for you. Both of you sit and wait a moment."

Zedd cleared the table; then, holding the plates in the crook of his arm, he strode to the house. Kahlan looked worried as she watched him go. Richard had thought that she would be happy to have found the wizard, but now she looked more frightened than anything else. Things were going differently from what he had expected.

When Zedd reappeared, he was carrying something long. Kahlan came to her feet. Richard realized Zedd's fist clutched the scabbard of a sword. Kahlan put herself in front of him before he reached the table, grabbing fistfuls of his robes.

"Don't do this, Zedd." Her voice was desperate.

107

"It is not my choice."

"Zedd, please no, choose someone else, not Richard. . . ."

Zedd cut her off. "Kahlan! I warned you about this. I told you; he picks himself. If I choose someone other than the true one, we all die. If you have a better way . . . put words to it!"

He swept her aside, came to the side of the table opposite Richard, and slammed the sword down in front of him. Richard jumped. He looked from the sword up into Zedd's fierce eyes as the other leaned over the table.

"This belongs to you," the wizard said. Kahlan turned her back to them.

Richard's gaze fell upon the sword. The silver scabbard gleamed with gold flourishes that embellished it in sweeps and waves. Steel crossguards swept out and down aggressively. Finely twisted silver wire covered the grip, and interwoven along the side of the braided silver, gold wire formed the word *Truth*. This, Richard thought, was the sword of a king. It was the finest weapon he had ever seen.

Slowly, he rose to his feet. Zedd picked up the scabbard by the point and held the hilt of the sword to Richard. "Draw it."

As if in a trance, Richard closed his fingers around the hilt and pulled the sword free, the blade making a ringing, metallic sound that hung in the air. Richard had never heard a sword make a sound quite like it. His hand closed tightly around the grip, and in his palm and on his fingers opposite he could feel the bumps of the gold wire that spelled out the word *Truth* on each side of the hilt pressing almost painfully into his flesh. Inexplicably, it felt precisely correct. The weight fit him exactly. He felt as if a part of him was now complete.

From deep within, he felt his anger stir, brought to life, searching direction. He was suddenly aware of the tooth against his chest.

As his rage rose, he felt an awakening power rushing into him from the sword: the twin to his own anger. His own feelings had always seemed independent, whole. This was like having an image in a mirror come to life. It was a terrifying specter. His anger fed on the force from the sword, and in return, the wrath from the sword fed on his anger. Together the twin storms spiraled through him. He felt like a helpless bystander, being dragged along. It was a frightening and at the same time seductive sensation that bordered on violation. Fearful perceptions of his own anger twisted with tantalizing promise. The bewitching emotions rushed headlong through him, seizing his anger, soaring with it. Richard struggled to control the rage. He was on the brink of panic. On the brink of abandon.

Zeddicus Zu'l Zorander threw his head back and spread his arms. To the sky, he called out, "Fair warning to those living and those dead! The Seeker is named!"

Thunder from the blue sky shook the ground and rolled off toward the boundary.

Kahlan fell to her knees in front of Richard, head bowed, hands held behind her back. "I pledge my life in the defense of the Seeker."

Zedd knelt beside her, his head bowed. "I pledge my life in the defense of the Seeker."

Richard stood gripping the Sword of Truth in his hand, eyes wide in breathless bewilderment.

"Zedd," he whispered, "what in the name of everything good is a Seeker?"

CHAPTER 9

WITH THE AID OF a hand to his knee, Zedd rose to his feet, rearranged his robes around his bony body, and held his hand out to Kahlan, who was staring at the ground. Noticing the hand, she took it, coming to her feet as well. Her face bore a distressed expression. Zedd considered her for a moment, and she nodded that she was all right.

Zedd turned to Richard. "What is a Seeker? A wise first question in your new capacity, but not one swiftly answered."

Richard gazed down at the gleaming sword in his hand, not at all sure he wanted anything to do with it. He slid it back into its scabbard, glad to be free of the feelings it invoked, and held it in both hands before him. "Zedd, I've never seen this before. Where have you kept it?"

Zedd smiled proudly. "In the cabinet, in the house."

Richard eyed him skeptically. "There's nothing in the cabinet but dishes and pans and your powders."

"Not that cabinet," he said, lowering his voice as if to thwart anyone who might be listening, "in my wizard's cabinet!"

Richard straightened with a frown. "I've never seen any other cabinet."

"Bags, Richard! You're not supposed to see it! It's a wizard's cabinet; it's invisible!"

Richard felt more than a little stupid. "And how long have you had this?"

"Oh, I don't know, maybe a dozen years or so." Zedd swept his slender hand in the air as if trying to brush the question away.

"And how did you come to have it?"

Zedd's tone hardened. "The naming of the Seeker is a wizard's task. The High Council wrongly took it upon itself to name the person. They didn't care anything about finding the right person. They gave the post to whoever suited them at the time. Or whoever offered the most. The sword belongs to the Seeker as long as he is alive, or as long as he chooses to be Seeker. In between, while a new Seeker is sought, the Sword of Truth belongs to the wizards. Or more precisely, it belongs to me, as naming Seekers is my responsibility. The last fellow who had it became . . ." His eyes turned up, as if searching the sky for the right word. ". . . entangled, with a witch woman. So, while he was distracted, I went into the Midlands and retrieved what is mine. Now it is yours."

Richard felt himself being drawn into something not of his own choosing. He looked to Kahlan. She seemed to have shed her anguish and was unreadable again. "This is what you came here for? This is what you wanted the wizard to do?"

"Richard, I wanted the wizard to name a Seeker. I did not know it would be you."

He was beginning to feel trapped as he looked from one to the other. "You two think I can somehow save us. That's what you both are thinking: that somehow I'm to stop Darken Rahl. A wizard can't do it, but I'm to try?" Terror rose with his heart into his throat.

Zedd came and put a reassuring arm around his shoulder. "Richard, look up in the sky. Tell me what you see." Richard looked and saw the snakelike cloud. He didn't need to answer the question. Zedd pressed his strong, bony fingers into Richard's flesh. "Come. Sit, and I will tell you what you need to know. Then you decide, for yourself, what it is you will do.

Come." He put his other arm around Kahlan's shoulder and guided them both to the bench at the table. He went to his place opposite them and sat. Richard laid the sword on the table between them to signify that the matter was yet to be decided.

Zedd pushed his sleeves up his arms a little. "There is a magic," he began, "an ancient and dangerous magic of immense power. It's a magic spawned from the earth, from life itself. It is held in three vessels called the three boxes of Orden. The magic is dormant until the boxes are put into play, as it is called. To do so is not easy. It requires a person who has knowledge gained from long scholarship and who can call upon considerable power on his own. Once a person has at least one of the boxes, the magic of Orden can be put in play. He then has one year from that time to open a box, but he must have all three before any will open. They work together; you can't simply have one and open it. If the person who puts them in play fails to acquire all three, and to open one within the allotted time, he forfeits his life to the magic. There is no going back. Darken Rahl must open one of the boxes, or die. On the first day of winter, his year is up."

Zedd's face was tight with hard wrinkles and determination. He leaned forward a little. "Each box holds a different power, which is released upon its opening. If Rahl opens the correct one, he gains the magic of Orden, the magic of life itself, power over all things living and dead. He will have unchallenged power and authority. He will be a master with immutable dominion over all people. Anyone he doesn't like, he will be able to kill with a thought, in any manner of his choosing, wherever that person is, no matter how far away."

"Sounds like a terribly evil magic," Richard said.

Zedd leaned back, taking his hands from the table. He shook his head. "No, not really. The magic of Orden is the power of life. Like all power, it simply exists. It's the user who determines what use it will be put to. The magic of Orden can just as easily be used to help crops grow, to heal the sick, to end conflict. It's all in what the user wants. The power is neither evil nor good; it simply exists. It is up to the mind of man to put it to use. I think we all know which use Darken Rahl would choose."

Zedd paused, as was his way, to let Richard ponder the meaning of what he had been told. His thin face fixed in resolve as he waited. Kahlan, too, had a look that told him she was determined to have him fully understand the ominous nature of what Zedd was saying.

Richard, of course, didn't need to ponder it, since he knew it all from the Book of Counted Shadows. The book was explicit. From the book, he knew Zedd was barely touching on the full extent of the cataclysm that would sweep the land if Darken Rahl opened the correct box. He knew, also, what would happen if one of the other boxes was opened, but he couldn't reveal his fore-knowledge, and so had to ask anyway. "And if he opens one of the others?"

Zedd came forward against the table in a blink. He had ex-pected that this would be the next question. "Open the wrong box, and the magic claims him. He's dead." Zedd snapped his fingers. "Just like that. We are all safe; the threat is removed." He leaned closer, his brow furrowed, and gave Richard a hard look. "Open the other wrong box, and every bug, every blade of grass, every tree, every man, woman, and child, every living thing, is incinerated into nothingness. It would be the end of all life. The magic of Orden is twin to the magic of life itself, and death is part of everything that lives, so the magic of Orden is tied to death, as well as life."

Zedd sat back, seeming to be overwhelmed by the telling of the choices of catastrophe. Though Richard already knew it all, he still swallowed hard at hearing it out loud. Somehow it seemed more real to him like this, more real when there was a name put to it. When he had learned the book, it was all so ab-stract, so hypothetical, that he had never given any thought to the possibility that it would come to pass. His only concern had been that the knowledge be preserved so as to be returned to its keeper. He wished he could tell Zedd what he knew, but his oath to his father prevented him from saying anything. It also required him to keep up the pretense by asking another question to which he already knew the answer.

"How will Rahl know which box to open?"

Zedd rearranged the sleeves of his robes and looked down at the table, watching his hands as he spoke. "Putting the boxes in play imparts to the person certain privileged information. It must be that this information tells him how he can discover which box is which."

That made sense. No one knew of the book but its keeper, and, it appeared, the person who put the boxes in play. The book made no reference to this, but it seemed logical. A sudden jolt went through him: Darken Rahl must be after him for the book. He almost didn't hear Zedd beginning to speak again.

"Rahl has done something out of the ordinary, though. He has put the boxes in play before he has all three."

Richard came to attention immediately. "He must be stupid, or very confident."

"Confident," the wizard said. "When I left the Midlands, it was for two main reasons. The first was because the High Council took the naming of the Seeker upon itself. The second was because they mishandled the boxes of Orden. People had come to believe that the power of the boxes was just a legend. They thought me an old fool for telling them it was no legend but the truth. They refused to heed my warnings."

He pounded his fist down on the table, causing Kahlan to jump. "They laughed at me!" His face was red with anger, making it stand out all the more against the mass of his white hair. "I wanted the boxes kept far apart from each other, and with magic, hidden and locked away so as to never be found again. The council, instead, wanted them given to important people, like trophies to be shown off. They used them as payments for favors or promises. This exposed the boxes to covetous hands. I don't know what happened to them in the intervening years. Rahl has at least one, but not all three. Not yet anyway." Zedd's eyes flashed with fervor. "Do you see, Richard? We don't have to go up against Darken Rahl, we have only to find at least one of the boxes before he does."

"And keep it from him, which may prove considerably harder than finding it," Richard pointed out, letting the words hang in the air a moment. He had a sudden thought. "Zedd, do you think one of the boxes could be here in Westland?"

"Not likely."

"Why not?"

Zedd hesitated. "Richard, I never told you I was a wizard, but you never asked before, so I didn't really lie about it. I did tell

114

you one lie, though. I told you I came here before the boundary went up. In reality I didn't come here before it went up, because I couldn't. You see, in order to create a Westland free of magic, there could be none here when the boundary went up. Magic could come here after the boundary was established, but not be here before. Since I have magic, my presence would have prevented it from happening, so I had to stay in the Midlands until after, and only then was I able to come through."

"Everyone has their little secrets. I don't begrudge you yours. But what's your point?"

"My point is, we know none of the boxes could have been here before the boundary went up, or their magic would have prevented it. So if they were all in the Midlands before the boundary, because of the magic, and I didn't bring one with me, they have to still be in the Midlands."

Richard thought about this awhile, feeling his spark of hope die. He turned his thoughts back to the matter at hand.

"You still have not told me what a Seeker is. Or my part in this."

Zedd folded his hands together. "A Seeker is a person who answers to no one but himself; he is a law unto himself. The Sword of Truth is his to wield as he wishes, and within the limits of his own strength, he can hold anyone to answer for anything." Zedd held up his hand to forestall Richard's objections and questions. "I realize this is vague. The problem with explaining it is that it is like all power. As I told you before, it's how the person uses power that makes it what it is. This is the core of why it is so important to find the right person, a person who will use the power wisely. You see, Richard, a Seeker does exactly as the name implies; he seeks. He seeks the answers to things. Things of his own choosing. If he is the right person, he will seek the answers that will help others, not just himself. The whole purpose of a Seeker is to be free to quest on his own, to go where he wants, ask what he wants, learn what he wants, find answers to what he wants to know, and if need be, do whatever it is the answers demand."

Richard straightened, his voice rising. "Are you telling me a Seeker is an assassin?"

115

"I won't lie to you, Richard; there have been times when it has turned out that way."

Richard's face was crimson. "I will not be an assassin!"

Zedd shrugged. "As I said, a Seeker is whatever he wants. Ideally, a Seeker is the standard-bearer of Justice. I can't tell you much more, because I've never been one. I don't know what goes on in their heads; however, I know the proper kind of person."

Zedd pushed his sleeves up again while he watched Richard. "But I don't pick a Seeker, Richard. A true Seeker picks himself. I only name them. You have been a Seeker for years without knowing it. I have watched you, and that is what you do. You are always seeking the truth. What do you think you were doing in the high Ven? You were seeking the answer to the vine, to your father's murder. You could have left that to others, others more qualified, and as it turned out, perhaps you should have, but that would have been against your nature, the nature of a Seeker. They don't leave it to others, because they want to know for themselves. When Kahlan told you she was looking for a wizard who was lost since before she was born, you had to know who it was, and you found him."

"But that's only because . . ."

Zedd cut him off. "It doesn't matter. It's irrelevant. Only one thing matters: that you did it. I saved you with the root I found. Does it matter that it was easy for me to find the root? No. Would you be any more alive if it had been extremely difficult for me to find the root? No. I found the root, you are well. That is all that matters. Same with the Seeker. It's of no importance how he finds an answer, only that he does. As I said, there are no rules. Right now there are answers you must find. I don't know how you will do so, and I don't care, only that you do. If you say, 'Oh, that's simple,' all the better, as we don't have much time."

Richard's guard went up. "What answers?"

Zedd smiled, and his eyes sparkled. "I have a plan, but you must first find a way to get us across the boundary."

"What!" Richard ran his fingers through his hair in exasperation, muttering his disbelief under his breath. He looked back to

Zedd. "You're a wizard; you had something to do with putting the boundary there in the first place. You have just said you have been through it to retrieve the sword. Kahlan has come through the boundary, sent by wizards. I know nothing of the boundary! If you expect me to find you the answer, well, here it is: Zedd, you are a wizard, send us through the boundary!"

Zedd shook his head. "No. I said across the boundary, not through it. I know how to go through it, but we can't do that. Rahl waits for us to do so. If we try to go through, he will kill us. If we are lucky. We must instead go across it, without going through it. There is a big difference."

"Zedd, I'm sorry, but it's impossible. I don't know anything about how to get us across. I don't see how it can be done. The boundary is the underworld. If we can't go through it, then we are stuck here. The whole purpose of the boundary is to prevent anyone from doing just what you are asking me to do." Richard felt helpless. They were depending on him, and he didn't have any answers.

Zedd's voice was kind and gentle. "Richard, you are too quick to criticize yourself. What is it you say when I ask how you must solve difficult problems?"

Richard knew what Zedd was talking about, but was reluctant to answer, as he felt answering only pulled him in deeper. Zedd lifted an eyebrow, waiting. Richard looked down at the table, picking at the wood with his thumbnail. "Think of the solution, not the problem."

"And right now you are doing it backwards. You are only concentrating on why the problem is impossible. You are not thinking of the solution."

Richard knew Zedd was right, but there was more to it. "Zedd, I don't think I'm qualified to be Seeker. I don't know anything about the Midlands."

"Sometimes it is easier to make a decision if you aren't burdened with a knowledge of history," the wizard said cryptically.

Richard let out a deep breath. "I don't know the place. I'd be lost there."

Kahlan put her hand on his forearm. "No, you wouldn't. I know the Midlands better than almost anyone. I know where it

117

is safe and where it is not. I'll be your guide. You will not be lost. I promise you that much."

Richard looked away from her green eyes and down at the table. It hurt to think that he might disappoint her, but her faith, and Zedd's, didn't seem justified. He didn't know anything about the Midlands, or the magic, or how to find some boxes, or how to stop Darken Rahl. He didn't know how to do any of it! And for the first trick, he was supposed to get them across the boundary!

"Richard, I know you think I'm thrusting this responsibility on you unwisely, but it is not me who chooses you. You are the one who has shown himself to be the Seeker. I have only recognized the fact. I have been a wizard a long time. You don't know what that entails, but you have to trust me when I say that I'm qualified to recognize the one." Zedd reached across the table, across the sword, and put his hand on Richard's. His eyes were somber. "Darken Rahl hunts you. Personally. The only reason I can fathom for this is that with the insight he has gained from the magic of Orden, he too knows you to be the one and so searches you out, to eliminate the threat."

Richard blinked in surprise. Maybe Zedd was right. Maybe this was the reason Rahl hunted him. Or maybe not. Zedd didn't know about the book. He felt as if his mind would explode with all the things filling his head, and suddenly he couldn't sit anymore. He stood up and began pacing, thinking. Zedd folded his arms across his chest. Kahlan leaned an elbow on the table. Both watched in silence as he paced.

The wisp had said to seek the answer or die. It didn't say it was necessary to become this Seeker. He could find the answers in his own way, as he always had. He hadn't needed the sword to figure out who the wizard was, although it hadn't been that hard.

But what was wrong with taking the sword? What could it hurt to have its help? Wouldn't it be foolish to turn down any assistance? Apparently the sword could be put to any use its owner wanted, so why not use it in the way he wanted? He didn't have to become an assassin, or anything else. He could use it to help them, that was all. That was all that was needed, or wanted; no more.

But Richard knew why he didn't want it. He didn't like the way it had felt when he had drawn the sword. It had felt good, and that bothered him. It had stirred his anger in a way that frightened him, made him feel like he had never felt before. The most disconcerting thing was that it felt right. He didn't want to feel right about anger, didn't want to lose his control of it. Anger was wrong. That's what his father had taught him. Anger had killed his mother. He kept his anger behind a locked door he didn't want opened. No, he would do this in his own way, without the sword. He didn't need it, didn't need the worry of it.

Richard turned to Zedd, who still sat with his arms folded across his chest, watching. The sunlight gave Zedd's wrinkles deep shadows. The lines and sharp angles of his familiar face seemed somehow different. He looked grim, resolute—somehow more like a wizard. Their eyes met and held each other. Richard was decided. He would tell his friend no. He would help, and would stand by them. His life, too, depended on this. But he would not be the Seeker. Before he could say so, Zedd spoke.

"Kahlan, tell Richard how Darken Rahl questions people." His voice was quiet, calm. He didn't look at her, instead continuing to hold Richard's eyes.

Her voice was barely audible. "Zedd, please."

"Tell him." This time his voice was harder, more forceful. "Tell him what he does with the curved knife he keeps at his belt."

Richard looked away from Zedd's eyes to her pale face. After a moment she held out her hand, and looked up at him with sad, green eyes, beckoning him to come to her. He stood a moment, wary, then came and took her hand. She pulled him down toward her. He sat, straddling the bench, facing her, waiting for what it was she was bidden to say, fearing it.

Kahlan shifted toward him, hooking some hair behind an ear, and looked down at his right hand as she held it in both of hers, stroking the back of it with her thumbs. Her fingers were gentle, soft, and warm against his palm. The size of her hands made his seem awkwardly large. She spoke quietly and didn't look up.

"Darken Rahl is a practitioner of an ancient form of magic

119

called anthropomancy. He divines the answers to questions by the inspection of living human entrails."

Richard felt his anger ignite.

"It's of limited use; he can at most get a yes or no to a single question, and sometimes, a name. Nonetheless, he continues to favor its use. I'm sorry, Richard. Please forgive me for telling you this."

Memories of his father's kindness, his laughter, his love, his friendship, their time together with the secret book, and a thousand other brief glimpses tore through him in a flood of anguish. The scenes and sounds converged into dim shadows and hollow echoes in Richard's mind and melted away. In its place, memories of the bloodstains on the floor, the white faces of the people there, images of his father's pain and terror, and the things Chase had told him flashed vividly in snatches through his mind. He didn't try to stop them, but instead pulled them onward, hungering for them. He washed himself in the detail of it all, felt the twisting torment. Pain flared up from a pit deep inside him. Invoked heedlessly, it came screaming forth. In his mind he added the shadowed figure of Darken Rahl, hands dripping crimson blood, standing over his father's body, holding the red, glinting blade. He held the vision before him, twisting it, inspecting it, drinking it into his soul. The picture was complete now. He had his answers. He knew how it had been. How his father had died. Until now that was all he had ever sought—answers. In his whole life, he had never gone beyond that simple quest.

In one white-hot instant that changed.

The door that held back his anger, and the wall of reason containing his temper, burned away in a flash of hot desire. A lifetime of rational thinking evaporated before his searing fury. Lucidity became dross in a cauldron of molten need.

Richard reached out to the Sword of Truth, curled his fingers around the scabbard, gripping it tighter and tighter until his knuckles were white. The muscles in his jaw flexed. His breathing came fast and sharp. He saw nothing else of what was around him. The heat of anger surged forth from the sword, not of its own volition, but summoned by the Seeker.

Richard's chest heaved with the burning hurt of his grief at knowing now what had happened to his father, and with that knowledge there was closure, too. Thoughts he had never permitted himself to have became his only desire. Caution and consequence vanished before a flood of lust for vengeance.

In that instant, his only want, his only desire, his only need, was to kill Darken Rahl. Nothing else had any significance.

With his other hand he reached out and seized the hilt of his sword to pull it free. Zedd's hand clamped down over his. The Seeker's eyes snapped up, livid at the interference.

"Richard." Zedd's voice was gentle. "Calm down."

The Seeker, his muscles flexing powerfully, glowered into the other's tranquil eyes. Some part of him, deep in the back of his mind, kept warning him, trying to regain control. He ignored the warning. He bent over the table to the wizard, his teeth gritted.

"I accept the position of Seeker."

"Richard," Zedd repeated calmly, "it's all right. Relax. Sit down."

The world came rushing back into his mind. He pulled his readiness to kill back a notch, but not his rage. Not only the door, but also the wall that had contained his anger, was gone. Even though the world about him had returned, it was a world seen through different eyes—eyes he had always had, but had been afraid to use: the eyes of a Seeker.

Richard realized that he was standing. He didn't remember getting up. He sat again next to Kahlan, removing his hands from the sword. Something inside him regained control of his anger. It wasn't the same as before, though. It didn't shut it away, didn't lock it behind a door, but pulled it back, unafraid, to make it ready when needed again.

Some of his old self seeped back into his mind, calming him, slowing his breathing, reasoning within him. He felt liberated, unafraid, unashamed of his temper for the first time. He allowed himself to sit there while he uncoiled, feeling his muscles relax.

He looked up into Zedd's calm, undisturbed face. The old man, his thatch of white hair framing an angular face set in a perceptive cast, studied him, assessed him with the slightest hint of a smile fixed at the corners of his thin mouth.

"Congratulations," the wizard said. "You have passed my final test to become Seeker."

Richard pulled back in confusion. "What do you mean? You already appointed me Seeker."

Zedd shook his head slowly. "I told you before. Weren't you listening? A Seeker appoints himself. Before you could become Seeker you had to pass one determinative test. You had to show me you could use all your mind. For many years, Richard, you have kept part of it locked away. Your anger. I had to know you could release it, call upon it. I've seen you angry, but you were unable to admit your anger to yourself. A Seeker who couldn't allow himself to use his anger would be hopelessly weak. It is the strength of rage that gives the heedless drive to prevail. Without the anger, you would have turned down the sword, and I would have let you, because you wouldn't have had what was required. But that is irrelevant now. You have proven you are no longer a prisoner to your fears. Be cautioned, though. As important as it is to be able to use your rage, it is equally important to be able to restrain it. You have always had that ability. Don't let yourself lose it now. You must be wise enough to know which path to choose. Sometimes letting out the anger is an even more grievous mistake than holding it in."

Richard nodded solemnly. He thought about the way it felt to hold the sword when he was in the rage, the way he felt its power, the liberating sensation of giving himself over to the primal urge, from within himself, and from the sword.

"The sword had magic," he said guardedly. "I felt it."

"It does. But Richard, magic is only a tool, like any other. When you use a whetstone to sharpen a knife, you are simply making the knife work better for its intended purpose. Same way with the magic. It's just a honing of the intent." Zedd's eyes were clear and sharp. "Some people are more terrified to die by magic, than, say, by a blade, as if somehow one is less dead if killed by a blow or cut than if killed by the unseen. But listen well. Dead is dead. The fear of the magic, though, can be a powerful weapon. Keep that in mind."

Richard nodded. The late-afternoon sun warmed his face and

out of the corner of his eye he could see the cloud. Rahl would be watching it, too. Richard remembered the man from the quad, on Blunt Cliff, how he had pulled his sword across his arm, drawing blood before he attacked. He remembered the look in the man's eyes. He hadn't understood it at the time; he understood it now. Richard hungered for the fight.

The leaves of the nearby trees fluttered in the light autumn wind, glimmering with their first touches of gold and red. Winter was coming; the first day of winter would soon be here. He thought about how he would get them across the boundary. They had to get one of the boxes of Orden, and when they found it, they would find Rahl.

"Zedd, no more games. I am Seeker now, no more tests. True?"

"True as toasted toads."

"Then we are wasting our time. I am sure Rahl is not wasting his." He turned to Kahlan. "I hold you to your pledge to be my guide when we reach the Midlands."

She smiled at his impatience and nodded. Richard turned to Zedd.

"Show me how the magic works, wizard."

CHAPTER 10

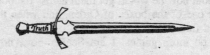

ZEDD'S IMPISH SMILE SPREAD across his face. He handed Richard the baldric. The finely tooled leather was old and supple. The gold and silver buckle matched the scabbard. It was adjusted too small, its last user having been smaller than Richard. Zedd helped readjust it as Richard strapped it across his right shoulder, and fit the Sword of Truth to it.

Zedd led them to the edge of the grass, amid long shadows stretching from the nearby trees, to where two small rock maples grew, one as thick as Richard's wrist, the other as thin as Kahlan's.

He turned to Richard. "Draw the sword." The unique ringing, metallic sound filled the late-afternoon air as the sword came free. Zedd leaned closer. "Now, I will show you the most important thing about the sword, but to do so I need you to briefly abdicate your post as Seeker, and allow me to name Kahlan Seeker."

Kahlan gave Zedd a suspicious glare. "I don't want to be Seeker."

"Just for the purpose of demonstration, dear one." He motioned for Richard to give her the sword. She hesitated before taking it in both hands. The weight was uncomfortable, and she allowed the point to lower until it rested on the grassy ground. Zedd waved his hands over her head with a flourish. "Kahlan Amnell, I name you Seeker." She continued to give him the same suspicious stare. Zedd put his finger under her chin, tilting her head up. His eyes had a fierce intensity. He put his face close to hers, speaking in a low voice.

"When I left the Midlands with this sword, Darken Rahl used his magic to place the larger of these two trees here, to mark me, to be able to come for me at a time of his choosing. So he could kill me. The same Darken Rahl who had Dennee killed." Her countenance became darker. "The same Darken Rahl who hunts you, to kill you like he killed your sister." Hate flared in her eyes. Her teeth clenched, making the muscles in her strong jaw line stand out. The Sword of Truth rose from the ground. Zedd stepped behind her. "This tree is his. You must stop him."

The blade flashed through the autumn air with speed and power Richard could scarcely believe. The arc of its sweep went through the larger tree with a loud crack, like a thousand twigs snapping at once. Splinters flew everywhere. The tree seemed to hang in the air a moment, then dropped down next to the ragged stump before toppling over with a crash. Richard knew it would have taken him at least ten blows with a good axe to have felled the maple.

Zedd slipped the sword from Kahlan's hands as she sank to her knees and rocked back on her heels, putting her hands over her face with a moan. Instantly, Richard crouched at her side, steadying her.

"Kahlan, what's wrong?"

"I'm all right." She laid a hand on his shoulder as he helped her to her feet. Her face was pale as she forced a small smile. "But I resign my post as Seeker."

Richard spun to the wizard. "Zedd, what is this nonsense? Darken Rahl didn't put that tree there. I've seen you water and care for those two trees. If you held a knife to my throat, I'd say you planted them there as a memorial to your wife and daughter."

Zedd gave only a small smile. "Very good, Richard. Here is

your sword. You are Seeker again. Now, my boy, you cut down the little tree, and then I will explain."

Annoyed, Richard took the sword in both hands, feeling the anger surge through him. He gave a mighty swing at the remaining tree. The tip of the blade whistled as it sliced through the air. Just before the blade hit the tree, it simply stopped, as if the very air about it had become too thick to allow it to pass.

Richard stepped back in surprise. He looked at the sword, and then tried again. Same thing. The tree was untouched. He glared over at Zedd, who stood with his arms folded and a smirk on his face.

Richard slid the sword back into its scabbard. "All right, what's going on."

Zedd lifted his eyebrows with an innocent expression. "Did you see how easily Kahlan cut through the bigger tree?" Richard frowned. Zedd smiled. "It could just as well have been iron. The blade would have cut through it the same. But you are stronger than she, and you couldn't even scratch the smaller tree."

"Yes, Zedd, I noticed."

Zedd's brows wrinkled in mock bewilderment. "And why do you think that is?"

Richard's irritation melted. This was the way Zedd often taught lessons, by making him come up with the answer on his own. "I would say it has something to do with intent. She thought the tree was evil, I didn't."

Zedd held up a bony finger. "Very good, my boy!"

Kahlan knitted her fingers together. "Zedd, I don't understand. I destroyed the tree, but it wasn't evil. It was innocent."

"That, dear one, is the point of the demonstration. Reality isn't relevant. Perception is everything. If you think it is the enemy, you can destroy it, whether true or not. The magic interprets only your perception. It won't allow you to harm someone you think innocent, but it will destroy whoever you perceive to be the enemy, within limits. Only what you believe, and not the truth of your thoughts, is the determining factor."

Richard was a little overwhelmed. "That leaves no room for error. But what if you aren't sure?"

Zedd lifted an eyebrow. "You had better be sure, my boy, or you are liable to find yourself in a lot of trouble. The magic

126

could read things in your mind you are not even aware of. It could go either way. You could kill a friend, or fail to kill a foe."

Richard drummed his fingers on the hilt of the sword, thinking. He watched the setting sun offer small golden flashes through the trees to the west. Overhead, the snakelike cloud had taken on a reddish cast on one side, deepening into darker purple on the other. It didn't really matter, he decided. He knew who he was after, and there was no doubt at all in his mind about him being the enemy. None whatsoever.

"There's one more thing. One more important thing," the wizard said. "When you use the sword against an enemy, there is a price to pay. Is that not true, dear one?" He looked to her. Kahlan nodded and lowered her eyes to the ground. "The more powerful the enemy, the higher the price. I am sorry it was necessary to do that to you, Kahlan, but it is the most important lesson Richard must learn." She gave him a small smile, letting him know that she understood the need. He turned back to Richard.

"We both know that sometimes, killing is the only choice, that it has to be classified as the right thing to do. I know you do not need to be told that any time you kill, though, it is a terrible thing. You live with it always, and once done, it cannot be undone. You pay a price within yourself; it diminishes you for having done it."

Richard nodded; it still made him uneasy that he had killed the man on Blunt Cliff. He wasn't sorry about what he had done; he had had no time or other choice, but in his mind he still saw the man's face as he went over the edge.

Zedd's eyes became intense. "It is different when you kill with the Sword of Truth, because of the magic. The magic has done your bidding, and it extracts a price. There is no such thing as pure good or pure evil, least of all in people. In the best of us there are thoughts or deeds that are wicked, and in the worst of us, at least some virtue. An adversary is not one who does loathsome acts for their own sake. He always has a reason that to him is justification. My cat eats mice. Does that make him bad? I don't think so, and the cat doesn't think so, but I would bet the mice have a different opinion. Every murderer thinks the victim needed killing.

"I know you don't want to believe this, Richard, but you

must listen. Darken Rahl does the things he does, because he thinks them right, just as you do the things you do because you think them right. The two of you are more the same in that than you think. You want revenge on him for killing your father, and he wants revenge on me for killing his. In your eyes he is evil, but to his eyes, you are the one who is evil. It is all just perception. Whoever wins thinks he was in the right. The loser will always believe himself wronged. It is the same as with the magic of Orden: the power is simply there; one use wins over the other."

"The same? Have you lost your mind? How could you think we are the same in any way! He craves power! He would chance destroying the world to get it! I don't want power, I just wanted to be left alone! He murdered my father! He ripped his guts out! He's trying to kill us all! How can you saw we are alike? You make it sound like he isn't even dangerous!"

"Haven't you been paying attention to what I have just been teaching you? I said you are the same in that you both think you are right. And that makes him more dangerous than you can imagine because in every other way you are different. Darken Rahl savors bleeding the life from people. He hungers for their pain. Your sense of right has bounds; his has none. His is twisted into an all-consuming lust to torture all opposition into submission, and he considers any who don't rush to bow before him as opposition. His conscience was clear when he used his bare hands to calmly extract your father's guts while he was still breathing. He found pleasure in the doing because his distorted sense of right gives him license. That is how he is very different from you. That is how dangerous he is." He pointed back at Kahlan. "Weren't you paying attention? Didn't you see what she was able to do with the sword? And how did she do what you could not? Hmm?"

"Perception," Richard said, in a much quieter voice. "She was able to do it because she thought she was right."

Zedd thrust a finger in the air. "Aha! Perception is what makes the threat even more dangerous." The wizard's finger came down and jabbed Richard's chest with each word. "Just ... like ... the sword."

Richard hooked a thumb under the baldric and let out a deep

breath. He felt as if he were standing in quicksand, but he had lived with Zedd too long to dismiss the things he said simply because they were hard to fathom. He longed for simplicity, though. "You mean that it's not only what he does that makes him dangerous, but also what he feels justified in doing?"

Zedd shrugged. "Let me put it another way. Who would you be more afraid of: a two-hundred-pound man who wants to steal a loaf of bread from you, and knows he is doing wrong, or a one-hundred-pound woman who believes, wrongly, but believes with all her heart, that you stole her baby?"

Richard folded his arms across his chest. "I would run from the woman. She wouldn't give up. She wouldn't listen to reason. She would be capable of anything."

Zedd's eyes were fierce. "So is Darken Rahl. Because he thinks he is right, he is that much more dangerous."

Richard returned the fierce expression. "I am in the right."

Zedd's expression softened. "The mice think they are in the right, too, but my cat eats them just the same. I am trying to teach you something, Richard. I don't want you to get caught in his claws."

Richard unfolded his arms and sighed. "I don't like it, but I understand. As I have heard you say, nothing is ever easy. While all of this in interesting, it isn't going to frighten me away from doing what it is I must, what I believe to be right. So what is this business about a price to using the Sword of Truth?"

Zedd held a thin finger to Richard's chest. "The payment is that you suffer the pain of seeing in yourself all your own evil, all your own shortcomings, all the things we don't like to see in ourselves, or admit are there. And you see the good in the one you have killed, suffer the guilt for having done so." Zedd shook his head sadly. "Please believe me, Richard, the pain comes not only from yourself, but more importantly, from the magic, a very powerful magic, a very powerful pain. Do not underestimate it. It is real, and it punishes your body, as well as your soul. You saw it in Kahlan, and that was from killing a tree. If it had been a man, it would have been profound. This is why anger is so important. Rage is the only armor you have against the pain; it gives a measure of protection. The stronger the enemy, the stronger the pain. But the stronger the rage, the stronger the shield. It makes you care less about the truth of what you have done. In some cases enough to not feel the pain. This is why I said the terrible things I did to Kahlan, things that hurt, and filled her with rage. It was to protect her when she used the sword. You see why I wouldn't have allowed you to take the sword, if you weren't able to use your anger? You would be naked before the magic; it would tear you apart."

Richard was a little frightened by this, by the look in Kahlan's eyes after she had used the sword, but it didn't dissuade him. He glanced up at the mountains of the boundary. They stood out, pale pink in the light of the setting sun. Behind them, from the east, darkness was coming. Darkness coming for them. He had to find a way across the boundary, into that darkness. The sword would help him, that was what mattered. There was much at stake. There was a cost to everything in life; he would pay this one.

His old friend placed his hands on Richard's shoulders and looked hard into his eyes. Zedd's features were set in grim warning.

"Now I have to tell you something you are not going to like." His fingers tightened, almost painfully. "You cannot use the Sword of Truth on Darken Rahl."

"What!"

Zedd gave him a shake. "He is too powerful. The magic of Orden protects him during the year of search. If you try to use the sword, you will be dead before it reaches him."

"This is crazy! First you want me to be the Seeker and take the sword, now you tell me I can't use it!" Richard was furious. He felt cheated.

"Just against Rahl, it won't work against him! Richard, I didn't make the magic, I only know how it works. Darken Rahl knows how it works too. He may try to make you use the sword against him. He knows it would kill you. If you give in to the rage and use the sword against him, he will win. You will be dead and he will have the boxes."

Kahlan's brow wrinkled in frustration. "Zedd, I agree with Richard. This makes it impossible. If he cannot use his most important weapon, then . . ."

Zedd cut her off. "No! This"—he rapped Richard on the head

with his knuckles—"this is a Seeker's most important weapon."
He jabbed his long finger at the center of Richard's chest. "And
this."

Everyone stood in silence for a moment.

"The Seeker is the weapon," Zedd said with emphasis. "The
sword is just a tool. You can find another way. You must."

Richard thought he should be upset, that he should feel angry,
frustrated, overwhelmed, but he didn't. His first view of his options lifted from him, letting him see beyond. He felt strangely
calm and determined.

"I'm sorry, my boy. I wish I could change the magic, but
I . . ."

Richard put his hand on Zedd's shoulder. "It's all right, my
friend. You're right. We must stop Rahl. That's all that matters.
I have to know the truth to succeed, and you have given me the
truth. Now it's up to me to use it. If we gain one of the boxes,
justice will have Rahl. I don't need to see it. I need only know
it is done. I said I wouldn't be an assassin, and so I shall not be.
The sword will be invaluable, I'm sure, but as you said, it's only
a tool, and that's the purpose I will put it to. The magic of the
sword isn't an end in itself. I can't allow myself to make that
mistake, or I will be only a pretend Seeker."

In the gathering gloom, Zedd patted Richard affectionately on
the shoulder. "You have gotten it all right, my boy. All of it." He
broke into a broad grin. "I have chosen the Seeker well. I am
proud of myself." Richard and Kahlan laughed at Zedd's self-
congratulation.

Kahlan's smiled faded. "Zedd, I cut down the tree you planted
in memory of your wife. That bothers me. I'm deeply sorry for
doing it."

"Don't be, dear one, her memory has aided us. She has helped
show the Seeker the truth, there could be no more fitting tribute
to her."

Richard didn't hear them talking. Already he was looking to
the east, to the massive wall of mountains, trying to think of so-
lutions. Cross the boundary, he thought, cross the boundary without going through it. How? What if it was impossible? What if
there was no way across the boundary? Would they be stuck here
while Darken Rahl searched for the boxes? Were they to die

without a chance? He wished there were more time and fewer limitations. Richard reprimanded himself for wasting time wishing.

If only he knew it could be done, then he could find out how. Something in the back of his mind nagged at him, insisting that it could be done, insisting he knew the truth of it. There was a way, there had to be. If he only knew that it was possible.

All around them, the night was coming alive with sounds. Frogs called from the ponds and streams, night birds from the trees, and insects from the grass. From the distant hills came the cry of wolves, mournful and plaintive against the dark wall of mountains. Somehow they had to cross those mountains, cross the unknown.

The mountains were like the boundary, he thought. You couldn't go through them, but you could cross them. You had only to find a pass. A pass. Was it possible? Could there be one?

Then it struck him like a bolt of lightning.

The book.

Richard spun on his heels, excited. To his surprise Zedd and Kahlan were both standing quietly, watching him, as if waiting for a pronouncement.

"Zedd, have you ever helped anyone other than yourself go through the boundary?"

"Like who?"

"Anyone! Yes or no!"

"No. No one."

"Can anyone other than a wizard send a person through the boundary?"

Zedd shook his head emphatically. "None but a wizard. And Darken Rahl, of course."

Richard frowned at him. "Our lives depend on this, Zedd. Swear. You have never, ever, sent anyone other than yourself through the boundary. True?"

"True as a boiling bog full of toasted toads. Why? What have you thought of? Do you have a way?"

Richard ignored the question, too deep in his own stream of thought to answer, and instead turned back to the mountains. It was true; there was a pass across the boundary! His father had found it, and used it! That was the only way the Book of

Counted Shadows could have been in Westland. He couldn't have brought it with him when he moved here, before the boundary, and he couldn't have found it in Westland; the book had magic. The boundary wouldn't have worked if magic had been here then. Magic could only be brought into Westland after the boundary was up.

His father had found a pass, gone into the Midlands, and brought the book back. Richard was shocked and excited at the same time. His father had done it! He had gone across the boundary. Richard was elated. Now he knew there was a way across; it could be done. He still had to find the pass, but that didn't matter for now. There was a pass; that was what mattered.

Richard turned back to the other two. "We will go have supper."

"I put a stew on, just before you awoke, and there is fresh bread," Kahlan offered.

"Bags!" Zedd threw his scarecrow arms up into the air. "It's about time someone remembered supper!"

Richard gave a little smile in the dark. "After we've eaten, we'll make preparations, decide what we need to take, what we can carry, get our provisions together and packed tonight. We'll need to get a good night's sleep. We leave at first light." He turned and headed for the house. The faint glow of the fire coming from the windows offered warmth and light.

Zedd held up an arm. "Where are we headed, my boy?"

"The Midlands," Richard called back over his shoulder.

Zedd was halfway through his second bowl of stew before he could bring himself to stop eating long enough to talk. "So, what have you figured out? Is there truly a way to cross the boundary?"

"There is."

"Are you sure? How can it be? How can we cross without going through?"

Richard smiled as he stirred his stew. "You don't have to get wet to cross a river."

The lamp light flickered on their faces as Kahlan and Zedd frowned in puzzlement. Kahlan turned and threw a small piece of meat to the cat, who was sitting on his haunches, waiting for any handout. Zedd ate another slab of bread before he was able to ask his next question.

"And how do you know there is a way across?"

"There is. That's all that matters."

Zedd had an innocent look on his face. "Richard." He ate two more spoonfuls of stew. "We are your friends. There are no secrets among us. You can tell us."

Richard looked from one big pair of eyes to the other, and laughed out loud. "I've had strangers tell me more of themselves."

Zedd and Kahlan both backed away a little at the rebuff and looked at each other, but neither dared repeat the question.

They talked on as they ate, of what they had at hand to take with them, how much they could do to prepare in such a short time, and what their priorities should be. They listed everything they could think of, each offering items to be taken. There was much to do and little time. Richard asked Kahlan if she traveled the Midlands often. She said that was almost all she ever did.

"And you wear that dress when you travel?"

"I do." She hesitated. "People recognize me by it. I don't stay in the woods. Wherever I go, I am always provided with food and a place to stay, and anything else I might require."

Richard wondered why. He didn't press, but he knew the dress she wore was more than something she bought in a shop. "Well, with the three of us being hunted, I don't think we want people to recognize you. I think we need to stay away from people as much as possible, keep to the woods when we can." She and Zedd both nodded their agreement. "We will need to find you some traveling clothes, forest garb, but there is nothing here that will fit you. We'll have to find something on the way. I have a hooded cloak here. It will keep you warm for now."

"Good," she said, smiling, "I'm tired of being cold, and I can tell you, a dress is not right for the woods."

Kahlan finished before the men and put her half-full bowl on the floor for the cat. The cat seemed to have the same appetite as Zedd and was eating out of the bowl before she could set it down.

They discussed each item they would take, and planned how they would do without others. There was no telling how long they would be gone, but Westland was a big place, and the Midlands bigger. Richard wished they could go to his house, since he often went on long treks and had the right kinds of provisions, but it was too big a risk. He would rather find the things they needed elsewhere, or go without, than go back to what waited there. He didn't know yet where they were going to cross the boundary, but he wasn't worried. He still had until morning to think about it. He was just relieved to know there was a way.

The cat's head came up. He crossed half the distance to the door and stopped, back and fur rising. Everyone noticed and fell silent. There was firelight in the front window, but it wasn't reflecting from the hearth. It was coming from outside.

"I smell burning pitch," Kahlan said.

In an instant the three were on their feet. Richard grabbed the sword from the back of his chair and had it on almost before he was to his feet. He went to look out the window, but Zedd didn't waste the time and went through the door in a rush with Kahlan in tow. Richard got only a glimpse of torches before he hurried out after the other two.

Spread out in the long grass in front of the house was a mob of about fifty men, some carrying torches, but most carrying crude weapons, axes, pitchforks, scythes, or axe handles. They were dressed in their work clothes. Richard recognized many of the faces, good men, honest, hardworking family men. They didn't look like good men this night, though. They looked to be in a foul mood, their faces grim and angry. Zedd stood in the center of the porch, hands on his skinny hips, smiling out at them, the red light from the torches making his white hair pink.

"What's this then, boys?" Zedd asked.

They mumbled among themselves, and several men in front took a step or two forward. Richard knew the one, John, who spoke for the rest.

"There's trouble about. Trouble caused by magic! And you're at the bottom of it, old man! You're a witch!"

"A witch?" Zedd asked in bewilderment. "A witch?"

"That's what I said, a witch!" John's dark eyes shifted to Richard and Kahlan. "This doesn't concern you two. Our business is with the old man. Leave now or you'll get the same as him." Richard couldn't believe the men he knew were saying this.

Kahlan came forward, stepping in front of Zedd, the folds of her dress swirling around her legs when she stopped. She held her fists at her sides. "Leave now," she warned menacingly, "before you come to regret what you have chosen to do."

The mob of men looked around at each other, some smirking, some making crude comments under their breath, some laughing. Kahlan stood her ground and stared them down. The laughter died out.

"So," John said with a sneer, "two witches to take care of." The men cheered and hollered, brandishing their weapons. John's round, heavyset face smiled defiantly.

Richard stepped slowly and deliberately in front of Kahlan, putting a hand behind as he did so, forcing her and Zedd to step back. He kept his voice calm, friendly. "John. How's Sara? I haven't seen you two for a while." John didn't answer. Richard surveyed the other faces. "I know many of you, know you to be good men. This isn't something you want to do." He looked back at John. "Take your men and go home to your families. Please, John?"

John pointed an axe handle at Zedd. "That old man's a witch! We're going to put an end to him." He pointed at Kahlan. "And her! Unless you want the same, Richard, be on your way!" The mob yelled their agreement. The torches sizzled and popped as they burned, and the air smelled of burning pitch and sweat. When they realized that Richard wasn't leaving, the rabble started to push forward.

The sword was free in a blink. The men took a step back as the metallic ringing filled the night air. John stood in red-faced anger. The ringing died out, and the only sound was from the burning torches. Grumbling broke out about Richard being in with the witches.

John charged, swinging the axe handle at Richard as he came. The sword flashed through the air, splintering John's weapon with a loud crack. Only two ragged inches of the axe handle

136

were left above his fist. The severed piece of wood spun off into the darkness, landing somewhere with a hollow thud.

John stood frozen, one foot on the ground, one on the porch, and the point of the Sword of Truth pressed to the underside of his ample chin. The polished blade glinted in the torchlight. Richard, his muscles hard with restrained need, slowly bent forward and with the sword point tilted John's face up to his own. In a voice barely more than a whisper, but so deadly cold it make John stop breathing, he said, "Another step, John, and your head follows." John didn't move, didn't breathe. "Back away," Richard hissed.

The man did as he was ordered, but when back with his fellows, regained his nerve. "You can't stop us, Richard, we're here to save our families."

"From what!" Richard yelled. He pointed the sword at one of the other men. "Frank! When your wife was sick, wasn't it Zedd who brought her a potion that made her well?" He pointed the sword to another. "And Bill, didn't you come and ask Zedd about the rains, when they would come so you fellows could harvest your crops?" He whipped the sword's point back to his attacker. "And John, when your little girl was lost in the woods, was it not Zedd who read the clouds all night and then went out himself and found her and brought her back, safe, to you and Sara?" John and a few others cast their eyes downward. Richard angrily drove the sword back into its scabbard. "Zedd has helped most of the men here. He has helped heal your fevers, find lost loved ones, and freely shared anything he has with you."

From the back someone yelled out, "Only a witch could do all those things!"

"He has done nothing to harm a single one of you!" Richard paced back and forth across the porch, facing the men down. "He has never harmed one of you! He's helped most of you! Why would you want to harm a friend!"

There was some confused grumbling for a few minutes, before they regained their conviction. "Most of the things he's done are magic!" John shouted. "A witch's magic! None of our families are safe with him around!"

Before Richard could answer, Zedd was pulling him back by his arm. He turned to the old man's smiling face. Zedd didn't seem to be bothered in the least. If anything, he seemed to be enjoying himself.

"Very impressive," he whispered, "both of you, very impressive. If you would, though, let me handle it from here?" He lifted an eyebrow, then turned to the men. "Gentlemen, good evening. How nice to see you all." Some of the men gave a greeting in return. A few lifted their hats self-consciously. "If you would be so kind, before you dispatch me, let me talk a moment with my two friends here?" There were nods all around. Zedd pulled Kahlan and Richard back a little toward the house, away from the crowd, and bent close.

"A lesson in power, my friends." He put a sticklike finger on Kahlan's nose. "Too little." Next he put the finger on Richard's nose. "Too much." He put the finger to his own nose, and with a twinkle in his eyes said, "Just right." He cupped Kahlan's chin in his hand. "If I were to let you do this, dear one, there would be graves to be dug this night. Our three would be among them. But very noble nonetheless. Thank you for your concern for me." He put his hand on Richard's shoulder. "If I were to let you do this, there would be a great many graves to be dug, and the three of us would be the only ones left to do the digging. I am too old to dig that many holes in the ground, and we have more important things to do. But you were very noble too; you handled yourself honorably." He patted Richard's shoulder and then put a finger under each of their chins.

"Now, I want you two to let me handle this matter. The problem is not what you are telling these men. The problem is they aren't listening. You have to get their attention before they will hear you." He lifted an eyebrow and looked to each in turn. "Watch and learn what you can. Listen to my words, but they will have no effect on you." He removed his finger and shuffled past them, smiling and waving to the men.

"Gentlemen. Oh, John, how is your little girl?"

"She's fine," he grumbled, "but one of my cows had a two-headed calf."

"Really? And how do you think that happened?"

"I think it happened because you're a witch!"

"There, you said it again." Zedd shook his head in confusion. "I don't understand. Do you gentlemen want to do away with me because you think I have magic, or is it simply your intention to demean me by calling me a woman?"

There was some confusion. "We don't know what you're talking about," someone said.

"Well, it's simple. Girls are witches. Boys are called warlocks. Do you see my point? If you call me a witch, you seem to be calling me a girl. If what you mean is that you think me a warlock, well, that is an altogether different insult. So, which is it? Girl or warlock."

There was more confused discussion, then John spoke up, angry. "We mean to say you're a warlock, and we intend to have your hide for it!"

"My, my, my," Zedd said, tapping his lower lip thoughtfully with the tip of his finger. "Why, I had no idea you men were so brave. So very brave indeed."

"How's that?" John asked.

Zedd shrugged. "Well, what is it you think a warlock capable of?"

There was more talk among themselves. They started shouting out suggestions. He could make two-headed cows, make the rains come, find people who were lost, make children be stillborn, make strong men weak and make their women leave them. Somehow this didn't seem to be sufficient, so more ideas were shouted out. Make water burn, turn people into cripples, change a man into a toad, kill with a look, call upon demons, and in general, everything else.

Zedd waited until they were done, and then held his arms out to them. "There you have it. Just as I said, you men are the bravest fellows I have ever seen! To think, armed only with pitchforks and axe handles, you come to do battle with a warlock who has these kinds of powers. My, my, how brave." His voice trailed off. Zedd shook his head in wonderment. Worry started to break out in the crowd.

Zedd went on, in a drawn-out, monotonous tone, suggesting the things a warlock could do, describing in great detail a variety of deeds from the frivolous to the terrifying. The men stood, transfixed, listening in rapt attention. He went on and on for a good half hour. Richard and Kahlan listened, shifting their weight as they became bored and tired. The eyes of the mob

139

were wide, unblinking. They stood like statues, the dancing flames from their torches the only motion among the men.

The mood had changed. There was no longer anger. Now there was fear. The wizard's voice changed, too; no longer kind and gentle, or even dull, it was harsh and threatening.

"And so, men, what do you think it is we should do now?"

"We think you should let us go home, unharmed," came the weak reply. The others nodded with agreement.

The wizard waggled a long finger in the air in front of them. "No, I don't think so. You see, you men came here to kill me. My life is the most precious thing I have, and you intended to take it from me. I can't let that go unpunished." Quaking and fear swept through the crowd. Zedd stepped to the edge of the porch. The men took a step back. "As punishment for trying to take my life, I take from you, not your life, but that which is most precious, most dear, most valuable!" With a flourish, he swept his hand dramatically over their heads. They gasped. "There. It is done," he declared. Richard and Kahlan, who had been leaning against the house, stood up straight.

For a moment no one moved; then a fellow in the midst of the mob thrust his hand into his pocket and felt around. "My gold. It's gone."

Zedd rolled his eyes. "No, no, no. I said the most precious, the most dear. That which you pride above all else."

Everyone stood a moment, confused. Then a few eyebrows went up in alarm. Another man suddenly thrust his hand into his pocket and felt around, eyes wide in fright. He moaned and then fainted. The ones near by drew back from him. Soon others were putting their hands in their pockets, cautiously feeling around. There were more moans and wails, and soon all the men were grabbing at their crotches in a panic. Zedd smiled in satisfaction. Pandemonium broke out among the mob. Men were jumping up and down, crying, grabbing at themselves, running around in little circles, asking for help, falling on the ground, and sobbing.

"Now, you men get out of here! Leave!" Zedd yelled. He turned to Richard and Kahlan; an impish grin on his face wrinkled his nose. He winked at them both.

"Please, Zedd!" a few men called out. "Please don't leave us

140

like this! Please help us!" There were pleas all around. Zedd waited a few moments and turned back to them.

"What's this? Do you men think I have been too harsh?" He asked with mock wonder and sincerity. There was quick agreement that he had been. "And why do you think this? Have you learned something?"

"Yes!" John yelled. "We realize now that Richard was right. You have been our friend. You have never done anything to harm any of us." Everyone shouted their agreement. "You have only helped us, and we acted stupidly. We want to ask your forgiveness. We know, just like Richard said, that we were wrong, that using magic doesn't make you bad. Please, Zedd, don't stop being our friend now. Please don't leave us like this." There were more pleas shouted out.

Zedd tapped a finger on his bottom lip. "Well—" He looked up, thinking. "—I guess I could put things back to the way they were." The men moved closer. "But only if you all agree to my terms. I think them quite fair, though." They were ready to agree to anything. "All right, then, if you agree to tell anyone who speaks up, from now on, that magic doesn't make a person bad; that their actions are what count; and if you go home to your families and tell them you almost made a terrible mistake tonight, and why you were wrong, then you will all be restored. Fair?"

There was nodding from everyone. "More than fair," John said. "Thank you, Zedd." The men turned and began to leave, quickly. Zedd stood and watched.

"Oh, gentlemen, one more thing." They froze. "Please pick up your tools from the ground. I'm an old man. I could easily trip and hurt myself." They kept a cautious eye to him as they reached out and snatched up their weapons, then turned and walked a ways before breaking into a run.

Richard came and waited to one side of Zedd, Kahlan to the other. Zedd stood with his hands on his bony hips, watching the men go. "Idiots," he muttered under his breath. It was dark. The only light came from the front window of the house behind them, and Richard could barely see Zedd's face, but he could see it well enough to see he wasn't smiling. "My friends," the old man said, "that was a stew stirred by a hidden hand."

"Zedd," Kahlan asked, diverting her eyes from his face, "did you really make . . . well, you know, make their manhood vanish?"

Zedd chuckled. "That would be quite the magic! Beyond me, I'm afraid. No, dear one, I only tricked them into thinking I had. Simply convinced them of the truth of it, let their own minds do the work."

Richard turned to the wizard. "A trick? It was just a trick? I thought you had done real magic." He seemed somehow disappointed.

Zedd shrugged. "Sometimes if a trick is done properly, it can work better than magic. In fact, I would go so far as to say a good trick is real magic."

"But still, it was just a trick."

The wizard held up a finger. "Results, Richard. That's what counts. Your way, those men would have all lost their heads."

Richard grinned. "Zedd, I think some of them would have preferred that over what you did to them." Zedd chuckled. "So is that what you wanted us to watch and learn? That a trick can work as well as magic?"

"Yes, but also something more important. As I said, this was a stew stirred by a hidden hand, the hand of Darken Rahl. But he has made a mistake tonight; it is a mistake to use insufficient force to finish the job. In so doing, you give your enemy a second chance. That is the lesson I want you to learn. Learn it well; you may not get a second chance when your time comes."

Richard frowned. "I wonder why he did it then?"

Zedd shrugged. "I don't know. Maybe because he doesn't have enough power in this land yet, but then it also was a mistake to try, because it only served to warn us."

They started toward the door. There was a lot of work to do before they could sleep. Richard began going through the list in his head but was distracted by an odd feeling.

Suddenly, realization washed over him like cold water. Richard inhaled in a gasp. He spun around, eyes wide, and grabbed a fistful of Zedd's robes.

"We have to get out of here! Right now!"

"What?"

"Zedd! Darken Rahl isn't stupid! He wants us to feel safe, to

142

feel confident! He knew we were smart enough to beat those men, one way or another. In fact he wanted us to, so we would sit around congratulating ourselves while he comes for us himself. He doesn't fear you—you said he's stronger than a wizard—he doesn't fear the sword, and he doesn't fear Kahlan. He's on his way here right now! His plan is to get us all at the same time, right now, this very night! He hasn't made a mistake, this was his plan. You said it yourself, sometimes a trick is better than magic. That's what he's doing; this was all a trick to distract us!"

Kahlan's face went white. "Zedd, Richard is right. This is how Rahl thinks, the mark of his way. He likes to do things in a manner you do not expect. We have to get out of here this very minute."

"Bags! I have been an old fool! You are right. We must leave now, but I can't leave without my rock." He started off around the house.

"Zedd, there's no time!"

The old man was already running up the hill, robes and hair flying, off into the darkness. Kahlan followed Richard into the house. They had been lulled into laziness. He couldn't believe how foolish he had been to underestimate Rahl. Snatching up his pack from the corner by the hearth, he ran into his room, checking under his shirt for the tooth. Finding it safe, he came back with his forest cloak. Richard threw it around Kahlan's shoulders and took a quick glance around to see if there was anything else he could grab, but there was no time to think, nothing worth their lives, so he took her by the arm and headed for the door. Outside, in the grass in front of the house, Zedd was already back, breathing hard.

"What about the rock?" Richard asked. There was no way Zedd could lift it, much less carry it.

"In my pocket," the wizard said with a smile. Richard couldn't spare the time to wonder at this. The cat was suddenly there, somehow aware of their urgency, rubbing up against their legs. Zedd picked it up. "Can't leave you here, Cat. There's trouble coming." Zedd lifted the flap of Richard's pack and tucked the cat inside.

Richard had an uneasy feeling. He looked about, scanning

the darkness, seeking something out of place, something hidden. He saw nothing, but felt eyes watching.

Kahlan noticed his searching. "What's wrong?"

Even though he could see nothing, he felt the eyes. It must be his fear, he decided. "Nothing. Let's go."

Richard led them through a sparsely wooded area he knew well enough to walk blindfolded, to the trail he wanted, and turned south. They moved along quickly in silence, with the exception of Zedd muttering occasionally about how stupid he had been. After a while, Kahlan told him he was too reproachful of himself. They had all been fooled, and each felt the sting of blame, but they had made good their escape, and that was all that mattered.

It was an easy trail, almost a road, and the company of three walked side by side, Richard in the middle, Zedd to his left, Kahlan to his right. The cat poked his head up from Richard's backpack and looked about as they walked. It was a mode of travel he had enjoyed since he was a kitten. The moonlight was enough to light their way. Richard saw a few wayward pines looming against the sky, but he knew there could be no stopping. They had to get away from here. The night was cold but he was warm enough with the effort of their rapid pace. Kahlan wrapped his cloak tightly around herself.

After about a half hour Zedd brought them to a halt. He reached into his robes and pulled out a small handful of powder. He threw it back down the path, the way they had come. Silver sparkles shot from his hand and followed their trail back into the darkness. The sparkles tinkled as they went, disappearing around a bend.

Richard started back up the trail. "What was that?"

"Just a little magic dust. It will cover our trail, so Rahl won't know where we went."

"He still has the cloud to follow us with."

"Yes, but that will only give him a general area. If we keep moving, it will be of little use to him. It's only when you stop, like you did at my house, that he can hunt you."

They continued on to the south, the trail taking them through sweet-smelling pines and higher into the hill country. At the top of a rise they all turned suddenly at a roaring sound behind. Off beyond the dark expanse of the forest, in the distance, they saw an immense column of flame shooting skyward, yellows and reds reaching up into the blackness.

"It's my house. Darken Rahl is there." Zedd smiled. "He looks to be angry."

Kahlan touched his shoulder. "I'm sorry, Zedd."

"Don't be, dear one. It's just an old house. It could have been us."

Kahlan turned to Richard as they started out again. "Do you know where we are going?"

Richard abruptly realized he did. "I do." He smiled to himself, glad to be telling the truth.

The three figures fled into the dark shadows of the trail, into the night.

Overhead, two huge winged beasts watched with hungry, glowing green eyes, and then pitched themselves into steep, silent dives. Wings tucked back for speed, they plummeted toward the backs of their prey.

CHAPTER 11

IT WAS THE CAT that saved him. He yowled and leapt over Richard's head in a fright, causing him to duck, not enough for the gar to miss him, but enough to deflect the full impact. Still, the claws raked his back painfully and knocked him sprawling facedown into the dirt, driving the wind from his lungs in a whoosh. Before he could take a breath the gar pounced on his back, its weight preventing him from breathing or reaching his sword. Before he went down he had seen Zedd sent tumbling into the trees by a second gar, and now it went crashing through the brush after him.

Richard braced himself for the claws he knew would come. Before the gar could rip him open, Kahlan heaved rocks at it from the side of the path. They bounced harmlessly off the beast's head, but it was distracted momentarily. The gar roared, mouth agape, seeming to split the night air with the sound, and held him pinned like a mouse beneath a cat's paw. Richard struggled mightily to lift himself, his lungs burning for air. Blood flies bit his neck. He reached behind, pulling out handfuls of fur, trying to get the great arm off his back. By its size he knew it had to be a short-tailed gar; it was much bigger than the long-tailed gar he had seen before. The sword was under him, digging painfully into his abdomen. He couldn't get to it. It felt as if the veins in his neck would burst.

Richard was beginning to black out. The sounds of yelling and roars from the gar were growing fainter as he struggled. Kahlan got too close in her flurry of rock throwing. The gar reached out with frightening quickness and snatched her by the hair. Doing so caused the beast to shift its weight enough to let Richard gasp desperately for air, but not enough to allow him to move. Kahlan screamed.

Out of nowhere, the cat, all teeth and claws, sprang to the gar's face. The cat howled, clawing furiously at the gar's eyes. With one arm holding Kahlan, it lifted the other to swipe at the the cat.

When it did, Richard rolled to the side and sprang to his feet, drawing his sword. Kahlan screamed again. Richard swung in fury, severing the arm that held her. She tumbled back, free. Howling, the gar backhanding him before he could bring the sword up. The force of the blow sent him flying through the air, landing on his back.

Richard sat up, the world spinning and tilting. The sword was gone, thrown into the brush somewhere. The gar was in the center of the trail, wailing in pain and rage as blood gushed from the stump. Glowing green eyes searched frantically for the object of its hate. They locked on Richard. He didn't see Kahlan anywhere.

Off to his right, in the trees, there was a sudden blinding flash, illuminating everything with intense, white light. The violent sound of an explosion hammered painfully into his ears as the concussion from the blast tumbled him against a tree and knocked the gar from its feet. Rolling flames whirled through gaps in the trees. Giant splinters and other debris hurtled past, streaming trailers of smoke.

Richard began a frantic search for the sword as the gar came to its feet with a howl. Richard felt around on the ground, desperate, and partially blinded from the flash of the explosion. He had enough vision, though, to see the gar coming. His anger flared. He could feel it flare in the sword, too. The sword's magic reached out to him, beckoned by its master. He called it forth, summoned it, hungered for it. It was there, across the trail. He knew it as surely as if he could see it. He knew exactly where it lay, as if he were touching it. He scrambled across the trail.

Halfway there the gar kicked him so hard he saw things moving past but couldn't understand what they were. All he knew for sure was that every breath caused intense pain in his left side. He didn't know where the trail was or where he was in relation to it. Blood flies were bumping into his face. He couldn't get his bearings. But he did know where the Sword of Truth was.

He dove for it.

For an instant his fingers touched it. For an instant he thought he saw Zedd. Then the gar had him. It picked him up by his right arm and wrapped its repulsive, warm wings about him, hugging him close, his feet dangling in midair. He cried out from the sharp pain in his left ribs. Glowing green eyes burned into his, and the giant mouth snapped, showing him his fate. The immense maw split open for him, its fetid breath on his face, its black throat waiting. Wet fangs glistened in the moonlight.

With all his strength, Richard kicked his boot into the stump of the gar's arm. It threw its head back, howled in pain, and dropped him.

Zedd emerged at the edge of the trees a dozen yards behind the gar. Richard, on his knees, grabbed the sword. Zedd threw his hands out, fingers extended. Fire, wizard's fire, shot from his fingers and came shrieking through the air. The fire grew and tumbled, illuminating everything it passed, becoming a blue and yellow ball of liquid flame that wailed and expanded as it came, a thing alive. It hit the gar's back with a thud, silhouetting the giant beast against the light. Within the space of a breath the blue-and-yellow flames washed over the gar, enveloping it, surging through it. Blood flies sparked into nothingness. Fire sizzled and snapped everywhere on the creature, consuming it. The gar disappeared into the blue heat and was gone. The fire swirled a moment and then it, too, was gone. The smell of burnt fur, and a hazy smoke, hung in the air. The night was suddenly quiet.

Richard collapsed, exhausted and in pain. The gashes on his back had dirt and gravel ground into them, and the pain in his left side seared into him with every breath. He wanted only to lie there, nothing more. The sword was still in his hand. He let the power of it wash through him, sustain him. He allowed the anger of it to let him ignore the pain.

The cat licked Richard's face with his rough tongue and nuzzled the top of his head against Richard's cheek. "Thank you, Cat," he managed. Zedd and Kahlan appeared over him. Both bent down to take his arms and help lift him up.

"No! You'll hurt me if you do that. Let me get up by myself."

"What's wrong?" Zedd asked.

"The gar kicked me in the left side. It hurts."

"Let me look." The old man bent over and gently felt Richard's ribs. Richard winced in pain. "Well, I don't see any bones sticking out. Can't be that bad."

Richard tried not to laugh, as he knew it would hurt. He was right. "Zedd, that was no trick. This time it was magic."

"This time it was magic," the wizard confirmed. "But Darken Rahl may have seen it too, if he was looking. We have to get out of here. Lie still, let me see if I can help."

Kahlan knelt on his other side and cupped her hand on his, on the hand that held the sword, held the magic. When her hand touched his, he felt a surge of power from the sword that startled him and nearly took his breath away. Somehow, he felt the magic was warning him, and trying to protect him.

Kahlan smiled down at him. She hadn't felt it.

Zedd put one hand on Richard's ribs and a finger under his chin as he spoke in a soft, calm, reassuring voice. As he listened to Zedd, Richard dismissed the sword's reaction to Kahlan's touch on his hand. His old friend told him that three of his ribs were injured and that he was putting magic around them to strengthen and protect them until they could heal. He continued to talk in his special way, telling Richard how the pain would be reduced, but not gone, until the ribs were healed. He spoke more, but the words seemed somehow not to matter. When Zedd finished at last, Richard felt as if he were waking from sleep.

He sat up. The pain had lessened greatly. He thanked the old man and got to his feet. He put the sword away and picked up the cat, thanking him again. He handed the cat to Kahlan for her to hold while he searched for his pack and found it near the side of the trail where it had been thrown in the fight. The gashes on his back were painful, but he would worry about them when they got to where they were going. When the other two weren't looking, he slipped the tooth from his neck and put it in his pocket.

Richard asked the other two if they were hurt. Zedd seemed insulted by the question. He insisted he wasn't as frail as he looked. Kahlan said she was fine, thanks to him. Richard told her he hoped never to get in a rock-throwing contest with her. She gave him a big smile as she put Cat in his backpack. He watched as she picked up the cloak and put it around her shoulders, wondering at the way the sword's magic had reacted when she had touched his hand.

"We had better be leaving," Zedd reminded them.

After about a mile, several smaller paths intersected theirs. Richard led them down the one he wanted. The wizard spread more of his magic dust to hide their trail. Their way was narrower now, so they walked single file, with Richard in the lead, Kahlan in the middle, and Zedd in the rear. The three of them kept a wary eye to the sky as they walked along. Even though it was uncomfortable to do so, Richard walked with his hand on the hilt of the sword.

Shadows in the moonlight swept back and forth across the heavy oak door and its iron strap hinges as the wind bowed branches close to the house. Kahlan and Zedd didn't want to climb the spiked fence, so Richard had left them on the other side to wait. He was just starting to reach up to knock on the door, when a big fist grabbed his hair and a knife pressed against his throat. He froze.

"Chase?" he whispered hopefully.

The hand released his hair. "Richard! What are you doing lurking about in the middle of the night! You know better than to sneak up to my place."

"I wasn't sneaking. I didn't want to wake the whole house."

"There's blood all over you. How much is yours?"

"Most of it, I'm sorry to say. Chase, go unlock your gate. Kahlan and Zedd are waiting out there. We need you."

Chase, cursing as he stepped on twigs and acorns with his bare feet, unlocked the gate, and shepherded them all into the house.

Emma Brandstone, Chase's wife, was a kind, friendly woman, always wearing a smile on her bright face. She seemed the complete opposite of Chase. Emma would be mortified if she thought she had intimidated anyone, while Chase's day wouldn't be complete unless he had. Emma was like Chase in one respect, though. Nothing ever seemed to surprise or fluster her. She was typically unruffled at this late hour as she stood in her long, white nightdress, her gray-streaked hair tied back, making tea as the rest of them sat at the table. She smiled, as if it were normal to have blood-streaked guests come visiting in the middle of the night. But then, with Chase, it sometimes was.

Richard hung his pack over the back of his chair, taking the cat out and handing him to Kahlan. She put him in her lap, where he immediately began purring as she stroked his back. Zedd sat to his other side. Chase put a shirt over his big frame and lit several lamps that hung from heavy oak beams. Chase had felled the trees, hewed the beams out, and placed them by himself. The names of the children were carved along the side of one. Behind his chair at the table was a fireplace made of stones he had collected in his travels over the years. Each had a unique shape, color, and texture. Chase would tell anyone who would listen where each had come from, and what sort of trouble he had encountered in retrieving it. A simple wooden bowl, full of apples, sat in the center of the stout pine table.

Emma removed the bowl of apples and replaced it with a pot of tea and a jar of honey, then passed around mugs. She told Richard to remove his shirt and turn his chair so she could clean his wounds, a task not unfamiliar to her. With a stiff brush and hot soapy water she scrubbed his back as if she were cleaning a dirty kettle.

Richard bit his bottom lip, holding his breath at times, and scrunched his eyes closed in pain as she worked. She apologized for hurting him, but said she had to get all the dirt out or it would be worse later. When she was finished cleaning the gashes, she patted his back dry with a towel and applied a cool salve while Chase got him a clean shirt. Richard was glad to put the shirt on, as it provided him at least a symbol of protection from her further ministering.

Emma smiled to the three guests. "Would anyone like something to eat?"

Zedd lifted a hand. "Well, I wouldn't mind . . ." Richard and Kahlan both shot him a withering glare. He shrank back into his chair. "No. Nothing for us. Thank you."

Emma stood behind Chase, combing her fingers affectionately through his hair. He sat in undisguised agony, barely able to tolerate her public display of sentiment. At last he leaned forward, using the excuse of pouring tea to put a stop to it.

With a frown, Chase pushed the honey across the table. "Richard, for as long as I've known you, you've had a talent for sidestepping trouble. But lately, you seem to be losing your footing."

Before Richard could answer, Lee, one of their daughters, appeared in the doorway, rubbing her sleepy eyes with her fists. Chase scowled at her. She pouted back.

Chase sighed. "You've got to be the ugliest child I've ever seen."

Her pout turned to a beaming grin. Lee ran over to him, threw her arms around his leg, put her head on his knee, and hugged it tight. He mussed her hair.

"Back to bed with you, little one."

"Wait," Zedd spoke up. "Lee, come here." She went around the table. "My old cat has been complaining that he has no children to play with." Lee stole a peek toward Kahlan's lap. "Do you know of any children he could visit?"

The girl's eyes widened. "Zedd, he could stay here! He would have fun with us!"

"Really? Well then, he will stay here for a visit."

"All right, Lee," Emma said, "off to bed with you."

Richard looked up. "Emma, could you do me a favor? Do you have any traveling clothes Kahlan could borrow?"

Emma looked Kahlan over. "Well, her shoulders are too big for my clothes, and her legs are too long, but the older girls have things I think would work nicely." She smiled warmly at Kahlan and held out a hand. "Come on, dear, let's see what we can find."

152

Kahlan handed Cat to Lee and took her other hand. "I hope Cat won't be a bother. He insists on sleeping on your bed with you."

"Oh, no," Lee said earnestly, "that will be fine."

As they left the room Emma knowingly shut the door.

Chase took a sip of tea. "Well?"

"Well, you know the conspiracy my brother was talking about? It's worse than he knows."

"That so," Chase said noncommittally.

Richard pulled the Sword of Truth from its scabbard and laid it on the table between them. The polished blade gleamed. Chase leaned forward and put his elbows on the table, lifting the sword with his fingertips. He let it roll into his palms, inspecting it closely, running his fingers over the word *Truth* on the hilt and down the fuller on each side of the blade, testing the sharpness of the edge. He betrayed nothing more than mild curiosity.

"Not unusual for a sword to be named, but typically the name is engraved on the blade. I've never seen the name on the hilt." Chase was waiting for someone else to say something consequential.

"Chase, you've seen this sword before," Richard admonished. "You know what it is."

"I have. But, I've never seen it this close." His eyes came up, dark and intense. "The point is, Richard, what are you doing with it?"

Richard peered back with equal intensity. "It was given to me by a great and noble wizard."

Chase's forehead wrinkled into a sober frown. He looked to Zedd. "What's your part in this, Zedd?"

Zedd leaned forward, a small smile on his thin lips. "I'm the one who gave it to him."

Chase leaned back in his chair, shaking his head slowly. "The spirits be praised," he whispered. "A real Seeker. At last."

"We don't have much time," Richard said. "I need to know some things about the boundary."

Chase let out a deep sigh as he rose and went to the hearth. He leaned an arm on the mantel, staring into the flames. The other two waited while the big man picked at the rough wood of the mantel as if trying to pick his words.

153

"Richard, do you know what my job is?"

Richard shrugged. "Keeping people away from the boundary, for their own good."

Chase shook his head. "Do you know how to get rid of wolves?"

"Go out and hunt them, I guess."

The boundary warden shook his head again. "That might get a few, but more would be born, and in the end, you have just as many. If you really want to have fewer wolves, you hunt their food. You trap rabbits, so to speak. It's easier. If there is less food, fewer pups will be born. In the end you have fewer wolves. That's my job. I hunt rabbits."

Richard felt a wave of fright ripple through him.

"Most people don't understand the boundary, or what we do. They think it's just some stupid law we enforce. Many are afraid of the boundary, mostly older people. Many others think they know what's best and go up there to poach. They aren't afraid of the boundary, so we make them afraid of the wardens. That's something real to them, and we keep it real. They don't like it, but out of fear of us, they stay away. To a few it's a game, to see if they can get away with it. We don't expect to catch them all; we don't really care. What we care about is scaring enough of them so the wolves in the boundary won't have enough rabbits to get stronger.

"We protect the people, but not by preventing them from going into the boundary. Anyone stupid enough to do that is beyond our help. Our job is to keep most away, keep the boundary weak enough so the things in there can't come out and get everyone else. The wardens have all seen things that have gotten loose. We all understand; others don't. Lately, more and more things have been getting loose. Your brother's government may pay us, but they don't understand, either; our allegiance is not to them, nor to any rule of law. Our only duty is to protect the people from the things that come out of the darkness. We consider ourselves sovereign. We take orders when it doesn't hinder our job. It keeps matters friendly. But if the time ever comes, well, we follow our own cause, our own orders."

He sat back at the table, leaning forward on his elbows. "Ultimately, there is only one whose orders we will follow, because our cause is a part of his larger cause. That one is the true Seeker." He picked up the sword in his big hands and held it out to Richard, looking him in the eyes. "I pledge my life and loyalty to the Seeker."

Richard sat back, moved. "Thank you, Chase." He looked to the wizard a moment, then back to the boundary warden. "Now we'll tell you what's been going on, and then I'll tell you what I want."

Richard and Zedd both shared in the telling of all that had happened. Richard wanted Chase to know it all, to understand that there could be no half efforts, that it had to be victory or death, not by their choice, but by Darken Rahl's. Chase looked from one to the other as they spoke, understanding the seriousness of what they were telling him, appearing grim at the telling of the story of the magic of Orden. They didn't have to convince him of the truth of it; he was a man who had seen more than they would probably ever know. He asked few questions, and listened carefully.

He did enjoy the story of what Zedd had done to the mob. His booming laugh filled the room until his laughter dissolved in tears.

The door opened, and Kahlan and Emma stepped into the light. Kahlan was outfitted in fine forest garb, dark green pants with a wide belt, tan shirt, dark cloak, and a good pack. The boots and waist pouch were her own. She looked ready to live a life in the woods. Still, her hair, her face, her figure, and mostly her bearing, spoke that she was more.

Richard introduced her to Chase. "My guide."

Chase lifted an eyebrow.

Emma saw the sword, and by her expression Richard knew she understood. She moved behind her husband again, not touching his hair, but simply resting a hand on his shoulder, wanting to be near him. She knew trouble visited this night. Richard sheathed the sword, and Kahlan came and sat next to him as he finished relating the rest of the events of the night. When he was done, they all sat in silence for a few minutes.

"What can I do to help you, Richard?" Chase finally asked.

Richard spoke softly, but firmly. "Tell me where the pass is."

Chase's eyes came up sharply. "What pass?" His old defensiveness was still in evidence.

"The pass across the boundary. I know about it, I just don't know exactly where it is, and I don't have time to search." Richard didn't have time to play these games and felt his anger rising.

"Who told you this?"

"Chase! Answer the question!"

The other smiled a little. "One condition. I take you there."

Richard thought about the children. Chase was used to danger, but this was different. "That isn't necessary."

Chase gave Richard an appraising look. "It is to me. It's a dangerous place. You three don't know what you're getting yourselves into. I won't send you there alone. And the boundary is my responsibility. If you want me to tell you, then I'm going."

Everyone waited while Richard considered this a moment. Chase didn't bluff, and time was dear. Richard had no choice. "Chase, we would be honored to have you with us."

"Good." He slapped his hand on the table. "The pass is called the Kings' Port. It's in a foul place called Southaven. Four, maybe five days' ride on horseback, if we take Hawkers Trail. Since you're in a hurry, that's the way you'll want to be going. It will be light in a few hours. The three of you need to get some sleep. Emma and I will get the provisions together."

CHAPTER 12

IT SEEMED THAT HE had just fallen asleep when Emma woke him and led them down to breakfast. The sun wasn't up yet, nor was anyone else in the house, but roosters were already crowing at the lightening of the new day. The aromas of cooking made him instantly hungry. Emma, smiling, but not as brightly as the night before, dished out a big breakfast and said Chase had already eaten and was loading the horses. Richard had always thought Kahlan looked alluring in her unusual dress. He decided her new outfit didn't lessen her appeal in the least. While Kahlan and Emma talked about the children, and Zedd gushed compliments about the food, Richard's mind fretted on what lay ahead.

The light dimmed a little as Chase's form filled the doorway. Kahlan gave a start when she saw him. He was wearing a chainmail shirt over a tan leather tunic, heavy black pants, boots, and cloak. Black gauntlets were tucked behind a wide black belt set with a large silver buckle emblazoned with the emblem of the boundary wardens. Strapped everywhere were enough armaments to outfit a small army. On an ordinary man the effect would have been silly; on Chase it was frightening. He was an image of overt threat, deadly with every weapon he carried. Chase had two basic expressions he wore most of the time; the first a look of feigned ignorant disinterest, the second, one that made him seem as if he was about to participate in a slaughter. He wore the second this day.

On their way out, Emma handed Zedd a bundle. "Fried chicken," she said. He gave her a big grin and kissed her forehead. Kahlan gave her a hug and promised to see that the clothes were returned. Richard bent and gave Emma a warm embrace. "Be careful," she whispered in his ear. She gave her husband a kiss on the cheek that he accepted graciously.

Chase handed Kahlan a sheathed long knife, telling her to wear it at all times. Richard asked if he could borrow a knife, too, as he had left his home. Chase's fingers deftly found the strap he wanted among the tangle, freed it, and handed a knife to Richard.

Kahlan eyed all the weaponry. "Do you think you will need all those?"

He gave her a crooked smile. "If I didn't take them, I know I would."

The small company, Chase leading, followed by Zedd, then Kahlan, with Richard bringing up the rear, settled into a comfortable pace through the Hartland Woods. It was a bright autumn morning with a chill to the air. A hawk wheeled in the sky over their heads, a sign of warning at the beginning of a journey. Richard thought to himself that the sign was totally unnecessary.

By midmorning they had left the Hartland Valley and passed into the upper Ven Forest, joining Hawkers Trail below Trunt Lake, and turned south, with the snakelike cloud in slow pursuit. Richard was glad to be leading it away from Chase's house and children. He was troubled that they had to travel so far to the south to cross the boundary, for time was dear. But Chase had said that if there was another pass, he didn't know about it.

Hardwood forests gave way to stands of ancient pines. Passing among them was like traveling through a canyon. The trunks soared to dizzying heights before the limbs branched out, and Richard felt small in the deep shade of the old trees. He had always been at ease traveling. He did it often, and the familiar places they passed made it seem to be just another trek, but this trip was not the same. They were going places he had never been. Dangerous places. Chase was concerned, and had warned them. This alone gave Richard pause, for Chase was not a man to worry over nothing; in fact, Richard had often thought he worried far too little.

Richard watched the other three as they rode: Chase, a black wraith upon his horse, armed to the teeth, feared by the people he protected as well as the ones he hunted, but somehow, not by children; the wisp of a wizard, sticklike Zedd, unassuming, hardly more than a smile, white hair, and simple robes, content to carry nothing more than a bundle of fried chicken, but wielder of wizard's fire and who knew what else; and Kahlan, courageous, determined, and keeper of some secret power, sent to threaten a wizard into naming the Seeker. The three of them were his friends, yet each in their own way made him uneasy. He wondered who was the most dangerous. They followed him unquestioningly, yet led him at the same time. The three of them, all, sworn to protect the Seeker with their lives. And yet, none of the small company, singly or together, was a match for Darken Rahl. The whole of their task seemed hopeless.

Zedd was already into the chicken. Periodically he would toss a bone over his shoulder. After a while he thought to offer a piece to the others. Chase declined, as he kept up a continual scan of their surroundings, paying particular attention to the left side of the trail, to the boundary. The other two accepted. The chicken had lasted longer than Richard thought it would. When the trail widened, he brought his horse up with Kahlan's and rode next to her. She took off her cloak as the day warmed, and smiled over to him with the special smile she never gave anyone else.

Richard had a thought. "Zedd, is there anything a wizard can do about that cloud?"

The old man squinted up at it, then peered back at Richard. "That idea has already come into my head. I think there might be, but I want to wait a while longer, until we are farther away from Chase's family. I don't want to lead a search to them."

In the late afternoon they came upon an old couple, woods people whom Chase knew. The four brought their horses to a halt while the boundary warden spoke with the couple. He sat relaxed on his mount, leather creaking, as he listened to them repeat rumors that they had heard about things coming out of the boundary. Richard now knew them to be more than rumors. Chase treated the couple with respect, as he did most people; nevertheless, they were clearly afraid of him. He told them he was looking into the matter and advised them to stay inside at night.

They rode until long after dark before making camp for the night in a stand of pine, and were on their way the next morning as the sky lightened behind the mountains of the boundary. Richard and Kahlan both yawned as they rode. The forest thinned, with open patches of meadow, bright and green and smelling sweet in the sunshine as they traveled through the hill country on their journey south, the road taking them temporarily farther from the mountains of the boundary. Occasionally they passed small farms, their owners making themselves scarce when they saw Chase.

The land became less familiar to Richard, who rarely traveled this far south. He kept a sharp lookout, making note of the landmarks they passed. After they ate a cold lunch in the warm sun, the road began angling steadily closer to the mountains, until in the late afternoon they were so close to the boundary that they began encountering the gray skeletons of trees killed by the snake vine. Even the sun did little to brighten the dense woods. Chase's demeanor became distant, harder, as he observed everything carefully. Several times he dismounted, walking his horse as he studied the ground, reading tracks.

They crossed a stream that flowed out of the mountains, the water churning sluggish, cold, and muddy. Chase stopped and sat, watching off into the shadows. The rest of them waited, looking at one another and toward the boundary. Richard recognized the dead smell of the vine drifting in the air. The boundary warden led them a little farther, then got off his horse and squatted, studying the ground. When he rose, he handed the reins of his horse to Zedd. He turned to them and said simply, "Wait." They watched him disappear into the trees as they sat quietly. Kahlan's big horse shivered flies off its hide as it nibbled grass.

Chase returned, pulling his black gauntlets on, and took the

160

reins from Zedd. "I want you three to keep going. Don't wait for me, and don't stop. Keep to the road."

"What is it? What did you find?" Richard asked.

Chase turned back and gave him a dark look. "The wolves have been feeding. I'm going to bury what's left, and then I'm going cross-country, between the boundary and you three. I need to check into something. Remember what I said. Don't stop. Don't run your horses, but keep up a good pace, and keep your eyes sharp. If you think I'm gone too long, don't you dare to think to come back looking for me. I know what I'm doing, and you would never find me. I'll be back with you when I can. Keep going until then, and stay on the road."

He mounted, turned his horse, and urged it into a run, its hooves kicking up clumps of sod. "Get moving!" Chase yelled back over his shoulder. As he disappeared through the trees Richard saw him reach up to a short sword strapped over his shoulder and pull it free. He knew Chase was lying. He wasn't going to bury anything. Richard didn't like to let his friend go off alone like this, but Chase spent most of his life alone out here by the boundary, and knew what he was doing, what was necessary to protect them. Richard had to trust his judgment.

"You heard the man," the Seeker said, "let's go."

As the three rode on through the boundary woods, rock outcroppings grew in size and twisted their route one way and then the other. The trees became so thick that the sunlight was all but banished from the still forest, the road a tunnel through the thicket. Richard didn't like how close everything felt, and as they moved quickly along they all kept watching the deep shadows to their left. Branches hung across the road, forcing them to duck under as they passed. He couldn't imagine how Chase could travel through a wood this thick.

When the way was wide enough, Richard rode up to Kahlan's left, wanting to keep himself between her and the boundary. He kept the reins in his left hand to leave his sword hand free. Her cloak was wrapped close around her, but he saw she kept a hand near her knife.

Off to their left, in the distance, came howling, something like a wolf pack, only it wasn't wolves. It was something from the boundary.

The three jerked their heads toward the sound. The horses were terrified and wanted to run. They had to keep reining in, but at the same time let them have enough freedom to trot. Richard understood the way the horses felt. He felt the urge to let them go, but Chase had said explicitly not to let them run. He must have had a reason, so they held back. When the howling was punctuated with bloodcurdling shrieks that made the hair on his neck stand on end, it became more difficult to force himself to prevent the horses from running. The shrieks were wild cries, cries of the need to kill, demanding, desperate. The three rode at a trot for almost an hour, but the sounds seemed to follow them. There was nothing they could do but continue, listening, as they went, to beasts from the boundary.

Unable to stand it any longer, Richard pulled his horse to a halt, and faced the woods. Chase was out there alone with the beasts. He couldn't bear any longer to let his friend face it alone. He had to help.

Zedd turned. "We have to keep moving, Richard."

"He may be in trouble. We can't let him do this alone."

"It's his job, let him do it."

"Right now, his job isn't to be boundary warden; it's to get us to the pass!"

The wizard rode back and spoke softly. "That's the job he's doing, Richard. He's sworn to protect you with his life. That is what he is doing, seeing to it you get to the pass. You have to get it through your head. What you are doing is more important than one man's life. Chase knows that. That's why he said not to come back for him."

Richard was incredulous. "You expect me to let a friend get himself killed if I can help prevent it?" The sounds of howling were getting closer.

"I expect you not to let him die for nothing!"

Richard stared at his old friend. "But maybe we can make the difference."

"And maybe not." The horses stamped about skittishly.

"Zedd is right," Kahlan said. "Going after Chase is not the brave thing to do, going on when you want to help is."

Richard knew they were right, but loathed admitting it. He

162

looked angrily toward Kahlan. "You may be in his position one day! Then what would you have me do?"

She looked at him evenly. "I would have you go on."

He glared at her, not knowing what to say. The shrieks from the woods were closer. Her face showed no emotion.

"Richard, Chase does this all the time, he will be all right," Zedd offered reassuringly. "I wouldn't be surprised if he was having a good time. Later on he will have a good tale to tell. You know Chase. Some of the tale might even be true."

Richard was angry at the two of them, and at himself. He kicked his horse out ahead, taking the lead, not wanting to talk anymore. They left him to his thoughts, let his horse trot ahead. It made him angry that Kahlan would think he could leave her like this. She was no boundary warden. He didn't like it that saving them might mean letting them get killed. It didn't make any sense. At least he didn't want it to make any sense.

He tried to ignore the shrieks and howls off in the woods. After a time the cries fell farther behind. The woods seemed devoid of life, no birds or rabbits or even mice, only the twisted trees and bramble and shadows. He listened carefully to make sure he heard the other two following. He didn't want to turn and look; didn't want to face them. After a while he realized the howls had stopped. He wondered if that was a good sign or not.

He wanted to tell them he was sorry, that he was just afraid for his friend, but he couldn't. He felt helpless. Chase would be all right, he told himself. He was the head of the boundary wardens, not a fool, and he wouldn't go into anything he couldn't handle. He wondered if there was anything Chase couldn't handle. He wondered if he would be able to tell Emma, if something happened to her husband.

He was letting his imagination run away with him. Chase was fine. Not only was he fine, but he would be furious with Richard for thinking these thoughts, for doubting him.

He wondered if Chase would return before nightfall. Should they stop for the night if he didn't? No. Chase had said not to stop. They would have to keep going, all night if necessary, until he rejoined them. He felt as if the mountains were looming over them, ready to pounce. He didn't think he had ever been this close to the boundary.

As concerned as he was about Chase, his anger faded. Richard turned and looked back at Kahlan. She gave him a warm smile, and he returned it, feeling better. He tried to imagine what the woods here had looked like before so many trees died. It might have been a beautiful place, green, snug, safe. Maybe his father had come this way when he had crossed the boundary, traveled this very road with the book.

He wondered if all the trees near the other boundary died before it fell. Maybe they could just wait until this one fell, too, and then go across. Maybe they didn't need to go so far out of their way to the south, to Kings' Port. But why should he think going south was out of the way? He didn't know where to go in the Midlands, so why was one place better than another? The box they sought could just as easily be in the south as farther north.

The woods were getting gloomier. Richard hadn't been able to see the sun for the last couple of hours, but there was no doubt it was setting. He didn't like the idea of traveling these woods at night, but the idea of sleeping in them seemed worse. He checked to make sure the other two were staying close.

The sound of running water came faintly through the evening stillness, swelling as they rode, and in a short distance they came to a small river with a wooden bridge over it. Just before they crossed, Richard stopped. He didn't like the look of it; inexplicably, something felt wrong. Being careful couldn't hurt. He led his horse down the bank and peered underneath. The support beams were anchored to iron rings in granite blocks. The pins were missing.

"Someone tampered with the bridge. It will support the weight of a man, but not a horse. Looks like we're going to have to get wet."

Zedd scowled. "I don't want to get wet."

"Well, do you have a better idea?" Richard asked.

Zedd drew his finger and thumb down opposite sides of his smooth chin. "Yes," he announced. "You two go across, I will hold up the bridge." Richard looked at him as if the wizard had lost his senses. "Go on, it will be all right."

Zedd sat up tall on his horse, held his arms out straight to his sides, palms up, tilted his head back, breathed deeply, and closed

164

his eyes. Reluctantly, cautiously, the other two crossed the bridge. On the other side they turned their horses and looked back. The wizard's horse began walking across unprompted while Zedd continued to hold his arms out, his head tilted back and his eyes closed. When he reached their side, he brought his arms down and looked at the other two. Richard and Kahlan stared at him.

"Maybe I was wrong," Richard said. "Maybe the bridge would hold the weight."

Zedd smiled. "Maybe you were." Without looking back, he snapped his fingers. The bridge collapsed into the water with a crash. The beams groaned as they were torn apart from one another in the current and swept downstream. "Then again, maybe you weren't. I couldn't leave it like that. Someone might come across and be hurt."

Richard shook his head. "Someday, my friend, we are going to sit down and have a long talk." He turned his horse and started off again. Zedd looked at Kahlan and shrugged. She smiled and gave him a wink, then turned and followed after Richard.

They continued down the dismal trail, watching the woods as they went. Richard wondered what else Zedd could do. He let his horse pick its own way in the gathering darkness, wondering how much longer this dead world went on, or if the road would ever take them away from it. The night was bringing life to the place, strange calls and scraping noises. His horse whinnied at things unseen. He patted its neck reassuringly and checked the sky for gars. It was hopeless; he couldn't see any sky. But if gars came they would have a hard time surprising the three of them, as the canopy of twisted, dead limbs and branches would prevent a silent approach. Maybe the things in the trees were more of a threat than gars. He didn't know anything about them, and he wasn't sure he wanted to. He realized his heart was pounding.

After about an hour, he caught the sound of something coming through the brush in the distance to their left. It was breaking branches as it came. He urged his horse into a canter, and checked to be sure Kahlan and Zedd were keeping up. Whatever it was, it was staying with them. They weren't going to be able to get ahead of it. They were going to be cut off. Maybe it was Chase, he thought. Then again, maybe it wasn't.

Richard pulled the Sword of Truth free as he leaned forward and pressed his legs around the horse, spurring it into a gallop. His muscles tensed as his horse raced down the road. He didn't know if Zedd and Kahlan were keeping up with him, and in fact he never gave it a thought. His mind focused on trying to see ahead in the darkness, trying to see anything that might come at him. Anger was slipping its bounds, heat and need coming forth. Jaw set tight, he charged ahead with lethal intent. The sound of his horse's hooves on the road prevented him from hearing the thing in the woods, but he knew it was there, knew it was coming.

Then he saw the black form moving against the barely discernible shapes of the trees. It broke from the woods into the trail a dozen yards in front of him. He raised the sword and went for it, picturing in his mind what he would do. It waited, motionless.

At the last instant he realized it was Chase, holding up an arm to halt him, the silhouette of a flanged mace in his fist.

"Glad to see you're keeping alert," the boundary warden said.

"Chase! You scared the wits out of me!"

"You gave me a moment of concern too." Kahlan and Zedd caught up with them. "Follow me, stay close. Richard, take the rear, keep your sword out."

Chase turned his horse and took off at a gallop, the rest following. Richard didn't know if something was after them or not. Chase didn't act as if there was about to be a fight, but he did tell him to keep his sword out. Richard kept a wary eye over his shoulder. They all hunched their heads down in case there were any low branches. It was dangerous to run the horses in the dark like this, but Chase knew that.

They came to a fork in the road, the first one all day, and without hesitation the boundary warden cut to the right, away from the boundary. Before long they were clear of the woods, moonlight showing an open country of rolling hills and few trees. Chase slowed after a time, letting the horses walk.

Richard sheathed his sword and pulled up close to the others. "What was that all about?"

Chase hooked the mace back onto his belt. "Things in the boundary are following us. When they came out of the boundary

166

for you, I was there to spoil their appetite. Some went back in. The ones left continue to follow from within the boundary, where I can't pursue them. That's why I didn't want you to go too fast. I wouldn't have been able to keep up through the woods, they would have gotten ahead of me, and then they would have had you. I took us away from the boundary now because I wanted to get our scent away from them for the night. It's too dangerous to travel that close to the boundary at night. We'll camp on one of those hills up there." He looked over his shoulder at Richard. "By the way, why did you stop back there? I told you not to."

"I was worried about you. I heard the howling. I was going to come and help. Zedd and Kahlan talked me out of it." Richard thought Chase would be angry, but he wasn't.

"Thanks, but don't do it again. While you were standing there thinking about it, they almost had you. Zedd and Kahlan were right. Don't argue with them the next time."

Richard felt his ears burning. He knew they were right, but it didn't make him feel any better about not helping a friend.

"Chase," Kahlan asked, "you said they had gotten someone, was that true?"

His face was cold stone in the moonlight. "Yes. One of my men. I don't know which one." He turned back to the trail and rode on in silence.

They set up camp on a high hill to give a clear view of anything that approached. Chase and Zedd tended to the horses while Richard and Kahlan started the fire, unpacked the bread, cheese, and dried fruit, and began cooking a simple stew. She went with him and scouted for firewood among the sparse trees, helping carry it back. He told her the two of them made a good team. She smiled a little smile and turned away. He took her arm and turned her back.

"Kahlan, if it had been you, I would have come after you," he said, meaning more than the words he spoke.

She studied his eyes. "Please, Richard, don't even say that." She gently pulled her arm away and went back to camp.

When the other two, back from tending the horses, came into the firelight, Richard could see that the scabbard strapped over Chase's shoulder was empty, the short sword missing. One of his battle axes and several long knives were gone, too. Not that this left him defenseless—far from it.

The mace hanging from his belt was covered in blood from one end to the other, his gauntlets were soaked with it, and it was splattered everywhere on him. Without comment he pulled a knife, pried a three-inch yellowish tooth from the mace where it was wedged between two of the blades, and threw the tooth over his shoulder into the darkness. After wiping the blood off his hands and face he sat down in front of the fire with the others.

Richard tossed a stick in the fire. "Chase, what were those creatures that were after us? And how could anything go in and out of the boundary?"

Chase picked up a loaf of bread and tore off about a third. He met Richard's eyes. "They're called heart hounds. They're about twice the size of a wolf, big barrel chests, heads are kind of flat, big snout full of teeth. Fierce. I'm not sure what color they are. They only prowl at night, until today, that is. But it was too dark in those woods to tell, and, anyway, I was kind of busy. There were more than I've ever seen together before."

"Why are they called heart hounds?"

Chase chewed a piece of bread as he stared back with intense eyes. "That's a matter of some debate. Heart hounds have big rounded ears, good hearing. Some say they can find a man by hearing the beating of his heart." Richard's eyes widened. Chase took another bite of bread, chewing for a minute. "Others say they're called heart hounds because that's how they kill. They come at your chest. Most predators go for the throat, but not heart hounds; they go straight for your heart, and they have big enough teeth to get the job done. It's the first thing they eat, too. If there's more than one hound, they'll fight over the heart."

Zedd dished himself a bowl of stew and handed the ladle to Kahlan.

Richard was losing his appetite, but he had to ask. "And what do you think?"

Chase shrugged. "Well, I've never sat real quiet in the dark next to the boundary, just to find out if they could hear my heart beating." He took another bite of bread, looking down at his chest as he chewed. He pulled the heavy mail away from himself. There were two long ragged rips in the chain. Broken pieces of yellow teeth were jammed into mangled links. The leather tunic behind it was soaked with hound's blood. "The one that did this had the blade of my short sword broken off in his chest, and I was still on my horse at the time." He looked back to Richard and raised an eyebrow. "That answer your question?"

Bumps ran up Richard's arms. "What about the way they can go in and out of the boundary?"

Chase took the bowl of stew from Kahlan as she handed it to him. "They have something to do with the magic of the boundary; they were created with it. They are the boundary's watchdogs, so to speak. They can go in and out without being claimed by it. But they're tied to it too, and can't go far from it. With the boundary weakening, they've been straying farther and farther all the time. That makes traveling Hawkers Trail dangerous, but to go another way would add a good week to the journey to Kings' Port. The cutoff we took is the only one that veers away from the boundary until we get to Southaven. I knew I had to reach you before you passed it, or we would have had to spend the night back there, with them. Tomorrow, in the daylight, when it's safer, I'll show you the boundary, how it's weakening."

Richard nodded as they all went back to their own thoughts.

"They are tan," Kahlan said softly. They all turned to her. She sat staring into the fire. "The heart hounds are tan, with short fur, like that on the back of a deer. They are seen everywhere now in the Midlands, having been released from their bonds when the other boundary failed. Crazed with lack of purpose, now they even come out in the daytime."

The three men sat motionless, considering her words. Even Zedd stopped eating.

"Great," Richard said under his breath. "And what else does the Midlands have that is even worse?"

He didn't mean it as a question, more as a curse of frustration. The fire crackled, warm on their faces.

Kahlan's eyes were in a faraway place. "Darken Rahl," she whispered.

CHAPTER 13

RICHARD SAT AWAY FROM the camp, leaning against a cold rock, his cloak wrapped tightly around himself as he looked out toward the boundary. What little wind there was bore a breath of ice. Chase had given him the first watch, Zedd was to have the second, and the warden the third. Kahlan had protested when she wasn't given a watch, but in the end went along with Chase's wishes.

Moonlight illuminated the open land between where he sat and the boundary. It was an expanse of gentle hills, a few trees and small streams; a pleasant-looking place, considering how near it was to the grim boundary woods. Of course, the woods had probably been pleasant at one time, too, before Darken Rahl had put the boxes in play, and started the destruction of the boundary. Chase had said he didn't think the heart hounds could stray this far, but if he was wrong, Richard intended to see them coming. He ran his hand over the hilt of his sword for reassurance, fingering the word *Truth* on it, tracing its raised letters absently while he scanned the night sky, vowing not to let the gars take him by surprise again. He was glad he was given the first watch, since he wasn't sleepy. He was fatigued, but not sleepy. Still, he yawned.

The mountains that were part of the boundary lay off at the edge of darkness, beyond the tangle mat of woods, rising up like the spine of a dark beast too big to hide itself. Richard wondered what manner of things were looking back at him from that black maw. Chase had said the boundary mountains diminished as they went south, and would be all but gone where they were going.

Unexpectedly, Kahlan, her cloak also wrapped snug about, slipped up silently in the darkness and wedged herself tight against him for warmth. She didn't talk, simply sat close. Stray wisps of her silky hair touched the side of his face. The handle of her knife jabbed into his side, but he didn't say anything for fear that if he did she would move away. He didn't want her to move.

"The others asleep?" he asked quietly, glancing over his shoulder. She nodded. "How can you tell?" he asked with a smile. "Zedd sleeps with his eyes open."

She smiled back. "All wizards do."

"Really? I thought it was just Zedd."

As he scanned the valley for any movement, he could feel her eyes on him. He looked back at her. "Aren't you sleepy?" She was so close he didn't have to speak in much more than a whisper.

She shrugged. The light breeze pulled some of her long hair across her face. She reached up and pulled it back. Her eyes found his. "I wanted to tell you I was sorry."

He wished she would lay her head on his shoulder, but she didn't. "About what?"

"About what I said to you before, that I wouldn't want you to come after me. I did not want you to think I don't appreciate your friendship; I do. It's just that what we are doing is more important than any one person."

He knew she had meant much more than she said, just as he had. He looked into her eyes, felt her breath on his face.

"Kahlan, do you have someone?" He feared the arrow to his heart, but had to ask. "Someone at home who waits for you, I mean? A love?"

He held the gaze of her green eyes for a long time. She didn't

171

look away, but her eyes filled with tears. More than anything he wanted to put his arms around her and kiss her.

She reached up, letting the backs of her fingers brush his face gently. She cleared her throat. "It is not that simple, Richard."

"Yes it is. Either you do or you don't."

"I have obligations."

For a time it seemed she was going to tell him something, tell him her secret.

She looked so beautiful in the moonlight, but it wasn't only the way she looked, it was what was inside her, everything from her intelligence and courage to her wit, and the special smile she gave only to him. He would slay a dragon, if there were such a thing, just to see that smile. He knew he would never want anyone else for as long as he lived. He would rather spend the rest of his life alone than with someone else. There could be no one else.

He desperately wanted to hug her close. He ached to taste her soft lips. But he was inexplicably getting the same feeling he had had before he crossed the bridge. It was a strong feeling of warning, stronger than his desire to kiss her. Something told him that if he did, it would be crossing one bridge too many. He remembered how the magic flared when she had touched his hand as he held the sword. He had been right about the bridge, so he didn't put his arms around her.

She broke the gaze with a glance to the ground. "Chase said the next two days are going to be rough. I guess I had better get some sleep."

He knew that whatever was going on in her head, he had no say in it. He couldn't force her. It was something she had to handle herself.

"You have an obligation to me too," he said. She looked back to him with a questioning frown, and he smiled. "You have promised to be my guide. I intend to hold you to that promise."

She smiled and could only nod, too close to tears to speak. She kissed the end of her finger and pressed it against his cheek, then slipped back into the night.

Richard sat in the dark, trying to swallow past the lump in his throat. Long after she was gone he could still feel the place on his cheek where she had put her finger, her kiss.

The night was so still that Richard felt as if he were the only one awake in the whole world. Stars flickered, looking like Zedd's magic dust frozen in place as the moon stared silently down at him. Not even the wolves sang tonight. Loneliness threatened to crush him.

He found himself wishing something would attack just so he would have something else to think about. He pulled out his sword, and for something to do, polished its already gleaming blade with the corner of his cloak. It was his sword to use as he saw fit; that's what Zedd had told him. Whether Kahlan liked it or not, he was going to use it to protect her. She was hunted. Anything that tried to touch her was going to have to come through his sword first.

The thought of her hunters, the quads, and Darken Rahl made his anger heat. He wanted them to come now so he could put an end to the threat. He hungered for them. His heart pounded. His jaws clenched.

He realized suddenly that it was the sword's anger awakening his. The sword was free from its scabbard and the mere thought of something threatening Kahlan was making its anger, and his anger, come forth. He was startled at how it had seeped into him, so quiet, so unseen, so seductive. Simply perception, the wizard had said. What was the sword's magic perceiving in him?

Richard slid the sword back into its scabbard, put back the anger, feeling the gloom seep through him once again as he resumed his scan of the countryside and sky. He stood and walked around to relieve the cramps in his legs, then sat once more against the rock, inconsolable.

An hour before his watch was due to end, he heard quiet footsteps he recognized. It was Zedd, a piece of cheese in each hand, with no cloak, wearing only his simple robes.

"What are you doing up? It's not time for your watch yet."

"I thought you might like the company of a friend. Here, I brought you a piece of cheese."

"No, thanks. About the cheese, I mean. I could use the friend part, though."

Zedd sat down next to him, folded his bony knees up to his chest, and pulled the robes down over them, making himself the center of a little tent. "What's the problem?"

Richard shrugged. "Kahlan, I guess." Zedd didn't say anything. Richard looked over. "She's the first thing in my mind when I wake and the last thing in my mind before I sleep. I've never felt like this before, Zedd, never felt this alone before."

"I see." Zedd laid the cheese on a rock.

"I know she likes me, but I get the feeling she's keeping me at arm's length. When we were setting up camp tonight, I told her that if it had been her, like Chase today, I would have come after her. A while ago she came out here to see me. She said she didn't want me coming after her, but she meant more than that. She meant she didn't want me coming after her, period."

"Good girl," Zedd said under his breath.

"What?"

"I said she's a good girl. We all like her. But Richard, she is other things, too. She has responsibilities."

Richard frowned at the old man. "And what are those other things?"

Zedd leaned back a little. "It's not for me to say. She is the one to answer that. I would have thought she would have done so by now." The old man put his arm around Richard's big shoulders. "If it makes you feel any better, the only reason she hasn't is because she cares for you more than she should. She is afraid of losing your friendship."

"You know about her secrets, and Chase knows; I can see it in his eyes. Everyone knows but me. She tried to tell me tonight, but she couldn't. She shouldn't worry about losing my friendship. That won't happen."

"Richard, she is a wonderful person, but she is not the one for you. She can't be that."

"Why?"

Zedd plucked something off his sleeve as he spoke, avoiding Richard's eyes. "I gave my word I would allow her to be the one to tell you. You will just have to trust me; she cannot be what you want. Find another girl. The land is awash with them. Why, half of all the people are girls; there are plenty to pick from. Pick another."

Richard drew his knees up, folding his arms across them, looking away. "All right."

174

Zedd looked up in surprise, then smiled and patted his young friend's back.

"All right on one condition," Richard added as he scanned the boundary woods. "You answer one question, honestly, toasted toads honest. If you can answer yes, then I will do as you ask."

"One? Only one question?" Zedd asked cautiously, putting a bony finger to his thin bottom lip.

"One question."

Zedd thought about it a minute. "Very well. One question."

Richard turned his fierce eyes to the old man. "Before you married your wife, if someone—tell you what, let's make it even easier for you to say yes—if someone you trusted, a friend, someone you loved like a father, if that person had come to you, and said pick another, would you have done so?"

Zedd looked away from Richard's eyes and took a deep breath. "Bags. You would think by now I would have learned not to let a Seeker ask me a question." He picked up the cheese and took a bite.

"I thought as much."

Zedd threw the cheese away into the darkness. "That doesn't change the facts, Richard! It will not work between you two. I'm not saying this to hurt you. I love you like a son. If I could change the way the world works, I would. I wish it were not so, for your sake, but there is no way for it to work. Kahlan knows it, and if you try, you will only hurt her. I know you don't want that."

Richard's voice was calm, quiet. "You said it yourself. I am the Seeker. There is a way, and I will find it."

Zedd shook his head sadly. "I wish it were so, my boy, but it is not."

"Then what am I to do?" Richard asked in a broken whisper.

His old friend put his skinny arms around him and hugged him close in the darkness. Richard felt numb.

"Just be her friend, Richard. That's what she needs. But you can be nothing more."

Richard nodded in Zedd's arms.

After a few minutes the Seeker, a suspicious look in his eye, pushed away, holding the wizard at arm's length.

"What is it you came out here for?"

"To sit with a friend."

Richard shook his head. "You came out here as wizard, away from the others, to counsel the Seeker. Now, tell me why you're here."

"Very well. I came here in my capacity as wizard, to tell the Seeker he almost made a serious mistake today."

Richard took his hands from Zedd's shoulders, but continued to hold his gaze. "I know that. A Seeker cannot put himself at risk when by so doing he puts everyone else at risk."

"But you were going to do it anyway," Zedd pressed.

"When you named me Seeker, you took the bad with the good. I'm new at the responsibilities of the position. It's hard for me to see a friend in trouble and not help. I know I can't afford that luxury anymore. Consider me reprimanded."

Zedd smiled. "Well, that part went well." He sat a minute, his smile faded. "But Richard, the issue is bigger than just what happened today. You must understand that, as Seeker, you may cause the death of innocent people. In order to succeed in stopping Rahl you may have to turn away from those who might be saved with your help. A soldier knows that on the battlefield, if he bends to help a downed comrade, he might take a sword in the back, and so, if he is to win, he must fight on despite the cries for help from his fellows. You must be able to do this to win; it may be the only way. You must steel yourself to it. This is a struggle for survival, and in this battle the ones crying for help probably won't be soldiers, but innocents. Darken Rahl will kill anyone to win. Those who fight on his side will do the same. You may have to do the same. Like it or not, the aggressor makes the rules. You must play by them, or you will surely die by them."

"How could anyone fight on his side? Darken Rahl wants to dominate everyone, to be the master of all. How could they fight for him?"

The wizard leaned back against the rock and looked out over the hills, as if seeing more than was there. His tone was sorrowful. "Because, Richard, many people must be ruled to thrive. In their selfishness and greed, they see free people as their oppressors. They wish to have a leader who will cut the taller plants so the sun will reach them. They think no plant should be allowed to grow taller than the shortest, and in that way give light to all. They would rather be provided a guiding light, regardless of the fuel, than light a candle themselves.

"Some of them think that when Rahl wins, he will smile on them, and they will be rewarded, and so they are as ruthless as he to gain his favor. Some are simply blind to the truth and fight for the lies they hear. And some find, once that guiding light is lit, that they are wearing chains, and then it is too late." Zedd smoothed his sleeves down his arms as he sighed. "There have always been wars, Richard. Every war is a murderous struggle between foes. And yet, no army has ever marched into battle thinking that the Creator had sided with their enemy."

Richard shook his head. "It doesn't make sense."

"I am quite sure that Rahl's followers think we are bloodthirsty monsters, capable of anything. They will have been told endless tales of their enemy's ruthless brutality. I'm sure none of them know much about Darken Rahl except what they have been told by Darken Rahl." The wizard frowned, his intelligent eyes sharp. "It may be a perversion of logic, but that makes it no less threatening, or deadly. Rahl's followers need only to crush us, they don't have to understand anything else. But for you to win, against a stronger foe, you must use your head."

Richard ran his fingers through his hair. "That leaves me stuck in an awfully tight crack. I may have to let innocent people die, yet I can't kill Darken Rahl."

Zedd gave him a meaningful look. "No. I never said you couldn't kill Darken Rahl; I said you couldn't use the sword to kill him."

Richard looked intently over at his old friend, the moonlight dim on the other's angular face. Sparks of thought lit in the darkness of his mood.

"Zedd," he asked quietly, "have you had to do that? Have you had to let innocent people die?"

Zedd's face turned hard, and pensive. "In the last war, and again now, as we speak. Kahlan told me Rahl kills people to get my name. No one can give it, but he continues to kill in the hope someone will finally offer it. I could turn myself over to him to stop the killing, but then I wouldn't be able to help defeat him,

177

and many more would die. It's a painful choice, let a few die horribly, or let even more die horribly."

"I'm sorry, my friend." Richard wrapped his cloak tighter about himself, chilled from without and from within. He looked back out over the still landscape, then back at Zedd. "I met the night wisp, Shar, before she died. She gave her life to get Kahlan here, so others might live. Kahlan also bears the burden of letting others die."

"She does," Zedd said softly. "It makes my heart ache to know the things that girl's eyes have seen. And the things your eyes may have to see."

"Makes my problem about the two of us seem pretty small."

Zedd's expression was gentle with compassion. "But not hurt any less."

Richard made another scan of the countryside. "Zedd, one more thing. Before we reached your house, I offered Kahlan an apple."

Zedd gave a surprised laugh. "You offered a red fruit to someone from the Midlands? That's tantamount to a death threat, my boy. In the Midlands, red fruit of any kind is deadly poison."

"Yes, I know that now, but I didn't at the time."

Zedd leaned over, lifting an eyebrow. "What did she say?"

Richard looked at him sideways. "It isn't what she said, it's what she did. She grabbed me by the throat. For a moment, I could see in her eyes that she was going to kill me. I don't know how she was going to kill me, but I'm sure she was going to do it. She hesitated long enough for me to explain. The point is, she was my friend, and she had saved my life several times, but in that instant she was going to kill me." Richard paused. "That's part of what you are saying, isn't it?"

Zedd let out a long breath and nodded. "It is. Richard, if you suspected I was a traitor, weren't sure, just suspected, and you knew that if it were true, our cause would be lost, would you be able to kill me? If you had no time or way to find the truth, only the strong belief I was a traitor, and only you knew, could you kill me on the spot? Could you come at me, your old friend, with lethal intent? With enough violence to see the job done?"

Zedd's stare burned into him. Richard was stunned. "I ... I don't know."

"Well, you had better know that you could, or you have no business going after Rahl. You won't have the resolve to live, to win. You may be called upon to make a life-and-death decision instantly. Kahlan knows this, she knows the consequences if she fails. She has the resolve."

"She hesitated, though. From what you're saying, she made a mistake. I could have overpowered her. She should have killed me before I had a chance to." Richard frowned. "And she would have been wrong."

Zedd shook his head slowly. "Don't flatter yourself, Richard. She had her hand on you. Anything you would have done wouldn't have been quick enough. All it would have taken is a thought on her part. She was in control and could afford to give you the chance to explain. She made no mistake."

A little shaken, Richard still wasn't ready to concede the issue. "But you wouldn't, you couldn't be a traitor to us, just as I would never hurt her. I don't see the point."

"The point is, even though I wouldn't, if I did, you have to be prepared to act. You have to have the strength to do even that, if necessary. The point is that even though Kahlan knew you were her friend, and wouldn't hurt her, when she thought you were trying to, she was prepared to act. If you hadn't quickly made her believe you, she would have."

Richard sat in silence for a moment, watching his friend. "Zedd, if it were the other way around, if you thought I was a danger to our cause, well, you know, could you ... ?"

The wizard leaned back, frowning, and without a hint of emotion in his voice, said, "In a twinkling."

The answer appalled Richard, but he understood what his friend was telling him, even if the whole idea seemed far-fetched; anything less than total commitment could spell their failure. If they faltered, Rahl would not be merciful. They would die. It was that simple.

"Still want to be Seeker?" Zedd asked.

Richard stared out at nothing. "Yes."

"Scared?"

"To the bone."

Zedd patted his knee. "Good. Me too. I would worry only if you were not."

The Seeker gave the wizard an icy glare. "I intend to make Darken Rahl afraid too."

Zedd smiled and nodded. "You are going to make a good Seeker, my boy. Have faith."

Richard gave a mental shudder at the thought of Kahlan killing him just for offering her an apple. He frowned. "Zedd? Why are all red fruits in the Midlands deadly poison? It isn't natural."

The wizard gave a sorrowful shake of his head. "Because, Richard, children like red fruit."

Richard's frown deepened. "That doesn't make any sense."

Zedd looked down, pushing a bony finger at the dirt for a moment. "It was about this time of year, in the last war. The harvests were in. I had found a constructed magic. That's a magic made by wizards of long ago. Something like the boxes of Orden. It was a poison magic, specific to color; and only able to cast one spell, one time. I wasn't sure how it was used, but I knew it was dangerous." Zedd took a deep breath and put his hands in his lap. "Anyway, Panis Rahl got his hands on it, and figured out how to make it work. He knew children loved fruit, and wanted to strike a blow at our hearts. He used the magic to poison all red fruit. It's a little like the poison of the snake vine. Slow at first. It took time for us to realize what caused the fever, and death. Panis Rahl deliberately chose something he could be sure children, not just the adults, would eat." His voice was barely audible as he looked out into the darkness. "A lot of people died. A lot of children."

Richard's eyes were wide. "If you found it, how did he get hold of it?"

Zedd looked into Richard's eyes with an expression that could have frozen a summer day. "I had a student, a young man I was training. One day I chanced upon him tinkering with something he shouldn't have been. I had an odd doubt about him. I knew something was wrong, but I was very fond of him and so I didn't act upon my suspicion. Instead, I decided to think on it for the night. The next morning, he was gone, and so was the constructed magic I had found. He had been a spy for Panis Rahl. If I had acted when I should have, and killed him, all those people, all those children, wouldn't have died."

Richard swallowed. "Zedd, you couldn't have known."

He thought that maybe the old man was going to yell, or cry, or storm off, but instead he only shrugged. "Learn from my mistake, Richard. If you do, then all those lives won't have been lost for nothing. Maybe their story can be a lesson that will help save everyone from what Darken Rahl will do if he wins."

Richard rubbed his arms, trying to work a bit of warmth back into them. "Why isn't the red fruit in Westland poison?"

"All magic has limits. This had a limit of distance from where it was used. It stretched as far as where the boundary between Westland and the Midlands went up. The boundary couldn't be put up where any of the poison spell was, or Westland would have had magic in it."

Richard sat in the dark, cold silence and thought for a time. At last he asked, "Is there any way to get rid of it? To make the red fruit no longer poison?"

Zedd smiled. Richard thought it an odd thing to do, but he was glad to see it. "Thinking like a wizard, my boy. Thinking how to undo magic." He frowned in thought as he looked out into the night again. "There might be a way to remove the spell. I would have to study it and see what I could do. If we can defeat Darken Rahl, I intend to put my mind to the task."

"Good." Richard tugged his cloak tighter. "Everyone should be able to eat an apple when they want. Especially children." He looked over at the old man. "Zedd, I promise I will remember your lesson. I won't let you down. I won't let all those people who died be forgotten."

Zedd smiled and gave Richard's back an affectionate rub.

The two friends sat in silence, sharing the stillness of the night and the quiet of each other's understanding, thinking about what they could not know: what was to come.

Richard thought about what needed to be done, about Panis Rahl, and about Darken Rahl. He thought about how hopeless everything seemed. Think about the solution, he told himself, not the problem; you are the Seeker.

"I need you to do something, wizard. I think it is time for us to disappear. Rahl has followed us long enough. What can you do about that cloud?"

"You know, I think you're right. I only wish I knew how it was hooked to you, so I could unhook it, but I can't figure it out.

So, I will have to do something else." He contemplatively drew his finger and thumb down the sharp sides of his jaw. "Has it rained, or been overcast since it first started following you?"

Richard thought back, trying to remember every day. Most of the time he had been in a fog over his father's murder. It seemed so long ago. "The night before I found the snake vine, it rained in the Ven, but by the time I got there, it had cleared off. No, no rain. I don't remember it being cloudy since my father's murder. At least, nothing more than a few high, thin clouds. What does that mean?"

"Well, it means I think there is a way to fool the cloud, even if I can't unhook it. Since the sky has been clear all that time, that means Rahl probably has been responsible. He has moved the other clouds away so he could easily find this one. Simple, but effective."

"How could he move the clouds away?"

"He put a spell on this one to repel other clouds, and somehow hooked this one to you."

"Then why don't you put a stronger spell on it to attract other clouds; before he realizes it, it will be lost, and he won't be able to find it to try to outdo your magic. If he does use stronger magic to move the clouds away to find this one, he won't know what you have done, and the stronger spell that pushes the clouds away will break the hook."

Zedd gave him an incredulous look, his eyes blinked. "Bags, Richard, you have gotten it exactly right! My boy, I think you would make an excellent wizard."

"No, thanks. I already have one impossible job."

Zedd drew back a little and frowned, but didn't say anything. His thin hand reached into his robes and pulled out a rock, tossing it on the ground in front of them. He stood and his fingers spun around in a circle over the little rock until, suddenly, it popped into a large rock.

"Zedd! That's your cloud rock!"

"Actually, my boy, it's a wizard's rock. My father gave it to me, long ago."

The wizard's finger stirred faster and faster until light came forth, sparkles and colors, swirling around. He continued to stir, mixing and blending the light. There was no sound, only the pleasant smell of a spring rain. At last the wizard seemed satisfied.

"Step up on the rock, my boy."

Unsure at first, Richard stepped into the light. It tingled and felt warm against his skin, as if he were lying in the hot summer sun without clothes, after a swim. He let himself bask in the warm, safe feeling, gave himself over to it. His hands floated outward from his sides until they were horizontal. He tilted his head back, took deep breaths, and closed his eyes. It felt wondrous, like floating in water, only he was floating in light. Exhilaration soaked through him. His mind felt a buoyant, timeless connection to everything around him. He was one with the trees, the grass, the bugs, the birds, the animals all around, the water, the very air itself; not a separate being, but part of a whole. He understood the interconnection of everything in a new way, saw himself as inconsequential and empowered at the same time. He saw the world through the eyes of all the creatures around him. It was a shocking, marvelous insight. He let himself soar into a bird that flew overhead, saw the world through its eyes, hunted with it, hungry and needful, for mice, watched the campfire below, the people sleeping.

Richard let his identity scatter to the wind. He became no one and everyone, felt the heat of their needs, smelled their fear, tasted their joy, understood their desires, and then let it all melt away into nothingness, until there was a void where he stood, alone in the universe, the only living thing, the only thing existing at all. Then he let the light flood through him, light that brought forth the others that had used this very rock: Zedd, Zedd's father, and the wizards before that, for untold years, thousands of years, one and all. Their essence flowed through him, shared themselves with him as tears streamed down his cheeks at the wonder of it all.

Zedd's hands sprang forward, loosing his magic dust. It swirled about Richard, glittering fluidly, until he was at the center of its vortex. The sparkles tightened their rotation and gathered at his chest. With a tinkling sound like a crystal chandelier in the wind, the dust climbed away into the sky as if climbing a kite string, taking the sound with it as it went, higher and higher, until it reached the cloud. The cloud took in the magic dust and was lit from within by roiling colors. All across the horizon lightning flashed, ragged streaks ripping this way and that, called forth, eager, expectant.

All at once the lightning stopped, the illumination in the cloud faded and was gone, and the light from the wizard's rock pulled itself inward until it was extinguished. There was sudden silence. Richard was there again, standing on a simple rock. He looked, wide-eyed, at Zedd's smiling face.

"Zedd," he whispered, "now I know why you stand on this rock all the time. I've never felt anything like that in my life. I had no idea."

Zedd smiled knowingly. "You're a natural, my boy. You held your arms just right, your head had the proper tilt, you even arched your back correctly. You took to it like a duckling to a pond. You have all the makings of a fine wizard." He leaned forward, gleefully. "Now just try to imagine doing it naked."

"It makes a difference?" Richard asked in amazement.

"Of course. The clothes interfere with the experience." Zedd put his arm around Richard's shoulder. "Someday I will let you try it."

"Zedd, why did you have me do that? It wasn't necessary. You could have done it."

"How do you feel now?"

"I don't know. Different. Relaxed. More clearheaded. I guess not as overpowered, not as depressed."

"That's why I let you do it, my friend, because you needed it. You have had a hard night. I can't change the problems, but I could help you feel better."

"Thank you, Zedd."

"Go get some sleep, it's my watch now." He gave Richard a wink. "If you ever change your mind about becoming a wizard, I would be proud to welcome you into the brotherhood."

Zedd help up his hand. Out of the darkness, the piece of cheese he had thrown away floated back to him.

CHAPTER 14

CHASE REINED IN HIS horse. "Here. This will be a good place."

He led the other three off the trail through an open tract of long-dead spruce, the silver-gray skeletons standing bare of all but a few branches and an occasional wisp of dull green moss. The soft ground was littered with the rotting corpses of the former monarchs. Brown bog weed, its broad, flat leaves laid down in haphazard fashion by past storms, looked like a tangled sea of dead snakes underfoot.

The horses picked their way carefully among the tangle. Warm air, heavy with humidity, carried the fetid smell of decay. A fog of mosquitoes followed them as they went, the only things alive as far as Richard could tell. As open as this place was, little brightness was offered by the sky, as a thick, uniform overcast of clouds hung oppressively close to the ground. Trailers of mist dragged across the silver spikes of the trees that remained standing, leaving them wet and slick.

Chase led the way for Zedd and then Kahlan, with Richard following behind, watching over them as they twisted their way along. Visibility was limited to less than a few hundred feet, and even though Chase didn't seem to be concerned, Richard kept a sharp lookout; anything could sneak up close before they would be able to see it. All four swatted at the mosquitoes, and except for Zedd, they kept their cloaks tight for protection. Zedd, who shunned wearing a cloak, nibbled on the remnants of lunch, looking about as if on a sightseeing excursion. Richard had an excellent sense of direction but was glad they had Chase to lead them. Everything in the bog looked the same, and he knew from experience how easy it would be to become lost.

Since Richard had stood on the wizard's rock the night before, he felt the weight of his responsibilities less of a burden, and more of an opportunity to be a part of something right. He didn't feel the danger any less, but felt more strongly his need to be part of stopping Rahl. He saw his part in the scheme of things as a chance to help others who had no chance to fight Darken Rahl. He knew he couldn't back away; that would be the end of him, and a lot of others.

Richard watched Kahlan's body sway as she rode, her shoulders moving to the horse's rhythm. He wished he could take her to places he knew of in the Hartland Woods, secret places of beauty and peace, far back in the mountains, show her the waterfall he had found, and the cave behind it, have lunch by a quiet forest pond with her, take her into town, buy her something pretty, take her someplace, any place, where she would be safe. He wanted her to be able to smile without having to worry every minute if her enemies were getting closer. After last night, he felt that the first part, his fantasy of being with her, was just an empty wish.

With a hand in the air, Chase brought them to a halt. "This is the place."

Richard looked around, there were still in the middle of an endless, dead, dried-up bog. He didn't see any boundary. It all looked the same in every direction. They tethered their horses to a fallen log and followed Chase a short distance farther on foot.

"The boundary," Chase announced, holding his arm out at the introduction.

"I don't see anything," Richard said.

Chase smiled. "Watch." He walked on, steadily, slowly. As he went forward, a green glow formed around him, at first hardly perceptible. It grew stronger, brighter, until after another twenty steps it became a sheet of green light pressing against him as he proceeded, stronger close to him and fading away about ten feet to the sides and above, growing larger with every step. It was like green glass, wavy and distorted, but Richard could see through it, see the dead trees beyond. Chase stopped and returned. The green sheet, and then the green glow, faded and vanished as he came back. Richard had always thought the boundary would be a wall of some sort, something that could be seen.

"That's it?" Richard felt a little let down.

"What more do you want? Now, watch this." Chase searched the ground, picking up branches, testing each for strength. Most were rotten and broke easily. Finally he found one, about a dozen feet long, that was strong enough to suit him. He carried it back into the glowing light until he reached the sheet of green. Holding the branch by the thick end, he passed the rest through the wall. Six feet away, the end of the stick disappeared as he pushed it forward, until he was holding what appeared to be a six-foot stick instead of a twelve-foot branch. Richard was perplexed. He could see beyond the wall, but not the other end of the stick. It didn't seem possible.

As soon as Chase had pushed the stick in as far as he dared, it jumped violently. There was no sound. He hauled it back and returned to the others. He held the splintered end of a now eight-foot stick toward them. The end was covered with slaver.

"Heart hounds," he said with a grin.

Zedd seemed bored. Kahlan was not amused. Richard was astounded. Since he seemed to have an audience of only one, Chase grabbed a fistful of Richard's shirt and dragged him off. "Come on, I'll show you what it's like." Chase locked his right arm together with Richard's left as they proceeded, cautioning Richard, "Go slow, I'll let you know when we've gone far enough. Keep hold of my arm." They walked ahead slowly.

Green light began. With each step it became more intense, but it was different from when Richard had watched Chase go in by himself. Then, the light had been to Chase's sides and above him, now it was all about. There was a buzzing sound, like a thousand bumblebees. With each step the sound became deeper, but not louder. The green light became deeper, too, and the surrounding wood darker, as if night were falling. Then the sheet of green was in front of them, materializing out of nothing, with the green glow everywhere else. Richard could hardly see the woods anymore; he looked back and couldn't see Zedd or Kahlan at all.

"Easy now," Chase warned. They pushed against the green sheet as they stepped slowly ahead. Richard could feel the pressure of it against his body.

Then everything else blacked out, as if he were in a cave at night, with a green glow around Chase and himself. Richard held Chase's arm tighter. The buzzing felt like it was vibrating his chest.

With the next step the green sheet of the wall changed suddenly. "Far enough," Chase said, his voice echoing. The wall had become darkly transparent, as if Richard were looking into a deep pond in the dark woods. Chase stood still, watching him.

There were forms on the other side.

Inky black shapes wavered in the gloom on the other side of the wall, specters floating in the deep.

The dead in their lair.

Something closer and faster moved nearer to them. "The hounds," Chase said.

Richard felt an odd sensation of longing. Longing for the blackness. The humming wasn't a sound, he realized, it was voices.

Voices that murmured his name.

Thousands of distant voices called out to him. The black shapes were gathering, calling to him, holding their arms out to him.

He felt a sudden, unexpected stab of loneliness, felt the solitude of his life, of all life. Why did he need the pain when they were waiting, waiting to welcome him? Never alone again. The black shapes drifted closer in the gloom, calling to him, and he began to see their faces. It was as if he were looking through murky water. They came closer. He longed to step through. To be there with them.

And then he saw his father.

Richard's heart pounded. His father called out to him mournfully in a long sorrowful cry. His arms thrust out, trying desperately to clutch for his son. He was just beyond the wall.

Richard's heart felt as if it were going to rip with yearning. It had been so long since he had seen his father. He wailed for him, hungered to touch him. He wouldn't have to be afraid ever again. He had only to reach his father. Then he would be safe.

Safe. Forever.

Richard tried to reach out to his father, tried to go to him, tried to step through the wall. Something was holding his arm. Irritated, he pulled harder. Someone held him from his father. He screamed for whoever held him to let go. His voice sounded hollow, empty.

Then he was being pulled away from his father.

His anger roared to life. Someone was trying to drag him back by his arm. In a rage he grabbed his sword. A big hand clamped over his with an iron grip. Screaming in unrestrained fury, he struggled mightily to free the sword, but the big hands held tight, dragging him, stumbling, from his father. Richard struggled, but was hauled away.

The green wall came up suddenly in place of the darkness as he was pulled back. Chase was dragging him away from it, through the green light. The world returned with a sickening jolt. The dry, dead bog returned.

Suddenly aware, Richard was appalled at what he had almost done. Chase released his sword hand. Shaking, Richard put it on the big man's shoulder for support, struggling to catch his breath as they stepped out of the green light. Relief washed over him.

Chase leaned over a little, searching his eyes. "All right?"

Richard nodded, too overwhelmed to speak. The sight of his father had brought back the devastating grief. He had to concentrate just to breathe, to stand. His throat hurt. He realized he had been choking, but hadn't been aware of it at the time.

Terror raced through Richard's mind as he realized how close he had come to stepping through the wall, to death. He had been totally unprepared for what had happened. If Chase hadn't been there holding on to him, he would be dead now. He had tried to give in to the underworld. He felt as if he didn't know himself. How could he have wanted to give himself over to it? Was he that weak? That frail?

Richard's head swirled with pain. He couldn't clear the vision of his father's face from his mind, the way his father longed for him, called to him, so desperate. He ached to be with him. It would have been so easy. The image haunted his mind, refusing to let go. He didn't want to let it go; he wanted to go back. He could feel the pull, even as he resisted.

Kahlan was there, waiting for them; at the edge of the green light as they emerged. She swept her arm protectively around his waist and tugged him away from Chase. With her other hand she grabbed hold of his jaw, turning his head, making him look at her.

"Richard. Listen to me. Think of something else. Concentrate. You have to think of something else. I want you to remember every intersection on every trail in the Hartland. Can you do that for me? Please? Do it now. Remember every one for me."

He nodded, and started to remember the trails.

Kahlan turned to Chase in a fury, slapping him across his face as hard as she could.

"You bastard!" she screamed. "Why would you do that to him!" Throwing all her weight into it, she slapped him again, her hair tossing across her face. Chase didn't try to stop her. "You did it on purpose! How could you do that!" She swung at him a third time, but this time, he grabbed her wrist in midswing.

"Do you want me to tell you or do you wish to go on hitting me?"

She jerked her hand away, glaring at him, her chest heaving. Some of her hair was stuck sideways across her face.

"Going through Kings' Port is dangerous. It isn't straight through; it twists and turns. Some places it's very narrow, the two walls of the boundary almost touching. One step either way and you're gone. You've been through the boundary; so has Zedd. You both understand. You can't see it until you start in, otherwise you don't know where it is. I only know because I've spent my life out here. It's even more dangerous now because it's failing, even easier to walk through it. When you get in the pass, if something started chasing you, Richard could run into the underworld without even knowing what it was."

"That's no excuse! You could have warned him!"

"I've never had a child yet who had the proper respect for fire until they put their hand in it once. No amount of telling is worth doing it once. If Richard didn't understand what it was like before he went into Kings' Port, he wouldn't come out the other side. Yes, I took him in there on purpose. To show him. To keep him alive."

"You could have told him!"

Chase shook his head. "No. He had to see it."

"Enough!" Richard said, his head clear at last. They all turned to him. "A day has yet to go by when one of you three doesn't scare the wits out of me. But I know you all have my best interests at heart. Right now we have more important things to worry about. Chase, how do you know the boundary is failing? What's different?"

"The wall is breaking down. Before, you couldn't see through the green into the darkness. You couldn't see anything on the other side."

"Chase is right," Zedd offered, "I could see it from here."

"How long until it fails?" Richard asked the wizard.

Zedd shrugged. "It's hard to tell."

"Then guess!" Richard shot back. "Give me some kind of idea. Your best guess."

"It will last at least two weeks. But not more than six or seven."

Richard thought a minute. "Can you use your magic to strengthen it?"

"I don't have that kind of power."

"Chase, do you think Rahl knows about Kings' Port?"

"How should I know?"

"Well, has anyone come through the pass?"

Chase thought about the question. "Not that I know of."

"I doubt it," Zedd added. "Rahl can travel the underworld; he doesn't need the pass. He's bringing the boundary down; I don't think he cares about a little pass."

"Caring is different from knowing," Richard said. "I don't think we should be standing here, and I'm worried he might know where we're going."

Kahlan pulled the hair off her face. "What do you mean?"

Richard gave her a sympathetic look. "Do you think it was your mother and sister you saw when you were in there?"

"I thought it was. Do you think otherwise?"

"I don't think that was my father." He looked to the wizard. "What do you think?"

"It's impossible to say. No one really knows all that much about the underworld."

"Darken Rahl knows about it," Richard said bitterly. "I don't think my father would want me in that manner. But I know Rahl would, so despite what my eyes tell me, it's more likely that it was Darken Rahl's disciples trying to take me. You said we couldn't go through the boundary because they were waiting for us to do so, waiting to get us. I think that was what I saw, his followers in the underworld. And they know right where I touched the wall. If I'm right that means Rahl will soon know where we are. I don't want to be here to find out if I'm right."

"Richard is right," Chase said. "And we have to get to Skow Swamp before nightfall, before the heart hounds come out. It's the only safe place between here and Southaven. We'll reach Southaven before tomorrow night and will be safe from the hounds there. The next day we will go see a friend of mine, Adie, the bone woman. She lives near the pass. We need her help to get through. But tonight, our only chance is the swamp."

Richard was about to ask what a bone woman was, and why they needed her help to cross the boundary, when a dark, shadowy form suddenly whipped out of the air, striking Chase so hard it threw him across several downed trees. With shocking speed the black form wrapped around Kahlan's legs, whiplike, pulling her feet from under her. She screamed Richard's name as he dove, grabbing for her. They locked their hands around each other's wrists. Both were dragged across the ground, toward the boundary.

Zedd's fingers threw fire over their heads. It shrieked past and vanished. Another black appendage struck out at the wizard with lightning speed, knocking the old man through the air. Richard hooked a foot around a branch on a log. Rotten, it tore from the stump. He twisted his body around, trying to dig his heels into the ground. His boots slid across the wet bog weed. He jammed his heels into the earth, but wasn't strong enough to hold the two of them from being dragged across the ground. He needed his hands free.

"Put your arms around my waist!" he yelled.

Kahlan lunged, throwing her arms around him, holding tight. The sinuous black thing wrapped around her legs undulated, getting a stronger grip on her. She screamed as it squeezed. Richard yanked the sword free, filling the air with its ringing.

The green light began to glow around them as they were dragged in.

Anger flooded through him. Richard's worst fear was coming to pass; something was trying to take Kahlan. The green light brightened. Being hauled across the ground, he couldn't reach the thing that pulled them. Kahlan held him hard by the waist; her legs were too far away, and the thing that held her legs was farther still.

"Kahlan, let go of me!"

She was too terrified to do it. She clutched him tightly, desperately, panting in pain. The green sheet came up as they were dragged in. The buzzing was loud in his ears.

"Let go!" he yelled again.

He tried to pry her hands from his waist. The trees of the bog started to fade into darkness. Richard could feel the pressure of the wall. He couldn't believe how strongly she held him. On his back, sliding across the ground, he tried to reach behind himself to pull her wrists away from him, but could not. Their only chance was for him to get up.

"Kahlan! You have to let go or we're dead! I won't let them get you! Trust me! Let go!" He didn't know if he was telling her the truth, but he was sure it was their only chance.

Her head pressed against his stomach as she clutched his body. Kahlan looked up at him, her face contorting in pain as the black thing squeezed. She screamed, then let go.

In a blink Richard was on his feet. As he jumped up, the dark wall materialized abruptly in front of him. His father reached out. He unleashed his rage, swinging the sword with every fiber of violence he possessed. The blade swept through the barrier, through the thing he knew wasn't his father. The dark shape wailed, exploding into a cloud of nothingness.

Kahlan's feet were at the wall, the dark thing enfolded tightly around her legs, compressing and pulling. He brought the sword up. Murderous need surged through him.

"Richard, no! It's my sister!"

He knew it wasn't, just as it wasn't his father. He gave himself over completely to the hot need and brought the sword down as hard as he could. Again it swept through the wall, slashed through the repulsive thing that held Kahlan. There was a confusion of flashes, unearthly wailing and keening. Kahlan's legs were free. She lay sprawled on her stomach.

Without looking to see what else was happening, Richard pushed his arm under her waist and lifted her in a single motion, scooping her off the ground. He held her tight against himself and held the sword toward the wall as he retreated from the boundary. Backing away steadily, he watched for any movement, any aggression. They left the green light.

He kept going until they were well clear, beyond the horses. When he stopped at last and released her, Kahlan turned and threw her arms around him, shaking. He had to struggle to restrain the rage that urged him to go back in and attack. He knew he would have to put the sword away to quell the anger, the need, but he didn't dare to.

"The others, where are they?" she asked in a panic. "We have to find them."

Kahlan pushed away from him and started to run back. Richard snatched her by the wrist, almost yanking her from her feet.

"Stay here!" he yelled far more angrily than required, pushing her to the ground.

Richard found Zedd in a heap, unconscious. As he bent to the old man, something swept out in a rush over his head. His anger erupted. He spun with the sword, the blade sweeping through the dark form. The stump reeled back into the boundary with a shrill screeching, the severed part vaporizing in midair. Richard picked up Zedd with one arm, threw him over his shoulder like a sack of grain, and carried him to Kahlan, where he laid him gently on the ground. She held the wizard's head in her lap, inspecting for wounds. Richard ducked low as he ran back, but the expected attack didn't come. He wished it would; he longed for the fight, hungered to strike. He found Chase jammed partway under a log. Richard seized the mail and pulled him over. Blood oozed from a gash on the side of Chase's head. Debris was stuck to the wound.

Richard's mind raced, trying to think what to do. He couldn't lift Chase with one arm, and he didn't dare to put the sword away. He did know he didn't want Kahlan to come help, he wanted her to stay safely away. Getting a good grip on the warden's leather tunic, Richard started dragging him. The slick bog weed eased the effort somewhat, but it was still difficult, because he had to go around several fallen trees. Surprisingly, nothing attacked. Maybe he had hurt it, or killed it. He wondered if it was possible to kill something already dead. The sword had magic. Richard wasn't sure what it was capable of; he wasn't even sure if the things in the boundary were dead. He finally reached Kahlan and Zedd, and dragged Chase close. The wizard was still unconscious.

Kahlan's face was white with worry. "What are we going to do?"

Richard scanned around. "We can't stay here, and we can't leave them. Let's put them over the horses and get out of here. We'll look to their wounds as soon as we're a safe distance away."

The clouds were thicker than before, and mist covered everything with a wet sheen. As he checked in every direction, Richard put the sword away and easily lifted Zedd over his horse. Chase was more difficult. He was big, and all his weapons were heavy. Blood throbbed from the wound on the side of his forehead, soaking his hair, and hanging him over the side of the horse made it bleed more. Richard decided he couldn't leave it untended. He quickly retrieved an aum leaf and a strip of cloth from a pack. He crumpled the leaf to make it seep its healing fluid, pressed it against the wound, and had Kahlan wrap the cloth around Chase's head. The cloth soaked through almost immediately, but he knew the aum leaf would stop the bleeding in a short time.

Richard helped Kahlan up onto her horse. He could tell that her legs hurt more than she would admit. He gave her the reins of Zedd's horse, mounted up, took Chase's horse, and then carefully got his bearings. He knew they would have a hard time finding the trail; the mist was getting heavy, visibility limited. There seemed to be ghosts watching from the shadows in every direction. He didn't know if he should lead or follow Kahlan, didn't know how best to protect her, so he rode beside her. Zedd and Chase weren't tied down and could easily slip off the horses, so they had to take it slow. The dead spruce looked the same in every direction, and they couldn't go in a straight line because they had to cut back and forth around fallen trees. Richard spat out mosquitoes that kept flying into his mouth.

The sky was the same dark steel gray everywhere; there was no chance to tell where the sun was, to get oriented. After a time, Richard wasn't at all sure they were going in the right direction; it seemed they should have reached the trail already. He took fixes from landmark trees, and when they reached each one he would pick a new one farther ahead, hoping they were traveling in a straight line. To do it properly he knew he had to be able to line up at least three trees to make sure the line of travel was straight, but he couldn't see that far in the mist. He couldn't be sure he wasn't leading them in circles. Even if he was going in a straight line, he wasn't sure the direction was toward the trail.

"Are you sure we're going the right way?" Kahlan asked. "It all looks the same."

"No. But at least we haven't run into the boundary."

"Do you think we should stop and tend to them?"

"We don't dare. For all I know we could be ten feet from the underworld."

Kahlan looked around, worried. Richard gave thought to having her wait with the other two while he went ahead and scouted for the trail, but dismissed the idea, as he was afraid he might not be able to find her again. They had to stay together. He started to wonder what they would do if they couldn't find their way out before dark. How would they protect themselves against the heart hounds? If there were enough of them, even the sword couldn't hold them all off at once. Chase had said they had to get to the swamp before nightfall. He hadn't said why, or how the swamp could protect them. The brown bog weed was an endless sea all around, with hulks of trees aground in it everywhere.

An oak appeared off to their left, then some more, some with leaves shimmering dark green and wet in the mist. This was not the way they had come in. Richard turned them to the right a little, following the edge of the dead bog, hoping it would lead them back to the trail.

Shadows from the brush among the oaks watched them. He

told himself it was his imagination that made the shadows seem to have eyes. There was no wind, no movement, no sound. He was angry with himself for being lost, despite how easily it could happen in this place. He was a guide; getting lost was unforgivable.

Richard breathed out in relief when he saw the trail at last. They quickly dismounted and checked their two charges. There was no change in Zedd, but at least Chase's wound had stopped bleeding. Richard had no idea what to do for them. He didn't know if they had been knocked unconscious, or if their condition was caused by some sort of magic from the boundary. Kahlan didn't know either.

"What do you think we should do?" she asked him.

Richard tried not to look as worried as he really was. "Chase said we had to get to the swamp or the hounds would get us. It won't do them any good to be laid out here and tended to while we wait for them to wake, only to have the hounds get us all. As I see it, we have only two choices: leave them here or take them with us. There is no way I'm leaving them. Let's tie them down on the horses so they don't fall off, and get to the swamp."

Kahlan agreed. They worked quickly to lash their friends to the horses. Richard changed Chase's bandage, and cleaned up the wound a little. The mist was changing to a light rain. He fished around in the packs, finding the blankets, and removed the oilcloth they were wrapped in. They put a blanket over each friend, then covered them with the oilcloth to keep them dry, crisscrossing rope over it all to hold it in place.

When they were finished, Kahlan unexpectedly put her arms around him, hugging him close and tight for a moment, separating before he could return her gesture.

"Thank you for saving me," she said softly. "The boundary terrifies me." She looked sheepishly up at him. "And if you remind me what I said about not coming after me, I'll kick you." She smiled as she looked up from under her eyebrows.

"Not a word. I promise."

He smiled back at her and pulled up the hood of her cloak, stuffing her hair into it, to keep her dry in the rain. He pulled up his own hood and they started off down the road.

The woods were deserted. Rain dripped down through the tangle overhead. Branches reached around the trail like talons reaching to snatch both people and horses. Even without their riders' direction, the horses trotted their way carefully down the center of the road, their ears pricking from one side to the other, as if listening to the shadows. So dense was the thicket to each side that there was no chance they could take to the trees if they had to. Kahlan drew her cloak tighter. It was go on, or go back. And there was no going back. They rode the horses hard the rest of the afternoon and evening.

When the day's death began stealing away the soft gray light, they still had not reached the swamp, and there was no way to tell how much farther it was. Off through the tangled woods, they caught the sound of howling. Their breath caught in their throats.

The heart hounds were coming.

CHAPTER 15

THE HORSES NEEDED NO encouragement to run. They fled down the road at full speed, their riders making no attempt to slow them, the howls of the heart hounds energizing the effort. Water and mud splashed as their hooves pounded the road, and rain ran in rivulets across their hides, but it was the mud that won out, streaking and caking on their legs and bellies. When the hounds shrieked, the horses returned a snort of fear.

Richard let Kahlan take the lead, wanting to stay between her and their pursuers. The sounds of the heart hounds were still distant, off toward the boundary, but he knew by the way they were angling in from the left that it was only a matter of time until they would be overtaken. If they could turn to the right and head away from the boundary, there was a chance they could outrun the hounds, but the woods were thick, impenetrable; it would be slow going if they could find an opening, a sure death if they tried. Their only chance was to stay on the road and reach the swamp before they were caught. Richard didn't know how far it was, or what they would do once they reached it, only that they had to.

The colors of day were washing out into a sullen gray as night approached. Rain pelted his face in small, cold pricks, heated and mingled with sweat, and ran down his neck. Richard watched the bodies of his two friends bounce and jostle on the horses, hoping they were tied down securely enough, hoping they were not badly hurt, hoping they would be conscious soon. The ride couldn't be doing them any good. Kahlan didn't turn or look back. She bent to her task, her dark form hunched forward over the horse as it ran.

The road curved back and forth as it threaded its way around imposing misshapen oaks and rock outcroppings. Dead trees became more infrequent. Leaves of the oak, ash, and maple trees sealed the riders away from the last vestiges of the sky, darkening the trail even more. The hounds were getting closer when the road began to descend into a sodden wood of cedar. A good sign, Richard thought: cedar often grew where the ground was wet.

Kahlan's horse disappeared over the edge of a drop. Richard reached the brink of the sharp slope and saw her again, descending into a bowl in the earth. The tangled tops of trees spread out into the distance, at least as much of it as he could see in the mist and dim light. It was the Skow Swamp, at last.

The smell of wet and rot assailed him as he followed her in a rush, down through swirling trailers of mist that moved and spun at their passing. Sharp calls and hoots came from the dense vegetation. The howls of the heart hounds came from behind, closer now. Woody vines hung from slick twisted limbs of trees that stood in the water on roots looking like claws, and smaller leafy vines spiraled around anything strong enough to hold them. Everything seemed to be growing on top of something else, seeking to gain an advantage. Water, dark and still, sat in stagnant expanses, sneaking in under clumps of bushes, enveloping stands of fat-bottomed trees. Duckweed drifted in thick mats on the water, looking like manicured lawn. The lush growth seemed to swallow the sound of their horse's hooves, allowing only the native calls to echo across the waters.

The road narrowed into a trail that struggled to remain above the black water, making it necessary to slow the horses for fear they would break a leg on the roots. Richard saw that as

Kahlan's horse passed, the surface of the water rolled in lazy ripples as things moved under it. He heard the hounds at the top of the bowl. Kahlan turned at the howls. If they stayed on the trail, the hounds would be at them in a matter of minutes. As Richard looked around he pulled the sword free. It sent its distinctive ringing across the murky water. Kahlan stopped and looked back to him.

"There"—he pointed with the sword across the water to their right—"that island. It looks high enough to be dry. Maybe the heart hounds can't swim."

He thought it a slim hope, but could think of nothing else. Chase had said they would be safe from the hounds in the swamp, but hadn't told them how. This was the only thing he could think of. Kahlan didn't hesitate. She led her horse right in, pulling Zedd's behind. Richard followed close after with Chase's, watching up the trail, seeing movement through gaps in the trees. The water seemed to be no more than three or four feet deep, with a muddy bottom. Weed broke from its anchoring and floated to the surface as Kahlan's horse waded through ahead of him, making steady progress to the island.

Then he saw the snakes.

Dark bodies wriggled in the water, just below the surface, heading toward them from every direction. Some lifted their heads, flicking red tongues out into the damp air. Their dark brown bodies had copper-colored splotches, almost invisible in the gloomy water, and barely disturbed the surface as they swam. Richard had never seen snakes this big. Kahlan was watching the island and hadn't noticed them yet. The dry land was too far away. He knew they weren't going to make it before the snakes reached them.

Richard turned and looked behind to see if they could make it back to high ground. Where they had left the trail, the dark shapes of the heart hounds were gathered, snarling and growling. Heads held low, the big black bodies paced back and forth, wanting to enter the water, to reach their prey, but only howling instead.

Richard lowered the tip of the sword into the water, letting it drag a small wake behind, as he prepared to strike at the first snake that came close enough. Then a surprising thing happened. When the sword dipped into the water, the snakes turned suddenly and squirmed away as fast as they could go. Somehow, the magic in the sword frightened them away. He wasn't sure why the magic would function this way, but was glad it did.

They worked their way among the large trunks of trees that stood like columns in the mire. Each in turn brushed aside vines and streamers of moss as they passed. When they crossed shallower areas of water, the tip of his sword no longer reached the water. The snakes returned immediately. He leaned lower, the sword's tip dipping back in the water, and the snakes turned once more, wanting nothing to do with them. Richard wondered what would happen when they reached dry land. Would the snakes follow them there? Would the sword's magic work to keep them away out of the water? The snakes might be as much trouble as the heart hounds.

Water ran off the underside of Kahlan's horse as it climbed up onto the island. There were a few poplar trees at the high point in the center and cedars at the water's edge on the far side of the small hump of dry ground, but mostly it was covered with reed and a smattering of iris. To see what would happen, Richard took the sword from the water before he needed to. The snakes began to come for him. When he left the water, some turned and swam away, some wandered the shoreline, but none followed onto dry land.

In near darkness, Richard laid Zedd and Chase on the ground beneath the poplars. He pulled a tarp from the packs and strung it between the trees to make a small shelter. Everything was wet, but since there was no wind, the makeshift structure kept most of the rain off them. There was no chance of a fire, for now, since all the wood that could be found was thoroughly soaked. At least the night wasn't cold. Frogs kept up a steady chirping from the wet darkness. Richard placed a pair of fat candles on a piece of wood so they could have some light under their shelter.

Together they checked Zedd. There didn't seem to be any sign of an injury, but he remained unconscious. Chase's condition was unchanged, too.

Kahlan stroked Zedd's forehead. "It is not a good sign for a wizard's eyes to be closed like this. I don't know what to do for them."

Richard shook his head. "Neither do I. We can be glad they don't have a fever. Maybe there's a healer in Southaven. I'll make litters the horses can pull. I think that would be better than having them ride again the way they did today."

Kahlan retrieved two more blankets to keep their friends warm; then she and Richard sat together by the candles, the water dripping around them. Glowing pairs of yellow eyes waited on the trail, in the blackness back through the trees. As the heart hounds paced, the eyes moved back and forth. Occasionally, Richard and Kahlan heard yelps of frustration. The two of them watched their hunters off across the dark water.

Kahlan stared at the glowing eyes. "I wonder why they didn't follow us."

Richard glanced sideways at her. "I think they're afraid of the snakes."

Kahlan jumped to her feet, quickly scanning around, her head pushing against the tarp. "Snakes, what snakes? I don't like snakes," she said in a rush.

He looked up. "Some kind of big water snakes. They swam off when I put the sword in the water. I don't think we have to worry; they didn't come up on the dry ground when we did. I think it's safe."

She looked around cautiously as she pulled her cloak tight and then sat down, closer to him this time. "You could have warned me about them," she said with a frown.

"I didn't know myself until I saw them, and the hounds were right behind us. I didn't think we had much choice in the matter, and I didn't want to scare you."

She didn't say anything more. Richard got out a sausage and a loaf of hard bread, their last one. He tore the bread in half and cut pieces off the sausage, handing her a few. They each held a tin cup under the rainwater that dripped off the tarp. They ate in silence, watching all around for any sign of threat, listening to the rhythm of the rain.

"Richard," she asked at last, "did you see my sister, in the boundary?"

"No. Whatever it was that had you didn't look like a person to me, and I would bet that the thing I struck down at first didn't look like my father to you." She shook her head that it didn't. "I think," he said, "they just appear in a form meant to re-create a person you want to see, to beguile you."

"I think you're right," she sighed, taking a bite of sausage. When she finished chewing, she added, "I'm glad. I would hate to think we had to hurt them."

He nodded his agreement and looked over. Her hair was wet, and some of it was stuck to the side of her face. "There's something else, though, that I think is odd. When that thing from the boundary, whatever it was, struck out at Chase, it was fast and it hit him square the first time, and before we could do anything it grabbed you with no trouble. Same with Zedd, it got him the first time. But when I went back for them, it tried for me and missed, then it didn't even try again."

"I noticed that when it happened," she said. "It missed you by a good distance. It was as if it didn't know where you were. It knew right where the three of us were, but it couldn't seem to find you."

Richard thought a moment. "Maybe it was the sword."

Kahlan shrugged. "Whatever it was, I am happy for it."

He wasn't at all sure it was the sword. The snakes had been afraid of the sword, and swam away from it. The thing in the boundary had shown no fear; it seemed as if it simply couldn't find him. There was one other thing that he wondered at. When he had struck down the thing in the boundary that looked like his father, he had felt no pain. Zedd had told him there would be a price to pay for killing with the sword, and that he would feel the pain of what he had done. Maybe there was no pain because the thing was already dead. Maybe it was all in his head, none of it was real. That couldn't be; it was real enough to strike down his friends. His self-assurance that it wasn't his father he had cut down began to waver.

They ate the rest of the meal in silence while he thought about what he could do for Zedd and Chase, which was nothing. Zedd had medicines along, but only Zedd know how to use them. Maybe it was magic from the boundary that had struck them

204

down. Zedd had magic along, too, but he was also the only one who knew how to use that.

Richard took out an apple and cut it into wedges, removed the seeds, and gave half to Kahlan. She moved closer and leaned her head on his arm as she ate it.

"Tired?" he asked.

She nodded, then smiled. "And I am sore in places I cannot mention." She ate another wedge of apple. "Do you know anything about Southaven?"

"I've heard other guides mention it when they've passed through Hartland. From what they say, it's a place of thieves and misfits."

"It doesn't sound like the kind of place that would have a healer." Richard didn't answer. "What will we do, then?"

"I don't know, but they'll get better, they'll be all right."

"And if not?" she pressed.

He took the apple away from his mouth, and looked at her. "Kahlan, what are you trying to say?"

"I am saying that we have to be prepared to leave them. To go on."

"We can't," he answered firmly. "We need them both. Remember when Zedd gave me the sword? He said he wanted me to get us across the boundary. He said he had a plan. He hasn't told me what that plan is." He looked out over the water at the hounds. "We need them," he repeated.

She picked at the skin of the apple wedge. "What if they were to die tonight? Then what would we do? We would have to go on."

Richard knew she was looking up at him, but he didn't look back. He understood her need to stop Rahl. He felt the same hunger, and would let nothing stop them, even if it meant leaving his friends, but it hadn't reached that point yet. He knew she was only trying to reassure herself that he had the necessary conviction, the required determination. She had given up much to her mission, lost much to Rahl, as he had. She wanted to know he had the ability to go on, at any cost, to lead.

The candles lit her face softly, a small glow in the darkness. Reflections of the flames danced in her eyes. He knew she didn't like saying these things to him.

"Kahlan, I'm the Seeker, I understand the weight of that responsibility. I will do anything required to stop Darken Rahl. Anything. You can place your faith in that. I will not, however, spend the lives of my friends easily. For now we have enough to worry about. Let's not invent new things."

Rain dripped into the water from trees, sending hollow echoes through the darkness. She put her hand on his arm, as if to say she was sorry. He knew she had nothing to be sorry for; she was only trying to face the truth, one possible truth, anyway. He wanted to reassure her.

"If they don't get better," he said, holding her eyes with his, "and if there is a safe place to leave them, with someone we can trust, then we will do so and go on."

She nodded. "That is all I meant."

"I know." He finished his apple. "Why don't you get some sleep. I'll keep watch."

"I couldn't sleep," she said, indicating the heart hounds with a nod of her head, "not with them watching us like that. Or with snakes all around."

Richard smiled at her. "All right, then, how about if you help me build the litters for the horses to pull? That way we can get out of here in the morning as soon as the hounds are gone."

She returned the smile and got up. Richard retrieved a wicked-looking war axe from Chase and found it worked as well on wood as on flesh and bone. He wasn't at all sure Chase would approved of putting one of his prize weapons to use in this fashion; in fact, he knew he wouldn't. He smiled to himself. He couldn't wait to tell him. In his mind he could picture his big friend's disapproving frown. Of course, Chase would have to embellish the story with every telling. To Chase, a story without embellishment was like meat without gravy; just plain dry.

His friends had to get better, he told himself. They just had to. He couldn't bear it if they died.

It was several hours before they were finished. Kahlan stayed close to him, as she was afraid of the snakes, and the heart hounds watched them the whole time. For a while Richard had thought to use Chase's crossbow to try to get some of the hounds, but finally decided against it: Chase would be angry at him for squandering valuable bolts to no purpose. The hounds couldn't get them, and would be gone with the light.

When they were finished, they checked the other two, then sat down together again by the candles. He knew Kahlan was tired—he could hardly keep his own eyes open—but she still didn't want to lie down to sleep, so he had her lean against him. In no time her breathing slowed and she was asleep. It was a fitful sleep; he could tell she was having bad dreams. When she started whimpering and jerking, he woke her. She was breathing rapidly, and almost in tears.

"Nightmares?" he asked, stroking her hair reassuringly with the backs of his fingers.

Kahlan nodded against him. "I was dreaming about the thing from the boundary that was around my legs. I dreamt it was a big snake."

Richard put his arm around her shoulders and hugged her tight against him. She didn't object, but pulled her knees up and put her arms around them as she nuzzled against him. He worried that she could hear his heart pounding. If she did, she didn't say anything and was soon fast asleep again. He listened to her breathing, to the frogs, and to the rain. She slept peacefully. He closed his fingers around the tooth under his shirt. He watched the heart hounds. They watched back.

She woke sometime near morning when it was still dark. Richard was so tired he had a headache. Kahlan insisted he lie down and sleep while she kept watch. He didn't want to; he wanted to continue holding her, but was too sleepy to argue.

When she gently shook him awake it was morning. Weak, gray light filtered through the dark green of the swamp and through heavy mist that made the world seem small and close. The water around them looked as if it had been steeped with decayed vegetation, a brew that rippled occasionally with unseen life beneath the surface. Unblinking black eyes pushed up through the duckweed, watching them.

"The heart hounds are gone," she said. She looked drier than she had last night.

"How long?" he asked, rubbing the cramps out of his arms.

"Twenty, maybe thirty minutes. When it got light they suddenly went off in a rush."

Kahlan gave him a tin cup of hot tea. Richard gave her a questioning look.

She smiled. "I held it over the candle until it was hot."

He was surprised at her inventiveness. She gave him a piece of dried fruit and ate some herself. He noticed the war axe leaning against her leg, and thought to himself that she knew how to stand watch.

It was still raining gently. Strange birds called out sharply in rapid, ragged shrieks from across the swamp, while others answered in the distance. Bugs hovered inches above the water, and occasionally there was an unseen splash.

"Any change in Zedd or Chase?" he asked.

She seemed reluctant to answer. "Zedd's breathing is slower."

Richard quickly went and checked. Zedd seemed hardly alive. His face had a sunken, ashen look. He put an ear to the old man's chest and found his heart to be beating normally, but he was breathing slower, and he felt cold and clammy.

"I think we must be safe from the hounds now. We had better get going, and see if we can find them some help," he said.

Richard knew she was afraid of the snakes—he was, too, and told her so—but she didn't let it interfere with that they had to do. She put her trust in what he said, that the snakes wouldn't come near the sword, and crossed the water without hesitation when he told her to go. They had to traverse the water twice, once with Zedd and Chase, and a second time to retrieve the parts for the litters, as they could only be used on dry land.

They hooked up the poles to the horses, but couldn't use them yet as the tangle of roots on the swamp trail would cause too jolting a ride. They would have to wait until they were on a better road, once they were clear of the swamp.

It was midmorning before they reached the better road. They stopped long enough to lay their two fallen friends in the litters and cover them with blankets and oilcloth. Richard was pleased to discover that the pole arrangement worked well; it didn't slow them at all, and the mud helped them slide along nicely. He and Kahlan ate lunch on their horses, passing food back and forth as they rode next to each other. They stopped only to check on Zedd and Chase, and continued on through the rain.

Before night came they reached Southaven. The town was little more than a collection of ramshackle buildings and houses fit crookedly in among the oaks and beech, almost as if to turn themselves away from the road, from queries, from righteous eyes. None looked ever to have seen paint. Some had tin patches that drummed in the steady rain. Set in the center of the huddle was a supply store, and next to it a two-story building. A clumsily carved sign proclaimed it to be an inn, but offered no name. Yellow lamplight coming from windows downstairs was the only color standing out from the grayness of the day and the building. Heaps of garbage leaned drunkenly against the side of the building, and the house next door tilted in sympathy with the rubbish pile.

"Stay close to me," Richard said as they dismounted. "The men here are dangerous."

Kahlan smiled oddly with one side of her mouth. "I'm used to their kind."

Richard wondered what that meant, but didn't ask.

Talking trailed off when they went through the door, and all faces turned. The place was about what Richard expected. Oil lamps lit a room filled with a fog of pungent pipe smoke. Tables, all arranged in a haphazard fashion, were rough, some no more than planks on barrels. There were no chairs, only benches. To the left a door stood closed, probably leading to the kitchen. To the right, in the shadows, leading up to the guest rooms, was a stairway minus a handrail. The floor, with a series of paths through the litter, was mottled with dark stains and spills.

The men were a rough collection of trappers and travelers and trouble. Many had unkempt beards. Most were big. The place smelled of ale and smoke and sweat.

Kahlan stood tall and proud next to him; she was a person not easily intimidated. Richard reasoned that perhaps she should be. She stuck out among the riffraff like a gold ring on a beggar. Her bearing made the room even more of an embarrassment.

When she pushed back the hood of her cloak, grins broke out

all around, revealing a collection of crooked and missing teeth. The hungry looks in the men's eyes didn't fit the smiles. Richard wished Chase were awake.

With a sinking feeling, he realized there was going to be trouble.

A stout man walked over and halted. He wore a shirt with no sleeves and an apron what looked like it could never have been white. The top of his shiny, shaved head reflected the lamplight, and the curly black hair on his thick arms seemed in competition with his beard. He wiped his hands on a filthy rag before flopping it over a shoulder.

"Something I can do for you?" the man asked in a dry voice. His tongue rolled a toothpick across his mouth as he waited.

With his own tone and eyes Richard let the man know he would brook no trouble. "There a healer in this town?"

The proprietor shifted his glance to Kahlan and then back to Richard. "No."

Richard noted the way, unlike the other men, the man kept his eyes where they belonged when he looked at Kahlan. It told him something important. "Then we would like a room." He lowered his voice. "We have two friends outside who are hurt."

Taking the toothpick out of his mouth, the man folded his arms. "I don't need any trouble."

"Nor do I," Richard said with deliberate menace.

The bald man looked Richard up and down, his eyes snagging for an instant on the sword. With his arms still folded, he appraised Richard's eyes. "How many rooms you want? I'm pretty full."

"One will do fine."

In the center of the room a big man stood. From a mass of long stringy red hair he looked out with mean eyes that were set too close together. The front of his thick beard was wet with ale. He wore a wolf hide over one shoulder. His hand rested on the handle of a long knife.

"Expensive-looking whore you got there, boy," the red-haired man said. "I don't suppose you'd mind if we came up to your room and passed her around some?"

Richard locked his glare on the man. He knew this was a challenge that would only be ended with blood. His eyes didn't move. His hand did—slowly, toward the sword. His rage pounded, fully awake even before his fingers reached the hilt.

This was the day he was going to have to kill other men.

A lot of other men.

Richard's grip tightened around the braided wire hilt until his knuckles were white. Kahlan gave a steady pull on the sleeve of his sword arm. She spoke his name in a low tone, raising the inflection at the end, the way his mother did when she was warning him to stay out of something. He stole a glance at her. She gave a luscious smile to the red-haired man.

"You men have it all wrong," she said in a throaty voice. "You see, this is my day off. I'm the one who hired him for the night." She smacked Richard on the rear. Hard. It surprised him so much he froze. She licked her top lip as she looked at the red-haired man. "But if he doesn't give me my money's worth, well, you will be the first I call to fill the breach." She smile lasciviously.

There was a thick moment of silence. Richard resisted mightily his need to pull the sword free. He held his breath as he waited to see which way it was going to go. Kahlan continued to smile at the men in a way that only made his anger deepen.

Life and death measured each other in the red-haired man's eyes. No one moved. Then a grin split his face and he roared with laughter. Everyone else hooted and hollered and laughed. The man sat down and the men started talking again, ignoring Richard and Kahlan. Richard breathed out in a sigh. The proprietor eased the two of them back a ways. He gave Kahlan a smile of respect.

"Thank you, ma'am. I'm glad your head is faster than your friend's hand. This place may not seem much to you, but it's mine and you just kept it in one piece for me."

"You are welcome," Kahlan said. "Do you have a room for us?"

The proprietor put the toothpick back in the corner of his mouth. "There's one, upstairs, at the end of the hall, on the right, that has a bolt on the door."

"We have two friends outside," Richard said. "I could use some help getting them up there."

The man gave a nod of his head back at the roomful of men. "It wouldn't do if that lot saw you were burdened with injured

211

companions. You two go up to the room, just like they expect. My son's in the kitchen. We'll bring your friends up the back stairs, so no one will see." Richard didn't like the idea. "Have a little faith, my friend," the other said in a low voice, "or you may be bringing harm to your friends. By the way, my name's Bill."

Richard looked at Kahlan; her face was unreadable. He looked back to the proprietor. The man was tough, hardened, but didn't appear to be devious. Still, it was his friends' lives at stake. He tried to keep his voice from sounding as threatening as he felt.

"All right, Bill, we will do as you ask."

Bill gave a small smile and a nod as he rolled the toothpick across his mouth.

Richard and Kahlan went up to the room and waited. The ceiling was lower than was comfortable. The wall next to the single bed was covered with years of spit. In the opposite corner were a three-legged table and short bench. A single oil lamp sat glowing weakly on the table. The windowless room was otherwise bare, and had a naked feel to it. It smelled rank. Richard paced while Kahlan sat on the bed, watching him, looking slightly uncomfortable. Finally, he strode over to her.

"I can't believe what you did down there."

She stood up and looked him in the eyes. "The result is what matters, Richard. If I had let you do what you were about to do, your life would have been at great risk. For nothing of value."

"But those men think . . ."

"And you care what those men think?"

"No . . . but . . ." He could feel his face redden.

"I am sworn to protect the life of the Seeker with my own. I would do anything required to protect you." She gave him a meaningful look, lifting an eyebrow. "Anything."

Frustrated, he tried to think how to put into words how angry he was without making it sound as if he was angry with her. He had been at the brink of lethal commitment. A brink only one wrong word away. Pulling back was agonizingly difficult. He could still feel his blood pounding with the lust for violence. It was difficult to understand the way the anger twisted his own rationality with hot need, much less explain it to her. Looking into her green eyes was making him relax, though, cooling his anger.

212

"Richard, you have to keep your mind where it belongs."

"What do you mean?"

"Darken Rahl. That is where your mind belongs. Those men downstairs are of no concern to us. We must only get past them, that's all. Nothing else. Don't expend your thoughts on them. It's a waste. Put your energy to our job."

He let out a breath, and nodded. "You're right. I'm sorry. You did a brave thing tonight. As much as I didn't like it."

She put her arms around him, her head against his chest, and gave him as slow hug. There was a soft knock at the door. After assuring himself it was Bill, he opened the door. The proprietor and his son carried Chase in and laid him carefully on the floor. When the son, a lanky young man, saw Kahlan, he fell instantly and hopelessly in love. Richard understood the feeling; nonetheless, he didn't appreciate it.

Bill pointed with his thumb. "This is my son, Randy." Randy was in a trance, staring at Kahlan. Bill turned to Richard, wiping the rain off the top of his head with the rag he kept over his shoulder. He still had the toothpick in his mouth.

"You didn't tell me your friend was Dell Brandstone."

Richard's caution flared. "That a problem?"

Bill smiled. "Not with me. The warden and me have had our disagreements, but he's a fair man. He gives me no trouble. He stays here sometimes when he's in the area on official business. But the men downstairs would tear him apart if they knew he was up here."

"They might try," Richard corrected.

A slight smile curled the corners of Bill's mouth. "We'll get the other one."

When they left, Richard gave Kahlan two silver coins. "When they come back, give the boy one of these to take the horses to the stables for us and tend to them. Tell him that if he will spend the night watching them and have them ready for us at sunrise, you will add the other."

"What makes you think he will do it?"

Richard gave a short laugh. "Don't worry, he'll do it, if you ask. Just smile."

Bill came back carrying Zedd in his husky arms. Randy followed, carrying most of their packs. Bill gently laid the old man

213

on the floor next to Chase. He gave Richard a look from under his curly eyebrows, then turned to his son.

"Randy, go get this young lady a basin, and a pitcher of water. And a towel. A clean towel. She might like to clean up."

Randy backed out of the room, smiling and tripping over his feet as he went. Bill watched him go, then turned to Richard with an intense look. He took the toothpick out of his mouth.

"These two are in bad shape. I won't ask you what happened to them because a smart fellow wouldn't tell me, and I think you're a smart fellow. We don't have a healer around here, but there's someone who may be able to help, a woman named Adie. They call her the bone woman. Most people are afraid of her. That bunch downstairs won't go near her place."

Richard remembered Chase saying Adie was his friend. He frowned. "Why?"

Bill glanced to Kahlan, and back to Richard, narrowing his eyes. "Because they're superstitious. They think she's bad luck of some sort, and because she lives near the boundary. They say that people she doesn't like have a bad habit of dropping dead. Mind you, I'm not saying it's true. I don't believe it myself. I think it's all made up in their own heads. She's not a healer, but I know of folks she's helped. She may be able to help your friends. At least you better hope she can, because they're not going to last much longer without help."

Richard combed his fingers through his hair. "How do we find this bone woman?"

"Turn left down the trail in front of the stables. It's about a four-hour ride."

"And why are you helping us," Richard asked.

Bill smiled and folded his muscled arms across his chest. "Let's just say I'm helping the warden. He keeps some of my other customers at bay, and the wardens bring me an income from the government with their business, here and from my dry goods store next door. If he makes it, you just be sure to tell him it was me that helped save his life." He chuckled. "That'll vex him good."

Richard smiled. He understood Bill's meaning. Chase hated to have anyone help him. Bill did indeed know Chase. "I will be sure to let him know you saved his life." The other looked pleased. "Now, since this bone woman lives by herself, way out by the boundary, and I'm to ask for her help, I think it would be a good idea if I took her some things. Can you get together a load of supplies for her?"

"Sure. I'm an approved supplier; I get reimbursed from Hartland. Of course, that thieving council takes most of it back in taxes. I can put it in my tally book for the government to pay, if this is official business."

"It is."

Randy came back with the basin, water, and towels. Kahlan put a silver coin in his hand and asked him about caring for the horses. He looked to his father for approval. Bill nodded.

"Just tell me which horse is yours, and I'll take extra good care of it," Randy said with a big grin.

Kahlan smiled back. "They are all mine. Take care with each, my life depends on it."

Randy's face turned serious. "You can count on me." Unable to decide what to do with his hands, he finally jammed them in his pockets. "I won't let anyone near them." He backed toward the door again, and when all but his head was through it, added, "I just want you to know I don't believe a word of what those men downstairs are saying about you. And I told them so."

Kahlan smiled in spite of herself. "Thank you, but I do not want you to endanger yourself on my account. Please stay away from those men. And do not mention that you talked to me, it will only embolden them."

Randy grinned and nodded and left. Bill rolled his eyes and shook his head. He turned to Kahlan with a smile.

"You wouldn't consider staying here and marrying the boy, would you? It would do him good to have a mate."

An odd look of pain and panic flashed across Kahlan's eyes. She sat on the bed, looking down at the floor.

"Just kidding, girl," Bill said apologetically. He turned back to Richard. "I'll bring you each a plate of supper. Boiled potatoes and meat."

"Meat?" Richard asked suspiciously.

Bill chuckled. "Don't worry, I wouldn't dare serve those men bad meat. I could lose my head."

In a few minutes he returned and set two steaming dishes of food on the table.

"Thank you for your help," Richard said.

Bill raised an eyebrow. "Don't worry, it will all be in my tally book. I'll bring it to you in the morning to sign. There anyone in Hartland who will recognize your signature?"

Richard smiled. "I think so. My name is Richard Cypher. My brother is First Councilor."

Bill flinched, suddenly shaken. "I'm sorry. Not that your brother is First Councilor. I mean that I'm sorry I didn't know. I mean that if I had known, I'd have given you better accommodations. You can stay at my house. It's not much but it's better than this. I'll take your things over right now. . . ."

"Bill, it's all right." Richard went to the man and put a hand on his back, reassuring him. The proprietor looked suddenly less fierce. "My brother is First Councilor; I am not. The room is fine. Everything is fine."

"You're sure? Everything? You're not going to send the army here, are you?"

"You've been a big help to us, honest. I have nothing to do with the army."

Bill didn't look convinced. "You're with the head of the boundary wardens."

Richard smiled warmly. "He's a friend of mine. For many years. The old man, too. They're my friends, that's all."

Bill's eyes brightened. "Well, if that's true, then how about if I add a couple of extra rooms to the tally book? Seeing as how they won't know you all stayed together."

Richard kept smiling, and patted the man's back. "That would be wrong. I won't put my name to it."

Breathing out with a sigh, Bill broke into a big grin. "So, you are Chase's friend." He nodded to himself. "Now I believe you. I haven't been able to get that man to fatten my tally book in all the time I've known him."

Richard put some silver in the man's hand. "But this wouldn't be wrong. I appreciate what you're doing for us. I would also appreciate it if you would water the ale tonight. Drunken men die too easy." Bill gave a knowing smile. Then Richard added, "You have dangerous customers."

216

The man studied Richard's eyes, glanced to Kahlan, then back again. "Tonight I do," he agreed.

Richard gave him a hard look. "If anyone comes through that door tonight, I will kill them, no questions asked."

Bill looked at him for a long moment. "I'll see what I can do to keep that from happening. Even if I have to knock some heads together." He went to the door. "Eat your supper before it gets cold. And take care of your lady, she has a good head on her shoulders." He turned to Kahlan and winked. "And a pretty one, too."

"One more thing, Bill. The boundary is failing. It will be down in a few weeks. Take care of yourself."

The man's chest rose as he took a deep breath. He held the doorknob as he looked into Richard's eyes for a long moment. "I think the council named the wrong brother First Councilor. But then, they didn't get to be councilors because they worry about doing right. I'll come get you in the morning when the sun is up and it's safe."

When he left, Richard and Kahlan sat close on the small bench and ate their meal. Their room was at the back of the building, and the men downstairs were at the front, so it was quieter than Richard thought it would be. All they could hear from the crowd was a muffled hum. The food was better than Richard expected, or maybe it was just that he was famished. The bed looked wonderful to him, too, as he was dead tired. Kahlan noticed.

"You only had an hour or two of sleep last night. I will stand first watch. If the men downstairs decide to come up here, it will not be until later that they work up the courage. If they come, it would be better if you were rested."

"Easier to kill people when you're well rested?" He was immediately sorry it came out the way it did; he hadn't meant it to sound harsh. He realized he was gripping his fork as if it were a sword.

"I'm sorry, Richard. I didn't mean it that way. I only meant I don't want you to get hurt. If you are too tired you will not be able to protect yourself as well. I'm afraid for you."

She pushed a potato around the plate with her fork. Her voice was hardly more than a whisper. "I'm so sorry you had to be pulled into this mess. I don't want you to have to kill people. I didn't want you to have to kill those men downstairs. That's the other reason I did what I did, so you would not have to kill them."

He looked over at her as she stared down at her plate. It hurt his heart to see the look of pain on her face. He gave her a playful shove with his shoulder.

"I wouldn't have missed this journey for anything. Gives me time to be with my friend." She looked at him out of the corner of her eye as he smiled.

She smiled back and put her head against the side of his shoulder for a second before eating the potato. Her smile warmed him.

"Why did you want me to ask the boy to take care of the horses?"

"Results. That's what you said was most important. The poor kid is hopelessly in love with you. Since you were the one who asked, he will guard the horses better than we could ourselves." She looked at him as if she didn't believe him. "You have that effect on men," he assured her.

Her smiled faded a little, taking on a haunted look. Richard knew he was getting too close to her secrets, so he said nothing else. When they finished eating, she walked to the basin, dipped the end of a towel in the water, and went to Zedd. She wiped his face tenderly, then looked over to Richard.

"He is the same, no worse. Please, Richard, let me have first watch, get some sleep?"

He nodded, rolled himself into the bed, and was asleep in seconds. Sometime in the early morning she woke him for his watch. As she went to sleep he washed his face with the cold water, trying to wake up, then sat on the bench, leaning against the wall, waiting for any sign of trouble. He sucked on a piece of dried fruit, trying to get the bad taste out of his mouth.

An hour before sunrise, there was an urgent knock at the door.

"Richard?" a muffled voice called. "It's Bill. Unbolt the door. There's trouble."

CHAPTER 16

KAHLAN SPRANG OUT OF bed, rubbing the sleep from her eyes as Richard unbolted the door. She pulled her knife. Bill, breathing hard, squeezed in and pushed the door shut with his back. Beads of sweat dotted his forehead.

"What is it? What's happened?" Richard asked.

"Everything was pretty quiet." Bill swallowed, catching his breath. "Then a little while ago these two fellows showed up. Right out of nowhere. Big men, thick necks, blond hair. Good-looking. Armed to the teeth. The kind of men you try not to look in the eye." He took a few deep breaths.

Richard stole a quick glance at Kahlan's eyes. There was no doubt in them as to who the men were. Apparently the wizard trouble the quad had run into wasn't trouble enough.

"Two?" Richard asked. "You're sure there weren't more?"

"Only saw two come in, but that was enough." Bill's wide eyes looked out from under his curly eyebrows. "One was tore up pretty good, arm in a sling, big claw cuts down his other arm. Didn't seem to bother him any, though. Anyway, they started asking about a woman that sounded a lot like your lady here. Except she isn't wearing a white dress like they described. They started for the stairs, and a quarrel broke out about who was going to do what with her. Your red-haired friend jumped the one with the sling and slit his throat from ear to ear. The other fellow cut down a bunch of my customers in a heartbeat. I've never seen anything like it. Then all of a sudden he just wasn't there anymore. Vanished into nothing. There's blood everywhere.

"The rest of the lot are down there right now arguing about who's going to be first to . . ." He glanced at Kahlan, leaving the rest unsaid. He wiped his forehead with the back of his arm. "Randy's bringing the horses to the back; you have to get out now. Head for Adie's. The sun's an hour away, the hounds two, so you'll be all right. But not if you delay."

Richard grabbed Chase's legs, Bill his shoulders. He told Kahlan to bolt the door and get their things together. With Chase in their arms they trudged down the back stairs and out into the darkness and rain. Lamplight coming from the windows reflected in the puddles, giving the wet, black forms of the horses yellow highlights. Randy was waiting, looking worried as he held the horses. They dropped Chase in a litter and ran as quietly as possible up the stairs. Bill scooped Zedd into his arms, while Richard and Kahlan threw on their cloaks and grabbed the packs. The three of them, Bill, Richard, then Kahlan, raced down the stairs and for the door.

As they burst out the door they almost tripped over Randy, sprawled on the ground. Richard looked up just in time to see the red-haired man lunging. He leapt back, narrowly missing the sweep of the long knife. The man went face-first into the mud. With surprising quickness he came to his knees, enraged, and then went rigid, the sword point an inch from his nose. The air rang with the sound of steel. The man looked up with vicious, black eyes. Water and mud ran from the strings of his hair. Richard flicked the sword a quarter turn in his hand and whacked him hard over the head with the flat of the blade. He went down in a limp heap.

Bill laid Zedd in the litter while Kahlan turned Randy over. One eye was swollen shut. Rain splattered on his face. He groaned. When he saw Kahlan with his one good eye he broke into a grin. Relieved that he wasn't hurt worse, she gave him a quick hug and helped him up.

"He jumped me," Randy said apologetically. "I'm sorry."

"You are a brave young man. You have nothing to be sorry for. Thank you for helping us." She turned to Bill. "You, too."

Bill smiled and gave a nod. Zedd and Chase were quickly covered with blankets and oilcloth and the packs loaded. Bill told them that Adie's supplies were already on Chase's horse. Richard and Kahlan mounted their horses. She flipped the silver coin to Randy.

"Payment on delivery, as promised," she told him. He caught the coin and grinned.

Richard bent down and clasped hands with Randy and thanked him earnestly, then pointed angrily at Bill.

"You! I want you to add everything to your tally book. Include all the damage, all your time and trouble, even the grave markers. I want you to add a fair fee for saving our lives. If the council doesn't want to approve payment, you tell them that you saved the life of the brother of the First Councilor, and Richard Cypher said if they don't pay, I'll personally have the head of the man responsible and I will put it on a pike on the front lawn of my brother's house!"

Bill nodded and laughed over the sound of the rain. Richard pulled back on the reins to keep his horse in place as it danced about, eager to go. He pointed down at the unconscious man in the mud. He was furious.

"The only reason I didn't kill this man is because he killed a man worse than himself, and in so doing may have unwittingly saved Kahlan's life. But he is guilty of murder, intent to murder, and intent to rape. I suggest you hang him before he wakes."

Bill looked up at him with hard eyes. "Done."

"Don't forget what I said about the boundary. Trouble comes. Take care with yourself."

Bill held Richard's eyes as he put his hairy arm around his son's shoulders. "We won't forget." A slight smile curled the corners of his mouth. "Long life to the Seeker."

Richard looked down at him in surprise and then grinned. Smiling quenched some of the fire of his rage. "When I first saw

221

you," Richard said, "my thought was that you were not a devious man. I find I was mistaken."

Richard and Kahlan pulled their hoods up and urged their horses on into the dark rain, toward the bone woman.

The rain had quickly drowned the lights from Southaven and left the travelers to grope their way through the blackness. Chase's horses had carefully picked their way down the trail; trained by the wardens for this kind of duty, they were comfortable in the adverse conditions. Dawn had struggled interminably at bringing light to the new day. Even after Richard knew the sun was up, the world still hung in half-light between night and day, a ghost of morning. The rain had helped to cool his hot rage.

Richard and Kahlan knew that the last member of the quad was loose somewhere, and they watched every movement as a potential threat. They knew that, sooner or later, he would come at them. The uncertainty of when ate at their concentration. Worry over what Bill had said, that Zedd and Chase wouldn't last long, gnawed at his spirit. If this woman, Adie, couldn't help, he didn't know what he would do. If she couldn't help, his two friends would die. He couldn't imagine a world without Zedd. A world without his tricks and help and comfort would be a dead world. He realized that he was getting a lump in his throat thinking about it. Zedd would tell him not to worry about what might be, but to worry about what was.

But what was seemed almost as bad. His father had been murdered. Darken Rahl was close to obtaining all the boxes. Richard's two oldest friends were near death. He was alone with a woman he cared about, but wasn't supposed to care about. She still kept her secrets closed to him, locked away.

He could tell she fought a constant battle over it in her mind. Sometimes when he felt he was getting closer to her, he saw pain and fear in her eyes. Soon they would be in the Midlands, where people knew what she was. He wanted her to be the one to tell him; he didn't want to learn it from someone he didn't know. If she didn't tell him soon, he would have to ask her. Against his nature or not, he would have to.

So deep was he in thought, he hadn't realized they had been on the trail for over four hours. The forest was drinking in the rain. Trees loomed dark and huddled in the mist; the moss on their trunks was vibrant and lush. It stood out on the bark of trees, and in round humps on the ground, green and spongy. The lichen on the rocks shone bright yellow and rust in the damp. In some places water ran down the trail, turning it into a temporary creek. The poles of Zedd's litter splashed through it, going over rocks and roots, rocking the old man's head from side to side on the rougher sections. His feet rode inches from water when they crossed runoff streams.

Richard smelled the sweetness of woodsmoke in the stillness. Birch wood. He realized that the area they were entering had changed somehow. It looked the same as it had for hours, yet it was different. Rain floated down in quiet reverence for the forest. The whole place felt somehow sacred. He felt like an intruder, disturbing the peace of timeless ages. He wanted to say something to Kahlan, but it seemed as if talking would be a sacrilege. He understood why the men from the inn wouldn't come up here; their foul presence would be a violation.

They came to a house that so blended with its surroundings, it was almost invisible next to the trail. A wisp of woodsmoke curled from its chimney, up into the misty air. The logs of the walls were weathered and ancient, matching the color of the surrounding trees, with nothing other than the ground it sat upon disturbed. The house seemed to be growing from the forest floor, with trees towering around it protectively. The roof was covered in a mass of ferns. A smaller, slanted roof covered a door and a porch large enough for only two or three people to stand on at once. There was a square, four-paned window in the front, and another on the side of the house Richard could see. None had curtains.

In front of the old house, a patch of ferns bowed and nodded when water from the trees dripped onto them. Mist turned their distinctive dusty pale green bright in the wetness. A narrow path slipped through their midst.

In the center of the ferns, in the center of the path, stood a tall woman, taller than Kahlan, not as tall as Richard. She wore a simple tan robe of a coarse weave, with red and yellow symbols and decorations at the neck. Her hair was fine and straight, a mix of black and gray, parted in the middle, chopped square with her strong jaw. Age had not stolen the handsome features of her weathered face. She leaned on a crutch. She had but one foot. Richard brought the horses to a slow halt in front of her.

The woman's eyes were completely white.

"I be Adie. Who be you?" Adie's voice had a harsh, throaty, raspy quality that sent a shiver up Richard's spine.

"Four friends," Richard said in a respectful tone. Light rain fell in a hushed, soft patter. He waited.

Fine wrinkles covered her face. She took the crutch from under her arm and folded both thin hands over the top, lending her weight to it. Adie's thin lips pulled tighter in a slight smile.

"One friend," she rasped. "Three dangerous people. I decide if they be friends." She nodded slightly to herself.

Richard and Kahlan stole a sidelong glance at each other. His guard went up. He felt somehow uncomfortable sitting on the horse, as if talking down to her suggested disrespect. He dismounted, Kahlan following his lead. With his horse's reins in his hand, he moved to stand in front of the animal, Kahlan next to him.

"I am Richard Cypher. This is my friend, Kahlan Amnell."

The woman studied his face with her white eyes. He had no idea if she could see, but he didn't know how it could be possible. She turned to Kahlan. The woman's raspy voice spoke a few words to Kahlan in a language he couldn't understand. Kahlan's eyes held the old woman's, and she gave Adie a slight bow of her head.

It had been a greeting. A greeting of deference. Richard hadn't recognized the words *Kahlan* or *Amnell* anywhere in it. The fine hairs on the back of his neck stiffened.

Kahlan had been addressed by title.

He had been around Kahlan long enough to know that by the way she was standing, with her back straight and her head held assertively up, she was on guard. Serious guard. If she had been a cat, her back would be arched, her fur standing on end. The two women faced each other; age had been dismissed for the moment by each. They measured each other on qualities he couldn't see. This was a woman who could bring them to harm, and he knew the sword wasn't going to protect him.

Adie turned back to Richard. "Put words to your need, Richard Cypher."

"We need your help."

Adie's head bobbed. "True."

"Our two friends are hurt. One, Dell Brandstone, told me he is your friend."

"True," Adie said again in her raspy voice.

"Another man, in Southaven, told us you may be able to help them. In return for your help, we brought you supplies. We thought it would be fair to offer you something."

Adie leaned closer. "Lie!" She thumped her crutch once on the ground. Richard and Kahlan both jerked back a little.

Richard didn't know what to say. Adie waited. "It's true. The supplies are right here." He turned a little, indicating Chase's horse. "We thought it would be fair . . ."

"Lie!" She thumped her crutch once again.

Richard folded his arms, his temper rising. His friends were dying while he played games with this woman. "What is a lie?"

" 'We' be a lie." She thumped her crutch again. "You be the one who thought to offer supplies. You be the one who decided to bring them. Not you and Kahlan. You. 'We' be a lie. 'I' be the truth."

Richard unfolded his arms, holding them out to his sides. "What difference does that make? 'I,' 'we,' what does it matter?"

She stared at him. "One be true, one be a lie. How much more difference could there be?"

Richard folded his arms across his chest again, frowning. "Chase must have a very difficult time telling you the stories of his adventures."

Adie's small smile came back. "True," she nodded. She leaned a little closer, motioning with her hand. "Bring your friends inside."

She turned, put the crutch back under her arm, and worked her way to the house. Richard and Kahlan looked at each other, and then went to get Chase, putting the blankets away first. He had

Kahlan take the boundary warden's feet; he took the heavy half. As soon as they lugged Chase through the door, Richard discovered why she was called the bone woman.

Bones of every kind stood out in stark relief against the dark walls. Every wall was covered. Against one were shelves that held skulls. Skulls of beasts Richard didn't recognize. Most were fearsome-looking, with long, curved teeth. At least none were human, he thought. Some of the bones were assembled into necklaces. Some were decorated into objects of purpose with feathers and colored beads, chalk circles drawn around them on the surface of the wall. There were stacks of bones in the corner, looking unimportant en masse. The ones on the wall were displayed carefully, with space around them to signify their importance. On the mantel over the fireplace was a rib bone as thick as Richard's arm, as long as he was tall, with symbols he didn't recognize carved in dark lines along its length. There were so many bleached bones around him that Richard felt as if he were in the belly of a dead beast.

They set Chase down while Richard's head swiveled around, looking. Rainwater dripped off Kahlan, Chase, and himself. Adie towered over him. She was as dry as the bones around her. She had stood outside in the rain, yet she was dry. Richard reconsidered the wisdom of his decision to come here. If Chase hadn't told him Adie was his friend, he would not be doing this.

He looked to Kahlan. "I'll go get Zedd." It was more of a question than a statement.

"I will help carry in the supplies," she offered, casting a glance at Adie.

Richard gently laid Zedd at the bone woman's feet. Together, he and Kahlan stacked the supplies on the table. When they had finished, both went and stood next to their friends, in front of Adie, both peering at the bones. Adie watched them.

"Who be this one?" she asked, pointing at Zedd.

"Zeddicus Zu'l Zorander. My friend," he said.

"Wizard!" Adie snapped.

"My friend!" Richard yelled, his anger unhinged.

Adie calmly looked at him with her white eyes while he glared back. Zedd was going to die if he didn't get help, and Richard was in no mood to allow that to happen. Adie leaned forward,

226

placing her wrinkled hand flat against his stomach. A little surprised, he stood still while she rubbed her hand in a slow circle, as if seeking to discern something. She took her hand back, carefully folding it over the other on the crutch. Her thin lips pulled to the sides in a slight smile as she looked up.

"The righteous rage of a true Seeker. Good." She looked over to Kahlan. "You have nothing to fear from him, child. It be the anger of truth. It be the anger of the teeth. The good need not fear it." With the aid of her crutch, she took a few steps to Kahlan. Adie placed her hand on Kahlan's stomach and repeated the procedure. When she was finished, she laid her hand over the crutch and nodded. She looked to Richard.

"She has the fire. The anger burns in her too. But it be the anger of the tongue. You have to fear it. All have to fear it. It be dangerous if she ever lets it out."

Richard gave Adie a leery look. "I dislike riddles; they leave too much room for misinterpretation. If you want to tell me something, then tell me."

"Tell me," she mocked. Her eyes narrowed. "What be stronger, teeth or tongue?"

Richard took a deep breath. "The answer is obviously teeth. Therefore I choose tongue."

Adie gave him a disapproving scowl. "Sometimes your tongue moves when it shouldn't. Make it be still," she commanded in a dry rasp.

Somewhat embarrassed, Richard kept quiet.

Adie smiled and gave a nod. "See?"

Richard frowned. "No."

"The anger of teeth be force by contact. Violence by touch. Combat. The magic of the Sword of Truth be the magic of the anger of teeth. Ripping. Tearing. The anger of the tongue need not touch, but it be force just the same. It cuts just as quick."

"I'm not sure what you mean," Richard said.

Adie reached out, her long finger stretching to him and lightly touching his shoulder. His head was suddenly filled with a vision, a vision that was a memory: a memory of the night before. He saw the men at the inn. He was standing in front of them with Kahlan, and the men were ready to attack. He was grasping the Sword of Truth, ready for the violence necessary to stop them, knowing that nothing short of blood would suffice. Then he saw Kahlan next to him, talking to the mob, stopping them, holding them with her words, running her tongue across her lip, giving meaning without speaking. She was taking the fire from them, disarming the depraved without touching them; doing what the sword could not. He began to understand what Adie meant.

Kahlan's hand swept up sharply and snatched Adie's wrist, pulling the hand away from Richard. There was a dangerous look in her eyes, one that wasn't lost on Adie.

"I am sworn to protect the life of the Seeker. I do not know what you are doing. You will forgive me if I overreact; I mean no disrespect, but I could not forgive myself if I failed in my task. There is much at risk."

Adie looked down at the hand around her wrist. "I understand, child. Forgive me for thoughtlessly giving you cause for alarm."

Kahlan held the wrist a moment longer to make her point, then released it. Adie laid the hand over her other on the top of the crutch. She looked back to Richard.

"Teeth and tongue work together. Same with the magic. You command the magic of the sword, the magic of the teeth. But that gives you magic of the tongue also. The magic of the tongue works because you back it with the sword." She turned her head slowly to Kahlan. "You have both, child. Teeth and tongue. You use them together, one backing the other."

"And what is a wizard's magic?" Richard asked.

Adie looked at him, considering the question. "There be many kind of magic, teeth and tongue be only two. Wizards know them all, save those of the underworld. Wizards use most of what they know." She looked down at Zedd. "He be a very dangerous man."

"He has never shown me anything but kindness and understanding. He is a gentle man."

"True. But he also be a dangerous one," Adie repeated.

Richard let it drop. "And Darken Rahl? Do you know of him, what kind he can use?"

Adie's eyes narrowed. "Oh, yes," she hissed. "I know of him. He can use all the magic a wizard does, and the magic a wizard cannot. Darken Rahl can use the underworld."

Icy bumps rippled up Richard's arms. He wanted to ask what

kind of magic Adie had, but decided better of it. She turned once more to Kahlan.

"Be warned, child, you have the true power of the tongue. You have never seen it. It will be a terrible doing if you ever let it loose."

"I don't know what you are talking about," Kahlan said, her eyebrows in a frown.

"True," Adie nodded. "True." She reached out and gently placed her hand on Kahlan's shoulder, working her fingers, bringing her closer. "Your mother died before you became a woman, before you were of the age when she could teach you of it."

Kahlan swallowed hard. "What can you teach me of it?"

"Nothing. I am sorry, but I have no understanding of its workings. It be something only your mother can teach, when you reached the age of woman. Since your mother did not show you, the teaching be lost. But the power be still there. Be warned. Just because you were not taught its use does not mean it cannot come out."

"Did you know my mother?" Kahlan asked in a painful whisper.

Adie's face softened as she looked at Kahlan. She nodded slowly. "I remember your family name. And I remember her green eyes; they not be easy to forget. You have her eyes. When she carried you, I knew her."

A tear rolled down Kahlan's cheek, and her voice came in the same painful whisper. "My mother wore a necklace, with a small bone on it. She gave it to me when I was a child. I wore it always, until . . . until, Dennee, the girl I called my sister . . . when she died, I buried it with her. She had always been fond of it. You gave that necklace to my mother, didn't you?"

Adie closed her eyes and nodded. "Yes child. I gave it to her to protect her unborn daughter, to keep her child safe, that she might grow to be strong, like her mother. I can see that she has."

Kahlan slipped her arms around the old woman. "Thank you, Adie," she said tearfully, "for helping my mother." Adie held the crutch with one hand, and with the other rubbed Kahlan's back in genuine sympathy. After a few moments Kahlan separated from the old woman and wiped the tears from her eyes.

Richard saw his opening, and went for it with single-minded determination.

"Adie," he said in a soft voice, "you helped Kahlan before she was born. Help her now. Her life and the lives of a great many others are at stake. Darken Rahl hunts her, hunts me. We need the help of these two men. Please help them. Help Kahlan."

Adie gave him her small smile. She nodded her head a little to herself. "The wizard chooses his Seekers well. Fortunately for you, patience be not a prerequisite for the post. Be at ease; I would not have had you bring them in if I did not intend to help them."

"Well, perhaps you cannot see," he pressed, "but Zedd especially is in bad shape. His breathing is hardly there at all."

Adie's white eyes regarded him with strained tolerance. "Tell me," she said in her dry rasp, "do you know Kahlan's secret, the one she keeps from you?"

Richard said nothing and tried to show no emotion. Adie turned to Kahlan.

"Tell me, child, do you know the secret he keeps from you?" Kahlan said nothing. Adie looked back to Richard. "Does the wizard know of the secret you keep from him? No. Do you know the secret the wizard keeps from you? No. Three blind people. Hmm? Seems I be able to see better than you."

Richard wondered what secret Zedd was keeping from him. He lifted an eyebrow. "And which of these secrets do you know, Adie?"

She pointed a thin finger at Kahlan. "Hers only."

Richard was relieved, but tried to let his face show nothing. He had been on the verge of panic. "Everyone has secrets, my friend, and has a right to keep them when there is need."

Her smile widened. "That be true, Richard Cypher."

"Now, what about these two?"

"Do you know how to heal them?" she asked.

"No. If I did, I obviously would have already done so."

"Your impatience is to be forgiven; it be only right for you to fear for the lives of your friends. I bear you no ill will for your concern. But be at ease, they have been receiving help from the moment you brought them in."

Richard gave her a confused look. "Really?"

She nodded. "They be struck down by underworld beasts. It will take time for them to wake, days. How many I cannot say. But they be dry. Lack of water will be the death of them, therefore they must be brought awake enough to drink, or they will die. The wizard breathes slow not because he be worse, but because that be the way wizards save strength in time of trouble—they go into a deeper sleep. I must bring them both awake to drink. You will not be able to talk to them, they will not know you, so be not afraid when you see it. Go to the corner, bring the water bucket."

Richard retrieved the water and then helped Adie lower herself to sit cross-legged at the heads of Zedd and Chase. She pulled Kahlan down next to her. She asked Richard to bring a bone implement from the shelf.

Part of it looked very much like a human thighbone. The entire object had a dark brown patina, and looked to be ancient. Down the shaft of the bone were carved symbols Richard didn't recognize. At one end were two skull tops, one to each side of the ball. They had been cut smoothly into half spheres, and covered with dried skin of some kind. In the center of each skin was a knot that looked like a navel. Spaced evenly around each skin, where it stretched across the skull edge, were tufts of coarse black hair tied on with beaded thread that matched that around the neck of Adie's robe. The skull tops looked like they could be human. Something inside rattled.

Richard handed it respectfully to Adie. "What makes the rattle?"

Without looking up, she said, "Dried eyes."

Adie shook the bone rattle gently from side to side over the heads of Zedd and Chase while mumbling a chant in the strange language in which she had spoken to Kahlan. The rattle made a hollow, wooden sound. Kahlan sat cross-legged next to her, head bowed. Richard stood back and watched.

After ten or fifteen minutes, Adie motioned with her hand for him to come closer. Zedd suddenly sat up and opened his eyes. Richard realized she wanted him to give him water. She continued to chant as he dipped the ladle in and held it up to Zedd's mouth. He drank thirstily. Richard was thrilled to see the old man sit up and open his eyes, even if he couldn't talk, even if he

231

didn't know where he was. Zedd drank half a bucket of water. When finished, he lay back down and closed his eyes. Chase was next, and he drank the other half of the water.

Adie handed Richard the bone rattle and asked him to return it to the shelf. Next she had him bring the bone pile from the corner and stack half over Zedd's body, half over Chase's, directing him on how to place each bone, to some alignment that only she could see or understand. Finally she had him stack rib bones in a wagon-wheel pattern with the hub centered over each man's chest. When he finished, she complimented him on doing a fine job, but he felt no pride, because she had directed his hand at each turn. Adie looked up at him with her white eyes.

"Can you cook?"

Richard thought about the time Kahlan had told him that his spice soup was like hers, and that their two lands were much the same. Adie was from the Midlands; maybe she would like something from her homeland. He smiled at her.

"I would be honored to make you some spice soup."

She put her hands together in a swoon. "That would be wonderful. I have not had a proper spice soup in years."

Richard went to the opposite corner of the room and sat at the table, cutting up vegetables and mixing spices. For over an hour, as he worked, he watched the two women sitting on the floor, talking in the strange language. Two women catching up on the news from home, he thought happily. He was in a good mood; someone was finally doing something to help Zedd and Chase. Someone who knew what the problem was. When he was finished and had the soup on the fire, he didn't want to disturb them—they looked like they were enjoying themselves—so he asked Adie if he could cut some firewood for her. She seemed pleased by the idea.

He went outside and removed the tooth from around his neck, putting it in his pocket, and left his shirt on the porch to keep it dry. He took the sword with him to the back of the house, where Adie had told him he would find the firewood pile. Placing logs on the sawbuck, he cut off pieces to length. Most of the wood was birch, easiest for an old woman to cut. He picked out the rock maple, excellent firewood but tough cutting. The woods nearby were dark and dense, but they didn't feel threatening.

They felt welcoming, enveloping, safe. Still, there was the last man of the quad out there somewhere, hunting Kahlan.

He thought about Michael, hoped he was safe. Michael didn't know what Richard was doing and probably wondered where he was. He was probably worried. Richard had planned on going to Michael's house after they left Zedd's place, but there had been no time. Rahl had almost caught them. He wished he had been able to get word to his brother. Michael was going to be in great danger when the boundary failed.

When he tired of sawing, he split what he had cut. It felt good to use his muscles, to sweat from labor, to do something that didn't require him to think. The cool rain felt good on his hot body, making the work easier. To amuse himself, he imagined the wood was Darken Rahl's head as he brought the axe down. For variation he sometimes imagined it to be a gar. When the piece of wood was particularly tough, he imagined it to be the red-haired man's head.

Kahlan came out, and asked him if he was ready to come eat. He hadn't even realized it was getting dark. After she left, he went to the well and poured a bucket of cold water over himself, washing off the sweat. Kahlan and Adie were sitting at the table, and since there were only two chairs, he brought in a log round to sit on. Kahlan set a bowl of soup in front of him as he sat down, and handed him a spoon.

"You have given me a wonderful gift, Richard," Adie said.

"And what would that be?" He blew on a spoonful of soup to cool it.

She looked at him with her white eyes. "Without taking offense, you have given me the time to talk to Kahlan in my native tongue. You cannot know what joy that be for me. So many years it has been. You are a very perceptive man. You are a true Seeker."

Richard beamed at her. "You have given me something very precious too. The lives of my friends. Thank you, Adie."

"And your spice soup be wonderful," she added, with a hint of surprise.

"Yes." Kahlan winked at him. "It's as good as I make."

"Kahlan has told me about Darken Rahl, and about the boundary failing," Adie said. "It explains much. She has told me that you know of the pass, and wish to cross into the Midlands. Now you must decide what you will do." She took a spoonful of soup.

"What do you mean?"

"They must be awakened every day to drink, and they must be fed a gruel. Your friends be asleep for many days, five, maybe ten. You must decide, as Seeker, if you are to wait for them, or go on. We cannot help you; you must decide."

"That would be a lot of work for you to do by yourself."

Adie nodded. "Yes. But it not be as much work as going after the boxes, as stopping Darken Rahl." She ate some more soup as she watched him.

Richard stirred his spoon around absently in his bowl. There was a long silence. He looked to Kahlan, but she showed nothing. He knew she didn't want to interfere with his decision. He looked back down at his soup.

"Every day that passes," he said quietly at last, "brings Rahl closer to the last box. Zedd told me he has a plan. That does not mean it is a good plan. And there may not be time to use it when he awakes at last. We could lose before we start." He looked up into Kahlan's green eyes. "We can't wait. We can't take the chance; too much is at risk. We must leave without him." Kahlan gave him a smile of reassurance. "I wasn't planning on letting Chase go with us anyway. I have a more important job for him."

Adie reached across the table and put her weathered hand on his. It felt soft and warm. "It not be an easy choice to make. It not be easy to be Seeker. That which lies ahead be difficult beyond your worst fears."

He forced a smile. "At least I still have my guide."

The three of them sat in silence, considering what must be done.

"You both will have a good sleep tonight," Adie said. "You will need it. After supper, I will tell you what you will need to know to get through the pass." She looked to each of them in turn; her voice became even raspier. "And I will tell you how I lost my foot."

CHAPTER 17

RICHARD PLACED THE LAMP on the side of the table, close to the wall, and lit it with a stick from the fire. The sound of gentle rain and night creatures drifted in from the window. The chirps and calls of small animals going about their nocturnal lives were familiar to him, comforting sounds of home. Home. His last night in his homeland, and then he was to cross into the Midlands. As his father had done. He smiled to himself at the irony. His father had brought the Book of Counted Shadows out of the Midlands, and now he was taking it back.

He sat down on the log round, across from Kahlan and Adie. "So, tell me, how do we find the pass?"

Adie leaned back in her chair and swept her hand through the air. "You already have. You be in the pass. The mouth of it anyway."

"And what do we need to know to get through it?"

"The pass be a void in the underworld, but it still be a land of the dead. You be living. The beasts hunt the living if the living be big enough to be of interest."

235

Richard looked at Kahlan's impassive face, then back to Adie. "What beasts?"

Adie's long finger pointed to each wall of the room in turn. "They be the bones of the beasts. Your friends were touched by things of the underworld. The bones confuse their powers. That be why I said your friends were being helped from the moment you brought them in here. The bones cause the magic poison to leave their bodies, letting the death sleep lift. The bones keep the evil away from here. The beasts cannot find me because they feel the evil of the bones and it blinds them, makes them think I be one of them."

Richard leaned forward. "If we took some of the bones with us, would that protect us?"

Adie smiled her little smile, making her eyes wrinkle. "Very good. That be exactly what you must do. These bones of the dead have the magic to help protect you. But there be more. Listen carefully to what I tell you."

Richard folded his fingers together and nodded.

"You cannot take your horses, the trail be too small for them. There be places they cannot fit. You must not wander from the trail—it be very dangerous to do so. And you must not stop to sleep. It will take one day, one night, and most of the next day to cross."

"Why can't we stop to sleep?" Richard asked.

Adie looked to each of them with her white eyes. "There be other things, besides the beasts, in the pass. They will get you if you stop long enough."

"Things?" Kahlan asked.

Adie nodded. "I go into the pass often. If you are careful, it be safe enough. If you are not careful, there be things that will get you." Her raspy voice lowered bitterly. "I became overconfident. One day I was walking a long time, and became very tired. I was sure of myself, sure I knew the dangers well, so I sat against a tree and took a small nap. For a few minutes only." She put her hand on her leg, rubbing it slowly. "When I was asleep, a gripper fixed itself on my ankle."

Kahlan scrunched up her features. "What's a gripper?"

Adie regarded her in silence for a minute. "A gripper be an animal that has armor all over his back, spikes all around the

236

bottom edge. Many legs underneath, each with a sharp, hooked claw at the end, a mouth like a leech with teeth all around. He wraps himself around, so only his armor is out. With his claws he digs into the flesh to hold tight so you cannot pull him off, and then he fixes his mouth to you, sucking the blood from you, tightening with the claws all the time."

Kahlan put her hand reassuringly on Adie's arm. The light from the lamp made the old woman's white eyes a pale shade of orange. Richard didn't move, his muscles tense.

"I had my axe with me." Kahlan closed her eyes as her head lowered. Adie went on. "I tried to kill the gripper, or at least get him off me. I knew that if I did not, he would suck all the life-blood from me. His armor be harder than the axe. I was very angry with myself. The grippers be one of the slowest creatures in the pass, but he be faster than a sleeping fool." She looked into Richard's eyes. "There be only one thing I could do to save my life. I could stand the pain no longer; his teeth were scraping into the bone. I tied a strip of cloth tight around my thigh, and laid my lower leg across a log. I used the axe to chop off my foot and ankle."

The silence in the small house was brittle. Only Richard's eyes moved, to meet Kahlan's. He saw sorrow there for the old woman, saw his own sorrow reflected. He couldn't imagine the resolve it would take to use an axe to cut off your own foot. His stomach felt sick. Adie's thin lips spread in a grim smile. With one hand she reached across the table to take Richard's hand, and with the other hand, took Kahlan's. She held their hands in a firm grip.

"I tell you this story not to have you feel sorry for me. I tell you only so you two will not become prey to something in the pass. Confidence can be a dangerous thing. Fear can keep you safe, sometimes."

"Then I think we shall be very safe," Richard said.

Adie continued to smile, and gave a single nod. "Good. There be one more thing. There be a place halfway through the pass, where the two walls of the boundary come very close together, almost touching. It be called the Narrows. When you come to a rock the size of this house, split down the middle, that be the place. You must pass through the rock. Do not go around it even

237

though you may want to; death be that way. And then beyond, you must pass between the walls of the boundary. It be the most dangerous place in the pass." She put a hand on Kahlan's shoulder, and squeezed Richard's hand tighter, looking to each in turn. "They will call to you from the boundary. They will want you to come to them."

"Who?" Kahlan asked.

Adie leaned closer to her. "The dead. It could be anyone you know who be dead. Your mother."

Kahlan bit her bottom lip. "Is it really them?"

Adie shook her head. "I don't know, child. But I do not believe it to be."

"I don't think so, either," Richard said, almost more to reassure himself.

"Good," Adie rasped. "Keep thinking so. It will help you resist. You will be tempted to go to them. If you do, you are lost. And remember, in the Narrows it be even more important to keep on the path the whole way through. A step or two off to either side and you have gone too far; the walls of the boundary be that close. You will not be able to step back. Ever."

Richard let out a deep breath. "Adie, the boundary is failing. Before he was struck down, Zedd told me he could see the change. Chase said you couldn't see into it before, and that now underworld beings were getting out. Do you think it will still be safe to go through the Narrows?"

"Safe? I never said it be safe. It never be safe to go through the Narrows. Many who were keen with greed, but not strong of will, have tried to go through and never come out the other side." She leaned closer to him. "As long as the boundary be there still, so too must be the pass. Stay on the trail. Keep in mind your purpose. Help each other if need be, and you will get across."

Adie studied his face. Richard turned to Kahlan's green eyes. He wondered if Kahlan and he could resist the boundary. He remembered what it felt like to want to go into it, to long for it. In the Narrows, it would be on both sides of them. He knew how frightened Kahlan was of the underworld, with good reason; she had been in it. He wasn't anxious to go anywhere near it himself.

Richard frowned in thought. "You said the Narrows were in

238

the center of the pass. Won't it be night? How will we see to stay on the trail?"

Adie put her hand on Kahlan's shoulder to help herself up. "Come," she said as she put the crutch under her arm. They followed slowly behind as she worked her way to the shelves. Her slender fingers clutched a leather pouch. She loosened the drawstring and dumped something in her palm.

She turned to Richard. "Hold out your hand."

He held his hand palm up in front of her. She put her hand over his, and he felt a smooth weight. In her native tongue she spoke a few words under her breath.

"The words say I give you this of my own free will."

Richard saw that in his palm rested a rock about the size of a grouse egg. Smooth and polished, it was so dark it seemed as if it could suck the light from the room. He couldn't even discern a surface, other than a layer of gloss. Beneath that was a void of blackness.

"This be a night stone," she said in a measured rasp.

"And what do I do with it?"

Adie hesitated, her gaze darting briefly to the window. "When it be dark, and you have need enough, take out the night stone and it will give off light so you may find your way. It only works for its owner, and then only if it be given of its last owner's free will. I will tell the wizard you have it. He has magic to find it, so he will be able to find you."

Richard hesitated. "Adie, this must be valuable. I don't feel right accepting it."

"Everything is valuable under the right conditions. To a man dying of thirst, water be more precious than gold. To a drowning man, water be of little worth and great trouble. Right now, you be a very thirsty man. I thirst for Darken Rahl to be stopped. Take the night stone. If you feel the weight of obligation, you may return it to me one day."

Richard nodded, slipped the stone into the leather pouch and then into his pocket. Adie turned to the shelf once more and retrieved a delicate necklace, holding it up for Kahlan to see. A few red and yellow beads were to each side of a small round bone. Kahlan's eyes brightened, her mouth opened in surprise.

"It is just like my mother's," she said with delight.

Adie placed it over her head while Kahlan lifted clear her mass of dark hair. Kahlan looked down at the necklace, touching it between her finger and thumb, smiling.

"For now it will hide you from the beasts in the pass, and someday, when you carry a child of your own, it will protect her, and help her to grow strong like you."

Kahlan put her arms around the old woman, hugging her tight for a long time. When they separated, Kahlan's face bore a distressed expression, and she spoke in the language Richard didn't understand. Adie simply smiled and patted her shoulder sympathetically.

"You two should sleep now."

"What about me? Shouldn't I have a bone to hide me from the beasts?"

Adie studied his face, then looked down at his chest. Slowly, she reached out. Her fingers uncurled and touched his shirt tentatively, touched the tooth underneath. She pulled her hand back and looked back up into his eyes. Somehow she knew about the tooth being there. Richard held his breath.

"You need no bone, Hartlander. The beasts cannot see you."

His father had told him the thing guarding the book had been an evil beast. He realized the tooth was the reason the things from the boundary hadn't been able to find him, as they had the others. If it hadn't been for the tooth, he would have been struck down as Zedd and Chase were, and Kahlan would be in the underworld now. Richard tried to keep his face from betraying any emotion. Adie seemed to get the hint and remained silent. Kahlan seemed confused but didn't ask.

"Sleep now," Adie said.

Kahlan refused Adie's offer of her bed. She and Richard laid their bedrolls near the fire, and Adie retired to her room. Richard put a few more logs in the fire, remembering how Kahlan liked to be by a fire. He sat by Zedd and Chase for a few minutes, smoothing the old man's white hair, listening to his even breathing. He hated to leave his friends behind. He was afraid of what was ahead. He wondered if Zedd had an idea of where to look for one of the boxes. Richard wished he knew what Zedd's plan was. Maybe it was some sort of wizard's trick to try on Darken Rahl.

Kahlan sat on the floor by the fire with her legs crossed, watching him. When he came back to his blanket, she lay down on her back, pulling the blanket up to her waist. The house was quiet and felt safe. Rain continued to fall outside. It felt good being by the fire. He was tired. Richard turned toward Kahlan, his elbow on the floor and his head propped in his hand. She stared up at the ceiling, turning the bone on the necklace between her finger and thumb. He watched her breast rise and fall with her breathing.

"Richard," she whispered while continuing to stare at the ceiling, "I'm sorry we have to leave them behind."

"I know," he whispered back. "Me too."

"I hope you do not feel I forced you to do it, because of what I said when we were in the swamp."

"No. It was the right decision. Every day brings winter closer. It will do us no good to wait with them, while Rahl gets the boxes. Then we will all be dead. The truth is the truth. I can't be angry at you for saying it."

He listened to the fire snap and hiss as he watched her face, the way her hair lay across the floor. He could see a vein in her neck pulsing with her heartbeat. He thought that she had the most delicious-looking neck he had ever seen. Sometimes she looked so beautiful, he could hardly stand to look at her, and at the same time, could not look away. She still held the necklace in her fingers.

"Kahlan?" She turned to his eyes. "When Adie told you the necklace would protect you and someday your child, what did you say to her?"

She gazed at him a long moment. "I thanked her, but I told her I did not think I would live long enough to have a child."

Richard felt bumps rise on the skin of his arms. "Why would you say that?"

Her eyes moved in little flicks as she studied different places on his face. "Richard," she said quietly, "madness is loose in my homeland, madness you cannot imagine. I am but one. They are many. I have seen people better than me go against it and be slaughtered. I am not saying I think we will fail, but I do not think I will live to know."

Even if she wasn't saying it, Richard knew she didn't think he would live either. She was trying not to frighten him, but she thought he would die in the effort, too. That was why she hadn't wanted Zedd to give him the Sword of Truth, to make him Seeker. He felt as if his heart were coming up into his throat. She believed she was leading them to their death.

Maybe she was right, he mused. After all, she knew more about what they were up against than he did. She must be terrified to go back to the Midlands. But then, there was no place to hide. The night wisp had said that to run was a sure death.

Richard kissed the end of his finger and then touched it against the bone on the necklace. He looked back up into her soft eyes.

"I add my oath of protection to the bone," he said in a whisper. "To you now and to any child you may bear in the future. I would trade no day I spend with you for a life of safe slavery. I accepted the post of Seeker of my own free will. And if Darken Rahl takes the whole world into madness, then we will die with a sword in our hands, not chains on our wings. We will not allow it to be easy for them to kill us; they will pay a high price. We will fight with our last breath if need be, and in our death, let us inflict a wound on him that will fester until it claims him."

A smile spread across her face, until her eyes were caught up in it. "If Darken Rahl knew you as I do, he would have reason to lose sleep. I thank the good spirits the Seeker has no cause to come after me in anger." She laid her head down on her arm. "You have an odd talent for making me feel better, Richard Cypher, even when telling me of my death."

He smiled. "That's what friends are for."

Richard watched her for a while after she closed her eyes, until sleep gently took him. His last thoughts before it came, were of her.

The first hint of morning was damp and dreary, but the rain had stopped. Kahlan had given Adie a parting hug. Richard faced the old woman, looking into her white eyes.

"I must ask you to do an important task. You must give Chase a message from the Seeker. Tell him he is to go back to Hartland and warn the First Councilor that the boundary will be down soon. Have him tell Michael to gather the army to protect Westland from Rahl's forces. They must be prepared to fight at any invasion. They must not let Westland fall as did the Midlands. Any forces that come across must be deemed invaders. Have him tell Michael that Rahl is the one who killed our father and those who come, do not come in peace. We are at war, and I am already joined in battle. If my brother or the army fails to heed my warning, then Chase is to abandon the service of the government and gather the boundary wardens to stand against Rahl's legions. His army was virtually unopposed when they took the Midlands. If they have to shed blood freely to take Westland, maybe they will lose their spirit. Tell him to show no mercy to the enemy, take no prisoners. I take no joy in giving these orders, but it's the way Rahl fights, and either we meet him on his terms or we die on them. If Westland is taken, I expect the wardens to extract a terrible price before they fall. After Chase has the army and wardens in place, he is free to come to my aid, if he chooses to do so, as above all else we must stop Rahl from getting all three boxes." Richard looked down at the ground. "Have him tell my brother that I love him and I miss him." He looked up and gauged Adie's expression. "Can you remember all that?"

"I do not think I could forget if I wanted to. I will tell the warden your words. What would you have me tell the wizard?"

Richard smiled. "That I'm sorry we couldn't wait for him, but I know he will understand. When he is able, he will find us by the night stone. I hope by then to have found one of the boxes."

"Strength to the Seeker," Adie said in a rasp, "and you too, child. Grim times lie ahead."

CHAPTER 18

THE TRAIL WAS WIDE enough to allow Richard and Kahlan to walk side by side after they left Adie's place. Clouds hung thick and threatening, but the rain held off. Both wrapped their cloaks tight. Damp, brown pine needles matted the path through the forest. There was little brush among the big trees, allowing an open view for a good distance. Ferns covered the ground in feathery swaths through the trees, and dead wood lay in it here and there as if asleep in a bed. Squirrels scolded the two of them as they hiked along, while birds sang with monotonous conviction.

Richard picked at the branch of a small balsam fir as they walked past, stripping the needles between his thumb and the crook of his first finger.

"Adie is more than she seems," he said at last.

Kahlan looked up at him as they walked. "She is a sorceress."

Richard glanced sideways at her in surprise. "Really? I don't know exactly what a sorceress is."

"Well, she is more than us, but less than a wizard."

Richard smelled the aromatic fragrance of the balsam needles, then cast them aside. Maybe she was more than he, Richard thought, but he wasn't at all sure she was more than Kahlan. He remembered the look on Adie's face when Kahlan had grabbed her by the wrist. It had been a look of fear. He remembered the look on Zedd's face when he had first seen her. What power did she have that could frighten a sorceress and a wizard? What had she done that had caused thunder without sound? She had done it twice that he knew of, once with the quad, and once with Shar, the night wisp. Richard remembered the pain that had followed. A sorceress greater than Kahlan? He wondered.

"What's Adie doing living here, in the pass?"

Kahlan pushed some of her hair back over her shoulder. "She became tired of people coming to her all the time, wanting spells and potions. She wanted to be left alone to study whatever it is a sorceress studies; some sort of higher summons, as she called it."

"Do you think she will be safe when the boundary fails?"

"I hope so. I like her."

"Me too," he added with a smile.

The trail, climbing sharply in places, forced them to go single file at times as it twisted along steep rocky hillsides and over ridges. Richard let Kahlan go first so he could keep an eye on her, make sure she didn't wander off the path. At times he had to point out the trail, his experience as a guide making it plain to him, but not to her unpracticed eye. Other times the trail was a well-defined rut. The woods were thick. Trees grew from splits in the rock that pushed up above the leaf litter. Mist drifted among the trees. Roots bulging from cracks provided handholds as they climbed the abrupt inclines. His legs ached from the effort of descending extreme drops in the dark trail.

Richard wondered what they were going to do once they reached the Midlands. He had depended on Zedd to let him know the plan once they crossed the pass, and now they were without Zedd, without a plan. He felt kind of foolish to be charging into the Midlands. What was he going to do once they crossed over? Stand there and look around, divine where the box was and then be off after it? Didn't sound like a good plan to him. They didn't have time to wander about aimlessly, hoping they would come across something. No one was going to be. waiting for him, waiting to tell him where to go next.

They reached a steep jumble of rock. The trail went straight up the face. Richard surveyed the terrain. It would be easier to go around, rather than climb over the jut of rock, but he finally decided against it, the thought that the boundary could be anywhere making up his mind. There must be a reason the trail went this way. He went first and took Kahlan's hand, helping to pull her up.

As he walked, Richard's thoughts continued nagging at him. Someone had hidden one of the boxes, or Rahl would have it already. If Rahl couldn't find it, how was Richard to? He didn't know anyone in the Midlands; he didn't know where to look. But someone knew where the last box was, and that was how they had to find it. They couldn't look for the box; they had to look for someone who would be able to tell them where it was.

Magic, he thought suddenly. The Midlands was a land of magic. Maybe someone with magic could tell where the box was. They had to look for someone with the right kind of magic. Adie could tell things about him without ever having seen him before. There had to be someone with the kind of magic that could tell him where the box was without ever having seen it. Then, of course, they had to convince that person to tell them. But maybe if someone was hiding their knowledge from Darken Rahl, he would be glad to help stop him. It seemed there were too many wishes and hopes in his thoughts.

But there was one thing he did know: even if Rahl got all the boxes, without the book he wasn't going to know which box was which. As they walked along, Richard recited the Book of Counted Shadows to himself, trying to find a way to stop Rahl. Since it was an instruction book for the boxes, it should have a way to stop their use, but there was nothing like that in the book. The actual explanation of what each box would do, directives to determine which box was which, and how to open one, took up only a relatively small portion at the end of the book. Richard understood this part well, as it was clear and precise. Most of the book, though, was taken up with directions for countering unforeseen eventualities, resolving problems that could prevent the holder of the boxes from succeeding. The book even started out with how to verify the truth of the instructions.

If he could create one of these problems, he could stop Rahl, since Rahl didn't have the book to help him. But most of the problems were things he had no way of bringing about, problems with sun angles and clouds on the day of opening. And a lot of it made no sense to him. It spoke of things he had never heard of. Richard told himself to stop thinking of the problem, and to think of the solution. He would go through the book again. He cleared his mind and started at the beginning.

Verification of the truth of the words of the Book of Counted Shadows, if spoken by another, rather than read by the one who commands the boxes, can only be insured by the use of a Confessor. . . .

By late afternoon, Richard and Kahlan were sweating freely with the effort of the hike. As they crossed a small stream, Kahlan stopped and dipped a cloth in the water and used it to wipe her face. Richard thought it was a good idea. When they came to the next stream, he stopped to do the same. The clear water was shallow as it ran over a bed of round stones. He balanced on a flat rock as he squatted to soak a cloth in the cold water.

When he stood up, Richard saw the shadow thing. He froze instantly.

Off through the woods there was something standing partly behind a tree trunk. It wasn't a person, but was about that size, with no definite shape. It looked like a person's shadow standing up in the air. The shadow thing didn't move. Richard blinked and squinted his eyes trying to tell if he was really seeing what he thought he was seeing. Maybe it was just a trick of the dim afternoon light, a shadow of a tree he mistook for something more.

Kahlan had continued to walk along the trail. Richard came quickly up behind her and put his hand on the small of her back, below her pack, so she wouldn't stop. He leaned over her shoulder and whispered in her ear.

"Look to the left, off through the trees. Tell me what you see."

He kept his hand on her back, kept her walking along as she turned her head, looking off to the trees. Her eyes searched as she held her hair back, out of the way. Then she saw the thing.

"What is it?" she whispered, looking back to his face.

He was a little surprised. "I don't know. I thought maybe you could tell me."

She shook her head. The shadow remained motionless. Maybe it was nothing, a trick of the light, he tried to tell himself. He knew that wasn't true.

"Maybe it's one of the beasts Adie told us about, and it can't see us," he offered.

She gave him a sidelong glance. "Beasts have bones."

Kahlan was right, of course, but he had been hoping she would have agreed with the idea. As they moved quickly down the trail, the shadow thing stayed where it was and they were soon out of sight of it. Richard breathed easier. It appeared that the bone necklace Kahlan wore, and his tooth, had hidden them.

They ate a supper of bread, carrots, and smoked meat as they walked. Neither enjoyed the meal. Their eyes searched off into the deep woods as they ate. Even though it hadn't rained all day, everything was still wet, and occasionally water dripped from the trees. The rock was slick with slime in places, needing care to be crossed safely. Both watched the surrounding forest for any sign of danger. They saw nothing.

The fact that they saw nothing began to worry Richard. There were no squirrels, no chipmunks, no birds, no animals of any kind. It was too quiet. Daylight was slipping away. Soon they would be at the Narrows. He worried about that, too. The idea of seeing the things from the boundary again was frightening. The idea of seeing his father again was terrifying. His insides cringed at what Adie had told them, that those in the boundary would call to them. He remembered how seductive their calls were. He had to be prepared to resist. He had to harden himself against it. Kahlan had almost been pulled back into the underworld when they were in the wayward pine, the first night he knew her. When they were with Zedd and Chase, something had tried to pull her in again. He was troubled that the bone might not protect her when they were that close.

The trail leveled out and widened, allowing them to walk side by side again. He was tired from the day's hike, and it would be another night and day before they could rest. Crossing the Narrows in the dark and when they were exhausted sounded like a bad idea, but Adie had been insistent they not stop. He could not question a person who knew the pass as well as she. He knew that the story of the gripper would keep him wide awake.

Kahlan looked around at the woods, turned to check behind. She stopped suddenly, grabbing his arm. In the trail, not ten yards behind, stood a shadow.

Like the other, this one did not move. He could see through it, see the woods behind, as if it were made of smoke. Kahlan kept a firm grip on his arm as both of them walked ahead in a sideways fashion, watching the shadow thing. They rounded a turn in the trail and were away from it. They walked on faster.

"Kahlan, do you remember when you told me of the shadow people that Panis Rahl sent forth? Could those be shadow people?"

She gave him a worried look. "I don't know. I have never seen one; they were in the last war, before I was born. But the stories were always told the same, that they floated along. I never heard anyone say they stood still like that."

"Maybe it's because of the bones. Maybe they know we're here, but can't find us, so they stay still to search."

She wrapped her cloak tighter, obviously afraid of his idea, but didn't say anything. In the gathering night they walked along, close to each other, sharing the same troubling thoughts. Another shadow stood at the side of the trail. Kahlan gripped his arm tight. They passed slowly, quietly, keeping their eyes on it. It didn't move. Richard felt like panicking, but knew he couldn't; they had to stay on the trail, had to use their heads. Maybe the shadows were trying to make them bolt, to run from the trail, and cross over accidentally into the underworld. They looked around, behind, as they went. When Kahlan was looking the other way, a branch brushed her face. She jumped against him with a start. She looked over and apologized. Richard gave her a reassuring smile.

Pine needles held droplets from the rains and mist, and when a light breeze swayed the branches, water from the trees above rained down. In the near darkness they had a hard time telling if there were shadow things around them or if it was just the dark shapes of tree trunks. Twice, they had no trouble telling; they were close to the trail and there was no doubt what they were. Still the shadows did not follow or move, but stood as if watching, even though they had no eyes.

249

"What are we going to do if they come for us?" Kahlan asked in a tense voice.

Her grip on his arm was becoming painful, so he pried her fingers off and put her hand in his. She gave his hand a squeeze. "Sorry," she said with a self-conscious smile.

"If they come for us, the sword will stop them," he answered confidently.

"What makes you so sure?"

"It stopped the things in the boundary."

She seemed satisfied with the answer—he wished he were. The forest was dead quiet, except for a soft rasp he couldn't quite figure out. There were none of the usual night sounds. Dark branches swayed near them with the breeze, making his heart race.

"Richard," Kahlan said quietly, "don't let them touch you. If they are shadow people, their touch is death. Even if they are not shadow people, we don't know what would happen. We must not let them touch us."

He gave her hand a squeeze of reassurance.

Richard resisted the temptation to pull the sword. There might be too many for the sword, if the sword's magic even worked against shadows. If there was no other choice he would use the sword, but for now, his instincts told him not to.

The woods were getting darker. Tree trunks stood like black pillars in the murk. Richard felt as if there were eyes everywhere, watching. The trail was beginning to traverse a hillside, and he could see dark rocks rising up to their left. Runoff from the rains trickled through the rock. He could hear it bubbling and dripping and splashing. The ground dropped away on the right. The next time they looked back, there were three shadows, barely visible in the path behind. The two of them kept moving. Richard heard the soft scraping sound again, off in the woods to either side. It wasn't a sound he was familiar with. He could feel, more than see, that there were shadow things on each side and behind them. A few were close enough to the trail that there was no doubt what they were. The only way that was clear was ahead.

"Richard," Kahlan whispered, "do you think you should take

out the night stone? I can hardly see the path." She was gripping his hand tightly.

Richard hesitated. "I don't want to until we absolutely need it. I'm afraid of what might happen."

"What do you mean?"

"Well, those shadows haven't come for us yet. Maybe because they can't see us, because of the bones." He paused a moment. "But what if they can see the light from the night stone?"

Kahlan bit her bottom lip in worry. They strained to pick out the trail as it twisted to go around trees and boulders, over rocks and roots, cutting its way across the hillside. The soft scraping sound was nearer, all around. It sounded like . . . It sounded like claws on rock, he thought.

Two shadows stood ahead, close, the trail between them. Kahlan pressed tight against him and held her breath as they squeezed past. She buried her face against his shoulder when they were even with the shadow things. Richard put his arm around her, holding her tight. He knew how she felt. He was terrified, too. His heart pounded. It seemed they were going too far with each step, getting in too deep. He looked behind, but in the darkness there was not enough light to see if the shadows were standing on the trail.

Abruptly, an inky black shape loomed up before them. It was an enormous boulder, split down the middle.

The Narrows.

They pressed their backs up against the boulder, at the split. It was too dark to see the trail anymore, or if there were any shadow things close. They couldn't follow the trail through the Narrows without the light of the night stone; it was far too dangerous. One wrong step in the Narrows and they were dead. In the stillness the scraping sound was closer, and all around them. Richard reached into his pocket and pulled out the leather pouch. He loosened the drawstring and dumped the night stone into his palm.

Warm light flared into the night, lighting the woods around, casting eerie shadows. He held the stone out, to see better.

Kahlan gasped.

In the warm yellowish illumination, they could see a wall of the shadow things, hundreds of them, not an inch between any two. They formed a half circle less than twenty feet away. On the ground were dozens and dozens of hump-shaped creatures, almost looking like rocks at first. But they weren't rocks. Gray armor bands interlocked across their backs, jagged spikes poked out around the bottom edge.

Grippers.

That was what the sound was, their claws on the rocks. The grippers were moving with an odd, waddling gait, their humped bodies swaying from side to side as they struggled forward. Not fast, but steady. Some were only a few feet away.

For the first time, the shadows began to move, floating, drifting, tightening their ring.

Kahlan stood frozen, her back against the boulder, her eyes wide. Richard reached across the split, grabbed a fistful of her shirt and pulled her into the opening. The walls were wet and slick. The tightness of the space made him feel as if his heart were coming up in his throat. He didn't like tight places. They backed through, turning occasionally to check their way. He held the night stone out, lighting the shadow things as they came. Grippers crawled into the split.

Richard could hear the sound of Kahlan's rapid breathing echoing in the confining, dank space. They continued backing up, their shoulders sliding against the sides of the rock. Cold, slimy water soaked their shirts. In one spot they had to duck down and turn sideways because the crack narrowed, almost closing together, open just enough for them to pass down low. Forest debris fallen into the split lay in the dampness, decomposing. The place smelled of sickening rot. They continued moving sideways, and at last reached the other side. The shadows stopped when they reached the opening in the rock. The grippers didn't.

Richard kicked one that got too close, sending it tumbling through the leaves and sticks on the floor of the split. Landing on its back, it clawed at the air, snapping and hissing, twisting and rocking, until it righted itself. When it did, the gripper rose up on its claw-tipped feet and let out a clicking growl before coming on once again.

Both turned quickly to follow the path. Richard held the night stone out to light the Narrows trail.

Kahlan drew a sharp breath.

The warm light illuminated the hillside where the Narrows path should have been. Spread out before them as far as they could see was a mass of rubble. Rocks, tree limbs, splintered wood, and mud, all tumbled together. A slide had recently plunged down the hillside.

The Narrows trail had been swept away.

They took a step beyond the rock to have a better look.

Green light of the boundary came on, surprising them. They stepped back as one.

"Richard . . ."

Kahlan clutched his arm. The grippers were at their heels. The shadows floated in the split.

CHAPTER 19

TORCHES SET IN ORNATE gold brackets lit the walls of the crypt with flickering light, reflected off the polished pink granite of the huge, vaulted room, lending their smell of pitch to the fragrance of roses in the dead, still air. White roses, replaced every morning without fail for the last three decades, filled each of the fifty-seven gold vases set in the wall beneath each of the fifty-seven torches that represented each year in the life of the deceased. The floor was white marble, so that any white rose petal that fell would not be a distraction before it could be whisked away. A large staff saw to it that no torch was allowed to go spent for longer than a few moments, and that rose petals were not allowed to rest long upon the floor. The staff was attentive and devoted to their tasks. Failure to be so resulted in an immediate beheading. Guards watched the tomb day and night to be sure the torches burned, the flowers were fresh, and no rose petal sat too long on the floor. And of course to carry out executions.

Staff positions were filled from the surrounding D'Haran countryside. Being a member of the crypt staff was an honor, by law. The honor brought with it the promise of a quick death if an

254

execution was in order. A slow death in D'Hara was greatly feared, and common. New recruits, for fear they would speak ill of the dead king while in the crypt, had their tongues cut out.

The Master, on the evenings when he was at home in the People's Palace, would visit the tomb. No staff or tomb guards were allowed to be present during these visits. The staff had spent a busy afternoon replacing the torches with freshly burning ones and testing each of the hundreds of white roses by gently shaking them to make sure none of the petals were loose, since any torch going out during the royal visit, or any rose petal falling to the floor, would result in an execution.

A short pillar in the center of the immense room supported the coffin itself, giving it the effect of floating in the air. The gold-enshrouded coffin glowed in the torchlight. Carved symbols covered its sides, and continued in a ring around the room, cut into the granite beneath the torches and gold vases: instructions in an ancient language from a father to a son on the process of going to the underworld, and returning. Instructions in an ancient language understood by only a handful other than the son; none but the son lived in D'Hara. All the others in D'Hara who understood had long ago been put to death. Someday, the rest would be.

The crypt staff and guards had been sent away. The Master was visiting his father's tomb. Two of his personal guards stood watch over him, one to each side of the massive, elaborately carved and polished door. Their sleeveless leather-and-mail uniforms helped display their bulky forms, the sharp contours of their heavy muscles, and the bands they wore around their arms just above their elbows, bands with raised projections sharpened to deadly edges, used in close combat to tear apart an adversary.

Darken Rahl ran his delicate fingers over the carved symbols on his father's tomb. An immaculate white robe, its only decoration gold embroidery in a narrow band around the neck and down the front, covered his lean frame to within an inch of the floor. He wore no jewelry, other than a curved knife in a gold scabbard embossed with symbols warning the spirits to give way. The belt that held it was woven of gold wire. Fine, straight, blond hair hung almost to his shoulders. His eyes were a pain-

255

fully handsome shade of blue. His features set off his eyes perfectly.

Many women had been taken to his bed. Because of his striking looks, and his power, some went eagerly. The others went despite his looks, but because of his power. Whether or not they were eager did not concern him. Were they unwise enough to be repulsed when they saw the scars, they entertained him in ways they could not have foreseen.

Darken Rahl, as had his father before him, considered women merely vessels for the man's seed, the dirt it grew in, unworthy of higher recognition. Darken Rahl, as his father before him, would have no wife. His own mother had been nothing more than the first to sprout his father's wondrous seed, and then she had been discarded, as was only fitting. If he had siblings, he didn't know, nor did it matter; he was firstborn, all glory fell to him. He was the one born with the gift, and the one to whom his father passed the knowledge. If he had half brothers or sisters, they were merely weeds, to be expunged if discovered.

Darken Rahl spoke the words silently in his mind as his fingers traced the symbols. Although it was of the utmost importance that the directives were followed exactly, he had no fear of making an error; the instructions were burned into his memory. But he enjoyed reliving the thrill of the passage, of hanging between life and death. He savored going into the underworld, commanding the dead. He was impatient for the next journey.

Footsteps echoed at someone's approach. Darken Rahl showed no concern, or interest, but his guards did; they drew their swords. No one was allowed to come into the crypt with the Master. When they saw who it was, they stood down, replacing their weapons. No one but Demmin Nass, that is.

Demmin Nass, the right hand of Rahl, the lightning of the Master's dark thoughts, was a man as big as those he commanded. As he strode in, ignoring the guards, his sharply chiseled muscles stood out in stark relief in the torchlight. His chest was covered with skin as smooth as that of the young boys he had a weakness for. In stark contrast, his face was riddled with pockmarks. His blond hair was cropped close enough to cause it to stand up in a collection of spikes. A streak of black hair started in the middle of his right eyebrow and continued back over his head, to the right of center. It made him recognizable from a distance, a fact appreciated by those who had cause to know of him.

Darken Rahl stood absorbed in the reading of the symbols, and did not look when his guards drew their weapons, or when they replaced them. Although his guards were formidable, they were unnecessary, mere accoutrements of his position. He had powers enough to put down any threat. Demmin Nass stood at ease, waiting for the Master to finish. When at last Darken Rahl turned, his blond hair and stark white robe swished around with him. Demmin gave a respectful bow of his head.

"Lord Rahl." His voice was deep, coarse. He kept his head bowed.

"Demmin, my old friend, how good to see you again." Rahl's quiet tone had a clear, almost liquid quality to it.

Demmin straightened, his face set in a frown of displeasure. "Lord Rahl, Queen Milena has delivered her list of demands."

Darken Rahl stared through the commander, as if he weren't there, slowly wetting the tips of the first three fingers of his right hand with his tongue and then carefully stroking his lips and eyebrows with them.

"Have you brought me a boy?" Rahl asked expectantly.

"Yes, Lord Rahl. He awaits you in the Garden of Life."

"Good." A small smile spread across Darken Rahl's handsome face. "Good. And he is not too old? He is still a boy?"

"Yes, Lord Rahl, he is but a boy." Demmin looked away from Rahl's blue eyes.

Darken Rahl's smile widened. "You are sure, Demmin? Did you take off his pants yourself, and check?"

Demmin shifted his weight. "Yes, Lord Rahl."

Rahl's eyes searched the other's face. "You didn't touch him, did you?" His smile vanished. "He must be unsoiled."

"No, Lord Rahl!" Demmin insisted, looking back to the Master, his eyes wide. "I would not touch your spirit guide! You have forbidden it!"

Darken Rahl again wet his fingers and smoothed his eyebrows as he took a step closer. "I know you wanted to, Demmin. Was it hard for you? Looking but not touching?" His smile came back, teasing, then melted again. "Your weakness has caused me trouble before."

"I took care of that!" Demmin protested in his deep voice, but not too forcefully. "I had that trader, Brophy, arrested for the murder of that boy."

"Yes," Rahl snapped back, "and then he submitted to a Confessor, to prove his innocence."

Demmin's face wrinkled in frustration. "How was I to know he would do that? Who could expect a man would willingly do that?"

Rahl held up his hand. Demmin fell silent.

"You should have been more careful. You should have taken the Confessors into account. And is that job finished yet?"

"All but one," Demmin admitted. "The quad that went after Kahlan, the Mother Confessor, failed. I had to send another."

Darken Rahl frowned. "Confessor Kahlan is the one who took the confession of this trader, Brophy, and found him innocent, is she not?"

Demmin nodded slowly, his face contorted in anger. "She must have found help, or the quad would not have failed."

Rahl remained silent, watching the other. At last Demmin broke the silence.

"It is but a small matter, Lord Rahl, not worthy of your time or thought."

Darken Rahl lifted an eyebrow. "I will decide what matters are worthy of my attention." His voice was soft, almost kind.

"Of course, Lord Rahl. Please forgive me." Demmin didn't need to hear an angry tone to know he was treading on dangerous ground.

Rahl licked his fingers again and rubbed them on his lips. He looked sharply back up into the other's eyes. "Demmin, if you touched the boy, I will know."

A bead of sweat rolled into Demmin's eye. He tried to blink it away. "Lord Rahl," he said in a coarse whisper, "I would gladly give my life for you. I would not touch your spirit guide. I swear."

Darken Rahl considered Demmin Nass for a moment, then nodded. "As I said, I would know anyway. And you know what

I would do to you if you ever lied to me. I can't tolerate anyone lying to me. It's wrong."

"Lord Rahl," Demmin said, anxious to change the subject, "what of Queen Milena's demands?"

Rahl shrugged. "Tell her I agree to all her demands in return for the box."

Demmin stared incredulously. "But Lord Rahl, you have not seen them listed."

Rahl shrugged innocently. "Now, *they* are truly a matter not worthy of my time or thought."

Demmin shifted his weight again, making the leather he wore creak. "Lord Rahl, I do not understand why you play this game with the queen. It is humiliating to be issued a list of demands. With no trouble, we could crush her like the fat toad she is. Just give me the word, allow me to issue my own demands, on your behalf. She will be made to regret not bowing down to you as she should have."

Rahl smiled a small private smile as he studied the pock-marked face of his loyal commander. "She has a wizard, Demmin," he whispered, his blue eyes intense.

"I know." Demmin's fists tightened. "Giller. You have only to ask, Lord Rahl, and I will bring you his head."

"Demmin, why do you think Queen Milena would enlist a wizard in her service?" Demmin only shrugged, so Rahl answered his own question. "To protect the box, that is why. It is her protection too, she believes. If we kill her or the wizard, we may find he has hidden the box with magic, and then we would have to spend time finding it. So why move too quickly? For now, the easiest path is to go along with her. If she gives me any trouble, I will deal with her, and the wizard." He walked slowly around his father's coffin, trailing his fingers along the carved symbols as he kept his blue eyes on Demmin. "And anyway, once I have the last box, her demands will be meaningless." He came back to the big man, stopping in front of him. "But there is another reason, my friend."

Demmin cocked his head to the side. "Another reason?"

Darken Rahl nodded, leaned closer, and lowered his voice. "Demmin, do you kill your little boyfriends before . . . or after?"

Demmin leaned back a little, away from the other, hooking a

259

thumb in his belt. He cleared his throat. At last he answered. "After."

"And why after? Why not before?" Rahl asked, his face in a coy, questioning frown.

Demmin avoided the Master's eyes, looked down at the floor, and shifted his weight to his other foot. Darken Rahl continued to keep his face close, watching, waiting. In a voice too low for the guards to hear, Demmin spoke.

"I like it when they squirm."

A slow smile spread over Rahl's face. "That is the other reason, my friend. I too enjoy it when they squirm, so to speak. I want to enjoy watching her squirm, before I kill her." He licked the ends of his fingers again, and stroked them on his lips.

A knowing grin grew across the pockmarked face. "I will tell Queen Milena that Father Rahl has graciously agreed to her terms."

Darken Rahl put his hand on Demmin's muscled shoulder. "Very good, my friend. Now, show me what manner of boy you have brought me."

Both wearing smiles, they strode toward the door. Before they reached it, Darken Rahl stopped suddenly. He spun on his heels, his robes flinging around him.

"What was that sound?" he demanded.

Except for the hiss of the torches, the crypt was as silent as the dead king. Demmin and the guards looked slowly around the chamber.

"There!" Rahl thrust out his arm.

The other three looked where he pointed. A single white rose petal sat on the floor. Darken Rahl's face reddened, his eyes fierce. Shaking, his hands clenched into white-knuckled fists, his eyes filled with tears of wrath. He was too furious to speak. Regaining his composure, he held out his hand toward where the white petal lay on the cold marble floor. As if touched by a breeze, it rose into the air and floated across the room, settling in Rahl's outstretched hand. He licked the petal, turned to one of the guards, and stuck it to the man's forehead.

The heavily muscled guard looked back impassively. He knew what the Master wanted, and gave a single grim nod before turning and going through the door in one fluid motion, pulling his sword as he went.

Darken Rahl straightened his body, smoothed his hair and then his robes with the flats of his hands. He took a deep breath, letting his anger out with it. Frowning, his blue eyes searched up at Demmin, who stood calmly beside him.

"I ask nothing else of them. Only that they care for my father's tomb. Their needs are seen to, they are fed and clothed and taken care of. It is a simple request." His face took on a hurt look. "Why do they mock me with their carelessness?" He looked over to his father's coffin, then back to the other's face. "Do you think I am too harsh with them, Demmin?"

The commander's hard eyes scowled back. "Not harsh enough. If you were not so compassionate, if you didn't allow them a quick punishment, maybe the others would learn to treat your heartfelt requests with more commitment. I would not be as lenient."

Darken Rahl stared off at nothing in particular, and nodded absently. After a time he took another deep breath and strode through the door, with Demmin at his side, and the remaining guard following at a respectful distance. They went down long corridors of polished granite lit by torches, up spiral stairs of white stone, down more corridors with windows that let the light out into the darkness. The stone smelled damp, stale. Several levels up, the air regained its freshness. Small tables of lustrous wood stationed at intervals along the halls held vases with bouquets of fresh flowers that lent a light fragrance to the rooms.

As they came to a pair of doors with a scene of hillsides and forests carved in relief, the second guard rejoined them, the task assigned him completed. Demmin pulled on the iron rings, and the heavy doors opened smoothly, silently. Beyond was a room of dark, brown oak panels. It gleamed in the light of the candles and lamps set about on heavy tables. Books lined two walls, and an immense fireplace warmed the two-story room. Rahl stopped for a short time to consult an old leather-bound book sitting on a pedestal; then he and his commander walked on through a labyrinth of rooms, most covered in the same warm wood panels. A few were plastered and painted with scenes of the D'Hara countryside, forests and fields, game and children. The guards followed at a distance, watching everywhere, alert but silent: the Master's shadows.

Logs crackled and popped as flames wavered in a brick hearth, providing the only light in one of the smaller rooms they passed into. On the walls hung trophies of the hunt, heads of every sort of beast. Antlers jutted out, lit by the light of the flames. Darken Rahl stopped suddenly in midstride, his robes made pink in the firelight.

"Again," he whispered.

Demmin had stopped when Rahl did, and now watched him with questioning eyes.

"Again she comes to the boundary. To the underworld." He licked his fingertips, smoothing them carefully over his lips and eyebrows as his eyes fixed in a stare.

"Who?" Demmin asked.

"The Mother Confessor. Kahlan. She has the help of a wizard, you know."

"Giller is with the queen," Demmin insisted, "not with the Mother Confessor."

A thin smile spread on Darken Rahl's lips. "Not Giller," he whispered, "the Old One. The one I seek. The one who killed my father. She has found him."

Demmin stood straight in surprise. Rahl turned and walked over to the window at the end of the room. Made up of small panes and round at the top, it stood twice his height. Firelight glinted off the curved knife at his belt. Clasping his hands behind him, he stood gazing down on the darkened countryside, on the night, on the things others couldn't see. He turned back to Demmin, his blond hair brushing his shoulders.

"That is why she went to Westland, you know. Not to run from the quad, as you thought, but to find the great wizard." His blue eyes sparkled. "She has done me a great favor, my friend; she has flushed out the wizard. It is fortunate she slipped past the ones in the underworld. Fate is truly on our side. You see, Demmin, why I tell you not to worry so? It is my destiny to succeed; all things have a way of working toward my ends."

Demmin's brow knitted into a frown. "Just because one quad failed, that does not mean she has found the wizard. Quads have failed before."

Rahl slowly licked his fingertips. He stepped closer to the big man. "The Old One has named a Seeker," he whispered.

Demmin unclasped his hands in surprise. "Are you sure?"

Rahl nodded. "The old wizard vowed never to help them again. No one has seen him in many years. No one has been able to offer his name, even to save their own lives. Now the Confessor crosses into Westland, the quad vanishes, and a Seeker is named." He smiled to himself. "She must have touched him, to make him help. Imagine his surprise when he saw her." Rahl's smile faded. He clenched his fists. "I almost had them. Almost had all three, but I was distracted by other matters, and they slipped away. For the time being." He considered this silently for a moment, then announced, "The second quad will fail too, you know. They will not be expecting to encounter a wizard."

"Then I will send a third quad, and I will tell them of the wizard," Demmin promised.

"No." Rahl licked his fingertips, thinking. "Not yet. For now, let's wait and see what happens. Maybe she is meant to help me again." He considered this a moment. "Is she attractive? The Mother Confessor?"

Demmin scowled. "I have never seen her, but some of my men have. They fought over who would be named to the quads, who would have her."

"Don't send another quad for now." Darken Rahl smiled. "It is time I had an heir." He nodded absently. "I will have her for myself," he declared.

"If she tries to go through the boundary, she will be lost," Demmin cautioned.

Rahl shrugged. "Maybe she will be smarter than that. She has already shown herself to be clever. Either way, I will have her." He glanced over at Demmin. "Either way, she will squirm for me."

"The two of them are dangerous, the wizard and the Mother Confessor. They could cause us trouble. Confessors subvert the word of Rahl; they are an annoyance. I think we should do as you first planned. We should kill her."

Rahl gave a wave of his hand. "You worry too much, Demmin. As you said, Confessors are an annoyance, nothing more. I will kill her myself, if she proves troublesome, but after she bears me a son. A Confessor son. The wizard cannot harm me, as he did my father. I will see him squirm and then I will kill him. Slowly."

"And the Seeker?" Demmin's face was lined with apprehension.

Rahl shrugged. "Even less than an annoyance."

"Lord Rahl, I need not remind you, winter approaches."

The Master lifted an eyebrow, the firelight flickering in his eyes. "The Queen has the last box. I will have it soon enough. There is no need for concern."

Demmin leaned his grim face closer. "And the book?"

Rahl took a deep breath. "After I have traveled to the underworld, I will search out the Cypher boy again. Worry yourself of it no more, my friend. Fate is on our side."

He turned and walked off. Demmin followed, the guards slipping through the shadows behind.

The Garden of Life was a cavernous room in the center of the People's Palace. Leaded windows high overhead let in light for the lush plants. This night they let in the moonlight. Around the outside of the room were flowers set in beds, with walkways winding through. Beyond the flowers were small trees, short stone walls with vines covering them, and well-tended plants completing the landscaping. Except for the windows overhead, it mimicked an outdoor garden. A place of beauty. A place of peace.

In the center of the expansive room was an area of lawn that swept around almost into a circle, the grass ring broken by a wedge of white stone, upon which sat a slab of granite, smooth but for grooves carved near the edge of the top, leading to a small well in one corner. It was held up by two short fluted pedestals. Beyond the slab stood a polished stone block set next to a fire pit. The block held an ancient iron bowl covered with beasts which served as legs to support the round bottom. The iron lid in the same half-sphere shape had but one beast upon it, a Shinga, an underworld creature, reared up on its two hind legs, serving as a handle. In the center of the lawn lay a round area of white sorcerer's sand, ringed with torches that burned with fluid flames. Geometric symbols crisscrossed in the white sand.

In the center of the sand was the boy, buried in an upright position to his neck.

Darken Rahl approached slowly, his hands clasped behind his back. Demmin waited off by the trees, before the grass. The Master stopped at the border of the grass and white sand, looking down at the boy. Darken Rahl smiled.

"What is your name, my son?"

The boy's lower lip quivered as he looked up at Rahl. His eyes shifted to the big man back by the trees. It was a fearful look. Rahl turned and looked to the commander.

"Leave us, and please take my guards with you. I wish not to be disturbed."

Demmin bowed his head and left, the guards following. Darken Rahl turned back, regarding the boy, then lowered himself to sit on the grass. He rearranged his robes once on the ground, and smiled again at the boy.

"Better?"

The boy nodded. His lip still quivered.

"Are you afraid of that big man?" The boy nodded. "Did he hurt you? Did he touch you where he shouldn't?"

The boy shook his head. His eyes, reflecting a mix of fear and anger, stayed locked on Rahl. An ant crawled from the white sand onto his neck.

"What is your name?" Rahl asked again. The boy did not answer. The Master watched his brown eyes closely. "Do you know who I am?"

"Darken Rahl," the boy answered in a weak voice.

Rahl smiled indulgently. "Father Rahl," he corrected.

The boy stared at him. "I want to go home." The ant inspected its way across his chin.

"Of course you do," Rahl said with a tone of sympathy and concern. "Please believe me, I'm not going to harm you. You are simply here to help me with an important ceremony. You are an honored guest, meant to represent the innocence and strength of youth. You were selected because people told me what a fine boy you are, what a very good boy you are. Everyone has spoken

265

highly of you. They tell me you are smart, and strong. Do they speak the truth?"

The boy hesitated, his shy eyes looking away. "Well, I guess they do." He looked back to Rahl. "But I miss my mother, and I want to go home." The ant went in a circle around his cheek.

Darken Rahl stared off wistfully and nodded. "I understand. I miss my mother also. She was such a wonderful woman, and I loved her so. She took good care of me. When I would do a chore that pleased her, she would make me a special supper, whatever I wanted."

The boys eyes got bigger. "My mother does that too."

"My father, mother, and I had wonderful times together. We all loved each other very much and had fun together. My mother had a merry laugh. When my father would tell a boastful story, she would poke fun at him and the three of us would laugh, sometimes until we got tears in our eyes."

The boy's eyes brightened, he smiled a little. "Why do you miss her? Is she gone away?"

"No," Rahl sighed, "she and my father died a few years ago. They were both old. They both had a good life together, but I still miss them. So I understand how you miss your parents."

The boy nodded a little. His lip had stopped quivering. The ant walked up the bridge of his nose. He scrunched up his face trying to get it off.

"Let's just try to have as good a time as we can for now, and you will be back with them before you know it."

The boy nodded again. "My name is Carl."

Rahl smiled. "Honored to meet you, Carl." He reached out and carefully picked the ant off the boy's face.

"Thanks," Carl said with relief.

"That's what I'm here for, Carl, to be your friend and help you in any way I can."

"If you're my friend, then dig me up and let me go home?" His eyes glistened wetly.

"Soon enough, my son, soon enough. I wish I could right now, but the people expect me to protect them from evil people who would kill them, so I must do what I can to help. You are going to be a part of that help. You are going to be an important part of the ceremony that will save your mother and father from the evil ones who would kill them. You do want to protect your mother from harm, don't you?"

The torches flickered and hissed as Carl thought.

"Well, yes. But I want to go home." His lip began quivering again.

Darken Rahl reached out and stroked the boy's hair reassuringly, combing it back with his fingers, then smoothing it down. "I know, but try to be brave. I won't let anyone harm, you, I promise. I will guard you and keep you safe." He gave Carl a warm smile. "Are you hungry? Would you like something to eat?"

Carl shook his head.

"All right, then. It is late, I will leave you to rest." He stood, straightening his robes, brushing off grass.

"Father Rahl?"

Rahl stopped, and looked back down. "Yes, Carl?"

A tear rolled down Carl's cheek. "I'm afraid to be here alone. Could you stay with me?"

The Master regarded the boy with a comforting expression. "Why, of course, my son." Father Rahl lowered himself back down to the grass. "For as long as you want, even all night if you want me."

CHAPTER 20

GREEN LIGHT GLOWED ALL about as they cautiously shuffled their feet through the rubble of the hillside, climbing over or under tree trunks, kicking limbs aside when necessary. The iridescent green sheet of the boundary walls pressed against them from both sides as they groped their way ahead. Blackness lay thick all about except for the uncanny illumination that made them feel as if they were in a cave.

Richard and Kahlan had come to the same decision at the same time. No choice had been left to the two of them; they couldn't go back, and they couldn't stay at the split rock, not with the grippers and shadow things coming for them, and so they were forced ahead, into the Narrows.

Richard had put the night stone away; it was useless for following the trail, as there was no trail to follow, and it made it difficult to tell where the boundary light changed to the green wall. He hadn't put it back into its leather pouch, in case it was needed again in a hurry, but had simply dropped it into his pocket.

"Let the walls of the boundary show us the way," he had said, his quiet voice echoing back from the blackness. "Go slow. If one wall turns dark, don't take another step, go a little more to the other side. That way we can stay between them, and get through the pass."

Kahlan had not hesitated, the grippers and shadows being a sure death; she had taken Richard's hand as they had stepped back into the green glow. Shoulder to shoulder, they had entered the invisible passage. Richard's heart pounded; he tried not to think about what it was they were doing—walking blindly between the walls of the boundary.

He knew what the boundary looked like from when he had been close to it with Chase, and again when the dark thing had tried to pull Kahlan in. He knew that if they stepped into the dark wall, there would be no return, but that if they could stay in the green glow before the wall, then they at least had a chance.

Kahlan stopped. She pushed him to the right. She was close to the wall. Then it appeared on his right. They centered themselves and continued forward, finding that if they went slowly, carefully, they could stay between the walls, walking a thin line of life, with death to each side. Years of being a guide were of no help to him. Richard finally stopped trying to find a trace of the trail, and let himself feel the force of the walls pressing from each side, let the pressure be his guide. It was slow going, with no sign of the trail in sight, no view of the hillside around them, only the tight world of the luminous green light, like a bubble of life floating helplessly through an endless sea of darkness and death.

Mud sucked at his boots, fear at his mind. Any obstacle they encountered had to be crossed, they couldn't go around; the boundary walls dictated where they went. Sometimes it was over fallen trees, sometimes over boulders, sometimes through wash-outs where they had to use exposed roots to pull themselves up the other side. They helped each other silently, giving only a squeeze of the hand for encouragement. Never was there more than a step or two to either side of their way that didn't bring up the dark walls. Each time the trail turned, the dark wall appeared, sometimes several times, until they could decipher which way it turned. Each time the wall loomed up, they pulled back as quickly as possible, and each time it scared him with a cold jolt.

Richard realized his shoulders ached. The tension of what they were doing was making his muscles tighten, his breathing shallow. He relaxed, took a deep breath, let his arms hang loose, shook his wrists to ease the stress away, and then took Kahlan's hand again. He smiled down at her face lit by the haunting green light. She smiled back, but he could see the controlled terror in her eyes. At least, he thought, the bones were keeping the shadow things and the beasts away from them, and nothing appeared beyond the walls when they accidentally encountered them.

Richard could almost feel his will to live draining from his soul with each careful step. Time took on an abstract dimension, holding no solid meaning. He could have been in the Narrows for hours, or days; he had trouble telling anymore. He found himself wishing only for peace, for it to be over, to be safe again. His fear was beginning to dull from the sheer level of tension he had maintained as they probed their way ahead.

Movement caught his attention. He looked behind. Shadow things, a flush of green light around each, floated in a line between the walls, close at their backs, following the two of them down the path, skimming above the ground, each lifting in turn to pass over a tree trunk that lay across the way. Richard and Kahlan stopped, frozen, watching. The shadows didn't stop.

"Lead the way," he whispered, "and keep hold of my hand. I'll watch them."

He could see that her shirt was soaked with sweat, same as his, even though it wasn't a warm night. Without so much as a nod, she started off. He walked backward, his back to hers, his eyes to the shadows, his mind in a panic. Kahlan went as fast as she could, having to stop and change direction several times, pulling him after by the hand.

She stopped again, at last groping her way to the right, when the unseen path made a sharp turn down the hill. Walking backward downhill was difficult; he stepped carefully to avoid falling. The shadows followed in a single file, turning with the path. Richard resisted his urge to tell Kahlan to go faster, as he didn't want her to make a mistake, but the shadows were getting closer.

It would only be a matter of minutes before they closed the distance, before they were on him.

Muscles tense, his hand gripped the hilt of his sword. He debated in his mind whether or not to draw it, not knowing if it could help them, or if it would bring them to harm. Even if the sword worked against the shadows, a fight in the confines of the Narrows would be a big risk, at best. But if there was no choice, if they came too close, he would have to use the sword.

The shadows seemed as if they had taken on faces. Richard tried to remember if they had faces before, but couldn't. His fingers gripped the hilt of the sword tighter as he walked backward, Kahlan's soft hand warm in his. The faces appeared sad, gentle, in the green glow. They regarded him with kind, pleading countenances. The raised lettering of the word *"Truth"* on the sword seemed to burn painfully into his fingers as he clutched it tighter. Anger seeped from the sword, searching his mind, searching for his own anger, but, finding only fear and confusion, the anger wilted. The forms no longer gained on him, but paced along, keeping him company in the lonely darkness. Somehow, they made him feel less afraid, less tense.

Their whispers calmed him. Richard's hand relaxed on the sword as he strained to make out the words. The slow, easy smiles reassured him, gentled his caution, his alarm, making him want to hear more, to understand the murmurs. Green light around the faint forms shimmered comfortingly. His heart pounded with the need for rest, for peace, for their company.

Like the shadows, his mind drifted, smoothly, quietly, gently. Richard thought of his father, longed for him. He remembered joyful, easy times with him, times of love, sharing, caring, times of safety when nothing threatened him, nothing frightened him, nothing worried him. He longed for those times again. He realized that that was what the whispers were saying, that it could be like that again. They wanted to help him reach that place again, that was all.

Small warnings burgeoned deep in his mind, but then withered and were gone. His hand slipped from the sword.

He had been so wrong, so blind, and hadn't been able to see it before. They weren't there to harm him, but to help him reach the peace he wanted. It wasn't what they wanted, but what he wanted, that's what they offered him. They wished only to help release him from loneliness. A wistful smile spread on his lips. How could he have not seen it before? How could he have been so blind? Whispers like sweet music washed over him in gentle waves, soothing his fears, giving him soft light in the dark places of his mind. He stopped walking so that he wouldn't step out of the bathing warmth of the enchanting murmurs, the breath of the music.

A cold hand tugged annoyingly at his, trying to pull him on, so he released it. It went without objection, to bother him no more.

The shadows drifted closer. Richard waited for them, watched their gentle faces, listened to their soft whispers. When they sighed his name it made him shudder with pleasure. He welcomed them as they came around in a comforting circle, floating closer, their hands reaching to him as they did so. Hands lifted to his face, almost touching him, seeking to caress him. He looked from one face to another, meeting the eyes of his saviors, each holding his gaze in turn, each whispering a promise of wonderment.

A hand almost brushed his face, and he thought he felt searing pain, but wasn't sure. The keeper of the hand promised that he would feel pain no more, after he joined with them. He wanted to speak, to ask them so many questions, but it seemed so suddenly unimportant, so trivial. He had only to give himself over to their care, and everything would be all right. He turned to each, offering himself to each, waiting to be taken.

As he turned, he looked for Kahlan, thinking to take her with him, to share the peace with her. Memories of her flamed into his mind, distracting his attention even though the whispers told him to ignore them. He scanned the hillside, peering off into the dark rubble. Faint light tinged the sky, morning materializing. Black voids of the trees ahead stood against the pale pink sky; he was almost to the end of the slide. He didn't see Kahlan anywhere. The shadows whispered insistently to him, calling his name. Memories of Kahlan blazed brightly into his mind. Sudden choking fear flamed up inside him, burning the whispers in his mind to ash.

"Kahlan!" he screamed.

There was no answer.

Dark hands, dead hands, reached for him. The faces of the shadows wavered like vapors rising from boiling poison. Gnarled voices called his name. He took a step back, away from them, confused.

"Kahlan!" he screamed again.

Hands reached for him, bringing searing pain even though they did not touch him. Again he took a step back, away from them, but this time the dark wall was there, at his back. The hands extended up, to push at him. He looked around for Kahlan, bewildered. This time the pain brought him fully awake. Terror raced through him as he realized where he was and what was happening.

And then his anger exploded.

Heat of rage from the magic surged through him as the sword came free, sweeping in an arc at the shadows. The ones caught by the blade flared into nothingness, the smoke of their form spinning, as if caught in a vortex of wind, before coming apart with a howl. More came at him. The sword flashed through them, and still more came, as if there were no end to their numbers. As he cut them down on one side, the ones on the other side would reach for him, the pain of their near touch burning into him before he turned with the sword. Richard wondered for an instant what it would feel like if they were able to finally touch him, if he would feel the pain or simply be dead in that moment. He stepped away from the wall, slashing with the sword as he did so. He took another step forward, cutting furiously as he moved, the blade whistling as he swung it.

Richard stood, feet dug in, destroying the shadows as fast as they came. His arms ached, his back hurt, his head pounded. Sweat poured from his face. He was exhausted. With nowhere to run, he was forced to stand his ground, but he knew he couldn't keep this up forever. Screams and howls filled the night air as the shadows seemed to fall eagerly on his sword. A knot of them rushed forward, forcing him back again before he could slash through them. Again the dark wall came up at his back. Black forms on the other side of it reached for him while giving out agonizing cries. Too many shadows were coming at once to allow him to step away from the wall; it was all he could do to hold where he was. Pain from the reaching hands was wearing him down. He knew that if they came at him fast enough and in enough numbers, he would be pushed through the wall, into the underworld. He fought on numbly, endlessly.

Anger was giving way to panic. The muscles of his arms burned with the effort of swinging the sword. It seemed the shadows' intent was simply to wear him down with their numbers. He realized that he had been right not to use the sword before, that it would bring them to harm. But there had been no choice. He had to use it to save them.

But there was no "them," he realized; Kahlan was nowhere to be found. It was only him. Swinging the sword, he wondered if it had been like this for her, if the shadows had seduced her with their whispers, and touched her, forced her into the wall. She had no sword to protect her; that was what he had said he would do. Fury erupted in him anew. The thought of Kahlan being taken by the shadows, by the underworld, brought the rage roaring forth again, the magic of the Sword of Truth rising to the summons. Richard cut through the shadows with renewed vengeance. Hatred, flaming into white-hot need, took him ahead through the forms, swinging the sword faster than they could come forward to meet it. So he went to them. Howls of their end joined in a mass cry of anguish. Richard's wrath at what they had done to Kahlan drove him forward in a frenzy of violence.

Without his realizing it at first, the shadows had stopped moving and instead hovered as Richard continued down the path between the walls, slashing at them. For a time, they made no attempt to avoid his blade, but simply floated in place. Then they began to glide, like trailers of smoke in a near still air. They drifted into the walls of the boundary, losing their green glow as they went through to become the dark things on the other side. At last, Richard came to a panting halt, his arms throbbing with weariness.

That was what they were, not shadow people, but the things from the other side of the boundary wall, the things that had been escaping and taking people, just as they had tried to take him.

Just as they had taken Kahlan.

A pain from deep inside welled up, and tears came to his eyes.

"Kahlan," he whispered into the cool morning air.

His heart ached with wrenching agony. She was gone, and it had been his fault; he had let down his guard, he had let her down, had not protected her. How could it have happened so fast? So easily? Adie had warned him, warned him that they would call to him. Why hadn't he been more cautious? Why hadn't he paid more attention to her warning? Over and over in his mind he imagined her fear, her confusion at why he wasn't there with her, her pleading for him to help her. Her pain. Her death. Desperately, his mind raced as he cried, trying to make time go backward, to do it again differently, to ignore the voices, to keep hold of her hand, to save her. Tears ran down his face as he let the tip of the sword lower and drag on the ground, too tired to put it away as he walked forward in a daze. Rubble of the slide was at an end. The green light faded and was gone as he stepped into the woods and onto the trail.

Someone whispered his name, a man's voice. He stopped and looked back.

Richard's father stood in the light of the boundary.

"Son," his father whispered, "let me help you."

Richard stared woodenly at him. Morning lit the overcast, washing everything in a wet gray light. The only color was the glowing green around his father, who held his hands open.

"You can't help me," Richard whispered back hoarsely.

"Yes, I can. She is with us. She is safe now."

Richard took a few steps toward his father. "Safe?"

"Yes, she is safe. Come, I will take you to her."

Richard took a few more steps, dragging the tip of the sword on the ground behind. Tears ran down his cheeks. His chest heaved. "You could really take me to her?"

"Yes, son," his father said softly. "Come. She waits for you. I will take you to her."

Richard walked numbly toward his father. "And I can be with her? Forever?"

"Forever," came the answer in the reassuring, familiar voice.

Richard trudged back into the green light, to his father, who smiled warmly at him.

When he reached him, Richard brought the Sword of Truth up,

and ran it through his father's heart. Wide-eyed, his father looked up at him as he was impaled.

"How many times, dear father," Richard asked through tears and gritted teeth, "must I slay your shade?"

His father only shimmered and then dissolved into the dim morning air.

Bitter satisfaction replaced the anger; then it, too, was gone as he turned once again to the path. Tears ran in streaks through the dirt and sweat on his face. He wiped them on his shirtsleeve as he swallowed back the lump in his throat. Woods enveloped him indifferently as he rejoined the trail.

Laboriously, Richard slid his sword home, into its scabbard. When he did so, he noticed the light from the night stone shining through his pocket, it still being just dark enough to cause it to glow weakly. He stopped and took the smooth stone out once more and replaced it in its leather pouch, quenching the dim yellow light.

His face set in grim determination, Richard slogged ahead, his fingers reaching up to touch the tooth under his shirt. Loneliness, deeper than he had never known, sagged his shoulders. All his friends were lost to him. He knew now that his life was not his own. It belonged to his duty, to his task. He was the Seeker. Nothing more. Nothing less. Not his own man, but a pawn to be used by others. A tool, same as his sword, to help others, that they might have the life he had only glimpsed for a twinkling.

He was no different from the dark things in the boundary. A bringer of death.

And he knew quite clearly who he was going to bring it to.

The Master sat straight-backed and cross-legged on the grass in front of the sleeping boy, his hands resting palm up on his knees, a smile on his lips, as he thought about what had happened with Confessor Kahlan at the boundary. Morning sunlight streamed crossways through the windows overhead, making the colors of the garden flowers vibrant. Slowly, he brought the fingers of his right hand to his lips, licking the tips and then smoothing his eyebrows before carefully returning the hand to its resting place. Thoughts of what he would do to the Mother Confessor had caused his breathing to quicken. He slowed it now, returning his mind to the matter at hand. His fingers wriggled, and Carl's eyes popped open.

"Good morning, my son. Good to see you again," he said in his most friendly voice. The smile, though for another reason, was still on his lips.

Carl blinked and squinted at the brightness of the light. "Good morning," he said in a groan. Then, his eyes looking about, thought to add, "Father Rahl."

"You slept well," Rahl assured the boy.

"You were here? Here all night?"

"All night. As I promised you I would be. I would not lie to you, Carl."

Carl smiled. "Thanks." He lowered his eyes shyly. "I guess I was kind of silly to be scared."

"I don't think it's silly at all. I am glad I could be here to reassure you."

"My father says I'm being foolish when I get afraid of the dark."

"There are things in the dark that can get you," Rahl said solemnly. "You are wise to know it, and to be on guard for them. Your father would do himself a favor to listen, and learn from you."

Carl brightened. "Really?" Rahl nodded. "Well, that's what I always thought too."

"If you truly love someone, you will listen to them."

"My father always says for me to keep my tongue still."

Rahl shook his head disapprovingly. "It surprises me to hear this. I had thought they loved you very much."

"Well, they do. Most of the time anyway."

"I'm sure you are right. You would know better than I."

The Master's long blond hair glistened in the morning light; his white robe shone brightly. He waited. There was a long moment of awkward silence.

"But I do get pretty tired of them always telling me what to do."

Rahl's eyebrows went up. "You seem to me to be of the age

277

where you can think and decide things for yourself. A fine boy like you, almost a man, and they tell you what to do," he added, half to himself, shaking his head again. As if he couldn't believe what Carl was telling him, he asked, "You mean they treat you like a baby?"

Carl nodded his earnest confirmation, then thought to correct the impression. "Most of the time, though, they're good to me."

Rahl nodded, somewhat suspiciously. "That is good to hear. It is a relief to me."

Carl looked up at the sunlight. "But I can tell you one thing, my parents are going to be madder than hornets that I've been gone so long."

"They get mad because of when you come home?"

"Sure. One time, I was playing with a friend, and I got home late, and my mother was real mad. My father took his belt to me. He said it was for worrying them so."

"A belt? Your father hit you with his belt?" Darken Rahl hung his head, then came to his feet, turning his back to the boy. "I'm sorry, Carl, I had no idea it was like this with them."

"Well, it's only because they love me," Carl hastened to add. "That's what they said, they love me and I caused them to worry." Rahl still kept his back to the boy. Carl frowned. "Don't you think that shows they care about me?"

Rahl licked his fingers and smoothed them over his eyebrows and lips before he turned back to the boy and sat once more in front of his anxious face.

"Carl"—his voice was so soft that the boy had to strain to hear—"do you have a dog?"

"Sure," he nodded, "Tinker. She's a fine dog. I had her since she was a pup."

"Tinker," Rahl rolled the name out pleasantly. "And has Tinker ever been lost, or run away?"

Carl scrunched up his eyebrows, thinking. "Well, sure, a couple times before she was grown. But she came back the next day."

"Were you worried, when your dog was gone? When she was missing?"

"Well, sure."

"Why?"

278

"Because I love her."

"I see. And so then when Tinker came back the next day, what did you do?"

"I picked her up in my arms and I hugged her and hugged her."

"You didn't beat Tinker with your belt?"

"No!"

"Why not?"

"Because I love her!"

"But you were worried?"

"Yes."

"So you hugged Tinker when she came back because you loved her and you were worried about her."

"Yes."

Rahl leaned back a little, his blue eyes intense. "I see. And if you had beaten Tinker with your belt when she came back to you, what do you think she would have done?"

"I bet she might not have come back the next time. She wouldn't want to come back so I could beat her. She'd have gone somewhere else where people loved her."

"I see," Rahl said meaningfully.

Tears streamed down Carl's cheeks. He looked away from Rahl's eyes as he cried. At last, Rahl reached out, stroking back the boy's hair.

"I'm sorry, Carl. I did not mean to upset you. But I want you to know that when this is all over, and you go home again, that if you ever need a home, you will always be welcome here. You are a fine boy, a fine young man, and I would be proud to have you stay here, with me. Both you and Tinker. And I want you to know I trust you to think for yourself, and you may come and go as you please."

Carl looked up with wet eyes. "Thank you, Father Rahl."

Rahl smiled warmly. "Now, how about some food?"

Carl nodded his approval.

"What would you like? We have anything you could want."

Carl thought a minute, and a smile came to him. "I like blueberry pie. It's my favorite." He cast his eyes down, the smile fading. "But I'm not allowed to have it for breakfast."

A big grin came to Darken Rahl's face. He stood. "Blueberry pie it is, then. I'll go get it and be right back."

The Master walked off through the garden to a small vine-covered door at the side. The door opened for him as he approached, the big arm of Demmin Nass holding it back as Rahl passed through into the dark room. Foul-smelling gruel boiled in an iron kettle hung over a fire in a small forge. The two guards stood silently against the far wall, a sheen of sweat covering them.

"Master Rahl." Demmin bowed his head. "I trust the boy meets with your approval."

Rahl licked his finger tips. "He will do nicely." He smoothed his eyebrows down. "Dish me out a bowl of that slop so it can cool."

Demmin picked up a pewter bowl and started ladling gruel into it with the wooden spoon from the kettle.

"If everything is all right"—a wicked grin came over his pockmarked face—"then I will be off to pay our respects to Queen Milena."

"Fine. On the way, stop and tell the dragon I want her."

Demmin stopped ladling. "She doesn't like me."

"She doesn't like anyone," Rahl said flatly. "But don't worry, Demmin, she will not eat you. She knows what I will do if she stretches my patience."

Demmin started ladling again. "She will ask how soon you will need her."

Rahl glanced at him out of the corner of his eye. "That is none of her concern, and tell her I said so. She is to come when I ask, and wait until I am ready." He turned and looked out a small slit, off through the foliage, at the side of the boy's head. "But I want you back here in two weeks."

"Two weeks, all right." Demmin set the bowl of gruel down. "But does it really need to take that long with the boy?"

"It does if I want to return from the underworld." Rahl continued to look out the slit. "It may take longer. Whatever it takes, it takes. I must have his complete trust, the freely given pledge of his unconditional loyalty."

Demmin hooked a thumb in his belt. "We have another problem."

Rahl glanced back over his shoulder. "Is that all you do, Demmin? Go around looking for problems?"

"It keeps my head attached to my shoulders."

Rahl smiled. "So it does, my friend, so it does." He sighed. "Get it off your tongue, then."

Demmin shifted his weight to his other foot. "Last night I received reports that the tracer cloud has vanished."

"Vanished?"

"Well, not so much vanished, as hidden." He scratched the side of his face. "They said clouds moved in and hid it."

Rahl laughed. Demmin frowned in confusion.

"Our friend, the old wizard. It sounds like he saw the cloud and has been up to his little tricks to vex me. It was to be expected. This one is not a problem, my friend. It is not important."

"Master Rahl, that was how you were to find the book. Other than the last box, what could be more important?"

"I did not say the book was unimportant. I said the cloud was unimportant. The book is very important, that is why I would not trust it only to a tracer cloud. Demmin, how do you suppose I hooked the cloud to the Cypher boy?"

"My talents lie in areas other than magic, Master Rahl."

"True enough, my friend." Rahl licked his fingertips. "Many years ago, before my father was murdered by that evil wizard, he told me of the boxes of Orden, and the Book of Counted Shadows. He was trying to recover them himself, but he was not well enough studied. He was too much a man of action, of battle." Rahl looked up into Demmin's eyes. "Much the same as you, my big friend. He didn't have the necessary knowledge. But he was wise enough to teach me the value of the head over the sword; how by using your head, you could defeat any number of men. He had the best instructors tutor me. Then he was murdered." Rahl pounded his fist down on the table. His face turned red. After a moment, he calmed himself. "So I studied harder, for many years, so that I might succeed where my father failed, and return the house of Rahl to its rightful place as rulers of all the lands."

"You have exceeded your father's deepest hopes, Master Rahl."

Rahl smiled his slight smile. He took another look through the slit as he went on. "In my studies, I found where the Book of

281

Counted Shadows lay hidden. It was in the Midlands, on the other side of the boundary, but I was not yet able to travel the underworld, to go there and retrieve it. So I sent a guard beast, to watch over it for me, until the day when I could go myself and liberate it."

He stood up straight, turning back to Demmin, a dark look on his face. "Before I could get the book, a man named George Cypher killed the guard beast, and stole the book. My book. He took a tooth from the beast as a trophy. A very stupid thing to do, as the beast was sent by magic, my magic"—he lifted an eyebrow—"and I can find my magic."

Rahl licked his fingers, stroking them over his lips, staring off absently. "After I put the boxes of Orden in play, I went to get the book. That's when I found it had been stolen. It took time, but I found the man who stole it. Unfortunately, he no longer had the book, and would not tell me where it was." Rahl smiled up at Demmin. "I made him suffer for not helping me." Demmin smiled back. "But I did learn that he had given the tooth to his son."

"So that is how you know the Cypher boy has the book."

"Yes, Richard Cypher has the Book of Counted Shadows. And he also wears the tooth. That's how I hooked the tracer cloud to him, by hooking it to the tooth his father gave him, the tooth with my magic. I would have recovered the book before now, but I have had many matters to attend to. I only hooked the cloud to him to help me keep track of him in the meantime. It was a mere convenience. But the matter is as good as settled; I can get the book at any time of my choosing. The cloud is of little importance. I can find him by the tooth."

Rahl picked up the bowl of gruel, handing it to Demmin. "Taste this, see if it is cool enough." He arched an eyebrow. "I wouldn't want to hurt the boy."

Demmin sniffed the bowl, his nose turning up in distaste. He handed it to one of the guards, who took it without objection and put a spoon of gruel to his lips. He gave a nod.

"Cypher could lose the tooth, or simply throw it away. Then you would not be able to find him, or the book." Demmin gave a submissive bow of his head as he spoke. "Please forgive me for saying so, Master Rahl, but it would seem to me you leave a lot to chance."

"Sometimes, Demmin, I leave things to fate, but never to chance. I have other ways of finding Richard Cypher."

Demmin took a deep breath, relaxing as he thought about Rahl's words. "I can see now why you haven't been worried. I didn't know all this."

Rahl frowned up at his loyal commander. "We have scarcely stroked the fur of what you do not know, Demmin. That is why you serve me, and not me you." His expression softened. "You have been a good friend, Demmin, since we were boys, so I will ease your mind on this subject. I have many pressing matters that require my time, matters of magic that cannot wait. Like this." His arm went out, indicating the boy. "I know where the book is, and I know my own talents. I can get the book at a time of my convenience. For now, I look upon it as if Richard Cypher is simply keeping it safe for me." Rahl leaned closer. "Satisfied?"

Demmin diverted his eyes to the ground. "Yes, Master Rahl." He looked back up. "Please know that I only bring my concerns to you because I want success for you. You are rightfully the master of all the lands. We all need you to guide us. I wish only to be part of delivering you victory. I fear nothing but that I should fail you."

Darken Rahl put his arm around Demmin's big shoulders, looking up at the pockmarked face, the streak of black hair through the blond. "That I had more like you, my friend." He took his arm away and picked up the bowl. "Go now and tell Queen Milena of our alliance. Don't forget to summon the dragon." His hint of a smile came back. "And don't let your little diversions make you late in returning."

Demmin bowed his head. "Thank you, Master Rahl, for the honor of serving you."

The big man left through a back door as Rahl went out the one into the garden. The guards stayed in the small, hot, forge room.

Picking up the feeding horn, Rahl went over to the boy. The feeding horn was a long brass tube, small at the mouthpiece, large at the other end. The big end was held up to shoulder height by two legs, so the gruel would slide down. Rahl set it down so the mouthpiece was in front of Carl.

"What's this thing?" Carl asked, squinting up at it. "A horn?"

"Yes, that's right. Very good, Carl. It's a feeding horn. It's a part of the ceremony you will be in. The other young men who have helped the people in the past have thought it a most fun way to eat. You put your mouth over the end there, and I serve you by pouring the food in the top."

Carl was skeptical. "Really?"

"Yes." Rahl smiled reassuringly. "And guess what, I got you a fresh blueberry pie, still warm out of the oven."

Carl's eyes lit up. "Great!" He eagerly put his mouth over the end of the horn.

Rahl passed his hand in a circle over the bowl three times to change the taste, then looked down at Carl. "I had to mash it up so it will go through the feeding horn, I hope that's all right."

"I always mash it up with my fork," Carl said with a grin, then put his mouth back over the horn.

Rahl poured a little gruel into the end of the horn. When it reached Carl's mouth, he ate it eagerly.

"It's great! The best I ever had!"

"I'm so pleased," Rahl said with a shy smile. "It's my own recipe. I feared it wouldn't be as good as your mother's."

"It's better. Can I have more?"

"Of course, my son. With Father Rahl, there is always more."

CHAPTER 21

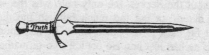

WEARILY, RICHARD SEARCHED THE ground where the trail resumed at the end of the slide, his hopes fading. Dark clouds scudded low overhead, occasionally bringing a few fat drops of cold rain to splatter on the back of his head as he hunted. It had occurred to him that maybe Kahlan had made it through the Narrows, that she had only become separated for him, and had continued on. She was wearing the bone Adie had given her, and it should have kept her safe. She should have been able to make it through. But he was wearing the tooth, and Adie had said he couldn't be seen either, yet the shadows had come from them anyway. It seemed odd; the shadows hadn't moved until it was dark, at the split rock. Why didn't they come for them before?

There were no tracks. Nothing had been through the Narrows for a long time. Fatigue and despair enveloped him again as fits of icy wind flapped his forest cloak around him, seeming to urge him on, away from the Narrows. All hope gone, he turned once more to the path, toward the Midlands.

He had taken only a few steps when a thought brought him to a sudden halt.

If Kahlan had become separated from him, if she thought the underworld had taken him, if she thought she had lost him and was alone, would she have continued on, to the Midlands? Alone?

No.

He turned to the Narrows. No. She would have gone back. Back to the wizard.

It would be no use for her to go to the Midlands alone. She needed help, that's why she had come to Westland in the first place. Without the Seeker, the only help was the wizard.

Richard dared not put too much faith in the thought, but it wasn't that far back to the place where he had fought the shadows, where he had lost her. He couldn't go on without checking, without knowing for sure. Fatigue forgotten, he plunged back into the Narrows.

Green light welcomed his return. Following his tracks back, in a short time he found the place where he had fought the shadows. His footprints wandered all about in the mud of the slide, telling the tale of his battle. He was surprised at how much ground he had covered in the fight. He didn't remember all the circling, the back and forth. But then he didn't remember much of the fight, until the last part.

With a jolt of recognition, he saw what he was looking for. The tracks of the two of them, together, then hers, alone. His heart pounded as he followed them, hoping so hard it hurt, that they wouldn't lead into the wall. Squatting, he inspected them, touched them. Her tracks wandered about a while, seemingly confused, and then they stopped, and turned. Where their pair of tracks led in from the other way, one set of tracks lead back.

Kahlan's.

Richard stood in a rush, his breathing rapid, his pulse racing. The green light glowed irritatingly about him. He wondered how far she could have gone. It had taken them most of the night to laboriously cross the Narrows. But they hadn't known where the trail was. He looked down at the footprints in the mud. He did now.

He would have to go fast; he couldn't be timid in following the way back. A memory of something Zedd had told him when the old man had given him the sword came into his mind. The strength of rage, the wizard had said, gives you the heedless drive to prevail.

The clear metallic ringing filled the dim morning air as the Seeker drew his sword. Anger flooded through him. Without a second thought, Richard dashed down the trail, following the tracks. The pressure of the wall buffeted him as he jogged through the cool mist. When the tracks turned, switching back and forth, he didn't slow, but set his feet to one side or the other to throw his weight the other way down the path.

Keeping a steady, sustainable pace, he was able to traverse the span of the Narrows before midmorning. Twice, he had come across a shadow floating in place on the path. They didn't move or seem to be aware of him. Richard charged through, sword first. Even without faces, they had seemed surprised as they howled apart.

Without slowing he went through the split rock, kicking a gripper out of the way. On the other side he stopped to catch his breath. He was overwhelmed with relief that her footprints went all the way. Now, back on the forest trail, her tracks would be harder to see, but it didn't matter. He knew where she was going, and he knew she was safely through the Narrows. He felt like crying with joy in the knowledge that Kahlan was alive.

He knew he was getting closer to her; the mist hadn't yet had time to soften the sharp edges of her footprints, the way it had when he had first found them. When it had gotten light, she must have followed their tracks instead of using the walls to show the way, or else he would have caught her long before now. Good girl, he thought, using your head. He would make a woods-woman of her yet.

Richard trotted off down the trail, keeping the sword—and his anger—out. He didn't waste time to stop and look for signs of her trail, but whenever there was a soft or muddy patch, he looked down, checking, as he slowed a little. After running over an area of mossy ground, he came to a small bare patch with footprints. He gave a cursory glance as he went by. Something he saw made him stop so suddenly that he fell. On his hands and knees, he peered down at the prints. His eyes widened.

Overlapping part of her footprint was a man's bootprint, nearly three times as large as hers. He knew without a doubt who it belonged to: the last man of the quad.

Rage brought him to his feet scrambling into a dead run. Branches and rock flashed by in a blur. His only concern was to stay on the trail and avoid accidentally running into the boundary, not out of fear for himself, but because he knew he couldn't help Kahlan if he got himself killed. His lungs burned for air as his chest heaved with exertion. The anger of the magic made him ignore his exhaustion, his lack of sleep.

Clambering to the top of a small jut of rock, he saw her at the bottom of the other side. For an instant, he froze. Kahlan stood on the left, feet apart, in a half crouch, a rock wall at her back. The last man of the quad stood in front of her, to Richard's right. Panic slashed through his anger. The man's leather uniform glistened in the wet. The hood of his chain-mail shirt covered his head of blond hair. His sword rose in his massive fists, and muscles stood out in knots along his arms. He howled a battle cry.

He was going to kill her.

Wrath exploded through Richard's mind. He screamed "No!" in a murderous rage as he leapt off the rock. With both hands he brought the Sword of Truth up while still in midair. When he hit the ground he recoiled, swinging it around from behind, in an arc. The sword whistled with its speed. The man had turned as Richard hit the ground. Seeing Richard's sword coming, he brought his own up defensively with lightning speed, the tendons in his wrists and hands making a popping sound as he did so.

Richard watched as if in a dream as his sword came around. Every ounce of his strength went into trying to make the sword go faster, go truer. Be deadlier. The magic raged with his need. Richard looked from the man's sword, hard into the steel blue eyes. The Seeker's sword followed the track of his eyes. He heard himself still screaming. The man held his sword straight up, to deflect the blow.

Everything else around the man dissolved in Richard's vision. His anger, the magic, was unleashed like never before. No power on earth could deny him the man's blood. Richard was beyond all reason. Beyond all other need. Beyond all other cause for living. He was death, brought to life.

Richard's entire life force focused lethal hatred into the drive of his sword.

With a beat of his heart that he could feel in the straining muscles of his neck, Richard watched out of his peripheral vision with expectant elation as he held the man's blue eyes, watched his sword finally sweep the rest of the agonizing distance around in a smooth arc, at long last contracting the enemy's raised sword. He saw the detail of it shattering ever so slowly in a burst of hot fragments, freeing the bulk of the severed blade to lift into the air, twisting as it went, its polished surface glinting in the light with a flash upon each of the three revolutions it made before the Seeker's sword, with all the power of his rage and the magic behind it, reached the man's head, contacting the chain mail, making the head deflect only the tiniest bit before the sword exploded through the steel links of the mail, through the man's head at eye level, filling the air with a shower of steel pieces and links.

The misty morning erupted with a burst of red fog that made Richard feel a flush of exhilaration as he watched clumps of blond hair and bone and brain tumble madly away as the blade continued its sweep through the crimson air, clearing the last ragged fragments of the enemy's skull, continuing its journey around, while the body with only a neck and jaw and little else recognizable above that, began dropping away as if all its bones had dissolved, leaving nothing to hold it up, finally hitting the ground with a hard jolt. Globs of blood were flung up into the air in long strings which finally arced and fell back to the ground and onto Richard, offering the victor the hot satisfying taste of it in his mouth where some of it had landed as he screamed his rage. More pumped thick and copious out into the dirt at the same time as bits of steel from the chain mail and shattered sword rained to earth while other bits of bone and steel that had already flown past Richard bounced and skittered across the rock behind him and still more bone and brain and blood from up in the air fell back at last onto the ground all about, tinting everything a rich red.

The bringer of death stood victorious over the object of his hate and rage, soaked in blood and the glory of joy such as he had never imagined. His chest heaved in rapture. Bringing the sword to the front again, he checked for any other threat. There was none.

And then the world imploded upon him.

Everything about jolted back into his sight. Richard saw a wide-eyed look of shock on Kahlan's face before the pain took him to his knees, ripping through him, doubling him over.

The Sword of Truth dropped from his hands.

Sudden realization of what he had done slashed through him. He had killed a man. Worse, he had killed a man he had wanted to kill. It didn't matter that he was protecting another life; he had wanted to kill. Had reveled in it. He would have allowed nothing to deny him the killing.

The vision of his sword exploding through the man's head flashed over and over in his mind. He couldn't make it stop.

In searing pain like none he had ever known, he clutched his arms across his abdomen. His mouth was open, but no scream came forth. He tried to let himself lose consciousness to stop the pain, but could not. Nothing else existed but the pain, just as nothing else had existed, in his desire to kill, but the man.

The pain whited his vision out. He was blind. Fire burned through every muscle, bone, and organ of his body, consuming him, taking his breath from his lungs, choking him in convulsing agony. He fell to his side on the ground, his knees pulled up to his chest, the screams coming at last in pain now as he had screamed in rage before. Richard felt the life being drawn from him. Through the anguish and hurt, he knew that if this went on he wasn't going to be able to retain his sanity, or worse, his life. The power of the magic was crushing him. He could never have imagined that this level of pain existed; now he couldn't imagine it ever leaving. He felt it stripping his sanity from him. In his mind, he begged for death. If something didn't change, and quick, he would have it, one way or another.

In the fog of agony, a realization came to him; he recognized the pain. It was the same as the anger. It coursed through him the same way as the anger from the sword. He knew that feeling well enough; it was the magic. Once he recognized it as the magic, he urgently tried to take control of it, the way he had learned to control the anger. This time he knew he must win control, or die. He reasoned with himself, came to comprehend the need of what he had done, horrible as it was. The man had sentenced himself to death with his own intent to kill.

At last, he was able to put away the pain, as he had learned to put away the anger. Relief washed over him. He had won both battles. The pain lifted, and was gone.

Lying on his back, panting, he felt the world come rushing back. Kahlan was kneeling beside him, wiping a cool, damp cloth over his face. Wiping off the blood. Her brow was wrinkled; tears ran down her cheeks. Splatters of the man's blood lay in long streaks across her face.

Richard rose to his knees and took the cloth from her hand, to wipe her face, as if to wipe from her mind the sight of what he had done. Before he could, she threw her arms around him, embracing him tighter than he would have thought her capable of. He hugged her back just as tight while her fingers went up the back of his neck, into his hair, holding his head to her as she cried. He couldn't believe how good it felt to have her back. He didn't want to let her go, ever.

"I'm so very sorry, Richard," she sobbed.

"For what?"

"That you had to kill a man on my account."

He rocked her gently, stroking her hair. "It's all right."

She shook her head against his neck. "I knew how much the magic would hurt you. That's why I didn't want you to have to fight the men back at the inn."

"Zedd told me the anger would protect me from the pain. Kahlan, I don't understand. There is absolutely no way I could have been any more angry."

She separated from him, her hands on his arms, squeezing as if to keep testing that he was real. "Zedd told me to watch out for you, if you used the sword to kill a man. He told me that what he said about the anger protecting you was true, but he said the first time was different, that the magic tested, took a measure of the Seeker with the pain, and nothing could protect you from it. He said that he couldn't tell you because if you knew, it would make you hold back, be more cautious in its use, and that could be disastrous. He said the magic has to join to the Seeker with its first ultimate use, to ascertain his intent when he kills." She squeezed his arms. "He said the magic could do terrible things to you. It tests with the pain, to see who will be the master, who the ruled."

Richard sat back on his heels, startled. Adie had said the wizard kept a secret from him. This must have been it. Zedd must have been very worried, and afraid for him. Richard felt sorry for his old friend.

For the first time, Richard truly understood the meaning of being Seeker, in a way no one else but a Seeker could. Bringer of death. He understood it now. Understood the magic, how he used it, how it used him, how they were now joined. For better or worse, he would never be the same again. He had tasted fulfillment of his darkest desire. It was done. There was no going back to being as he was before.

Richard brought the cloth up and wiped the blood from Kahlan's face.

"I understand. I know now what he was talking about. You were right to not tell me." He touched the side of her face, his voice gentle. "I was so afraid you were killed."

She put her hand over his. "I thought you were dead. One minute I was holding your hand, and then I realized I wasn't." Her eyes filled with tears again. "I couldn't find you. I didn't know what to do. The only thing I could think of was to go get Zedd, to wait for him to wake, to get him to help me. I thought you were lost to the underworld."

"I thought that's what happened to you too. I almost went on, alone." He grinned. "Seems I have to keep coming back for you."

She smiled for the first time since he had found her, then put her arms around him again. Quickly, she pushed away.

"Richard, we have to get out of here. There are beasts about. They will come for his body; we can't be here when they do."

He nodded, turned, picked up his sword, and got to his feet. He reached down for her, to help her up. She took his hand.

The magic ignited in a rage, warning its master.

Startled, Richard stared at her in shock. Just as the last time, when she had touched his hand when he held the sword, the magic had come to life, only this time it was stronger. Smiling,

292

she didn't seem to feel anything. Richard forced the anger down. It went with great reluctance.

She hugged him once more, a quick hug with her free arm. "I still can't believe you are alive. I was so sure I had lost you."

"How did you get away from the shadows?"

Kahlan shook her head. "I don't know. They were following us, and when we became separated and I went back, I didn't see them anymore. Did you see any?"

Richard nodded solemnly. "Yes, I saw them. And my father again. They came for me, tried to push me into the boundary."

Concern came over Kahlan's face. "Why just you? Why not both of us?"

"I don't know. Last night at the split rock, and later, when they started following us, it must have been me they were after, not you. The bone protected you."

"The last time at the boundary, they came for everyone but you," she said. "What's different this time?"

Richard thought a moment. "I don't know, but we have to get across the pass. We're too tired to have to spend tonight fighting shadows again. We must get to the Midlands before dark. And this time, I promise I won't let go of your hand."

Kahlan smiled and squeezed his hand.

"I won't let go of yours either."

"I ran back through the Narrows. It didn't take long that way. You up to that?"

She nodded and they started running at an easy pace he thought she could keep up. As the last time he crossed, no shadows followed, although several floated above the path. And as before, Richard went through them sword-first without waiting to find out what they would do. Kahlan flinched at their howls. He watched the tracks as he ran, pulling her through the turns, keeping her on the trail.

When they were clear of the slide, and on the forest path on the other side of the Narrows, they slowed to a fast walk to catch their breath. Drizzle wet their faces and hair. Happiness over finding her alive dimmed his worry about the difficulties that lay ahead. They shared bread and fruit as they kept moving. Even though his stomach was grumbling with hunger, he didn't want to stop for anything more elaborate.

Richard was still confused by the reaction of the magic when Kahlan had taken his hand. Was it something the magic felt in her, or was the magic reacting to something in his own mind? Was it because he was afraid of her secret? Or was it something more, something the magic itself felt in her? He wished Zedd was around, so he could ask him what he thought. But then, Zedd had been there the last time, and he hadn't asked him about it then. Was he afraid of what Zedd might tell him?

After they had eaten a little and the afternoon had worn on, they heard growls off in the woods. Kahlan said it was the beasts. They decided to run again, to get clear of the pass as soon as possible. Richard was beyond being tired. He was simply numb as they ran through the thick wood. Light rain on the leaves washed out the sound of their footfalls.

Before dark they came to the edge of a long ridge. Below, the trail descended in a series of switchbacks. They stood at the top of the ridge, in the woods, as if at the mouth of a cave, looking out over an open grassland swept with rain.

Kahlan held herself erect, rigid. "I know this place," she whispered.

"So what is it?"

"It is called the Wilds. We are in the Midlands." She turned to him. "I am returned home."

He lifted an eyebrow. "The place doesn't look that wild to me."

"It is not named after the land. It is named after those who live in it."

After descending the steep ridge, Richard found a small protected spot under a slab of rock, but it wasn't deep enough to keep out all the rain, so he cut pine boughs and leaned them against the jut of rock, making a small, reasonably dry shelter where they could spend the night. Kahlan crawled inside, and Richard followed, pulling boughs over the entrance, sealing out most of the rain. Both slumped down, wet and exhausted.

Kahlan took her cloak off and shook out the water. "I've never seen it be overcast so long, or rain so much. I can't even remember what the sun looks like. I'm becoming weary of it."

"Not me," he said quietly. She frowned, so he explained. "Remember the snakelike cloud that followed me, the one sent by Rahl to track me?" She nodded. "Zedd cast a wizard's web to bring other clouds to hide it. As long as it's cloudy, and we can't see the snake cloud, neither can Rahl. I prefer the rain to Darken Rahl."

Kahlan thought this over. "From now on, I will be happier about the clouds. But next time, could you ask him to bring clouds that are not so wet?" Richard smiled and nodded. "Do you want anything to eat?" she asked.

He shook his head. "I'm too tired. I just want to sleep. Is it safe here?"

"Yes. No one lives near the boundary in the Wilds. Adie said we are protected from the beasts, so the heart hounds should not bother us."

The sound of steady rain was making him all the more sleepy. They wrapped themselves in their blankets, the night being cold already. In the dim light Richard could just make out the features of Kahlan's face as she leaned up against the rock wall. The shelter was too small for a fire, and everything too wet anyway. He reached into his pocket, fingering the pouch with the night stone, considering if he should take it out, to see better, but at last decided against it.

Kahlan smiled over at him. "Welcome to the Midlands. You have done as you said you would: you got us here. Now the hard work begins. What would you have us do?"

Richard's head was throbbing; he leaned back next to her. "We need someone with magic who can tell us where the last box is, where to find it. Or at least where to look for it. We can't just go running around blindly. We need someone who can point us in the right direction. Who do you know like that?"

Kahlan gave him a sideways glance. "We are a long way from anyone who would want to help us."

She was avoiding telling him something. His anger jumped. "I didn't say they had to want to help us, I said they had to be able to. You just take me to them and I'll worry about the rest!" Richard immediately regretted his tone of voice. He leaned his head back against the rock wall and put the anger down. "Kahlan, I'm sorry." He rolled his head away from her. "I've had a hard day. Besides killing that man, I had to run my sword through my father again. But the worst of it was I thought my best friend was lost to the underworld. I just want to stop Rahl, to end this nightmare."

He turned his face to hers, and she gave him one of her special, tight-lipped smiles. Kahlan watched his eyes in the near darkness for a few minutes.

"Not easy, being Seeker," she said softly.

He smiled back at her. "Not easy," he agreed.

"The Mud People," she said at last. "They may be able to tell us where to search, but there is no guarantee they will agree to help us. The Wilds are a remote part of the Midlands, and the Mud People are not used to dealing with outsiders. They have strange customs. They do not care about the problems of others. They wish only to be left alone."

"If he succeeds, Darken Rahl will not respect their wishes," he reminded her.

Kahlan took a deep breath, letting it out slowly. "Richard, they can be dangerous."

"Have you dealt with them before?"

She nodded. "A few times. They do not speak our language, but I speak theirs."

"Do they trust you?"

Kahlan looked away as she wrapped her blanket tighter. "I guess so." She looked up at him from under her eyebrows. "But they are afraid of me, and with the Mud People, that may be more important than trust."

Richard had to bite the inside of his lip to keep from asking why they were afraid of her. "How far?"

"I'm not sure exactly where we are in the Wilds. I didn't see enough to tell for certain, but I'm sure they are no more than a week to the northeast."

"Good enough. In the morning we head northeast."

"When we get there, you must follow my lead, and if I tell you something, you must pay heed. You must convince them to help you, or they will not, sword or no sword." He gave her a nod. She took her hand out from under the blanket and put in on his arm. "Richard," she whispered, "thank you for coming back for me. I'm sorry for what it cost you."

"I had to—what good would it do to go to the Midlands without my guide?"

Kahlan grinned. "I will try to live up to your expectations."

He gave her hand a squeeze before they both lay down. Sleep took him as he thanked the good spirits for protecting her.

CHAPTER 22

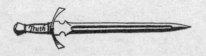

ZEDD'S EYES POPPED OPEN. The aroma of spice soup was thick in the air. Without moving, he looked cautiously about. Chase lay next to him, there were bones hung on the walls, and it was dark outside the window. He looked down at his body. Bones were piled upon him. Without moving, he carefully caused them to rise slowly into the air, then he silently made them float aside, and finally to set down. Making no sound, he rose. He was in a house full of bones, bones of beasts. He turned around.

He was surprised to come face-to-face with a woman just as she also turned around.

In a fright, they both screamed and threw their skinny arms into the air.

"Who are you?" he asked, leaning forward, peering into her white eyes.

She snatched her crutch just before it toppled over and put it back under her arm. "I be Adie," she answered in a raspy voice. "You gave me a scare! You awoke sooner than I expected."

Zedd straightened his robes. "How many meals have I missed?" he demanded.

Scowling, Adie looked him up and down. "Too many, by the looks of it."

A grin creased Zedd's cheek. He in turn eyed Adie from top to bottom. "You are a fine-looking woman," he announced. With a bow he took her hand and kissed it lightly, then stood up proud and straight, holding one bony finger skyward. "Zeddicus Zu'l Zorander, humbly at your whim, my dear lady." He leaned forward. "What's wrong with your leg?"

"Nothing. It be perfectly fine."

"No, no," he said with a frown, pointing. "Not that one, the other."

Adie looked down at the missing foot, then back up to Zedd. "It does not go all the way to the ground. What be the matter with your eyes?"

"Well, I hope you learned your lesson; you only have one foot left, you know." Zedd's frown melted back to a grin. "And the problem with my eyes," he said in his thin voice, "is that they have been famished, but now they are feasting."

Adie smiled a little smile. "Would you like a bowl of soup, wizard?"

"I thought you would never ask, sorceress."

He followed her as she worked her way across the room to the kettle hanging in the fireplace and, after she had dished out two bowls of soup, carried them to the table. Leaning her crutch against the wall, she sat opposite him, and cut a thick slice each of bread and cheese, pushing them across the table to him. Zedd bent over and dug right in, but stopped after one swallow of soup and looked up at her white eyes.

"Richard made this soup," he said in an even voice, the second spoonful hanging midway between the bowl and his mouth.

Adie tore off a piece of bread and dunked it in the soup as she watched him. "That be true. You be fortunate; mine would not be this good."

Zedd looked around as he put the spoon down in the bowl. "And where is he?"

Adie took a bite of the bread and chewed, watching Zedd. When she had swallowed, she answered. "He and the Mother Confessor have gone through the pass, to the Midlands. Although he knows her only as Kahlan; she still hides her identity from him." She went on to tell the wizard the story of how Richard and Kahlan had come to her, seeking her help for their stricken friends.

Zedd picked up the cheese in one hand, the bread in the other, taking alternating bites as he listened to Adie's tale, wincing at hearing that he had been sustained on gruel.

"He told me to tell you he could not wait for you," she said, "but that he knew you would understand. The Seeker gave me instructions to pass on to Chase, for him to return and make preparations for when the boundary fails, for the coming of Rahl's forces. He was sorry he did not know what your plan be, but feared he could not wait."

"Just as well," the wizard said under his breath. "My plan does not include him."

Zedd went back to eating in earnest. When he had finished the soup, he went to the kettle and helped himself to another bowlful. He offered to get Adie more, but she was not yet finished with her first, since she had spent most of the time with her eyes on the wizard. As he sat back down, she pushed more bread and cheese at him.

"Richard keeps a secret from you," she said in a low voice. "If it were not for this business with Rahl, I would not speak of it, but I thought you should know."

The light from the lamp lit his thin face and white hair, making him look stark and all the more thin in the sharp shadows. He picked up his spoon, looked down at the soup a moment, then back up at her face.

"As you well know, we all have secrets, wizards more than most. If we all knew each other's secrets, it would prove a very strange world. Besides, it would take all the fun out of the telling of them." His thin lips widened in a smile, his eyes sparkled. "But I fear no secret of a person I trust, and he has no need to fear mine. It is part of being friends."

Adie leaned back in her chair, her blank white eyes stared at him, her small smile came back. "For his sake, I hope you be right in your trust. I would not want to give a wizard cause to be angry."

Zedd shrugged. "As wizards go, I'm pretty harmless."

She studied his eyes in the lamplight.

"That be a lie," the sorceress whispered in a low rasp.

Zedd cleared his throat, and thought to change the subject. "It would seem I owe you thanks for tending to me, dear lady."

"That be true."

"And for helping Richard and Kahlan"—he looked over to Chase, pointing with his spoon—"and the boundary warden too. I am in your debt."

Adie's smile widened. "Perhaps, someday you can return the favor."

Zedd pushed up the sleeves of his robes and went back to eating the soup, but not quite as voraciously as before. He and the sorceress watched each other. The fire in the hearth crackled, and outside night bugs chirped. Chase slept on.

"How long have they been gone?" Zedd asked at last.

"This be the seventh day he has left you and the boundary warden to my care."

Zedd finished his meal, pushing the bowl carefully away. He folded his thin hands on the table, looking down as he tapped his thumbs together. The light from the lamp flickered and danced on his mass of white hair.

"Did Richard say how I was to find him?"

For a moment Adie didn't answer. The wizard continued to wait, tapping his thumbs, until at last she spoke. "I gave him a night stone."

Zedd jumped to his feet. "You did what!"

Adie calmly looked up at him. "Would you have me send him through the pass, at night, without a way to see? To be blind in the pass is a sure death. I wanted him to make it through. It be the only way for me to help him."

The wizard put his knuckles on the table and leaned forward, his wavy white hair falling around his face. "And did you warn him?"

"Of course I did."

His eyes narrowed. "How? With a sorceress's riddle?"

Adie picked up two apples and tossed one to Zedd. He caught it in the air with a silent spell. It floated, spinning slowly while he continued to glare at the old woman.

"Sit down, wizard, and stop showing off." She took a bite of her apple, chewing slowly. Zedd sat down in a huff. "I did not want to frighten him. He already be fearful enough. Had I told him what a night stone could do, he might have been afraid to use it, and the result would have been that the underworld would have had him sure. Yes, I warned him, but with a riddle, so he would figure it out later, after he be through the pass."

Zedd's sticklike fingers snatched the apple out of the air. "Bags, Adie, you don't understand. Richard hates riddles, always has. He considers them an insult to honesty. He won't brook them. He ignores them as a matter of principle." The apple snapped as he took a big bite.

"He be Seeker; that be what Seekers do: they solve riddles."

Zedd held up a bony finger. "Riddles of life, not words. There is a difference."

Adie set her apple down and leaned forward, putting her hands on the table. A look of concern softened her face. "Zedd, I was trying to help the boy. I want him to succeed. I lost my foot in the pass; he would have lost his life. If the Seeker loses his life, we all lose ours too. I did not mean him harm."

Zedd put his apple down and dismissed his anger with a wave of his hand. "I know you meant no harm, Adie. I did not mean to suggest you did." He took Adie's hands in his. "It will be all right."

"I be a fool," she said bitterly. "He told me he disliked riddles, but I never thought more of it. Zedd, seek him through the night stone? See if he has made it through?"

Zedd nodded. He closed his eyes and let his chin sink to his chest as he took three deep breaths. Then he stopped breathing for a long time. From the air about came the low, soft sound of distant wind, wind on an open plain: lonely, baleful, haunting. The sound of the wind left at last, and the wizard began breathing again. His head came up, and his eyes opened.

"He is in the Midlands. He has made it through the pass."

Adie gave a nod of relief. "I will give you a bone to carry, so that you may go safely through the pass. Will you go after him now?"

The wizard looked down at the table, away from her white eyes. "No," he said in a quiet voice. "He will have to handle this, among other things, on his own. As you said, he is the

302

Seeker. I have an important task to attend to, if we are to stop Darken Rahl. I hope he can stay out of trouble in the meantime."

"Secrets?" the sorceress asked, smiling her little smile.

"Secrets." The wizard nodded. "I must leave right away."

She took one hand out from under his and stroked his leathery skin.

"It be dark outside."

"Dark," he agreed.

"Why not stay the night? Leave with the light."

Zedd's eyes snapped up, looking at her from under his eyebrows. "Stay the night?"

Adie shrugged as she stroked his hands. "It be lonely here sometimes."

"Well," Zedd's impish grin lit his face, "as you say, it is dark outside. And I guess it would make more sense to start out in the morning." A sudden frown broke out, wrinkling his brow. "This isn't one of your riddles, is it?"

She shook her head, and his grin came back.

"I have my wizard's rock along. Could I interest you?"

Adie's face softened in a shy smile. "I would like that very much." She watched him as she sat back, taking a bite of her apple.

Zedd arched an eyebrow. "Naked?"

Wind and rain bowed the long grass in broad slow waves as the two of them made their way across the open, flat plain. Trees were few and far between, mostly birch and alder in clusters along streams. Kahlan watched the grass carefully; they were near the Mud People's territory. Richard followed silently behind, keeping her under his watchful eye, as always.

She didn't like taking him to the Mud People, but he was right, they had to know where to look for the last box, and there was no one else anywhere near who could point them in the right direction. Autumn was wearing on, and their time was dwindling. Still, the Mud People might not help them, and then the time would be wasted.

Worse, although she knew they probably would not dare to kill a Confessor, even one traveling without the protection of a wizard, she had no idea if they would dare to kill the Seeker. She had never traveled the Midlands before without a wizard. No Confessor did; it was too dangerous. Richard was better protection than Giller, the last wizard assigned her, but Richard was not supposed to be her protection, she was supposed to be his. She couldn't allow him to put his life at risk for her again. He was more important than she to stopping Rahl. That was what mattered, above all else. She had pledged her life in defense of the Seeker . . . in defense of Richard. She had never meant anything more ardently in her life. If a time came that called for a choice, it must be she who died.

The path through the grasses came to two poles, one set to each side of the trail. They were wrapped in skins dyed with red stripes. Richard stopped by the poles, looking up at the skulls fixed atop them.

"This meant to warn us away?" he asked as he stroked one of the skins.

"No, they are the skulls of honored ancestors, meant to watch over their lands. Only the most respected are accorded such recognition."

"That doesn't sound threatening. Maybe they won't be so unhappy to see us after all."

Kahlan turned to him and lifted an eyebrow. "One of the ways you get to be revered by the Mud People is by killing outsiders." She looked back at the skulls. "But this is not meant as a threat to others. It is simply a tradition of honor among themselves."

Richard took a deep breath as he withdrew his hand from the pole. "Let's see if we can get them to help us, so they can go on revering their ancestors, and keeping outsiders away."

"Remember what I told you," she warned. "They may not want to help. You have to respect that if it is their decision. These are some of the people I am trying to save. I don't want you to hurt them."

"Kahlan, it's not my desire or intention to hurt them. Don't worry, they will help us. It's in their own interest."

"They may not see it that way," she pressed. The rain had stopped, replaced by a light, cold mist she felt on her face. She

304

pushed the hood of her cloak back. "Richard, promise me you won't hurt them."

He pushed his hood back also, put his hands on his hips, and surprised her with a little smile out of one side of his mouth. "Now I know how it feels."

"What?" she asked, a tone of suspicion in her voice.

As he looked down at her, his smile grew. "Remember when I had the fever from the snake vine, and I asked you not to hurt Zedd? Now I know how you felt when you couldn't make that promise."

Kahlan looked into his gray eyes, thinking of how much she wanted to stop Rahl, and thought of all those she knew whom he had killed.

"And now I know how you must have felt when I could not make that promise." She smiled in spite of herself. "Did you feel this foolish for asking?"

He nodded. "When I realized what was at stake. And when I realized what kind of person you were, that you wouldn't do anything to harm anyone unless there was no choice. Then I felt foolish. For not trusting you."

She did feel foolish for not trusting him. But she knew he trusted her too much.

"I'm sorry," she said, the smile still on her lips. "I should know you better than that."

"Do you know how we can get them to help us?"

She had been to the village of the Mud People several times, none of them by invitation; they would never request a Confessor. It was a common chore among Confessors, paying a professional call on the different peoples of the Midlands. They had been polite enough, out of fear, but they had made it clear that they handled their own affairs, and did not want outside involvement. They were not a people who would respond to threats.

"The Mud People hold a gathering, called a council of seers. I have never been allowed to attend, maybe because I am an outsider, maybe because I am a woman. This group divines the answers to questions that affect the village. They will not hold a gathering at swordpoint; if they are to help us, they must do so willingly. You must win them over."

He gazed intently into her eyes. "With your help, we can do it. We must."

She nodded, and turned to the path once more. Clouds hung low and thick above the grassland, seeming to boil slowly as they rolled along in an endless procession. Out on the plains, there seemed to be much more sky than there was anywhere else. It was an overpowering presence, dwarfing the unchanging, flat land.

Rains had swollen the streams until the churning, muddy water pounded and frothed with a roar at the bottoms of the crossing logs that were used as bridges. Kahlan could feel the power of the water making the logs shudder under her boots. She stepped carefully, as the logs were slippery, and there was no hand rope to aid her crossing. Richard offered her his hand, to steady her, and she was glad for the excuse to take it. She found herself looking forward to the stream crossings, to being able to take his hand. But as deeply as it hurt, she couldn't allow herself to encourage his feelings for her. She wished so much she could just be a woman, like any other. But she wasn't. She was a Confessor. Still, sometimes for brief moments, she could forget, and pretend.

She wished Richard would walk next to her, but he instead stayed behind, scanning the countryside, watching out for her. He was in a strange land, taking nothing for granted, seeing threat in everything. In Westland, she had felt the same way, so she understood the feeling. He was putting his life at great peril against Rahl, against things he had never encountered before, and was right to be wary. The wary died quick enough in the Midlands, the unwary faster still.

After crossing another stream and plunging back into the wet grass, eight men sprang up suddenly in front of them. Kahlan and Richard came to an abrupt halt. The men were wearing animal skins over most of their bodies. Sticky mud that didn't wash away in the rain was smeared over the rest of their skin and faces, and their hair smoothed down with it. Clumps of grass were tied to their arms and to the skins, and stuffed under headbands, making them invisible when they had been squatted down. They stood silently in front of the two of them. All wore grim expressions. Kahlan recognized several of the men; it was a hunting party of Mud People.

The eldest, a fit, wiry man she knew as Savidlin, approached her. The others waited, spears and bows relaxed but ready. Kahlan could feel Richard's presence close behind her. Without turning, she whispered for him to stay calm and do as she did. Savidlin stopped in front of her.

"Strength to Confessor Kahlan," he said.

"Strength to Savidlin and the Mud People," she answered in their language.

Savidlin slapped her across the face, hard. She slapped him back just as hard. Instantly Kahlan heard the ringing sound of Richard's sword being pulled free. She spun on her heels.

"No, Richard!" He had the sword up, ready to strike. "No!" She grabbed his wrists. "I told you to stay calm and do as I do."

His eyes flicked from Savidlin's to hers. They were filled with unleashed anger, the magic that was ready to kill. The muscles in his jaw flexed as he clenched his teeth. "And if they slit your throat, would you have me let them slit mine as well?"

"That is the way they greet people. It is meant to show respect for another's strength."

He frowned, hesitating.

"I'm sorry I did not warn you. Richard, put the sword away."

His eyes went from hers to Savidlin, and then back to hers again, before he yielded and angrily thrust the sword back into its scabbard. Relieved, she turned back to the Mud People as Richard stepped up protectively next to her. Savidlin and the others had been watching calmly. They didn't understand the words, but they seemed to grasp the meaning of what had happened. Savidlin looked away from Richard, to Kahlan. He spoke in his dialect.

"Who is this man with the temper?"

"His name is Richard. He is the Seeker of Truth."

Whispers broke out among the other members of the hunting party. Savidlin's eyes sought Richard's.

"Strength to Richard, the Seeker."

Kahlan told him what Savidlin had said. There was still a hot look on his face.

Savidlin stepped up and hit Richard, not with an open hand as he had hit her, but with his fist. Immediately Richard unleashed a powerful blow of his own that knocked Savidlin from his feet and sent him sprawling on his back. He lay dazed on the ground with his limbs strewn awkwardly out. Fists tightened on weapons. Richard straightened, giving the men a dangerous look that kept them rooted firmly in place.

Savidlin propped himself up on one hand, rubbing his jaw with the other. A grin spread across his face. *"None has ever shown such respect for my strength! This is a wise man."*

The other men broke out in laughter. Kahlan held her hand over her mouth, trying to hide her own. The tension evaporated.

"What did he say?" Richard demanded.

"He said you have great respect for him, that you are wise. I think you have made a friend."

Savidlin held his hand out for Richard to help him up. Warily, Richard complied. Once on his feet, Savidlin slapped Richard on the back, putting an arm around his big shoulders.

"I am truly glad you recognize my strength, but I hope you do not come to respect me any more." The men laughed. *"Among the Mud People, you shall be known as 'Richard With The Temper.'"*

Kahlan tried to hold back her laughter while she translated. The men were still snickering. Savidlin turned to them.

"Maybe you men would like to greet my big friend, and have him show you his respect for your strength."

They all held their hands out in front of themselves and shook their heads vigorously.

"No," one of them said between fits of laughter, *"he has already shown you enough respect for all of us."*

He turned back to Kahlan. *"As always, Confessor Kahlan is welcome among the Mud People."* Without looking over, he gave a nod of his head, indicating Richard. *"Is he your mate?"*

"No!"

Savidlin tensed. *"Then you have come here to choose one of our men?"*

"No," she said, her voice regaining its calmness.

Savidlin looked greatly relieved. *"The Confessor chooses dangerous traveling companions."*

"Not dangerous to me, only to those who would think to harm me."

Savidlin smiled and nodded, then looked Kahlan up and down. *"You wear odd things. Different from before."*

"Underneath, I am the same as before," Kahlan said as she leaned a little closer to make her point. *"That is what you need to know."*

Savidlin backed away a little from her intense expression and gave a nod. His eyes narrowed. *"And why are you here?"*

"So that we might help each other. There is a man who would rule your people. The Seeker and I would have you rule yourselves. We came seeking your people's strength and wisdom to aid us in our fight."

"Father Rahl," Savidlin announced knowingly.

"You know of him?"

Savidlin nodded. *"A man came. He called himself a missionary, said he wanted to teach us of the goodness of one called Father Rahl. He talked to our people for three days, until we became tired of him."*

It was Kahlan's turn to stiffen, she glanced to the other men, who had started smiling at the mention of the missionary. She looked back to the elder's mud streaked face. *"And what happened to him after the three days?"*

"He was a good man." Savidlin smiled meaningfully.

Kahlan straightened herself. Richard leaned closer to her.

"What are they saying?"

"They want to know why we are here. They said they have heard of Darken Rahl."

"Tell them I want to talk to their people, that I need them to call a gathering."

She looked up at him from under her eyebrows. "I am getting to that. Adie was right, you are not a patient person."

Richard smiled. "No, she was wrong. I am very patient, but I am not very tolerant. There is a difference."

Kahlan smiled at Savidlin as she spoke to Richard. "Well, please do not become intolerant just now, or show them any more respect for the moment. I know what I am doing, and it is going well. Let me do it my way, all right?"

He agreed, folding his arms in frustration. She turned once

309

more to the elder. He peered at her sharply and asked something that surprised her.

"Did Richard With The Temper bring us the rains?"

Kahlan frowned. *"Well, I guess you could say that."* She was confused by the question and didn't know what to say, so told him the truth. *"The clouds follow him."*

The elder studied her face intently and nodded. She didn't feel comfortable under his gaze, and sought to bring the conversation back to the reason for her visit.

"Savidlin, the Seeker has come to see your people on my advice. He is not here to harm or interfere with your people. You know me. I have been among you before. You know of my respect for the Mud People. I would not bring another to you unless it was important. Right now, time is our enemy."

Savidlin considered what she had said for a while, then at last spoke.

"As I said before, you are welcome among us." He looked up with a grin at the Seeker, then back to her. *"Richard With The Temper is most welcome in our village too."*

The other men were pleased with the decision; they all seemed to like Richard. They gathered up their things, including two deer and a wild boar, each tied to a carrying pole. Kahlan hadn't seen the result of their hunt before because it had been hidden in the tall grass. As they all started off down the path, the men gathered about Richard, touching him cautiously and jabbering questions he couldn't understand. Savidlin clapped him on the shoulders, looking forward to showing off his big new friend to the village. Kahlan went along beside him, for the most part ignored, and happy that so far they liked Richard. She understood the feeling—it was hard to dislike him—but there was some other reason for their ready acceptance of him. She worried about what that reason could be.

"I told you I would win them over," Richard said with a grin as he looked at her over their heads. "I just never thought I would do it by laying one of them out."

CHAPTER 23

CHICKENS SCATTERED AT THEIR feet as the hunting party surrounding Kahlan and Richard led them into the Mud People's village. Set on a slight rise that passed for a hill in the grasslands of the Wilds, the village was a collection of buildings constructed of a kind of mud brick, surfaced with a tan clay plaster and topped with grass roofs that leaked as they became dry, and had to be replaced constantly to keep the rain at bay. There were wood doors, but no glass in the windows of the thick walls, only cloth hanging in some to keep out the weather.

Set in a rough circle around an open area, the buildings were one-room family homes clustered tightly on the south side, most sharing at least one common wall, narrow walkways passing between the homes here and there, and communal buildings grouped together on the north. A variety of structures placed loosely on the east and west separated them. Some of these were nothing more than four poles with grass roofs, used as places to eat, or as work areas for making weapons and pottery, or as food preparation and cooking areas. In dry times the whole village was shrouded in a fog of dust that clogged the eyes, nose, and tongue, but now its buildings were washed clean by the rain, and on the ground a thousand footprints were turned to puddles that reflected the drab buildings above.

Women wrapped in simple dresses of brightly colored cloth sat in the work areas, grinding tava root, from which they made the flat bread that was the staple of the Mud People. Sweet-smelling smoke rose from the cooking fires. Adolescent girls with short-cropped hair smoothed down by sticky mud sat by the women, helping.

Kahlan felt their shy eyes on her. She knew from being here before that she was the object of great interest among the young girls, a traveler who had been to strange places and seen all sorts of things. A woman whom men feared and respected. The older women abided the distraction with understanding indulgence.

Children ran from every corner of the village to see what manner of strangers Savidlin's hunting party had brought back. They crowded around the hunters, squealing with excitement, stomping their bare feet in the mud, and splashing the men. Ordinarily, they would be interested in the deer and boar, but now those were ignored in favor of the strangers. The men tolerated them with good-natured smiles; little children were never scolded. When they were older, they would be put into strict training where they would be taught the disciplines of the Mud People—of hunting, food gathering, and the ways of spirits—but for now they were allowed to be children, with almost free rein to play.

The knot of children offered up scraps of food as bribes for stories of who the strangers might be. The men laughed, declining the offerings in favor of saving the tale for the elders. Only slightly disappointed, the children continued to dance about, this being the most exciting thing that had happened in their young lives; something very much out of the ordinary, with a distinct tinge of danger.

Six elders stood under the leaky protection of one of the open pole structures, waiting for Savidlin to bring the strangers to them. They wore deerskin pants, and were bare-chested; each had a coyote hide draped around his shoulders. Despite their grim faces, Kahlan knew them to be more friendly than they ap-

312

peared. Mud People never smiled at outsiders until greetings had been exchanged, lest their souls be stolen.

The children stayed back from the pole building, sitting in the mud to watch as the hunting party brought the outsiders to the elders. The women had halted their work at the cooking fires, as had the young men their weapons making, and all fell silent, including the children sitting in the mud. Business among the Mud People was conducted in the open, for all to see.

Kahlan stepped up to the six elders, Richard to her right but back a pace, Savidlin to his right. The six surveyed the two outsiders.

"Strength to Confessor Kahlan," said the eldest.

"Strength to Toffalar," she answered.

He gave her face a gentle slap, hardly more than a pat. It was their custom to give only small slaps in the village proper. Heartier ones like Savidlin had delivered were reserved for chance meetings out on the plain, away from the village. The gentler custom helped preserve order, and teeth. Surin, Caldus, Arbrin, Breginderin, and Hajanlet each in turn offered strength and a small slap. Kahlan returned the greetings and the gentle slaps. They turned to Richard. Savidlin stepped forward, pulling his new friend with him. He proudly displayed his swollen lip to the elders.

Kahlan spoke Richard's name under her breath with a rising inflection and a cautionary tone. "These are important men. Please do not loosen their teeth."

He gave her a quick glance out of the corner of his eye, and a mischievous smile.

"This is the Seeker, Richard With The Temper," Savidlin said, proud of his charge. He leaned closer to the elders, his voice heavy with meaning. *"Confessor Kahlan brought him to us. He is the one you spoke of, the one who brought the rains. She told me so."*

Kahlan began to worry; she didn't know what Savidlin was talking about. The elders remained stone-faced, except Toffalar, who lifted an eyebrow.

"Strength to Richard With The Temper," Toffalar said. He gave Richard a gentle slap.

"Strength to Toffalar," he answered in his own language, having recognized his name, and immediately returned the slap.

Kahlan breathed out in relief that it was gentle. Savidlin beamed, showing his fat lip again. Toffalar at last smiled. After the others had given and received a greeting, they smiled, too.

And then they did something very odd.

The six elders and Savidlin each dropped to one knee and bowed their heads to Richard. Kahlan instantly tensed.

"What's going on?" Richard asked out of the side of his mouth, alerted by her anxiety.

"I do not know," she answered in a low voice. "Maybe it's their way of greeting the Seeker. I have never seen them do this before."

The men rose to their feet, all smiles. Toffalar held his hand up and motioned over their heads to the women.

"Please," Toffalar said to the two of them, *"sit with us. We are honored to have you both among us."*

Pulling Richard down with her, Kahlan sat cross-legged on the wet wooden floor. The elders waited until they were seated before seating themselves, paying no attention to the fact that Richard kept his hand near his sword. Women came with woven trays stacked high with loaves of round, flat tava bread and other food, offering them first to Toffalar and then the other elders, as they kept their eyes and smiles on Richard. They chatted softly among themselves about how big Richard With The Temper was, and what odd clothes he wore. They mostly ignored Kahlan.

Women in the Midlands tended not to like Confessors. They saw them as a menace who could take their men, and a threat to their lifestyle; women were not supposed to be independent. Kahlan disregarded their cool glances; she was more than used to them.

Toffalar took his bread and tore it into three sections, offering a third to Richard first and then a third to Kahlan. With a smile, another woman offered a bowl of roasted peppers to each. Kahlan and Richard both took one, and following the elder's example, rolled them in the bread. She noticed just in time that Richard was keeping his right hand near his sword and was about to eat with his left.

"Richard!" she warned in a harsh whisper. "Don't put food in your mouth with your left hand."

He froze. "Why?"

"Because they believe that evil spirits eat with their left hand."

"That's foolish," he said, an intolerant tone in his voice.

"Richard, please. They outnumber us. All their weapons are tipped with poison. This is a poor time for theological arguments."

She could feel his gaze on her as she smiled at the elders. Out of the corner of her eye she saw with relief that he switched the food to his right hand.

"Please forgive our meager offering of food," Toffalar said. *"We will call a banquet for tonight."*

"No!" Kahlan blurted out. *"I mean, we do not want to impose upon your people."*

"As you wish," Toffalar said with a shrug, a little disappointed.

"We are here because the Mud People, among others, are in great danger."

The elders all nodded and smiled. *"Yes,"* Surin spoke up. *"But now that you have brought Richard With The Temper to us, all is well. We thank you, Confessor Kahlan, we will not forget what you have done."*

Kahlan looked around at their happy, smiling faces. She didn't know what to make of this development, and so took a bite of the flat-tasting tava bread with roasted peppers to gain time to think it over.

"What are they saying?" Richard asked before he took a bite himself.

"For some reason, they are glad I brought you here."

He looked over at her. "Ask them why."

She gave him a nod, and turned to Toffalar. *"Honored elder, I am afraid I must admit that I am without your knowledge of Richard With The Temper."*

He smiled knowingly. *"I am sorry, child. I forget you were not here when we called the council of seers. You see, it was dry, our crops were withering, and our people were in danger of starvation. So we called a gathering, to ask the spirits for help. They told us one would come, and bring the rain with him. The rains came, and here is Richard With The Temper, just as they promised."*

"And so you are happy that he is here, because he is an omen?"

"No," Toffalar said, eyes wide with excitement, *"we are happy that one of the spirits of our ancestors has chosen to visit us."* He pointed at Richard. *"He is a spirit man."*

Kahlan almost dropped her bread. She sat back in surprise.

"What is it?" Richard asked.

She stared into his eyes. "They had a gathering, to bring rain. The spirits told them someone would come, and bring the rain. Richard, they think you are a spirit of their ancestors. A spirit man."

He studied her face a moment. "Well, I'm not."

"They think you are. Richard, they would do anything for a spirit. They will call a council of seers if you ask."

She didn't like asking him to do this; she didn't feel at all right about deceiving the Mud People, but they needed to know where the box was. Richard considered her words.

"No," he said quietly while holding her gaze.

"Richard, we have an important task to attend to. If they think you are a spirit, and that will help us get the last box, what does it matter?"

"It matters because it's a lie. I won't do it."

"Would you rather have Rahl win?" she asked quietly.

He gave her a cross look. "First of all, I will not do it because it's wrong to deceive these people about something as important as this. Secondly, these people have a power; that is why we are here. They have proven it to me by the fact that they said one would come with the rains. That part is true. In their excitement, they have jumped to a conclusion that is not. Did they say the one who would come would be a spirit?" She shook her head. "People sometimes believe things simply because they want to."

"If it works to our advantage, and theirs, what harm is there?"

"The harm is in their power. What if they call the gathering and they see the truth, that I'm not a spirit? Do you think they will be pleased that we lied to them, tricked them? Then we will be dead, and Rahl wins."

She leaned back and took a deep breath. The wizard chooses his Seekers well, she thought.

"Have we aroused the temper of the spirit?" Toffalar asked, a look of concern on his weathered face.

"He wants to know why you are angry," she said. "What shall I tell him?"

Richard looked at the elders, then to her. "I will tell them. Translate my words."

Kahlan nodded her agreement.

"The Mud People are wise, and strong," he began. "That is why I have come here. Your ancestor spirits were right that I would bring the rains." They all seemed pleased when Kahlan told them his words. Everyone else in the village was stone silent as they listened. "But they have not told you everything. As you know, that is the way of spirits." The elders nodded their understanding. "They have left it to your wisdom to find the rest of the truth. In this way you remain strong, as your children become strong because you guide them, not because you provide them their every want. It is the hope of every parent that their children will become strong and wise, to think for themselves."

There were nods, but not as many. *"What are you saying, great spirit?"* asked Arbrin, one of the elders in the back.

Richard ran his fingers through his hair after Kahlan translated. "I am saying that, yes, I brought the rains, but there is more. Perhaps the spirits saw a greater danger for your people, and that is the more important reason I have come. There is a very dangerous man who would rule your people, make you his slaves. His name is Darken Rahl."

There were snickers among the elders. *"Then he sends fools to be our masters,"* Toffalar said.

Richard regarded them angrily. The laughter died out. "It is his way, to lull you into overconfidence. Do not be fooled. He has used his power and his magic to conquer peoples of greater numbers than you. When he chooses, he will crush you. The rains came because he sends clouds to follow me, to know where I am, that he might try to kill me at a time of his choosing. I am not a spirit, I am the Seeker. Just a man. I want to stop Darken Rahl, so that your people, and others, may live their own lives, as they wish."

Toffalar's eyes narrowed. *"If what you say is true, then the one called Rahl sent the rains, and has saved our people. That is what his missionary tried to teach us, that Rahl would save us."*

"No. Rahl sent the clouds to follow me, not to save you. I chose to come here, just as your spirit ancestors said I would. They said the rains would come, and a man would come when they did. They did not say I would be a spirit."

There was great disappointment in the expressions of the elders as Kahlan interpreted; she hoped it wouldn't turn to anger.

"Then maybe the message of the spirits was a warning about the man that would come," Surin said.

"And maybe it was a warning about Rahl," Richard answered right back. "I am offering you the truth. You must use your wisdom to see it, or your people are lost. I offer you a chance to help save yourselves."

The elders considered in silence. *"Your words seem to flow true, Richard With The Temper, but it is yet to be decided,"* Toffalar said at last. *"What is it you want from us?"*

The elders sat quietly, the joy gone from their faces. The rest of the village waited in quiet fear. Richard regarded the face of each elder in turn, then spoke quietly.

"Darken Rahl looks for a magic that will give him the power to rule everyone, including the Mud People. I look for this magic also, so that I might deny him the power. I would like you to call a council of seers, to tell me where I might find this magic, before it is too late, before Rahl finds it first."

Toffalar's face hardened. *"We do not call gatherings for outsiders."*

Kahlan could tell that Richard was getting angry and straining to control himself. She didn't move her head, but her eyes swept around, gauging where everyone was, especially the men with weapons, in case they had to fight their way out. She didn't judge their chances of escape to be very good. Suddenly, she wished she had never brought him here.

Richard's eyes were full of fire as he looked around at the people of the village and then back to the elders. "In return for bringing you the rain, I ask of you only that you do not decide right now. Consider what manner of man you find me to be." He was keeping his voice calm, but there was no mistaking the import of his words. "Think it over carefully. Many lives depend upon your decision. Mine. Kahlan's. Yours."

As Kahlan translated, she was suddenly suffused with the cold feeling that Richard was not talking to the elders. He was speaking to someone else. She suddenly felt the eyes of that other on her. Her own gaze swept the crowd. All eyes were on the two of them; she didn't know whose gaze she still felt.

"Fair," Toffalar proclaimed at last. *"You both are free to be among our people as honored guests while we consider. Please enjoy all we have, share our food and our homes."*

The elders departed, through the light rain, toward the communal buildings. The crowd went back to their business, shooing the children as they went. Savidlin was the last to leave. He smiled and offered his help in anything they might need. She thanked him as he stepped off into the rain. Kahlan and Richard sat alone on the wet wooden floor, dodging the drips of rainwater leaking through the roof. The woven trays of tava bread and the bowl of roasted peppers remained behind. She leaned over and took one of each, wrapping the bread around the pepper. She handed it to Richard and made herself another.

"You angry with me?" he asked.

"No," she admitted with a smile. "I am proud of you."

A little-boy grin spread on his face. He began eating, with his right hand, and made short work of it. After he swallowed the last bite, he spoke again.

"Look over my right shoulder. There is a man leaning against the wall, long gray hair, arms folded across his chest. Tell me if you know who he is."

Kahlan took a bite of the bread and pepper, chewing as she glanced over his shoulder.

"He is the Bird Man. I don't know anything about him, except that he can call birds to himself."

Richard took another piece of bread, rolled it up, and took a bite. "I think it's time we went and had a talk with him."

"Why?"

Richard looked up at her from under his eyebrows. "Because he's the one who is in charge around here."

Kahlan frowned. "The elders are in charge."

Richard smiled with one side of his mouth. "My brother always says that real power is not brokered in public." He watched her intently with his gray eyes. "The elders are for show. They are respected, and so are put on display for others to see. Like the skulls on the poles, only they still have the skin on them. They have authority because they are esteemed, but they are not in charge." With a quick flick of his eyes, Richard indicated the Bird Man leaning against the wall behind him. "He is."

"Then why has he not made himself known?"

"Because," he said, grinning, "he wants to know how smart we are."

Richard stood and held his hand out to her. She stuffed the rest of the bread in her mouth, brushed her hands on her pants, and took his hand. As he hoisted her up, she thought about how much she liked the way he always offered her his hand. He was the first person who had ever done that. It was just one part of why it felt so easy being with him.

They walked across the mud, through the cold rain, toward the Bird Man. He still leaned against the wall, his sharp brown eyes watching them come. Long hair, mostly silver-gray, lay on his shoulders, flowing partway down the deerskin tunic that matched his pants. His clothes had no decoration, but a bone carving hung on a leather thong around his neck. Not old, but not young, and still handsome, he was about as tall as she. The skin of his weathered face was as tough-looking as the deerskin clothes he wore.

They stopped in front of him. He continued to lean his shoulders against the wall, and his right knee stuck out as his foot propped against the plastered brick. His arms lay folded across his chest as he studied their faces.

Richard folded his arms across his own chest. "I would like to talk to you, if you are not afraid I might be a spirit."

The Bird Man's eyes went to hers as she translated, then back to Richard's.

"I have seen spirits before," he said in a quiet voice. *"They do not carry swords."*

Kahlan translated. Richard laughed. She liked his easy laugh.

"I also have seen spirits, and you are right, they do not carry swords."

A small smile curled the corners of the Bird Man's mouth. He unfolded his arms and stood up straight. *"Strength to the Seeker."* He gave Richard a gentle slap.

"Strength to the Bird Man," he said, returning the easy slap.

The Bird Man took the bone carving that hung on the leather thong at his neck, and put it to his lips. Kahlan realized it was a whistle. His cheeks puffed out as he blew, but there was no sound. Letting the whistle drop back, he held his arm out while he continued to hold Richard's eyes. After a moment, a hawk wheeled out of the gray sky and alighted on his outstretched arm. It fluffed its feathers, then let them settle as its black eyes blinked and its head swiveled about in short, jerky movements.

"Come," the Bird Man said, *"we will talk."*

He led them among the large communal buildings, to a smaller one at the back, set away from the others. Kahlan knew the building with no windows, although she had never been in it. It was the spirit house, where the gatherings were held.

The hawk stayed on his arm as the Bird Man pulled the door open and motioned them inside. A small fire was burning in a pit at the back end, offering a little light to the otherwise dark room. A hole in the roof above the fire let the smoke out, although it did a poor job of it, and left the place with a sharp smoky smell. Pottery bowls left from past meals lay about the floor, and a plank shelf along one wall held a good two dozen ancestral skulls. Otherwise, the room was empty. The Bird Man found a place near the center of the room where the rain wasn't dripping, and sat down on the dirt floor. Kahlan and Richard sat side by side, facing him, as the hawk watched their movements.

The Bird Man looked at Kahlan's eyes. She could tell he was used to having people be afraid when he looked at them, even if it wasn't warranted. She could tell because she was used to the same thing. This time he found no fear.

"Mother Confessor, you have not yet chosen a mat ." He gently stroked the hawk's head while he watched her.

Kahlan decided she didn't like his tone. He was testing. *"No. Are you offering yourself?"*

He smiled slightly. *"No. I apologize. I did not mean to offend you. Why are you not with a wizard?"*

"All the wizards, save two, are dead. Of those two, one sold

321

his services to a queen. The other was struck down by an underworld beast, and lies in a sleep. There are none left to protect me. All the other Confessors have been killed. We are in dark times."

His eyes looked genuinely sympathetic, but his tone still was not. *"It is dangerous for a Confessor to be alone."*

"Yes, and it is also dangerous for a man to be alone with a Confessor who is in great want of something. From where I sit, it would seem that you are in greater danger than I."

"Perhaps," he said, stroking the hawk, his slight smile returning. *"Perhaps. This one is a true Seeker? One named by a wizard?"*

"Yes."

The Bird Man nodded. *"It has been many years since I have seen a true Seeker. A Seeker who was not a real Seeker came here one time. He killed some of my people when we would not give him what he wanted."*

"I am sorry for them," she said.

He shook his head slowly. *"Do not be. They died quickly. Be sorry for the Seeker. He did not."* The hawk blinked as it looked at her.

"I have never seen a pretend Seeker, but I have seen this one in the rage. Believe me, you and your people do not want to ever give this one cause to draw his sword in anger. He knows how to use the magic. I have even seen him strike down evil spirits."

He studied her eyes for a moment, seeming to judge the truth of what she said. *"Thank you for the warning. I will remember your words."*

Richard spoke up at last. "Are you two about done threatening each other?"

Kahlan looked at him in surprise. "I thought you couldn't understand their language."

"Can't. But I can understand eyes. If looks caused sparks, this place would be ablaze."

Kahlan turned back to the Bird Man. *"The Seeker wishes to know if we are finished threatening each other."*

He glanced at Richard and then back to her. *"He is an impatient man, is he not?"*

She nodded. *"I have told him so myself. He denies it."*

322

"It must be a burden traveling with him."

Kahlan broke into a smile. *"Not at all."*

The Bird Man returned her smile, and then addressed his gaze to Richard. *"If we choose not to help you, how many of us will you kill?"*

Kahlan interpreted the words as they spoke.

"None."

The Bird Man studied the hawk as he asked, *"And if we choose not to help Darken Rahl, how many of us will he kill?"*

"Sooner or later, a great many."

He took his hand away from the hawk, and looked at Richard with his sharp eyes. *"It would seem you argue for us to help Darken Rahl."*

A smile spread across Richard's face. "If you choose not to help me and remain neutral, foolish as that would be, it is your right, and I will harm none of your people. But Rahl will. I will press on and fight against him with my last breath if need be."

His face took on a dangerous expression. He leaned forward. "If, on the other hand, you choose to help Darken Rahl, and I defeat him, I will come back, and . . ." He pulled his finger across his throat in a quick gesture that needed no translation.

The Bird Man sat stone-faced, no quick retort at hand. *"We wish only to be left alone,"* he said at last.

Richard shrugged, looking down at the ground. "I can understand that. I too wished only to be left alone." His eyes came up. "Darken Rahl killed my father, and sends evil spirits that haunt me in my father's guise. He sends men to try to kill Kahlan. He brings down the boundary, to invade my homeland. His minions have struck down my two oldest friends. They lie in a deep sleep, near death, but at least they will live . . . unless he is successful the next time. Kahlan has told me of many he has killed. Children; stories that would make your heart sick." He nodded, his voice soft, hardly more than a whisper. "Yes, my friend, I too wished only to be left alone. On the first day of winter, if Darken Rahl gains the magic he seeks, he will have a power no one can stand against. Then it will be too late." His hand went to his sword. Kahlan's eyes widened. "If he were here, in my place, he would pull this sword and have your help or have your head."

He took his hand away. "That, my friend, is why I cannot harm you if you choose not to help me."

The Bird Man sat quiet and still for a while. *"I can see now that I do not want Darken Rahl for an enemy. Or you."* He got up and went to the door, casting the hawk into the sky. The Bird Man sat once more, sighing heavily with the weight of his thoughts. *"Your words seem to flow true, but I cannot know for sure yet. It would also seem that although you want us to help you, you also wish to help us. I believe you are sincere in this. It is a wise man who seeks help by helping, and not by threats or tricks."*

"If I wanted to get your help by tricks, I would have let you believe me to be a spirit."

The corners of the Bird Man's mouth turned up in a small smile. *"If we had held a gathering, we would have discovered you were not. A wise man would suspect that too. So which reason is it that made you tell the truth? You did not want to trick us, or you were afraid to?"*

Richard smiled back. "In truth? Both."

The Bird Man nodded. *"Thank you for the truth."*

Richard sat quietly, took a deep breath, and let it out slowly. "So, Bird Man, I have told you my tale. You must judge it true or not. Time works against me. Will you help?"

"It is not that simple. My people look to me for direction. If you asked for food, I could say 'Give him food,' and they would do so. But you have asked for a gathering. That is different. The council of seers are the six elders you spoke to, plus myself. They are old men, firm in the ways of their past. An outsider has never been given a gathering before, never been permitted to disturb the peace of our ancestors' spirits. Soon these six will join the ancestors' spirits, and they do not want to think they will be called from the spirit world for an outsider's needs. If they break the tradition, they will be forever burdened with the results. I cannot order them to do this."

"It is not only an outsider's needs," Kahlan said, telling them both her words. "Helping us also helps the Mud People."

"Maybe in the end," the Bird Man said, *"but not in the beginning."*

324

"What if I were one of the Mud People?" Richard asked, his eyes narrowing.

"Then they would call the gathering for you, and not violate the tradition."

"Could you make me one of the Mud People?"

The Bird Man's silver-gray hair glistened in the firelight as he considered. *"If you were to first do something that helped our people, something that benefited them, with no advantage to you, proved you were a man of good intentions toward us, doing so without promise of aid for your help, and the elders wished it, I could."*

"And once you named me as one of the Mud People, I could ask for a gathering, and they would call it?"

"If you were one of us, they would know you had our interests in your heart. They would call a council of seers to help you."

"And if they called the council, would they be able to tell me where the object I seek is located?"

"I cannot answer that. Sometimes the spirits will not answer our questions, sometimes they do not know the answers to our questions. There is no guarantee that we could help you, even if we held a gathering. All I could promise is that we would try our best."

Richard looked down at the ground, thinking. With his finger, he pushed some dirt into one of the puddles where the rain dripped.

"Kahlan," he asked quietly, "do you know of anyone else who would have the power to tell us where to look for the box?"

Kahlan had been giving this consideration all day. "I do. But of all the ones I know of, I do not know of any who would be any more eager to help us than the Mud People are. Some would kill us just for asking."

"Well, of the ones who wouldn't kill us just for asking, how far away are they?"

"Three weeks, at least, north, through very dangerous country controlled by Rahl."

"Three weeks," Richard said out loud with a heavy tone of disappointment.

"But Richard, the Bird Man is able to promise us precious little. If you could find a way to help them, if it pleases the elders,

325

if they ask the Bird Man to name you one of the Mud People, if the council of seers can get an answer, if the spirits even know the answer ... if, if, if. Many opportunities for a wrong step."

"Was it not you who told me I would have to win them over?" he asked with a smile.

"It was."

"So, what do you think? Do you think we should stay and try to convince them to help, or we should go to find the answers elsewhere?"

She shook her head slowly. "I think you are the Seeker, and you will have to decide."

He smiled again. "You are my friend. I could use your advice."

She hooked some hair behind her ear. "I don't know what advice to give, Richard, and my life, too, depends upon you making the right choice. But as your friend, I have faith that you will decide wisely."

"Will you hate me," he grinned, "if I make the wrong choice?"

She looked into his gray eyes, eyes that could see into her, eyes that made her weak with longing. "Even if you choose wrong, and it costs me my life," she whispered, swallowing back the lump in her throat, "I could never hate you."

He looked away from her, back down at the dirt awhile, then once again up to the Bird Man. "Do your people like having roofs that leak?"

The Bird Man raised an eyebrow. *"Would you like it if water dripped on your face when you were asleep?"*

Smiling, Richard shook his head. "Then why don't you make roofs that don't leak?"

The Bird Man shrugged. *"Because it cannot be done. We have no materials at hand to use. Clay bricks are too heavy and would fall down. Wood is too scarce; it must be carried long distances. Grass is all we have, and it leaks."*

Richard took one of the pottery bowls and turned it upside down under one of the drips. "You have clay from which you make pottery."

"Our ovens are small, we could not make a pot that big, and

besides, it would crack, then it too would leak. It cannot be done."

"It is a mistake to say something cannot be done simply because you don't know how to do it. I would not be here otherwise." He said this gently, without malice. "Your people are strong, and wise. I would be honored if the Bird Man would allow me to teach his people how to make roofs that do not leak, and also let the smoke out at the same time."

The Bird Man considered this without showing any emotion. "If you could do this, it would be a great benefit to my people, and they would give you many thanks. But I can make no promises beyond that."

Richard shrugged. "None asked for."

"The answer may still be no. You must accept that, if that is the answer, and bring no harm to my people."

"I will do my best for your people, and hope only that they judge me fairly."

"Then you are free to try, but I cannot see how you will make a roof of clay that will not crack and leak."

"I will make you a roof for your spirit house that will have a thousand cracks, but will not leak. Then I will teach you to make more for yourselves."

The Bird Man smiled and gave a nod.

CHAPTER 24

"I HATE MY MOTHER."

The Master, sitting cross-legged on the grass, looked down at the bitter expression on the boy's face and waited a moment before he answered in a quiet voice. "That is a very strong thing to say, Carl. I would not want you to say something you would come to regret when you had thought it over."

"I've thought it over plenty," Carl snapped. "We've talked about it a long time. I know now how they've twisted me around, deceived me. How selfish they are." He squinted his eyes. "How they are enemies of the people."

Rahl glanced up at the windows, at the last tinge of fading sunlight turning the wisps of clouds a beautiful deep reddish purple, frosted with tips of gold. Tonight. Tonight, at long last, would be the night he returned to the underworld.

For most of long days and nights he had kept the boy awake with the special gruel, allowing him to sleep for only brief spells, kept him awake to hammer away at him until his mind was empty, and could be molded. He had talked to the boy endlessly, convincing him how others had used him, abused him, and lied

328

to him. Sometimes he had left the boy to think over what he had been told, and used the excuse to visit his father's tomb and read the sacred inscriptions again, or to snatch some rest.

And then, last night, he had taken that girl to his bed, to get some relaxation; a small, momentary diversion. An interlude of gentleness to feel another's soft flesh against his, to relieve his pent-up excitement. She should have been honored, especially after he had been so tender with her, so charming. She had been anxious enough to be with him.

But what did she do? She laughed. When she saw the scars, she laughed.

As he thought of it now Rahl had to strain to control his rage, strain to show the boy a smile, strain to hide his impatience to get on with it. He thought of what he had done to the girl, the exhilaration of his violence unleashed, her ripping screams. The smile came more easily to his lips. She would laugh at him no more.

"What's the big grin for?" Carl asked.

Rahl looked down at the boy's big brown eyes. "I was just thinking about how proud I am of you." His smile widened as he remembered the way her hot sticky blood pumped and spurted as she screamed. Where was her haughty laughter then?

"Me?" Carl asked, smiling shyly.

Rahl's blond head nodded. "Yes, Carl, you. Not many young men of your age would be intelligent enough to see the world as it really is. To see beyond their own lives to the wider dangers and wonders all about. To see how hard I work to bring safety and peace to the people." He shook his head sadly. "Sometimes it hurts my heart to see the very ones for whom I struggle so hard turn their backs to me, reject my tireless efforts, or worse yet, join with the enemies of the people.

"I have not wanted to burden you with worry for me, but right now, as I speak with you, there are evil people who plot to conquer us, to crush us. They have brought down the boundary that protected D'Hara, and now the second boundary too. I fear they plot an invasion. I have tried to warn the people of the danger from Westland, to get them to do something to protect themselves, but they are poor and simple people, they look to me for protection."

Carl's eyes widened. "Father Rahl, are you in danger?"

Rahl brushed the matter away with a wave of his hand. "It's not me I fear for, it's the people. If I were to die, who would protect them?"

"Die?" Carl's eyes filled with tears. "Oh, Father Rahl! We need you! Please don't let them get you! Please let me fight at your side. I want to help protect you. I couldn't stand the thought of you getting hurt."

Rahl's breathing quickened, his heart raced. The time was near. It would not be long now. He smiled warmly at Carl as he remembered the girl's hoarse screams. "I could not stand the thought of you being in danger for me. Carl, I have come to know you these last days; you are more to me than simply a young man who was chosen to help me with the ceremony, you have become my friend. I have shared my deepest concerns with you, my hopes, my dreams. I don't do that with many. It's enough to know you care."

Tears in his eyes, Carl looked up at the Master. "Father Rahl," he whispered, "I'd do anything for you. Please let me stay? After the ceremony, let me stay and be with you? I'll do anything you need, I promise, if I could just stay with you."

"Carl, that's so like you, so kind. But you have a life, parents, friends. And Tinker, don't forget your dog. Soon you will be wanting to go back to all that."

Carl slowly shook his head while his eyes stayed on Rahl. "No I won't. I only want to be with you. Father Rahl, I love you. I'd do anything for you."

Rahl considered the boy's words, a serious look on his face. "It would be dangerous for you to stay with me." Rahl could feel his heart pounding.

"I don't care. I want to serve you, I don't care if I might get killed. I only want to help you. I don't want to do anything else but help you in your fight with those enemies. Father Rahl, if I got killed helping you, it would be worth it. Please, let me stay, I'll do whatever you ask. Forever."

To help control his rapid breathing, Rahl took a deep breath, and let it out slowly. His face was grave. "Are you sure of what you are saying, Carl? Are you sure you really mean it? I mean, are you really sure you would give your life for me?"

"I swear. I'd die to help you. My life is yours, if you'll have it."

Rahl leaned back a little, put his hands on his knees, and nodded slowly, his blue eyes riveted on the boy.

"Yes, Carl. I will have it."

Carl didn't smile, but shook slightly with the excitement of acceptance, his face set in determination. "When can we do the ceremony? I want to help you and the people."

"Soon," Rahl said, his eyes getting wide and his speech slow. "Tonight, after I have fed you. Are you ready to begin?"

"Yes."

Rahl rose, feeling the surge of blood through his veins; he strained to control the flush of arousal. It was dark outside. The torches gave off a flickering light that danced in his blue eyes, gleamed on his long blond hair, and made his white robes seem to glow. Before going to the forge room, he placed the feeding horn near Carl's mouth.

Inside the dark room, his guards waited, their massive arms folded across their chests. Sweat rolling from their skin left little trails in the light covering of soot. A crucible sat in the fire of the forge, an acrid smell rising from the dross.

Eyes wide, Rahl addressed his guards. "Is Demmin back?"

"For several days, Master."

"Tell him to come and wait," Rahl said, unable to manage more than a whisper. "And then I would like you two to leave me alone for now."

They bowed and left through the back door. Rahl swept his hand over the crucible, and the smell changed to an appetizing aroma. His eyes closed as he offered silent prayers to the spirit of his father. His breathing was a shallow pant. In the fervor of his emotions he was unable to control it. He licked his shaking fingertips and rubbed them on his lips.

Affixing wooden handles to the crucible so as to lift it without burning himself, he used the magic to make its weight easy to maneuver, and went back through the door with it. The torches lit the area around the boy, the white sand with the symbols traced in it, the ring of grass, the altar set on the wedge of white stone. Torchlight reflected off the polished stone block that held the iron bowl with the Shinga on its lid.

331

Rahl's blue eyes took it all in as he approached the boy. He stopped in front of him, by the mouth of the feeding horn. There was a glaze in his eyes as he looked down to Carl's upturned face.

"Are you sure about this, Carl?" he asked hoarsely. "Can I trust you with my life?"

"I swear my loyalty to you, Father Rahl. Forever."

Rahl's eyes closed as he drew a sharp breath. Sweat beaded on his face, stuck his robes to his skin. He could feel waves of heat rolling off the crucible. He added the heat of his magic to the vessel, to keep its contents boiling.

Softly, he began chanting the sacred incantations in the ancient language. Charms and spells whispered their haunting sounds in the air. Rahl's back arched as he felt power surging through his body, taking him with hot promise. He shook as he chanted, offering up his words to the spirit of the boy.

His eyes opened partway, the visage of wanton passion burning in them. His breathing was ragged; his hands trembled slightly. He gazed down at the boy.

"Carl," he said in a husky whisper, "I love you."

"I love you, Father Rahl."

Rahl's eyes slid closed. "Put your mouth over the horn, my boy, and hold tight."

While Carl did as he was told, Rahl chanted the last charm, his heart pounding. The torches hissed and spit while they burned, the sound intertwining with that of the spell.

And then he poured the contents of the crucible into the horn.

Carl's eyes snapped wide, and he both inhaled and swallowed involuntarily when the molten lead hit him, searing into his body.

Darken Rahl shuddered with excitement. He let the empty crucible slip from his hands to the ground.

The Master went on to the next set of incantations, the sending of the boy's spirit to the underworld. He said the words, every word in the proper order, opening the way to the underworld, opening the void, opening the dark emptiness.

As his hands extended upward, dark forms swirled around him. Howls filled the night air with the terror of their calls. Darken Rahl went to the cold stone altar, knelt in front of it, stretched his arm across it, put his face to it. He spoke the words in the ancient language that would link the boy's spirit to him. For a short while he cast the needed spells. When finished, he stood, fists at his side, his face flushed. Demmin Nass stepped forward, out of the shadows.

Rahl's vision focused on his friend. "Demmin," he whispered, his voice coarse.

"Master Rahl," he answered in greeting, bowing his head.

Rahl stepped to Demmin, his face drawn and sweat-streaked. "Take his body from the ground, and put it on the altar. Use the bucket of water to wash him clean." He glanced down at the short sword Demmin wore. "Crack his skull for me, no more, and then you may stand back, and wait."

He passed his hands over Demmin's head; the air about shuddered. "This spell will protect you. Wait for me then, until I return, just before dawn. I will need you." He looked away lost in his thoughts.

Demmin did as asked, going about the grim task while Rahl continued to chant the strange words, rocking back and forth, his eyes closed, as if in a trance.

Demmin wiped his sword clean on his muscular forearm and returned it to its scabbard. He took one last look at Rahl, who was still lost in the trance. "I hate this part," he muttered to himself. He turned and went back into the shadows of the trees, leaving the Master to his work.

Darken Rahl went to stand behind the altar, breathing in deeply. Suddenly, he cast his hand down at the fire pit, and flames leapt up with a roar. He held out both hands, fingers contorted, and the iron bowl lifted and floated over, setting itself down on the fire. Rahl pulled his curved knife from its sheath and laid it on the boy's wet belly. He slipped his robes from his shoulders and let them drop to the ground, kicking them back out of the way. Sweat covered his lean form, ran down his neck in rivulets.

His skin was smooth and taut over his well-proportioned muscles, except on his upper left thigh, across part of his hip and abdomen, and the left side of his erect sex. That was where the scar was; where the flames sent by the old wizard had tasted him: the flames of the wizard's fire that had consumed his father as he stood at his right hand; flames that had licked him also, giving him the pain of the wizard's fire.

It had been a fire unlike any other, burning, sticking, searing, alive with purpose, as he had screamed until he had lost his voice.

Darken Rahl licked his fingers, and reaching down ran them wetly over the bumpy scars. How he had so badly wanted to do that when he had been burned, how he had so badly wanted to do it to stop the terror of the unrelenting pain and burning.

But the healers wouldn't let him. They said he mustn't touch the burn, and so they bound him by his wrists, to keep him from reaching down. He had licked his fingers and instead rubbed them on his lips as he shook, to try to stop his crying, and on his eyes to try to wipe away the vision of having seen his father burned alive. For months he had cried and panted and begged to touch and soothe the burns, but they would not let him.

How he hated the wizard, how he wanted to kill him. How he wanted to push his hand into the wizard's living body while he looked into his eyes—and pull his heart out.

Darken Rahl took his fingers away from the scar and, picking up the knife, put the thoughts of that time out of his mind. He was a man now. He was the Master. He put his mind back to the matter at hand. He wove the proper spell, and then plunged the knife into the boy's chest.

With care, he removed the heart and put it into the iron bowl of boiling water. Next he removed the brain and added it to the bowl. Last, he took the testicles and added them, too; then, finally, he put the knife down. Blood mixed with the sweat that covered him. It dripped from his elbows.

He laid his arms across the body and offered prayers to the spirits. His face lifted to the dark windows above as he closed his eyes and continued the incantations, rolling them out without having to think. For an hour he went on with the words of the ceremony, smearing the blood on his chest at the proper time.

When he had finished with the runes from his father's tomb, he went to the sorcerer's sand where the boy had been buried for the time of his testing. With his arms he smoothed the sand; it stuck to the blood in a white crust. Squatting, he carefully began drawing the symbols, radiating from the center axis, branching in intricate patterns learned in years of study. He concentrated as he worked into the night, his straight blond hair hanging down, his brow wrinkled with intensity as he added each element, leaving out no line or stroke or curve, for that would be fatal.

At last finished, he went to the sacred bowl and found the water almost boiled away, as it should be. With magic, he floated the bowl back to the polished stone block and let it cool a little before he took a stone pestle and began grinding. He mashed, sweat running from his face, until he had worked the heart, brain, and testicles into a paste, to which he added magic powders from pockets in his discarded robes.

Standing in front of the altar, he held up the bowl with the mixture while he cast the calling spells. He lowered the bowl when finished, and looked around at the Garden of Life. He always like to look upon beautiful things before he went to the underworld.

With his fingers, he ate from the bowl. He hated the taste of meat, and never ate anything but plants. Now, though, there was no choice, the way was the way. If he wanted to go to the underworld, he had to eat the flesh. He ignored the taste, and ate it all, trying to think of it as vegetable paste.

Licking his fingers clean, he set the bowl down and went to sit cross-legged on the grass in front of the white sand. His blond hair was matted in places with dried blood. He placed his hands palm up on his knees, closed his eyes, and took deep breaths, preparing himself for meeting the spirit of the boy.

At last ready, all preparations done, all charms spoken, all spells cast, the Master raised his head and opened his eyes.

"Come to me, Carl," he whispered in the secret ancient language.

There was a moment of dead silence, and then a wailing roar. The ground shook.

From the center of the sand, the center of the enchantment, the boy's spirit rose, in the form of the Shinga, the underworld beast.

The Shinga came, transparent at first, like smoke rising from the ground, turning, as if unscrewing itself from the white sand, lured by the drawing. Its head reared as it struggled to pull itself through the drawing, snorting steam from its flared nostrils. Rahl calmly watched as the fearsome beast rose, becoming solid as it came, ripping the ground and pulling the sand up with it, its powerful hind legs pulling through at last as it reared with a wail. A hole opened, black as pitch. Sand around the edges fell away into the bottomless blackness. The Shinga floated above it. Piercing brown eyes looked down at Rahl.

"Thank you for coming, Carl."

The beast bent forward, nuzzling its muzzle against the Master's bare chest. Rahl came to his feet and stroked the Shinga's head as it bucked, calming its impatience to be off. When at last it quieted, Rahl climbed onto its back and held its neck tight.

With a flash of light, the Shinga, Darken Rahl astride its back, dissolved back into the black void, corkscrewing itself down as it went. The ground shuddered and the hole closed with a grating sound. The Garden of Life was left in the sudden silence of the night.

From the shadows of the trees, Demmin Nass stepped forward, forehead beaded with sweat. "Safe journey, my friend," he whispered, "safe journey."

CHAPTER 25

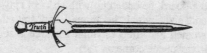

THE RAIN HELD OFF for the time being, but the sky remained thickly overcast, as it had been for almost as long as she could remember. Sitting alone on a small bench against the wall of another building, Kahlan smiled to herself as she watched Richard construct the roof of the spirit house. Sweat ran off his bare back, over the swell of his muscles, over the scars where the gar's claws had raked his back.

Richard was working with Savidlin and some other men, teaching them. He had told her he didn't need her to translate, that working with one's hands was universal, and if they had to partly figure it out themselves, they would understand it better and have more pride in what they had done.

Savidlin kept jabbering questions Richard didn't understand. Richard just smiled and explained things in words the others couldn't understand, using his hands in a sign language he invented as needed. Sometimes the others thought it hilarious, and all would end up laughing. They had accomplished a lot for men who didn't understand each other.

At first, Richard hadn't told her what he was doing; he just smiled and said she would have to wait and see. First, he took blocks of clay, about one by two feet, and made wavelike forms. Half the block's face was a concave trough, like a gutter, the other half a long rounded hump. He hollowed them out and asked the women who worked the pottery to fire them.

Next, he attached two uniform strips of wood to a flat board, one to each side, and put a lump of soft clay into the center. Using a rolling pin, he flattened the clay, the two strips of wood acting as a thickness gauge. Slicing off the excess at the top and bottom of the board, he ended up with slabs of clay of a uniform thickness and size, which he draped and smoothed over the forms the women had fired for him. He used a stick to poke a hole in the two upper corners.

The women followed him around, inspecting his work closely, so he enlisted their help. Soon he had a whole crew of smiling, chatting women making the slabs and forming them, showing him how to do it better. When the slabs were dry, they could be pulled from the forms. While these were being fired, the women, by then buzzing with curiosity, made more. When they asked how many they should make, he said to just keep making them.

Richard left them to their new work and went to the spirit house and began making a fireplace out of the mud bricks that were used for the buildings. Savidlin followed him around, trying to learn everything.

"You're making clay roofing tiles, aren't you?" Kahlan had asked him.

"Yes," he had said with a smile.

"Richard, I have seen thatched roofs that do not leak."

"So have I."

"Then why not simply make their grass roofs over properly, so they don't leak?"

"Do you know how to thatch roofs?"

"No."

"Neither do I. But I know how to make tile roofs, so that's what I have to do."

While he was building the fireplace, and showing Savidlin how to do it, he had other men strip the grass off the roof, leaving a skeleton of poles that ran the length of the building, poles that had been used to tie down each course of grass. Now they would be used to secure the clay tiles.

The tiles spanned from one row of poles to the next, the bottom edge laid on the first pole, the top edge laid on the second, with the holes in the tiles used to lash them tight to the poles. The second course of tiles was laid so its bottom edge overlapped the top of the first, covering the holes that tied the tiles down, and owing to their wavelike form, each interlocked with the one before. Because the clay tiles were heavier than the grass, Richard had first reinforced the poles from underneath with supports running up the pitch of the roof, with cross members bracing them.

It seemed as if half the village was engaged in the construction. The Bird Man came by from time to time to watch the work, pleased with what he saw. Sometimes he sat with Kahlan, saying nothing, sometimes he talked with her, but mostly he just watched. Occasionally he slipped in a question about Richard's character.

Most of the time while Richard was working, Kahlan was alone. The women weren't interested in her offers of help; the men kept their distance, watching her out of the corners of their eyes; and the young girls were too shy to actually bring themselves to talk to her. Sometimes she found them standing, staring at her. When she would ask their names, they would only give their shy smiles, and run away. The little children wanted to approach, but their mothers kept them well clear. She wasn't allowed to help with the cooking, or the making of the tiles. Her approaches were politely turned down with the excuse that she was an honored guest.

She knew better. She was a Confessor. They were afraid of her.

Kahlan was used to the attitude, the looks, the whispers. It no longer bothered her, as it had when she was younger. She remembered her mother smiling at her, telling her it was just the way people were, and it could not be changed, that she must not let it bring her to bitterness; and that she would come to be above it someday. She had thought she was beyond caring, that it didn't matter to her, that she had accepted who she was, the way life was, that she could have none of what other people had, and that it was all right. That was before she met Richard; before he became her friend, accepted her, talked to her, treated her like a normal person. Cared about her.

But then, Richard didn't know what she was.

Savidlin, at least, had been friendly to her. He had taken her and Richard into his small home with him, his wife, Weselan, and their young boy, Siddin, and had given them a place to sleep on the floor. Even if it was because Savidlin had insisted, Weselan had accepted Kahlan into her home with gracious hospitality, and did not show coldness when she had the chance, unseen by her husband, to do so. At night, after it was too dark to work, Siddin would sit wide-eyed on the floor with Kahlan as she told him stories of kings and castles, of far-off lands, and of fierce beasts. He would crawl into her lap and beg for more stories, and give her hugs. It brought tears to her eyes now to think of how Weselan let him do that, without pulling him away, how she had the kindness not to show her fear. When Siddin went to sleep, she and Richard would tell Savidlin and Weselan some of the stories of their journey from Westland. Savidlin was one who respected success in struggle, and listened with eyes almost as wide as his son's had been.

The Bird Man had seemed pleased with the new roof. Shaking his head slowly, he had smiled to himself when he had seen enough to figure out how it would work. But the other six elders were less impressed. To them, a little rain dripping in once in a while seemed hardly enough to become concerned about; it had done so their whole life, and they were resentful of an outsider coming in and showing them how stupid they had been. Someday, when one of the elders died, Savidlin would become one of the six. Kahlan wished he were one now, for they could use such a strong ally among the elders.

Kahlan worried about what would happen when the roof was finished, about what would happen if the elders refused to ask to have Richard named one of the Mud People. Richard had not given her his promise that he wouldn't hurt them. Even though he was not the kind of person to do something like that, he was the Seeker. More was at stake than the lives of a few of these people. Much more. The Seeker had to take that into account. She had to take that into account.

340

Kahlan didn't know if killing the last man of the quad had changed him, made him harder. Learning to kill made you weigh matters differently; made it easier to kill again. That was something she knew all too well.

Kahlan wished so much he had not come to her aid when he had; wished he had not killed that man. She didn't have the heart to tell him it was unnecessary. She could have handled it herself. After all, one man alone was hardly a mortal danger to her. That was why Rahl always sent four men after Confessors: one to be touched by her power, the other three to kill him and the Confessor. Sometimes only one was left, but that was enough after a Confessor had spent her power. But one alone? He had almost no chance. Even if he was big, she was faster. When he swung his sword, she would have simply jumped out of the way. Before he could have brought it up again, she would have touched him, and he would have been hers. That would have been the end of him.

Kahlan knew there was no way she could ever tell Richard that there had been no need for him to kill. What made it doubly bad was that he had killed for her, had thought he was saving her.

Kahlan knew another quad was probably already on its way. They were relentless. The man Richard had killed knew he was going to die, knew he didn't stand a chance, alone, against a Confessor, but he came anyway. They would not stop, did not know the meaning of it, never thought of anything but their objective.

And, they enjoyed what they did to Confessors.

Even though she tried not to, she couldn't help remembering Dennee. Whenever she thought of the quads, she couldn't help remembering what they had done to Dennee.

Before Kahlan had became a woman, her mother had been stricken with a terrible sickness, one no healer was able to turn back. She had died all too quickly of the awful wasting disease. Confessors were a close sisterhood; when trouble struck one, it struck all. Dennee's mother took in Kahlan and comforted her. The two girls, best friends, had been thrilled that they were to be sisters, as they called themselves from then on, and it helped ease the pain of losing her mother.

Dennee was a frail girl, as frail as her mother. She did not

341

have the strength of power that Kahlan did, and over time, Kahlan became her protector, guardian, shielding her from situations that required more force than she could bring from within. After its use, Kahlan could recover the strength of her power in an hour or two, but for Dennee, it sometimes took several days.

On one fateful day, Kahlan had been away for a short time, taking a confession from a murderer who was to be hanged, a mission that was to have been Dennee's. Kahlan had gone in her sister's place because she wanted to spare Dennee the torment of the task. Dennee hated taking confessions, hated seeing the look in their eyes. Sometimes she would cry for days after. She never asked Kahlan to go in her stead, she wouldn't, but the look of relief on her face when Kahlan told her she would do it was words enough. Kahlan, too, disliked taking confessions, but she was stronger, wiser, more reflective. She understood, and accepted, that being a Confessor was her power; it was who she was, and so it didn't hurt her the way it did Dennee. Kahlan had always been able to place her head before her heart. And she would have done any dirty job in Dennee's place.

On the trail home, Kahlan heard soft whimpers from the brush at the side of the road, moans of mortal pain. To her horror, she discovered Dennee, thrown there, discarded.

"I was ... coming to meet you. ... I wanted to walk back with you," Dennee had said as Kahlan cradled the girl's head in her lap. "A quad caught me. I'm sorry. I got one of them, Kahlan. I touched him. I got one of them. You would have been proud of me."

In shock, Kahlan held Dennee's head, comforted her, telling her it would be all right.

"Please, Kahlan ... pull my dress down for me?" Her voice sounded as if it were coming from a faraway place. Wet and weak. "My arms don't work."

Past panic, Kahlan saw why. Dennee's arms had been brutally broken. They lay useless at her sides, bent in places where they shouldn't be bent. Blood trickled from one ear. Kahlan pulled what was left of the blood-soaked dress over her sister, covering her as best she could. Her head spun with the horror of what the men had done. The choking feeling in her throat wouldn't let words come out. She strained to hold back her screams, fearful of frightening her sister any more. She knew she had to be strong for her this one last time.

Dennee whispered Kahlan's name, beckoning her closer. "Darken Rahl did this to me ... he wasn't here, but he did this to me."

"I know," Kahlan said with all the tenderness she could gather. "Lie still, it will be all right. I will take you home." She knew it was a lie, knew Dennee would not be all right.

"Please, Kahlan," she whispered, "kill him. Stop this madness. I wish I were strong enough. Kill him for me."

Anger boiled up in her. It was the first time Kahlan had ever wanted to use her power to hurt someone, to kill someone. She had gone to the brink of feeling something she had never felt before or since. A terrible wrath, a force from deep within; a frightening birthright. With shaking fingers, she stroked Dennee's bloody hair.

"I will," she promised.

Dennee relaxed back in her arms. Kahlan took off the bone necklace and placed it around her sister's neck.

"I want you to have this. It will help protect you."

"Thank you, Kahlan." She smiled, tears rolling from her wide eyes, down the pale skin of her cheeks. "But nothing can protect me now. Save yourself. Don't let them get you. They enjoy it. They hurt me so much ... and they enjoyed it. They laughed at me."

Kahlan closed her eyes against the sickening sight of her sister's pain, rocked her in her arms, and kissed her forehead.

"Remember me, Kahlan. Remember the fun we had."

"Bad memories?"

Kahlan's head snapped up, jolted out of her thoughts. The Bird Man stood beside her, having come up silently, unnoticed. She nodded, looking away from his gaze.

"Please forgive me for showing weakness," she said, clearing her throat as her fingers wiped the tears from her face.

He regarded her with soft brown eyes and sat lightly beside her on the short bench.

"It is not a weakness, child, to be a victim."

She wiped her nose on the back of her hand and swallowed back the wail that was trying to fight its way out of her throat.

She felt so alone. She so missed Dennee. The Bird Man put his arm tenderly around her shoulder and gave her a short, fatherly hug.

"I was thinking of my sister, Dennee. She was murdered by order of Darken Rahl. I found her. . . . She died in my arms. . . . They hurt her so bad. Rahl is not content to kill. He must see to it that people suffer before they die."

He nodded his understanding. *"Though we be different peoples, we hurt the same."* With his thumb, he brushed a tear from her cheek, then reached into his pocket. *"Hold out your hand."*

She did as he asked, and he poured some small seeds in it. Surveying the sky, he blew the whistle that made no sound, the one that hung from his neck, and shortly a small, bright yellow bird lit with a flutter upon his finger. He placed his hand next to hers so it could climb over and eat the seeds. Kahlan could feel its tiny little feet gripping her finger while it pecked away at the seeds. The bird was so bright and pretty it made her smile. The Bird Man's leathery face smiled with her. When it finished eating, the bird fluffed itself up and sat contentedly, without fear.

"I thought you might like to gaze upon a small vision of beauty among the ugliness."

"Thank you," she smiled.

"Do you wish to keep him?"

Kahlan watched the bird a moment longer, its bright yellow feathers, the way it cocked its head, and then cast it into the air.

"I have no right," she said, watching the bird flit away. *"It should be free."*

A small smile brightened the Bird Man's face as he gave a single nod. Leaning forward and resting his forearms on his knees, he looked over at the spirit house. The work was almost done, maybe one more day. Long, silver-gray hair slipped off his shoulders and down around his face, hiding his expression from her. Kahlan sat awhile and watched Richard working on the roof. She ached to have him hold her right now, and hurt all the more because she knew she couldn't allow it.

"You wish to kill him, this man, Darken Rahl?" he asked without turning to her.

"Very much."

"And is your power enough?"

"No," she admitted.

"And does the Seeker's blade have enough power to kill him?"

"No. Why do you ask?"

The clouds were getting darker as the day was drawing to an end. Light rain was beginning to fall once more, and the gloom among the buildings was deepening.

"As you said yourself, it is dangerous to be with a Confessor who is in great want of something. I think this is also true of the Seeker. Maybe even more so."

She paused a moment, then spoke softly. *"I do not wish to put words to what Darken Rahl did with his own hands to Richard's father; it would make you fear the Seeker all the more. But know that Richard would also have let the bird fly free."*

The Bird Man seemed to laugh without sound. *"You and I are too smart for these tricks with words. Let us speak without them."* He sat back and folded his arms across his chest. *"I have tried to tell the other elders what a wonderful thing the Seeker is doing for our people, how good it is that he is teaching us these things. They are not so sure, as they are set in their ways and can be stubborn, sometimes almost beyond my tolerance. I fear what you and the Seeker will do to my people if the elders say no."*

"Richard has given you his word that he will not harm your people."

"Words are not as strong as a father's blood. Or as strong as a sister's."

Kahlan leaned back against the wall, pulling her cloak around her, shutting out the wet breeze. *"I am a Confessor because I was born so. I did not seek the power. I would have chosen otherwise, would have chosen to be like other people. But I must live with what I was given, and make the best of it. Despite what you may think of the Confessors, despite what most people think, we are here to serve the people, to serve the truth. I love all the people of the Midlands, and would give my life to protect them, to keep them free. That is all I wish to do. And yet I am alone."*

"Richard keeps his eyes on you, he watches over you, cares for you."

She looked over out of the corner of her eye. *"Richard is from Westland. He does not know what I am. If he knew . . ."*

The Bird Man lifted his eyebrow at hearing this. *"For one who serves the truth . . ."*

"Please do not remind me. It is trouble of my own making, with consequences I must bear, and fear greatly. And that only proves my words. The Mud People live in a land distant from the other peoples. That has given them the luxury of being out of reach of trouble in the past. This trouble has long arms; it will reach you. The elders can argue against helping all they want, but they will not be able to argue against the fangs of truth. All of your people will pay the price if these few put pride before wisdom."

The Bird Man listened carefully, respectfully. Kahlan turned to him.

"I cannot honestly say at this moment what I will do if the elders say no. It is not my wish to harm your people, but to save them from the pain I have seen. I have seen what Darken Rahl does to people. I know what he will do. If I knew I could somehow stop Rahl by killing Savidlin's precious little boy, I would do it without hesitation, with my bare hands if need be, because as much as the doing of it would wound my heart, I know I would be saving all the other precious little children. It is a terrifying burden I carry, the burden of the warrior. You are one who has killed other men to save others, and I know you take no joy in it. Darken Rahl takes joy in it, believe me. Please, help me save your people without hurting any of them." Tears ran down her cheeks. *"I want so much not to hurt anyone."*

Tenderly he drew her to him and let her sob against his shoulder. *"The people of the Midlands are fortunate to have you as their warrior."*

"If we can find the thing we seek, and keep it from Darken Rahl until the first day of winter, he will die. No one else will have to be hurt. But we must have help to find it."

"The first day of winter. Child, that is not much time. This season withers away, the next will be here soon."

"I do not make the rules of life, honored elder. If you know the secret to stopping time, please tell me, that I might make it so."

He sat quietly, without an answer. *"I have watched you among our people before. You have always respected our wishes, never acted to bring us harm. It is the same with the Seeker. I am on your side, child. I will do my best to win over the others. I only hope my words to them will be enough. I wish my people to come to no harm."*

"It is not the Seeker or me you must fear if they say no," she said as she lay against his shoulder, staring off at nothing in particular. *"It is the one from D'Hara. He will come like a storm and destroy you. You have no chance against him. He will butcher you."*

That night in the warmth of Savidlin's home, sitting on the floor, Kahlan told Siddin the story of the fisherman who turned into a fish and lived in the lake, cleverly stealing bait from hooks without ever being caught. It was an old story her mother had told her when she was as little as he. The wonder in his face made her remember her own excitement when she had first heard it.

Later, while Weselan cooked sweet roots, the pleasant aroma mingling with the smoke, Savidlin showed Richard how to carve proper arrow points for different animals, harden them in the coals of the cooking fire, and apply poison to their tips. Kahlan lay on a skin on the floor with Siddin curled up in a ball, snuggled asleep against her stomach as she stroked his dark hair. She had to swallow back the lump in her throat as she thought about how she had told the Bird Man she would even be willing to kill this little boy.

She wished she could take back those words. She hated that it was true, but wished she had not put words to it. Richard hadn't seen her talking to the Bird Man, and she did not tell him of their conversation. She saw no point in worrying him; what would happen would happen. She only hoped the elders would listen to reason.

The next day was windy and exceptionally warm, with occasional periods of driving rain. By early afternoon a crowd had gathered at the spirit house as the roof was completed and a fire started in the new fireplace. Cries of excitement and wonder rose from the people when the fist wisps of smoke emerged from the chimney. They peeked in the doorway to see the fire burning without filling the room with smoke. The idea of living without smoke in their eyes seemed as thrilling as living without water dripping on their heads. A wind-driven rain like this was the worst. It went right through the grass roofs.

Everyone watched with glee as water ran off the tiles of the roof and none went inside. Richard was in a good mood as he climbed down. The roof was finished, it didn't leak, the fireplace drew well, and everyone was joyous because of what he had done for them. The men who had helped were proud of what they had accomplished, what they had learned. They acted as guides, excitedly showing off the finer points of the construction.

Ignoring the onlookers, stopping only to strap on his sword, Richard headed for the center of the village, where the elders waited under one of the open pole buildings. Kahlan fell in to his left, Savidlin to the right, intending to stand up for him. The crowd watched him go, then swept behind, spilling around the buildings, laughing and shouting. Richard's jaw was set tight.

"Do you think you need to take the sword?" she asked.

He looked to her as he continued his long strides. He smiled crookedly. Rainwater ran from his wet, matted hair. "I am the Seeker."

She gave him a disapproving look. "Richard, don't play games with me. You know what I mean."

His smile widened. "I'm hoping it will serve as a reminder of why they should do the right thing."

Kahlan had a bad feeling in the pit of her stomach, that things were spinning beyond her control, that Richard was going to do something terrible if the elders turned him down. He had been working hard, from when he woke until he fell into bed, the whole time with the single thought that he would win them over. He had won over most people, but they were not the people who counted. She was afraid he hadn't given rational thought to what he would do if the word was no.

Toffalar stood tall and proud at the center of the leaking pole structure. The rain dripping around him splashed in little puddles on the floor. Surin, Caldus, Arbrin, Breginderin, and Hajanlet stood to his sides. They each wore their coyote hides, something

348

Kahlan had learned they did only when official events were taking place. It seemed as if the whole village was out. They spread around the open area, sitting under roofs of the open buildings, filling windows, all watching as work stopped and they waited to hear the elders speak of their future.

Kahlan caught sight of the Bird Man standing among some armed men to the side of a pole that held up the roof over the elders' heads. When their eyes met, her heart sank. She grabbed the sleeve of Richard's shirt, leaning toward him.

"Don't forget, no matter what these men say, we must get out of here if we are to have a chance of stopping Rahl. We are two, they are many, sword or no sword."

He ignored her. "Honored elders," he started in a loud, clear voice. She translated as he spoke. "It is my privilege to report to you that the spirit house has a new roof that does not leak. It has also been my privilege to teach your people how to build these roofs so they may improve the other buildings of your village. I did this out of respect for your people, and I expect nothing in return. I only hope you are pleased."

The six stood grim-faced as Kahlan translated. There was a long silence when she finished.

At last Toffalar spoke in a determined voice. *"We are not pleased."*

Richard's expression turned dark when she told him Toffalar's words. "Why?"

"A little rain does not melt the strength of the Mud People. Your roof may not leak, but only because it is clever. Clever as the ways of outsiders. They are not our ways. It would only be the beginning of outsiders telling us what to do. We know what you want. You want to be named one of us so we will call a gathering for you. Just another clever trick of an outsider to get from us what will serve you. You wish to draw us into your fight. We say no!" He turned to Savidlin. *"The roof of the spirit house will be put back to the way it was. The way our honored ancestors wanted it."*

Savidlin was livid, but he did not move. The elder, a slight smile on his pinched lips, turned back to Richard.

"Now that your tricks have failed," he said with disdain.

"would you think to harm our people, Richard With The Temper?" It was a taunt, aimed to discredit Richard.

Richard looked as dangerous as she had ever seen him. His glare turned briefly to the Bird Man, then back to the six under the shelter. She held her breath. The crowd was dead quiet. He turned slowly to them.

"I will not harm your people," he said in an even voice. There was a collective sigh of relief when Kahlan spoke his words. When it was quiet again, he went on. "But I will mourn for what is going to happen to them." Without turning back to the elders, his arm slowly lifted as he pointed to them. "For you six, I will not mourn. I do not mourn the death of fools." His words came out like poison. The crowd gasped.

Toffalar's face twisted into bitter rage. Whispers and fear spread through the onlookers. Kahlan glanced over to the Bird Man. He seemed to have aged years. She could see in his heavy brown eyes how sorry he was. For a moment their eyes locked and they shared the grief of what they both knew was going to sweep over all their lives; then his gaze sank to the ground.

In a sudden flash of movement, Richard spun toward the elders, pulling free the Sword of Truth. It was so fast almost everyone, including the elders, flinched back a step in shock and then froze in place, the six faces reflecting the fear that kept them paralyzed. The crowd began creeping back; the Bird Man had not moved. Kahlan feared Richard's anger, and understood it, too. She decided not to interfere, but to do what was necessary to protect the Seeker, whatever he did next. Not even a whisper was uttered; the only sound in the dead silence was the distinctive ringing of steel. With his teeth gritted, Richard pointed the glinting sword at the elders, its tip inches from their faces.

"Have the courage to do one last thing for your people." Richard's tone sent a chill through her. Kahlan translated out of reflex, too transfixed to do anything else. Then, unbelievably, he turned the sword around, holding it by the point, holding the hilt out to the elders. "Take my sword," he commanded. "Use it to kill the women and children. It will be more merciful than what Darken Rahl will do to them. Have the courage to spare them the torture they will suffer. Give them the charity of a quick death." His countenance withered their expressions.

Kahlan could hear women starting to cry softly as they clutched their children. The elders, in the grip of a terror they hadn't expected, did not move. At last their eyes fled from Richard's glare. When it was clear to all they did not have the courage to take the sword, Richard painstakingly slid it back into its scabbard, as if slowly extinguishing their last chance at salvation—an unequivocal gesture that the elders had forfeited forever the aid of the Seeker. The finality of it was frightening.

Then at last he broke his hot glare at them and turned to her, his face changing. When she saw the look in his eyes, she swallowed hard. It was a look of heartache for a people he had come to love, but could not help. All eyes stayed on him as he closed the distance between them and took her gently by the arm.

"Let's collect our things and get moving," he said softly. "We've wasted a lot of time. I only hope it wasn't too much." His gray eyes were wet. "I'm sorry, Kahlan ... that I chose wrong."

"You did not choose wrong, Richard; they did." Her anger at the elders had a finality to it, too, a door closing on any hope for these people. She cut off her concern for them; they were the walking dead. They had been offered a chance, and had chosen their own fate.

When they passed Savidlin, the two men locked arms for a moment without looking at each other. No one else made a move to leave; they stayed and watched the two outsiders walk quickly among them. As they passed, a few reached out and touched Richard, he returning the wordless sympathy with a squeeze of his hand on their arms, unable to bear meeting their eyes.

They gathered up their things from Savidlin's house, stuffing their cloaks into the packs. Neither spoke. Kahlan felt empty, drained. When their eyes met at last, they suddenly came together in a wordless embrace, a shared grief for their new friends, for what they both knew would happen to them. They had gambled with the only thing they had—time. And lost.

When they separated, Kahlan put the last of her things in the pack and closed the flap. Richard pulled his cloak back out. She watched as he pushed his hand inside and rummaged around, an urgency to his search. He went to the doorway for light, and looked inside as he moved items roughly about. The arm holding the pack lowered and his face came up to hers, alarm in his expression.

"The night stone is gone."

The way he said it frightened her. "Maybe you left it out somewhere. . . ."

"No. I never took it out of my pack. Never."

Kahlan didn't understand why he seemed so panicked about it. "Richard, we don't need it now, we are through the pass. I'm sure Adie will forgive its loss. We have more important things to worry about."

He took a step closer to her. "You don't understand. We have to find it."

"Why?" she frowned.

"Because I think that thing can wake the dead." Her mouth fell open. "Kahlan, I've been thinking about it. Do you remember how nervous Adie was when she gave it to me, how she kept looking around until it was put away? And when did the shadow things in the pass start coming for us? After I took it out. Remember?"

Her eyes were wide. "But, even if someone else used it, she said it would only work for you."

"She was talking about it giving off light. She said nothing about waking the dead. I can't believe Adie wouldn't warn us."

Kahlan looked away, thinking. Her eyes closed as a wave of realization swept over her. "Yes, she did, Richard. She warned you with a sorceress's riddle. I'm sorry, I never gave it a thought. That is the way of a sorceress. She will not always come right out with what she knows, with a warning. She will sometimes put it in the form of a riddle."

Richard turned to the door, glaring out. "I can't believe it. The world is being sucked into oblivion, and that old woman gives us riddles." He pounded his fist against the doorframe. "She should have told us!"

"Richard, maybe she had a reason, maybe it was the only way."

He stared out the door, thinking. "If you have need enough. That's what she said. Like water. It is valuable only under the right conditions, that to a drowning man it is of little worth and

352

great trouble. That was how she was trying to warn us. Great trouble." He turned back to the room, picking up the pack again, taking another look inside. "It was here last night, I saw it. What could have happened to it?"

Together they looked up, their eyes meeting.

"Siddin," they both said at once.

CHAPTER 26

Dropping their packs, they both ran out the door, heading for the open area where they had last seen Savidlin. Both screamed out Siddin's name. As they ran, splashing through the mud, people scattered out of the way. By the time they reached the open area, the crowd was in a panic, not knowing what was happening, and were sweeping back for the shelter of the buildings. The elders retreated on the platform. The Bird Man stretched up, trying to see. The band of hunters behind him nocked arrows to their bowstrings.

She saw Savidlin, frightened and confused that they were calling out his son's name.

"Savidlin!" Kahlan screamed. *"Find Siddin! Don't let him open the pouch he has!"*

Savidlin paled, whirled around, searching, then ran off in a half crouch, looking for his son, his head darting among the running people. Kahlan didn't see Weselan anywhere. Richard and Kahlan separated, widening their search. The area was turning to mass confusion; she had to push people out of her way. Kahlan's heart was in her throat. If Siddin opened the pouch . . .

And then she saw him.

As people cleared the center of the village, there he was, paying no attention to the panic all around him as he sat in the mud, shaking the leather pouch in his little fist, trying to get the stone out.

"Siddin! No!" she yelled at him over and over, running toward him.

He couldn't hear her screams. Maybe he wouldn't be able to get it out. He was just a defenseless little boy. Please, she begged in her mind, let the fates be kind to him.

The stone dropped from the pouch and plopped into the mud. Siddin smiled and picked it up. Kahlan felt her skin go cold.

Shadow things began to materialize all around. They turned like wisps of mist in the damp air, as if looking about. Then they floated for Siddin.

Richard ran for him, screaming over at her, "Get the stone! Put it back in the pouch!"

His sword flashed through the air, cutting through the shadows as he ran in a straight line for Siddin. When the sword sliced through them, they howled in agony and spun apart. Upon hearing the terrifying wails Siddin looked up and froze, wide-eyed.

Kahlan yelled at him to put the stone back in the pouch, but he could not move. He was hearing other voices. She ran faster than she had ever run, weaving back and forth around the dense knots of shadows as they floated toward the boy.

Something dark and small zipped past her, making her breath catch in her throat. Then another, behind her. Arrows. The air suddenly became thick with arrows, the Bird Man having ordered his hunters to bring down the shadows. Every one went true and found its mark, but they simply passed through the shadow things as if they were whizzing through smoke. Poison-tipped arrows were flying wildly everywhere. She knew that if one even nicked her or Richard, they were dead. Now she had to dodge the arrows as well as the shadows. She heard another whistle past her ear as she ducked at the last second. One skipped in the mud and flew past her leg.

Richard had reached the boy, but couldn't grab the stone. All he was able to do was frantically strike down the advancing shadows. He couldn't pause to try for the stone.

355

Kahlan was still a long way off, not able to run in as Richard had, cutting through them. She knew that if she inadvertently touched a shadow, she was dead. There were so many materializing around her the very air was like a gray maze. Richard fought around the boy in a circle that got smaller all the time. He held the sword in both hands, swinging it wildly. He dared not slow for an instant or they would close over him. There was no end to the shadow things.

Kahlan couldn't make any headway. The shadows, floating past her from all around, and the arrows streaking by, cut her off at every turn, the arrows forcing her to jump back just as she went for an opening. She knew Richard wouldn't be able to hold out much longer. Hard as he fought, he was falling back in a tighter and tighter circle, closer to the boy. She was their only chance, and she wasn't even close.

Another arrow zipped past, the feather flicking her hair.

"Stop the arrows!" she yelled angrily at the Bird Man. *"Stop shooting the arrows! You're going to kill us!"*

Frustrated, he recognized her plight and reluctantly called a halt to the archers. But then they all drew knives and quickly advanced on the shadows. They had no idea what they were up against. They would be killed to the last man.

"No!" she screamed, shaking her fists. *"If you touch them you will die! Stay back!"*

The Bird Man held his arm up, stopping his men. She knew how helpless he felt as he watched her dart back among the shadows, angling slowly closer to Richard and Siddin.

She heard another voice. It was Toffalar, yelling.

"Stop them! They are destroying our ancestors' spirits! Shoot them with your arrows! Shoot the outsiders!"

Hesitantly, looking at one another, the archers nocked arrows to their bows once again. They could not disobey one of the elders.

"Shoot them!" he yelled, red-faced, shaking his fist. *"You heard me! Shoot them!"*

They brought up their bows. Kahlan crouched, preparing to try to jump out of the way once the arrows were loosed. The Bird Man stepped in front of his men, holding his arm out, across them, countermanding the order. There were words she couldn't hear between him and Toffalar. She wasted no time, and took the opportunity to work her way forward, ducking under the outstretched arms of the floating shadow things.

Out of the corner of her eye she caught sight of Toffalar. He had a knife and was running toward her. She dismissed the danger; sooner or later he would run into a shadow and be killed. He stopped here and there to plead with the shadow things. She couldn't hear his voice above the wails. The next time she looked he had closed most of the distance. It was unbelievable that he hadn't run into one. Somehow the gaps just opened for him as he ran heedlessly, recklessly, for her, his face contorted in rage. Still, she didn't worry that he could make it; soon he had to touch one, and would be dead.

Kahlan gained the rest of the open ground, but found the ring of shadows around Richard and Siddin an impenetrable gray wall. There was no opening. She dodged right, and left, trying to find a way in, but couldn't get through. She was so close, yet so far, and the trap was closing around her, too. Several times she barely escaped by stepping back before shadows converged. Richard snatched glimpses to see where she was. He tried to fight through to her a number of times, but was forced to turn to the other side to keep the shadows from Siddin.

With a start, she saw the knife slashing through the air. Toffalar had reached her. Lost in hate, he screamed things she couldn't even understand. But she understood the knife, what he intended. He intended to kill her. She dodged his slash. It was her opening.

And then she made a mistake.

She started to reach to touch Toffalar, but caught sight of Richard looking toward her. She faltered at the thought of him seeing her use her power. She hesitated, and let Toffalar have the instant he needed. Richard screamed her name in warning, then turned to fight back the shadows from behind him.

Toffalar's knife came up, hitting her right arm, deflecting off the bone.

Shock and pain ignited her rage. Rage at her own stupidity. She did not miss the opening a second time. Her left hand came up and caught Toffalar by the throat. She felt her grip shut off his

357

air for an instant. She needed only to touch him; grabbing him by the throat was a reflex of her rage, not her power.

Though there were terrified screams and shouts coming from people all around, and the horrifying wails from the shadows Richard was destroying wholesale, her mind went suddenly quiet, calm. There was no sound in her head. Only silence. The silence of what she was going to do.

In the calm spark of an instant that to her twisted for an eternity, she saw the look of fear in Toffalar's eyes, the realization of his fate. She saw in his eyes his railing against that end, felt his muscles beginning to tense, to fight her, his hands starting the ever so slow, hopeless journey to her grip at his throat.

But he had no chance, not the slightest glimmer. She was in control now. Time was hers. He was hers. She felt no pity. No remorse. Only deadly calm.

As she had done countless times before, in her calm, the Mother Confessor relaxed her restraint. Released at last, her power slammed into Toffalar's body.

There was a hard impact to the air; thunder with no sound. Water in the puddles around her danced and flung muddy droplets into the air.

Toffalar's eyes went wide. The muscles of his face went slack. His mouth fell open.

"Mistress!" he called out in a reverent whisper.

The calm expression on her face contorted with anger. With all her strength she shoved Toffalar backward, at the ring of shadows around Richard and Siddin. Arms flung in the air, he fell into the shadows and screamed at the contact before falling to the mud. Somehow, the contact opened a brief, small gap in the ring of shadows. Without hesitation she dove for it, flinging herself through an instant before it closed behind her.

Kahlan threw herself over Siddin.

"Hurry!" Richard yelled.

Siddin didn't look at her; his face was fixed on the shadows, his mouth open, all his muscles locked. She tried to get the stone from his tight little fist, but his fingers were fastened around it with the strength of his fright. She snatched the pouch from his other hand. Gripping the pouch and his wrist with her left hand, she started prying his little fingers off the stone with the right, begging him the whole time to let go. He didn't hear her. Blood ran down her arm to her shaking hand, mixing with the rain, making her fingers slippery.

A shadowy hand reached for her face. She flinched back. The sword hissed past her face, through the shadow. It added its wail to the others. Siddin's eyes were transfixed on the shadows, all his muscles rigid. Richard was right over her, swinging the sword in weaving patterns all around. There was no more ground to give. It was just the three of them now. Siddin's slippery fingers wouldn't open.

Gritting her teeth with an effort that sent searing pain through the wound in her right arm, she finally raked the stone out of Siddin's hand. Because of the blood and mud, it shot from her fingers like a melon seed, plopping in the mud by her knee. Almost instantly her hand was over it, snatching it back up in a scoopful of mud. She jammed it in the pouch and yanked the drawstring closed. Gasping, she looked up.

The shadows stopped. She could hear Richard's heavy breathing as he continued slashing at them. Slowly, at first, the shadows began moving back, as if confused, lost, searching. Then they dissolved back into the air, retreating to the underworld whence they had come. In a moment, they were gone. Except for Toffalar's body, the three of them were in an empty expanse of mud.

Kahlan, rain running off her face, took Siddin into her arms, hugging him tight against her as he began crying. In exhaustion, Richard closed his eyes and collapsed to his knees, sitting back on his heels. His head hung down as he panted.

"Kahlan," Siddin whimpered, *"they were calling my name."*

"I know," she whispered in his ear, kissing it, *"it's all right now. You were very brave. Brave as any hunter."*

He hugged his arms around her neck as she comforted him. She felt weak, shaky. They had almost lost their lives, to save a single one. Something she had told him the Seeker must not do, yet they had done it without a second thought. How could they not have tried? Having Siddin's arms around her made it all worth it. Richard was still holding the sword in both hands; its tip sunk in the mud. She reached over and put a hand on his shoulder.

At the touch of her hand, his head instantly snapped up and the sword whipped around toward her, stopping in front of her face. Kahlan jumped with surprise. Fury lit Richard's wide eyes.

"Richard," she said, startled, "it's just me. It's over. I didn't mean to frighten you."

He let his muscles go limp, let himself fall over onto his side in the mud.

"Sorry," he managed, still trying to catch his breath. "When your hand touched me . . . I guess I thought it was a shadow."

Legs were suddenly all about them. She peered up. The Bird Man was there, as were Savidlin and Weselan. Weselan was sobbing loudly. Kahlan stood and handed her her son. Weselan passed the boy to her husband and threw her arms around Kahlan, kissing her face all over.

"Thank you, Mother Confessor, thank you for saving my boy," she bawled. *"Thank you, Kahlan, thank you."*

"I know, I know." Kahlan hugged her back. *"It's all right now."*

Weselan turned tearfully back to take Siddin in her arms. Kahlan saw Toffalar lying close by, dead. She flopped down in the mud, exhausted, and pulled her knees up with her arms around them.

She put her face against her knees and, losing control, started crying. Not because she had killed Toffalar, but because she had hesitated. It had almost cost her her life; almost cost Richard and Siddin—everyone—their lives. She had almost given victory to Rahl because she hadn't wanted Richard to see what she was going to do, and had hesitated. It was the stupidest thing she had ever done, other than not telling Richard she was a Confessor. Tears of frustration poured out as she cried in choking sobs.

A hand reached under her good arm, pulling her up. It was the Bird Man. She bit her quivering lip, forcing herself to stop crying. She could not let these people see her showing weakness. She was a Confessor.

"Well done, Mother Confessor," he said as he took a strip of cloth from one of his men and started wrapping it around her wounded arm.

Kahlan held her head up. *"Thank you, honored elder."*

360

"This will need to be stitched together. I will have the gentlest healer among us do the work."

She stood numbly as he tightened the bandage, sending flames of pain through the deep cut. He looked down at Richard, who seemed content to lie there on his back in the mud, as if it were the most comfortable bed in the world.

The Bird Man lifted an eyebrow to her, and gave a nod, indicating Richard. *"Your warning that I should not want to give the Seeker cause to draw his sword in anger was as true as an arrow from my finest archer."* There was a twinkle in his sharp brown eyes; the corners of his mouth curled in a smile. He looked down at the Seeker. *"You made a good showing of yourself too, Richard With The Temper. Fortunately the evil spirits still have not learned to carry swords."*

"What'd he say?" Richard asked.

She told him, and he gave a grim smile at their private joke as he came to his feet and put away the sword. He reached out and took the pouch from her hand. She hadn't even realized it was still clutched there. Richard put it in his pocket. "May we never encounter spirits armed with swords."

The Bird Man nodded his agreement. *"And now we have business."*

He reached down and grabbed a fistful of the coyote hide around Toffalar. The body rolled over in the mud as he tore it off. He turned to the hunters.

"Bury the body." His eyes narrowed. *"All of it."*

The men looked at each other, unsure. *"Elder, you mean all of it except the skull?"*

"I said what I meant. All of it! We only keep the skulls of honored elders, to remind us of their wisdom. We do not keep the skulls of fools."

This sent a chill through the crowd. It was just about the worst thing you could do to an elder, a dishonor of the highest order. It meant his life had mattered for nothing. The men gave a nod. No one spoke up for the dead elder, including the five standing nearby.

"We are short an elder," the Bird Man announced. He turned, looking slowly to the eyes around him, then made his back

361

straight and shoved the coyote hide against Savidlin's chest. *"I choose you."*

Savidlin put his hands around the muddy hide with the reverence due a gold crown. He gave a small, proud smile and a nod to the Bird Man.

"Do you have anything to say to our people, as their newest elder?" It was not a question, it was a command.

Savidlin walked over and turned, standing between Kahlan and Richard. He put the hide around his shoulders, beaming with pride at Weselan, and then addressed the gathered people. Kahlan looked out and realized that the whole village surrounded them.

"Most honored among us," he addressed the Bird Man, *"these two people have acted selflessly in the defense of our people. In my life, I have never witnessed anything to compare with it. They could have left us to fend for ourselves when we foolishly turned our backs on them. Instead, they have shown us what manner of people they be. They are as fine as the best of us."* Almost everyone in the crowd was nodding agreement. *"I demand that you name them Mud People."*

The Bird Man smiled a small smile. The smile evaporated as he turned to the other five elders. Though he hid it well, Kahlan could see the Bird Man's eyes flash with the ghost of his anger. *"Step forward."* They gave one another sidelong glances, then did as ordered. *"The demand made by Savidlin is extraordinary. It must be unanimous. Do you make the same demand?"*

Savidlin strode to the archers and snatched a bow from the hands of one. He smoothly nocked an arrow while he kept his squinted eyes on the elders. He put tension to the string, locking the arrow in place with the bow hand, then stepped in front of the five. *"Make the demand. Or we will have new elders who will."*

They stood grimly, facing Savidlin. The Bird Man made no movement to interfere. There was a long silence as the crowd waited, spellbound. At last, Caldus took a step forward. He put his hand on Savidlin's bow and gently lowered its point to the ground.

"Please, Savidlin, allow us to speak from our hearts, not from the point of an arrow."

"Speak then."

Caldus walked to Richard, stopping in front of him, looking him in the eye.

"The hardest thing for a man to do, especially an old man," he said in a soft voice, waiting for Kahlan to translate, *"is to admit he has acted foolishly, and selfishly. You have acted neither foolishly nor selfishly. The two of you are better examples of Mud People for our children than I. I demand of the Bird Man that you be named Mud People. Please, Richard With The Temper, and Mother Confessor, our people need you."* He held his palms out in an open gesture. *"If you deem me unworthy of making this demand upon your behalf, please strike me down that one better than I might make the demand."*

Head bowed, he dropped to his knees in the mud in front of Richard and Kahlan. She translated it all word for word, omitting only her title. The other four elders came and knelt beside him, adding their sincere request to that of Caldus. Kahlan sighed in relief. At last, they had what they wanted; what they needed.

Richard stood over the five men with his arms folded, looking down at the tops of their heads, saying nothing. She couldn't understand why he wasn't telling them it was all right, and to get to their feet. No one moved. What was he doing? What was he waiting for? It was over. Why wasn't he acknowledging their contrition?

Kahlan could see the muscle in his jaw tighten and flex. She went cold. She recognized the look in his eyes. The anger. These men had crossed a line against him. And against her. She remembered how he had slid the sword away when he had last stood with them, this very day. It had been final, and Richard meant it. He was not thinking. He was thinking of killing.

Richard's arms unfolded; his hand went to the hilt. The sword slid out as slowly, smoothly, as it had slid away for them the last time. The high-pitched sound of steel announced the blade's arrival in the silent air, sending a painful shiver through her shoulders and up the back of her neck. She could see Richard's chest beginning to heave.

Kahlan stole a glance at the Bird Man. He did not move, nor did he have any intention of moving. Richard did not know it, but under the law of the Mud People, these men were his to kill if he so wished. It was no false offer they had made. Savidlin had not been bluffing either; he would have killed them. In a blink. Strength, to the Mud People, meant the strength to kill your adversary. These men were already dead in the eyes of the village, and only Richard could give them back their lives.

Even so, their law was irrelevant; the Seeker was a law unto himself, answering ultimately to no one but himself. There was no one present who could stop this.

Richard's knuckles were white as he held the Sword of Truth level in both hands, over the heads of the five elders. Kahlan could see the rage building in him, the hot need, the fury. The whole scene felt like a dream, a dream she could only watch helplessly, one she couldn't stop.

Kahlan thought of all those she knew who had already died, both the innocent and those who had given their lives trying to stop Darken Rahl. Dennee, all the other Confessors, the wizards, Shar the night wisp, perhaps Zedd and Chase.

She understood.

Richard was not deciding if he should kill them, but if he dared let them live.

Could he trust these men with his chance of stopping Rahl, trust that they were sincere? Could Richard trust them with his life? Or should he have a new council of elders, ones who might be more intent on his success?

If he couldn't trust these men to send him in the right direction against Rahl, he would have to kill them and have ones he thought would be on his side. Stopping Rahl was all that mattered. The lives of these men must be forfeited if there was a chance they would jeopardize success. Kahlan knew that what Richard was doing was right. It was no less than she herself would do, no less than what the Seeker must do.

She watched him as he stood over the elders. The rain had stopped. Sweat ran from his face. She remembered the pain he suffered when he had killed the last man of the quad. She watched the anger building, hoping it would be enough to protect him from what he was about to do.

Kahlan understood why a Seeker was so feared. This was no game; he meant this. He was lost within himself, within the magic. If anyone were to try to stop him right now, he would kill them, too. If, that was, they got past her.

The blade of the sword came up in front of Richard's face. His head tilted back. His eyes closed. He shook with wrath. The five did not move as they knelt before the Seeker.

Kahlan remembered the man Richard had killed, remembered the way the sword had exploded through the man's head. The blood everywhere. Richard had killed him because of a direct threat. Kill or be killed, no matter that the threat was to her and not him.

But this was an indirect threat, a different kind of killing. Very different. This was an execution. And Richard was both judge and executioner.

The sword lowered again. Richard glowered at the elders, then made a fist and pulled the blade in a slow sweep across the inside of his left forearm. He turned the blade, wiping both sides in the blood, until it ran down, dripping off the tip.

Kahlan snatched a quick glance around. The Mud People stood transfixed, gripped by the mortal drama playing out before their eyes, not wanting to watch, yet unable to turn away. No one spoke. No one moved. No one even blinked.

Every eye followed as Richard brought the sword up again, touching it to his forehead.

"Blade, be true this day," he whispered.

His left hand glistened with blood. She could see him shaking with need. The sword flashed in places between the red. He looked down at the men.

"Look at me," he said to Caldus. The elder did not move. "Look at me while I do this!" he yelled. "Look into my eyes!" Still Caldus did not move.

"Richard," she said. His eyes came angrily to hers. Eyes looking at her from a different world. The magic danced in them. She kept her voice even, showed no emotion. "He cannot understand you."

"Then you tell him!"

"Caldus." He looked to her blank face. *"The Seeker wishes you to look into his eyes while he does this."*

He didn't answer, but simply looked at Richard, held by the Seeker's glare.

Richard inhaled sharply as the sword rose swiftly into the air. She watched the tip as it paused for only an instant. Some people turned away; others shielded their children's eyes. Kahlan held her breath and half turned to brace for an aftermath of fragments.

The Seeker screamed as he brought down the Sword of Truth. Its tip whistled through the air. The crowd gasped.

The sword stopped dead in the air, a scant inch from Caldus's face, just as it had stopped the first time Richard had used it, when Zedd had him try to cut down the tree.

For what seemed an eternity, Richard stood, unmoving, the muscles in his arms hard as steel; then at last they relaxed, and he withdrew the blade from over Caldus, withdrew his burning stare.

His eyes unmoving, he asked Kahlan, "How do you say 'I return your lives and your honor to you' in their language?"

She answered quietly.

"Caldus, Surin, Arbrin, Breginderin, Hajanlet," he announced loud enough for all to hear, *"I return your lives and your honor to you."*

There was a brief moment of silence; then the Mud People erupted in a wild cheer. Richard slid the sword back into its scabbard and then helped the elders to their feet. Pale, they gave him smiles, pleased with his action, and in no small measure relieved. They turned to the Bird Man.

"We make a unanimous demand of you, most honored elder. What have you to say?"

The Bird Man stood with his arms folded. He looked from the elders to Richard and Kahlan. His eyes showed the strain of the emotional ordeal he had just witnessed. Dropping his arms to his sides, he approached Richard. The Seeker looked drained, exhausted. The Bird Man put an arm around each of their shoulders as if to congratulate them on their courage, then put a hand on each of the elders' shoulders to let them know all was set straight. He turned and headed off, intending for them to follow. Kahlan and Richard walked behind him, Savidlin and the other elders followed behind, a royal escort.

"Richard," she said in a low voice, "did you expect the sword to stop?"

He looked ahead as he walked, letting out a deep breath. "No."

She had thought as much. She tried to imagine what this was

doing to him. Even if he hadn't executed the elders, he had committed to it, expected it. Though he didn't have to live with the deed, he still had to live with the intent.

She wondered if he had done the right thing, not killing them. She knew what she would have done in his place; she would not have allowed the option of clemency. Too much was at stake. But then, she had seen more than he had. Maybe she had seen too much, was too ready to kill. You couldn't kill every time there was a risk; risk was constant. It had to stop somewhere.

"How's the arm?" he asked, bringing her out of her thoughts.

"It throbs like mad," she admitted. "The Bird Man says it must be stitched together."

Richard looked deliberately ahead as he walked next to her. "I need my guide," he said quietly, without emotion. "You gave me a fright."

It was as close as he would come to a reprimand. Her face burned, and she was glad he wasn't looking at her to see it. He didn't know what it was she could do, but he knew she had hesitated. She had almost made a fatal mistake, had put them all at risk because she hadn't wanted him to see. He hadn't pressed her when he had the chance, the right, just as now, he put her feelings first. Her heart felt as if it would break.

The little group stepped onto the platform of the pole building. The elders stood in the back, the Bird Man between the two of them as they faced the crowd.

The Bird Man regarded her with an intense expression. *"Are you prepared to do this?"*

"What do you mean?" she asked, suspicious of his tone.

"I mean that if the two of you want to become Mud People, then you must do that which is required of Mud People: respect our laws. Our ways."

"I alone know what we are up against. I expect to die in the quest." She kept her tone deliberately hard. *"I have already escaped death more times than anyone has a right to. What we want is to save your people. We are sworn on our lives to do so. What more could be asked of us than our lives?"*

The Bird Man knew she was avoiding the question and didn't let her get away with it. *"This is not something I do lightly. I do it because I know you are true in your struggle, that you mean* to shield my people from the storm that comes. But I must have your help in this. You must agree to our ways. Not to please me, but out of respect for my people. They expect it."

Her mouth was so dry she could hardly swallow. *"I do not eat meat,"* she lied. *"You know that from when I have been here before."*

"Though you are a warrior, you are also a woman, therefore it may be excused. That much is within my power. Being a Confessor excludes you from the other." His eyes showed that this was as far as his compromise would go. *"Not the Seeker. He must do these things."*

"But . . ."

"You have said you will not choose him as your mate. If he will call a gathering, it must be as one of us."

Kahlan felt trapped. If she turned him down now, Richard would be furious, for good reason. They would lose to Rahl. Being from Westland, Richard was not used to the ways of the different peoples of the Midlands. He might not willingly go along. She couldn't take the chance. Much was at stake. The Bird Man's eyes waited.

"We will do what your law requires," she said, trying not to show what she really thought.

"Don't you wish to consult the Seeker on his feelings about these things?"

She looked away, over the heads of the waiting crowd. *"No."*

He took her chin in his hand and turned her face back to his. *"Then it will be your responsibility to see to it that he does as required. By your word."*

She could feel the heat of her anger rising. Richard leaned around the Bird Man.

"Kahlan, what's going on? What's wrong?"

Her eyes went from Richard back to the Bird Man, and she gave him a nod. "Nothing. It's all right."

The Bird Man released her chin and turned to his people, blowing the silent whistle he carried around his neck. He began talking to them of their history, their ways, why they avoided the influence of outsiders, how they had the right to be a proud people. As he talked, doves began coming in, landing among the people.

Kahlan listened without hearing, standing still on the platform, feeling like a trapped animal. When she had thought they could win over the Mud People, and have themselves named Mud People, she hadn't contemplated having to agree to these things. She had thought their initiation to be a mere formality, after which Richard could ask for a gathering. She hadn't given consideration to events going this way.

Maybe she could simply not tell him some of it. He wouldn't even know. After all, he didn't understand their language. She would just keep quiet. It was for the best.

But other things, she thought despondently, would be all too obvious. She could feel her ears turning red, could feel a knot in the pit of her stomach.

Richard sensed that the words of the Bird Man were not yet something he needed to understand and didn't ask for a translation. The Bird Man finished his introductory remarks, and arrived at the important part.

"When these two came to us, they were outsiders. By their actions, they have proved their caring for our people, proved their worth. From this day forward, let all know that Richard With The Temper and Confessor Kahlan are Mud People."

Kahlan translated, dropping her title, as the crowd cheered. Smiling, Richard held his hand up to the people, and they cheered all the more. Savidlin reached out and gave him a friendly slap on the back. The Bird Man put a hand on each of their shoulders, giving hers a sympathetic squeeze, trying to relieve the sting of the agreement he had forced upon her.

She took a deep breath, resigning herself to it. It would be over soon enough, and then they would be gone, on their way to stop Rahl. That was all that mattered. Besides, she, of all people, had no right to be upset about it.

"There is one more thing," The Bird Man went on. *"These two were not born Mud People. Kahlan was born a Confessor, a matter of blood, not choosing. Richard With The Temper was born in Westland, across the boundary, of ways that are a mystery to us. Both have agreed to be Mud People, to honor our laws and ways from this day on, but we must understand that our ways may be a mystery to them. We must have patience with them, understand that they are trying for the first time to be Mud*

People. We have lived our lives as Mud People, this is their first day. They are as new children to us. Give them the understanding you would give our children, and they will do their best."

The crowd buzzed with talk, heads nodding, all agreeing the Bird Man was wise. Kahlan let out a sigh; the Bird Man had given himself, and the two of them, a sliver of room if things went wrong. He was indeed wise. He gave her shoulder another squeeze, and she placed her hand over his, giving her own appreciative squeeze.

Richard didn't waste a second. He turned to the elders.

"I am honored to be one of the Mud People. Wherever I may travel, I will uphold the honor of our people, to make you proud of me. Right now, there is danger to our people. I need help so I might protect them. I request a council of seers. I request a gathering."

Kahlan translated, and each elder in turn nodded his agreement.

"*Granted,*" the Bird Man said. "*It will take three days to prepare for the gathering.*"

"Honored elder," Richard said, restraining himself, "the danger is great. I respect your ways, but is there any way it can be done faster? The lives of our people depend on this."

The Bird Man took a deep breath, his long silver hair reflecting the gloomy light. "*In this special circumstance, we will do our best to help you. Tonight we will hold the banquet, tomorrow night we will hold the gathering. This is as fast as it can be done. There are preparations that must be made for the elders to bridge the gap to the spirits.*"

Richard, too, took a deep breath. "Tomorrow night then."

The bird man blew the whistle again and the doves took to the air. Kahlan felt as if her hopes, impossible and foolish as they had been, took wing with them.

Preparations were quickly set underway, and Savidlin took Richard to his home, to care for his cuts and clean him up. The Bird Man took Kahlan to the healer, to have her wound treated.

370

Blood had completely soaked the bandage, and the cut hurt in earnest. He guided her through narrow passageways with his arm protectively around her shoulders. She was thankful he didn't speak of the banquet.

He left her in the care of a stooped woman named Nissel, instructing her to care for Kahlan as if she were his daughter. Nissel smiled little, mostly at the oddest times, and spoke little, other than instructions. Stand here, hold your arm up, put it down, breathe, don't breathe, drink this, lie here, recite the Candra. Kahlan didn't know what the Candra was. Nissel shrugged and instead had her balance flat stones atop one another on her stomach while the wound was inspected. When it hurt and the stones started slipping. Nissel admonished her to try harder to keep the stones balanced. She was given bitter-tasting leaves to chew while Nissel removed Kahlan's clothes and bathed her.

The bath did more for her than the leaves. She couldn't remember a bath feeling so good. She tried to let her depressing thoughts slough away with the mud. She tried very hard. While she was left to soak, Nissel washed her clothes and hung them by the fire, where a little pot of brown paste bubbled, smelling of pine pitch. Nissel dried her off, wrapped her in warm skins, and sat her on a bench built into the wall near the raised fire pit. The taste of the leaves seemed to get better the more she chewed them, but her head was beginning to spin.

"Nissel, what are the leaves for?"

Nissel turned from studying Kahlan's shirt, which she thought very curious. *"It will make you relax, so you will not feel what I do. Keep chewing. Do not worry, child. You will be so relaxed, you will not care when I stitch."*

Kahlan immediately spit out the leaves. The old woman looked at them on the floor, lifting an eyebrow to Kahlan.

"Nissel, I am a Confessor. If I am relaxed in a manner like that, I might not be able to hold back the power. When you touch me, I could release it without wanting to."

Nissel frowned with curiosity. *"But you sleep, child. You relax then."*

"That is different. I have slept from birth, before my power grew in me. If I were to be too relaxed or distracted in a way I

do not know, as with your leaves, I could touch you without intending it."

Nissel gave a crooked nod. Then her eyebrows came up. She leaned closer. *"Then how do you . . ."*

Kahlan gave a blank expression that said nothing and everything.

A look of sudden understanding came over Nissel's face. The healer straightened up. *"Oh. I see now."*

She stroked Kahlan's hair sympathetically, then went to the far corner and came shuffling back with a piece of leather. *"Put this between your teeth."* She patted Kahlan's good shoulder. *"If you are ever hurt again, be sure to have them bring you to Nissel. I will remember, and know what not to do. Sometimes, when you are a healer, it is more important to know what not to do. Maybe when you are a Confessor too. Hmm?"* Kahlan smiled and gave a nod. *"Now, child, make teeth marks in this leather for me."*

When she was finished, Nissel wiped the sweat from Kahlan's face with a cold, wet cloth. Kahlan was so dizzy and nauseated she couldn't even sit up. Nissel kept her lying down as she applied the brown paste and wrapped the arm with clean bandages.

"You should sleep for a while. I will wake you before the banquet."

Kahlan put her hand on the old woman's arm, and made herself smile. *"Thank you, Nissel."*

She woke to the feel of her hair being brushed. It had dried while she slept. Nissel smiled at her.

"You will find it hard to brush your pretty hair until your arm is better. Not many have the honor to have hair such as yours. I thought you would like it brushed for the banquet. It starts soon. A handsome young man waits for you outside."

Kahlan sat up. *"How long has he been out there?"*

"Almost the whole time. I tried to chase him away with a broom." Nissel frowned. *"But he would not go. He is very stubborn. Yes?"*

"Yes." Kahlan grinned.

Nissel helped her put on her clean clothes. Her arm didn't hurt as much as before. Richard was leaning impatiently against the outside wall and stood up straight when she came out. He was washed and clean and fresh-looking, the mud all gone, and was dressed in simple buckskin pants and tunic, and of course his sword. Nissel was right: he did look handsome.

"How are you doing? How's the arm? Are you all right?"

"I'm fine." She smiled. "Nissel has made me well."

Richard kissed the top of the old woman's head. "Thank you, Nissel. I forgive you the broom."

Nissel smiled at the translation, leaned closer, and gave him a deep look he found uncomfortable.

"Shall I give him a potion," Nissel asked, turning to her, *"to give him stamina?"*

"No," Kahlan said bristling. *"I am sure he will do just fine."*

CHAPTER 27

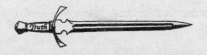

Laughter and the sound of drums drifted from the center of the village as Richard and Kahlan walked among the huddled, dark buildings. Black skies held back their rain, and the damp, warm air brought in the smell of the wet grasses that surrounded the village. Torches lit the platforms of the pole buildings, and large fires set about the open area snapped and popped, throwing off fluttering shadows. Kahlan knew it was a lot of work to haul in wood for cooking and kiln fires, and most were kept small. This was an extravagance the Mud People rarely witnessed.

Wonderful aromas from the cooking fires drifted to her through the night air, but failed to spark her appetite. Women dressed in their brightest dresses rushed around, with young girls at their sides, tending to errands, seeing to it that all went well. The men wore their finest skins, ceremonial knives hung at their waists, and their hair was slicked down with sticky mud in traditional fashion.

Cooking went on nonstop as people wandered by, sampling the fare, talking, sharing stories. Most people, it seemed, were either cooking or eating. There were children everywhere, playing and running and laughing, overflowing with excitement at the unexpected nighttime, firelit gathering.

Under grass roofs, musicians pounded drums and scraped paddles up and down ripples carved on boldas, long bell-shaped hollow tubes. The eerie strains, music meant to call ancestors' spirits to the banquet, carried far out into the grasslands. Other musicians sat on the opposite side of the open area, the sounds of the two groups sometimes joining, sometimes separating, calling to one another in haunting and occasionally frantic beats and knells. Men in costume, some dressed as animals, others painted as stylized hunters, jumped and danced, acting out stories of Mud People legends. Gleeful children surrounded the dancers, imitating them and stamping their feet in time with the drumming. Young couples off in darker areas watched the activities as they nuzzled close together. Kahlan had never felt so alone.

Savidlin, his freshly cleaned coyote hide around his shoulders, found her and Richard, and dragged them off, slapping Richard's back the whole way, to sit with the elders under their shelter. The Bird Man was dressed in his usual, plain buckskin pants and tunic. He was important enough not to have to wear anything more. Weselan was there, as were the wives of the other elders, and she came to sit next to Kahlan, taking her hand and asking with sincere concern how her arm was. Kahlan wasn't used to having people care about her. It felt good to be one of the Mud People, even if it was only pretense. Pretense, because she was a Confessor, and as much as she wished it otherwise right now, it was not, and no decree could make it so. She did as she had learned to do at a young age: she put her emotions away, and thought about the job that lay ahead, about Darken Rahl and how little time they had left. And she thought about Dennee.

Richard, resigned to the fact that they would have to wait another day for the gathering, tried to make the best of it, smiling and nodding at chattered advice he couldn't understand. People streamed past the elders' shelter in a steady procession, to greet the newest Mud People with gentle slaps. In all fairness, Kahlan had to admit that they paid as much regard to her as to Richard.

Woven trays and pottery bowls filled with various foods lay on the floor in front of where they sat cross-legged, greeting people, some of whom sat with them for a time. Richard sampled most of the food, remembering to use his right hand. Kahlan nibbled on a piece of tava bread so as not to appear impolite.

"This is good," Richard said, taking another rib. "I think it's pork."

"It is wild boar," she said, watching the dancers.

"And the venison, it's good too. Here, have a piece." He tried to hand her a strip.

"No. Thank you."

"You all right?"

"Fine. I'm just not hungry."

"You haven't eaten any meat since we've been with the Mud People."

"I'm just not hungry, that's all."

He shrugged and ate the venison.

After a time, the crowd of people greeting them thinned out, finally going off to other activities. From the corner of her eye, she saw the Bird Man raise his hand in a signal to someone in the distance. Kahlan put a brake to her feelings, and made her face betray nothing of the effort, as her mother had taught her: a Confessor's face.

Four young women, all with shy smiles and short hair slicked down with mud, timidly approached. Richard greeted them with smiles and nods and gentle slaps, as he had the other people. They stood, pushing against each other, giggling, whispering how fine he was to look upon. Kahlan glanced back at the Bird Man. He gave her a single nod.

"Why aren't they leaving?" Richard asked out of the side of his mouth. "What do they want?"

"They are for you," she said in an even voice.

The flickering firelight lit his face as he looked blankly at the four women. "For me. And what am I to do with them?"

Kahlan took a deep breath as she looked at the fires for a moment. "I am only your guide, Richard. If you need instruction in this, you will have to seek it elsewhere."

There was a moment of silence.

"All four? For me?"

She turned back to him and saw a mischievous grin spreading on his face. She found his smile irritating.

"No, you are to pick one."

"Pick one?" he repeated, the stupid grin still on his face.

She consoled herself with the fact that at least he wasn't going to cause trouble over this part. He looked from one girl to another.

"Pick one. Now that will be hard. How long do I have to decide?"

She looked off at the fire again and closed her eyes for a moment, then turned to the Bird Man. *"The Seeker wishes to know when he must decide which woman to pick."*

The Bird Man looked a little surprised by the question. *"Before he goes to his bed. Then he must pick one, and give our people his child. In that way he will be joined to us by blood."*

She told him what the Bird Man said.

Richard considered carefully what he was told. "Very wise." He looked back at the Bird Man and smiled and nodded. "The Bird Man is very wise."

"The Seeker says you are very wise," she said to him, trying to control her voice.

The Bird Man and the other elders seemed pleased. Events were going as they wished.

"Well, this will be a difficult decision. I'll have to think about it. It's not something I want to rush into."

Kahlan pushed some of her hair back and turned to the girls. *"The Seeker is having difficulty deciding."*

He gave the four a big grin and eagerly motioned them up on the platform. Two sat to the far side of him, the other two squeezed between Kahlan and Richard, forcing her to move over as they sat down. They leaned against him, putting their hands on his arms, and felt his muscles as they giggled. They commented to Kahlan about how big he was, like her, and how he would make big children. They wanted to know if he thought they were pretty. Kahlan said she didn't know. They begged her to ask him.

She took another deep breath. "They want to know if you think they are pretty."

"Of course! They're beautiful! All of them. That's why I can't decide. Don't you think they're beautiful?"

She didn't answer his question, instead assuring the four that the Seeker found them appealing. They gave their typical shy laughs. The Bird Man and the elders seemed pleased. They were still all smiles; they were in control of events. She stared numbly at the celebration, watched the dancers without seeing them.

The four girls fed Richard with their fingers and giggled. He told Kahlan it was the best banquet he had ever been to, and asked if she didn't think so, too. She swallowed the lump in her throat and agreed it was wonderful as she looked away blankly, at the fiery sparks swirling up into the blackness.

After what seemed like hours, an older woman with her head bowed approached carrying a large round woven tray in front of her. It was neatly arranged with dark strips of dried meat.

Kahlan snapped out of her distant thoughts.

With her head still bowed, the woman respectfully approached the elders, silently offering each the tray. The Bird Man took some first, pulling off a piece with his teeth as each of the other elders took a strip. A few of the wives took some as well. Weselan, sitting beside her husband, declined.

The woman held the tray in front of Kahlan. She politely declined. The woman held the tray out to Richard. He took a strip. The four young women shook their bowed heads, declining, then watched Richard. Kahlan waited until he took a bite, met the Bird Man's eyes briefly, then turned once more to watch the fires.

"You know, I'm having a hard time deciding which one of these fine young women to pick," Richard said after he swallowed the first bite. "Do you think you could help me, Kahlan? Which one should I choose? What do you think?"

Struggling to slow her breathing, she looked over at his grinning face. "You are right, it is a difficult choice. I think I would rather leave it to you."

He ate some more meat as she clenched her teeth and swallowed hard.

"This is kind of strange, I've never had anything like it before." He paused, his voice changed. "What is it?" The question had an edge to it that frightened her, almost made her jump. He had a threatening, hard look in his eyes. She hadn't intended to tell him, but the way he looked at her made her forget that pledge.

She asked the Bird Man, then turned back to him. "He says it is a firefighter."

"A firefighter." Richard leaned forward. "What kind of animal is a firefighter?" Kahlan looked into his piercing gray eyes. In a soft voice she answered, "One of Darken Rahl's men."

"I see." He leaned back.

He knew. She realized he had known before he asked her the question. He wanted to see if she would lie to him.

"Who are these firefighters?"

She asked the elders how they had come to know about the firefighters. Savidlin was only too eager to tell the story. When he finished, she turned back to Richard.

"Firefighters are enforcers who travel the country to bring Rahl's decree that people are not allowed to use fire. They can be quite brutal in their task. Savidlin says two of them came here a few weeks back, told them fire was outlawed, and then threatened them when the Mud People wouldn't agree to follow the new law. They feared the two would go back and bring more men. So they killed them. The Mud People believe they can gain their enemies' wisdom by eating them. To be a man among the Mud People, to be one of them, you must eat it also, so you will have the knowledge of their enemies. It is the main purpose of banquets. That, and to call the ancestors' spirits."

"And have I eaten enough of it to satisfy the elders?" The expression in his eyes cut through her.

She wished she could run away. "Yes."

With deliberate care, Richard laid down the piece of flesh. The smile returned to his lips, and he looked to the four young women as he spoke to her, wrapping his arms around the two closest to him.

"Kahlan, do me a favor. Go and get me an apple out of my pack. I feel like I need something familiar to clear this taste out of my mouth."

"Your legs work," she snapped.

"Yes, but I need to devote some time to deciding which one of these beautiful young women I will lie with."

Rising to her feet, she shot the Bird Man a furious glare, and then stormed off toward Savidlin's house. She was glad to be away from Richard, to be away from watching those girls pawing him.

Her fingernails dug into her palms, but she didn't notice as she marched past the happy people. The dancers danced, the drummers drummed, the children laughed. People she passed wished her well. She wanted one of them to say something mean so she would have an excuse to hit someone.

When she reached Savidlin's house, she went inside and flopped down on the skin that covered the floor, trying unsuccessfully to keep from crying. Just a few minutes, she told herself, that was all she needed to bring herself back under control. Richard was doing what the Mud People demanded, what she herself had promised the Bird Man he would do. She had no right to be angry, none at all; Richard was not hers. She cried with deep pain. She had no right to feel this way, no right to be angry with him. But she was; she was furious.

She remembered what she had told the Bird Man—trouble of her own making, with consequences she must bear, and feared greatly.

Richard was just doing what was necessary to get a gathering, what was necessary to find the box and stop Rahl. Kahlan wiped the tears from her eyes.

But he didn't have to be so delighted about it. He could do it without acting like . . .

She snatched an apple from his pack. What did it matter. She couldn't change the way things were. But she didn't have to be happy about it. She bit her lip as she stomped out the door, trying to make her face once again show nothing. At least it was dark.

When she had crossed the gauntlet of celebration, she found Richard with his shirt off. The girls were painting him with Mud People symbols of the hunter. Their fingers were applying the black and white mud in jagged lines across his chest, in rings around his upper arms. They stopped when she stood over them, glaring down.

"Here." She slapped the apple in his hand and sat down in a huff.

"I still haven't been able to decide," he said, polishing the apple on his pants leg, looking from one girl to another. "Kahlan,

380

are you sure you don't have a preference? I could use your help." His voice lowered meaningfully, the hard edge returning. "I'm surprised you didn't just pick one for me in the first place."

Stunned, her eyes came up to his. He knew. He knew this, too, was a commitment she had made on his behalf. "No. Whatever you decide will be fine, I'm sure." She looked away again.

"Kahlan," he asked, waiting until she turned back to him, "are any of these girls related to the elders?"

She looked again at their faces. "The one at your right arm. The Bird Man is her uncle.

"Uncle!" His smile widened as he continued to polish the apple on his leg. "Well, then, I guess I'll pick her. It will be a sign of respect for the elders, that I pick the Bird Man's niece."

He took the girl's head in both of his hands, kissing her on the forehead. She beamed. The Bird Man beamed. The elders beamed. The other girls left.

Kahlan glanced back at the Bird Man, and he gave her a look of sympathy, a look that said he was sorry. She turned, staring absently, painfully, out into the night. So now Richard had picked. So now, she though bleakly, the elders would perform a ceremony and the happy couple would be going off somewhere to make a baby. She watched the other couples walking, hand in hand, happy to be together. Kahlan swallowed back the lump, the tears. She heard the snap as Richard bit into his stupid, stupid apple.

And then she heard a collective gasp from the elders and their wives, then shouts.

The apple! In the Midlands, red fruit was poison! They didn't know what an apple was! They thought Richard was eating poison! She spun around.

Richard was holding his arm back to the elders, commanding silence, and for them to stay put. But he was looking right into her eyes.

"Tell them to sit down," he said in a quiet voice.

Wide-eyed, she looked back at the elders and told them what Richard had said. They lowered themselves uncertainly back in place. He leaned back, turning casually to them, an innocent expression on his face.

"You know, back in Hartland, in Westland, where I am from,

we eat these things all the time." He took a couple more bites. Their eyes were wide. "Have for as long as anyone knows. Men and women both eat them. We have healthy children." He snapped off another piece, turning and watching her as she translated. He chewed slowly, prolonging the tension. He looked over his shoulder at the Bird Man. " 'Course, it could be that it makes a man's seed poison to any woman other than one of our own. Never been put to the test, far as I know."

He let his gaze settle back on Kahlan as he took another bite, letting his words sink in after she translated. The girl next to him was getting nervous. The elders were getting nervous. The Bird Man showed no emotion. Richard had his arms half folded, one elbow resting in his other hand, so he could hold the apple near his mouth, where everyone could see it. He started to take a bite, then stopped, thinking to offer a bite to the Bird Man's niece. She turned her head away. He looked back at the elders.

"I find them quite good. Really." He shrugged. "But then, there is the thing about them maybe making my seed poison. But I don't want you to think I'm not willing to try. I just thought you should know, that's all. I wouldn't want it to be said I wasn't willing to go along with the duties that go with becoming a Mud Person. I am. More than willing." He ran the back of his finger down the girl's cheek. "I assure you, it would be an honor. This fine young woman will make a splendid mother for my child, I am sure." Richard let out a sigh. "If she lives, of course." He took another bite.

The elders looked apprehensively from one to another. None spoke. The mood on the platform had definitely changed. They were no longer in control; Richard was. It had happened in a blink. They were now afraid to move much more than their eyes. Without looking at them, Richard went on.

" 'Course, it's up to you. I'm willing to give it a try, but I thought you should know of the ways of my homeland. I didn't think it would be fair not to tell you." Now Richard turned to them, his eyebrows set in a menacing frown, his voice carrying a thread of threat. "So, if the elders, in their wisdom, wish to ask me not to perform this duty, I will understand, and with regret, comply with their wishes."

He held them in his hard gaze. Savidlin grinned. The other

five were of no mind to challenge Richard, and turned to the Bird Man beseeching direction. He sat still, a bead of sweat rolling down the leathery skin of his neck, silver hair limp on the buckskin shoulders of his tunic, holding Richard's eyes for a short time. His mouth turned up in a small smile that showed in his eyes, too, and he nodded slightly to himself.

"Richard With The Temper," his voice was even, and strong, for not only the elders, but also the crowd that had gathered around the platform, were listening, *"since you are from a different land, and your seed could be poisonous to this young woman ..."* he lifted one eyebrow, leaning the slightest bit forward, *" ... my niece,"* he looked to her, then back to Richard, *"we beg that you not hold us to this tradition; that you not take her as your wife. I am sorry to have to ask this of you. I know you were looking forward to giving us your child."*

Richard nodded seriously. "Yes, I was. But I will just have to live with my failing, and try to make the Mud People, my people, proud of me in other ways." He was closing the deal with a condition of his own: they were not going to be allowed to back out now; he was, a Mud Person and this would not change it.

There was a collective sigh of relief from the other elders. They all nodded, only too happy to have the matter settled to his liking. The young woman smiled with relief at her uncle and left. Richard turned to Kahlan; his face showed no emotion.

"Are there any other conditions that I don't know about?"

"No." Kahlan felt confused. She didn't know if she felt happy because Richard had gotten out of taking a wife, or if she was heartbroken because he felt she had betrayed him.

He turned to the elders. "Is my presence required any longer tonight?"

The five were delighted to grant him his wish to leave. Savidlin seemed a little disappointed. The Bird Man said that the Seeker had been a great savior of his people, had performed his duties with honor, and that if he was tired from the struggles of the day, he could be excused.

Richard stood slowly, towering over her. His boots were right in front of her. Kahlan knew he was looking down at her, but she fixed her eyes on the floor.

"Piece of advice," he said in a voice that surprised her with its gentleness, "since you have never had a friend before. Friends don't bargain away another friend's rights. Or their hearts."

She couldn't bring herself to look up at him.

He dropped the apple core in her lap and walked off, disappearing in the crowd.

Kahlan sat on the elders' platform, in a fog of loneliness, watching her fingers shake. The others watched the dancers. With supreme effort she counted the drumbeats and used the count to help her control her breathing and keep from crying. The Bird Man came and sat next to her. She found herself cheered by the company.

He raised an eyebrow to her, leaning closer. *"Someday, I would like to meet the wizard who named that one. I would like to know where he finds such Seekers."*

Kahlan was surprised she could still laugh.

"Someday," she said, smiling at him, *"if I live, and we win, I promise I will bring him here, to meet you. In many ways, he is as remarkable as Richard."*

He lifted an eyebrow. *"I shall hone my wits to defend myself in the encounter."*

She leaned her head against him and laughed until she started to cry. He put his arm protectively around her shoulders.

"I should have listened to you," she sobbed. *"I should have asked him his wishes. I had no right to do as I did."*

"Your desire to stop Darken Rahl made you do what you thought necessary. Sometimes, making the wrong choice is better than making no choice. You have the courage to go forward, that is rare. A person who stands at the fork, unable to pick, will never get anywhere."

"But it hurts so much to have him angry at me," she cried.

"I will tell you a secret you might not otherwise learn until you are too old to benefit from the knowledge." Wet eyes looked up at his smile. *"It hurts him just as much to be angry at you, as it hurts you when he is that angry."*

"Really?"

He laughed silently and nodded. *"Take it on faith, child."*

"I had no right, I should have seen that before. I am so sorry I did it."

"Don't tell me. Tell him."

She pushed away, looking at his weathered face. *"I think I will. Thank you, honored elder."*

"And while you are offering apologies, offer mine also."

Kahlan frowned. *"For what?"*

He sighed. *"Being old, being an elder, does not exclude you from holding foolish ideas. Today, I too made a mistake, for Richard, and for my niece. I, too, had no right. Thank him for me, for keeping me from imposing deeds I should have questioned, but did not."* He took his whistle from around his neck. *"Give him this gift, with my thanks, for opening my eyes. May it serve him well. Tomorrow, I will show him how to use it."*

"But, you need it to call the birds."

He smiled. *"I have others. Go now."*

Kahlan took the whistle, clutching it tightly in her hand. She wiped the tears from her face. *"In my whole life, I've hardly ever cried. Since the boundary to D'Hara came down, it seems as if that's all I do."*

"We all do, child. Go."

She kissed his cheek quickly and left. Searching the open areas, she found no sign of Richard. People she asked hadn't seen him. She walked around in circles, looking. Where was he? Children tried to draw her into their dancing, people offered her food, others wanted to talk to her. She politely turned them all down.

At last she went off to Savidlin's home, deciding that that was where he would be. But the house was empty. She sat down on the floor skin, thinking. Would he leave without her? Her heart panicked. Her eyes searched around the floor. No. His pack was still there, where she had left it when she had gotten him the apple. Besides, he wouldn't leave before the gathering.

Then it came to her. She knew where he was. She smiled to herself, took an apple out of his pack, and headed through the dark walkways between the buildings of the Mud People's village, headed for the spirit house.

Light flared suddenly in the darkness, lighting the walls

around her. At first, she didn't realized what it was; then, looking out between the buildings, she saw lightning. Lightning at the horizon, in every direction, all around, lacing its angry fingers into the sky, into the dark clouds, lighting them from inside with boiling colors. There was no thunder. And then it was gone, leaving darkness once more.

Was there no end to this weather, she wondered. Would she ever again see stars, or the sun? Wizards and their clouds, she thought, shaking her head. She wondered if she would ever see Zedd again. At least the clouds protected Richard from Darken Rahl.

The spirit house sat in the dark, away from the sound and activity of the banquet. Cautiously, Kahlan pulled back the door. Richard sat on the floor in front of the fire, his sword, in its scabbard, lay at his side. He didn't turn at the sound.

"Your guide wishes to speak with you," she said meekly.

The door squeaked closed behind her as she kneeled down, sitting back on her heels next to him, her heart pounding.

"And what does my guide wish to tell me?" He smiled, she thought in spite of himself.

"That she made a mistake," she said softly, picking at a string on her pants. "And that she is sorry. Very, very sorry. Not just for what she did, but mostly for not trusting you."

The insides of his elbows were hooked around his knees, one hand holding the other. He turned to face her, the warm, red glow of firelight reflecting in his gentle eyes.

"I had a whole speech rehearsed in my mind. But now I can't remember a word of it. You have that effect on me." He smiled again. "Apology accepted."

Relief swept through her. She felt as if her heart were mending. From under her eyebrows, she looked up at him. "Was it a good speech?"

His grin widened. "It seemed so at the time, but now I don't think so."

"You are pretty good at speeches. You nearly scared the wits out of the elders, including the Bird Man." Reaching out, she placed the whistle over his head, around his neck.

Unclasping his hands, he touched it with his fingers. "What's this for?"

"It is a gift from the Bird Man, with his apology for what he tried to make you do. He said he, too, had no right, and wishes to thank you, with this gift, for opening his heart's eyes. Tomorrow he will teach you to use it." Kahlan turned to sit with her back to the fire, facing him, close against him. It was a warm night, and with the heat of the fire, Richard glistened with sweat. The symbols painted across his chest and around his upper arms gave him a wild, savage appearance. "You have a way of opening people's eyes," she said in a coy voice. "I think you must have used magic."

"Maybe I did. Zedd says that sometimes a trick is the best magic."

The sound of his voice resonated with something deep inside her, made her feel weak. "And Adie said you have the magic of the tongue," she whispered.

The look in his gray eyes penetrated her, impaling her with its power, making her breathing quicken. Haunting sounds of the boldas carried in from the distance, mingling with the sound of the fire, of his breathing. She had never felt this safe, this relaxed, and this tense, all at the same time. It was confusing.

Her gaze wandered from his eyes, feasting on other places on his face: the shape of his nose, the angle of his cheeks, the line of his chin. Her eyes stopped on his lips. Suddenly she was aware of how hot it was in the spirit house. She felt lightheaded.

Probing his gaze again, she withdrew the apple from her pocket and took a slow, juicy bite, dragging her teeth across the meat. The iron look in his eyes never wavered. Fluidly, impulsively, she put the apple to his mouth and held it there as he took a big, wet bite. If only it were possible for him to put his lips on her like that, she thought.

And why not? Was she to die in this quest without being allowed to be a woman? Must she be only a warrior? Fight for everyone's happiness but her own? Seekers, in the best of times, died all too quickly, and these were not the best of times.

These were the end of times.

She ached at the thought of him dying.

She pushed the apple harder against his teeth as she watched his eyes. Even if she took him, she reasoned, he could still fight on, at her side, maybe with even more resolve than he had now.

387

It would be for different reasons, but he would be just as deadly, maybe more so. He would be different, though, not the same person he was now. That person would be gone forever. That person would be hers. She wanted him so desperately, in a way she had never wanted anything before, a way that was painful. Were they both to die without being allowed to live? She felt a tingling weakness with the need of him.

Teasingly, she took the apple from his mouth. Juice ran down his chin. Slowly, deliberately, she leaned over and licked the sweet juice from his chin. He didn't move. Their faces were inches apart; she shared his breath, quick and warm. So close was she that her eyes could scarcely focus on his. She had to swallow the wetness in her mouth.

Reason was rapidly evaporating from her mind, being replaced with feelings that tantalized her with promise, gripped her with hot need.

She released the apple, brought her wet fingers to his lips, and watched, her own tongue on her upper lip, as he let each finger slide into his mouth, slowly sucking the juice from them one at a time as she offered them. The feeling of the inside of his mouth, wet and warm, sent shivers through her.

A small sound escaped her lips. Her heart pounded in her ears. Her chest heaved. She ran her wet fingers down his chin, his neck, to his chest, lightly gliding them over the symbols painted on him, tracing them with her fingers, feeling the hills and valleys of him.

Coming to her knees above him, she circled a fingertip around the hardness of one of his nipples, firmly caressed his chest as she let her eyes slide closed for a moment while gritting her teeth. Gently, but forcefully, she pushed him down on his back. He went easily, without protest. She leaned over him with her hand still on his chest for support. The feeling of him surprised her, the rigid hardness of his muscles, sheathed with yielding, velvety soft skin, the wetness of his sweat, the coarseness of his hairs, the heat. His chest rose and fell with his heavy breathing, with the life in him.

Leaving one knee next to his hip, she put the other between his legs as she looked down into his eyes, her thick hair cascading down around his face as she continued to support herself with the hand on his chest, not wanting to move it, to lose the connection with his moist flesh. A connection that was igniting her with its heat.

Between her knees, the muscles of his thigh flexed, sending her pulse racing even faster. She had to open her mouth to get her breath. She lost herself in his eyes, eyes that felt as if they were probing her soul, stripping it bare. They sent fire raging through her.

With her other hand she smoothly unbuttoned her shirt and pulled out the tails.

She put her hand behind his strong neck, still holding herself up, away from him, with the other on his chest. Her fingers slid into his damp hair, tightened into a fist, held his head to the ground.

A big, powerful hand slipped under her shirt, to the small of her back, stroking in little circles, then slowly slid up the line of her spine, sending shivers through her, before coming to a stop between her shoulder blades. Her eyes half closed as she flexed her back against his hand, wanting him to draw her against him. Her breathing was so fast, she was almost panting.

She drew her knee up his leg until it wouldn't go any father. Little sounds escaped with some of her breaths. His chest heaved against her hand. As he lay under her, she thought he had never seemed so big to her before.

"I want you," she panted in a breathless whisper.

Her head lowered. Her lips brushed against his.

A look of pain seemed to cross his eyes. "Only if you first tell me what you are."

The words cut through her, bringing her eyes open wide. Her head moved back a little. But she was touching him; he could not stop her, she thought, she didn't want him to stop her. She barely had a grasp on the power as it was, and it was slipping from her hold. She could feel it. She brought her lips back to his, another small sound escaping with her breath.

The hand on her back moved up under her shirt, took a fistful of her hair, gently pulling her head away.

"Kahlan, I mean it. Only if you tell me first."

Reason flooded back into her mind, washing coldly through her, drowning her passion. She had never cared for anyone like this. How could she touch him with her power? How could she do this to him? She pushed back. What was she doing? What was she thinking?

She sat back on her heels, taking her hand from his chest, putting it over her mouth. The world crashed in around her. How could she tell him? He would hate her; she would lose him. Her head spun sickeningly.

Richard sat up, put his hand gently on her shoulder. "Kahlan," he said softly, drawing her panicked eyes to his, "you don't have to tell me if you don't want to. Only if you want to do this."

Her eyebrows wrinkled together as she tried to keep from crying. "Please." She could hardly get the words out. "Just hold me?"

He drew her tenderly to him, held her head to his shoulder. Pain, pain of who she was, reached its icy fingers back into her. His other arm wrapped protectively around her, holding her tight against him as he rocked her.

"That's what friends are for," he whispered in her ear.

She was too drained even to cry.

"I promise, Richard, I will tell you. But not tonight? Tonight, just hold me. Please?"

He slowly lay back down, embracing her tightly against him with his strong arms as she bit one of her knuckles and clutched him with her other hand.

"When you want to. Not before," he promised.

The horror of what she was wrapped her in its cold embrace, too. She shook with the chill of it. Her eyes refused to close for a long time, until at last she went to sleep, her last thoughts of him.

CHAPTER 28

"Try once more," the Bird Man said. *"And stop thinking of the bird you want"*—he tapped Richard's head with his knuckles—*"from here."* He jabbed a finger in Richard's abdomen. *"Think of it here!"*

Richard nodded at Kahlan's translation and put the whistle to his lips. His cheeks puffed out as he blew. As usual, there was no sound. The Bird Man, Richard, and Kahlan looked around the flat country. The hunters who had escorted them out onto the plain, their heads swiveling nervously, leaned against spears planted point up in the grassy ground.

Seemingly from nowhere, starlings, sparrows, and small field birds, thousands of them, descended, diving and swooping, on the small company. The hunters ducked, laughing, as they had all day. The air was filled with small birds flying wildly about in a frenzy. The sky was black with them. The hunters fell to the ground, covering their heads, laughing hysterically. Richard rolled his eyes. Kahlan turned her face from him as she laughed. The Bird Man frantically put his own whistle to his lips and blew over and over again, his silver hair flying, trying desperately to send the birds back. At last they heeded his calls and vanished once more. Quiet returned to the grassland except, of course, for the hunters, who still rolled on the ground in laughter.

The Bird Man took a deep breath and put his hands on his hips. *"I give up. We have been trying all day, and it is the same now as when we started. Richard With The Temper,"* he announced. *"you are the worst bird caller I have ever seen. A child could learn it in three tries, but there is not enough breath in you for the rest of your life to learn. It is hopeless. The only thing your whistle says is, 'Come, there is food here.'"*

"But I was thinking 'hawk,' I really was. Every kind of bird you named, I thought it hard as I could, honest."

When Kahlan translated, the hunters laughed all the more. Richard scowled over at them, but they kept laughing. The Bird Man folded his arms with a sigh.

"It is no use. The day ends, the gathering will be soon." He put his arm around the shoulders of a frustrated Seeker. *"Keep the gift of the whistle anyway. Though it will never aid you, let it serve as a reminder that while you may be better at some things than most people, in this, even a child is better than you."*

The hunters roared. Richard sighed and gave the Bird Man a nod. Everyone collected their things and headed back to the village.

Richard leaned toward her. "I was trying my best. Really. I don't understand it."

She grinned, taking his hand in hers. "I am sure you were."

Though the light was fading, the cloudy day had been the brightest in longer than she could remember, and it had helped to lift her spirits. Mostly, though, what helped her was the way Richard had treated her. He had let her have time to recover from last night without asking her anything. He had just held her, let her be.

Even though nothing more had happened, she felt closer to him than she ever had, but at the same time, she knew that was not a good thing. It only deepened her dilemma. She had almost made a very big mistake last night. The biggest mistake of her life. She was relieved that he had pulled her back from the brink. At the same time, part of her wished he hadn't.

When she woke this morning, she didn't know how he would

feel about her, if he would be hurt, angry, or hate her. Even though she lay bare-chested against him all night, she turned her back to him in embarrassment while she buttoned her shirt. As her fingers slipped the buttons back in place, she told him that no one had ever had a friend as patient as the one she had. She said she only hoped that someday she could prove to be as good a friend as he was.

"You already have. You have placed your trust, your life, in my hands. You have pledged your life in defense of me. What more proof could I have?"

She turned, and resisting mightily the urge to kiss him, thanked him for putting up with her.

"I will have to admit, though," he said, smiling, "that I will never look at an apple in quite the same way."

That made her laugh, partly in embarrassment, and they both laughed together a long time. Somehow, it made her feel better, and took away what could have been a thorn.

Suddenly Richard stopped in his tracks. She stopped, too, as the others walked on.

"Richard, what is it?"

"The sun." He looked pale. "For a moment, a shaft of sunlight was on my face."

She turned to the west. "All I see are clouds."

"It was there, a small opening, but I don't see it either, now."

"Do you think it means something?"

He shook his head. "I don't know. But it's the first time I've seen even the slightest break in the clouds since Zedd put them there. Maybe it's nothing."

They started walking again, the eerie sounds of the boldas carrying to them across the windswept, flat grasslands. By the time they reached the village, it was dark. The banquet was still going on, as it had all last night, as it would tonight, until the gathering was over. Everyone was still going strong, except the children; many of whom walked around in a sleepy stupor or slept contentedly in corners here and there.

The six elders were on their platform, their wives gone. They were eating a meal being served by special women; cooks who were the only ones allowed to prepare the gathering feast. Kahlan watched them pour a drink for each of the elders. It was red, different from any other drink at the banquet. The eyes of the six were glazed, far off, as if they were seeing things others didn't. Kahlan felt a chill.

Their ancestors' spirits were with them.

The Bird Man spoke to them. When he seemed satisfied by whatever it was they told him, he nodded and the six rose, walking in a line toward the spirit house. The sound of the drums and the boldas changed in a way that ran bumps up her arms. The Bird Man strode back to them, his eyes as sharp and intense as ever.

"It is time," he told her. "Richard and I must go now."

"What do you mean, 'Richard and I'? I'm going too."

"You cannot."

"Why?"

"Because a gathering is only men."

"I am the Seeker's guide, I must be there to translate."

The Bird Man's eyes shifted about in an uncomfortable manner. "But a gathering is only men," he repeated, seemingly unable to come up with a better reason.

She folded her arms. "Well, this one will have a woman."

Richard looked from her face to the Bird Man's and back again, knowing by the tone of her voice that something was going on, but deciding not to interfere. The Bird Man leaned a little closer to her and lowered his voice.

"When we meet the spirits, it must be as they are."

Her eyes narrowed. "Are you trying to tell me that you can't wear clothes?"

He took a deep breath and nodded. "And you must be painted with mud."

"Fine," she said, holding her head up. "I have no objections."

He leaned back a little. "Well, what about the Seeker? Maybe you would like to ask him what he feels about you doing this."

She held his eyes for a long time, then turned to Richard. "I need to explain something to you. When a person calls a gathering, they are sometimes asked questions by the spirits, through the elders, to be sure they are acting of noble intent. If you answer a question in a way that a spirit ancestor finds dishonorable or untruthful . . . they may kill you. Not the elders, the spirits."

"I have the sword," he reminded her.

"No, you won't. If you want a gathering, you must do as the elders do, face the spirits with nothing but yourself. You can wear no sword, no clothes, and you must have mud painted on you." She took a breath, pushed some hair back over her shoulder. "If I am not there to translate, you may get killed simply because you cannot answer a question you don't understand. Then Rahl wins. I must be there to interpret. But if I'm there, I, too, can wear no clothes. The Bird Man is in a fret, and wishes to know what you think of this. He is hoping you will forbid me from doing this."

Richard folded his arms, looking her in the eye. "I think you are bound and determined, one way or another, to have your clothes off in the spirit house."

The corners of his mouth turned up, and his eyes sparkled. Kahlan had to bite her lower lip to keep from laughing. The Bird Man looked from one to the other, confused.

"Richard!" She spoke his name in a rising tone of caution. "This is serious. And don't get your hopes up. It will be dark." Still, she could hardly keep from laughing.

Richard's face regained its seriousness as he turned to the Bird Man. "I called the gathering. I need Kahlan there."

She could almost see him flinch at the translation. *"You two have been stretching my limits from the moment you arrived."* He gave a loud sigh. *"Why should it change now? Let's go."*

Kahlan and Richard walked side by side, following the Bird Man's silhouette as he led them off through the dark passageways of the village, turning to the right several times, then the other way. Richard's hand found hers. Kahlan was a lot more nervous about this than she let on, about sitting naked with eight naked men. But she was not about to let Richard go into the gathering without her. This was no time to let it all slip away from them: they had worked too hard; time was too short.

She put on her Confessor's face.

Before they reached the spirit house, the Bird Man took them through a narrow doorway, into a small room in a building nearby. The other elders were there, sitting cross-legged on the floor, staring blankly ahead. She smiled at Savidlin, but he didn't respond. The Bird Man picked up a small bench and two clay pots.

"When I call your name, come out. Wait until then."

As the Bird Man took his bench and pots with him, squeezing sideways out the door, Kahlan told Richard what he had said. In a while he called Caldus's name, and after a time, each of the other elders in turn, Savidlin last. Savidlin did not speak to them or even acknowledge that he knew they were there. The spirits were in his eyes.

Kahlan and Richard sat in silence in the empty, dark room, waiting. She picked at the heel of her boot, trying not to think about what it was she had committed herself to, yet unable to think of anything else.

Richard would be unarmed, without his sword, his protection. But she would not be without her power. She would be his protection. Though she had not spoken it, that was the other reason she had to be in there. If anything went wrong, it was going to be she who died, not him, that much she knew. She would see to it. She steeled herself, went into herself. She heard the Bird Man call out Richard's name. He rose to his feet.

"Let's hope this works. If it doesn't, we're in a lot of trouble. I'm glad I'll have you there." It was a warning, to stay alert.

She nodded. "Just remember, Richard, these are our people now, we belong. They want to help us; they will be doing their best."

Kahlan sat hugging her knees, waiting, until her name was called, then went out into the cool, dark night. The Bird Man sat against the wall of the spirit house, on the little bench. She could see in the dark that he was naked, symbols painted in jagged lines, stripes and whorls all over his body, his silver hair down around his bare shoulders. Chickens roosted on a short wall nearby, watching. A hunter stood near the Bird Man. Coyote hides, clothes, and Richard's sword lay at his feet.

"Remove your clothes," the Bird Man said.

"What is this?" she asked, pointing at the hunter.

"He is here to take the clothes. They are taken to the elders' platform, for the people to see that we are in a gathering. Before dawn, he will return them, to let the people know that the gathering is at an end."

"Well, tell him to turn around."

The Bird Man gave the order. The hunter turned around. She

gripped the tongue of her belt, yanked it free from the catch. She paused, looking down at the Bird Man.

"*Child,*" he said softly, "*tonight you are neither man nor woman. You are a Mud Person. Tonight, I am neither man nor woman. I am a spirit guide.*"

She nodded, removed her clothes, and stood before him, the cold night air on her naked flesh. He scooped a handful of white mud from one of the pots. His hands paused before her. She waited. He was clearly skittish about doing this, despite what he said. Seeing was one thing, touching quite another.

Kahlan reached out, took his hand, and pulled it firmly against her belly, feeling the cold mud squish against her.

"*Do it,*" she ordered.

When finished, they pulled the door open and went inside, he sitting among the circle of painted elders, she opposite him, next to Richard. Black and white lines swept diagonally across Richard's face in dramatic tangles, a mask they all wore for the spirits. The skulls that had sat on the shelf were arranged in the center of the circle. A small fire burned slowly in the fireplace behind her, giving off an odd, acrid smell. The elders stared fixedly ahead as they rhythmically chanted words she couldn't understand. The Bird Man's far-off eyes came up. The door closed of its own accord.

"*From now, until we are finished, near dawn, no one may go out, no one may come in. The door is barred by the spirits.*"

Kahlan's eyes swept the room, but saw nothing. A shiver ran up her spine. The Bird Man took a woven basket sitting near him and reached inside. He pulled out a small frog, then passed the basket to the next elder. Each took a frog and began rubbing its back against the skin of his chest. When the basket reached her, she held it between her hands and looked up at the Bird Man.

"*Why do we do this?*"

"*These are red spirit frogs, very hard to find. They have a substance on their backs that makes us forget this world, and allows us to see the spirits.*"

"*Honored elder, I may be one of the Mud People, but I am also a Confessor. I must always hold back my power. If I forget this world, I may not be able to do that.*"

"*It is too late to back out now. The spirits are with us. They*

397

have seen you, seen the symbols on you that open their eyes. You may not leave. If one is here who is blind to them, they will kill that person, and steal their spirit. I understand your problem, but I cannot help you. You will just have to do your best to hold back your power. If you cannot do so, then one of us will be lost. It is a price we will have to pay. If you want to die, then leave your frog in the basket. If you want to stop Darken Rahl, take it out."

She stared wide-eyed into his grim face, then reached into the basket. The frog wriggled and kicked in her hand as she passed the basket to Richard, telling him what to do. Swallowing hard, she pushed the cold slimy back of the frog against her chest, between her breasts, to the one place on her where there were no symbols painted, pushed it around in circles as the others had done. Where the slime touched her skin, it felt tingly, tight. The feeling spread through her. The sounds of the drums and the boldas grew in her ears until it seemed as if the sound was the only thing in the world. Her body vibrated with the beat. In her mind, she took hold of her power, held it tightly, concentrated on her control of it; then, hoping it was enough, she felt herself drift away.

Everyone took the hand of the person to each side. The walls of the room swam away from her vision. Her consciousness undulated, like ripples on a pond, floating, bobbing, pitching. She felt herself beginning to spin in a circle with the others, around and around the skulls in the center. The skulls brightened, lighting the faces of everyone in the circle. They were all swallowed into a soft void of nothingness. Shafts of light, from the center, spun with them.

All around, shapes closed in. In terror, she recognized what they were.

Shadow things.

Unable to get a scream out, her breath caught in her throat, she squeezed Richard's hand. She had to protect him. She tried to get up, to throw herself over him so they couldn't touch him. But her body wouldn't move. She realized with horror that it was because hands, hands of the shadow things, were on her. She struggled, struggled to get up, to protect Richard. Her mind raced with panic. Had they already killed her? Was she dead? Was she no more than a spirit now? Unable to move?

The shadow things stared down at her. Shadow things didn't have faces. These did. Mud People faces.

They weren't shadow things, she realized with a wave of relief, the were the ancestors' spirits. She caught her breath, eased the panic back down. Relaxed herself.

"Who calls this gathering?"

It was the spirits speaking. All of them. Together. The sound, hollow, flat, dead, almost took her breath away. But it was the Bird Man's mouth that moved.

"Who calls this gathering?" they repeated.

"This man does," she said, *"this man beside me. Richard With The Temper."*

They floated between the elders, gathering into the center of the circle.

"Release his hands."

Kahlan and Savidlin let go of Richard's hands. The spirits spun in the center of the circle; then, in a rush, they came out in a line, passing through Richard's body.

He inhaled sharply, threw his head back, and screamed in agony as they swept through him.

Kahlan jumped. The spirits all hovered behind him. The elders all closed their eyes.

"Richard!"

His head came back down. "It's all right. I'm all right," he managed in a hoarse voice, but he was clearly still in pain.

The spirits moved around the circle, behind the elders, then settled into their bodies, both spirit and man, in the same place at the same time. It gave the elders a soft, indefinite appearance around the edges. Their eyes come open.

"Why have you called us?" the Bird Man asked, in their hollow, harmonic voices.

She leaned a little toward Richard, keeping her eyes on the Bird Man. "They want you to say why you called this gathering."

Richard took a few deep breaths, recovering from what they had done to him.

"I called this gathering because I must find an object of magic before Darken Rahl finds it. Before he can use it."

Kahlan translated as the spirits talked to Richard through the elders.

"How many men have you killed?" Savidlin asked with spirit voices.

Richard answered without hesitation. "Two."

"Why?" Hajanlet asked in their haunting tones.

"To keep them from killing me."

"Both?"

He thought a moment. "The first one I killed in self-defense. The second I killed in defense of a friend."

"Do you think the defense of a friend gives you the right to kill?" Arbrin's mouth moved this time.

"Yes."

"Suppose he was going to kill your friend only to defend the life of his friend?"

Richard took a deep breath. "What's the point of the question?"

"The point is, according to what you believe, that you think it is justified to kill in the defense of a friend, then if he was killing to defend a friend, he had the right to kill your friend. He was justified. Since he was justified, that would void your right, would it not?"

"Not all questions have answers."

"Maybe not all questions have answers you like."

"Maybe."

Kahlan could tell by his tone that Richard was getting angry. All the eyes of the elders, the spirits, were on him.

"Did you enjoy killing this man?"

"Which one?"

"The first."

"No."

"The second."

Richard's jaw muscles tightened. "What is the point of these questions?"

"All questions have a different reason for being asked."

"And sometimes the reasons have nothing to do with the question?"

"Answer the question."

"Only if you first tell me the reason for it."

"You came here to ask us questions. Shall we ask your reasons?"

"It would seem you are."

"Answer our question or we will not answer yours."

"And if I answer it, will you promise to answer mine?"

"We are not here to make bargains. We are here because we were called. Answer the question or the gathering is over."

Richard took a deep breath and let it out slowly as he stared up at the void. "Yes. I enjoyed killing him, because of the magic of the Sword of Truth. That is how it works. If I had killed him in another manner, without the sword, I would not have enjoyed it."

"Irrelevant."

"What?"

" 'If' is irrelevant. 'Did' is not. So, now you have given two reasons for killing the second man: to defend a friend; and because you enjoyed it. Which is the true reason?"

"Both. I killed him to protect a friend's life, and because of the sword, I enjoyed it."

"What if you did not need to kill to protect your friend? What if you were wrong in your assessment? What if the life of your friend was not in fact in danger?"

Kahlan tensed at this question. She hesitated a moment before translating it.

"In my mind, the deed is not as important as the intent. I truly believed my friend's life was in danger, therefore I felt justified in killing to protect her. I had only a moment to act. In my mind, indecision would have resulted in her death.

"If the spirits think I was wrong in killing, or that the one I killed may have been justified, voiding my right, then we have a disagreement. Some problems have no clear solution. Some problems don't provide the time to analyze them. I had to act with my heart. As a wise man once told me, every murderer thinks he is justified in killing. I will kill to prevent myself or a friend, or an innocent, from being killed. If you feel that is wrong, tell me now so we can put an end to these painful questions, and I may go in search of the answers I need."

"As we said, we are not here to make bargains. You said that

401

to your mind, the deed is not as important as the intent. Is there anyone you have intended to kill, but have not?"

The sound of their voices was painful; Kahlan felt as if it was burning her skin.

"You have misinterpreted the context of what I said. I said I killed because I thought I had to, that I thought his intent was to kill her, therefore I thought I had to act or she would die. Not that my intent equates to the deed. There is probably a long list of people who, at one time or another, I have wanted to kill."

"If you wanted to, why have you not done so?"

"Many reasons. For some, I had not true justification, it was only a mind game, a fantasy, to counter the sting of an injustice. For some, though I felt justified, I was able to escape without killing. Some, well, it just turned out that I didn't that's all."

"The five elders?"

Richard sighed. "Yes."

"But you intended to."

Richard didn't answer.

"Is this a case where the intent is as the deed?"

Richard swallowed hard. "In my heart, yes. That I intended it wounds me almost as much as the deed would have."

"So then we have not, it would seem, gotten what you said entirely out of context."

Kahlan could see tears in Richard's eyes. "Why are you asking me these questions!"

"Why do you want the object of magic?"

"To stop Darken Rahl!"

"And how will getting this object stop him?"

Richard leaned back a little. His eyes went wide. He understood. A tear ran down his cheek. "Because, if I can get the object, and keep it from him," he whispered, "he will die. I will kill him in that way."

"What you are really asking us, then, is for our aid in killing another." There voices echoed around her in the darkness.

Richard only nodded.

"That is why we are asking you these questions. You are asking for our aid in killing. Do you not think it fair we should know what kind of person it is we would be helping in his attempt to kill?"

Sweat was rolling off Richard's face. "I guess so." He closed his eyes.

"Why do you want to kill this man?"

"Many reasons."

"Why do you want to kill this man?"

"Because he tortured and killed my father. Because he has tortured and killed many others. Because he will kill me if I don't kill him. Because he will torture and kill many more if I don't kill him. It is the only way to stop him. He cannot be reasoned with. I have no option but to kill him."

"Consider the next question carefully. Answer with the truth, or this gathering will end."

Richard nodded.

"What is the reason, above all others, why you want to kill this man?"

Richard looked down and closed his eyes again. "Because," he whispered at last, tears running down his face, "if I don't kill him, he will kill Kahlan."

Kahlan felt as if she had been hit in the stomach. She could barely bring herself to translate the words. There was a long silence. Richard sat naked, in more ways than one. She was angry at the spirits for doing this to him. She was also deeply distraught by what she was doing to him. Shar had been right.

"If Kahlan were not a factor, would you still try to kill this man?"

"Absolutely. You asked the reason above all others. I told you."

"What is the object of magic you seek?" they asked suddenly.

"Does that mean you agree with my reasons for killing?"

"No. It means that for our own reasons, we have decided to answer your question. If we can. What is the object of magic you seek?"

"One of the three boxes of Orden."

When Kahlan translated, the spirits suddenly howled as if in pain. *"We are not allowed to answer that question. The boxes of Orden are in play. This gathering is over."*

The elders' eyes began to close. Richard jumped to his feet. "You would let Darken Rahl kill all those people when you have the power to help?"

403

"Yes."

"You would let him kill your descendants? Your living flesh and blood? You aren't spirit ancestors to our people, you are spirit traitors!"

"Not true."

"Then tell me!"

"Not allowed."

"Please! Don't leave us without your help. Let me ask another question?"

"We are not allowed to disclose where the boxes of Orden are. It is forbidden. Think, and ask another question."

Richard sat down, pulling his knees up. He rubbed his eyes with the tips of his fingers. The symbols painted all over him made him look like some kind of wild creature. He put his face in his hands, thinking. His head snapped up.

"You can't tell me where the boxes are. Are there any other restrictions?"

"Yes."

"How many boxes does Rahl already have?"

"Two."

He looked at the elders evenly. "You have just disclosed where two of the boxes are. That is forbidden," he reminded them. "Or maybe it is simply a gray shade of intent?"

Silence.

"That information is not restricted. Your question?"

Richard leaned forward like a dog on scent. "Can you tell me who knows where the last box is?"

Richard already knew the answer to this question, she suspected. She recognized his manner of slicing the loaf the other way.

"We know the name of the person who has the box, and the names of several other people nearby, but we cannot tell you the names because that would be the same as telling you where it is. That is forbidden."

"Then, can you tell me the name of a person, other than Rahl, who is not in possession of the last box, who is not near it, but who knows where it is?"

"There is one we can name. She knows where the box is. If we tell you her name, that would not lead you to the box, only to

404

her. This is allowed. It will be up to you, not us, to get whatever information you might."

"That is my question, then: who is it? Name her."

When they uttered the name, Kahlan froze with a jolt. She didn't translate. The elders shook at the mere name, spoken aloud.

"Who is it? What's her name?" Richard demanded of her.

Kahlan looked up at him.

"We are as good as dead," she whispered.

"Why? Who is it?"

Kahlan sank back, into herself. "It is the witch woman, Shota."

"And do you know where she is?"

Kahlan nodded, her brow wrinkled in terror. "In the Agaden Reach." She whispered the name as if even the words tasted of poison. "Not even a wizard would dare to go into the Reach."

Richard studied the visage of fear in her face, and looked to the elders as they shook.

"Then we go to Agaden Reach, to this witch woman, Shota," he said in an even voice, "and find out where the box is."

"We wish you kind fates," the spirits said, through the Bird Man. *"The lives of our descendants depend upon you."*

"Thank you for your help, honored ancestors," Richard said. "I will do my best to stop Rahl. To help our people."

"You must use your head. That is Darken Rahl's way. Meet him on his terms, and you will lose. It will not be easy. You will have to suffer, as will our people, as will other people, before you have even a chance to succeed. And in all probability, you will still fail. Heed our warning, Richard With The Temper."

"I will remember the things you say. I pledge to do my best."

"Then we will test the truth of your pledge. There is something else we would tell you." They paused for a moment. *"Darken Rahl is here. He looks for you."*

Kahlan translated in a rush, jumping to her feet. Richard came up beside her.

"What! He is here now? Where is he, what is he doing?"

"He is in the center of the village. He is killing people."

Fear raged through Kahlan. Richard took a step forward. "I

405

have to get out of here. I have to get my sword. I have to try to stop him!"

"*If you wish. But hear us out first. Sit,*" they commanded.

Richard and Kahlan sank back down, looking wide-eyed at each other, clutching each other's hands. Tears welled up in her eyes. "Hurry, then," Richard said.

"*Darken Rahl wants you. Your sword cannot kill him. Tonight, the balance of power is on his side. If you go out there, he will kill you. You will have no chance. None. In order to win, you must change the balance of power, something you cannot do this night. The people he kills tonight will die whether or not you go out to fight him. If you do go out, more will die in the end. Many more. If you are to succeed, you must have the courage to let these die tonight. You must save yourself to fight at another time. You must suffer this pain. You must heed your head rather than your sword, if you are to have a chance to win.*"

"But I have to go out sooner or later!"

"*Darken Rahl has loosed many dark terrors. He must balance many things, including his time. He does not have the time to wait all night. He is confident, with good reason, that he can defeat you at any time of his choosing. He has no reason to wait. He will be gone soon, to tend to other dark matters, to look for you another day.*

"*The symbols painted upon you open our eyes to you, so we may see you. They close his eyes to you; he cannot see you. Unless you draw your sword. That, he will be able to see; then he would have you. As long as the symbols are upon you, and the magic of your sword remains in its scabbard, while you are in Mud People territory, he cannot find you.*"

"But I can't stay here!"

"*Not if you wish to stop him. When you leave our territory, the power of the symbols will be gone, and he will be able to see you again.*"

Richard's clenched fists shook. Kahlan could see by the look on his face that he was close to disregarding the warning, close to going out to fight.

"*The choice is yours,*" the spirits said. "*Wait in here while he kills some of our people, and when he is gone, go after the box, to kill him. Or go out now, and accomplish nothing.*"

Richard closed his eyes tight. His chest rose and fell with his labored breathing.

"I will wait," he said in a voice she could barely hear.

Kahlan threw her arms around his neck, putting her head against his, as they both cried. The circle of elders began spinning around again.

That was the last thing she remembered until she and Richard were shaken awake by the Bird Man. She felt as if she were coming out of a nightmare as she recalled the things the spirits said, about the killing of the Mud People, and that to find the box they had to go into Agaden Reach, to Shota. She recoiled at the thought of the witch woman. The other elders were standing over them, and helping both of them up. All wore grim faces. Tears tried to come to her again. She forced them back.

The Bird Man pushed the door open to the cold night air, to a clear, starlit sky.

The clouds were gone. Even the snakelike cloud.

Dawn was less than an hour away, and already the eastern sky had a hint of color to it. A solemn-faced hunter handed them their clothes, and Richard his sword. Wordlessly, they dressed and went out.

A phalanx of hunters and archers protectively surrounded the spirit house. Many were bloodied. Richard pushed in front of the Bird Man.

"Tell me what happened," he ordered in a quiet voice.

A man with a spear stepped forward. Kahlan waited next to Richard, to translate. Rage flared in the man's eyes.

"The red demon came from the sky, carrying a man. He wanted you." Fire in his eyes, he pushed his spearpoint against Richard's chest. The Bird Man, stonefaced, put his hand on the spear, raising the point away from Richard. *"When he could only find your clothes, he began killing people. Children!"* His chest was heaving with anger. *"Our arrows would not touch him. Our spears would not touch him. Our hands would not touch him. Many of those who tried were killed by magic fire. Then he became even more angry when he saw that we use fire. He made all the fires go out. Then he climbed back on the red demon and told us that if we use fire again, he will come back and kill every child in the village. With magic, he floated Siddin into the air,*

407

and took him under his arm. A gift, he said, for a friend. Then he flew away. And where were you and your sword!"

Savidlin's eyes filled with tears. Kahlan put her hand against the ripping pain in her heart. She knew who the gift was for.

The man spat on Richard. Savidlin went for him, but Richard held his arm out, held Savidlin back.

"I heard the voices of our ancestors' spirits," Savidlin said. *"I know this is not his failing!"*

Kahlan put her arms around Savidlin, and comforted him. *"Be strong. We have saved him once when it seemed he was lost. We will save him again."*

He nodded bravely as she pulled back. Richard asked softly what she had told Savidlin.

"A lie," she answered, "to ease his pain."

Richard nodded his understanding, and turned to the man with the spear.

"Show me the ones he killed," he said without emotion.

"Why?" the man demanded.

"So I will never forget why I am going to kill the one who did this."

The man gave the elders an angry glance and then led them all to the center of the village. Kahlan put on her blank expression, to shield herself from what she knew she would see. She had seen it too many times before, in other villages, other places. And as she expected, it was the same as she had seen before. Lined up in terrible disarray beside a wall were the torn and ripped bodies of children, the burned bodies of men and dead women, some without arms, or jaws. The Bird Man's niece was among them. Richard showed no emotion as he walked among the chaos of screaming and wailing people, past the dead, looking, the calm in the eye of the hurricane. Or maybe, she thought, the lightning about to strike.

"This is what you brought us," the man hissed. *"This is your fault!"*

Richard watched as others nodded their agreement, then turned his eyes on the man with the spear. His voice was gentle.

"If it eases your pain to think so, then blame me. I choose to blame the one whose hands have the blood on them." He addressed the Bird Man and the other elders. "Until this is over, don't use fire. It will only invite more killing. I swear to stop this man or die in the attempt. Thank you, my friends, for helping me."

His eyes turned to Kahlan. They were intense, reflecting his anger over what he had just seen. He gritted his teeth. "Let's go find this witch woman."

They had no choice, of course. But she knew of Shota.

They were going to die.

They might as well go ask Darken Rahl to tell them where they could find the box.

Kahlan walked up to the Bird Man, then suddenly threw her arms around him.

"Remember me," she whispered.

When they separated, the Bird Man looked around at the people, his face drawn. *"These two need some men to guard them safely to the edge of our land."*

Savidlin stepped forward instantly. Without hesitation, a band of ten of his best hunters came to stand with him.

CHAPTER 29

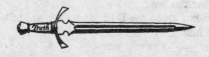

PRINCESS VIOLET TURNED SUDDENLY and slapped Rachel's face. Hard. Rachel had done nothing wrong, of course; the Princess just liked to slap her when she least expected it. The Princess thought it was fun. Rachel didn't try to hide how much it hurt; if it didn't hurt enough, the Princess would slap her again. Rachel put her hand over the sting, her bottom lip quivering, tears welling up in her eyes, but she said nothing.

Turning back to the shiny, polished wall of little wooden drawers, Princess Violet put her stubby finger through a gold handle and slid open another drawer, taking out a sparkling silver necklace studded with large blue stones.

"This one's pretty. Hold my hair up."

She turned to the tall wood-framed mirror, admiring herself as her fingers hooked the clasp behind her plump neck while Rachel held her long, dull, brown hair out of the way for her. Rachel eyed herself in the mirror, inspecting the red mark on her face. She hated looking at herself in the mirror, hated seeing her hair, how it looked when the Princess chopped it off short. She wasn't allowed to let her hair grow, of course, she was a nobody, but she wished so much it could at least be cut even. Almost everyone else had their hair cut short, but it was even. The Princess liked chopping it for her, liked making it all jagged. Princess Violet liked it when other people thought Rachel was ugly.

Rachel shifted her weight to her other foot and rolled her free ankle around to ease its stiffness. They'd been in the Queen's jewel room all afternoon, the Princess trying on one piece of jewelry after another, then primping and turning in front of the tall mirror. It was her favorite thing to do, trying on the Queen's jewelry and looking at herself in the mirror. Being her playmate, Rachel was required to be with her, to make sure the Princess was enjoying herself. Dozens of the little drawers stood open, some a little, some a lot. Necklaces and bracelets hung halfway out of some, like sparkling tongues. More were scattered around the floor, along with brooches, tiaras, and rings.

The Princess looked down her nose and pointed to a blue stone ring on the floor. "Give me that one."

Rachel slipped it over the finger held in front of her face; then the Princess watched herself in the mirror as she turned her hand this way and that. She ran her hand over the pretty pale blue satin dress, admiring the ring. Letting out a long, bored sigh, she walked over to the fancy white marble pedestal that stood by itself in the opposite corner of the jewel room. She was looking up at her mother's favorite object, one she fawned over at every opportunity.

Princess Violet's pudgy fingers reached up, pulling the gold, jewel-encrusted box off its honored resting place.

"Princess Violet!" Rachel blurted out before she had a chance to think. "Your mother said you mustn't touch that."

The Princess turned with an innocent expression, then tossed her the box. Rachel gasped, catching the box, horrified it might crash against the wall. Terrified that she had it in her hands, she immediately set it down on the floor as if it were a hot coal. She backed away, fearful of getting whipped just for being caught near the Queen's precious box.

"What's the big deal?" Princess Violet snapped. "Magic keeps it from being taken from this room. It's not like anyone's going to steal it or anything."

411

Rachel didn't know anything about any magic, but she knew she didn't want to be caught touching the Queen's box.

"I'm going down to the dining room," the Princess said, lifting her nose, "to watch the guests arrive, and wait for dinner. Clean up this dreadful mess, then go to the kitchen and tell the cooks I don't want my roast cooked like leather, like the last time, or I'll tell my mother to have them beaten."

"Of course, Princess Violet." Rachel curtsied.

The Princess held her big nose up. "And?"

"And . . . thank you, Princess Violet, for bringing me, and letting me see how pretty you look in the jewelry."

"Well, it's the least I can do; you must get tired of looking at your ugly face in the mirror. My mother says we must do kind things for the less fortunate." She reached in a pocket and brought out something. "Here. Take the key and lock the door when you're finished putting everything back."

Rachel curtsied again. "Yes, Princess Violet."

While the key was dropping into Rachel's outstretched hand, the Princess's other hand came out of nowhere, slapping Rachel's face unexpectedly, and unexpectedly hard. She stood stunned as Princess Violet walked out of the room, laughing a high, squeaky, snorting laugh. Princess Violet's laugh hurt almost as much as the slap.

Tears fell from her face as she crawled around on the floor on her hands and knees, picking up fingerfuls of rings from the carpets. She stopped and sat back a moment, carefully touching her fingertips to the place where she had been slapped. It hurt like anything.

Rachel deliberately worked around the Queen's box, giving it sidelong glances, afraid to touch it, yet knowing she would have to, because she had to put it back. She worked slowly, meticulously laying the jewelry in its place, carefully pushing the drawers closed, hoping somehow she wouldn't finish, so she wouldn't have to pick up the box, the Queen's favorite thing in the whole world.

The Queen wouldn't be happy at all if she knew that some nobody had touched it. Rachel knew the Queen was always having somebody's head chopped off. Sometimes, the Princess made

412

Rachel go with her to watch, but Rachel always closed her eyes. The Princess didn't.

When all the jewelry was put away, the last drawer closed, she looked out of the corner of her eye, down at the box sitting on the floor. She felt as if it were looking back, as if it might somehow tell the Queen. Finally, squatting down, eyes wide, she picked it up. Holding it at arm's length, she carefully shuffled her feet over the edges of carpets, terrified she might drop it. She set the box in its place as slowly as she could, carefully, gingerly, fearing a jewel might fall out or something. She quickly drew her fingers away, relieved.

Turning back, she caught sight of the hem of a silver robe that touched the floor. Her breath caught in her throat. She hadn't heard footsteps. Her head slowly, almost involuntarily, rose up the line of the robe; to the hands stuck in the opposite sleeves, to the long, pointed, white beard, to the bony face, the hooked nose, the bald head, and the dark eyes looking down at her startled face.

The wizard.

"Wizard Giller," she whined, fully expecting to be struck dead any second, "I was only putting it back. I swear. Please, please don't kill me." Her face wrinkled up as she tried to make herself back away, but her feet wouldn't move. "Please." She stuck the hem of her dress in her mouth, biting it as she whimpered.

Rachel scrunched her eyes closed and shook as the wizard began sinking, lowering himself to the floor.

"Child," he said in a soft voice. Rachel cautiously opened one eye, surprised to find he was sitting on the floor, his face even with hers. "I am not going to hurt you."

She opened the other eye, just as cautiously. "You're not?" She didn't believe him. She saw with a start that the big heavy door was closed, her only escape route blocked.

"No," he smiled, shaking his bald head. "Who took the box down?"

"We were playing. That's all, just playing. I was putting it back for the Princess. She's very good to me, so very good, I wanted to help her. She's a wonderful person. I love her, she's so kind to me ..."

He put a long finger over her lips, to gently silence her. "I get the point, child. So, you are the Princess's playmate then?"

She nodded in earnest. "Rachel."

His grin got bigger. "That's a pretty name. Glad to meet you, Rachel. I'm sorry I frightened you. I was only coming to check on the Queen's box."

No one had ever told her that her name was pretty. But he had shut the big door. "You're not going to strike me dead? Or change me into something horrid?"

"Oh, dear, no." he laughed. He turned his head, peering at her with one eye. "Why are there red marks on your cheeks?"

She didn't answer, too scared to say. Slowly, carefully, he reached out, his fingers touching one cheek, then the other. Her eyes opened wide. The sting was gone.

"Better?"

She nodded. His eyes seemed so big, the way they looked at her up close like this. They made her feel like telling him, so she did. "The Princess hits me," she admitted, ashamed.

"So? She is not so kind to you, then?"

She shook her head, casting her eyes downward. Then the wizard did something that absolutely stunned her. He reached around and gave her a gentle hug. She stood stiffly for a moment, then put her arms around his neck, hugging him back. His long white whiskers tickled the side of her face and neck, but she still liked it.

He looked at her with sad eyes. "I'm sorry, dear child. The Princess and the Queen can be quite cruel."

His voice sounded so nice, she thought, like Brophy's. A big grin spread beneath his hook nose.

"Tell you what, I have something here that might help." A thin hand reached into his robes, and he looked up into the air while his hand felt around. Then his hand found what it was looking for. Her eyes went wide as he pulled out a doll with short hair the same yellow color as hers. He patted the doll's tummy. "This is a trouble doll."

"Trouble doll?" she whispered.

"Yes." He nodded. There were deep wrinkles at the ends of his smile. "When you have troubles, you tell them to the doll, and she takes them away for you. She has magic. Here. Try it out."

Rachel could hardly take a breath as she reached out with both hands, her fingers carefully clutching the doll. She pulled it to her chest cautiously and hugged it. Then, tentatively, slowly, she held it out, looking at its face. Her eyes got all watery.

"Princess Violet says I'm ugly," she confided in the doll.

The face on the doll smiled. Rachel's mouth dropped open.

"I love you, Rachel," it said in a tiny little voice.

Rachel gasped in surprise, she giggled in glee, she hugged the doll to her as tight as she could. She laughed and laughed, swinging her body back and forth as she hugged the doll to her chest.

Then, she remembered. She pushed the doll back at the wizard, turning her face away.

"I'm not allowed to have a doll. The Princess said so. She would throw it in the fire, that's what she said. If I had a doll, she would throw it in the fire." She could hardly speak, because of the lump in her throat.

"Well, let me think," the wizard said, rubbing his chin. "Where do you sleep?"

"Most of the time, I sleep in the Princess's bedroom. She locks me in the box at night. I think that's mean. Sometimes, when she says I've been bad, she makes me leave the castle for the night, so I have to sleep outside. She thinks that's even meaner, but I really like it, because I have a secret place, in a wayward pine, where I sleep.

"Wayward pines don't have locks on them, you know. I can go potty whenever I have to. It's pretty cold sometimes, but I got a pile of straw, and I climb under it to keep warm. I have to come back in the morning, before she sends the guards to look for me, so they won't find my secret place. I don't want them to find it. They would tell the Princess and she wouldn't send me out anymore."

The wizard tenderly cupped his hands around her face. It made her feel special. "Dear child," he whispered, "that I could have been a party to this." His eyes were wet. Rachel didn't know wizards could get tears. Then his big grin came back, and he held up a finger. "I have an idea. You know the gardens, the formal gardens?"

Rachel nodded. "I go through them to go to my secret place,

415

when I'm put out at night. The Princess makes me go through the outer wall at the garden gate. She doesn't want me to go out the front, past the shops and people. She's afraid someone might take me in for the night. She told me I mustn't go to the town or the farmland. I must go to the woods, as punishment."

"Well, as you walk down the central path of the garden, there are short urns, on both sides, with yellow flowers in them." Rachel nodded. She knew where they were. "I will hide your doll in the third urn on the right. I will put a wizard's web over it— that's magic—so no one but you will find it." He took the doll and carefully tucked it away back in his robes as her eyes followed it. "The next time you are put out for the night, you go there and you will find your doll. Then you can keep it at your place, your wayward pine, where no one will find it, or take it from you.

"And I will also leave you a magic fire stick. Just build a little stack of sticks, not too big now, with stones around it, and then hold the magic fire stick to it and say 'Light for me,' and it will burn, so you can keep warm."

Rachel threw her arms around him, hugging and hugging him as he patted her back. "Thank you, wizard Giller."

"You may call me Giller when we are alone, child, just Giller, that is what all my good friends call me."

"Thank you so much for my doll, Giller. No one ever gave me anything so nice before. I'll take the bestest care of her. I have to go now. I'm to scold the cooks for the Princess. Then I have to sit and watch her eat." She grinned. "Then I have to think of something bad to do so the Princess will put me out to-. night."

The wizard laughed a deep laugh as his eyes sparkled. He mussed her hair with his big hand. Giller helped her with the heavy door and locked it for her, then handed the key back to her.

"I so hope we can talk again sometime," she said, looking up at him.

He smiled at her. "We will, Rachel, we will. I'm sure of it."

Waving back at him, she ran off down the long, empty hall, happier than she had been since she first came to live at the castle. It was a long way, through the castle, down to the kitchen, down stone stairs and halls with rugs on the floors and paintings on the walls, through big rooms with tall windows hung with gold and red drapery, and chairs of red velvet with gold legs, long carpets with pictures on them of men fighting on horseback, past guards who stood still as stone at some of the big fancy doors or marched in twos, and by servants who rushed everywhere carrying linens, trays, or brooms and rags and buckets of soapy water.

None of the guards or servants gave her a second look, even though she was running. They knew she was Princess Violet's playmate, and had seen her running through the castle many times before on errands for the Princess.

She was winded when she finally reached the kitchens, which were steamy and smoky and filled with noise. Helpers were scurrying around carrying heavy sacks, big pots, or hot trays, all trying not to bump into one another. People chopped things she couldn't see on the high tables and huge chopping blocks. Pans clanged, cooks yelled orders, helpers took pans and metal bowls off hooks overhead and put others back. There was a constant rapping of spoons mixing and whipping food, the sharp hiss of oil and garlic and butter and onions and spices in hot pans, and everyone seemed to be yelling at the same time. This chaotic place smelled so good it made her head spin.

She tugged on the sleeve of one of the two head cooks, trying to tell him she had a message from the Princess, but he was arguing with another cook and told her to go sit and wait until they were finished. She sat down nearby, on a little stool by the ovens, her back pressed against the hot brick. The kitchen smelled so good, and she was so hungry. But she knew she would get in trouble if she asked for food.

The head cooks were standing over a big crock, waving their arms around, yelling at each other. Suddenly, the crock fell to the floor with a big thunk, splitting in two, sending light brown liquid flooding all over. Rachel jumped up on the stool so it wouldn't get on her bare feet. The cooks stood still, their faces almost as white as their coats.

"What're we going to do now?" the short one asked. "We don't have any more of the ingredients Father Rahl sent."

417

"Wait a minute," the tall one said, holding his hand to his forehead. "Let me think."

He put both hands to his face, squishing it together. Then he put both arms in the air.

"All right. All right. I've got an idea. Get me another crock, and just keep your mouth shut. Maybe we can keep our heads. Get me some other ingredients."

"What ingredients!" the short one yelled, red-faced.

The tall cook leaned over him. "Brown ingredients!"

Rachel watched while they ran around snatching up things, pouring in bottles of liquid, adding ingredients, stirring, tasting. At last they both smiled.

"All right, all right, it'll work. I think. Just let me do the talking," the tall one said.

Rachel stepped tiptoed across the wet floor and tugged on his sleeve again.

"You! You still here? What do you want?" he snapped.

"Princess Violet said not to make her roast dry again, or she would have the Queen make those men beat you." She looked down at the ground. "She made me say that."

He looked down at her a minute, then turned to the short cook, shaking his finger. "I told you! I told you! This time, slice hers from the center, and don't mix up the plates or we'll both end up losing our heads!" He looked back down at her. "And you didn't see any of this," he said, stirring his finger in the air over the crock.

"Cooking? You don't want me to tell anyone I saw you cooking? All right," she said, a little confused, and started tiptoeing across the wet floor again. "I won't tell anyone, I promise. I don't like to see people getting hurt by those men with the whips. I won't tell."

"Wait a minute," he called after her. "Rachel, isn't it?"

She turned and nodded.

"Come back here."

She didn't want to, but she tiptoed back anyway. He took out a big knife that scared her at first, then turned to a platter on the table behind him and cut off a big, juicy piece of meat. She had never seen such a piece of meat, without fat and gristle all over it, at least not up close. It was a piece of meat like the Queen and the Princess ate. He handed it down to her, put it right into her hand.

"Sorry I yelled at you, Rachel. You sit on that stool over there and eat this, and then let us be sure you're cleaned up, so no one will be the wiser. All right?"

She nodded and ran off to the stool with her prize, forgetting to tiptoe. It was the best, most delicious thing she had ever eaten. She tried to eat it slowly while she watched all the people running around, clanging pots and carrying things, but she couldn't. Juice ran down her arms and dripped off her elbows.

When she was finished, the short cook came and wiped her hands and arms and face with a towel, then he gave her a slice of lemon pie, placing it right in her hands the way the tall cook had done with the meat. He said he baked it himself and he wanted to know if it was good. She told him, quite truthfully, that it was just about the bestest thing she had ever had. He grinned.

This had been just about the best day she could ever remember. Two good things in the same day: the trouble doll, and now the food. She felt like a queen herself.

Later, as she sat in the big dining room on her little chair behind the Princess, it was the first time, ever, that she hadn't been so hungry that her stomach made noises while the important people ate. The head table, where they sat, was three steps higher than all the other tables, so if she sat up straight she could see the whole room even from her little chair. Servers were dashing all about, bringing in food, taking out dishes with food still left on them, pouring wine, and exchanging half-full trays on the tables with full ones from the kitchen.

She watched all the fine ladies and gentlemen dressed in pretty dresses and colorful braided coats, sitting at the long tables, eating from the fancy plates, and for the first time she knew how the food tasted. She still didn't understand, though, why they needed so many forks and spoons to eat with. One time when she had asked the Princess why there were so many forks and spoons and things, the Princess had said it was something a nobody like her would never need to know.

Mostly Rachel was ignored at the banquets. The Princess only turned to look at her once in a while; she was just there because

419

she was Princess Violet's playmate, for looks, she guessed. The Queen had people standing or sitting behind her when she ate, too. The Queen said Rachel was for the Princess to practice on, to practice leadership.

She leaned forward and whispered, "Is your roast juicy enough, Princess Violet? I told the cooks it was mean to give you bad meat, and you said not to do it again."

Princess Violet looked back over her shoulder, gravy dripping from her chin. "It's good enough to keep them from getting whipped. And you're right, they shouldn't be so mean to me. It's about time they learned."

Queen Milena sat at the table, as she always did, with her tiny little dog held in one arm. It kept pushing its skinny little stick legs against her fat arm as it shook, making little dents with its feet. The Queen fed it scraps of meat that were better than any Rachel had ever been fed. Before today, that is, she thought with a smile.

Rachel didn't like the little dog. It barked a lot, and sometimes when the Queen set it on the floor, it would run over to her and bite her legs with its tiny sharp teeth, and she didn't dare to say anything. When the dog bit her, the Queen always told it to be careful, not to hurt itself. She always used a funny, high, sweet voice when she talked to the dog.

While the Queen and her ministers talked about some kind of alliance, Rachel sat jiggling her legs, knocking her knees together, thinking about her trouble doll. The wizard stood behind and to the right of the Queen, offering his advice when asked. He looked grand in his silver robes. She had never paid much attention to Giller before; he had just been another one of the Queen's important people, always there with her, like her little dog. People were afraid of him, too, the way she was afraid of the dog. Now, as she watched him, he seemed like just about the nicest man she had ever seen.

He ignored her through the whole dinner, never once looking her way. Rachel figured he didn't want to draw attention to her, and make the Princess mad. That was a good idea. Princess Violet would be cross if she knew Giller had said he thought Rachel's name was pretty. The Queen's long hair hung down behind her fancy carved chair, shaking in waves when her important people talked to her and she nodded her head.

When the meal was finished, servers rolled out a cart with the crock she had seen the cooks mixing. Goblets were filled from a ladle and carried to all the guests. Everyone seemed to think it was pretty important.

The Queen stood, holding her goblet in the air, and the little dog in her other arm. "Lords and ladies, I present you with the drink of enlightenment, that we may see the truth. This is a very precious commodity; few are offered the opportunity of enlightenment. I have availed myself of it many times, of course, that I might see the truth, the way of Father Rahl, in order to lead my people to the common good. Drink up."

Some people looked like they didn't want to, but only for a minute. Then they all drank. The Queen drank, after she saw that everyone else had, then sat back down with a funny look on her face. She leaned to a server, whispering. Rachel started to get worried; the Queen was frowning. When the Queen frowned, people got their heads chopped off.

The tall cook came out, smiling. The Queen motioned to him with her finger hooked, to lean closer. There was sweat on his forehead. Rachel guessed it was because the kitchen was so hot. She was sitting behind the Princess, who sat at the left arm of the Queen, so she could hear them talking.

"This does not taste the same," she said in her mean voice. She didn't always talk in her mean voice, but when she did, people got scared.

"Ah, well, Your Majesty, you see, in truth, uh, well, it's not, you see. Not the same, that is." Her eyebrows lifted and he talked faster. "You see, uh, in truth, well, I knew this was a very important dinner. Yes, I knew, you see, that you wouldn't want anything to go wrong. You see. Wouldn't want anyone to fail to be enlightened, to fail to see your brilliance, about all this, uh, business, so, you see, well," he leaned a little closer and lowered his voice to speak confidentially, "so I took the liberty of making the drink of enlightenment stronger. Much stronger, actually, you see. So no one would fail to see the rightness of what you say. I assure you, Your Majesty, it is so strong, no one will fail to be enlightened."

He leaned even closer, lowered his voice even more. "In fact, Your Majesty, it is so strong that anyone who fails to be enlightened, and opposes you after drinking it, well, they could only be a traitor."

"Really," the Queen whispered in surprise. "Well, I thought it was stronger."

"Very perceptive, Your Majesty, very perceptive. You have a very refined palate. I knew I wouldn't be able to fool you."

"Indeed. But are you sure it isn't too powerful? I can feel the enlightenment sweeping through me already."

"Your Majesty," his eyes shifted among the guests. "Where your mandate is concerned, I feared to make it any weaker." His eyebrows lifted up. "Lest any traitor go unfound."

She smiled at last, and nodded. "You are a wise and loyal cook. From now on, I put you, exclusively, in charge of the drink of enlightenment."

"Thank you, Your Majesty."

He bowed a bunch of times and left. Rachel was glad he didn't get in trouble.

"Lords and ladies, a special treat. Tonight, I had the cook prepare the drink of enlightenment extra strong, so none loyal to their queen could fail to see the wisdom of Father Rahl's ways."

The people all smiled and nodded how pleased they were about this. Some told how they could already feel the special insights the drink was giving them.

"A special treat, lords and ladies, for your entertainment." She snapped her fingers. "Bring in the fool."

Guards brought in a man, and made him stand in the center of the room, directly in front of the Queen, all the tables around him. He was big and strong-looking, but he was bound with chains. The Queen leaned forward.

"We here have all agreed that an alliance with our ally, Darken Rahl, will bring great benefits to all our people, that we all will profit, together. That the little people, the workers, the farmers, will benefit the most. That they will be freed from the oppression of those who would only exploit them for profit, for gold, for greed. That from now on, we all will be working for the common good, not individual goals." The Queen frowned. "Please tell all these ignorant lords and ladies"—she swept her hand around the room—"how it is that you are smarter than they, and why you should be allowed to work only for yourself, instead of your fellow man."

The man had an angry look on his face. Rachel wished he would change it, before he got in trouble.

"The common good," he said, sweeping his hand around the room like the Queen had done, except his hands had chains on them. "This is what you call the common good? All you fine people look to be enjoying the good food, the warm fire. My children go hungry tonight because most of our crops have been taken, for the common good, for those who have decided not to bother to work, but to eat the fruit of my labor instead."

The people laughed.

"And you would deny them food, simply because you are fortunate that your crops grew better?" the Queen asked. "You are a selfish man."

"Their crops would grow better if they would plant seeds in the ground first."

"And so you have so little care for your fellow man, that you therefore would condemn them to starve?"

"My family starves! To feed others, to feed Rahl's army. To feed you fine lords and ladies, who do nothing but discuss and decide what to do with my crop, how to divide the product of my labor among others."

Rachel wished the man would keep still. He was going to get his head chopped off. The people and the Queen thought he was funny, though.

"And my family goes cold," he said, and his face looked even more angry, "because we aren't allowed to have fire." He pointed at a few of the fireplaces. "But here there is fire, to warm the people who tell me we are all equal now, how there will no longer be some put before others and I must therefore not be allowed to keep what is mine. Isn't it odd, that the people who tell me how we are to all be the same under the alliance with Darken Rahl and do no work other than to divide up the fruit of my labors, are all well fed, and warm, and have fine clothes on their backs. But my family goes hungry and cold."

Everyone laughed. Rachel didn't laugh. She knew what it was like to be hungry, and cold.

"Lords and ladies," the Queen said, with a chuckle. "did I not promise you royal entertainment? The drink of enlightenment lets us see what a selfish fool this man truly is. Just think, he actually believes it is right to profit while others starve. He would put his profit above the lives of his fellow man. For his greed, he would murder the hungry."

Everyone laughed with the Queen.

The Queen smacked her hand down on the table. Plates jumped and a few glasses fell over, spilling a red stain across the white tablecloth. Everyone fell quiet, except the little dog, who barked at the man. "This is the kind of greed that will be ended, when the People's Peace Army comes to help rid us of these human leeches that suck us all dry!" The Queen's round face was as red as the stains on the tablecloth.

Everyone cheered and clapped for a long time. The Queen sat back, smiling at last.

The man's face was as red as hers. "Odd, isn't it, now that all the farmers, the workers in town, are all working for the common good, that there isn't enough good to go around, like there used to be, or enough food."

The Queen jumped to her feet. "Of course not!" she shouted. "Because of greedy people like you!" She took some deep breaths, until her face wasn't quite so red, then turned to the Princess. "Violet dear, you must learn matters of state sooner or later. You must learn how to serve the public good for all our people. Therefore, I will put this matter in your hands, so you may gain experience. What would you do with this traitor to our people? You choose, dear, and it will be done."

Princess Violet stood. Smiling, she looked around at the people.

"I say," she said, as she leaned forward a little, across the table, to look at the big man in chains, "I say, off with his head!"

Everyone cheered and clapped again. Guards dragged the man away as he called them names Rachel didn't understand. She was sad for him, and for his family.

After the assembled crowd talked for a while longer, they all decided to go watch the man get his head chopped off. When the Queen left and Princess Violet turned to her and said it was time to go watch, Rachel stood up in front of her with fists at her side.

"You're really mean. You're really mean to say to chop off that man's head."

The Princess put her hands on her hips. "Is that so? Well you can just spend the night outside tonight!"

"But Princess Violet, it's so cold out tonight!"

"Well, while you're freezing you can just think about how you dared speak to me in that tone! And so you remember the next time, you are to stay out all day tomorrow, and tomorrow night, too!" Her face looked mean, like the Queen's did sometimes. "That should teach you some respect."

Rachel started to say something else; then she remembered the trouble doll, and that she wanted to go out. The Princess pointed at the archway toward the door.

"Go on. Right now, with no supper." She stomped her foot.

Rachel looked at the ground, to pretend she was sad. "Yes, Princess Violet," she said, as she curtsied.

She walked with her head down, through the archway and down the big hall with all the rugs hung on the high walls. She liked to look at the pictures on the rugs, but she kept her head down this time, in case the Princess was watching; she didn't want to look happy about being put out. Guards, wearing shiny armor breastplates and swords and holding pikes, opened the great, tall, iron doors for her without saying anything. They never said anything to her when they let her out, or when they let her back in. They knew she was the Princess's playmate: a nobody.

When she got outside, she tried not to walk too fast, in case anyone was watching. The stone was as cold as ice on her bare feet. Carefully, and with each hand under the other armpit to keep her fingers warm, she went down the wide steps and terraces, taking them one at a time so she wouldn't fall, at last reaching the cobblestone walk at the bottom. More guards patrolled outside, but they ignored her. They saw her all the time. The closer she got to the gardens, the faster she walked.

Rachel slowed on the main garden path, waiting until the guards' backs were turned. The trouble doll was right where Giller had said it would be. She put the fire stick in her pocket, then hugged the doll to her as tight as she could before hiding it behind her back. She whispered to it, a warning to be still. She couldn't wait to get to her wayward pine so she could tell the

425

doll how mean Princess Violet was to have that man's head chopped off. She looked around in the darkness.

There was no one watching, no one to see her take the doll. At the outer wall, more men were patrolling the high walks, and the Queen's guards were at the gate, standing stiffly in their armor. They wore their fancy uniforms over the armor, sleeveless red tunics with the Queen's mark, a black wolf's head, emblazoned in the center. As they lifted the heavy iron bar and two of them pulled the squeaky door open for her, they didn't even look to see what she had behind her back. When she heard the clang of the bar dropping back in place, and turned around to see the backs of the guards on the wall, then at last she smiled and started to run; it was a long way.

In a high tower, dark eyes watched her go. Watched her pass through the heavy guard without raising the slightest suspicion, or interest, like a breath through fangs, through the outer wall garden gate that had kept determined armies out, and traitors in, watched her cross the bridge where hundreds of foes had died in battle, yet failed to gain, watched her run across the fields, barefoot, unarmed, innocent, and into the forest. To her secret place.

Furious, Zedd slapped his hand to the cold metal plate. The massive stone door slowly grated closed. He had to step over the bodies of D'Haran guards as he walked to the low wall. His fingers came to rest on the familiar, smooth stone as he leaned forward, looking out over the sleeping city below.

From this high wall on the mountainside, the city looked peaceful enough. But he had already slipped through the darkened streets and seen the troops everywhere. Troops that were there at the cost of many lives, on both sides.

But that wasn't the worst of it.

Darken Rahl had to have been here. Zedd pounded his fist to the stone. It had to be Darken Rahl who had taken it.

The intricate web of shields should have held, but they hadn't. He had been away too many years. He had been a fool.

"Nothing is ever easy," the wizard whispered.

CHAPTER 30

"KAHLAN," RICHARD ASKED, "REMEMBER, when we were back with the Mud People, and that man said Rahl had come, riding a red demon? Do you know what he was talking about?"

They had traveled three days across the plains, with Savidlin and his hunters, then had bid him good-bye with a promise to his sad eyes to do whatever they could to find Siddin, and they had spent the past week climbing up into the high country, into the Rang'Shada, the vast spine of rock that Kahlan had said ran northeast across the back of the Midlands, and cradled in its mountains the remote place known as Agaden Reach. A place she said was surrounded by jagged peaks, like a wreath of thorns, meant to keep all away.

"You don't know?" She looked a little surprised.

When he shook his head, she slumped down on a hump of rock to take a break. Richard slipped his pack off with a tired groan and flopped on the ground, leaning against a short rock, putting his arms back on it to stretch them into a different position. She looked different to him, now that the black and white

427

mud had been washed off her face. He had gotten used to it over those three days.

"So what was it?" he asked again.

"A dragon."

"A dragon! There are dragons in the Midlands? I didn't think there really were such things!"

"Well, there are." She frowned over at him. "I thought you knew." He gave a single shake of his head. "I guess you wouldn't, since Westland has no magic. Dragons have magic. I believe that's how they fly, with the aid of magic."

"I thought dragons were just legends, old tales." He flicked a pebble between his thumb and second finger, watching it bounce off a boulder.

"Old tales of things remembered, maybe. Anyway, they are real enough." With her thumbs, she lifted her hair away from the back of her neck, to cool it, and closed her eyes. "There are different kinds. Gray, green, red, and a few others, less common. The gray ones are the smallest, rather shy. The green are a lot bigger. The smartest and the biggest are the red ones. Some peoples of the Midlands keep the gray ones as pets, and for hunting. No one keeps green ones; they're rather dumb, have bad tempers and can be quite dangerous." Her eyelids slid open and she tilted her head to look up from under her arched eyebrows. "The red ones are something altogether different; they will fry you and eat you in a blink. And, they are smart."

"They eat people!" Richard pressed the heels of his hands to his eyes and gave a groan.

"Only if they are hungry enough, or angry enough. We wouldn't make much of a meal for them." When he took his hands away and opened his eyes, her green eyes were looking at him. "The thing I don't understand is what Rahl was doing on one."

Richard remembered the red thing in the sky that flew over him in the upper Ven Forest, just before he found Kahlan. He tossed another pebble at the boulder. "That must be how he covers so much territory."

She shook her head slowly. "No, I mean I don't understand why a red dragon would submit to it. They are fiercely independent, take no sides in human affairs, in fact, couldn't care less. They would rather die than be subjugated. And they would make a good fight of it, believe me. As I said, they have magic, and could deal even the one from D'Hara quite a match, for a time anyway. Even if he threatened them with death from some of his own magic, they wouldn't care; they would rather die than be ruled.

"They would simply fight until they killed, or were killed." She leaned a little toward him and lowered her voice meaningfully. "The idea of one flying Rahl around on its back is very odd. It's impossible for me to imagine anyone ruling a red dragon."

She watched him a moment, then straightened and picked at the lichen on a rock.

"Are these dragons a threat to us?" He felt stupid asking if a dragon was dangerous.

"Not likely. I have only seen red ones up close a few times. Once, I was walking on a road, and one swooped down, close, in the field right next to me, and grabbed two cows. Carried them off, one in each claw. If we came upon one, a red one, and it was in a foul temper, I suppose it could be big trouble, but that is not very likely."

"We have already come upon a red one," he reminded her in a quiet voice, "and it was big trouble."

She didn't answer. By her expression, the memory obviously pained her as much as it did him.

"Well, there you two are!" a stranger's voice called out.

They both jumped. Richard sprang to his feet with his hand on the sword; Kahlan was in a half crouch ready for anything.

"Sit, sit." The old man motioned with both hands as he walked down the path toward them. "I didn't mean to give you a fright!" His white beard shook when he laughed. "It's just Old John, come looking for the two of you. Sit. Sit."

His large round belly jiggled under his dark brown robes as he laughed. White hair was parted neatly down the middle, and long curly eyebrows and drooping lids shaded his brown eyes. His jolly round face wrinkled with a wide smile as he waited. Kahlan cautiously eased herself back down. Richard lowered himself partway, to sit lightly on the rock he had been leaning against. He kept his hand on his sword.

"What do you mean you have been looking for us?" Richard asked in a not entirely friendly tone.

"My old friend, the wizard, sent me looking for you. . . ."

Richard jumped back to his feet. "Zedd! Zedd sent you?"

Old John held his stomach as he laughed. "How many old wizards do you know, my boy? Of course old Zedd." He gripped his beard, pulling it a little as he peered at them with one eye. "He had important business to attend to, but he needs you, needs you with him, now. So he came and asked me if I'd go get you. Had nothing better to do, so I told him I'd do it. He told me where I'd find you. Looks like he was right, as usual."

Richard smiled at that. "Well, how is he? Where is he, what's he want us for?"

Old John pulled a little harder on his beard, nodding and smiling. "He told me. Told me you asked a lot of questions. He's just fine. Thing is, I don't know why he wants you. When old Zedd's in a fret, you don't ask questions, you just do as he asks. So I did. And here I am."

"Where is he? How far?" Richard was excited about seeing Zedd again.

Old John scratched his chin and leaned forward a little. "Depends. How long you plan on standing there wagging your tongue?"

Richard grinned, then snatched up his pack, his weariness forgotten. Kahlan gave him one of her special tight-lipped smiles as they followed Old John up a rocky trail. Richard let Kahlan walk ahead of him as he watched the surrounding woods. She had told him that they weren't far from the witch woman.

He was excited about seeing Zedd again. He hadn't realized how tense he had been, deep down inside, with worry about his old friend. He knew Adie would have taken good care of him, but she had made no promise that he would be all right. He hoped this meant Chase was well, too. He felt overwhelmed with cheer about seeing Zedd again. He had so much to tell him, to ask him. His mind raced.

"So he's all right then?" Richard called ahead to Old John.

"He's recovered? He didn't lose any weight, did he? Zedd can't afford to lose any weight."

"No," Old John laughed without turning as he walked, "he looks the same as always."

"Well, I hope he didn't eat you out of your larder."

"Not to worry, my boy. How much could one skinny old wizard eat?"

Richard smiled to himself. Zedd might be all right, but he couldn't be fully recovered, or Old John wouldn't have a scrap of food left.

After a couple of hours during which they hurried to keep pace with Old John, the woods became thicker, darker, the trees bigger and closer together. The trail was rocky, hard to walk over, especially at this pace. Calls of strange birds echoed from the murk. The three came to a fork in the trail. Old John took to the right without a pause and kept going. Kahlan followed him. Richard stopped, uncertain about something, but he couldn't quite seem to squeeze it out of the back of his mind. Every time he tried, he found himself thinking again of Zedd. Kahlan heard him stop, and turned, then walked back.

"Which way to the witch woman?" he asked her.

"Left," Kahlan answered, a note of relief in her voice because the old man had gone right. She hooked a thumb under the front of her pack's shoulder strap and pointed with her chin to several stark spines of rock he could just see through the upper branches of the trees. "Those are some of the peaks that surround Agaden Reach." The snow-covered caps shone brightly in the high thin air. He had never seen such inhospitable-looking mountains. Ring of thorns indeed.

Richard looked off down the left trail. It looked to be little traveled, and disappeared quickly into the thick forest. Old John stopped and turned, his hands on his hips.

"You two coming?"

Richard looked back down the left trail. They had to get the last box before Rahl did. Even if Zedd needed them, they had to find out where the box was. That was his first duty.

"Do you think Zedd could wait?"

Old John shrugged, then pulled on his beard. "Don't know.

431

But he wouldn't have sent me if it wasn't important. It's up to you, my boy. But Zedd is this way."

Richard wished he didn't have to make this decision. He wished he knew if Zedd could wait. He wished he knew what Zedd wanted. Stop wishing and start thinking, he told himself.

He frowned up at the old man. "How far?"

Old John looked up at the late-afternoon sun off through the trees as he tugged some more on his beard. "If we don't stop early, and don't sleep late, we'll be there by midday tomorrow." He looked back to Richard, waiting.

Kahlan said nothing, but he knew what she was thinking. She would rather not go anywhere near Shota, and even if they went to Zedd first, it wasn't that far, they could always come back if they had to. And maybe Zedd knew where the box was, maybe he even had the last box, and they wouldn't have to go into Agaden Reach. It made more sense to go after Zedd. That was what she would say.

"You're right," he said to her.

She looked confused. "I said nothing."

Richard gave her a big grin. "I could hear you thinking. You're right. We'll go with Old John."

"I didn't know my thoughts were that loud," she muttered.

"If we don't stop at all," he called up to Old John, "we could be there before morning."

"I'm an old man," he complained, then sighed loudly. "But I know how anxious you are. And I know how badly he needs you." He wagged his finger at Richard. "I should have listened when Zedd warned me about you."

Richard laughed a little as he let Kahlan walk ahead of him. She strode fast to catch up with the old man, who was already on his way. He watched her absently as she walked, watched as she pulled a spiderweb off her face, spit some of it out of her mouth. Something nagged at him; something was wrong. He wished he could figure out what it was. He tried for a minute, but all he could think about was Zedd, how much he wanted to see him again, how he couldn't wait to talk to him. He ignored the feeling that there were eyes watching him.

"Mostly, I miss my brother," she said to her doll. She looked away. "They said he died," she confided softly.

Rachel had been telling her doll her troubles for most of the day. All her troubles she could think of. When she got tears, the doll said she loved her, and it made her feel good. Sometimes it made her laugh.

Rachel put another small stick in the fire. It felt so good to be able to get warm, and have light. But she kept the fire small, just like Giller had told her. The fire kept her from being so afraid in the woods, especially at night. It would be night again soon. Sometimes there were noises in the woods at night that made her scared, made her cry. But being out here in the lonely woods was still better than being locked in the box.

"That was when I lived in that place I told you about. With the other children, before the Queen came and picked me. I liked it there a lot better than living with the Princess. They were nice to me there." She looked over at the doll to see if she was listening. "There was a man, Brophy, who came sometimes. People said mean things about him, but he was nice to us children. He was nice, like Giller. He gave me a doll, too, but the Queen wouldn't let me take it with me when I went to live at the castle. I didn't care, though, because I was so sad my brother died. I heard some people say he got murdered. I know that means he got killed. Why do people kill children?"

The doll just smiled. Rachel smiled back.

She thought about the new little boy she had seen the Queen having locked up. He talked funny, and looked funny, but his presence still had reminded her of her brother. That was because he seemed so afraid. Her brother was always getting afraid, too. Rachel could always tell when her brother was getting afraid because he would fidget and squirm. She felt so sorry for the new boy; she wished she was important so she could help him.

Rachel put her hands toward the fire to warm them for a minute, then stuck one in her pocket. She was hungry. A few berries were all she had been able to find to eat. She held a big one out,

433

offering it to her doll. The doll didn't seem hungry, so she ate it herself, then a handful more, until they were gone. She was still hungry, but she didn't want to look for more. The place where they grew wasn't close, and it was getting dark. She didn't want to be out in the woods when it was dark. She wanted to be in her wayward pine with her doll. By the warm fire; by the light.

"Maybe the Queen will be nicer when she gets her alliance, whatever that is. That's all she talks about, how she wants her alliance. Maybe she'll be happier then, and won't say to chop off people's heads. The Princess makes me go with her, you know, but I don't like to watch, I close my eyes. Now even Princess Violet says to chop off people's heads. She gets meaner every day. Now I'm afraid that she'll say to chop off my head. I wish I could run away." She looked over at her doll. "I wish I could run away and never come back. And I'd take you with me."

The doll smiled. "I love you, Rachel."

She picked up the doll and gave it a long hug, then kissed it on its head.

"But if we run away, Princess Violet would send the guards to find me, and then she would throw you in the fire. I don't want her to throw you in the fire. I love you."

"I love you, Rachel."

Rachel hugged her doll tight, and crawled into the hay, with the doll next to her. Tomorrow she had to go back, and the Princess would be mean to her some more. She had to leave her doll when she went back, she knew, or it would get thrown in the fire.

"You're the bestest friend I ever had. You and Giller."

"I love you, Rachel."

She started to worry, to worry what would happen to her doll, all alone here in the wayward pine. The doll would be lonely. What if the Princess never sent her out again; what if she somehow found out that she wanted to be sent out, and kept her in the castle just to be mean?

"Do you know what I should do?" she asked the doll as she looked up at the firelight flickering on the dark branches inside the tree.

"Help Giller," the doll said.

She rolled over on one elbow and looked at the doll. "Help Giller?"

The doll nodded. "Help Giller."

Rays from the setting sun ahead reflected off the layer of leaves, making the path bright and shiny between the dark mass of woods to each side. Richard could hear Kahlan's boots scuffing across rocks hidden under the colorful mat. A light scent of rot was in the air: fallen leaves beginning to decompose in the low damp places and the thick piles in the laps of rocks, where the wind had collected them.

Even though it was getting cold, neither Richard nor Kahlan wore their cloaks, being warm from the exertion of the pace Old John was setting. Richard kept trying to think about Zedd, but his train of thought was constantly being interrupted by having to lope to keep up. The realization that he was getting winded finally made him push Zedd from his mind. But one thought wouldn't leave him: something didn't feel right.

At last, he allowed that caution to blossom in his mind. How could an old man be out walking him like this, yet look fresh and relaxed? Richard felt his forehead, wondering if he was sick, or had a fever. He did feel hot. Maybe he wasn't well; maybe there was something wrong with him. They had been pushing hard for days, but not this hard. No, he felt fine, simply winded.

For a while, he watched Kahlan walking ahead of him. She, too, was having difficulty keeping up. She pulled another spiderweb off her face, then trotted to keep up. He could see that, like him, she was breathing hard. For some reason, Richard's caution was igniting into foreboding.

He caught a brief glimpse of something off to the left, in the woods, keeping pace. Just a small animal, he thought. But it looked like something with long arms, skittering along the ground; then it was gone. His mouth felt dry. It must just be his imagination, he told himself.

He turned his attention back to Old John. The path was wide in some places, narrow in others with branches that reached in tight. When Kahlan and Richard went past, they both sometimes brushed against them, or simply pushed them out of the way. Not the old man. He stayed to the center of the trail, avoiding any errant limb, his arms clutching his cloak tightly to him.

Richard's eye was caught by the strands of a spiderweb, glistening golden in the setting sun, stretched across the path in front of Kahlan. The web parted against her upper leg when she walked through it.

The sweat on his face instantly turned ice cold against his skin.

How could Old John not have broken the web?

He looked up and saw a branch, its tip sticking out in the path. The old man skirted it. But not the tip. The tip passed through his arm as it would pass through smoke.

Breathing faster, he glanced down at the footprints Kahlan made through an open patch of soft ground. There were none from Old John.

Richard's left hand shot forward, seized a fistful of Kahlan's shirt, and yanked her behind him, causing her to cry out in surprise. He tossed her backward as his right hand pulled the sword free.

Old John stopped and half turned at the sound of the sword's ringing.

"What is it, my boy? See something?" His voice came like the hiss of a snake.

"Indeed." Richard gripped the sword in both hands, his legs set in a defensive stance, his chest heaving. He felt the anger flooding his fear. "How is it that you don't break spiderwebs when you walk through them, or leave footprints?"

Old John gave a slow, sly smile, appraising him with one eye. "Did you not expect that an old friend of a wizard would have special talents?"

"Maybe," Richard said, his eyes darting left and right, checking. "But tell me, Old John, what is your old friend's name?"

"Why, it's Zedd." His eyebrows lifted. "How else would I know, if he weren't my old friend." His cloak was pulled tightly around him. His head had sunken into his shoulders.

"I'm the one who foolishly told you his name was Zedd. Now, you tell me your old friend's last name."

Old John watched him with a dark frown, his eyes moving slowly, appraising, measuring. Eyes of an animal.

With a sudden roar that made Richard flinch, the old man turned, his cloak flinging open. In the time it took to complete the turn, he mushroomed to twice his previous size.

An impossible nightmare came to life: fur and claws and fangs, where an old man had been an instant before.

A creature of snarl and snap.

Richard gasped as he looked up at the gaping maw of the beast. It roared and abruptly took a giant step forward. Richard took three back. He gripped the sword so hard it hurt. The woods echoed with the earsplitting cry of the thing, deep, savage, vicious. The mouth stretched wide with each roar. It leaned over him, deep-set red eyes glowing, snapping its huge teeth. Richard urgently backed up, retreating behind the sword. He took a quick glance, but didn't see Kahlan behind him.

All at once, it came for him. Richard didn't have a chance to swing the sword. He tripped on a root, falling backward, sprawling across the ground. He couldn't get his breath. Instinctively, he brought the sword up to impale the thing, expecting it to fall on him.

Sharp, wet teeth reached over the sword, snapping viciously at his face. He drove the sword up, but the beast stayed clear. Furious red eyes glared at the sword. It backed away and looked toward the woods to its right. Its ears lay back as it snarled at something.

It picked up a rock twice the size of Richard's head, put its blunt snout high in the air, took a deep breath, and with a roar squeezed the rock in its claw. Corded muscles tightened. The rock split with a loud crack that reverberated through the forest. Dust and flakes of rock filled the air. The beast looked about, turned, and swiftly slipped into the trees.

Richard lay on his back, panting, watching the woods with wide eyes, expecting the beast to reappear. He called out Kahlan's name. She didn't answer.

Before he could scramble fully to his feet, something ashen, with long arms, leapt on him, knocking him to his back again. It screamed with rage. Powerful gnarled hands gripped his, trying to pry the sword from his grip. One of the arms backhanded him across the jaw, nearly slamming him senseless. Bloodless white lips curled back, exposing sharp teeth, as it howled. Bulging yellow eyes snatched glances back at him. It tried frantically to kick his face. Richard held on to the sword with all his strength, trying to twist away from the painful grip of the long fingers.

"My sword," it snarled. "Gimme. Gimme my sword."

Locked desperately together, the two of them rolled across the ground, leaves and sticks flying. One of the powerful hands reached back, grabbing Richard by the hair, whacking his head on the ground, aiming for a rock. With a grunt, suddenly it reached again for the hilt, pulling one of Richard's sweating hands from the sword, slapping its own hand to the hilt with Richard's other. Its shrill screams split the forest quiet. Sinewy fingers started clawing his left hand off the hilt; sharp nails dug into the flesh.

Richard knew he was losing. The wiry little creature, despite its size, was stronger than he was. He had to do something or he would soon lose the sword.

"Gimme," it hissed, in a flash turning its pallid head back to his, snapping, trying to bite his face. Spaces between its teeth were packed with spongy, gray debris. Its heavy breath reeked of rot. Dark splotches covered the hairless, waxy head.

The next time they rolled across the ground, Richard desperately reached to his belt and pulled his knife. In a rush he had it to the folds of the thing's neck.

"Please!" it howled. "No kill! No kill!"

"Then let go of the sword! Now!"

The thing slowly, reluctantly, released its grip. Richard was on his back, the putrid-smelling creature on his chest. It went limp against him.

"Please, no kill me," it repeated in a whimper.

Richard untangled himself from the disgusting creature, laying it on its back. He put the point of the sword hard against its chest. Its yellow eyes went wide.

The anger from the sword, which had somehow seemed confused and lost, at last charged into him.

"If I even think you're about to do something I don't like"— Richard jabbed—"I'll push. Understand?" It nodded vigorously. Richard leaned closer. "Where did your friend go?"

438

"Friend?"

"That big thing that almost had me before you did!"

"The Calthrop. Not friend," it whined. "Lucky man. Calthrop kills at night. Was waiting till night. To kill you. It has power in the night. Lucky man."

"I don't believe you! You were with it."

"No," it winced. "I only followed. Till it kills you."

"Why?"

Bulging eyes went to the sword. "My sword. Gimme. Please?"

"No!"

Richard looked around for Kahlan. Her pack lay on the ground a short distance behind him, but he didn't see her. Suddenly Richard was cold with worry. His eyes swept the area in quick jerks. He knew the Calthrop didn't have her; it had gone into the woods alone. He continued to hold the point of the sword against the creature on the ground while he yelled out her name, hoping she would return his desperate calls. No answer.

"Mistress has the pretty lady."

Richard's face snapped back to the yellow eyes. "What're you talking about?"

"Mistress. She took pretty lady." Richard pushed the sword harder, indicating that he wanted to hear more, and right now. "We were following you. Watching the Calthrop play with you. To see what would happen." His bulging yellow eyes went to the sword again.

"To steal the sword," Richard glared.

"Not steal! Mine! Gimme!" Its hands started to go for it again until Richard pushed the sword a little, making the creature freeze.

"Who's your mistress!"

"Mistress!" it shook, pleading for rescue. "Mistress is Shota."

Richard's head twitched back a little. "Your mistress is the witch woman, Shota?"

The creature nodded vigorously.

His hand tightened on the hilt. "Why did she take the pretty lady?"

"Don't know. Maybe, to play with her. Maybe, to kill her." The thing peered up at him. "Maybe, to get you."

439

"Turn over," Richard said. The creature cringed. "Turn over, or I'll run you through!"

It flipped over, trembling. Richard leaned his boot into the small of its back, below the sharp, raised projections of its spine. He reached in his pack, pulling out a length of rope. He ran a loop with a slip knot around its neck.

"Do you have a name?"

"Companion. I am Mistress's companion. Samuel."

Richard pulled him to his feet; leaves stuck to the gray skin of his chest. "Well, Samuel, we're going after your mistress. You're going to lead the way. If you make one wrong move, I'll snap your neck with this rope. Understand?"

Samuel nodded quickly, then, giving a sidelong glance at the rope, nodded slowly. "Agaden Reach. Companion take you there. No kill me?"

"If you take me there, to your mistress, and if the pretty lady is all right, I won't kill you."

Richard put tension to the rope to let Samuel know who was in charge, then put away the sword.

"Here, you carry the pretty lady's pack."

Samuel snatched the pack out of Richard's hands. "Mine! Gimme!" Big hands started rummaging through it.

Richard gave a sharp tug on the rope. "That doesn't belong to you. Keep your hands out of it!"

Bulging yellow eyes filled with hate looked up at him. "When Mistress kills you, then Samuel eats you."

"If I don't eat you first," Richard sneered. "I'm pretty hungry. Maybe I'll have a little Samuel stew along the way?"

The look of hate changed to a look of wide, yellow-eyed terror. "Please! No kill me! Samuel take you to Mistress, to pretty lady. Promise." He put the pack to his shoulder and took a few steps, until he ran out of slack. "Follow Samuel. Hurry," he said, wanting to prove his worth alive. "No cook Samuel, please," he muttered over and over as they went back down the trail.

Richard couldn't begin to imagine what sort of creature Samuel was. There was something familiar, unsettling, about him. He wasn't very tall, but he was powerfully strong. Richard's jaw still throbbed from where Samuel had hit him, and his neck and head ached from having his head pounded on the ground.

Long arms nearly reached the ground as Samuel walked along in an odd waddle, muttering over and over that he didn't want to be cooked. Short, dark pants held up with straps were all he wore. His feet were as disproportionately large as his hands and arms. His belly was round and full, with what, Richard could only wonder. There was no hair on him anywhere, and his skin looked as if it hadn't been in the sunlight in years. From time to time, Samuel would snatch up a stick, or a rock, and say "Mine! Gimme!" to no one in particular, only to soon lose interest and drop his latest find.

Keeping a sharp eye on both the woods and Samuel, Richard followed the companion, prodding him to move faster. He was afraid for Kahlan, and he was furious at himself. Old John, or the Calthrop, whatever it was, had completely taken him in. He couldn't believe how stupid he had been. He had fallen for the story because he had wanted to believe, had wanted so badly to see Zedd. The very thing he had always told others not to do. And there he was, giving the monster the information it then repeated back to him as proof. He was furious at how stupid he had been. He was also painfully ashamed.

People believe things because they want to, he had told Kahlan, and so had he, and now the witch woman had her. The very thing she had been so afraid of, and because he had been so stupid, had let his guard down. It seemed that every time he let his guard down, she was the one who paid the price. If the witch woman harmed Kahlan, she would find out what the wrath of a Seeker was all about, he vowed to himself.

Once again he reprimanded himself. He was letting his imagination get away from him. If Shota wanted to kill her, she would have done so on the spot. She wouldn't be taking her back to Agaden Reach. But why take her back to the Reach? Unless, as Samuel put it, she wanted to play with her. Richard tried to put that thought out of his mind. It had to be him she wanted, not Kahlan. That was probably why the Calthrop left so quickly; the witch woman had scared it off.

When they reached the fork they had passed before, Samuel took them immediately down the left path. It was getting dark, but the companion didn't slow. The trail started climbing up steep switchbacks, and soon they were out of the trees, onto an open trail across the rock, climbing steadily toward the jagged, snow-covered peaks.

In the moonlit snow, Richard could see two sets of footprints, one of them Kahlan's. A good sign, he thought; she was still alive. It didn't look like Shota intended to kill her. At least not right away.

Skirting the bottom of the snowcaps, the path led over the bottom fringes of the snow, which was wet, heavy, and hard to walk through. Without Samuel leading the way, knowing where this pass was, Richard realized it would take days to make it over these peaks. The cold wind whipped through the gaps in the rock, pulling away long thin clouds of their breath in the frigid air. Samuel was shivering. Richard put on his cloak, then pulled Kahlan's out of the pack Samuel was carrying.

"This belongs to the pretty lady. You may wear it, for now, to keep warm."

Samuel snatched the cloak out of his hands. "Mine! Gimme!"

"If you're going to be like that, then I won't let you wear it." Richard pulled the rope taut and yanked the cloak back.

"Please! Samuel cold," he whined. "Please? Wear the pretty lady's cloak?"

Richard handed it back. This time the companion took it slowly, and put it around his shoulders. The little creature made Richard's skin crawl. He took out a piece of tava bread and ate it as they walked along. Samuel kept looking over his shoulder, watching Richard eat. When he could stand it no longer, Richard offered Samuel a piece.

The big hands reached out. "Mine! Gimme!" Richard pulled the bread back, out of reach. Pleading yellow eyes looked up at him in the moonlight. "Please?" Richard carefully put the bread into his eager hands.

Samuel made small talk as he they trudged through the snow. He had eaten the bread in one bite. Richard knew if given the chance, Samuel would slit his throat without a second thought. He seemed to be a creature devoid of any redeeming qualities.

"Samuel, why does Shota keep you around?"

He looked back over his shoulder, his yellow eyes set in a puzzled frown. "Samuel companion."

"And won't your mistress be angry with you for leading me to her?"

Samuel made a gurgling sound that Richard took for laughter. "Mistress not afraid of Seeker."

Near dawn, at the edge of a descent into a dark wood, Samuel's long arm pointed downward. "Agaden Reach," he gurgled. He looked back over his shoulder with a taunting grin. "Mistress."

The heat was oppressive in the wood. Richard took off his cloak and put it in his pack, then stuffed Kahlan's back in hers. Samuel watched without protest. He seemed happy, confident, to be back in the Reach. Richard pretended he could see where they were going, not wanting to give the companion any idea that he was almost blind in the thick darkness. Richard let himself be guided along by the rope, like a blind man. Samuel loped along as if it were bright as midday. Whenever he turned his hairless head back to Richard, his yellow eyes shone like twin lanterns.

As the light of dawn slowly suffused the wood, Richard could begin to see large trees all about, trailers of moss wafting down, boggy patches with vapor rising from the black, murky water, pairs of eyes that watched and blinked from the shadows. Hollow calls echoed through the mist and vapor as he stepped carefully over the tangle of roots. The place reminded him a little of the Skow Swamp. It smelled just as rank.

"How much farther?"

"Close." Samuel grinned.

Richard took up the slack on the rope. "Just remember, if anything goes wrong, you die first."

The grin faded from the bloodless lips.

Here and there in the mud Richard could see the same pair of footprints that he had seen in the snow. Kahlan was still walking. Dark forms followed, keeping to the shadows, the thick brush, sometimes letting out whoops and howls. Richard wondered, and worried, if they were more things like Samuel. Or worse. Some followed in the treetops, just beyond sight. Despite his best efforts to halt it, a shiver went up his spine.

Samuel skirted off the path, around the twisted roots of a squat, fat-trunked tree.

"What're you doing?" Richard asked, pulling the companion to a halt.

Samuel grinned back at him. "Watch." He picked up a stout stick, big as his wrist, and threw it with an underhand swing into the roots of the tree. The roots whipped out, knotting around the stick, pulling it under the tangled mass. Richard heard it snapping apart. Samuel gurgled with laughter.

As the sun climbed higher, the woods of Agaden Reach seemed to become even darker. Dead branches twisted together overhead, and mist occasionally drifted across their way. At times Richard couldn't even see Samuel on the other end of the wet rope. But always he could hear things: scratching, clawing, whistling, things clicking at them from just out of sight. Sometimes the mist twirled and spun at the passing of creatures darting by, near but unseen.

Richard remembered what Kahlan had said: they were going to die. He tried to put the thought out of his head. She had told him she had never met the witch woman, only heard others speak of her. But what she had heard had terrified her. Those who went in never came out. Not even a wizard would go into Agaden Reach, she had said. But still, it was secondhand knowledge; she hadn't ever met Shota. Maybe the stories were exaggerated. His eyes scanned the menacing, forbidding woods. And maybe not.

From ahead, through the tangles mass of trees, came light, sunlight, and the sound of rushing water. The farther they went, the brighter it became. Soon they reached the edge of the dark wood. The trail simply ended. Samuel gurgled with glee.

Spread out far below was a long valley, green, bright, lit by the sun. Gigantic rocky peaks soared almost straight up all around it. Fields of golden grasses among stands of oak, beech, and maple set in rich autumn colors rippled in the breeze. In the dark forest where they stood, it felt like standing in night, looking out on day. Water tumbled off the rocks beside them, down

444

the vertical drop, disappearing soundlessly through the air until it reached the clear pools and streams below, where it made a distant roar and a hiss. Spray drifted up past them, wetting their faces.

Samuel pointed down into the valley. "Mistress."

Richard nodded and had him move on. Samuel led them through a labyrinth of brush, tight trees, and fern-covered boulders, to a place Richard would never have found without his little guide: a trail hidden behind rocks and vines, at the edge of the precipice, leading down the wall of the valley. As they descended, the trail offered panoramic views of the beautiful country below: the trees looking small in patches over the gentle hills, the streams meandering among the fields and banks, the sky a bright blue overhead.

In the center of it all, set among a carpet of grand trees, was a beautiful palace of breathtaking grace and splendor. Delicate spires stretched into the air, wispy bridges spanned the high gaps between towers, stairs spiraled around turrets. Colorful flags and streamers atop every point snapped lightly and flew lazily in the wind. The magnificent palace seemed to be reaching joyously to the sky.

Richard stood silent for a moment, mouth agape, staring, hardly able to believe what he was seeing. He loved his home of Hartland, but there was no place there to compare to this. This was, quite simply, the most beautiful place he had ever seen. He never would have imagined that a vision of such exquisite loveliness even existed.

The two of them started off again, down the valley's edge. In places, there were steps, thousands of them, cut from the stone of the wall, twisting, tunneling and turning downward, sometimes spiraling back on themselves, going underneath the ones above. Samuel sprang down them as if he had done it a thousand times before. He was obviously thrilled to be home again, near the protection of his mistress.

At the bottom, in the sunlight, a road led off through the tree-dotted hills and warm grass fields. Samuel bounded along in his odd gait, gurgling to himself. Richard took in the slack once in a while to remind him who still held the other end of the rope.

445

As they crossed the valley floor, following a clear stream for a time, moving ever closer to the palace, the trees became a little thicker, closer together, each a magnificent specimen, shading road or field from the bright sun. The road took them gently uphill. At the top of a rise, the trees seemed as if they were gathered, sheltering, surrounding a place before them. Richard could see the spires of the palace off through the branches ahead.

They entered a shady, still, enveloping cathedral of trees.

Richard could hear the gentle sound of water running through mossy rock. Hazy streamers of sunlight penetrated the quiet, muted area. There was the sweet smell of grass and leaves.

Samuel's arm stretched out. Richard looked where he pointed, to the center of the open, sheltered place. There sat a rock; water bubbling up from a spring in its center ran down the sides into a little stream dotted with rich, green, mossy rocks. A woman in a long white dress, soft brown hair, with her back to him, sat on the edge of the rock, in the dappled sunlight, running her fingers through the clear water. Even from the back, she looked somehow familiar.

"Mistress," Samuel said, glassy-eyed. He pointed again, off to the side of the road, closer to them. "Pretty lady."

Richard could see Kahlan standing stiffly. There was something odd about her. Something was on her, moving. Samuel turned his blotchy head back, pointing a long gray finger at the rope. He looked up at Richard with one yellow eye.

"Seeker promises," he said in a low growl.

Richard untied the rope, took Kahlan's pack off the companion's shoulder, and laid it on the ground. Samuel curled his bloodless lips up at Richard, hissing, then abruptly skittered off into the shadows, sitting in a squat to watch.

Richard swallowed hard as he walked to Kahlan, a tight knot in his stomach. With a jolt, he saw at last what it was that was moving on her.

Snakes.

Kahlan was covered by a writhing mass of snakes. The ones he recognized were all poisonous. Big, fat ones were wrapped around her legs, one coiled tightly around her waist, constricting; others were wrapped around her arms, which hung at her sides.

446

Small snakes squiggled, tunneling through her thick hair, flicking their tongues out; others curled around her neck; still more slithered down the front of her shirt, poking their heads out between the buttons. He struggled to control his breathing as he approached her. His heart was pounding. Tears ran down Kahlan's cheeks, and she shook the slightest bit.

"Be still," he said in a quiet voice. "I'll get them off."

"No!" she whispered back. Her eyes, wide with panic, met his. "If you touch them, or if I move, they will bite me."

"It's all right," he tried to reassure her, "I'll get you out of this."

"Richard," she said in a pleading whisper, "I'm dead. Leave me. Get out of here. Run."

He felt as if an invisible hand were constricting his throat. In her eyes, he could see how she was struggling to control her panic. He tried to look as calm as he could, to hearten her. "I'm not leaving you," he breathed.

"Please, Richard," she whispered hoarsely, "for me, before it's too late. Run."

A thin, poisonous banded viper, its tail coiled in her hair, dropped its head down in front of her face. The red tongue flicked at her. Kahlan closed her eyes, and another tear ran down her cheek. The snake wriggled around the side of her face, down over her collarbone. The banded body disappeared into her shirt. She gave out the slightest whimper.

"I'm going to die. You can't save me now. Please, Richard, save yourself. Please. Run. Run while you still have a chance."

Richard was afraid she would move deliberately, to be bitten, to try to save him, thinking he then would have no reason to stay. He had to convince her that that would do no good. He gave her a sober look.

"No. I came here to find out where the box is. I'm not leaving until I know. Now be still."

She opened her eyes wide at what the snake was doing in her shirt. She bit her bottom lip; her eyebrows wrinkled together. Richard swallowed back dryness in his mouth.

"Kahlan, just hold on. Try to think of something else."

In a rage, he strode over to the woman sitting on the rock with her back still to him. Something inside warned him not to pull

447

the sword, but he could not, would not, hold back his anger at what she was doing to Kahlan. He breathed through gritted teeth.

When he reached her, she stood and gently turned to him, speaking his name in a voice he recognized.

His heart leapt into his throat when he saw the face that matched the voice.

CHAPTER 31

IT WAS HIS MOTHER.

Richard felt as if a bolt of lightning had struck him. His whole body went rigid. His rage flinched, and the anger dropped its grip from him, recoiling at the idea of lethal intent and his mother in the same mental image.

"Richard." She smiled sadly at him, showing in that smile how much she loved and missed him.

His mind raced, trying to grasp what was happening, unable to fit what he was seeing with what he knew. This couldn't be. It was simply impossible.

"Mother?" he breathed in a whisper.

Arms he knew, remembered, slipped around him, comforted him, brought tears to his eyes, a lump to his throat.

"Oh, Richard," she said soothingly, "how I've missed you." She ran her fingers through his hair, gentling him. "How I've missed you so."

Reeling, he fought to regain control of his emotions. He struggled to focus his mind on Kahlan. He couldn't let her down again, let himself be fooled again. She was in this trouble because he had allowed himself to be fooled. This wasn't his mother, it was Shota, a witch woman. But what if he was somehow wrong?

"Richard, why have you come to me?"

Richard put his hands on her small shoulders, gently pushing her back a little. Her hands slipped to his waist, squeezing with familiar affection. She was not his mother, he forced himself to say in his mind, she was a witch woman, a witch woman who knew where the last box of Orden was, and he had to know the answer to that. But why would she be doing this? And what if he was wrong? Could this somehow be true?

His finger went to the little scar above her left eyebrow, tracing the familiar bump. A scar he had put there. He had been at swordplay with Michael, with their wooden swords, and had just jumped off the bed, taking a foolish and wild swing at his older brother, when his mother came through the door. His sword had caught her across the forehead. Her cry had terrified him.

Even the whipping his father had given him didn't hurt as much as the thought of what he had done to his mother. His father had sent him to bed without supper, and that night, when it was dark, she had come to sit on the side of his bed, run her fingers through his hair as he cried. He had sat up and asked her if it hurt a lot. She had smiled at him and said . . .

"Not as much as it hurts you," the woman in front of him whispered.

Richard's eyes went wide; bumps ran up his arms. "How do you . . ."

"Richard," came an even, cautioning voice from behind him, jolting him again. "Stand away from her." It was Zedd's voice.

His mother's hand cupped the side of his face. He ignored it and turned his head, looking back up the road, to the top of the rise. It was Zedd, or at least he thought it was Zedd. It looked just like Zedd, but then, this looked just like his mother. Zedd was standing there, with a look he recognized, a look of cold danger, warning.

"Richard," came Zedd's voice again. "Do as I say. Stand away from her. Now."

"Please, Richard," his mother breathed, "don't leave me. Don't you know me?"

450

Richard turned to her soft face. "Yes. You are Shota."

He took her wrists, pulled her hands from his waist, and stepped back from her. Near tears, she watched him move away.

Suddenly, she spun toward the wizard. Her hands snapped up. With an earsplitting crack, blue lightning erupted from her fingers, streaking toward Zedd. The wizard's hands instantly brought up a shield, like glass, reflecting light in its gloss. The lightning from Shota hit it with a thunderous peal and glanced off, striking a huge oak, snapping its trunk in a shower of splinters. The tree crashed to earth. The ground shuddered.

Zedd's hands were already up. Wizard's fire shot from his curled fingers. It shrieked as it came, tumbling through the air with howling fury.

"No!" Richard screamed.

The ball of liquid flame harshly illuminated the shady area with intense blue and yellow light.

He couldn't let this happen! Shota was the only way to find the box! The only way to stop Rahl!

The fire wailed as it expanded, heading right for Shota. She stood motionless.

"No!" Richard yanked the sword free and jumped in front of her. Gripping the hilt in one hand, the point in the other, with arms locked, he held it up horizontally in front of himself, as a shield.

The magic raced through him. Wrath took him. The fire was upon him. The roar filled his ears. He turned his face, closed his eyes, held his breath and gritted his teeth, fully expecting that he might die. But there was no choice. The witch woman was their only chance. He couldn't let her be killed.

The impact staggered him back a step. He felt the heat. Even with his eyes tightly closed, he could see the light. The wizard's fire wailed in rage as it struck the sword, exploding around him.

And then there was silence. He opened his eyes. The wizard's fire was gone. Zedd wasted no time. Already he was throwing a handful of magic dust. It sparkled as it came. Richard saw something coming from behind him, magic dust from the witch woman. It shimmered like ice crystals, taking the sparkle from Zedd's dust, and slammed into him.

Zedd stood frozen, unmoving, one hand in the air.

"Zedd!"

There was no reply. Richard spun to the witch woman. She was no longer his mother. Shota wore a wispy dress with variegated shades of gray across its gauzy surface, its folds and loose points floating in the light breeze. Her full, thick hair was a wavy auburn, her smooth skin flawless. Almond eyes shone up at him. She was as beautiful as the palace that stood behind her, the valley around her. She was so attractive, it almost took his breath away, and would have, were it not for the rage he was feeling.

"My hero," she said in a voice that was no longer his mother's, but silky, clear, easy. A sly smile came to her full lips. "Totally unnecessary, but it's the thought that counts. I am impressed."

"And who is this supposed to be? Another vision from my mind? Or is this the real Shota?" Richard was enraged. He recognized all too well the anger from the sword, but decided to keep the weapon out.

Her smile widened. "Are those clothes really you?" she teased. "Or are they something you wear for a time, to serve a purpose?"

"What's the purpose of who you are now?"

Her eyebrow lifted. "Why, to please you, Richard. That's all."

"With some illusion!"

"No." Her voice softened. "This is no illusion, it's the way I appear to myself, most of the time anyway. This is real."

Richard ignored her answer, pointing up the road with the sword. "What have you done to Zedd?"

She shrugged, looking away with a demure smile. "Merely prevented him from harming me. He is all right. For the moment anyway." Almond eyes sparkled up from under her eyebrows. "I will kill him later, after you and I have talked."

His grip on the sword tightened. "And Kahlan?"

Shota redirected her gaze to Kahlan, who stood still, pale, her mouth trembling, her eyes locked on Shota's every move. Richard knew Kahlan feared this woman more than she feared the snakes. Shota frowned; then it melted back into her coy smile as she returned her gaze to him.

"She is a very dangerous woman." Her eyes flashed with knowing that went well beyond the years she appeared to be.

452

"More dangerous than even she knows. I have to protect myself from her." She shrugged again, deftly catching the corner of a floating wisp of her dress. When she did, the rest of the dress settled down, as if the breeze had died. "So I did that to keep her still. If she moves, they will bite her. If she doesn't, they won't," Shota thought a moment. "I will kill her later, too." Her voice seemed too gentle, too pleasant for the words she spoke.

Richard considered using the sword to take off the witch woman's head. His rage demanded it. He visualized it powerfully in his mind, hoping Shota could see it, too. Then he put the fury down a little, but still at the ready.

"And me? Are you not afraid of me?"

Shota gave a little laugh, a smile. "A Seeker?" Her fingers went to her lips as if to try to hide her amusement. "No, I don't think so."

Richard could barely contain himself. "Perhaps you should be."

"Perhaps. Perhaps in normal times. But these are not normal times. Otherwise why would you be here? To kill me? You have just saved me." She gave him a look that said he should be ashamed of himself for saying something so stupid, then walked around him, one full turn. He turned with her, keeping the sword between them, although she seemed unconcerned by it. "These are times that demand strange alliances, Richard. Only the strong are wise enough to recognize this." She stopped and folded her arms, appraising him with a thoughtful smile. "My hero. Why, I can't remember the last time anyone thought to save my life." She leaned toward him. "Very gallant. It truly was." She slipped an arm around his waist. Richard wanted to stop her, but somehow he didn't.

"Don't flatter yourself. I had my motives." He found her easy manner unnerving, and fiercely attractive. He knew he had no reason to feel attracted to her. She had just said she was going to kill his two best friends, and by Kahlan's manner he knew it was no vain boast. Worse, he had the sword out, the sword's anger out. He realized that even its magic was being bewitched. He felt as if he were drowning, and to his surprise, was finding the experience pleasant.

Her smile widened, making her almond eyes sparkle. "As I

said, only the strong are wise enough for the alliances needed. The wizard wasn't wise enough; he tried to kill me. She isn't wise enough; she would also. She didn't even want to come here. Only you were wise enough to see that these times demand an alliance such as ours."

Richard struggled to maintain a level of outrage. "I make no alliances with those who would kill my friends."

"Even if they try to kill me first? Have I no right to defend myself? Am I to lay down and die, because it's your friends who would do the killing? Richard," she said, shaking her head with a frown and a smile, "think about what you are saying. Look at it from my eyes."

He thought about it, but said nothing. She gave his waist an affectionate squeeze.

"But you were very gallant. You, my hero, have done a very rare thing. You have put your life at risk for me, a witch woman. That kind of thing does not go unrewarded. You have earned a wish. Anything you want, simply name it, and it will be granted." With her free hand she made gliding motions in the air. "Anything, on my word."

Richard started to open his mouth, but Shota put a finger gently to his lips. Her warm body, firm beneath the thin dress, pressed against him. "Don't spoil my opinion of you by answering too quickly. You may have anything you want. Don't waste the wish. Think it over carefully before you ask. It's an important wish, offered for a reason, and perhaps the most important wish you will ever have. Haste could mean death."

Richard was seething, in spite of how strangely attracted he was to this woman. "I don't have to think it over. My wish is for you not to kill my friends. To leave them unharmed, and let them go."

Shota sighed. "I'm afraid that would complicate things."

"Oh? So, your word means nothing?"

She gave him a reproachful glare. Her voice had a hint of harshness to it. "My word means everything. I simply want you to know it would complicate matters. You came here for the answer to an important question. You have a wish coming. You have merely to ask the question as your wish, and I will grant it.

"Isn't that what you really want? Ask yourself what's more

454

important; how many will die if you fail in your duty." She squeezed his waist again, her beautiful smile returning. "Richard, the sword is confusing you. The magic is interfering with your judgment. Put it away, then think again. If you are wise, you will heed my warning; it is not without reason."

Richard angrily thrust the sword back into its scabbard to show her he wouldn't change his mind. He looked back at Zedd, standing frozen in place. He looked over at Kahlan, snakes writhing all over her. When their eyes met, his heart ached for her. He knew what Kahlan wanted him to do; he could see it in her eyes; she wanted him to use the wish to find the box. Richard turned away from her, unable to witness her torment another moment. He regarded Shota with determination.

"I've put the sword away, Shota. It changes nothing. You are going to answer my question anyway. Your life, too, depends upon my knowing the answer. You have as much as admitted it. I'm not wasting my wish. To use it to get an answer you already intend to give me would be a waste of my friends' lives. Now, grant my wish!"

Shota regarded him with ancient eyes. "Dear Richard," she said softly, "a Seeker needs his anger, but don't let it fill your head to the exclusion of wisdom. Do not judge too quickly actions you do not fully understand. Not all acts are as they seem. Some are meant to save you."

Her hand came up slowly to the side of his face, reminding him again of his mother. Her gentleness made him feel calm, and somehow sad. In that moment, he felt his fear of her wane.

"Please, Shota," he whispered. "I have made my wish. Grant it."

"Your wish, dear Richard, is granted," she said in a sad whisper.

He turned to Kahlan. The snakes were still on her. "Shota, you made a promise."

"I promised I would not kill her, and that she could leave. When you go, she may go with you, I will not kill her. But she is still a danger to me. If she remains still the snakes will not harm her."

"You said Kahlan would have tried to kill you. That isn't true; she guided me here seeking your help, the same as me. Even though she intended you no harm, you would have killed her. And now you do this to her!"

"Richard," she touched a finger to her chin, thinking, "you come here thinking me evil, didn't you? Even though you knew nothing of me, you were ready to bring harm to me, based on what you invented in your head. You have committed to belief that which you have heard from others." There was no malice in her voice. "People who are jealous or afraid say these things. People also say that to use fire is wrong, and that those who use fire are evil. Does that make it true? People say the old wizard is evil, and that people die because of him. Does that make it true? Some of the Mud People say you brought death to their village. Does that make it true, because fools say it is so?"

"What kind of person would try to make me think she was my dead mother?" he asked bitterly.

Shota looked genuinely hurt. "Do you not love your mother?"

"Of course."

"What greater gift could anyone give, than the return of a passed loved one? Did it not give you joy to see your mother again? Did I ask for anything in return? Did I demand payment? For a moment, I gave you something beautiful, pure, a living memory of your love for your mother, and hers for you, at a cost to myself you could never fathom, and you see this, too, as evil? And in payment, you would think to take my head off with your sword?"

Richard swallowed hard, but didn't answer. He looked away from her eyes, feeling suddenly, unexpectedly, ashamed.

"Is your mind that poisoned by the words of others? Their fears? All I ask is to be judged by my deeds, to be seen for who I am, not what others say of me. Richard, don't be a soldier in this silent army of fools."

Richard stood speechless at hearing the words of his own beliefs coming back at him.

"Look around," Shota said, sweeping her hand through the air. "Is this a place of ugliness? Evil?"

"It's the most beautiful place I've ever seen," Richard admitted in a soft voice. "But that doesn't prove anything, and what about the place up there?" He pointed with his chin, toward the dark wood above.

She took a brief glance. "Think of it as my moat." Shota smiled proudly. "It keeps away fools who would harm me."

Richard saved the hardest question for last. "And what of him?" He glanced toward the shadows, where Samuel sat, watching, with glowing yellow eyes.

She held Richard's gaze as she spoke, her voice heavy with regret. "Samuel, come here."

The disgusting creature skittered across the grass, to his mistress's side, pushing against her, making an odd, throaty gurgle. Samuel's eyes locked on the sword, and stayed there. Her hand reached down, stroking his gray head affectionately. Shota gave Richard a warm, brave smile.

"I guess a formal introduction is in order. Richard, may I introduce Samuel, your predecessor. The former Seeker."

Richard looked down, wide-eyed, speechless, to the companion.

"My sword! Gimme!" Samuel started to reach out. Shota spoke his name in caution without taking her gaze from Richard, and the little creature instantly withdrew his arms, nuzzling back against her hip. "My sword," he complained to himself in a low voice.

"Why does he look like that?" Richard asked cautiously, afraid of the answer.

"You really don't know, do you?" Shota lifted an eyebrow as she studied his face. Her sad smile returned. "The magic. Did the wizard not warn you?"

Richard shook his head slowly, unable to form words. His tongue stuck to the roof of his mouth.

"Well, I suggest you have a talk with him."

He forced himself to speak, but barely. "You mean, the magic will do this to me?"

"I'm sorry, Richard, I can't answer that." She gave a heavy sigh. "One of my talents is that I have vision for the flow of time, the way events flow into the future. But this is a type of magic, wizard's magic, that I cannot see; I am blind to it. I can't see how it flows forward.

"Samuel was the last Seeker. He came here many years back, desperate for help. But I could do nothing for him, other than take pity on him. Then the old wizard came, suddenly, one day,

457

and took the sword." She lifted an eyebrow meaningfully. "It was a very unpleasant experience—for both of us. I'm afraid I must admit I do not think kindly of the old wizard." Her face softened again. "To this day, Samuel thinks of the Sword of Truth as his. But I know better. The wizards, for all ages, are the caretakers of the sword, and therein its magic, and only assign it to mere Seekers for a time."

Richard remembered Zedd telling him that while the last pretend Seeker was distracted by a witch woman, he had gone and taken the sword back. This was the Seeker; this was the witch woman. Kahlan was wrong. There was at least one wizard who would dare to go into Agaden Reach.

"Maybe, it's because he wasn't a real Seeker," Richard managed, trying to reassure himself. His tongue still felt thick.

Her face was set in a frown of true concern. "Maybe. I just don't know."

"That must be it," he whispered. "It has to be. Zedd would have warned me otherwise. He's my friend."

She gave him a grave expression. "Richard, there are more important things at stake than friendship. Zedd knows this, and so do you; after all, you chose these things over his life when you had to."

Richard looked up at Zedd. How he wanted to talk to him. He needed him so badly right now. Could that be true, could he have chosen the box over Zedd's life that easily, without a second thought? "Shota, you promised to let him go."

Shota's eyes studied his face a moment. "I'm sorry, Richard." She waved her hand through the air in the direction of Zedd. Zedd wavered, and then disappeared. "That was only a little deception. A demonstration. It wasn't really the old wizard."

Richard thought he should feel angry, but he didn't. He felt just a little hurt at the deception, yet sad that Zedd wasn't here, with him. Then a wave of icy dread washed through him, raising bumps on his arms again.

"Is that really Kahlan? Or have you already killed her, and presented me with her image, another trick? Another demonstration?"

Shota's breast rose and fell as she took a deep breath. "I'm afraid," she sighed, "that she is real enough. And therein lies the problem."

Shota put her arm through his, taking him to stand in front of Kahlan. Samuel followed and stood by them. His arms were so long that as he stood erect, his yellow eyes moving warily back and forth between them, he casually drew lines and circles in the dirt of the road with his fingers.

Shota regarded Kahlan for a moment, seemingly lost in thought, as if pondering a dilemma. Richard just wanted the snakes off her. Despite the witch woman's words of help and friendship, Kahlan was still terrified, and it wasn't the snakes. It was Shota that her eyes followed, the way the eyes of an animal in a trap follow the trapper, not the trap.

"Richard," Shota asked, while she held Kahlan's stare, "would you be able to kill her if you had to? If she was a threat to your success, would you have the courage to kill her? If it meant the lives of everyone else? The truth, now."

Despite the disarming tone of Shota's voice, her words went through him like an ice dagger. Richard met Kahlan's widening eyes, then looked to the woman beside him. "She is my guide. I need her," he said simply, offhandedly.

Big almond eyes stared back at him. "That, Seeker, is not the question I asked."

Richard didn't say anything; he tried to betray nothing with his face.

Shota gave a smile of regret. "As I thought. And that is why you made a mistake with your wish."

"I made no mistake," Richard protested. "If I hadn't used it as I did, you would have killed her!"

"Yes," Shota nodded grimly, "I would have. The image of Zedd was a test. You passed the test, and as a reward, I gave you a wish, not that you might have something you want, but that I might do an onerous deed for you, because you lack the required courage. That was your second test. That test, dear boy, you failed. I must honor your wish. That is your mistake; you should have let me kill her for you."

"You're mad! First you try to tell me how you're not evil, how I should judge you by your actions, and now you prove your true self by telling me how I made a mistake by not allowing you to

459

kill Kahlan! And for what! Some perceived threat? She has done nothing to threaten you, nor would she. She wishes only to stop Darken Rahl, same as me. Same as you!"

Shota listened patiently until he finished. The timeless look passed across her eyes again. "Were you not listening when I said not all acts are as they seem? That some are meant to save you? Once again you judge too quickly, without knowing all the facts."

"Kahlan is my friend. That is the only fact that matters."

Shota took a breath, as if she were trying to remain patient, as if she were trying to teach something to a child. Her expression made him feel somehow stupid.

"Richard. Listen to me. Darken Rahl has put the boxes of Orden in play. If he succeeds, there will be no one with the power to restrain him. Ever. A great many people will die. You. Me. It's in my own interest to help you because you are the only one who has a chance to stop him. How, or why, I don't know, but I can see the flow of power. You are the only one with a chance.

"That does not mean you will succeed, only that you have the chance. No matter how small, it is within you. Know also that there are forces to defeat you before you could bring your chance to bear. The old wizard does not have the power to stop Rahl. That's why he gave you the sword. I do not have the power to stop Rahl. But I do have the power to be of aid to you. That's all I wish to do. In so doing I help myself. I do not want to die. If Rahl wins, I will."

"I know all this. That's why I said you would answer my question without my having to use the wish."

"But there are other things I know, Richard, that you do not."

Her beautiful face studied him with a sadness that hurt. Her eyes had the same fire in them that Kahlan's had; the fire of intelligence. Richard felt the need in her, the need to help him. He feared suddenly what it was she knew, because he realized that it wasn't meant to hurt him, it was simply truth. Richard saw Samuel watching the sword and became aware of his own left hand, resting around the hilt, aware of how tightly he was gripping it, and how the raised letters of the word *Truth* were pressing painfully into his palm.

"Shota, what are these things you know?"

"The easiest first," she sighed. "You know the way you stopped the wizard's fire with the sword? Practice the move. I gave you that test for a reason. Zedd will use the wizard's fire against you. Only the next time, it will be for real. The flow of time does not say who will prevail, only that you have a chance to beat him."

Richard's eyes widened. "That can't be true. . . ."

"True," she said, clipping off his words, "as a tooth given by a father to show the keeper of the book, to show the truth of how it was taken."

That rattled him to his bones.

"And no, I don't know who the keeper is." Her eyes burned into him. "You will have to find him yourself."

Richard could hardly draw a breath, could hardly make himself ask the next question. "If that was the easy part, then what is the hard?"

Auburn hair tumbled off her shoulder as Shota looked away from his eyes, to Kahlan, who stood stone still while the snakes writhed on her. "I know what she is, and how it is she is a threat to me. . . ." Her voice trailed off. She turned back to him. "It is obvious you do not know what she is, or perhaps you would not be with her. Kahlan has a power. Magic power."

"That much I know," Richard offered cautiously.

"Richard," Shota said, trying to find the words for something she found difficult, "I am a witch woman. As I said, one of my powers is that I can see things as they will come to pass. It is one reason fools fear me." Her face drew closer to his, uncomfortably close. Her breath smelled of roses. "Please, Richard, don't be one of these fools; don't fear me because of things I have no control over. I'm able to see the truth of events that will come to be; I do not dictate or control them. And just because I see them, that does not mean I'm at all happy about them. It is only by action in the present that we can change what otherwise will come to pass. Have the wisdom to use the truth to your advantage, don't simply rail against it."

"And what truth do you see, Shota?" he whispered.

Her eyes had an intensity that halted his breath, her voice the sharp edge of a blade.

"Kahlan has a power, and if she isn't killed, she will use that power against you." She watched his eyes carefully as she spoke. "There can be no doubt of the truth of this. Your sword can protect you from the wizard's fire, but it will not protect you from her touch."

Richard felt the stab of her words, as if they cut through his heart.

"No!" Kahlan whispered. They both looked at her, her face wrinkled with pain at Shota's words. "I wouldn't! Shota, I swear, I couldn't do that to him."

Tears ran down her cheeks. Shota stepped close to her and reached through the snakes, touching her face tenderly, to comfort her.

"If you are not killed, child, I am afraid you will." As a tear rolled down, her thumb brushed it back. "You have already come close, once," Shota said with surprising compassion. "Within a breath." She nodded slightly to herself. "This is true, is it not? Tell him. Tell him if I am speaking the truth."

Kahlan's eyes snapped to Richard. He looked into the depths of her green eyes and remembered the three times she had touched him when he had been holding the sword, and how that touch made the magic jump in warning. The last time, with the Mud People when the shadow things had come, the magic's reaction had been so strong that he almost put the sword through her before he realized who it was. Kahlan's eyebrows wrinkled together, her eyes shrinking from his gaze. She bit her bottom lip as a little moan escaped her throat.

"Is this true?" Richard asked in a whisper, his heart in his throat. "Have you come within a breath of using your power against me, as Shota says?"

Kahlan's face drained of color. She let out a loud, painful moan. She closed her eyes and cried in a long, agonizing wail, "Please, Shota. Kill me. You must. I am sworn to protect Richard, to stop Rahl. Please," she cried in choking sobs. "It's the only way. You must kill me."

"I cannot," Shota whispered. "I have granted a wish. A very foolish one."

Richard could hardly stand the pain of seeing Kahlan like this, asking to die. The lump in his throat threatened to choke him.

Kahlan suddenly cried out and threw up her arms, to make the snakes bite her. Richard lunged for them, but they were gone. Kahlan held out her arms, looking for snakes that were no longer there.

"I'm sorry, Kahlan. If I were to let them bite you, it would break the wish I granted."

Kahlan collapsed to her knees, crying with her face against the ground, her fingers digging into the earth. "I'm so sorry, Richard," she wept. Her fists grabbed at the grass, then his pants legs. "Please, Richard," she sobbed. "Please. I'm sworn to protect you. So many have already died. Take the sword and kill me. Do it. Please. Please, Richard, kill me."

"Kahlan ... I could never ..." He couldn't make any more words come.

"Richard," Shota said, nearly in tears herself, "if she isn't killed, then before Rahl opens the boxes, she will use her power against you. There is no doubt of this. None. It cannot be changed if she lives. I granted your wish, I cannot kill her. So you must."

"No!" he shrieked.

Kahlan wailed again in anguish and pulled her knife. As she brought it up to plunge it into herself, Richard grabbed her wrist.

"Please, Richard," she cried, falling against him, "you don't understand. I have to. If I live I will be responsible for what Rahl will do. For everything that will happen."

Richard pulled her up by her wrist and held her to him with one arm as she cried, keeping her arm twisted behind her back so she couldn't use the knife on herself. He glared angrily at Shota, who stood with her hands loose at her sides, watching. Was any of this possible? Could it be true? He wished he had listened to Kahlan and never come here.

He relaxed his pressure on Kahlan's arm when he realized by the way she cried that he was hurting her. He wondered numbly if he should let her kill herself. His hand shook.

"Please, Richard," Shota said, tears in her own eyes, "hate me for who I am if you will, but do not hate me for telling you the truth."

"The truth as you see it, Shota! But maybe not the truth as it will be. I will not kill Kahlan on your word."

Shota nodded sadly, looking at him through wet eyes.

"Queen Milena has the last box of Orden." She spoke in a voice barely more than a whisper. "But heed this warning: she will not have it for long. If, that is, you choose to believe the truth, as I see it." She turned to her companion, "Samuel," she said gently, "guide them out of the Reach. Do not take anything that belongs to them. I would be very displeased if you did. That includes the Sword of Truth."

Richard saw a tear run down her cheek as she turned without looking at him and began walking up the road. She stopped in midstride and stood a moment; her beautiful auburn hair lay upon her shoulders and partway down the back of the wispy dress. Her head came up, but didn't turn back to him.

"When this is over," she said in a voice that broke with emotion, "and if you should happen to win . . . don't ever come here again. If you do . . . I will kill you."

She walked on, toward her palace.

"Shota," he whispered hoarsely, "I'm sorry."

She did not stop or turn, but continued on.

CHAPTER 32

WHEN SHE CAME AROUND the corner, she almost bumped into his legs, he was walking so quietly. She looked up the long silver robes to his face, far up in the air.

"Giller! You scared me!"

His hands were each stuck in the other sleeve. "Sorry, Rachel, I didn't mean to frighten you." He looked both ways down the hall and then lowered himself to the floor. "What are you about?"

"Errands," she told him, letting out a deep breath. "Princess Violet says I'm to go yell at the cooks for her, and then I'm to go to the washwomen and tell them that she found a gravy stain on one of her dresses, and that she would never get gravy on one of her dresses, and that they must have done it, and if she ever finds they do that again, she'll have their heads chopped off. I don't want to say that to them, they're nice." She touched the pretty silver braiding on the sleeve of Giller's robes. "But she said that if I don't say it, I'll be in a lot of trouble."

Giller nodded. "Well, just do as she says, I'm sure the washwomen will know they aren't really your words."

Rachel looked in his big dark eyes. "Everyone knows she gets her own gravy on her own dresses."

Giller laughed a quiet laugh. "You're right, I've seen her do it myself. But it brings no fortune to pull the tail of a sleeping badger." She didn't understand, and made a face. "That means you will get in trouble if you point it out to her, so it's best to keep still."

Rachel nodded; she knew that that was true. Giller looked up and down the hall again, but there was no one else there.

He leaned closer and whispered, "I'm sorry I haven't been able to talk to you, to check. Did you find your trouble doll?"

She nodded with a smile. "Thank you so much, Giller. She's wonderful. I've been put out twice more since you gave her to me. She told me how I mustn't talk to you unless you say it's safe, so I just waited, like she said. We talked and talked, and she made me feel so much better."

"I'm glad, child." He smiled.

"I named her Sara. A doll's got to have a name, you know."

"Is that so?" He lifted an eyebrow. "I never knew that. Well, Sara is a fine name for her then."

Rachel grinned; she was happy that Giller liked her doll's name. She put one arm around his neck and her face by his ear. "Sara's been telling me her troubles too," she whispered. "I promised her I would help you. I never knew you wanted to run away too. When can we leave, Giller? I'm getting so afraid of Princess Violet."

His big hand patted her back when she hugged him. "Soon, child. But there are things we must prepare first, so we aren't found out. We wouldn't want anyone to follow us, to find us and bring us back, now, would we?"

Rachel shook her head against his shoulder; then she heard footsteps. Giller stood up, looking down the hall.

"Rachel, it would be very bad if we were seen talking. Someone might . . . find out about the doll. About Sara."

"I better go," she said in a hurry.

"No time. Stand against the wall, show me how brave, and quiet you can be."

She did what he told her and he stood in front of her, hiding her behind his robes. Rachel heard the clinking of armor. Just some guards, she thought. Then she heard the little barks. The Queen's dog! It must be the Queen and her guards! They would be in a fine mess if the Queen found her hiding behind the wizard's robes. She might find out about the doll! She scrunched up tighter in the dark folds. The robes moved a little when Giller bowed.

"Your Majesty," Giller said as he stood back up.

"Giller!" she said in her mean voice. "What are you doing lurking about up here?"

"*Lurking*, Your Majesty? It was my understanding I was in your employ to see to it there was no *lurking* going on. I was merely checking the magic seal on the jewel room to make sure it hadn't been tampered with." Rachel heard the little dog sniffing around the bottom of Giller's robes. "If it is your wish, Your Majesty, I will leave matters to the fates, and not investigate where I feel a worry." The little dog came around the side of the robes, close to her; she could hear the sniff, sniff, sniff. Rachel wished he would leave, before she got found out. "We will all just go to bed at night with a simple prayer to the good spirits that when Father Rahl arrives, all will be well. And if anything is amiss, well, we can simply tell him we didn't want to have any *lurking about*, so we didn't check. Perhaps he will be understanding."

The little dog started to growl. Rachel was getting tears in her eyes.

"Don't get your feathers ruffled, Giller, I was simply asking." Rachel could see the little black nose sticking under the robes. "Precious, what have you found there? What is it, my little Precious?"

The dog growled and gave out a little bark. Giller backed up a little, pushing her tighter to the wall. Rachel tried to think about Sara, wishing she were with her right now.

"What is it, Precious? What do you smell?"

"I'm afraid, Your Majesty, I have also been *lurking about* in the stables, I'm quite sure that is what your dog smells." Giller's hand went into his robes right by her head.

"The stables?" Her mean voice wasn't quite gone. "What could there possibly be for you to investigate in the stables?" Ra-

467

chel could hear her voice getting louder; the Queen was bending over, to get her dog. "What *are* you doing there, Precious?"

Rachel sucked the hem of her dress, to keep from making a noise as she shook. Giller's hand came out of his robe. She saw a pinch of something between his thumb and finger. The dog pushed his head under the robe and started barking. Giller opened his fingers, and sparkling dust dropped down on the dog's head. The dog started sneezing. Then Rachel saw the Queen's hand come and pull him away.

"There, there, my little Precious. It's all right now. Poor little thing." Rachel could hear her kissing the dog's nose the way she liked to do all the time; then she sneezed, too. "As you were saying, Giller? What business does a wizard have in the stables?"

"As I was saying, Your Majesty"—Giller's voice could get kind of mean, too, but Rachel thought it was funny when it was the Queen he was sounding mean to—"if you were an assassin, and you wanted to come into a Queen's castle and put a big fat arrow through her, do you think you would rather walk right in the main gate, bold as day? Or would you rather ride with your long bow in a wagon, hiding, maybe under some hay, or behind some sacks? Then come out in the dark of the stables."

"Well . . . I . . . but, are there, do you think . . . have you found something. . . ."

"But, since you don't want me *lurking about* in the stables either, well, I'll just scratch that off my list too! But if you don't mind, from now on, when we are in public view I will be standing well clear of you. I don't want to be in the way if some of your subjects choose to show their love for their Queen from afar."

"Wizard Giller"—her voice got real nice, like when she talked to the dog—"please forgive me. I have been on edge lately, what with Father Rahl coming soon. I just want everything to go well; then we will all have what we want. I know you only have my best interest at heart. Please, do carry on, and forget the momentary foolishness of a lady."

"As you wish, Your Majesty." He bowed again.

The Queen started hurrying away, down the hall, sneezing; then Rachel heard her thumping footsteps and the clinking armor stop.

"By the way, wizard Giller," she called back, "did I tell you? A messenger came. He said Father Rahl will be here sooner than expected. Much sooner. Tomorrow in fact. He will be expecting the box, of course, to seal the alliance. Please see to it."

Giller's leg jerked so hard it almost knocked Rachel over. "Of course, Your Majesty." He bowed again.

Giller waited until the Queen was gone and then pulled Rachel up with big hands around her waist and held her against his hip with an arm. His cheeks weren't red, as they usually were; they were more white. He put his finger against her lips, and she knew he wanted her to keep quiet. He stretched his neck, looking up and down the hall again.

"Tomorrow!" he muttered to himself. "Curse the spirits, I'm not ready."

"What's wrong, Giller?"

"Rachel," he whispered, his big hook nose close to hers, "is the Princess in her room right now?"

"No," Rachel whispered back. "She went to pick out fabric for a new dress, for when Father Rahl comes to visit."

"Do you know where the Princess keeps her key to the jewel room?"

"Yes. If she doesn't have it with her, she keeps it in the desk. In the drawer on the side by the window."

He started off down the hall, toward Princess Violet's room. His feet were so quiet on the carpets that she couldn't even hear his footsteps as he carried her. "Change of plans, child. Can you be brave for me? And Sara?"

She nodded that she could and put her arms around his neck to hold on as he walked fast. He went past all the dark wooden doors that were pointed at the tops, until he got to the biggest one, a double door set back in a little hall, with stone carving all around. That was the Princess's room. He squeezed her tight.

"All right," he whispered, "you go in and get the key. I'll stay out here and stand guard."

He set her down on the floor. "Hurry now." He closed the door behind her.

The curtains were pulled back, letting in the sunlight, so she could see right away that the room was empty. None of the servants were cleaning or anything. The fire was burned out, and

469

the servants hadn't yet come and made another for tonight. The Princess's big canopy bed was already made up. Rachel liked the bedcover with all the pretty flowers. It matched the gathered canopy and curtains. She always wondered why the Princess needed such a big bed. It was big enough for ten people. Where she came from, six girls slept together in a bed half the size of this one, and the bedcover was plain. She wondered what the Princess's bed felt like. She had never once even sat on it.

She knew Giller wanted her to hurry, so she crossed the room, walking over the fur rug, to the polished desk with the pretty swirled wood. She put her fingers through the gold handle and slid the drawer open. It made her nervous to do it, even though she had done it before when the Princess had sent her to get the key, but she had never done it before without being told to by the Princess. The big key to the jewel room was lying in the red velvet pocket, right next to the little key to her sleeping box. She put the key in her pocket and slid the drawer closed again, making sure it was shut all the way.

As she started for the door, she looked at the corner where her sleeping box was. She knew Giller wanted her to hurry, but she ran over to the box anyway—she had to check. She crawled inside, into the dark, and went to the back corner where the blanket was pushed up in a pile. Carefully, she pulled the blanket back.

Sara looked back at her. The doll was right where she had left her.

"I have to go quick," she whispered. "I'll be back later."

Rachel kissed the doll's head and covered her back up with the blanket, hiding her in the corner so no one would find her. She knew it was trouble to bring Sara to the castle, but she couldn't bear to leave her in the wayward pine, all alone. She knew how lonely and scary it got in the wayward pine.

Finished, she ran to the door, pulled it open a crack, and looked up at Giller's face. He nodded to her and motioned with his hand that it was all right to come out.

"The key?"

She pulled it out of the pocket where she kept her magic fire stick, to show him. He smiled and called her a good girl. No one had ever called her a good girl before, at least not for a long time. He picked her up again and walked fast down the hall and then down the dark, narrow servants' stairs. She could hardly ever hear his footsteps on the stone. His whiskers tickled her face. At the bottom he set her down again.

"Rachel," he said, squatting down close to her, "listen carefully, this is very important, this is no game. We must get out of the castle, or we will both get our heads chopped off, just like Sara told you. But we must be smart about it, or we will get caught. If we run away too quickly, without doing the right things first, we will be found out. And if we are too slow, well, we just better not be too slow."

She started to get tears in her eyes. "Giller, I'm afraid to get my head chopped off, people say it hurts terrible bad."

Giller hugged her tight. "I know, child. I'm afraid too." He put his hands on her shoulders, holding her up straight while he looked in her eyes. "But if you trust me, and do exactly as I say, and are brave enough, we will get away from here, and go to where no one ever chops off people's heads, or locks them in boxes, and where you can have your doll and people will let you, and they will never take Sara away from you or throw her in the fire. All right?"

Her tears started to go away. "That would be wonderful, Giller."

"But you must be brave, and do just as I tell you. Some of it will be hard."

"I will, I promise."

"And I promise, Rachel, that I will do whatever I must to protect you. We are in this together, you and me, but a lot of other people are depending on us too. If we do a good job, we will be able to fix it so a lot of other people, innocent people, won't get their heads chopped off anymore."

Her eyes got wide. "Oh, I would like that, Giller. I hate it when people get their heads chopped off. It scares me fierce."

"All right then, the first thing I need you to do is to go scold the cooks, just like you are supposed to, and while you are down in the kitchen, get a big loaf of bread, the biggest you can find. I don't care how you get it, steal it if you have to. Just get it. Then bring it up to the jewel room. Use the key and wait inside for me. I must tend to some other things. I'll tell you more then. Can you do that?"

471

"Sure," she nodded. "Easy."

"Off with you then."

She went through the door into the big hall on the first floor while Giller disappeared up the steps without making a sound. The stairs to the kitchen were at the other end, on the other side of the grand stairs in the middle that the Queen used. Rachel liked going up the grand stairs with the Princess because they had carpets, and weren't cold like the stone steps she was supposed to use when she was on errands. The hall was open in the middle, where the grand stairs came down to a big room with black and white marble squares on the floor. They were very cold under her feet.

She was trying to think of a way she could get a big loaf of bread without stealing it, when she saw Princess Violet coming across the room to the grand stairs. The royal seamstress and two of her helpers were following behind, carrying bolts of pretty, pink cloth. Rachel looked quick for a place to hide, but the Princess had already seen her.

"Oh good, Rachel," the Princess said. "Come here."

Rachel went and curtsied. "Yes, Princess Violet?"

"What are you doing?"

"I was doing my errands. I was just going to the kitchen now."

"Well . . . don't bother."

"But Princess Violet, I have to!"

The Princess frowned. "Why? I just said you didn't."

Rachel bit her lip; the Princess's frown scared her. She tried to think of how Giller would answer. "Well, if you don't want me to, I won't," she said. "But your lunch was simply dreadful, and I would hate to see you eating another dreadful meal. You must be starving for something good. But if you don't want me to go tell them, I won't."

The Princess thought this over a minute. "On second thought, go ahead, it was dreadful. Just be sure to tell them how angry I am, too!"

"Yes, Princess Violet." She curtsied. She turned and started to leave.

"I'm going for a fitting." Rachel turned back to her. "Then I want to go to the jewel room, and try on some things, to go with

472

my new dress. When you're finished with the cooks, go get the key and wait for me in the jewel room."

Rachel's mouth felt as if it were stuck together. "But Princess, wouldn't you rather wait until tomorrow, when the dress is finished, to see how pretty the jewelry will look with the dress?"

Princess Violet looked surprised. "Well, yes, that would be good, to see the jewels with the dress." She thought another minute, then started up the steps. "I'm glad I thought of that."

Rachel let out a breath, then headed off to the servants' stairs. The Princess called down to her.

"On second thought, Rachel, I need to pick out something for tonight's dinner, so I need to go to the jewel room anyway. Meet me there in a little while."

"But, Princess . . ."

"But nothing. After you deliver my message to the cooks, go get the key and wait for me in the jewel room. I'll be there as soon as I'm done with the fitting."

The Princess went up the grand stairs and disappeared.

What was she going to do now? Giller was going to meet her in the jewel room, too. She was breathing hard, as if she was going to cry. What was she going to do?

She was going to do as Giller said, that's what. She was going to be brave. So those people didn't get their heads chopped off. She stopped herself from crying and went down the steps to the kitchen. She wondered what Giller wanted a big loaf of bread for.

"Well, what do you think?" he whispered. "Any ideas?"

Kahlan was lying close, next to him on the ground, frowning while she looked over the edge to the scene below.

"I can't even imagine," she whispered back. "I have never seen so many short-tailed gars together in one place."

"What could they be burning?"

"They're not burning anything. The smoke is coming from the ground. This place is called Fire Spring. Those are vents where steam comes up from the ground, and from other openings water boils up from below, and more over there where other things boil, foul-smelling yellow liquid and thick mud. The fumes keep people away from this place. I have no idea what gars would be doing here."

"Well, look there, near the back where the hill rises up, where the biggest vent is. There's something on top of it, something egg-shaped, with steam coming out around it. They keep going up to look at it, to touch it."

She shook her head. "Your eyes are better than mine. I can't tell what it is, or even that it's round."

Richard could hear and feel rumbles from the ground, some followed by great belches of steam roaring from the vents. The awful suffocating smell of sulfur wafted up to where they hid in the stunted trees of the high ridge.

"Maybe we should go have a closer look," he whispered, half to himself, as he watched the gars moving about below.

"That would be beyond foolhardy," she whispered harshly. "It would be just plain stupid. One gar would be trouble enough, or have you forgotten so quickly. There must be dozens down there."

"I guess," he complained. "What's that behind them, just above, on the side of the hill? A cave?"

Her eyes went to the dark maw. "Yes. It's called the Shadrin's Cave. Some say it goes all the way through the mountain, to the valley on the other side. But I don't know of anyone who knows for sure, or who would want to find out."

He watched the gars tearing an animal apart, fighting over it. "What's a Shadrin?"

"The Shadrin is a beast that is supposed to live in the caves. Some say it's just a myth, others swear it is real, but nobody wants to go find out for sure."

He looked over at her as she watched the gars. "And what do you think?"

Kahlan shrugged. "I don't know. There are many places in the Midlands where there are supposed to be beasts. I have been to many, and found no beasts. Most of these stories are just that, stories. But not all."

Richard was glad she was talking. It was the most she had said in days. The odd behavior of the gars seemed to have overwhelmed her with curiosity, and brought her, for the moment, out of her withdrawal. But they couldn't lie there talking; they were wasting time. Besides, if they stayed too long, the gars' flies would find them. They both crawled backward, clear of the edge, then crept farther away, keeping their heads down and their movements quiet. Kahlan withdrew once again into silence.

Once away from the gars, they started down the road again, to Tamarang, the border land of the Wilds, the land ruled by Queen Milena. Before they had gone far, they came to a divide in the road. Richard assumed they would go to the right, as Kahlan had said that Tamarang lay to the east. The gars and Fire Spring had been off to their left. Kahlan went down the left road.

"What're you doing?" He had had to watch her like a hawk since leaving Agaden Reach. He couldn't trust her anymore. All she wanted to do was die, and he knew she would manage it if he didn't watch her every move.

She looked back at him with the same blank expression she had worn for days. "This is called an inverted fork. Up ahead, where it's hard to see because of the lay of the land and the heavy woods, the roads cross over each other and switch directions. Because of the thick trees, it's hard to tell where the sun is, which direction you are going. If we take the right fork here, we will end up with the gars. This one, to the left, goes to Tamarang."

He frowned. "Why would anyone go to the trouble to build a road like that?"

"It's just one little way the old rulers of Tamarang used to help confuse invaders from the Wilds. Sometimes it slowed them down a little, gave the defenders time to retreat and regroup if they needed to, then to fall on the attackers again."

He studied her face a moment, trying to judge if she was telling the truth. It infuriated him that he had to worry about whether Kahlan was telling him the truth.

"You're the guide," he said at last. "Lead on."

At his word, she turned without comment and walked on. Richard didn't know how much more of this he could take. She would only talk when it was required, wouldn't listen when he tried to make conversation, and backed away whenever he got close. She acted as if his touch would be poison, but he knew it was really her touch she worried about. He had hoped that the way she was talking when they had spotted the gars signaled a change, but he was wrong. She had quickly reverted to her dark mood.

She had reduced herself to a prisoner on a forced march; had reduced him to a reluctant jailer. He kept her knife in his belt. He knew what would happen if he gave it back to her. With every step, she was drifting farther and farther from him. He knew he was losing her, but didn't have the slightest idea what to do about it.

At night, when it was time for her watch, for him to sleep, he had to tie her hands and feet to prevent her from killing herself when he wasn't watching. When he bound her, she endured it limply. He endured it with great pain. Even then, he had to sleep with one eye open. He slept by her feet so if she saw or heard something, she could wake him. He was dead tired from the strain.

He wished they had never gone to Shota. The idea that Zedd would turn on him was unthinkable; the idea that Kahlan would was unbearable.

Richard took out some food. He kept his voice cheerful, hoping to perk her up. "Here, have some of this dried fish?" He smiled. "It's really awful."

She didn't laugh at his joke. "No, thank you. I'm not hungry."

Richard struggled to keep the smile on his face, struggled to keep his voice from betraying his anger. His head was pounding. "Kahlan, you've hardly eaten for days. You have to eat."

"I said I don't want any."

"Come on, for me?" he coaxed.

"What are you going to do next? Hold me down and force it in my mouth?"

The calmness in her voice infuriated him, but he covered it as best he could with his tone, if not his words. "If I have to."

She spun at him, her chest heaving. "Richard, please! Just let me go? I don't want to be with you! Just let me go!" It was the first emotion she had shown since leaving Agaden Reach.

It was his turn to hide his emotions. "No."

She glared at him with fire in her green eyes. "You can't watch me every minute. Sooner or later . . ."

"Every minute . . . if I have to."

They stood glaring angrily at each other; then the emotion on her face was gone, and she turned back to the road, walking on.

They had only stopped for a few minutes, but it had been enough for the thing that followed them to make another mistake, a rare one. It had let its guard down briefly, and let itself get too close—close enough for Richard to see its fierce yellow eyes again, if only for an instant.

He had been aware that they were being followed since the second day out of the Reach. Years spent alone in the woods made him aware when he was being followed, tracked. It was a game he and the other guides had played sometimes in the Hartland Woods, seeing how far they could follow each other without being detected. Whatever followed now was good at the game. But not as good as Richard. Three times now, he had seen the yellow eyes, when no one else would have.

He knew it wasn't Samuel; the yellow was different, darker, and the eyes were closer together—and it was smarter. It couldn't be a heart hound; they would have been attacked long before now. Whatever it was, it only watched.

Richard was sure Kahlan hadn't seen it; she was too far lost in her own dark thoughts. Sooner or later, the thing would make itself known, and Richard would be ready. But with Kahlan the way she was right now, he had his hands full, and he didn't need more trouble.

So he didn't turn and look, to show it that he suspected, didn't backtrack, and didn't snap a circle, as he and the other guides had called the maneuver, but rather, he let his eyes catch the glimpses when they did, without forcing a glance. He was reasonably sure the thing that followed didn't know he was aware of it. For now, that's the way he wanted to keep it. It left the advantage with him.

He watched Kahlan as she walked with her shoulders slumped, and wondered what he was going to do in a few days, when they reached Tamarang. Whether he liked it or not, she was winning this slow battle, simply because things couldn't go on like this. She could fail time and again; she had only to succeed once. He had to win every time. To slip just once would let her end her life. In the end, he knew he couldn't win, knew he was going to lose, and could think of nothing to change that.

Rachel sat on the short footstool in front of the tall chair that was covered with red velvet and buttons and gold carving, waiting, knocking her knees together. Hurry, Giller, she kept saying to herself, hurry, before the Princess comes. She looked up at the Queen's box. She hoped that when Princess Violet came to try on jewelry, she didn't touch the box again. Rachel hated it when she did that; it scared her.

The door opened a little. Giller poked his head in.

"Hurry, Giller," she whispered loudly.

The rest of him came in. He stuck his head back out, looking up and down the hall, then he shut the door. He looked down at her.

"Did you get the bread?"

She nodded. "I got it here." She pulled the bundle out from under the chair and set it on the footstool. "I took a towel and wrapped it around the bread so no one would see."

"Good girl." He smiled as he turned around, away from her.

She smiled up at him, then frowned. "I had to steal it. I never stole anything before."

"I assure you, Rachel, it's for a good cause." He was looking at the box.

"Giller, Princess Violet is coming here."

He turned back, his eyes big. "When?"

"She said after she has the fitting for her new dress. She's pretty fussy, so it may take a while, but maybe not. She likes to try jewelry on and look at herself in the mirror."

"Curse the spirits," Giller whispered, "nothing is ever easy." He turned around again and snatched the Queen's box off the marble stand.

"Giller! You mustn't touch that! It's the Queen's!"

He looked a little mad when he looked down at her. "No! It's not! Just wait, and I will explain."

He set the box down on the stool next to the bread. His hand reached into his robes and pulled out another box. "How's it look?" With a smile on one side of his mouth, he held the new box toward her.

"It looks just the same!"

"Good." He put it on the stand where the real one had been, then sat down on the floor next to her and the footstool. "Now listen to me very carefully, Rachel. We don't have much time, and it is very important that you understand."

She could tell by the way his face looked that he meant it. She nodded. "I will, Giller."

He laid his hand on the box. "This box has magic, and it does not belong to the Queen."

She frowned. "It doesn't? Who does it belong to?"

"I don't have time to explain that right now. Maybe after we are away from here. The important thing is that the Queen is a bad person." Rachel nodded; she knew that was true. "She chops off people's heads just because she wants to. She doesn't care about anyone but herself. She has power. Power means she can do whatever she wants. This box has magic and it helps give her power. That is why she took it."

"I understand. Like the way the Princess has power, so she can slap me, and chop my hair crooked, and laugh at me."

He nodded. "That's right. Very good, Rachel. Now. There is a man who is even meaner than the Queen. His name is Darken Rahl."

"Father Rahl?" She was confused. "Everyone say he's nice. The Princess says he is the nicest man in the world."

"The Princess also says she doesn't spill gravy on her dresses." He lifted an eyebrow.

"That's a lie."

Giller put his hands on her shoulders, real soft. "You listen very carefully. Darken Rahl, Father Rahl, is the meanest man that ever was. He hurts more people than the Queen could even think of. He is so mean that he even kills children. Do you know what that means, to kill someone?"

She felt sad, and scared. "It means you chop off their head or something, and make them dead."

"Yes. And just as the Princess laughs when she slaps you, Darken Rahl laughs when he kills people. You know the way

479

when the Princess is at dinner with all the lords and ladies, she is real nice, and polite? But when she is alone with you, she slaps you?"

Rachel nodded; she had a lump in her throat. "She doesn't like them to know she's really mean."

Giller held his finger up. "That's right! You're a very bright girl! Well, Father Rahl is the same way. He doesn't want people to know he is really mean, so he can be very polite, and make it seem like he is the nicest man in the world. Whatever you do, Rachel, you stay away from him, if you can."

"I will, for sure."

"But if he talks to you, just be polite right back, don't let him know that you know. You must not let people know all the things you know. That keeps you safe."

She smiled. "Like Sara. I don't let people know about her so they can't take her away from me. It keeps her safe."

He put his arms around her and gave her a quick hug. "The spirits be praised, you are a smart child." It made her feel really good that he said that. No one ever told her that she was smart. "Now, listen close. This is the important part."

She nodded again. "I will, Giller."

He put his hand back on the box. "This box has magic. When the Queen gives it to Father Rahl, he will be able to use the magic to hurt even more people. He will chop off a lot more people's heads. The Queen is a mean person, and wants him to do it, so she is going to give him the box."

Her eyes got real big. "Giller! We mustn't let her give him the box! Or all those people will get their heads chopped off!"

A big smile spread under his hook nose. He held her chin in his hand. "Rachel, you are the smartest girl I have ever met. You truly are."

"We have to hide it, hide the box, like I hide Sara!"

"And that's just what we are going to do." He pointed up at the box he had put on the stand. "That is a fake. That means it's not the real thing, it's just pretend, so they will be fooled for a while, and we can get away before they find out the real one is gone."

She looked up at the fake box. It looked just like the real one. "Giller, you're the most clever man I ever did know."

His smile went away a little. "I'm afraid, child, that I am too clever for my own good." His smile came back. "Here is what we are going to do."

Giller took the loaf of bread she had stolen from the kitchen and broke it in half. With his big hands, he scooped out some of the insides. Part of it he stuffed in his mouth; his cheeks puffed out, there was so much. He stuffed some in her mouth. She chewed as fast as she could. It was good, still warm. When they finished eating the middle, he took the real box and pushed it into the middle of the bread and put the two halves back together. He held it up for her to look at.

"What do you think?"

She made a face. "It's all cracked. People will know it's been broken."

He shook his head. "Smart. You are really smart. Well, since I'm a wizard, perhaps I could do something about that. What do you think?"

She nodded. "Maybe."

He put the bread in his lap and made his hands go all around in the air over it. He took his hands away and held the bread up in front of her face again. The cracks were gone! It looked just like new!

"No one will know now for sure." She giggled.

"Let's hope you're right, child. I have put a wizard's web, a magic spell, in the bread, to be sure no one will be able to see the magic of the box inside it."

He spread the cloth out on top of the stool and put the bread on it, then pulled up all four corners and tied them in the middle on top. He lifted up the bundle by the knots and put it in the palm of his other hand, in front of her. He looked her in the eyes and he didn't smile; he looked almost sad.

"Now, here's the hard part, Rachel. We have to get this box away from here. We can't hide it in the castle, or it might be found. You remember where I hid your doll, in the garden?"

She smiled proudly, she remembered. "Third urn on the right."

He nodded. "I will hide this there, just like I hid your doll. You must go and get it, just like you did with your doll, and then take it out of the castle." He leaned a little closer. "You have to do it tonight."

481

She started twisting her finger in the hem of her dress. She started to get tears in her eyes. "Giller, I'm scared to touch the Queen's box."

"I know you're afraid, child. But remember? It's not the Queen's box. You do want to help keep all those people from getting their heads chopped off, don't you?"

"Yes," she whined. "But, couldn't you take it away from the castle?"

"If I could, I swear to you, Rachel, I would. But I can't. There are some who watch me, and don't want me to go out of the castle. If they found me with the box, then Father Rahl would get it, and we can't have that, now, can we?"

"No . . ." Then she got real scared. "Giller, you said you were going to run away with me. You promised."

"And I mean to keep that promise, believe me. But it may take a couple of days for me to sneak out of Tamarang. It's very dangerous for the box to be here another day, and I can't get it out myself. You must get it away. Take it to your secret place, your wayward pine. You wait there for me, until I can cover our escape, and I will come get you."

"I guess I can. If you say it's important, I'll try."

Giller moved up and sat on the stool. He pulled her up with his hands around her waist, and set her on his knee.

"Rachel, you listen to me. If you live to be a hundred years old, you will never again do anything as important as this. You must be brave, braver than you have ever been before. You must not trust anyone. You must not let anyone get the box. I will come get you in a few days, but if something goes wrong, and I don't come, you must hide with the box until winter. Then everything will be all right. If I knew of anyone else to help you, I would get them to do it. But I don't. You are the only one who can do this."

She watched him with big eyes. "I'm just little," she said.

"That is why you will be safe. Everybody thinks you are a nobody. But that isn't true. You are the most important person in the world, but you can trick them because they don't know. You must do this, Rachel. I need your help so much, and so does everyone else. I know you're smart enough, and brave enough to do it."

She could see that his eyes were wet. "I'll try, Giller. I'll be brave and do it. You're the bestest man in the whole world, and if you say to do it, I will."

He shook his head. "I have been a very foolish man, Rachel, I have been far from the bestest man in the world. If only I had been wiser before, and remembered the things I was taught, my true duty, the reason I became a wizard in the first place, maybe I wouldn't have to ask you to do this. But just as this is the most important thing you will ever do, it is also the most important thing I will ever do. We must not fail, Rachel. You must not. No matter what happens, you must not let anyone stop you. Not anyone."

He put a finger on each side of her forehead and she felt a safe feeling in her head. She knew she would be able to do it and she would never have to do as the Princess said again. She would be free. Giller suddenly pulled his fingers away.

"Someone comes," he whispered. He kissed her head real quick. "Good spirits protect you, Rachel."

He stood up and put his back to the wall, behind the door. He slipped the loaf of bread into his robes, and put his finger over his lips. The door opened, and Rachel jumped to her feet. It was Princess Violet. Rachel curtsied. When she came back up, the Princess slapped her, then laughed. Rachel looked down at the ground, and while she rubbed her cheek, holding back the tears, she saw a piece of bread between Princess Violet's feet. She took a quick glance at Giller, who stood pressed against the wall behind the door. His eyes went to the bread. Quieter than a cat, he bent down and snatched up the bread, put it it his mouth, then slipped out the door behind Princess Violet's back without her ever seeing him.

Kahlan held her arms out to him, hands made into fists, the insides of her wrists pressed together, waiting for him to bind them with the rope. Her unblinking eyes stared off at nothing. She had said she wasn't tired, but Richard surely was—his head pounded so hard it made him feel sick—so she was going to take the first watch. What good her watch was, the way she stared blankly, he didn't know.

He held the rope taut between his shaking fist, his mind feeling the last of his hope finally abandoning him. Nothing was changing, nothing was getting any better, as he had hoped; it was one long endless battle with her—she wanting to die, he trying constantly to prevent it.

"I can't do this anymore," he whispered, looking down at her wrists in the light of the small fire. "Kahlan, you may be the one who wishes to die, but it is me you are killing."

Her green eyes came up to his; the firelight flickered in them. "Then let me go, Richard. Please, if you care at all for me, then show it. Let me go."

He lowered the rope and let it drop. With trembling hands, he slowly pulled her knife from his belt, and looked at it for a minute in the palm of his hand. The glint of the blade was blurred in his vision. He clenched the handle tightly in his fist and jammed the knife in the sheath at her belt.

"You win. Get out of here. Get out of my sight."

"Richard . . ."

"I said get out of here!" He pointed back the way they had come. "Go back and let the gars do the job. You may botch it with that knife! I'd hate to think you slipped and didn't finish it properly. I'd hate to think that after all this, you might not be dead."

He turned his back to her and sat on a windfall spruce that lay in front of the fire. She stood watching him in silence, then moved off a few paces.

"Richard . . . after all we have been through together, I don't want it to be finished like this."

"I don't care what you want. You have forfeited that right." He struggled to make the words come out. "Get out of my sight."

Kahlan nodded, and looked down at the ground. Richard leaned over, elbows on his knees, his face in his shaking hands. He thought he might throw up.

"Richard," she said in a soft voice, "when this is all ended, I hope you can think well of me, remember me more fondly than you do right now."

That was it. He came over the log with a boost of one boot on top. In a blink he had her shirt in his fists.

"I will only remember you for what you are! A traitor! A traitor to all those who have died, all those who will die!" Her eyes were wide as she tried to back away from him, but he held her with a vengeance. "A traitor to all the wizards who have given their lives, to Shar, to Siddin and all the Mud People who were killed! A traitor to your sister!"

"That's not true. . . ."

"A traitor to all those and more! If I fail and Rahl wins, we will all have you to thank, and so will Darken Rahl. It is you who aids him!"

"I do this to help you! You heard what Shota said!" She was getting angry now, too.

"That won't work. Not for me. Yes, I heard what Shota said. She said that both Zedd and you would turn against me somehow. She did not say you both would be wrong!"

"What do you mean . . ."

"This is not a quest for me! It's to stop Rahl! How do you know that once we have the box it might not be me who would deliver it to him? What if it's me who would betray us, and the only chance to keep the box from Rahl is for you and Zedd to stop me?"

"That doesn't make any sense."

"Does it make any more sense that both you and Zedd would try to kill me? That would require two to be wrong, this would require only one. It's just the stupid riddle of a witch woman! You're letting yourself die for a stupid riddle! We can't know how the future will come about. We can't know the meaning of what she said, how it will be true! Or if. Not until it happens! Only then can we know what it means, and deal with it."

"I only know I cannot allow myself to live to carry out the prophecy. You are the thread that weaves this struggle together."

"And thread can't get there without the needle! You're my needle. Without you I wouldn't have gotten this far. At every turn, I needed you. Today, at the inverted fork, I would have chosen wrong without you. You know the Queen, I don't. Even if I manage to get the box without you, what then? Where will I go? I don't know the Midlands. Where will I go, Kahlan, tell me?

485

How will I know where it's safe? I could walk right into Rahl's hands, carry the box right to him."

"Shota said you are the only one with a chance. Without you all is lost. Not me. You. She said that if I live . . . Richard, I can't allow that. I won't."

"You are a traitor to us," he whispered viciously.

She shook her head slowly. "Despite what you think, Richard, I do this for you."

Richard screamed and threw her backward as hard as he could. She fell to the ground on her back. He came and stood above her, glaring down, dust rising around his boots.

"Don't you dare say that!" he yelled, both hands in fists. "You do this for yourself, because you haven't got the stomach for what victory entails! Don't you dare to say you do this for me!"

She came to her feet, keeping her eyes on him. "I would give almost anything, Richard, for you not to remember me in this way. But what I do, I do because I must. For you. For you to have a chance. I have sworn to protect the Seeker with my life. The payment has come due." Tears ran down her face, through the dust on her cheeks.

As he watched her turn and vanish into the darkness, Richard felt as if a plug inside him had been pulled and his whole self was draining away.

He went to the fire, slid his back down the log until he sat on the ground. He pulled his knees up with his arms around them, put his face against them, and cried as he had never cried.

CHAPTER 33

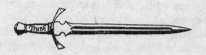

RACHEL SAT ON HER little chair behind the Princess, knocking her knees together, thinking about how she would get the Princess to put her out so she could take the box away with her and never come back. She kept thinking about the loaf of bread with the box in it, waiting for her in the garden. She was afraid, but excited, too. Excited that she was going to be helping all those people so they wouldn't get their heads chopped off. It was the first time she had ever felt like an important person. She twisted the hem of her dress. She could hardly wait to get away.

All the lords and ladies were drinking their special drink. They all seemed happy to be doing it. Giller was standing behind the Queen with her other advisors. He was talking quietly to the court artist. She didn't like the artist, he scared her, he always smiled funny at her. And he only had one hand. She had heard the servants talking before, that they were afraid the artist would draw a picture of them.

The people started getting scared looks on their faces. They were looking at the Queen. They started to stand up. Rachel looked over at the Queen and saw that the people weren't looking at her, they were looking at something else, behind her. Her eyes got wide when she saw the two big men.

They were the biggest men she had ever seen. Their shirts didn't have sleeves but their arms had metal bands on them, with sharp things sticking out. The men had big muscles all over, and yellow hair. They looked like the meanest men she had ever seen, meaner even than any of the dungeon guards. The men looked around the room at the people, then went and stood on each side of the big archway behind the Queen and folded their arms. The Queen huffed and turned around in her chair to see what was happening.

A man with blue eyes, and long yellow hair and white robes, and a gold-handled knife at his belt, came through the archway. He was the handsomest-looking man she had ever seen. He smiled at the Queen. She jumped to her feet.

"What an unexpected surprise!" she said in her nicest dog voice. "We are honored. But we weren't expecting you until tomorrow."

The man again smiled a pretty smile at her. "I couldn't wait to get here, to see your lovely face again. Forgive me for being early, Your Majesty."

The Queen giggled as she held her hand out for him to kiss. She was always having people kiss her hand. Rachel was surprised at what the nice-looking man had said. She never knew anyone who thought the Queen was lovely. The Queen took his hand in hers and brought him forward.

"Lords and ladies, may I introduce Father Rahl."

Father Rahl! She looked around to see if anyone had seen her jump, but no one had; they were all looking at Father Rahl. She was sure he was going to look at her, and see that she was going to run away with the box. She looked at Giller, but he didn't look back. His face was white. Father Rahl was here before she had run away with the box! What was she going to do?

She was going to do what Giller had told her to do, that's what. She was going to be brave and save all those people. She had to think of a way to get out.

Father Rahl looked around at all the people who were standing up now. The little dog barked. He turned to the source of the sound and it stopped barking; instead it began to whine softly. He turned back to the people. It got real quiet.

"Dinner is over. You will excuse us now," he said in a soft voice.

Everyone started whispering. His blue eyes watched. The whispering stopped and they started to leave, first slow, then faster. Father Rahl looked at some of the royal advisors, and they left, looking glad to be doing it. A few he didn't look at, including Giller, stayed. Princess Violet stayed, too, and Rachel tried to stay behind her so she wouldn't be noticed. The Queen smiled and held her arm out to the table.

"Won't you sit, Father Rahl, I'm sure you have had a strenuous journey. Let us bring you something to eat. We have a lovely roast tonight."

He looked at her with blue eyes that didn't blink. "I don't approve of butchering helpless animals and then consuming their flesh."

Rachel thought the Queen was going to choke. "Well, then . . . we also have a lovely turnip soup, and some other things, I'm sure . . . there must be something . . . if there isn't, the cooks, will make whatever . . ."

"Perhaps some other time. I am not here to eat, I am here for your contribution to the alliance."

"But . . . this is sooner than expected, we haven't finished drawing up the agreements, there are many papers to be signed, and you will want to have them looked over first, surely."

"I will be only too happy to sign anything you have ready, and offer my word that I will sign whatever additional documents you might have drawn up. I trust your honesty to deal with me fairly." He smiled. "You don't have any intention of tricking me somehow with these agreements, do you?"

"Well, no, Father Rahl, of course not. Of course not."

"There you have it, then. Why would I need anyone to look over these papers, if you are being fair with me? You are being fair, you say?"

"Well, of course I am. I guess there is no need . . . but this is most unusual."

"So is our alliance. Let's be on with it, then."

"Yes. Yes, of course." She turned to one of her advisors. "Go get whatever of the alliance treaty you have ready and bring it. Bring ink and pens. And my seal." He bowed and left. The Queen turned to Giller. "Wherever you have secreted the box, go and get it."

He bowed. "Of course, Your Majesty." Rachel felt alone and afraid when she saw him go through the door, his silver robes flying behind him.

While they waited, the Queen introduced the Princess to Father Rahl. Rachel stood behind Princess Violet's chair after she went to have her hand kissed. Father Rahl bowed to her and kissed her hand and told her how she was as pretty as her mother. The Princess grinned and grinned and held the hand he had kissed to her breast.

The advisor came back with his helpers; they each carried armfuls of papers. They moved plates aside and laid the papers all over the head table, pointing to where the Queen and Father Rahl should sign their names. One of the helpers dripped red wax on the papers, and the Queen pressed her seal into it. Father Rahl said he didn't have a seal, and that his written name would do, that he was sure he would recognize his own writing in the future. When Giller came back, he stood off to the side and waited until they finished. The men started gathering up all the papers, arguing with each other about which order they went in. The Queen motioned Giller forward.

"Father Rahl," Giller said with his finest smile, "may I present you with Queen Milena's box of Orden." He held the fake box out in both hands, careful, just as if it were the real one. The jewels all sparkled real pretty.

Father Rahl smiled a little smile as he reached out and carefully lifted the box from Giller's hands. He turned it around a minute, looking at the pretty jewels. Then he motioned one of the big men with all the muscles to come forward. When he did, Father Rahl looked him in the eye and handed him the box.

With one hand, the man squeezed the box. It shattered. The Queen's eyes got real big.

"What is the meaning of this!" she asked.

Father Rahl's face got scary-looking. "That would be my question, Your Majesty. This box is a counterfeit."

"Why, that's simply not possible . . . there is no way . . . I know for a fact . . ." The Queen turned her head to Giller. "Giller! What do you know of this?"

He held his hands in the opposite sleeves of his robes. "Your Majesty . . . I don't understand . . . no one has tampered with the magic seal, I saw to that myself. I assure you, this is the same box I have guarded ever since you put it in my hands. It must have been a fake from the first. We have been tricked. That is the only possible explanation."

Father Rahl's blue eyes stayed on the wizard the whole time he talked. Then they slid to one of his men. The man came and grabbed the robes at the back of Giller's neck. He lifted Giller off the ground with that one hand.

"What are you doing! Let go of me, you big ox! Have respect for a wizard or you will regret it. I can assure you!" His feet were dangling in the air.

Rachel had a lump in her throat, tears in her eyes. She tried to be brave and not cry. She knew that if she did, they might notice her.

Father Rahl licked his fingertips. "Not the only possible explanation, wizard. The real box has magic, a particular type of magic. The magic of this box is wrong. A Queen would not be able to see it, to know if it was the real box. But a wizard would."

Father Rahl smiled a small smile to the Queen. "The wizard and I are going to go now, and have a private conversation." He turned and walked out of the room, white robes flying behind him. The man holding Giller up in the air followed Father Rahl. The other man stepped in front of the door and folded his arms. Giller's feet didn't touch the ground as he was carried away.

Rachel wanted to run after Giller, she was so scared for him. She saw his head turn back and look at the people. His dark eyes were wide, and for a second, they looked right at her, right into her eyes. When they did, she heard his voice in her head, as clear as if he had yelled to her. The voice in her head screamed only one word.

Run.

Then he was gone. Rachel wanted to cry. Instead, she sucked the hem of her dress. All the people around the Queen started talking at once. James, the court artist, started picking up some

491

of the pieces of the fake box, turning them over in his one hand, looking at them, holding them against the stump of his other. Princess Violet took one of the big pieces from him and looked at the jewels, running her fingers over them.

Rachel kept remembering the voice in her head, Giller's voice, yelling at her to run. She looked around; no one was paying any attention to her. She went around the tables, keeping her head down, below the tabletops, so they wouldn't be able to see her. When she got to the other side of the room, she poked her head up to see if anyone was looking. They weren't.

She reached up and took some food off the plates: a piece of meat, three bread rolls, and a big piece of hard cheese. She stuffed them all in her pockets, then checked the people again.

Then she ran for the hall. She kept herself from getting tears, to be brave for Giller. Her bare feet ran down the carpets, past the picture rugs hanging on the walls. Before she got to the guards at the doors, she slowed down, so they wouldn't see her running. When they saw her coming, they pulled up the big bolt and didn't say anything as she went through the door. The guards on the outside of the door just glanced at her as she came through, then looked back out, watching the grounds.

Rachel wiped some tears off her face as she went down the cold stone steps. She had tried to keep them from coming, but a few got out before she could stop them. The guards on patrol ignored her as she walked fast over the cobblestones, toward the garden.

Away from the torches hung on the walls outside the castle it was dark, but she knew her way. The grass was wet on her bare feet. At the third urn, she knelt down, looking to see that no one was watching, then reached under the flowers. She felt the cloth around the bread, and pulled it out. Untying the knots, she laid the four corners back, then reached in her pockets and put the meat, the three hard rolls, and the cheese on top of the bread and tied the corners of the cloth back up.

Just before she started running for the outer-wall gate, she remembered, and made a little gasp. She froze stiff, her eyes wide.

She had forgotten Sara! Her doll was still in her sleeping box! Princess Violet would find her doll, she would throw Sara in the fire! Rachel couldn't leave her doll there; she was running away and not coming back. Sara would be afraid without her. Sara would get burned up.

She pushed the bundle with the bread back under the flowers, looked around, and ran for the castle. She had to slow down and walk when she got close, back into the torchlight. One of the guards at the door looked down at her.

"I just let you out," he said.

She swallowed hard. "I know. But now I have to go back in for a few minutes."

"Forget something?"

She nodded and managed to make herself say, "Yes."

He shook his head and lifted the little window. "Open the door," he said to the guard inside. She heard the heavy bolt open.

Once back inside, she looked down the hall. The big room with the black-and-white floor and the grand stairs was ahead, a few turns down some long halls and through a couple of big rooms. One of the big rooms was the dining room. That was the shortest way. But the Queen, or the Princess, might be there, or even Father Rahl. They might see her. She couldn't let them see her. Princess Violet might take her up to her room and lock her in the sleeping box; it was late.

She turned and went through the little door on the right. That was the servants' passageway. It was a lot longer, but no one important would be in the servant halls or on the servant stairs. None of the servants would stop her; they all knew she was the Princess's playmate, and they didn't want the Princess mad at them. She would have to go down through the place where the servants stayed, down under the big rooms and under the kitchen.

The stairs were all stone, worn smooth on the front edges. One window at the top was uncovered and it let in rain, and the steps always had water leaking from the stone walls, running down them. Some places it was just a little, some places more, and there was green slime on some of the steps. She always had to step careful to keep from stepping in the slime. Torches in iron brackets made the stone and the steps look red and yellow.

There were some people in the halls on the bottom floor, servants carrying linens and blankets, washwomen with buckets of water and mops, and men carrying bundles of firewood for the

493

fireplaces upstairs. Some of the people stopped and whispered to each other. They seemed excited. She heard Giller's name and it made her get a lump in her throat.

When she went past the servants' quarters, all the oil lamps were burning, hung from the big beams of the low ceilings, and there were bunches of people gathered around, telling each other what they had seen. Rachel saw one of the men talking loud, with mostly women, but some men, too, standing around him. It was Mr. Sanders, the man who wore the fancy coat and greeted the fine ladies and gentlemen when they came to dinner, and announced their names when they came in.

"Heard it myself, from those two that stand watch over the dining room. You know who I'm talking about, the young one, Frank and the other, with the limp, Jenkins. Said the D'Haran guards told them personal that there's going to be a search of the castle, top to bottom."

"What're they lookin' for?" a woman asked.

"Don't know. Least they didn't tell Frank and Jenkins. But I wouldn't want to be the one that had whatever they're after. Those men from D'Hara could give you nightmares when you were wide awake."

"Wish they'd find whatever it is under Violet's bed," somebody else said. "It'd do her up right to get a nightmare for a change, 'stead of givin' 'em." Everyone laughed.

Rachel went on, through the big storeroom with all the columns. Barrels were on one side, all piled up in rows on top of one another; boxes and crates and sacks were stacked up on the other side. The room smelled damp and musty, and she could always hear mice scratching about. She went down the middle, past the lamps hung on the side of columns, to the heavy door at the other end. The iron strap hinges creaked when she strained and pulled on the iron ring and opened the door. Rust from the ring got on her hands, so she wiped them on the stone. Another big door to the right led to the dungeon. She went up the stairway. It was dark, with only one torch at the top, and she could hear water go plink, plink, plink and echo. Through the door at the top that stood open a crack, she went down the stone block halls like the wind that was always in them. She was too scared to cry. She wanted Sara to be safe, with her, and away from here.

On the top floor, at last, she peeked her head around the door, looking up and down the hall that ran past Princess Violet's room. The hall was empty. Tiptoeing across the carpet with the pictures of the boats on it, she reached the entryway set back from the hall. She snuck into it, checking the hall again. Carefully, she opened the door a sliver. The room was dark. She slipped in and shut the door tight.

There was a fire in the fireplace, but no lamps were lit. She sneaked across the floor, feeling the fur rug on her bare feet. She got down on her hands and knees and crept into her sleeping box, and pulled the blanket back with one hand. She gasped. Sara wasn't there. She felt just as if a cold wind had blown across her skin.

"Looking for something?" It was Princess Violet's voice.

For a minute, she couldn't move. She started to breathe hard, but she kept the tears from coming. She couldn't let Princess Violet see her cry. She backed out of the box and saw there was a black form standing in front of the fire. It was the Princess. She took a step forward, away from the fireplace, toward Rachel. Her hands were behind her back. Rachel couldn't see what she had.

"I was just coming up to get in my box. To go to sleep."

"Is that so." Rachel could see better in the dark now, could see the smile on Princess Violet's face. "You wouldn't happen to be looking for this, would you?"

She slowly pulled her hands out from behind her back. She had Sara. Rachel's eyes went wide and she suddenly felt like she had to go potty.

"Princess Violet, please . . ." she whined. Her hands reached out, pleading.

"Come here, and we'll talk about it."

Rachel stepped slowly to the Princess, stopping in front of her, twisting her finger in the hem of her dress. The Princess suddenly slapped her, harder than she had ever slapped her before. It was so hard that it made Rachel give out a little scream as she was knocked a step backward. She put her left hand over the stinging pain. Tears welled up in her eyes. She jammed her fist into her pocket, determined that she would not cry this time.

The Princess stepped to her and hit her across the other cheek with the back of her hand. Her knuckles hurt more than the first

495

slap. Rachel gritted her teeth and clutched her fist around something in her pocket to keep from letting the tears come.

Princess Violet stepped back to the fireplace. "What did I tell you I would do if you ever had a doll?"

"Princess Violet, please don't. . . ." She was shaking because her face hurt so much, and because she was so scared. "Please, let me keep her? She's no harm to you."

The Princess laughed her awful laugh. "No. I'm going to throw it in the fire, just like I told you I would. To teach you a lesson. What's her name?"

"She doesn't have a name."

"Well, no matter, she'll burn just as well."

She turned around to the fire. Rachel's fist was still clutched around the thing in her pocket. It was the magic fire stick Giller had given her. She pulled it out of her pocket and looked at it.

"Don't you dare throw my doll in the fire or you'll be sorry!"

The Princess spun around. "What did you say? How dare you speak to me in that tone of voice. You're just a nobody. I'm a Princess."

Rachel touched the magic fire stick to the doily on a small round marble table next to her. "Light for me," she whispered.

The doily burst into flames. The Princess's face looked surprised. Rachel touched the fire stick to a book on a short marble table. She looked quickly to the Princess's eyes to make sure she was watching, then whispered again, and with a roar it, too, burst into flames. Princess Violet's eyes were wide. Rachel picked up the book by a corner and threw it in the fireplace while the Princess watched her. Rachel spun around, took a step, and put the fire stick against the Princess.

"Give me my doll, or I'll burn you up."

"You wouldn't dare. . . ."

"Right now! If you don't, I'll set you on fire, and your skin will burn up."

Princess Violet pushed the doll at her. "Here. Please, Rachel, don't burn me. I'm afraid of fire."

Rachel took the doll with her left hand, hugging it to her, still holding the fire stick against the Princess. Rachel was starting to feel sorry for her. Then she thought about how much her face hurt. More than it had ever hurt before.

"Let's just forget all about this, Rachel. You may keep the doll, all right?" Her voice was getting real nice now, not mean like before.

Rachel knew it was a trick. As soon as there were guards around, she knew the Princess would say to chop her head off. Then Princess Violet would really laugh at her, and burn Sara up too.

"Get in the box," Rachel said. "Then you can see how you like it."

"What!"

Rachel pushed the fire stick a little harder. "Right now, or I'll burn you up."

Princess Violet walked across the floor slow, with the fire stick at her back. "Rachel, think about what you're doing, are you really . . ."

"Be quiet and get inside. Unless you want me to burn you."

The Princess got down on her knees and crawled inside. Rachel looked in at her.

"Go to the back."

She did as she was told. Rachel shut the door with a clang and went to the drawer and got the key. She locked the iron door on the iron box, then put the key in her pocket. She got down on her knees and looked inside through the little window. She could hardly see the Princess's eyes looking back in the dark.

"Good night, Violet. Go to sleep. I'm going to sleep in your bed tonight. I'm sick of your voice. If you make any noise at all, I'll come over and light your skin on fire. Do you understand?"

"Yes," came back the weak voice from the dark hole in the door.

Rachel set Sara down while she pulled the fur rug close and turned it over on the box, covering it all up. She went and bounced on the bed to make it squeak, to make Princess Violet think she was going to sleep in it.

Rachel smiled and tiptoed all the way to the door as she hugged Sara.

After she had gone all the way back the way she had come, through the servants' passageways and to the door at the end, she looked carefully into the hall, and went down to the big door with the guards. Rachel didn't say anything. She couldn't think of anything to say; she just stood and waited for them to open the door.

"So that's it, a doll you forgot," the guard said.

She just nodded.

She heard the door clang shut behind as she went into the dark, to the garden. There were more guards than she was used to seeing. The regular guards had new ones with them, dressed different. The new ones looked at her more than the old ones did, and she could hear the regular ones telling them who she was. She tried not to let them see her looking back as she walked with her doll, holding it tight against her, trying to keep her feet from running.

The bundle with the bread with the box in it was where she had left it, under the flowers. Rachel pulled it out, holding it in one hand by the knot, while she held Sara to her chest with her other. As she walked through the garden, she wondered if Princess Violet still thought she was sleeping in the big bed, or if she knew it was a trick and was yelling for help. If she yelled for help, and the guards had come and found her in the box, they might already be looking for her. She had had to go the long way; it had taken a lot of time for her legs to take her under the whole castle and back up again. Rachel listened carefully for shouts, to see if they were looking for her yet.

She could hardly breathe, hoping she could get out of the castle before they chased after her. She remembered Mr. Sanders saying they were going to search the castle. She knew what they were looking for. They wanted the box. She had promised Giller she would get it away, so they couldn't have it and hurt all those people.

A lot of men were on the walk at the top of the wall. When she got almost to the door through the wall, she slowed down. Before, there were always two of the Queen's guards there. Now there were three men. Two she recognized—they wore the red tunics with the black wolf's head, the Queen's guard—but the other was dressed different, in dark leather, and he was a lot bigger. He was one of the new men. Rachel didn't know if she should keep going or run away. But run away where? She had to get through the wall before she could really run away.

Before she could decide what to do, they saw her, so she kept going. One of the regular guards turned to lift the bolt. The new man put his arm up to stop him.

"It's just the Princess's playmate. The Princess puts her out sometimes."

"No one goes out," the new man said to him.

The regular guards stopped opening the door. "Sorry, little one, but you heard him, no one goes out."

Rachel stood there with her mouth stuck shut. Her eyes stared at the new man while he looked down at her. She swallowed. Giller was depending on her to get the box out. There was no other way out. She tried to think what Giller would do.

"Well, all right," she said at last, "it's cold tonight, I'd rather stay in anyway."

"Well, there you go then. You get to stay in tonight," the regular guard said.

"What's you name?" Rachel asked.

He looked a little surprised. "Queen's lancer Reid."

With her doll in her hand, Rachel pointed at the other regular guard. "What's yours?"

"Queen's lancer Walcott."

"Queen's lancer Reid and Queen's lancer Walcott," she repeated to herself. "All right, I think I can remember." She pointed at the new man, the doll swinging back and forth by its arm when she did. "And what's your name?"

He hooked his thumbs in his belt. "What do you want to know for?"

She hugged Sara back to her chest. "Well, the Princess yelled at me, to tell me to be put out tonight. If I don't go out, she'll be spitting mad, and want to chop my head off for not doing as she said, so I want to tell her who wouldn't let me be put out. I want your names so she won't think I'm making it up, so she can come and ask you herself. She scares me. She's been starting to say to have people's heads chopped off."

All three of them stood back up a little and looked at each other. "That's true enough," Queen's lancer Reid said to the new man. "The Princess is turning into her mother's daughter. A little handful, what with the Queen letting her cut her teeth on the axe now."

"No one goes out, those are our orders," the new man repeated.

"Well, the two of us are for doing as the Princess orders." Queen's lancer Reid turned a little and spat. "Now, if you want her kept in, that's fine by us, so long as it's clear whose neck's on the block. If it comes down to it, we told you to let her out, just like the Princess said. We're not going to the block with you." The other guard, Walcott, nodded that he agreed. "Not for the threat from a little girl, no taller than that." He held his hand out, level with the top of her head. "I'll not tell them we three big strong soldiers all agreed we thought she was dangerous. It's your call, but it'll be your head, not ours, if you go against the Princess. You'll answer to the Queen's axeman, not us."

The new man looked down at her; he seemed a little mad. He looked back at the other two a minute, then down at her again. "Well, it's obvious she's no threat. The orders were meant to protect from threat, so I guess . . ."

Queen's lancer Walcott started lifting up the heavy bolt on the door.

"But I want to know what she's got there," the new man said.

"Just my supper and my doll," Rachel said, trying to make it sound unimportant.

"Let's have a look."

Rachel laid the bundle down on the ground and untied the knots, laying the corners back. She handed Sara up to him.

He took Sara in his big hand, turning her around, looking. He turned her upside down and lifted her dress with his big finger. Rachel kicked him in the leg, hard as she could.

"Don't you do that! Don't you have no respect?" she yelled.

The other two guards laughed. "You find anything dangerous under there?" Queen's lancer Reid asked.

The new man looked over at the other two, handing Sara back down to her. "What else have you got there?"

"I told you. My supper."

He started to bend over. "Well, a little thing like you has no need for a whole loaf of bread."

"That's mine!" she yelled. "Leave it be!"

"Leave it alone," Queen's lancer Walcott told the new man.

"She gets little enough. It look to you like the Princess overfeeds her?"

The new man straightened up. "I guess not." He let out a deep breath. "Go on. Get out of here."

Rachel tied the cloth back over the bread and other food as fast as she could. She held Sara tight to her with one hand, and held the bundle just as tight with the other as she went between the men's legs and out the door.

When she heard it clang shut, she started running. She ran fast as she could, not looking back, too afraid to know for sure if anyone was chasing her. After a time, she had to know, and finally stopped to check. No one. Out of breath, she sat down to rest on a fat root in the path.

She could see the outline of the castle against the starry sky, the notched top edge of the wall, the towers with lights in them. She was never going back there again, never. Her and Giller were going to run away to where people were nice and they were never going to come back. While she was panting, she heard a voice.

"Rachel?" It was Sara, she realized.

She laid Sara in her lap, on top of the bundle. "We're safe now, Sara. We got away."

Sara smiled. "I'm so glad, Rachel."

"We're never going back to that mean place again."

"Rachel, Giller wants you to know something."

She had to lean close; she could hardly hear Sara's voice. "What?"

"That he can't come with you. You must go on without him."

Rachel started to get tears. "But I want him to come with me."

"He would like to, more than anything, child, but he must stay and keep them from finding you, so you can get away. It's the only way to keep you safe."

"But I'll be afraid by myself."

"You won't be by yourself, Rachel, you will have me with you. Always."

"But what am I to do? Where am I to go?"

"You must run away. Giller says not to go to your old wayward pine, they will find you there." Rachel's eyes got big when she heard this. "Go to a different wayward pine, then the next

501

day, another, just keep running away and hiding until the winter comes. Then find some nice people who will take good care of you."

"All right, if Giller says so, that's what I'll do."

"Rachel, Giller wants you to know he loves you."

"I love Giller too," Rachel said, "more than anything."

The doll smiled.

All at once, the woods lit up with blue and yellow light. She looked up. Then came a sudden loud bang that made her jump. Her mouth dropped open; her eyes were wide as they would go.

A giant ball of fire came up from the castle, from behind the walls.

The ball of fire lifted into the air. Sparks dropped from it, and black smoke rolled away. The fire turned to black smoke as it went higher, until it was all dark again.

"Did you see that?" she asked Sara.

Sara didn't say anything.

"I hope Giller is all right."

She looked down at the doll, but she didn't say anything, or even smile back.

Rachel hugged Sara to her and picked up the bundle.

"We better get going, like Giller said."

When she went past the lake, she threw the key to her sleeping box as far as she could, out into the water, and smiled when she heard it splash.

Sara didn't say anything as they rushed away from the castle, down the path. Rachel remembered what Giller said, that she shouldn't go to the same wayward pine. She turned and went down a deer trail, through the bramble, in a new direction.

West.

CHAPTER 34

THERE WAS A SOUND. Small, soft, spitting.

In the fog of half sleep, half wake, it made no sense, no matter how hard he tried to understand it. Slowly at first, then with accelerating urgency, he came awake, aware of the aroma of cooking meat. Immediately, he regretted the experience of being conscious, the memories of what had happened, his longing for Kahlan. His knees were pulled up to his chest with his head resting against them. The bark of the tree at his back dug painfully into his flesh, and his muscles were cramped to near paralysis from sleeping in the same position all night. With his head against his knees he couldn't see anything, except that it was only just beginning to lighten with dawn.

There was someone, or something, near him.

Continuing to feign sleep, he took assessment of where his hands were in relation to his weapons. The sword was a goodly reach, and then a long pull to draw it. The knife wasn't. His fingertips were touching the hickory handle. Flexing his fingers slowly, carefully, he worked the handle into his palm, tightening his grip around it. Whatever it was was near to his left side. A spring and a thrust with the knife, he thought.

He took a careful peek. With a shock, he saw that it was Kahlan. She was sitting, leaning against the log, watching him. A rabbit was cooking on the fire. He sat up straight.

"What are you doing here?" he asked cautiously.

"Is it all right if we talk?"

Richard slid the knife back into its sheath, stretched his legs, rubbing the cramps from them. "I thought we did all our talking last night." He immediately winced at his own words. She gave him an unreadable look. "I'm sorry," he said, softening his tone. "Of course we can talk. What do you want to talk about?"

She shrugged in the dim light. "I've been doing a lot of thinking." She had a length of birch branch that he had cut the night before for the fire, and was stripping off pieces of white bark. "Last night, after I left, well, I knew you had a headache . . ."

"How did you know that?"

She shrugged again. "I can always tell, by the look in your eyes, when you have a headache." Her voice was soft, gentle. "I knew you hadn't been getting much sleep lately, and that it was my fault, so I decided that before I . . . before I left, I would stand watch for you while you slept. So I went over there," she pointed with the branch, "in those trees, where I could keep my eye on you." She looked down at the branch as she peeled off strips of bark. "I wanted to make sure you got some sleep."

"You were there the whole night?" Richard was afraid to hope at what this meant.

She nodded, but didn't look up. "While I was watching, I decided to make a snare, like you taught me, to see if I could catch you some breakfast. While I was sitting there, I did a lot of thinking. Mostly, I cried for a long time. I couldn't stand it that you thought those things about me. It hurt that you thought of me like that. It made me angry too."

Richard decided it was best not to say anything while she struggled to find the words. He didn't know what to say, and was afraid if he said anything it might make her leave again. Kahlan pulled off a curl of birch bark and tossed it in the fire, where it sizzled and flared to flame.

"Then I thought about what you said, and I decided there were

504

some things I needed to tell you, about how to conduct yourself when you are with the Queen. And then I remembered some things I needed to tell you about which roads to avoid, and about where you might go. I just keep thinking about things I needed to tell you, things you need to know. Before I knew it, I realized you were right. About everything."

Richard thought she looked like she was near tears, but she didn't cry. Instead, she picked at the branch with her fingernail, and avoided his eyes. Still he kept quiet. Then she asked him a question he wasn't expecting.

"Do you think Shota is pretty?"

He smiled. "Yes. But not as pretty as you."

Kahlan smiled and pushed some hair back over her shoulder. "Not many would dare to say that to a . . ." She caught herself again. Her secret stood between them like a third person. She started again. "There is an old women's proverb, maybe you have heard it before. 'Never let a beautiful woman pick your path for you when there is a man in her line of sight.'"

Richard laughed a little and stood to stretch his legs. "No, I've not heard that before." He half leaned, half sat against the log, as he folded his arms. He didn't think Kahlan needed to worry about Shota stealing his heart; Shota had said she would kill him if she ever saw him again. Even without Shota's vow, Kahlan had no cause for worry.

She tossed the branch aside and stood next to him, leaning her hip against the log. She looked into his eyes at last, her eyebrows wrinkled together. "Richard"—her voice was low, almost a whisper—"last night I figured out I was being very stupid. I had been afraid the witch woman would kill me, and all of a sudden, I realized, she was about to succeed. Only I was doing it for her; letting her pick my path for me.

"You were right about it all. I should have known better than to disregard the things a Seeker says." She looked back down at the ground before her green eyes came back up to his. "If . . . if it is not too late, I would like my job back, as your guide."

Richard couldn't believe it was over. He had never been this happy, this relieved, in his life. Instead of answering, he reached out and pulled her into his arms, hugged her tight to him. Her arms slipped around him as she laid her head against his chest for a moment. Then she pushed away.

"Richard, there is one other matter. Before you can say you will take me back, you must hear the rest of it. I can't go on anymore without telling you about me. About what I am. It's cleaving my heart, because I'm supposed to be your friend. I should have told you from the beginning. I have never had a friend like you before. I didn't want it to end." Her gaze left his. "But now it must," she added faintly.

"Kahlan, I've told you before; you're my friend, and nothing can change that."

"This secret can." Her shoulders were slumped. "This is about magic."

Richard wasn't sure anymore that he wanted to hear her secret. He had just gotten her back; he didn't want to lose her again. He squatted down in front of the fire, picking up the roasting stick with the rabbit. Sparks swirled up into the waning darkness. He felt proud of her, for catching the rabbit on her own, the way he had taught her.

"Kahlan, I don't care what your secret is. I care about you, that's all that matters. You don't have to tell me. Come on, the rabbit is done, come and have some."

Cutting off a piece with his knife, he handed it to her as she sat on the ground next to him, pulling her hair back off her face. The meat was hot, so she held it lightly with her fingertips, and blew to cool it. Richard cut a piece for himself and sat back.

"Richard, when you first saw Shota, did she really look like your mother?"

He looked over to Kahlan's face, lit by the fire, and nodded before he took a bite.

"Your mother was very pretty. You have her eyes, and her mouth."

Richard smiled a little at the memory. "But it wasn't really her."

"So you felt angry that Shota was pretending to be someone she could not be? That she was deceiving you?" She took a bite of the rabbit, breathing in through her mouth because the meat was still hot. She watched him carefully.

Richard shrugged, feeling the sting of sorrow. "I guess. It wasn't fair."

Kahlan chewed a minute, and then swallowed. "That is why I must tell you who I am, even if you hate me for it, because you have been my friend. Although I have not been the kind of friend you deserve. That is the other reason I came back, because I didn't want someone else to tell you. I wanted you to hear it from me. After I tell you, if you want me to I will leave."

Richard looked up at the sky, at the color coming slowly to it. He suddenly wished Kahlan weren't telling him what she was; he wished things could stay the way they were. "Don't worry, I'm not sending you away. We have a job to do. Remember what Shota said? The Queen won't have the box long; that can only mean someone will take it from her. Better us than Darken Rahl."

Kahlan put her hand on his arm. "I don't want you to decide until you hear what I have to say, until you hear what I am. Then, if you want me to leave I will understand." She looked intently into his eyes. "Richard, I just want you to know that I have never cared for anyone the way I care for you, nor will I ever again. But it is not possible for it to go beyond that. Nothing can ever come of it. Nothing good anyway."

He refused to believe that. There was a way, there had to be. Richard took a heavy breath, letting it out slowly. "All right then, out with it."

She nodded. "Remember when I told you that some who lived in the Midlands were creatures of magic? And that they couldn't give up that magic, because it was part of them?" He nodded to her. "Well, I am one of those creatures. I am more than a woman."

"So, what are you?"

"I am a Confessor."

Confessor.

Richard knew that word.

Every muscle in his body went stiff. His breath caught in his throat. The Book of Counted Shadows suddenly flooded through his mind. *Verification of the truth of the words of the Book of Counted Shadows, if spoken by another, rather than read by the one who commands the boxes, can only be insured by the use of a Confessor. . . .*

His mind raced, as if flipping the pages in his mind's eye, scanning the words, trying to remember the whole book, trying to remember if *Confessor* was mentioned again. No, it wasn't. He knew every word in the book, and Confessor was in it only once, at the beginning. He could remember puzzling over what a Confessor could be. He hadn't even been sure, before, that it was a person. He felt the weight of the tooth hanging around his neck.

Kahlan frowned at the look on his face. "Do you know what a Confessor is?"

"No," he managed. "I heard the word before, that's all . . . from my father. But I don't know what it means." He struggled to regain control of himself. "So, what does it mean, to be a Confessor?"

Kahlan pulled her knees up, hugging her arms around them, withdrawing just a little. "It's a power, magic power, that is passed from mother to daughter, going back almost as far as there have been the lands, back beyond the dark time."

Richard didn't know what the "dark time" was, but didn't interrupt. "It is something we are born with, magic that is part of us, and cannot be separated from us any more than you could be separated from your heart. Any woman who is a Confessor will bear children who are Confessors. Always. But the power is not the same in all of us; in some it is weaker, in some, stronger."

"So you can't get rid of it, even if you wanted to. But what sort of magic is it?"

She looked away, to the fire. "It's a power invoked by touch. It's always there, inside us. We don't bring it out to use it; instead, we must always hold it in, and use it by releasing our grip of it, relaxing our hold and letting it come forth."

"Sort of like holding your stomach in?"

She smiled at his analogy. "Sort of."

"And what does this power do?"

She twisted the corner of her cloak. "It does not reveal itself well in words. I never thought it would be this troublesome to explain, but to someone who is not from the Midlands, well, it's difficult to put into words. I have never had to do this before, and I'm not even sure it can be done, accurately. It's a little like trying to explain fog to a blind person."

"Try."

She nodded and stole a look into his eyes.

"It is the power of love."

Richard almost laughed. "And I'm supposed to be afraid of the power of love?"

Kahlan's back stiffened; indignation flared in her eyes: indignation and the kind of timeless look Adie and Shota had flashed him, one that said that his words were disrespectful, that even his small smile was insolent. It was a countenance he was not used to seeing her direct at him. He felt a cold realization that Kahlan was not used to having anyone smile about her power, and who she was. Her look said more to him about her power than any words could have. Whatever her magic was, it was definitely not something to be smiled about. His small grin withered. When she seemed sure he was not about to say anything else flippant, she went on.

"You don't understand. Do not take it lightly." Her eyes narrowed. "Once touched by it, you are no longer the person you were. You are changed forever. Forevermore you are devoted to the one who touches you, to the exclusion of all else. What you wanted, what you were, who you were, no longer means anything to you. You would do anything for the one who touches you. Your life is no longer yours, it is hers. Your soul is no longer yours, it is hers. The person you were no longer exists."

Richard felt bumps on the skin of his arms. "How long does this, this, magic, whatever it is, how long does it last?"

"As long as the one I touch is alive," she said evenly.

Richard felt the chill run the rest of the way through him. "So, it's sort of like you bewitch people?"

She let out a breath. "Not exactly, but if it helps you to understand, I guess you could put it that way. But the touch of a Confessor is much more. Much more powerful, and final. A bewitching could be removed. My touch cannot. Shota was bewitching you, even though you did not realize it. It's an incremental thing. Witches cannot help it, it's their way. But your anger, and the anger from the sword, protected you.

"The touch of my power is all at once, and final. Nothing

509

could protect you. The person I touch cannot be brought back, because once I touch them, that person is no longer there. That person is gone forever. Their free will is gone forever. One reason I was afraid to go to Shota was because witches hate Confessors. They are fiercely jealous of our power; jealous that once touched, the person is totally devoted. The one touched by a Confessor would do anything she says." She gave him a hard look. "Anything."

Richard felt his mouth go dry as his thoughts scattered in every direction at once, trying desperately to hold on to his hopes, his dreams. The only way he could hold it together, and gain time to think, was to ask questions. "Does it work on everyone?"

"Everyone human. Except Darken Rahl. The wizards warned me that the magic of Orden protects him from our touch. He has nothing to fear from me. On those who are not human, it mostly doesn't work because they don't have the capacity for compassion, which the magic requires in order to work. A gar, for example, would not be changed by my touch. It works on some other creatures, but not exactly the same as it does a human."

He watched her from under his eyebrows. "Shar? You touched her, didn't you?"

Kahlan nodded and leaned back a little, the slump settling back into her shoulders. "Yes. She was dying, and lonely. She was suffering the pain of being away from her kind, the pain of dying alone. She asked me to touch her. My touch took her fear, and replaced it with a love for me that left no room for her own pain, for her own loneliness. Nothing was left of her except her love for me."

"What about when I first met you, when the quad was chasing us? You touched one of those men too, didn't you?"

Kahlan nodded, leaning back the rest of the way against the log, pulling her cloak around her, looking into the fire. "Even though they are sworn to kill me, once I touch one of them, they are mine," she said with finality. "They will fight to the death to protect me. That is the reason Rahl sends four men to kill a Confessor; it's expected she will touch one, then there are three left to kill him, and her. It takes the three left because the one will fight so fiercely he usually kills one, often two, but that still leaves at least one to kill the Confessor. On a rare occasion, he

510

will kill the remaining three. That happened to me with the quad that chased me before the wizards sent me across the boundary. A quad is the most economical unit to send, they almost always succeed, and if they don't, Rahl will simply send another.

"We weren't killed on the cliff because you separated them. The one I touched killed the other with him while you held off the other two; then he went after the remaining two, but you had pushed one off the edge, so he used his own life to take the leader over the cliff. He did that because then there wouldn't be any chance of losing in a sword fight. It meant his life too, but that didn't matter to him after I touched him. It was the only way for him to be sure he protected me."

"Can't you simply touch all four?"

"No. The power is expended with each use. It takes time for it to recover."

He felt the hilt of his sword against his elbow and a sudden thought came to him. "When we came through the boundary, and that last man of the quad was after you, and I killed him . . . I wasn't really saving you, was I."

She was silent for a moment before answering. "One man, no matter how big, or strong, is no threat to a Confessor, even a weak Confessor, much less me. If you hadn't come when you did . . . I would have dealt with him. I'm sorry, Richard," she whispered, "but there was no need for you to have killed him. I could have handled it."

"Well," he said dryly, "at least I saved you from having to do it."

She didn't answer, only looked sadly at him. It seemed she had nothing to say that could bring him any comfort.

"How much time?" he asked. "How much time does it take to recover after a Confessor has used her power?"

"In every Confessor the power is different. In some it is weaker, and it may take several days and nights to recover. In most, it takes about one day and one night."

Richard looked over at her. "And in you?"

She looked up at his eyes, almost as if she wished he hadn't asked the question. "About two hours."

He turned back to the fire, not liking the sound of her answer. "Is that unusual?"

511

She let out a breath. "So I have been told." Her voice sounded weary. "Shorter time to recover the power also means the power is stronger, works more powerfully in the one touched. That is why some of the quad members I touch are able to kill the other three. It would not be so for a Confessor with a weaker power.

"Confessors have position according to their power, because the ones with the strongest power will bear daughters who have the best chance of having that stronger power. There is no jealousy among the Confessors for those with the strongest power, only deeper affection and devotion in times of trouble; like since Rahl came through the boundary. The lower ranks will protect the higher, with their lives if need be."

He knew she wasn't going to say it unless he asked, so he did. "And what is your rank?"

Her eyes stared unblinking at the fire. "All Confessors follow me. Many laid down their lives to protect mine . . ." Her voice caught for a moment. ". . . that I might survive, and somehow use my power to stop Rahl. Of course, there are none to follow me now. I am the only one left. Darken Rahl has killed every last one."

"I'm sorry, Kahlan," he said softly. He was only just beginning to comprehend the importance of the woman she was. "So, do you have a title? What do people call you?"

"I am the Mother Confessor."

Richard tensed. The sound of "Mother Confessor" had the chill of terrible authority to it. Richard felt a little overwhelmed. He had always known Kahlan was important, but he had dealt with important people when he was a guide, and had learned not to be awed by them. But he never knew she was someone of such prominence. Mother Confessor. Even if he was just a guide, and she was this important, he didn't care, he could live with that. Surely, she could, too. He wasn't going to lose her, or send her away because of who she was.

"I don't know what that means. Is it something like a princess, or a queen?"

Kahlan lifted an eyebrow to him. "Queens bow down to the Mother Confessor."

Now he felt intimidated.

"You are more than a queen?" he winced.

"The dress I wore when you first saw me? That is a Confessor's dress. We all wear them so there can be no mistaking who we are, although most people of the Midlands would recognize us no matter how we were to dress. All Confessors, no matter their age, wear a Confessor's dress that is black—except the Mother Confessor; her dress is white." Kahlan seemed a little annoyed by having to explain her eminence. "It feels very odd to me to explain all this, Richard. Everyone in the Midlands knows it all, so I have never had to think about how to put it all into words. It sounds so . . . I don't know, so arrogant when I put words to it."

"Well, I'm not from the Midlands. Just try, I need to understand."

She nodded and looked back up at him. "Kings and queens are masters of their land; they each have their own domain. There are a number of them in the Midlands. Other lands are ruled in different manners, such as by councils. Some are places of magic creatures. The night wisps, for example—no humans live in their lands.

"The place where the Confessors live, my home, is called Aydindril. It is also the home of the wizards, and the Central Council of the Midlands. Aydindril is a beautiful place. It's been a long time since I have been home," she said wistfully. "The Confessors and the wizards are closely linked, bonded; much the way the Old One, Zedd, is linked with the Seeker.

"No one holds claim to Aydindril. No ruler would dare to lay claim to it; they all fear it, fear the Confessors and the wizards. All the lands of the Midlands contribute to the support of Aydindril. They all pay tribute. Confessors are above the law of any one land, much the same way the Seeker is ultimately above any law but his own. Yet at the same time, we serve all the people of the Midlands through the Central Council.

"In the past, arrogant rulers had thought to make the Confessors submit to their word. In those times, there were farsighted Confessors, now revered as legends, who knew they must lay the foundation for our independence, or forever submit to domination; so the Mother Confessor took the rulers with her power. The rulers were removed from their thrones, and replaced with new rulers who understood that Confessors were to be left alone.

The old rulers, those who were taken, were kept in Aydindril as little more than slaves. The Confessors took these old rulers with them when they traveled to the different lands, made them carry the provisions and luxuries of travel. Back then, there was more ceremony surrounding the Confessors than there is now. Anyway, it made the intended impression."

"I don't understand," Richard said. "Kings and queens must be powerful leaders. Didn't they have protection? Didn't they have guards, and others, to keep them safe? How could a Confessor get near to a king or queen to touch them?"

"Yes, they have protection, a lot, in fact, but it's not as difficult as it sounds. A Confessor touches one person, maybe a guard, then she has an ally, he takes her to another, he is taken, soon she is inside. Each person she touches can get her close to one of higher rank, and gains her more allies. Working her way up through the trusted positions and advisors, she can be at the king or queen sooner than you would think, and often before so much as an eyebrow is raised, much less an alarm. Any Confessor could do it. The Mother Confessor even easier.

"The Mother Confessor with a band of her sisters would sweep through a castle like the plague. Not that such an effort is without danger, many Confessors died, but the goal was seen as worth it. This is the reason no land is closed to a Confessor, though it may be to every other.

"Closing a land to a Confessor is tantamount to an admission of guilt, and is sufficient cause for the leader to be taken from power. This is why the Mud People, for example, allow me in, even though they do not often let other outsiders in. Not allowing a Confessor access would raise questions and suspicions. A leader involved in any sort of plot would gladly grant a Confessor free access, to try to hide their involvement in any subversion.

"In those times, there were some among the Confessors who were more than willing to use their power as they wanted, to root out wrongdoing, as they saw it. The wizards exerted their influence to bring this under control, but the Confessors' zeal showed the people what a Confessor was capable of. But those were different times."

Taking a ruler from power. Different times or not, Richard

found all this hard to take, to justify. "What gave these Confessors the right?"

She shook her head slowly. "What we are doing now, you and I, is it much different from what has been done in the past? Taking a ruler from power? We all do what we think we must, what we think is right."

He shifted his weight uncomfortably. "I see your point," he admitted. "Have you done this before? Removing a ruler?"

She shook her head. "Still, the leaders of the lands are all keen to avoid my attention. It is much the same way with the Seeker. At least, it used to be, before you and I were born. Then, Seekers were more feared and respected than Confessors." She gave him a meaningful look. "They, too, have dethroned kings. Now, though, because the Old One was ignored, and the sword had become a political favor, they are seen as less; little more than pawns, thieves."

"I'm not sure that has changed," Richard said, more to himself than to her. "Much of the time, I feel as if I am nothing more than a pawn, being moved by others. Even by Zedd, and . . ."

He shut his mouth and didn't finish; she did it for him.

"And by me."

"I don't mean it that way. It's just that, sometimes, I wish I had never heard of the Sword of Truth. But at the same time, I can't allow Rahl to win, so I'm stuck with my duty. I guess I have no choice, and that's what I hate."

Kahlan smiled sadly as she folded her legs under her. "Richard, as you come to understand what I am, I hope you can remember it's the same with me. I, too, have no choice. But with me, it's worse, because I was born with my power. At least when this is all done, you can give the sword back if you want. I am a Confessor for as long as I live." She paused, then added, "Since I have come to know you, I would pay any price to be able to give it up, and just be a normal woman."

Richard didn't know what to do with his hands, so he picked up a stick and started drawing lines in the dirt. "I still don't understand, why are you called 'Confessors'? What does 'Confessor' mean?" He was able to look up at her only with great difficulty.

Kahlan took on an expression of pain that made him feel sorry

515

for her. "It is what we do. We are the final arbiters of truth. It is the reason the wizards gave us the power, back in times long forgotten. It is how we serve the people."

"Final arbiter of truth," he repeated with a frown. "Something like a Seeker."

She nodded. "Seekers and Confessors are linked in purpose. In a way, we are the opposite ends of the same magic. The wizards of long ago were almost like rulers, and they became frustrated by the corruption about them. They hated the lies and deception. They wanted a way to prevent corrupt leaders from using their power to deceive and subvert the people. You see, these unscrupulous leaders would simply accuse their political enemies of a crime, and have them executed for it, at once dishonoring them and eliminating them.

"The wizards wanted a way to put a stop to this. They needed a way that left no room for doubt. So they created a magic, and gave it a life of its own. They created the Confessors from a select group of women. They picked the women carefully, because once brought to life in these women, the power had a life of its own, and would pass to their offspring—forever." She looked down at the stick, idly watching him draw lines. "We use our power to find the truth, when the truth is important enough. Mostly, now, it is used to make sure a person sentenced to death is really guilty. When a person is condemned to death, we touch them, and then, once they are ours, we have them confess."

Richard found himself leaning over, the stick frozen in place. He forced himself to move it as she went on.

"Once touched, even the most vile of murderers will do as we command, and will confess his crimes. Occasionally, the courts are not sure they have the right man, and so a Confessor is called in to find the truth. In most lands, the law states that none can be put to death without first giving a confession, so all can be sure they are putting the right man to death, and not letting the guilty escape, and that it's not an act of political revenge.

"Some peoples of the Midlands won't use a Confessor; the Mud People, for example. They don't want what they see as outside interference. But they still fear us, because they know what we can do. We respect the wishes of these people; there is no law forcing them to use our services. But still, we would force it on

516

them if we suspected there was deception involved. Most lands, though, do use us. They find it expedient.

"The Confessors were the ones who first uncovered the plotting and subversion taking place on behalf of Darken Rahl. Discovering important truths, such as this, is the very reason wizards created Confessors, and Seekers, in the first place. Darken Rahl was not happy we discovered his scheming.

"In rare cases, someone who is to be put to death without the use of a Confessor will call for a Confessor to be brought in, so that he may give a true confession, and thus prove his innocence. In all of the Midlands, this is the right of the condemned."

Her voice became softer, weaker. "I hate that the most. No one who is guilty would call for a Confessor; it would only prove them to be guilty. Even before I touch these men, I know they are innocent, but I must do it anyway. If you ever saw the look in their eyes when I touch them . . . you would understand. So when we are called, and even though these men are innocent, they are left . . ."

Richard swallowed. "How many confessions have you . . . taken."

She shook her head slowly. "Too many to count. I have spent half my life in prisons and dungeons, with the most vicious and loathsome animals you could imagine, yet most look to be nothing more than a kindly shopkeeper, or brother, or father, or neighbor. After I touch them, I have heard them all tell me the things they have done. For a long time, in the beginning, it gave me such nightmares I feared sleeping. The stories of the things they had done . . . you can't even imagine . . ."

Richard tossed the stick aside and took her hand in his, squeezing it tightly. She was starting to cry. "Kahlan, you don't have to . . ."

"I remember the first man I killed." Her lip quivered. "I still have dreams about him. He confessed to me the things he had done to his neighbor's three daughters . . . the oldest was only five . . . he looked up at me with wide eyes after he told me the most ghastly things you could imagine . . . and he said, 'What is your wish, my mistress' . . . and without thinking, I said, 'My wish is for you to die.' " She wiped some of the tears off her cheek with trembling fingers. "He dropped dead on the spot."

517

"What did the people there say?"

"What would they dare to say to a Confessor who has just made a man drop dead in front of their eyes simply by her command? They all just backed up and got out of our way when we left. It is not something every Confessor can do. It even scared my wizard speechless."

Richard frowned. "Your wizard?"

She nodded as she finished wiping the tears away. "Wizards see it as their duty to protect us, as we are universally feared and hated. Confessors almost always travel with the protection of a wizard. One is ... well, one was, assigned to each of us when we were called to take a confession. Rahl managed to separate us from our wizards, and now they are dead too. Except Zedd, and Giller."

Richard picked up the rabbit. It was getting cold. He cut off another piece and handed it to her, then tore off a piece for himself. "Why would the Confessors be feared and hated?"

"The relatives and friends of the man to be executed hate us because they often don't believe their loved one would do the things they confess to. They would rather believe we somehow trick them in to confessing." She picked at the meat, pulling off little pieces and chewing them slowly. "I have found that people do not often want to believe the truth. It is of little value to them. Some have tried to kill me. This is one of the reasons a wizard was always with us, to protect us until our power is recovered."

Richard swallowed his mouthful. "That doesn't sound like enough reason to me."

"It is more than simply what we do. This must all sound very strange to someone who has not lived with it. The ways of the Midlands, of magic, must seem very odd to you."

Odd was not the right word, he thought. *Frightening* was more like it.

"Confessors are independent; people resent that. Men resent that none of them can rule us, or even tell us what to do. Women resent that we do not live the kind of life they do, that we do not live in the traditional role of women; we do not take care of a man, or submit to one. We are seen as privileged. Our hair is long, a symbol of our authority; they are made to keep their hair short, as a sign of submission to their man and every other per-

518

son of higher status than they. It may seem a small matter to you, but to our people, no matter having to do with power is small. A woman who allows her hair to grow beyond the length appropriate to her status is forced to forfeit some of that status in punishment. In the Midlands, long hair on a woman is a sign of authority, bordering on defiance. It is a sign that we have the power to do as we wish, and that none may command us; that we are a threat to all. Much as your sword tells people the same thing. No Confessor would wear her hair short, and that rankles people, that none could dare make us do so. It is ironic that we are less free than they, yet they don't see that part of it. We do their distasteful tasks for them, and yet we are not free to choose what we will do with our own lives. We are prisoners of our power."

Kahlan ate the rest of the meat he had given her while he thought about how ironic it also was that the Confessors brought love to the most hateful of criminals, yet they could not bring it to ones with whom they would choose closeness. He knew there was something else she was trying to explain.

"I think your long hair is pretty," he said. "I like the way it is."

Kahlan smiled. "Thank you." She tossed the bones into the fire, watching it for a time, then looked down at her hands as she clicked her thumbnails together. "And then there is the matter of choosing a mate."

Richard finished his piece of meat and threw the bone in the fire. He leaned back against the log, not liking the sound of this. "Choosing a mate? What do you mean?"

She studied her hands as if trying to find refuge in them. "When a Confessor reaches the age to be a proper mother, she must choose a mate. A Confessor may choose any man she wishes, even one already married. She may roam the Midlands, searching for a proper father to her daughters, one who is strong, and maybe one who is handsome to her eyes. Whatever she wants.

"Men are terrified of a Confessor who is looking for a mate, because they don't want to be chosen, to be touched by her. Women are terrified because they don't want their man, or their brother, or their son to be taken. They all know they have no say

519

in the matter; any who stood in the way of a Confessor's choosing would be taken by her. People are afraid of me, first because I am the Mother Confessor, and second because I am long past the time I should have chosen a mate."

Richard still clung tenaciously to his hopes and dreams. "But what if you care about someone, and they care for you?"

Kahlan shook her head sadly. "Confessors have no friends but other Confessors. It is not a problem; no one would ever have feelings for a Confessor. Every man is afraid of us." She left unsaid that it was a problem now. Her voice was choking up again. "We are taught from a young age that the mate we choose must be a man of strength, so that the children we bear will be strong. But it must not be someone we care for, because we would destroy him. That is why nothing can come of . . . of us."

"But . . . why?" He felt himself fighting against her words, her power.

"Because . . ." She looked away, her face unable to mask her pain, her green eyes filling with tears. "Because in the throes of passion, a Confessor's hold on the power would relax, and she would release it into him, even though she didn't mean to, and then he would no longer be the person she cared for. There is no way for her to prevent herself from doing it. None. He would be hers, but not in the same way. The very one she cared for would be with her, but only because of the magic, no longer by his choice, and not because he wanted to. He would only be a shell, holding what she had put into him. No Confessor would want that for a man for whom she cared.

"That is why Confessors, since time long forgotten, have shut themselves away from men, for fear they would grow to care for one. Though we are seen as heartless, it is not true; we all fear what our touch would do to a man we held dear. Some Confessors choose men who are disliked, or even hated, so as not to destroy a kind heart. Though it is only the choice of a few, it is the way they deal with it, and is their right. No other Confessor would criticize one who has chosen in this manner; we all understand it." Her tearful eyes looked at him, pleading for him to understand.

"But . . . I could . . ." He could think of no defense for his heart.

"I could not. For me, it would be the same as you wanting to be with your mother, and instead having Shota, appearing to be your mother. But she wasn't. It would just be an illusion of love. Do you understand?" she cried. "Would that bring you any true joy?"

Richard felt the hopes of his world collapsing in the flames of his understanding. His heart sank into the ashes.

"The spirit house," he asked in a dry voice, "is that what Shota was talking about? Is that when you came within a breath of using your power on me?" His tone was a little colder than he wished it to be.

"Yes." Her voice broke with emotion as she tried to keep from crying. "I'm sorry, Richard." She knitted her fingers together. "I have never before cared for anyone the way I care for you. I wanted to be with you so badly. I almost forgot who I was. I almost didn't care." Tears started running down her cheeks. "Do you see now how dangerous my power is? Do you see how easily I could destroy you? If you hadn't stopped me when you did . . . you would have been lost."

He felt an agony of compassion for her, for what she was, and for the fact that she couldn't do anything about it, and he felt the ache of his own pain at the feeling of loss, even though he realized now that there was nothing to lose, she could never have been his, or more precisely, he hers; it all had just been a fantasy in his mind.

Zedd had tried to warn him, tried to save him this pain. Why couldn't he have listened? Why did he have to be so stupid and think he would be smart enough to figure something out? He knew why. He stood slowly and took a step to the fire so she wouldn't see his tears. He kept swallowing so he could try to talk.

"Why do you always say 'she,' 'her,' 'daughter'? Why always women? What of the men, don't Confessors bear male children?" He realized his voice sounded as if it were scraping over gravel.

He listened to the fire crackling for a long time as she didn't answer. He turned back to her when he heard her crying. She looked up and held her hand out for him to help her up. Once up, she leaned against the log, pulled her long hair back from her face, and then folded her arms below her breasts.

521

"Yes, Confessors bear male children. Not as often as in the past, but they still do." She cleared her throat. "But the power is stronger in them; they need no time to recover. Sometimes, the power becomes everything to them, corrupts them. This is the mistake the wizards made.

"They chose women for this very reason, but didn't give sufficient thought to how the power would take on a life of its own. They didn't foresee how the power would be passed on to the offspring, and be so different in men.

"Long ago, a few male Confessors joined forces, and brought about a terrible reign of cruelty. It was called the dark time. They were the cause of it. It was a time something like now, with Darken Rahl. At last, the wizards hunted them all down and killed them. Many of the wizards died too. From that time, the wizards withdrew from trying to rule the lands. Too many of them had been killed anyway. Instead, now they only try to serve the people, to help where they can. But they no longer interfere with rulers if they can help it. They have learned bitter lessons."

Kahlan looked down, away from his eyes as she went on. "For some reason, it takes the unique compassion of a woman to handle the power, to be free from its corrupting influence. The wizards don't know the reason for this. It is similar with the Seeker: he must be the right one, one found by a wizard, or he will use the power for corrupt reasons. That is why Zedd was so angry at the council of the Midlands for taking the naming away from him. Male Confessors, not all, but most, cannot retain their sense of balance with the power. They don't have the strength to hold it back when they should." She peered up at him.

"When they wanted a woman, they simply used the power and took her. Many women. They had no restraint, no sense of responsibility for what they were doing. From what I have been told, the dark time was one long night of terror. Their reign lasted for years. The wizards had to do a lot of killing. They eventually killed all the offspring of this lust, to prevent the power from spreading, uncontrolled. To say the wizards were displeased would not touch it."

"So what happens now?" he asked warily. "What happens when a Confessor bears a male child?"

She cleared her throat again, swallowing back her sobs.

"When a boy is born to a Confessor, he is brought to a special place in the center of Aydindril, where his mother places him on the Stone." She shifted her weight; she was clearly having difficulty telling him about this. He took her soft hand in both of his and rubbed the back of it with his thumbs, even though he felt for the first time that he had no business touching her in a familiar manner. "As I told you, a man touched by a Confessor will do whatever she tells him." He could feel her hand trembling. "The mother commands her husband in what she is to do . . . and he . . . he places a rod over the baby's throat . . . and . . . and he steps on both ends."

Richard released her hand. Running the fingers of both hands through his hair, he turned to the fire. "Every boy child?"

"Yes," she admitted in a voice he could hardly hear. "No chance can be taken that any male Confessor lives, because he might be one who could not handle the power, and would use it to gain dominance for himself, bring back the dark times. The wizards and the other Confessors watch carefully any Confessor who is with child, and do everything they can to comfort her if it is a boy, and therefore must be . . ." Her voice trailed off.

Richard suddenly realized that he hated the Midlands—hated it with a vengeance second only to what he felt toward Darken Rahl. For the first time, he understood why those in Westland had wanted a place to live without magic. He wished he could be back there, away from any magic. Tears came to his eyes when he thought of how much he missed the Hartland Woods. He vowed to himself that if he stopped Rahl, he would see to it that the boundary was put back up. Zedd would help with that, there was no doubt. Richard understood now why Zedd, too, had wanted to be away from the Midlands. And when the boundary went back up, Richard would be on the other side. For as long as he lived.

But first, there would be the matter of the sword; he would not give back the Sword of Truth. He would destroy it.

"Thank you, Kahlan," he forced himself to say, "for telling me. I wouldn't have wanted to hear this from another." He felt his world withering to nothing. He had always seen stopping Rahl as the beginning of his life, a point from where he went forward and anything was possible. Now stopping Rahl was an end.

Not only of Rahl, but of him, too; there was nothing beyond that, everything beyond was dead. When he stopped Rahl, and Kahlan was safe, he would go back to the Hartland Woods, alone, and his life would be over.

He could hear her crying behind him. "Richard, if you want me to leave, please do not be afraid to tell me so. I will understand it. It is something a Confessor is used to."

He looked down at the dying fire for a moment and then closed his eyes tight, forcing back the lump in his throat, the tears. Pain seared through his chest as it sank with his labored breathing.

"Please, Kahlan, is there any way," he asked, "any way at all . . . that we could . . . for us . . ."

"No," she moaned.

He rubbed his shaking hands together. Everything was lost to him.

"Kahlan," he managed at last, "is there any law, or rule or something, that says we can't be friends?"

She answered in a whining cry. "No."

He turned numbly to her and put his arms around her. "I could really use a friend right now," he whispered.

"Me too," she cried against his chest as she hugged him back. "But I can be no more."

"I know," he said as tears ran down his cheeks. "But Kahlan, I love . . ."

She put her fingers to his lips to silence him. "Don't say that," she cried. "Please, Richard, don't ever say that."

She could stop him from saying it out loud, but not in his mind.

She clung to him, sobbing, and he remembered when they had been in the wayward pine after they first met, and the underworld had almost reclaimed her; she had clung to him, and he had thought at the time that she was not used to having anyone hold her. Now he knew why. He laid his cheek against the top of her head.

A small flame of his anger flickered in the ashes of his dreams. "Have you picked your mate yet?"

She shook her head. "There are more important things to

worry about right now. But if we win, and I live . . . then I must."

"Make one promise for me."

"If I can."

His throat felt so hot he had to swallow twice to talk. "Promise me you won't pick him until I'm back in Westland. I don't want to know who it is."

She sobbed for a moment before she answered, her fingers clutching tighter at his shirt. "I promise."

After a time of standing, holding her, trying to get control of himself, fighting back the blackness, he forced a smile. "You're wrong about one thing."

"And what would that be?"

"You said no man can command a Confessor. You are wrong. I command the Mother Confessor herself. You are sworn to protect me, I hold you to your duty as my guide."

She laughed a painful little laugh against his chest. "It would appear you are right. Congratulations—you are the first man ever to have done so. And what does my master command of his guide?"

"That she doesn't give me any more trouble about ending her life; I need her. And that she gets us to the Queen, and the box, before Rahl, and then sees us safely away."

Kahlan nodded her head against his chest. "By your command, my lord." She separated from him, put her hands on his upper arms, and gave them a squeeze as she smiled through her tears. "How is it that you can always make me feel better, even at the worst times of my life?"

He shrugged, forcing himself to smile for her, even though he was dying inside. "I am the Seeker. I can do anything." He wanted to say more, but his voice failed him.

Her smile widened as she shook her head. "You are a very rare person, Richard Cypher," she whispered.

He only wished he were alone so he could cry.

Chapter 35

With his boot, Richard pushed little piles of dirt over the dying embers of the fire, snuffing out the only heat in the dawn of the cold new day. The sky was brightening into an icy blue, and a sharp wind blew from the west. Well, at least the wind would be at their backs, he thought. Near his other boot lay the roasting stick that Kahlan had used to cook the rabbit—the rabbit she had caught herself, with a snare he had taught her to make.

He felt his face flush with the thought of that, the thought of him, a woods guide, teaching her things like that. The Mother Confessor. More than a queen. Queens bow to the Mother Confessor, she had said. He felt as foolish as he had ever felt in his life. Mother Confessor. Who did he think he was? Zedd had tried to warn him, if he had only listened.

Emptiness threatened to consume him. He thought of his brother, his friends Zedd and Chase. Though it didn't fill the void, at least he had them. Richard watched Kahlan shouldering her pack. She had no one, he thought; her only friends, the other Confessors, were dead. She was alone in the world, alone in the Midlands, surrounded by people she was trying to save, who feared and hated her, and enemies who wanted to kill her, or worse, and not even her wizard to protect her.

He understood why she had been afraid to tell him. He was her only friend. He felt even more foolish for thinking only of himself. If her friend was all he could be, then that's what he would be. Even if it killed him.

"It must have been hard to tell me," he said as he adjusted the sword at his hip.

She pulled her cloak around herself, against the gusts of cold wind. Her face had resumed once more the calm expression that showed nothing, except that, as well as he knew her, he could now read the trace of pain in it. "It would have been easier to have killed myself."

He watched as she turned and started off, then followed after her. If she had told him in the beginning, he wondered, would he still be with her? If she had told him before he had come to know her, would he have been too afraid to be near her, same as everyone else? Maybe she had been right in being afraid to tell him sooner. But then, if she had, it might have spared him what he was feeling now.

Near to midday, they came to a juncture of trails, marked with a stone half again as tall as he. Richard stopped, studying the symbols cut into the polished faces.

"What do they mean?"

"They give direction to different towns and villages, and their distances," she said, warming her hands under her armpits. She inclined her head toward a trail. "If we want to avoid people, this trail is best."

"How much farther?"

She looked at the stone again. "I usually travel the roads between towns, not these less-traveled trails. The stone does not give the distance by the trail, only by the roads, but I would guess a few more days."

Richard drummed his fingers on the hilt of his sword. "Are there any towns near?"

She nodded. "We are an hour or two from Horners Mill. Why?"

"We could save ourselves time if we had horses."

She looked up the trail toward the town, as if she could some-

527

how see it. "Horners Mill is a lumber town, a sawmill. They would have a lot of horses, but it may not be a good idea. I have heard their sympathies lie with D'Hara."

"Why don't we go have a look; if we had horses, it could save us a day at least. I have some silver, and a piece or two of gold. Maybe we could buy some."

"I guess if we are careful, we could go have a look. But don't you dare pull out any of your silver or gold. It is Westland-marked, and these people view anyone from across the western boundary as a threat. Stories and superstition."

"Well, how will we get horses then? Steal them?"

She lifted an eyebrow. "Have you forgotten so soon? You are with the Mother Confessor. I have but to ask."

Richard covered his displeasure as best he could with a blank face. "Let's go have a look."

Horners Mill sat hard on the edge of the Callisidrin River, drawing both power for the sawmills and transportation for the logs and lumber from the muddy brown water. Spillways snaked through the work areas, and ramshackle mill buildings loomed over the other structures. Stickered stacks of lumber lay row upon row under roofs of open buildings, and even more lay under tarps, waiting for either barges to take them by river or wagons to take them by road. Houses squatted close together on the hillside above the mill, looking as if they had started life as temporary shelter and as the years had worn on, became unfortunately permanent.

Even from a distance, Richard and Kahlan both knew that something was wrong. The mill was silent, the streets empty. The whole town should have been alive with activity. There should have been people at the shops, on the docks, at the mill, and in the streets, but there was no sign of beast or man. The town hunched in quiet, except for some tarps flapping in the wind, and a few squeaking and banging tin panels on the mill buildings.

When they got close enough, the wind brought something other than flapping tarps and banging tin; it brought the putrid smell of death. Richard checked that his sword was loose in its scabbard.

Bodies, puffy and swollen, nearly ready to burst, stretched buttons, and oozed fluid that attracted clouds of flies. The dead lay in corners and up against buildings, like autumn leaves blown into piles. Most had ghastly wounds; some were pierced through with broken lances. The silence seemed alive. Doors, smashed in and broken, hung at odd angles from a single hinge, or lay in the street with personal belongings and broken pieces of furniture. Windows in every building were shattered. Some of the buildings were nothing more than cold, charred piles of beams and rubble. Richard and Kahlan both held their cloaks across their noses and mouths, trying to shield themselves against the stench as their eyes were pulled to the dead.

"Rahl?" he asked her.

She studied different tumbled bodies from a distance. "No. This is not the way Rahl kills. This was a battle."

"Looks more like a slaughter to me."

She nodded her agreement. "Remember the dead among the Mud People? That is what it looks like when Rahl kills. It is always the same. This is different."

They walked along through the town, staying close to the buildings, away from the center of the street, occasionally having to step over the gore. Every shop was looted, and what wasn't carried off was destroyed. From one shop, a bolt of pale blue cloth, with evenly spaced dark stains, had unwound itself across the road, as if it had been thrown out because its owner had ruined it in death. Kahlan pulled his sleeve, and pointed. On the wall of a building was written a message—in blood. DEATH TO ALL WHO RESIST THE WESTLAND.

"What do you suppose that means?" she whispered, as if the dead might hear her.

He stared at the dripping words. "I can't even imagine." He started off again, turning back twice to frown at the words on the wall.

Richard's eye was caught by a cart sitting in front of a grain store. The cart was half loaded with small furniture and clothes, the wind whipping at the sleeves of little dresses. He exchanged a glance with Kahlan. Someone was left alive, and it looked as if they were preparing to leave.

He stepped carefully through the empty doorframe of the grain store, Kahlan close at his back. Streamers of sunlight coming through the door and window sent shafts through the dust inside the building, falling on spilled sacks of grain and broken barrels. Richard stood just inside the doorway, to one side, with Kahlan to the other, until his eyes adjusted to the dark. There were fresh footprints, mostly small ones, through the dust. His eyes followed them behind a counter. He gripped the hilt of his sword, but didn't draw it, and went to the counter. People cowered behind, trembling.

"I'm not going to hurt you," he said in a gentle voice, "come out."

"Are you a soldier with the People's Peace Army, here to help us?" came a woman's voice from behind the counter.

Richard and Kahlan frowned at each other. "No," she said. "We are . . . just travelers, passing through."

A woman with a dirty, tearstained face and short, dark, matted hair pushed her head up. Her drab brown dress was ragged and torn. Richard took his hand away from his sword so as not to frighten her. Her lip quivered, and her hollow eyes blinked at them in the dim light as she motioned others to come out. There were six children—five girls and one boy—another woman, and an old man. Once they were out, the children clinging woodenly to the two women, the three adults glanced at Richard, then stared openly at Kahlan. Their eyes were wide, and they all shrank back as one against the wall. Richard frowned in confusion; then he realized what they were staring at. Her hair.

The three adults collapsed to their knees, heads bowed, each with their eyes to the floor; the children buried their faces silently in the women's skirts. With a sideways glance at Richard, Kahlan quickly motioned with her hands for them to get up. They had their eyes fixed on the floor and couldn't see her frantic gesturing.

"Get up," she said, "there is no need for that. Get up."

Their heads came up, confused. They looked at her hands, urging them to get to their feet. With great reluctance, they complied.

"By your command, Mother Confessor," one woman said in a shaking voice. "Forgive us, Mother Confessor, we . . . did not recognize you . . . by your clothes, at first. Forgive us, we are only human people. Forgive us for . . ."

Kahlan gently cut her off. "What is your name."

The woman bowed deeply from the waist, remaining bent. "I am Regina Clark, Mother Confessor."

Kahlan grabbed her by her shoulders and straightened her. "Regina, what has happened here?"

Regina's eyes filled with tears, and she cast a shrinking glance toward Richard as her lip trembled. Kahlan looked back to him.

"Richard," she said softly, "why don't you take the old man and the children outside?"

He understood; the women were too afraid to talk in front of him. He gave a helping arm to the stooped old man, and herded four of the children out. Two of the youngest girls refused to leave the women's skirts, but Kahlan nodded to him that it was all right.

The four children clung together in a clump as they sat on the step outside, eyes empty and distant. None would answer when he asked their names, or even look at him except with frightened peeks to make sure he didn't come any closer. The old man only stared blankly ahead when Richard asked his name.

"Can you tell me what happened here?" Richard asked him.

His eyes widened as he looked out over the street. "Westlanders . . ."

Tears welled up and he wouldn't say anything else. Fearing to get any more forceful, he decided to let the old man be. Richard offered him a piece of dried meat from his pack, but he ignored it. The children shrank back from his hand as he held it out with the same offer. He put the meat back in his pack. The oldest girl, just nearing womanhood, looked at him as if he might slay them, or eat them, on the spot. He had never seen anyone so terrified. Not wanting to frighten her or the other children more than they were, he kept his distance, smiled reassuringly, and promised he wouldn't hurt them, or even touch them. They didn't look as if they believed him. Richard turned toward the door often; he was uncomfortable and wished Kahlan would come out.

At last she did, her face an intense mask of calmness, a spring wound too tight. Richard stood and the children ran back into the building. The old man stayed where he was. She took Richard's arm, walking him away.

531

"There are no horses here," she said, watching fixedly ahead as she walked back the way they had come. "I think it best if we stay off the roads, stay to the less-traveled trails."

"Kahlan, what's going on?" He looked back over his shoulder. "What happened here?"

She glared at the bloody message on the wall as they went past. DEATH TO ALL WHO RESIST THE WESTLAND.

"Missionaries came, telling the people of the glory of Darken Rahl. They came often, telling the town council of the things they would have when D'Hara rules all the lands. Telling everyone of Rahl's love for all the people."

"That's crazy!" Richard whispered harshly.

"Nonetheless, the people of Horners Mill were won over. They all agreed to declare the town a territory of D'Hara. The People's Peace Army marched in, treating everyone with the utmost respect, buying goods from the merchants, spending silver and gold with abandon." She pointed back at the rows of lumber under tarps. "The missionaries were as good as their word; orders came down for lumber. A lot of lumber. To build new towns where people would live in prosperity under the glowing rule of Father Rahl."

Richard shook his head in wonderment. "Then what?"

"Word spread; there was more work here than the town people could handle. Work for Father Rahl. More people came in to work the orders for lumber. While all this was going on, the missionaries told the people of the threat to them from Westland. The threat to Father Rahl from Westland."

"From Westland!" Richard was incredulous.

She nodded. "Then the People's Peace Army moved out, saying they were needed to fight the Westland forces, to protect the other towns that had sworn allegiance to D'Hara. The people begged for some to stay, for protection. In return for their loyalty and devotion, a small detachment was left behind."

Richard ushered her back onto the trail ahead of him as he gave one last puzzled glance over his shoulder. "So it wasn't Rahl's army that did this?"

The trail was wide enough, so she waited until he was next to her before she went on. "No. They said everything was fine for a while. Then, about a week ago, at sunrise, a military unit of the

Westland army swept in, killing the D'Hara detachment to a man. After that, they went on a rampage, killing people indiscriminately, and sacking the town. As the Westland soldiers killed, they yelled that this was what happens to anyone following Rahl, to anyone who resists Westland. Before the sun set, they were gone."

Richard grabbed a fistful of shirt at her shoulder, jerking her to face him.

"That's not true! Westlanders wouldn't do this! It wasn't them! It couldn't be!"

She blinked at him. "Richard, I did not say it was true. I am merely telling you what I was told, what those people back there believe."

He released his grip of her shirt, his face having a second reason for its flush. He couldn't help himself from adding, "No Westland army did this." He started to turn back to the trail, but she took his arm, halting him.

"That is not the end of it."

By her eyes, he knew he didn't want to hear the end of it. He nodded for her to go on.

"Those left alive began leaving at once, taking what they could carry. More left the next day, some after burying members of their families. That night, a detachment of Westlanders came back, maybe fifty men. There were only a handful of townspeople left by that time. The people were told that resisters to Westland are not allowed to be buried, that they are to be left, for animals to pick clean, as a reminder to all of what will happen to any who resist the rule of Westland. To make their point, they collected all the men still left, even the boys, and executed them." By Kahlan's inflection of the word *executed*, and making no mention of the manner, he knew he didn't want to know. "The little boy and the old man back there were somehow overlooked or they would have been killed too. The women were made to watch." She paused.

"How many women were left?"

She shook her head. "I don't know, not many." She peered back up the trail, staring off toward the town a moment before her intensely angry eyes returned to his. "The soldiers raped the

533

women. And the girls." Her eyes burned into his. "Each one of those girls you saw back there was raped by at least . . ."

"Westlanders did not do this!"

She studied his face. "I know. But who? Why?" Her expression cooled back to calm.

He stared back at her in frustration. "Isn't there anything we can do for them?"

"Our job is not to protect a few people, or the dead; it is to protect the living, by stopping Darken Rahl. We do not have the time to give; we must get to Tamarang. Whatever trouble is about, we had best stay off the roads."

"You're right," he admitted reluctantly. "But I don't like it."

"Nor do I." Her features softened. "Richard, I think they will be safe. Whatever army it was that did this is not likely to return for a couple of women and children; they will be off to hunt bigger game."

Some solace that was, that the killers would be off to hunt larger groups of people to hurt, in the name of his homeland. Richard thought about how he hated all this, and remembered how when he was back in Hartland, his biggest trouble was his brother always telling him what to do.

"A group of soldiers that big isn't going to be traveling by trail through a thick wood such as this, they'll stay to the roads, but I think it best if we start looking for wayward pines at night. No telling who could be watching."

She nodded her agreement. "Richard, many people of my homeland have joined with Rahl, and done unspeakable crimes. Does that make you think less of me?"

He frowned. "Of course not."

"And I would think no less of you were it Westland soldiers. It is no crime upon you, to have your countrymen do things you abhor. We are at war. We are trying to do as our ancestors have done in the past, Seekers and Confessors alike; dethrone a ruler. In this, there are only two we can count on. You and me." She studied him with an intense, timeless expression. He realized he was gripping the hilt of his sword tightly. "A time may come when it is only you. We all do as we must." It was not Kahlan who had spoken; it was the Mother Confessor.

It was a hard, uncomfortable moment before she released his

eyes, turning at last and starting off. He pulled his cloak tight, chilled from without, and within.

"It was not Westlanders," he muttered under his breath, following behind her.

"Light for me," Rachel said. The little pile of sticks with rocks all around burst into flame, lighting the inside of the wayward pine with a bright red glow. She put the fire stick back in her pocket and with a shiver warmed her hands at the fire as she looked down at Sara lying in her lap.

"We'll be safe here tonight," she told her doll. Sara didn't answer—she hadn't talked since the night they ran away from the castle—so Rachel just pretended the doll was talking, telling her she loved her. She gave Sara's silent words an answering hug.

She pulled some berries from her pocket, eating them one at a time, warming her hands in between each one. Sara didn't want any berries. Rachel nibbled on the piece of hard cheese; all the other food she had brought from the castle was gone. Except the loaf of bread, of course. But she couldn't eat that; the box was hidden inside it.

Rachel missed Giller something fierce, but she had to do as he had said; she had to keep running away, finding a new wayward pine every night. She didn't know how far she was from the castle; she just kept going while it was day, the sun at her back in the morning and in her face at evening. She had learned that from Brophy. He called it traveling by the sun. She guessed that was what she was doing. Traveling.

A pine bough moved by itself, making her start. She saw a big hand holding it back. Then the shiny blade of a long sword. She stared, her eyes wide. She couldn't move.

A man stuck his head in. "What have we here?" He smiled.

Rachel heard a whine, and realized it was coming from her own throat. Still, she couldn't move. A woman pushed her head in beside the man's. She pulled the man back behind her. Rachel clutched Sara to her chest.

535

"Put the sword away," the woman scolded, "you're scaring her."

Rachel pulled the partly unbundled loaf of bread close to her hip. She wanted to run, but her legs didn't work. The woman pushed into the wayward pine, came close and knelt down, sitting back on her heels, the man right behind her. Rachel's eyes looked up at her face; then she saw the woman's long hair, lit by the firelight. Her eyes went even wider, and another cry came from her throat. At last her legs worked, at least a little: they scooted her backward against the trunk of the tree, pulling the bread with her. Women with long hair were always trouble. She bit down on Sara's foot, panting, a whine coming with each breath. She squeezed Sara with all her strength. She tore her eyes from the woman's hair; she darted glances to the sides, looking for a place to run.

"I'm not going to hurt you," the woman said. Her voice sounded nice, but Princess Violet said the same thing, sometimes, just before she slapped her.

The woman reached out and touched Rachel's arm. She jumped with a cry, pulling back.

"Please," she said, her eyes filling with tears, "don't burn Sara up."

"Who's Sara?" the man asked.

The woman turned and made him hush. She turned back, her long hair falling from her shoulder, Rachel's eyes fixed on it. "I won't burn Sara," she said in a nice voice. Rachel knew that when a woman with long hair talked in a nice voice, it meant she was probably lying. Still, her voice did sound like it was really nice.

"Please," she whined, "can't you just leave us be?"

"Us?" The woman glanced around. She looked back, right to Sara. "Oh. I see. So this is Sara?" Rachel nodded, biting down harder on Sara's foot. She knew she would get a hard slap if she didn't answer a woman with long hair. "She's a very nice-looking doll." She smiled. Rachel wished she wouldn't smile. When women with long hair smiled, it usually meant there was going to be trouble.

The man stuck his head around the woman. "My name's Richard. What's yours?"

She liked his eyes. "Rachel."

"Rachel. That's a pretty name. But I have to tell you, Rachel, you have the ugliest hair I've ever seen."

"Richard!" the woman squawked. "How could you say such a thing!"

"Well, it's true. Who cut it all crooked like that, Rachel, some old witch?"

Rachel giggled.

"Richard!" the woman squawked again. "You're going to frighten her."

"Oh, nonsense. Rachel, I have a little scissors here in my pack, and I'm pretty good at cutting hair. Would you like me to fix your hair for you? At least I could make it straight. If you leave it like that, you might scare a dragon or something."

Rachel giggled again. "Yes, please. I would like to have my hair straight."

"All right then, come over here and sit on my lap and we'll fix it right up."

Rachel got up and walked around the woman, watching her hands, keeping far away, at least as far away as she could inside the wayward pine. Richard picked her up with a big hand on each side of her waist and set her on his lap. He pulled some strands of hair out. "Let's have a look at what we have here."

Rachel kept an eye toward the woman, fearing a slap. He looked over, too. He pointed with the scissors.

"This is Kahlan. She scared me at first, too. She's awfully ugly, isn't she."

"Richard! Where did you learn to speak to children like this!"

He smiled. "Picked it up from a boundary warden I know."

Rachel giggled at him; she couldn't help it. "I don't think she's ugly, I think she's the prettiest lady I ever saw." That was the truth. But Kahlan's long hair scared her something fierce.

"Well, thank you, Rachel, and you are very pretty, too. Are you hungry?"

Rachel wasn't ever supposed to tell anyone with long hair, any lord or lady, that she was hungry. Princess Violet said it was improper, and punished her one time for telling someone she was hungry when she was asked. She looked at up Richard's face. He smiled, but still she was too afraid to tell Kahlan she was hungry.

Kahlan patted her arm. "I bet you are. We caught some fish, and if you let us share your fire, we would share some fish with you. What do you say?" She smiled real pretty.

Rachel looked up at Richard again. He gave her a wink, then sighed. "I'm afraid I caught more than we can eat. If you don't help us, we'll just have to throw some out."

"All right then. If you're just going to throw them out, I'll help you eat them."

Kahlan started taking off her pack. "Where are your parents?"

Rachel told the truth because she couldn't think of anything else to say. "Dead."

Richard's hands stopped working, then started again. Kahlan got a look like she was sad, but Rachel didn't know if it was real or not. She gave her a squeeze on her arm with a soft hand. "I'm sorry, Rachel." Rachel didn't feel too sad; she didn't remember her parents, only the place she lived with the other children.

Richard snipped at her hair while Kahlan took out a pan and started to fry the fish. Richard was right, there were a lot of fish. Kahlan put some kind of spices on them while they cooked, as Rachel had seen cooks doing. It smelled so good, and her stomach was making noises. Little pieces of hair were falling down around her. She smiled to herself at how mad Princess Violet would be if she knew Rachel's hair was cut straight. Richard snipped off one of the longer curls, and tied a thin little vine around one end of it. He put it in her hand. She frowned up at him.

"You're supposed to keep that. Then someday if you like a boy, you can give him a lock of your hair, and he can keep it in his pocket, right next to his heart." He winked at her. "To remember you by."

Rachel giggled. "You're the silliest man I ever saw." He laughed. Kahlan smiled while she looked over at him. Rachel stuffed the lock of hair in her pocket. "Are you a lord?"

"Sorry, Rachel, I'm just a woods guide." His face got a little sad then. She was glad he wasn't a lord. He turned and dug a little mirror out of his pack and handed it to her. "Have a look. Tell me what you think."

She held it up, trying to see herself in the mirror. It was the littlest mirror she ever saw, and it took a minute to get it in the right place so she could see herself in the firelight. When she did, her eyes went wide, and she got tears.

She threw her arm around Richard. "Oh, thank you, Richard, thank you. It's the prettiest my hair has ever been." He gave her back a hug that felt as good as any Giller had ever given her. One of his big, warm hands rubbed her back. It was a long hug, too, the longest she had ever got, and she wished it would never end. But it did.

Kahlan shook her head to herself. "You are a very rare person, Richard Cypher," she whispered to him.

Kahlan stuck a big piece of fish on a stick for her, and told her to blow on it until it was cool enough not to burn her mouth. Rachel blew a little, but she was too hungry to blow for long. It was the bestest fish she ever had. It was as good as the piece of meat the cooks had given her that one time.

"Ready for another piece?" Kahlan asked. Rachel nodded. Then she pulled a knife from her belt. "Should we all have a slice of your bread with the fish?" She started to reach for it.

Rachel dove for the loaf of bead, snatching it away just before Kahlan got her hand on it. Rachel hugged it to her with both arms. "No!" She pushed with her heels, scooting back, away from Kahlan.

Richard stopped eating; Kahlan frowned. Rachel reached one hand into her pocket, her fingers clutching the fire stick Giller had given her.

"Rachel? What's the matter?" Kahlan asked.

Giller had told her, told her not to trust anyone. She had to think of something. What would Giller say?

"It's for my grandmother!" She could feel a tear run down her cheek.

"Well then," Richard said, "since it's for your grandmother, we won't touch it. Promise. Isn't that right, Kahlan?"

"Of course. I'm sorry, Rachel, we didn't know. I promise, too. Forgive me?"

Rachel took her hand back out of her pocket, and nodded. The lump in her throat was too big to talk past.

"Rachel," Richard asked, "where is your grandmother?"

Rachel froze stiff; she didn't really have a grandmother. She tried to think of the name of a place she had heard of. She thought about places she had heard the Queen's advisors name. She said the first one that came into her head.

"Horners Mill."

Before the words were finished coming out of her mouth, she knew it was a mistake. Richard and Kahlan both got scared looks on their faces and turned to look at each other. It was real quiet for a minute; Rachel didn't know what was going to happen. She looked to the sides of the wayward pine, the spaces between the branches.

"Rachel, we won't touch your grandmother's bread," Richard said in a soft voice, "we promise."

"Come, have another piece of fish," Kahlan said. "You can leave the loaf of bread over there; we won't bother it."

Rachel still didn't move. She thought about running away, fast as she could, but she knew they could run faster, and would catch her. She had to do as Giller told her, hide with the box until winter, or all those people would get their heads chopped off.

Richard picked up Sara, and put her on his lap. He pretended to give her a piece of fish. "Sara's going to eat all the fish. If you want any, you better get over here and have your share. Come on, you can sit on my lap and eat. All right?"

Rachel searched their faces, trying to decide if they were telling the truth. Women with long hair could lie easily. She looked at Richard; he didn't look like he was lying. She got up and ran over to him. He pulled her into his lap, then put Sara on her lap.

Rachel snuggled up against him while they all ate fish. She didn't look at Kahlan. Sometimes when you looked at a lady with long hair, it was improper, Princess Violet said. She didn't want to do anything that would get her a slap. Or anything to get taken off Richard's lap. It was warm in his lap, and made her feel safe.

"Rachel," Richard said, "I'm sorry, but we can't let you go to Horners Mill. There's no one left in Horners Mill. It's not safe there."

"That's all right. I'll go somewhere else then."

"I'm afraid it's not safe anywhere, Rachel," Kahlan said. "We will take you with us, so you will be safe."

"Where?"

Kahlan smiled. "We are going to Tamarang, to see the

Queen." Rachel stopped chewing. She couldn't breathe. "We will take you with us. I'm sure the Queen will be able to find someone to take care of you, if I ask."

"Kahlan, are you sure about this?" Richard whispered. "What about the wizard?"

Kahlan nodded and spoke softly to him. "We will see to her before I skin Giller."

Rachel forced herself to swallow, so she could breathe. She knew it! She knew she shouldn't trust a woman with long hair. She almost cried; she was just starting to like Kahlan. Richard was so nice. Why would he be nice to Kahlan? Why would he even be with a woman mean enough to hurt Giller. It must be like when she was nice to Princess Violet, so she wouldn't get hurt. He must be afraid of getting hurt, too. She felt sorry for Richard. She wished he could run away from Kahlan like she was running away from Princess Violet. Maybe she should tell Richard about the box, and he could run away from Kahlan with her.

No. Giller said not to trust anyone. He might be too afraid of Kahlan, and tell her. She had to be brave for Giller. For all the other people. She had to get away.

"We can deal with it in the morning," Kahlan said. "We better get some sleep so we can be off at first light."

Richard nodded as he hugged her. "I'll take the first watch. You get some sleep."

He picked her up and handed her to Kahlan. Rachel bit her tongue to keep from screaming. Kahlan hugged her tight. Rachel looked down at her knife; even the Princess didn't have a knife. She put her arms out to Richard with a whine. Richard smiled and put Sara in her hands. That wasn't what she wanted, but she hugged Sara tight, and bit down on her foot to keep from crying.

Richard mussed her hair. "See you in the morning, little one."

And then he was gone, and she was alone with Kahlan. She squeezed her eyes shut. She had to be brave, she couldn't cry. But then she did.

Kahlan held her tight. Rachel shook. Fingers stroked her hair. Kahlan rocked her while Rachel eyed a dark gap in the boughs on the other side of the wayward pine. Kahlan's chest was making funny little movements, and Rachel realized with wonder that she was crying, too. Kahlan put her cheek against the top of her head.

She almost started to believe ... but then she remembered what Princess Violet said sometimes, that it hurt more to punish than to be punished. Her eyes went wide at what Kahlan must be planning that would make her cry. Even Princess Violet never cried when she dealt out a punishment. Rachel cried harder, and shook.

Kahlan took her hands away and wiped the tears from her cheeks. Rachel's legs were too wobbly to run.

"Are you cold?" Kahlan whispered. Her voice sounded like there were still tears in it.

Rachel was afraid that no matter what she said she would get a slap. She gave a nod, ready for what might happen. Instead, Kahlan took a blanket out of her pack and wrapped it around the both of them, she guessed so it would be harder to get away.

"Come, lie close and I will tell you a story. We will keep each other warm. All right?"

Rachel lay on her side, her back against Kahlan, who curled all around her and put her arm over her. It felt nice, but she knew it was a trick. Kahlan's face was close to her ear, and as she lay there, Kahlan told her a story about a fisherman who turned into a fish. The words made pictures in her head, and for a while she forgot about her troubles. Once, she and Kahlan even laughed together. When she was finished with the story, Kahlan kissed the top of her head and then stroked the side of her forehead.

She pretended Kahlan wasn't really mean. It couldn't hurt to pretend. Nothing had ever felt as good as those fingers on her, and the little song Kahlan sang in her ear. Rachel thought this must be what it felt like to have a mother.

Against her will, she fell asleep, and had wonderful dreams.

She came awake in the middle of the night when Richard woke Kahlan, but she pretended she was still asleep.

"You want to keep sleeping with her?" he whispered real soft.

Rachel held her breath.

"No," Kahlan whispered back, "I'll take my watch."

Rachel could hear her putting on her cloak and going outside. She listened to which way Kahlan's feet went. After he put some more wood in the fire, Richard lay down, close. She could see the inside of the wayward pine brighten. She knew Richard was watching her; she could feel his eyes on her back. She wanted so much to tell him how mean Kahlan really was, and ask him to run away with her. He was such a nice man, and his hugs were the bestest things in the whole world. He reached over and pulled the blanket up around her tighter, tucking it under her chin. Tears ran down her cheeks.

She could hear him lie on his back and pull his blanket up. Rachel waited until she heard his even breathing and she knew he was asleep before she slipped out from under the blanket.

CHAPTER 36

KAHLAN TURNED EXPECTANTLY WHEN he batted a limb out of the way as he pushed into the wayward pine and flopped down in front of the fire. He pulled his pack across the ground and started jamming things in it.

"Well?"

Richard shot her an angry glare. "I found her tracks, going west, back the way we came. They join the trail a few hundred yards out. They're hours old." He pointed to the ground at the back of the wayward pine. "That's where she went out. She circled around you through the woods, well clear of us. I've tracked men who didn't want to be found, and their trails were easier to follow. She walks on top of things, roots, rocks, and she's too little to make a print where another would. Did you see her arms?"

"I saw long bruises. They are from a switch."

"No, I mean scratches."

"I saw no scratches."

"Exactly. Her dress had burrs on it; she's been through the bramble, yet she had no scratches on her arms. She's tender, so she avoids brushing up against anything. An adult would just

544

push past, leave a trail of disturbed or broken branches. She almost never touches anything. You should see the trail I left, going through the bushes trying to track her; a blind man could follow it. She moves through the underbrush like air. Even when she was back on the trail, I couldn't tell for a while. Her feet are bare; she doesn't like stepping in water or mud—it makes her feet colder—so she steps where it's dry, where you can't see her passing."

"I should have seen her leaving."

He realized Kahlan thought he was blaming her. He let out an exasperated breath. "It's not your fault, Kahlan. If I had been standing watch, I wouldn't have seen her go either. She didn't want to be seen. She's one smart little girl."

It didn't seem to make her feel any better. "But you can track her, right?"

He gave her a sidelong glance. "I can." He reached to his breast. "I found this in my shirt pocket." He lifted an eyebrow. "By my heart." He pulled out the lock of Rachel's hair, tied with the vine. He twisted it in his fingers. "To remember her by."

Kahlan's face was ashen as she rose. "This is my fault." She pushed out of the wayward pine. He tried to grab her arm, but she tore away from him.

Richard set his pack aside and followed. Kahlan stood off a ways, her arms folded below her breasts, her back to him. She stared off into the woods.

"Kahlan, it isn't your fault."

She nodded. "It was my hair. Didn't you see the fear in her eyes when she looked at my hair? I have seen that look a thousand times. Do you have any idea what it's like to frighten people, even children, all the time?" He didn't answer. "Richard? Cut my hair for me?"

"What?"

She turned to him, pleading in her eyes. "Cut it off for me?"

He watched the hurt in her eyes. "Why haven't you just cut it yourself?"

She turned away. "I cannot. The magic will not allow a Confessor to cut her own hair. If we try, it brings pain so great, it prevents us from doing so."

"How could that be?"

"Remember the pain you suffered, from the magic of the sword, when you killed a man the first time? It is the same pain. It will render a Confessor unconscious before the task can be accomplished. I tried only once. Every Confessor tries once. But only once. Our hair must be cut by another when it needs trimming. But none would dare to cut it all of." She turned to him once more. "Will you do it for me? Will you cut my hair?"

He looked away from her eyes, to the brightening slate blue sky, trying to understand what it was he was feeling, what it was she must be feeling. There was so much he didn't know about her, still. Her life, her world, was a mystery to him. There had been a time when he wanted to know it all. Now he knew he never could; the gulf between them was filled with magic. Magic, designed, it seemed, explicitly to keep them apart.

His eyes returned to her. "No."

"May I know why?"

"Because I respect you for who you are. The Kahlan I know wouldn't want to fool people by trying to make them think she is less than she is. Even if you did fool some, it would change nothing. You are who you are: the Mother Confessor. We all can be no more, or less, than who we are." He smiled. "A wise woman, a friend of mine, told me that once."

"Any man would leap for the chance to cut a Confessor's hair."

"Not this one. This one is your friend."

She gave a nod, her arms still folded against her stomach. "She must be cold. She didn't even take a blanket."

"She didn't take any food either, other than that loaf of bread she's saving for some reason, and she was starving."

Kahlan smiled at last. "She ate more than you and me together. At least her belly is full. Richard, when she gets to Horners Mill . . ."

"She isn't going to Horners Mill."

Kahlan came closer. "But that's where her grandmother is."

Richard shook his head. "She doesn't have a grandmother. When she said her grandmother was in Horners Mill, and I told her she couldn't go there, she didn't even falter. She simply said she would go somewhere else. She never gave it a thought, never

546

asked about her grandmother, or even raised an objection. She's running from something."

"Running? Maybe from whoever put those bruises on her arms."

"And on her back. Whenever my hand touched one, she flinched, but she didn't say anything. She wanted to be hugged that badly." Kahlan's brow wrinkled with sorrow. "I'd say she was running from whoever cut her hair like that."

"Her hair?"

He nodded again. "It was meant to mark her, maybe as property. No one would cut someone's hair like that, except to give a message. Especially in the Midlands, where everyone pays so much attention to hair. It was deliberate, a message of power over her. That's why I cut it for her, to remove the mark."

Kahlan stared at nothing in particular. "That was why she was so happy to have it cut even," she whispered.

"There is more to it, though, than simply running away. She lies easier than a gambler. She lies with the ease of someone who has a powerful need."

Her eyes came to his again. "Like what?"

"I don't know." He sighed. "But it has something to do with that loaf of bread."

"The bread? Do you really think so?"

"She had no shoes, no cloak, nothing but her doll. It's her most precious possession, she's devoted to it, yet she let us touch it. But she wouldn't let us get within an arm's length of that loaf of bread. I don't know much about the magic in the Midlands, but where I come from, a little girl will not value a loaf of bread more than her doll, and I don't think it's any different here. Did you see the look in her eyes when you reached for the bread, and she snatched it away? If she had had a knife, and you hadn't backed off, she would have used it on you."

"Richard," she admonished, "you can't really believe that about a little girl. A loaf of bread couldn't be that important to her."

"No? You said yourself she ate as much as both of us put together. I was beginning to think she was related to Zedd. Explain why if she was half starved, she hadn't even nibbled on that loaf of bread." He shook his head. "There is something going on, and that loaf of bread is at the center of it."

Kahlan took a step toward him. "So, we're going after her?"

Richard felt the weight of the tooth against his chest. He took a deep breath, letting it out slowly. "No. As Zedd is fond of saying, nothing is ever easy. How can we justify going after one little girl, to solve the riddle of her loaf of bread, while Rahl goes after the box?"

She took his hand in one of hers, looked down at it. "I hate what Darken Rahl does to us, the way he twists us." She squeezed his hand. "She got into our hearts awfully quick."

Richard gave her a one-armed hug. "That she did. She's one special little girl. I hope she finds what she's after, and that she is safe." He let go of Kahlan and started for the wayward pine, to get their things. "Let's get moving."

Neither wanted to think about how they felt, that they were deserting Rachel, condemning her to the embrace of dangers she knew nothing about and was defenseless against, and so both set their minds to covering as much ground as fast as they could. The bright day wore on with an endless expanse of rugged forest, and with their exertion they didn't notice the cold.

Richard was always glad when he saw a spiderweb stretched across the trail; he had begun to think of spiders as his guardians. When he had been a guide, he had always been annoyed to have them tickle his face. Thank you, sister spider, he said to himself every time he passed one now.

Near midday, they stopped for a break on sunlit rocks in an icy stream. Richard splashed the frigid water on his face, trying to work up some energy. He was tired already. Lunch was cold, too, and lasted only as long as it took to bolt it down. They both stuffed the last bites in their mouths, brushed their hands off on their pants, and hopped down off the flat, pink rock.

As much as he tried not to think about Rachel, he found himself frowning with worry before he realized he was doing it again. He saw Kahlan's brow wrinkle sometimes when she turned, checking to the sides. One time he asked if she thought he had made the right decision. She didn't have to ask which decision he was talking about. She asked how long he thought it would have taken to catch her. He thought two days, if everything went right, at least one to catch her and another back. Two days, she had told him, was more than they could afford. It felt reassuring to hear her say it.

Late in the afternoon, the sun slipped behind a distant peak of one of the mountains of the Rang'Shada, muting and softening the colors of the woods, calming the wind, and settling a stillness over the countryside. Richard was able to set aside his thought of Rachel as he concentrated on what they would do when they reached Tamarang.

"Kahlan, Zedd told us we both had to stay away from Darken Rahl, that we have no power against him, no defense."

She gave a short glance over her shoulder. "That's what he said."

Richard frowned. "Well, Shota said the Queen wouldn't have the box for long."

"Maybe when she said that, she meant we would get it soon."

"No, it was a warning, that the Queen wouldn't have it long, meaning we must hurry. So what if Darken Rahl is already there?"

She looked over her shoulder, then slowed, and walked next to him. "So what if he is? There is no other way. I'm going to Tamarang. Do you wish to wait behind for me?"

"Of course not! I'm only saying we should keep in mind what we are walking into; that Darken Rahl might be there."

"I have had that thought in my mind for a long time now."

He walked next to her for a minute without saying anything. At last he asked, "And what have you concluded? What will we do if he is there?"

She stared straight ahead as she spoke. "If Darken Rahl is in Tamarang, and we go there, then in all likelihood—we will die."

Richard lost a stride; she didn't wait for him, but walked on.

As the woods grew darker, a few small clouds glowed red, the dying embers of day. The trail had begun following the Callisidrin River, sometimes taking them close enough for a view of it, and even when it didn't, they could still hear the rush of its brown waters. Richard hadn't seen a wayward pine all afternoon. Glancing about at the treetops, he saw no sign of one now, either. As it grew dark, he gave up hope of finding one before nightfall, and so began looking for other shelter. Off the trail a safe distance, he found a short, cleft face of rock at the bottom of a rise. Trees were sheltering all about, and he felt it a well-hidden camp, even if it was open to the sky.

The moon was well up by the time Kahlan had a stew cooking on the fire, and by a bit of luck that surprised him, Richard had two rabbits in the snare before he expected to, and was able to add them to the pot.

"I think we have enough to feed Zedd," she said.

As if bidden by her words, the old man, white hair in disarray, strode into the circle of light, stopping on the other side of the fire, hands on his hips, his robes looking a little tattered.

"I'm starved!" he announced. "Let's eat."

Richard and Kahlan both blinked, wide-eyed, and came to their feet. The old man blinked, too, when Richard drew the sword. In a heartbeat, Richard was over the fire, the sword's point to his ribs.

"What's this?" the old man asked.

"Back up," Richard ordered. They moved, the sword between them, to the trees. Richard eyed the trees carefully.

"Mind if I inquire as to what we're doing, my boy?"

"I've been called by you once, and seen you once, yet neither was you. Third time tricked, marks the fool," Richard quoted. He saw what he was looking for. "I'll not be tricked the third time, I'll not be the fool. Over there." He pointed with his chin. "Walk between those two trees."

"I will not!" the old man protested. "Sheath your sword, my boy!"

"If you don't walk between those two trees," Richard said through gritted teeth, "I'll sheath my sword in your ribs."

The old man lifted his elbows in surprise, then picked up his robes as he stepped through the low brush, muttering to himself while Richard prodded him along with the sword. He took only a quick glance back before stepping between the trees. Richard watched as the spiderweb parted. A grin spread on his face.

"Zedd! Is it truly you?"

Zedd, hands on his hips, peered at him with one eye. "True as toasted toads, my boy."

Richard sheathed the sword and threw his arms around his old friend, nearly squeezing the life out of him. "Oh, Zedd! I'm so glad to see you!"

Zedd's arms flailed as he tried to get a breath. Richard let up, looked him in the eye, beaming, then squeezed again.

"I fear what would have happened had you been any more glad to see me."

Richard walked him back to the fire, an arm around his shoulders. "Sorry about that, but I had to know for sure. I can't believe you're here! I'm so glad to see you! I'm so happy you're all right. We have so much to talk about."

"Yes, yes. Can we eat now?"

Kahlan came and gave him a hug, too. "We were so worried about you."

Zedd longingly eyed the cooking pot over her shoulder as he hugged her back. "Yes, yes. But this would all go better on a full stomach."

"But it isn't done yet," she smiled.

Zedd gave a look of disappointment. "Not done? Are you sure? Perhaps we could check."

"Quite sure. We've only just started it."

"Not done," he said to himself, holding an elbow with one hand, rubbing his chin with the other. "Well, we'll just see about that. Stand back, the both of you."

The wizard pushed the sleeves of his robes up his arms while he eyed the fire as if it were a child who had misbehaved. His skinny arms stretched out, fingers extended. Blue light sizzled around his bony hands, seeming to gather momentum. With a hiss, it shot out in a jagged blue streak, striking the cooking pot, making it jump. The blue fire cradled the pot, twisting around it, caressing it, stroking it. The stew bubbled with blue light, churned and sloshed. The wizard pulled his hands back and the blue fire sizzled out.

Zedd smiled in satisfaction. "There, now it's done. Let's eat!"

Kahlan kneeled, tasting the stew with a wooden spoon. "He's right. It is done."

"Well, don't just stand there staring, my boy. Get some plates!"

Richard shook his head and did as he was told. Kahlan dished up a plate full, putting some dried biscuits on the side, and Richard handed it to Zedd. The old man didn't sit, but stood next to them, by the fire, shoveling in the stew by the forkful. Kahlan spooned stew on the other two plates, and by the time she was done, Zedd was handing her his empty plate to be refilled.

Having finished one helping, Zedd was able to spare himself the time to sit. Richard sat on a small outcropping of ledge; Kahlan sat next to him, folding her legs under her; Zedd sat on the ground facing them.

Richard waited until Zedd had swallowed down half the stew on his plate, and finally allowed himself a pause before asking, "So, how did you get along with Adie? Did she take good care of you?"

Zedd looked up at him, blinking. Even in the firelight, Richard could have sworn Zedd's face reddened. "Adie? Well we . . ." He looked at Kahlan's puzzled face. "Well, we . . . we got along . . . fine." He scowled at Richard. "What kind of question is that to ask?"

Richard and Kahlan glanced at each other. "I didn't mean anything by it," he said. "It's just that I couldn't help noticing that Adie is a handsome woman. And interesting. I just meant you would find her interesting." Richard smiled a small smile to himself.

Zedd put his face back to his plate. "She's a fine woman." He rolled something around his plate with the end of his fork. "What is this? I've eaten three, and I still don't know what it is."

"Tava root," Kahlan said. "Don't you like it?"

Zed grunted. "Didn't say I didn't like it. Just wanted to know what it was, that's all." He looked up from his plate. "Adie told me she gave you a night stone. That's how I found you, by the night stone." He shook his fork at Richard. "I hope you are being careful with that thing. Don't take it out unless there is great need. Exceptionally great need. Night stones are extremely dangerous. Adie should have warned you. And I told her so!" He stabbed a tava root with his fork. "It would be best to be rid of it."

Richard pushed at a piece of meat. "We know."

Richard's mind was awash with questions he wanted to ask; he didn't know where to start. Zedd beat him to it, asking first.

"Have you two been doing as I said? Have you been staying out of trouble? What have you been doing?"

"Well," Richard said, taking a deep breath, "we spent a good deal of time with the Mud People."

"The Mud People?" Zedd mulled this over. "Good," he proclaimed at last, holding a forkful of meat in the air. "You can't get in much trouble with the Mud People." He took the meat off the fork with his teeth and dipped it back in his plate for more stew and a bite of dried biscuit. He spoke and chewed at the same time. "So, you two had a nice stay with the Mud People." He noticed that they weren't saying anything, and his eyes went from one to the other. "You can't get in much trouble with the Mud People." It sounded like an order.

Richard glanced over at Kahlan. She dipped her biscuit in the stew. "I killed one of the elders," she said, putting the biscuit in her mouth without looking up.

Zedd dropped his fork, then caught it in midair just before it hit the ground. "What!"

"It was self-defense," Richard protested to her. "He was trying to kill you."

"What?" Zedd stood with his plate, then sat back down. "Bags! Why would an elder dare to try to kill a . . ." He snapped his mouth shut, with a glance to Richard.

"Confessor," Richard finished for him. His mood withered.

Zedd looked from one bowed head to the other. "So. You finally told him."

Kahlan nodded. "A few days ago."

"Just a few days ago." Zedd grunted an acknowledgment, then ate more stew in silence, eyeing them suspiciously from time to time. "Why would an elder dare to try to kill a Confessor?"

"Well," Richard said, "that was when we found out what a night stone could do. Just before they named us as Mud People."

"They named you Mud People? Why?" Zedd's eyes widened. "You took a wife!"

"Well . . . no." Richard pulled the leather thong out of his shirt and showed Zedd the Bird Man's whistle. "They settled for giving me this."

Zedd gave a cursory glance to the whistle. "Why would they

agree to you not ... And why would they name you Mud People?"

"Because we asked them. We had to. It was the only way to get them to call a gathering for us."

"What! They called a gathering for you?"

"Yes. That was just before Darken Rahl came."

"What!" Zedd yelled again, jumping to his feet. "Darken Rahl was there! I told you; stay away from him!"

Richard looked up. "We didn't exactly invite him."

"He killed a lot of them," Kahlan said in a quiet voice, still looking down at her plate, chewing slowly.

Zedd stared at the top of her head, then slowly sank back down. "I'm sorry," he said softly. "So, what did the ancestors' spirits tell you?"

Richard gave a shrug. "That we had to go to see a witch woman."

"Witch woman!" Zedd's eyes narrowed. "What witch woman? Where?"

"Shota. In Agaden Reach."

Zedd winced, almost dropping his plate, the air making a sound going through his bared, gritted teeth as he drew a sharp breath. "Shota!" He looked around as if someone might hear. He lowered his voice, directing a harsh whisper to Kahlan as he leaned closer to her. "Bags! What would possess you to guide him into Agaden Reach! You are sworn to protect him!"

"Believe me," she said, looking him in the eye, "I did not want to do it."

"We had to," Richard said, coming to her defense.

Zedd cast an eye to him. "Why?"

"To find out where the box is. And we did, too, Shota told us."

"Shota told you," Zedd mocked, scowling at him. "And what else did she tell you? Shota tells you nothing you want to know without telling you something you don't."

Kahlan gave Richard a sidelong glance. He didn't return it. "Nothing. She told us nothing else." He held Zedd's eyes without backing down. "She told us that Queen Milena, in Tamarang, has the last box of Orden. She told us because her life too depends on this."

Richard held Zedd's glare. He doubted that his old friend believed him, but he didn't want to tell him what Shota had said. How could he tell Zedd that one, or two, of them might end up being traitors? That Zedd would use wizard's fire against him, that Kahlan would touch him with her power? He feared that maybe it would be justified; after all, he was the one who knew about the book. They didn't.

"Zedd," he said softly, "you told me you wanted me to get us to the Midlands, and that you had a plan once we were here. You were struck down by that underworld beast, you were unconscious, we didn't know when, or if, you would wake. I didn't know what to do, I didn't know what your plan was. Winter is coming. We have to stop Darken Rahl."

His voice turned harder as he went on. "I have been doing the best I could without you. I've lost track of the number of times we have nearly been killed. All I knew to do was try to find the box. Kahlan helped me, and we found out where it is. It has cost us both dearly. If you don't like what I have done, then take your cursed Sword of Truth back, I am near to being fed up with it! With everything!"

He threw his plate on the ground, walking off a ways into the dark, standing with his back to them, a lump growing in his throat. The dark trees in front of him became watery. It surprised him the way the anger had reached up and taken him. He had wanted to see Zedd so badly, and now that he was here, he was angry with him. He let the ire rage, waiting for it to die of its own accord.

Zedd and Kahlan exchanged a look. "Yes," he said softly to her, "I can see that you have indeed told him." He set his plate on the ground, stood, and gave her a pat on the shoulder. "I'm sorry, dear one."

Richard didn't move when he felt Zedd's hand on his shoulder.

"I'm sorry, my boy. I guess you have been having a hard time of it."

Richard nodded as he stared into the darkness. "I killed a man with the sword. With the magic."

Zedd waited a short while before he spoke. "Well, I know you, I'm sure you had to."

"No," Richard said in a painful whisper. "I didn't have to. I thought I was protecting Kahlan, protecting her life. I didn't know she was a Confessor, that she needed no protection. But I surely wanted to. And I surely enjoyed it."

"You only thought you did. That was the magic."

"I'm not so sure. I'm not sure what is becoming of me."

"Richard, forgive me for sounding as if I were angry with you. It is myself I'm angry with. You have done well, it is I who have failed."

"What do you mean?"

Zedd patted his shoulder. "Come and sit. I will tell you both what has happened."

They walked back to the fire, Kahlan watching them together, looking lonely. Richard sat next to her again and gave her a small smile, which she returned.

Zedd picked up his plate, gave it a hard look, and set it back down. "I'm afraid we're in a lot of trouble," he said in a soft voice.

A sarcastic remark immediately sprang to Richard's mind, but he stifled it and asked instead, "Why, what's happened? What of your plan?"

"My plan." Zedd gave a wry smile, drew his knees up, and pulled his robes over his legs, making a little tent over them. "My plan was to stop Rahl without having to deal with him, and without you two having to get in danger's way. My plan was for you two to stay out of trouble while I dealt with this. It would seem as if your own plans may be our only way now. I have not told you all there is to know of the boxes of Orden, because it was not for you to know. It was none of your business; it was only for me to know." He looked at each of them, anger flashing in his eyes for an instant before it faded. "But I guess it doesn't matter now."

"What was not for us to know?" Kahlan asked with a frown, her own anger flashing a little. Apparently, she didn't like it any more than Richard did that they were in danger without knowing it all.

"Well, you see," Zedd said, "the three boxes work just as I said, each with their own purpose, but you have to know which to open. That is the part I know. It's all in a book, called the

Book of Counted Shadows. The Book of Counted Shadows is an instruction book for the boxes. I'm its keeper."

Richard went rigid. The tooth felt as if it would jump right off his chest. He couldn't move a muscle, could hardly breathe.

"You know which box is which?" Kahlan asked. "You know which he must open?"

"No. I'm the keeper of the book. That information is all in the book. But I've never read it. I don't know which box is which, or even how to figure it out. If I were to open the book, it would risk spreading the knowledge. It must not be opened; that could be very dangerous. So I never did. I am the keeper of many books, this only one among them, but a very important one."

Richard realized that his eyes were open wide and tried to relax them back to normal with a few blinks. Almost his whole life he had been looking forward to the day he would find the keeper of the book, and it had been Zedd the whole time. The shock left him frozen.

"Where was it?" Kahlan asked. "What happened?"

"It was in my Keep. The Wizard's Keep. In Aydindril."

"You went to Aydindril?" Kahlan asked, her voice anxious. "How is Aydindril? Is it safe?"

Zedd averted his eyes. "Aydindril has fallen."

Kahlan's hand went to her mouth; tears filled her eyes. "No."

Zedd nodded. "I'm afraid so." He picked at his robes. "It is not going well for them. At least I gave the occupiers something to think about," he added under his breath.

"Captain Riffkin? Lieutenants Delis and Miller? The Home Guard?"

Zedd kept his eyes to the ground and shook his head as she named each in turn. Kahlan put her hands to her breast as she took deep breaths and bit her lip. Whoever these men were, she looked to be pretty upset by the news.

Richard thought he should cover his own shock by saying something. "What's this Wizard's Keep?"

"It's a refuge, a place where the wizards preserve important things of magic, such as the books of prophecies, and books of even more importance—books of magic and instruction, such as the Book of Counted Shadows. Some of the books are used to teach new wizards, some are used as reference, and some are used as weapons. Other items of magic are kept there also, such as the Sword of Truth, between Seekers. The Keep is sealed by magic; none can enter but a wizard. At least none but a wizard was supposed to be able to enter. But someone did. How they did without being killed is beyond me. It must have been Darken Rahl. He must have the book."

"Maybe it wasn't Darken Rahl," Richard managed, his back straight as a board.

Zedd's eyes narrowed. "If it wasn't Darken Rahl, then it was a thief. A very clever thief, but a thief nonetheless."

Richard swallowed back the dryness in his mouth. "Zedd . . . I . . . Do you think this book, the Book of Counted Shadows, would be able to tell us how to stop Rahl? How to keep him from using the boxes?"

Zedd shrugged his bony shoulders. "As I said, I've never opened the cover. But from what I know from other books of instruction, it would only be of aid to the person with the boxes; it's designed to help use magic, not to help another in stopping its use. In all likelihood, it wouldn't have helped us. My plan was to simply get the book, and destroy it, to keep Rahl from getting the information. Having the book lost to us leaves us with no alternative; we must find the last box."

"But without the book, can Rahl still open the boxes?" Kahlan asked.

"With as much as he knows, I am sure he can. But he still wouldn't know which one."

"Then, with or without the book, he's going to open a box." Richard said. "He has to. If he doesn't, he dies. He has nothing to lose. Even if you had recovered the book, he would still open a box—after all, there is a chance he will pick right."

"Well, if he has the book, then he will know which to open. I was hoping that if we couldn't find the last box, at least I could destroy the book, and keep it from Rahl, give us at least that one chance. The chance he might pick right—for us." Zedd's face soured. "I would give anything to destroy that book."

Kahlan put her hand on Richard's arm; he almost jumped. "Then Richard has done as the Seeker should; he has found where the box is. Queen Milena has it." She gave Richard a smile of reassurance. "The Seeker has done his job well." His mind was spinning too fast to return the smile properly.

Zedd drew a finger and thumb down opposite sides of his chin. "And how do you propose we get it from her? Knowing is one thing, getting is quite another."

Kahlan gave Zedd a smooth smile. "Queen Milena is the one to whom the snake in the silver robes sold his services. He is about to have an unpleasant meeting with the Mother Confessor."

"Giller? Queen Milena is the one Giller went to?" The wrinkles on Zedd's face deepened with his scowl. "I think he will be astonished to meet my eyes again."

She frowned. "You just leave this task to me. He is my wizard. I will deal with him."

Richard's eyes went back and forth between the two of them. He felt suddenly out of place. The great wizard and the Mother Confessor discussing how they would deal with an upstart wizard, as if they were talking of pulling weeds in a garden. He thought of his father, of how his father had told him he had taken the book to prevent it from falling into covetous hands. Darken Rahl's hands. He spoke without thinking.

"Maybe he had a good reason for doing what he did."

They both turned and looked at him, as if they had forgotten he was there.

"A good reason?" Kahlan snapped. "Greed was his good reason. He deserted me, and left me to the quads."

"Sometimes people do things for reasons that aren't what they seem." Richard gave her an even look. "Maybe he thought the box was more important."

Kahlan looked too surprised to speak.

Zedd frowned, his white hair looking wild in the firelight. "Perhaps you are right. It could be that Giller knew about the Queen having the box, and wanted to protect it. He certainly knew what the boxes were about." He gave Richard an ironic smile. "Maybe the Seeker has given us a new perspective. Maybe we have an ally in Tamarang."

"And maybe not," Kahlan said.

"We will know soon enough," the wizard sighed.

"Zedd," Richard asked, "yesterday, we went to a place called Horners Mill."

Zedd nodded. "I saw it. And I have seen many more just like it."

Richard leaned forward. "It wasn't Westlanders, was it? It couldn't have been Westlanders. I told Michael to get the army together and protect Westland. I didn't tell him to attack anyone. Certainly not helpless people. It couldn't have been Westlanders; they wouldn't do that."

"No, it wasn't anyone from Westland. I haven't seen or heard from Michael."

"Then who?"

"It was Rahl's own men who did it, by his command."

"That does not make any sense," Kahlan said. "The town was loyal to D'Hara. There were forces of the People's Peace Army there, and they were killed to a man."

"That's the very reason he did it."

They both gave him puzzled looks. "That doesn't make any sense," Kahlan said.

"Wizard's First Rule."

Richard frowned. "What?"

"Wizard's First Rule: people are stupid." Richard and Kahlan frowned even more. "People are stupid; given proper motivation, almost anyone will believe almost anything. Because people are stupid, they will believe a lie because they want to believe it's true, or because they are afraid it might be true. People's heads are full of knowledge, facts, and beliefs, and most of it is false, yet they think it all true. People are stupid; they can only rarely tell the difference between a lie and the truth, and yet they are confident they can, and so are all the easier to fool.

"Because of the Wizard's First Rule, the old wizards created Confessors, and Seekers, as a means of helping find the truth, when the truth is important enough. Rahl knows the Wizard's Rules. He is using the first one. People need an enemy to feel a sense of purpose. It's easy to lead people when they have a sense of purpose. Sense of purpose is more important by far than the truth. In fact, truth has no bearing in this. Darken Rahl is providing them with an enemy, other than himself, a sense of purpose. People are stupid; they want to believe, so they do."

"But they were his own people," Kahlan protested. "He was killing his supporters."

"You will notice not all the people were killed; some were raped, tortured, but left alive to flee, to spread the news. You will also note how none of the soldiers were left alive to dispute the story. That it isn't the truth doesn't matter, and the ones hearing the story will believe it because it provides them with a sense of purpose, an enemy to rally against. The survivors will spread the word like a wildfire. Even though Rahl has destroyed a few towns that were loyal to him, and a few of his soldiers, he has gained many more towns to his side, a hundredfold over. Even more people will rally around him and support him because he has told them he wants to protect them from this enemy. Truth is hard to sell; it gives no sense of purpose. It is simply truth."

Richard sat back, a little stunned. "But it isn't true. How can Rahl get away with it? How could everyone believe it?"

Zedd gave him a stern look. "You knew better, you knew it wasn't Westlanders, yet even you doubted your knowledge. You were afraid it was true. Being afraid something is true is accepting the possibility. Accepting the possibility is the first step to believing. At least you are smart enough to question. Think of how easy it is to believe, for people who don't question, who don't even know how to question. For most people, it's not the truth that is important, it's the cause. Rahl is intelligent; he has given them a cause." His eyes glinted with purpose. "It is the Wizard's First Rule because it is the most important. Remember it."

"But the ones who did the killing, they knew. It was murder. How could they do it?"

Zedd shrugged. "Sense of purpose. They did it for the cause."

"But that goes against nature. Murder goes against nature."

The wizard smiled. "Murder is the way of nature, of all living things."

Richard knew Zedd was sucking him in—it was his way to draw you in with an outrageous statement—but his blood was up and he couldn't help protesting. "Only some of nature. Like predators. And that's only to survive. Look about at these trees, they can't even think of murder."

"Murder is the way of all things, the way of nature," Zedd repeated. "Every living thing is a murderer."

Richard looked to Kahlan for support. "Don't look at me," she said. "I learned a long time ago not to debate with wizards."

Richard looked up, at the beautiful big pine spreading over them, illuminated in the firelight. A spark of understanding lit in his mind. He saw the branches, stretched out with murderous intent, in a years-long struggle to reach the sunlight and dispatch its neighbors with its shade. Success would give space for its offspring, many of which would also shrivel in the shade of the parent. Several close neighbors of the big pine were withered and weak, victims all. It was true: the design of nature was success by murder.

Zedd watched Richard's eyes. This was a lesson, the way the old man had taught Richard since he was young. "You have learned something, my boy?"

Richard nodded. "Life for the strongest. There is no sympathy for the slain, only admiration for the winner's strength."

"But people don't think that way," Kahlan said, unable to hold her tongue.

Zedd gave a sly smile. "No?" He pointed to a small, withered tree near them. "Look at this tree, dear one." He pointed to the big pine. "And this. Tell me which you admire more."

"This one," she said, pointing at the big pine. "It's a beautiful tree."

"This one. You see? People do think this way. It's beautiful, you said. You chose the tree that murders, not the one murdered." Zedd smiled triumphantly. "The way of nature."

Kahlan folded her arms. "I knew I should have kept my mouth shut."

"You may keep your mouth closed if you wish, but don't close your mind. To defeat Darken Rahl, we must understand him to know how to destroy him."

"This is how he's winning so much territory," Richard said, tapping his finger on the hilt of his sword. "He's letting others do it for him, giving them a cause; then all he has to worry about is going after the boxes. There is no one to interfere."

Zedd nodded. "He uses the Wizard's First Rule to do most of the work for him. This is what makes our job so hard. He gets people on his side because people don't care about the truth; they do his bidding because they believe what they want to, and fight to the death for these beliefs, despite how false they are."

Richard slowly stood, looking off into the night. "All this time, I thought we were fighting evil. Evil on the loose, run amok. But that's not it at all. What we're up against is more like a plague. A plague of fools."

"You have gotten it right, my boy. A plague of fools."

"Directed by Darken Rahl," Kahlan noted.

Zedd peered at her a moment. "If someone digs a hole, and it fills with rainwater, where is the fault? Is it the rain's fault? Or is it the fault of the person who digs the hole? Is it Darken Rahl's fault, or the fault of those who dig the hole, and let him rain in?"

"Maybe both," Kahlan said. "That leaves us with a lot of enemies."

Zedd lifted a finger. "And very dangerous ones. Fools who won't see the truth are deadly. As a Confessor, perhaps you have already learned this lesson, yes?" She nodded. "They don't always do what you think they will, or should, and you can be caught off guard. People you don't think should be trouble can kill you quick."

"This doesn't change anything," Kahlan said. "If Rahl gets all the boxes, and opens the right one, he is the one who will kill us all. He is still the head to the snake; it is still this head we must remove."

Zedd shrugged. "You are correct. But we must stay alive to have a chance to kill this snake, and there are plenty of small snakes that can kill us first."

"This is a lesson we already learned," Richard said. "But as Kahlan said, it doesn't change anything. We must still get the box to kill Rahl." He sat down again, next to her.

Zedd's face turned deadly serious. "Just remember: Darken Rahl can kill you," he pointed a bony finger at Richard, then Kahlan, "and you," then at himself, "and me—easy."

Richard sat back a little. "Then, why hasn't he?"

Zedd lifted an eyebrow. "Do you go around a room, and kill all the flies in it? No. You ignore them. They don't merit your attention. Until they bite. Then you swat them." He leaned closer to the two of them. "We are about to bite him."

Richard and Kahlan gave each other a sideways glance.

"Wizard's First Rule." Richard felt a trickle of sweat run down his back. "I'll remember."

"And don't repeat it to anyone," the wizard admonished. "Wizard's Rules are for none but a wizard to know. The Wizard's Rules may seem cynical or trivial to you, but they are powerful weapons if you know how to use them, because they are true. Truth is power. I have told you two because I'm the head of the wizards, and I think it important for you to understand. You must know what Rahl is doing, since it is the three of us who must stop him."

Richard and Kahlan both nodded their oath.

"It's late." Zedd yawned. "I have been traveling a long time to reach you. We will talk more later."

Richard jumped up. "I'll take first watch." He had something to do, and wanted it done before anything else happened. "Use my blankets, Zedd."

"Done. I'll take second watch." Second watch of three was the least pleasant: it split your sleeping in two. Kahlan began to protest. "I spoke first, dear one."

Richard pointed to the rock outcropping where he would be, after he scouted the area, and headed off. His mind churned with a thousand thoughts, but with one above all the rest. The night was still, and cold, yet not uncomfortably so. He left his cloak open as he picked his way through the trees, intent on where he was going. Night creatures called to one another, but he hardly noticed. At one point, he scrambled to the top of a boulder and peered back through the gaps in the trees, watching the fire, waiting until he saw the other two roll themselves in the blankets; then he slid off the rock and continued on toward the sound of rushing water.

At the edge of the river, he cast about until he found a chunk of driftwood big enough for his purpose. Richard remembered Zedd telling him that he must have the courage to do what was necessary for their goal, and he must be prepared to kill any one of them if it came to that. Richard knew Zedd, and he knew that Zedd wasn't just making a point—he meant what he said. He knew that Zedd was capable of killing him, or, more important, Kahlan.

He took the tooth from his shirt, pulling the leather cord over his head. He held the triangular-shaped tooth in his hand, feeling the weight of it, looking at it in the moonlight, and thought about his father. The tooth was the only way for Richard to prove to Zedd that his father wasn't a thief, that he had taken the book to keep it from Darken Rahl. Richard wanted so badly to tell Zedd, to tell him that his father had been a hero, had given his life to stop Rahl and died a hero to protect them all. He wanted his father to be remembered for what he had done. He wanted to tell Zedd.

But he couldn't.

The wizard wanted the Book of Counted Shadows destroyed. Richard was the Book of Counted Shadows now. Shota had warned him that Zedd would use the wizard's fire against him, but that he had a chance to beat him. Perhaps this was the way. To destroy the book, Zedd would have to kill him. Richard didn't care about himself, he had nothing to live for; he no longer cared if he died.

But he did care if Kahlan died. If Zedd knew that Richard had the book inside him, he would make him tell what it said, and then he would know that to make sure the book was true, Rahl would have to use a Confessor. And there was only one Confessor left alive. Kahlan. If Zedd knew, he would kill her to prevent Rahl from getting the knowledge.

Richard couldn't allow the chance of Zedd knowing, of killing Kahlan.

He wrapped the cord around the piece of driftwood and jammed the tooth into a long crack, wedging it into the wood so it wouldn't come out. Richard wanted the tooth as far away from him as he could get it.

"Forgive me, Father," he whispered.

Hard as he could, he threw the wood with the tooth attached. He watched it arc through the air, and splash into the dark water with a distant sound. In the moonlight, he could see it bob to the surface. He stood with a lump in his throat as he watched it being carried downriver. Richard felt naked without the tooth.

When it was no longer in sight, he circled the camp, his mind in a daze. He felt empty. Richard sat on the rock outcropping where he had told them he would be, and watched their camp below.

He hated this. Hated having to lie to Zedd, to feel that he couldn't trust him. What was he coming to, to no longer be able to trust his oldest friend? The hand of Rahl was reaching out to him, even at this distance, and making him do things he didn't want to.

When this was ended, and Kahlan was safe, and if he lived, he could go home.

Near the middle of his watch, he became suddenly aware again of the thing that followed them. He couldn't see its eyes, but he could feel them. It was on the hill opposite the camp, watching. He felt a chill run through him, at being watched.

A distant sound made him sit bolt upright. A snarl, a growl, followed by a yelp. Then silence again. Something had died. Richard's eyes were wide, trying to see, but he saw only blackness. The thing that followed had killed something. Or been killed itself. He felt an odd worry for it. As long as it had followed, it had never tried to hurt them. Of course, that didn't really mean anything. It could simply be waiting for the right time. For some reason, though, Richard didn't think it meant them any harm.

He felt the eyes again. Richard smiled; it was still alive. He had the urge to go after it, to find out what it was, but dismissed the idea. This was not the time. This was a creature of the dark. Better to meet it on his own terms.

Once more on his watch, he heard something die. Closer.

Without Richard having to go wake him, Zedd appeared for his watch, looking rested and refreshed, eating a piece of dried meat. Zedd came and sat next to him, offering a piece of meat. Richard declined.

"Zedd, what about Chase, is he all right?"

"He is well. Far as I know, he went off to follow your instructions."

"Good. I'm glad he's well." Richard hopped down off the rock, ready for some sleep.

"Richard, what did Shota tell you?"

Richard studied his friend's face in the dim light of the moon. "What Shota said to me is private. It is not for others to hear."

The edge to his own voice surprised him. "And that is the way it will remain."

Zedd took a bite while he watched Richard. "The sword has a lot of anger to it. I see you are having trouble controlling it."

"All right. All right, I'll tell you one thing Shota said. She told me she thought I ought to have a talk with you about Samuel!"

"Samuel?"

Richard gritted his teeth and leaned closer. "My predecessor!"

"Oh. That Samuel."

"Yes, that Samuel. Would you like to explain that to me? Would you like to tell me that's the way I too will end up? Or had you planned on keeping it from me until I was done doing wizard's work and you have to give the sword to some other fool!" Zedd watched calmly as Richard became more and more upset. He grabbed Zedd's robes and pulled his face close. "Wizard's First Rule! Is that how wizards find someone to take the sword? Just find someone stupid enough not to know better and there you go! A new Seeker! Do you have any other little things you forgot to tell me? Any other little unpleasant things I ought to know!"

Richard released his robes with a shove. He had to resist mightily the urge to draw the sword. His chest heaved with his anger. Zedd watched calmly.

"I'm truly sorry, my boy," he whispered, "that she has hurt you so."

Richard stared back, everything that had happened pushing in on him, extinguishing the anger. Everything seemed so hopeless. He burst into tears and fell against Zedd, throwing his arms around him. He cried in choking sobs, unable to control himself.

"Zedd, I just want to go home."

Zedd held him, patted his back gently, spoke tenderly. "I know, Richard. I know."

"I wish I had listened to you. But I can't help myself. I can't make myself stop feeling this way, no matter how hard I try. I feel like I'm drowning and can't get any air. I want this nightmare to end. I hate the Midlands. I hate the magic. I just want to go home. Zedd, I want to be rid of this sword and its magic. I never want to hear about magic again."

Zedd held him and let him cry. "Nothing is ever easy."

567

"Maybe it wouldn't be so bad if Kahlan hated me or some-thing, but I know she cares for me too. It's the magic. The magic keeps us apart."

"Believe me, Richard, I know how you feel."

Richard sank to the ground, leaned against the rock, crying. Zedd sat next to him.

"What is to become of me?"

"You will go on. There is nothing else you can do."

"I don't want to go on. And what of Samuel? Is that what is to become of me?"

Zedd shook his head. "I'm sorry, Richard. I don't know. I gave you the sword against my own heart, because I had to, for everyone else. The magic of the Sword of Truth does that to a Seeker, in the end. The prophecies say that the one who truly masters the sword's magic, and in so doing makes the blade turn white, will be protected from that fate. But I don't know how it's to be done. I don't even know what it means. I didn't have the courage to tell you. I'm sorry. If you want, you may strike me dead for what I've done to you. Only, promise me first that you will go on and stop Darken Rahl."

Richard laughed bitterly through the tears. "Strike you dead. That's a joke. You're all I have, all I'm allowed to love. How could I kill that? It's myself I should kill."

"Don't say such a thing," Zedd whispered. "Richard, I know how you feel about the magic. I walked away from it too. Some-times events happen that you have to deal with. You are all I have left. I went after the book because I didn't want you to be in danger. I would do anything to spare you hurt. But I cannot spare you this. We must stop Darken Rahl, not just for ourselves, but for all the others who have no chance."

Richard scrubbed his eyes. "I know. I won't quit until it's fin-ished. I promise. Then maybe I can give up the sword, before it's too late for me."

"Go and get some sleep. Each day will get a little better for you. If it's any consolation, although I don't know why Seekers end up like Samuel, I truly don't believe it will happen to you. But if it does, it won't happen for some time, and therefore, that can only mean you have defeated Darken Rahl, and all the peo-ple of the lands will be safe. Know that if it happens I will always take care of you. If we can stop Rahl, maybe I can help you find the secret to turning the blade white."

Richard nodded and rose to his feet, pulling his cloak around himself. "Thank you, my friend. Sorry I've been so hard on you tonight. I don't know what's gotten into me. Maybe the good spirits have deserted me. I'm sorry I can't tell you what Shota said.

"And Zedd, be careful tonight. There's something out there. It's been following us for days. I don't know what it is, I haven't had the time to snap a circle on it. But I don't think it means us harm, at least it hasn't so far, but you never know in the Midlands."

"I will be careful."

Richard started to walk away. Zedd called his name. He stopped and turned.

"Just be glad she cares for you as much as she does. If she didn't, she might have touched you."

Richard stared back at him a long moment. "I'm afraid, in a way, she already has."

Kahlan picked her way along in the dark among the rocks and trees, and found Zedd sitting on a rock, watching her come, his legs crossed under him.

"I would have come and woke you when it was time," he said.

She went and sat next to him, hugging her cloak around herself. "I know, but I couldn't sleep, so I thought I would come and sit with you."

"Did you bring anything to eat?"

She reached in her cloak, pulling out a small bundle. "Here." She smiled. "Some rabbit and biscuits."

While Zedd rubbed his hands together and started right in, she watched out into the night, thinking how to put the question she had come to ask him. It didn't take him long to finish the snack.

"Wonderful, dear one, wonderful. That's all you brought?"

Kahlan laughed. "I also brought some berries." She pulled out a cloth bundle. "I thought you might like something sweet. Can I share them with you?"

He eyed her up and down. "I guess you're small enough, you couldn't eat that many."

She laughed again and took a small handful from the open bundle in his hands. "I think I know why Richard is so good at finding food. Growing up around you, he had to be good, or he would starve."

"I would never let him starve," he protested. "I care for him too much."

"I know. Me, too."

He chewed a few berries. "I want to thank you for keeping your word."

"My word?"

Zedd peered up at her as he hunched over the bundle, eating berries one at a time. "Your word not to touch him, not to use your power on him."

"Oh." She looked off into the night, gathering her courage. "Zedd, you are the only wizard left, other than Giller. I am the last Confessor. You have lived in the Midlands, you have lived in Aydindril. You are the only one who knows what it is like to be a Confessor. I tried to explain it to Richard, but it takes a lifetime to truly understand, and then, I think none but another Confessor or a wizard can really understand."

Zedd patted her arm. "You may be right."

"I have no one. I can have no one. You can't imagine what that's like. Please, Zedd." Her eyebrows wrinkled together. "Please, can you use your magic to remove this from me? Can you take the Confessor's magic from me, and let me be a normal woman?"

She felt as if she was hanging by a thin strand over a gaping, dark, bottomless pit. She twisted on the end of the strand while she watched his eyes.

His head bent. He didn't look up. "There is only one way to release you from the magic, Mother Confessor."

Her heart leapt into her throat. "How?" she whispered.

His eyes came to hers. They were filled with pain. "I could kill you."

She felt the strand of hope break. She put all her effort to making her face show nothing, a Confessor's face, as she felt herself disappearing down into the blackness. "Thank you, wizard Zorander, for hearing my request. I didn't really think there was, I just thought I would ask. I appreciate your honesty. You better go get some sleep now."

He nodded. "First, you must tell me what Shota said."

She maintained her expression. "Ask the Seeker. It is to him she spoke; I was covered with snakes at the time."

"Snakes." Zedd lifted an eyebrow. "Shota must have liked you. I have seen her do worse."

Kahlan held his eyes. "She did worse to me, too."

"I asked Richard. He won't tell me. You must."

"You would have me step between two friends? You would ask me to betray his trust? No, thank you."

"Richard is smart, perhaps the smartest Seeker I have ever seen, but he knows very little of the Midlands. He has seen only a tiny portion of it. In some ways it's his best defense and strongest asset. He found where the last box is by going to Shota. No Seeker from the Midlands would have done that. You have spent your whole life here, you know many of the dangers. There are creatures here who could use the magic of the Sword of Truth against him. There are creatures who would suck the magic from him and kill him with it. There are dangers of every kind. We don't have the time to teach him all he needs to know, so we must protect him, so he can do his job. I must know what Shota said so I can judge if it's important; if we need to protect him."

"Zedd, please, he is my only friend. Don't ask me to betray his trust."

"Dear one, he is not your only friend. I'm your friend too. Help me protect him. I will keep it from him that you told me."

She gave him a meaningful glare. "He has an uncanny way of finding out things you wish him not to know."

Zedd gave a knowing smile at that; then his face hardened. "Mother Confessor, this is not a request, this is an order. I expect you to treat it as such."

Kahlan folded her arms, half turning away from him as she bristled. She could hardly believe he was doing this to her. She no longer had a say in the matter. "Shota said Richard was the only one who has a chance to stop Darken Rahl. She doesn't know how, or why, but he is the only one with a chance."

Zedd waited in silence. "Go on."

Kahlan gritted her teeth. "She said you would try to kill him, that you would use wizard's fire against him, and that he has a chance to beat you. There is a chance you will fail."

Silence settled around them again. "Mother Confessor . . ."

"She said that I too will use my power on him. But he has no chance against it. If I live, I will not fail."

Zedd took a deep breath. "I see why he didn't want to tell me." He thought in silence a moment. "Why didn't Shota kill you?"

Kahlan wished he would stop asking questions. She turned back to him. "She planned on it. You were there. Well, it wasn't really you, it was just an illusion, but we thought it was you. You, I mean, your image, tried to kill Shota. Richard knew she was the only way to find the box, so he, well, he protected her. He . . . well, he turned back your wizard's fire, and gave Shota a chance to . . . to use her power on you."

Zedd lifted an eyebrow. "Really . . ."

Kahlan nodded. "In return for 'saving' her, she granted him a wish. He used it to save us. He made her spare our lives. Richard wouldn't back down. Shota was not happy. She said that if he ever comes back to Agaden Reach, she will kill him."

"That boy never fails to amaze me. He really picked the information over my life?"

She was a little surprised by his smile. She nodded. "He jumped right in front of the wizard's fire. He used his sword to turn it away."

Zedd rubbed his chin. "How wondrous. That's precisely what he should have done. I had always feared he wouldn't be able to do what was necessary, if it came right down to it. I guess I need fear no longer. Then what?"

Kahlan looked down at her hands. "I wanted Shota to kill me, but she wouldn't, because she had granted him the wish. Zedd, I . . . I couldn't stand the thought of doing that to him. I begged him to kill me. I didn't want to live to carry out the prophecy, to hurt him."

She paused, and for a moment silence hung between them.

"He wouldn't do it. So I tried to. For days I tried. He took my knife away, he tied me up at night, he watched me every second. I felt like I had lost my mind. Maybe for a time, I had. At last, he convinced me that we couldn't know what the prophecy meant, or even that it wasn't he who would turn against us, and would have to be killed in order to defeat Darken Rahl. He made me see that I couldn't act on a prophecy we didn't yet understand."

"I'm very sorry, dear one, that I had to make you tell me, and for what you two have been through. But Richard is right. Prophecies are dangerous things to take too seriously."

"But a witch woman's prophecies are always true, aren't they?"

"Yes." He shrugged as he spoke softly. "But not always in the way you think. Sometimes, prophecies can even be self-fulfilling."

She gave him a puzzled look. "Really?"

"Sure. Just imagine, for the sake of illustration, that I tried to kill you because I wanted to protect Richard, from this prophecy coming true. He sees this, we fight, one of us wins, say it's him. That part of the prophecy is fulfilled, so he fears the other part will be too, and thinks he must kill you. You don't want to be killed, so you touch him to protect yourself. There you have it; prophecy fulfilled.

"The problem is, it's a self-fulfilling prophecy. Without it, none of these things would have happened. There was no outside influence other than the prophecy. Prophecies are always true, but we seldom know how." He gave her a look as if asking if she understood.

"I always thought prophecies were to be taken seriously."

"They are, but only by those who understand such things; prophecies are dangerous. The wizards guard books of prophecies, as you know. When I was at my Keep, I reread some of the pertinent books. But I don't understand most of them. There used to be wizards who did nothing else but study the books of prophecies. There are prophecies in them I have read that would scare you blind, if you knew them. They sometimes make even me wake at night in a sweat. There are things in them I think might be about Richard, that frighten me, and there are things in them

I know are about Richard, but I don't know what they will turn out to mean, and I dare not act on what I have read. We can't always know what the prophecies mean, and so they must be kept secret. Some of these could cause great trouble if people heard them."

Kahlan's eyes were wide. "Richard is in the books of prophecies? I have never met anyone before who was in the books."

He gave her an even gaze. "You are in the books too."

"Me! My name is in the books of prophecies!"

"Well, yes and no. That's not how it works. You seldom know for sure. But in this case, I do. It says things like, 'The last Mother Confessor' this, and 'The last Mother Confessor' that, but there can be no doubt who the last Mother Confessor is. It is you, Kahlan. There can also be no doubt who 'the Seeker who commands the wind against the heir to D'Hara' is. It is Richard. Heir to D'Hara is Rahl."

"Commands the wind! What does that mean?"

"I haven't the slightest idea."

Kahlan frowned and looked down as she picked at the rock. "Zedd, what does it say about me in the books of prophecies?"

He was watching her when her eyes came back up. "I'm sorry, dear one, I can't tell you that. You would be too frightened to ever sleep again."

She nodded. "I feel very foolish now, for wanting to kill myself because of Shota's prophecy. To keep it from coming true, I mean. You must think me stupid."

"Kahlan, until it comes to be, we can't know. But you shouldn't feel foolish. It could be that it's just as it says, that Richard is the only one with a chance, and you will betray us, and take him, and thus give victory to Rahl. There is a chance you should have done it to save us all."

"You are not making me feel any better."

"It could also be that Richard will somehow be a traitor, and you will save us all."

She gave him a dark look. "Either way, I don't like it."

"Prophecies are not meant for people to see. They can cause more trouble than you could believe; there have been wars over them. Even I don't understand most of them. If we had the wizards of old, the experts in the prophecies, maybe they could help us, but without them to guide us, it is best to leave Shota's prophecy be. The first page of one of the books of prophecies says: 'Take these Prophecies to mind, not to heart.' It is the only thing on the whole page, in a book half as big as a good-size table. Each letter is gilded. It is that important."

"The prophecy from Shota is different somehow, from those in books, isn't it?"

"Yes. Prophecy given directly from one to another, is meant to be an aid to that person. Shota was trying to help Richard. Shota herself wouldn't even know how it is meant to help, though; she was only the channel. Someday, it may mean something to Richard, it may aid him. There is no way to tell, though. I was hoping I would be able to understand it, and help him. He doesn't take to riddles. Unfortunately, it is of the kind called a Forked Prophecy, and I can be of no aid."

"Forked, that means it can go different ways?"

"Yes. It could mean what it says, or just about anything else. Forked Prophecies are almost always useless. Hardly better than a guess. Richard was right in his choice not to be guided by it. I would like to think it's because I have taught him well, but it could be his instinct. He had the instincts of a Seeker."

"Zedd, why don't you just tell him these things, like you have told me? Doesn't he have a right to know all this?"

Zedd stared off into the night for a long time. "It's difficult to explain. You see, Richard has a feel for things." He made an odd frown. "Have you ever shot a bow?"

Kahlan smiled. She drew her knees up, folded her fingers together over them, and rested her chin on her fingers. "Girls are not supposed to do such things. So I took it up as a diversion when I was young. Before I began taking confessions."

Zedd gave a little laugh. "Have you ever been able to feel the target? Have you ever been able to ignore all the noise in your head and hear the silence, and know where the arrow is going to go?"

She nodded with her chin still resting on her fingers. "Only a couple of times. But I know what you're talking about."

"Well, Richard can feel the target like that almost at will. Sometimes I think he could even hit it if he closed his eyes.

When I have asked him how he does it, he shrugs and can't explain. He simply says he can feel where the arrow is to go. He can do it all day long. But if I start telling him things, like how fast the wind is, how many feet away the target is, or that the bow was outside the night before and it was a humid night, affecting the draw, well, then he can't even hit the ground. The thinking interferes with the feeling.

"He does the same thing with people. He's relentless in the search for an answer. He has been heading for the box like an arrow. He has never been to the Midlands before, yet he found a way through the boundary, and has found the answers he needed to keep going, to seek out the target. That is the way of a true Seeker. The problem is, if I give him too much information, he starts doing what he thinks I want him to do, instead of what he feels. I have to point him in the right direction, toward the target, and then let him go. Let him find it himself."

"That's pretty cynical. He is a human being, not an arrow. He only does that because he thinks so much of you, and he would do anything to please you. You are an idol to him. He loves you very much."

He gave her a somber look. "There is no way I could be any more proud of him, or love him any more, but if he doesn't stop Darken Rahl, I will be a dead idol. Sometimes, wizards must use people to accomplish what must be done."

"I guess I know how you feel, not telling him what you wish you could."

Zedd rose. "I'm sorry the two of you have had a hard time of it. Maybe with me here, it will be easier. Good night, dear one." He started off into the darkness.

"Zedd?" He stopped and looked back toward her, a dark form against the moonlit forest. "You had a wife."

"I did."

She cleared her throat and swallowed. "What was it like? Loving someone more than life itself, and being able to be with them, and having them love you back?"

Zedd stood still and silent for a long time, staring at her in the darkness. She waited, wishing she could see his face. She decided he wasn't going to answer.

Kahlan held her chin up. "Wizard Zorander, I am not making a request. This is an order. You will answer the question."

She waited. His voice came softly. "It was like finding the other half of myself, and being complete, whole, for the first time in my life."

"Thank you, Zedd." She was glad he couldn't see her tears as she struggled to hold her voice steady. "I was just wondering."

CHAPTER 37

RICHARD WOKE WHEN HE heard Kahlan come back and toss some wood in the fire. Light was just starting to creep across the tips of distant mountains, casting them in a soft pink glow, dark clouds behind making the snowcapped peaks stand out all the more. Zedd lay on his back, eyes wide open, snoring. Richard rubbed the sleep from his eyes and yawned.

"How about some tava-root porridge?" he whispered, wanting to let Zedd sleep.

"Sounds good," she whispered back.

Richard pulled the roots from his pack and began peeling them with his knife while Kahlan retrieved a pot.

When he finished cutting them up, he tossed the roots in with the water she had added from a skin. "This is the last of them. We'll have to start digging some more roots tonight, but I doubt we'll find tava. Not in this rocky ground."

"I picked some berries."

Together they warmed their hands at the fire. More than a queen, he thought. He tried to imagine a queen in fine robes and a crown, picking berries.

"You see anything while you were on watch?"

She shook her head. Then she seemed to remember something and her face came up. "But one time, I did hear something strange. It was down here, near the camp. It was like a growl, then a yelp. I almost came and woke you, but it was gone as soon as it started, and I didn't hear it again."

"Really." He glanced over each shoulder. "Down here. Wonder what that was about. I guess I was so tired it didn't wake me."

Richard mashed the pot of roots when they were done and added a little sugar. Kahlan dished up the porridge and added a big handful of berries on top of each.

"Why don't you wake him," she said.

Richard smiled. "Watch this."

He tapped his spoon a few times against the side of the tin bowl. Zedd made a short snort, and sat bolt upright.

The old man blinked twice. "Breakfast?"

With their backs to him, they both giggled.

"You're in a good mood this morning," she said, looking over.

He smiled. "Zedd's back with us."

Richard walked over and handed Zedd a bowl of porridge, then sat with his own on the low ledge. Kahlan made herself comfortable on the ground, wrapping a blanket around her legs while she balanced her bowl with one hand. Zedd didn't bother to unwrap himself from his blanket as he ate. Richard waited, biding his time, eating slowly while Zedd bolted his porridge.

"Good!" Zedd proclaimed as he rose to get himself another bowlful from the pot.

Richard waited until his old friend was spooning from the pot, then said, "Kahlan told me what happened. I mean, she told me about how you made her tell you about Shota."

Kahlan froze with a look as if she had been struck by lightning.

Zedd flinched up straight and spun to her. "Why did you tell him! I thought you didn't want him to know you . . ."

"Zedd . . . I never . . ."

Zedd's face grimaced. He turned slowly to Richard, who hunched over his bowl, methodically spooning porridge into his mouth.

579

He didn't bother to look up. "She didn't tell me. But you just did."

Richard put the last spoonful in his mouth, and after he swallowed he licked his spoon clean and dropped it in the tin bowl with a clank.

His face, calm and triumphant, came up to the wizard's squinting eyes. "Wizard's First Rule," Richard announced with a wisp of a smile. "The first step to believing something is wanting to believe it is true . . . or being afraid it is."

"I told you," Kahlan fumed at Zedd. "I told you he would find out."

Zedd paid her no attention; his eyes were locked on Richard.

"I thought about it last night," Richard explained as he set down his bowl. "I decided you were right, that you should know what Shota said. After all, you're a wizard, maybe there's something in it you could help us with to stop Darken Rahl. I knew you wouldn't rest until you knew what had happened. I decided I would tell you today, but then I figured you would get it out of Kahlan first, one way or another."

Kahlan fell back on the blanket, laughing.

Zedd straightened his back and put his fists on his hips. "Bags! Richard, do you have any idea what you have just done?"

"Magic," Richard smiled. "A trick, if done properly, is magic." He shrugged. "Or so I've been told."

Zedd nodded slowly. "Indeed." He pointed a thin finger skyward, the sparkle returning to his intense hazel eyes. "You have tricked a wizard with his own rule. Not one of my wizards was ever able to do that." He stepped closer, a grin spreading on his face. "Bags, Richard! You have it! You have the gift, my boy! You can be a wizard of the First Order, like me."

Richard frowned. "I don't want to be a wizard."

Zedd ignored his words. "You have passed the first test."

"You just said none of the other wizards was able to do it, so how could they be wizards if they couldn't pass the test?"

Zedd gave him a one-sided smile. "They were wizards of the Third Order. One, Giller, is of the Second Order. None were able to pass the tests to be a wizard of the First Order. They didn't have the gift. Only the calling."

Richard made a smirk. "It was just a trick. Don't make something out of it that it wasn't."

"A very special trick." Zedd's eyes narrowed again. "I'm impressed. I'm also very proud of you."

"And how many of these tests are there, if this is the first?"

Zedd shrugged. "Oh, I don't know. Maybe a few hundred or so. But you have the gift, Richard." A shadow of worry passed across his eyes, as if he hadn't expected it. "You must learn to control it, or . . ." His eyes lit up again. "I will teach you. You really could be a wizard of the First Order."

Richard realized he was starting to listen too closely, and shook his head to clear it. "I told you, I don't want to be a wizard." He added under his breath, "I don't want anything to do with magic ever again when this is over." He realized that Kahlan was staring at him. He looked from one wide-eyed face to another. "It was just a stupid little trick. Nothing more."

"Just a stupid little trick if done on someone else. No small trick, if done on a wizard."

Richard rolled his eyes. "The both of you are . . ."

Zedd leaned forward eagerly, cutting him off. "Can you command the wind?"

Richard leaned back a little. "Of course I can," he said, playing along. He held both hands up to the sky. "Come to me, brother wind! Gather about! Blow a gale for me!" He spread his arms dramatically.

Kahlan wrapped her cloak around herself expectantly. Zedd looked about. Nothing happened. The two of them seemed a little disappointed.

"What's the matter with the two of you?" Richard scowled. "Did you eat some bad berries?"

Zedd turned to her. "He must learn that later."

Kahlan considered what Zedd said, then looked up at Richard. "Richard . . . to be a wizard, it's not an offer made to many."

Zedd scrubbed his hands together. "Bags! I wish I had the books here with me now. I'd bet a dragon's tooth they have something to say about this." His face darkened. "But then there is the matter of the pain . . . and . . ."

Richard squirmed uncomfortably. "And just what kind of wizard are you anyway? You don't even have a beard."

Zedd came out of his own thoughts and frowned. "What?"

"A beard. Where's your beard? I've been wondering about it ever since I found out you were a wizard. Wizards are supposed to have beards, you know."

"Who told you this?"

"Well . . . I don't know. Everybody knows it. Wizards are supposed to have beards. It's common knowledge. I'm surprised you don't know it."

Zedd made a face as if he had just sucked on a lemon. "But I hate beards. They itch."

Richard shrugged. "Seems you don't know as much as you think you do about being a wizard, if you don't even know wizards are supposed to have beards."

Zedd folded his arms. "A beard is it?" He unfolded his arms, and began drawing his fingers and thumb down opposite sides of his chin. As he drew his fingers repeatedly, whiskers began appearing. The more he did this, the longer the whiskers grew. Richard watched, wide-eyed, until a snow white beard reached to the middle of Zedd's chest.

Zedd cocked his head and gave Richard an intent look. "Will this do, my boy?"

Richard realized his mouth was open. He made it shut, but could only nod.

Zedd scratched his chin and neck. "Good. Now give me your knife, so I can shave this thing off. It itches like ants."

"My knife? What do you need my knife for? Why don't you just make it disappear like you made it appear?"

Kahlan gave a little laugh, then made her face straight when he glanced at her.

"It doesn't work that way. Everyone knows it doesn't work that way," Zedd mocked. He turned to Kahlan. "Doesn't everyone know? You tell him."

"Magic can only do things that use what is there. It cannot undo things that have happened."

"I don't understand."

Zedd peered at him with sharp eyes. "Your first lesson, should you ever decide to become a wizard. The three of us all have magic. It is all Additive Magic. Additive Magic uses what is there, and adds to it, or uses it somehow. The magic Kahlan has uses the spark of love in a person, no matter how small, and adds to it until it's changed into something else. The magic of the Sword of Truth uses your anger, and adds to it, takes power from it, until it becomes something else.

"I do the same thing. I can use whatever I need in nature to change things. I can change a bug to a flower, I can change a fear to a monster, I can make a broken bone knit, I can take heat from the air around us and add to it, multiply it, into wizard's fire. I can make my beard grow. But, I can't make it ungrow." A rock big as his fist started rising into the air. "I can lift something. I can change it." The rock crushed to dust.

"Then, you can do anything," Richard whispered.

"No. I can lift or crush or move the rock, but I can't make it vanish. Where would it go? That's called Subtractive Magic: the undoing of things. My magic, Kahlan's magic, the sword's magic, is from this world. All magic from this world is Additive Magic. Darken Rahl can do any of it I can." Zedd's expression turned dark. "Subtractive Magic is from the underworld. Darken Rahl knows how to use that too. I don't."

"Is it as powerful as Additive Magic?"

"Subtractive Magic is the counter to Additive. As night is to day. Yet it is all part of the same thing. The Magic of Orden is the magic of both. Additive and Subtractive. It can add to the world, and it can take the world to nothing. To open the boxes, you must be a master of both magics. People never worried about it ever happening, because no one was ever able to tap Subtractive Magic. But Darken Rahl commands it as easily as I command the Additive."

"And how do you suppose that came to be?" Richard asked with a frown.

"I have no idea. But it troubles me greatly."

Richard drew a deep breath. "Well, I still think you are getting worked up over nothing. All I did was a little trick."

Zedd gave him a serious glare. "If done on a normal person, it would have been as you say. But I'm a wizard. I know how the Wizard's Rules work. You would not have been able to do this to me, except with magic of your own. I have taught many to be wizards. I have had to teach them to do what you have done. They could not do it without learning it first. Once in a great while, one is born with the gift. I was one such as this. Richard, you have the gift too. Sooner or later you will have to learn to control it." He put out his hand. "Now, give me the knife so I can rid myself of this ridiculous beard."

Richard put the knife handle in Zedd's hand. "The blade is dull. I've been digging roots with it. It's too dull to shave with."

"Really?" Zedd pinched the edge of the blade between his thumb and forefinger, drawing them along the length of the knife. He turned the knife around and held it delicately between his thumb and two fingers. Richard grimaced at him shaving dry. With a light stroke, a swath of beard fell away.

"You just used Subtractive Magic! You made some of the edge go away to sharpen it."

Zedd arched an eyebrow. "No, I used what was already there, and re-formed the edge, making it sharp again."

Richard shook his head and went about gathering up their things while Zedd shaved off the beard. Kahlan helped put things away.

"You know, Zedd," Richard said as he picked up the bowls, "I think you're getting too obstinate in your ways. I think when this is over, you need someone. Someone to take care of you, help keep your perspectives straight. Put the light of day to your imagination. I think you need a wife."

"A wife?"

"Sure. I think that's what you need. Maybe you should go back and take another look at Adie."

"Adie?"

"Yes, Adie," Richard scolded. "You remember Adie. The woman with one foot."

"Oh, I remember Adie quite well." He gave Richard his most innocent look. "But Adie has two good feet, not one."

Richard and Kahlan both came to their feet in a rush. "What?"

"Yes," Zedd smiled, turning away. "Seems it grew back." He bent, pulling an apple from Richard's pack. "Quite unexpectedly."

Richard took Zedd's sleeve and turned him around. "Zedd, you ..."

The wizard smiled. "Are you thoroughly sure you wouldn't like to be a wizard?" He took a bite of the apple, pleased at seeing the astonishment on Richard's face. Zedd handed him the knife, the blade as sharp as he had ever seen it.

Richard shook his head and turned to his work. "I just want to go home and be a guide. Nothing more." He thought awhile, then asked, "Zedd, all the time I grew up with you, you were a wizard and I never knew. You didn't use the magic. How could you stand not to? Why didn't you?"

"Ah, well, there are dangers to using the magic. Also, pain."

"Dangers? Like what?"

Zedd regarded him for a moment. "You have used magic, with the sword. You tell me."

"But that's the sword, that's different. What dangers are there for a wizard in using the magic? And what pain?"

Zedd gave a small, sly smile. "Only just finished with the first lesson, and already he is eager for the second."

Richard straightened. "Never mind." He hoisted the pack onto his back. "All I want to be is a woods guide."

Apple in hand, Zedd started toward the trail. "So you have told me." He took a big bite. "Now, I want you two to tell me everything that has happened since I was knocked unconscious. Don't leave out a thing, no matter how trivial."

Richard and Kahlan exchanged a crimson look. "I won't tell if you don't," he whispered.

She held him back with a hand on his arm. "I swear, not a word about what happened in the spirit house."

By the look in her eyes, he knew she meant to keep her word.

For the rest of the day as they trudged along the trails, keeping off the main roads, the two of them told Zedd the stories of everything that had happened since they were attacked that day at the boundary. Zedd made them go back to previous events at the oddest places in a story. Working off each other's words, Richard and Kahlan managed to weave the story of the Mud People without mention of anything that happened between them in the spirit house.

As they drew nearer to Tamarang, they crisscrossed roads, and began to see refugees carrying their belongings on their backs, or on small carts. Richard saw to it that they didn't stay long in the sight of people, and placed himself between them and Kahlan whenever he could. He didn't want anyone recognizing the

Mother Confessor. He was relieved each time they were back in the woods. The forest was where he was most comfortable, even though it had proven its dangers to them.

Late in the day, they had to take to the main road in order to cross the Callisidrin River. It was too big and swift to risk fording, so they took the big wooden bridge. Zedd and Richard kept Kahlan protectively between them as they walked among the people crossing the bridge. Kahlan kept the hood of her cloak up so people wouldn't see her long hair. Most of the people were headed for Tamarang, seeking shelter and safety from the marauding forces, supposedly sweeping in from Westland. Kahlan said that they would reach Tamarang by the middle of the next day. From now on they would have to travel most of the time on the road. Richard knew that they would have to move far from the road at night to be clear of any people. He began watching the sun so as to leave them time to move deep enough into the forest before it became too dark.

"Does that feel good?"

Rachel pretended Sara answered that it did, and tucked a little more grass around her doll to be doubly sure she was warm enough. She nestled the loaf of bread with the cloth tied around it next to Sara.

"You'll be warm for now. I have to go get some wood before it's too dark, and then we'll have a fire. Then we can both be warm."

She left Sara with the bread in the wayward pine and went outside. The sun was down, but it was still light enough to see. The clouds were a pretty pink. She looked at them once in a while as she picked up sticks, holding them against her body with the other arm. She checked her pocket to be sure the fire stick was still there. She had almost forgotten it last night, and was scared now, unless she checked to make sure she hadn't forgotten it again.

She looked up again at the pretty clouds. Just as she did, some big dark thing swooped low over the trees a little way up the hill.

It must be some big bird, she thought. Ravens were big, and dark. It must be one of those noisy ravens. She picked up some more sticks. Then she saw a bunch of blueberry bushes, low against the ground in an open place, their leaves starting to turn a flaming red. She threw the sticks down.

She was so hungry, she sat down on the berry bushes and started eating them as fast as she could pick. It was getting late in the year, and the berries were starting to get dry and shriveled, but they were still good. In fact, they tasted wonderful. She started putting one in her pocket for each one she ate. She moved on her hands and knees, picking berries, eating them, and putting them in her pocket. It was getting darker. Once in a while, she looked up at the pretty clouds. They were getting a darker color. Purple.

When her stomach felt better, and her pocket was full, she picked the sticks up and went back to the wayward pine. Once back inside, she untied the cloth that was around the bread and dumped the berries from her pocket onto the cloth. She sat down and ate the berries off the cloth as she chatted with Sara, offering to share her berries as she ate. Sara didn't eat many. Rachel wished she had a mirror. She wished she could look in a mirror at her hair. Earlier in the day, she had seen herself in a dark pool. Her hair looked so wonderful, all even. Richard was such a nice man to cut it for her.

She missed Richard. She wished he were here now, to run away with her, to hug her. He gave the bestest hugs in the whole world. If Kahlan weren't so mean, he could give her hugs too. Kahlan would find out then how wonderful his hugs were. For some reason, Rachel missed her, too. Her stories, and her songs, and her fingers on her forehead. Why did she have to be so mean and say she was going to hurt Giller? Giller was one of the nicest men in the world. Giller gave her Sara.

Rachel broke the sticks as best she could, so they would fit in the circle of stones she had made. After stacking them carefully, she pulled out the fire stick.

"Light for me."

She set the fire stick down on the cloth with the berries and then warmed her hands and ate a few berries while she told Sara some of her troubles, how she wished Richard were hugging her, how she wished Kahlan weren't mean, how she hoped Kahlan didn't hurt Giller, how she wished she had something other than berries to eat.

Some bug bit her on the neck. She let out a little squeal and swatted it. There was a little bit of blood on her hand when she took it away. And a fly.

"Look, Sara. Look at how that stupid fly bit me. It made blood."

Sara seemed sorry for her sting. Rachel ate a few more berries.

Another fly bit her neck. Rachel swatted it, not squealing this time. There was another spot of blood on her hand.

"That hurt!" she told Sara. With a frown, she threw the squished fly in the fire.

The fly that bit her on the arm made her jump. She slapped it flat. Another bit her neck. Rachel flailed at the flies in the air around her face. Two more bit her neck, making blood before she smacked them. Tears welled up in her eyes from the pain of the stings.

"Get away!" she yelled as she waved her hands around.

Some were inside her dress, biting her chest and back. More bit her neck.

Rachel started screaming as she batted at the flies, trying to get them off. Tears streamed down her cheeks. A fly bit the inside of her ear, making her scream even louder. The sound of it buzzing in her ear made her cry and scream as she dug with her finger, trying to get it out. She thrashed her arms as she yelled.

Rachel screamed in a high pitch as she stumbled out of the wayward pine, wiping flies off her eyes. She ran, arms lashing out, trying to get the flies away. The flies followed her as she ran and screamed.

Something in front of her made her stop dead in her tracks.

Her wide eyes worked their way up the giant, fur-covered body of the thing. Its belly was pink, and had flies on it.

Against the fading colors of the sky, it slowly unfolded huge wings, spreading them wide. Not wings covered with feathers, wings covered with skin. Rachel could see big blood veins in them, throbbing.

With all her courage, she put her shaking hand in her pocket. The fire stick wasn't there. Her legs wouldn't move. She didn't even feel the flies that were biting her. She heard a sound like a cat purring, but a lot louder. Her eyes went up further.

Glowing green eyes glared down at her. The purring sound was a low growl.

The mouth opened with a louder growl, lips pulling back, showing its long, curved teeth.

Rachel couldn't run. She couldn't move. She couldn't even scream. She shook as her wide eyes looked up into those mean eyes that glowed green. She forgot how to move her feet.

A big claw reached for her.

She felt something warm running down her legs.

CHAPTER 38

RICHARD FOLDED HIS ARMS and leaned back against the rock. "Enough!"

Zedd and Kahlan both turned their heads, seeming to have forgotten he was even there. He had been listening to the two of them arguing for at least the last half hour as they sat in front of the fire, and was tired of it. In fact, he was just plain tired. Dinner was long since done and they should be getting some sleep, but instead they were trying to decide what they would do tomorrow when they reached Tamarang. Now, instead of arguing, they started presenting their cases to him.

"I say we march in there and I deal with Giller. He is my student. I will get him to tell me what's going on. I'm still Wizard of the First Order. He will do as I say. He will give me the box."

Kahlan pulled her Confessor's dress from her pack and held it up to Richard. "This is the way we deal with Giller. He is my wizard and he will do as I say because he knows the consequences."

Richard let out a deep breath as he rubbed his eyes with his fingertips. "You both want to eat a chicken we haven't even plucked yet. We aren't even sure whose chicken it is."

"What do you mean?" Kahlan asked.

Richard leaned forward. Now he had their attention, at last. "At the very least, Tamarang is giving a sympathetic ear to D'Hara. At the very worst, Darken Rahl is there. Most likely, the fact is somewhere between the two. If we march in there and tell them what we want, they might not like it. Tamarang has a whole standing army to express to us how much they don't like it. Then what? Are the three of us going to fight a war with their army? How is this going to get us the box? How is it going to even get us to Giller? If we have to fight, I'd rather it be on the way out, not on the way in."

Richard expected one of them to express some sort of objection while they sat as if being scolded, but neither did, so he went on.

"Maybe Giller is waiting and hoping someone will come, so he can help them get away with the box. Then again, maybe he will not be so willing to part company with it. But we won't know if we never make it to him, now, will we?" He addressed Zedd. "You told me the box has magic, and a wizard, or Rahl, can feel that magic, but a wizard can also cover the feeling of that magic with a wizard's web, so the box can't be detected. That could be why Queen Milena wanted a wizard—to hide the box from Rahl, and use it as a bargaining tool. If we create a big commotion, and scare Giller, no matter how he feels about us, he may be frightened, and use the opportunity to escape. It could also be that Rahl is just waiting for the quarry to be flushed from cover, and then he will pounce."

Zedd turned to Kahlan. "I think the Seeker has some good points. Perhaps we should hear him out?"

Kahlan smiled a little. "I believe you are correct, good wizard." She turned to Richard. "What is your way?"

"You've dealt with this Queen Milena before, right? What sort of person is she?"

Kahlan needed no time to give it any thought. "Tamarang is a minor and relatively insignificant land. Still, Queen Milena is as pompous and arrogant as any queen comes."

"A small snake, but a snake that can kill us nonetheless," Richard noted.

Kahlan nodded. "But a snake with a big head."

"Small snakes have to be careful, cautious, when they don't know what they are up against. The first thing we have to do, is to give her a worry. Make her unsure enough not to bite us."

"What do you mean?" Kahlan asked.

"You said you've dealt with her before. Confessors go to the lands to take confessions, and to inspect the prisons, to find out what they will. She wouldn't want to close Tamarang to a Confessor, would she?"

"Not if she has half a brain," Zedd chuckled.

"Well, that's what we do then. You put your dress back on, and do your duty. Simply a Confessor doing what Confessors are expected to do. She may not like it, but she will treat you well; she will want you to be happy. She will want you to see what you will, and then be on your way. The last thing she will want is to raise a fuss. So, you inspect her dungeon, smile, or frown, or whatever it is you do, and then before we're on our way, you say you want to speak to your former wizard."

"You think she should go alone?" Zedd protested.

"No. Kahlan doesn't have a wizard with her; the Queen would see that as a tempting vulnerability. We don't want her mouth to water."

Zedd folded his arms. "I will be her wizard."

"No, you will not be her wizard! Darken Rahl is killing people as we speak, looking for you. If you remove the wizard's web, let them know who you are, we'll have trouble down around our ears before we can get away with the box. Who knows what reward there is on your wrinkled hide. You will be her protection, but you will be anonymous protection. You will be . . ." Richard tapped the sword hilt, thinking. His eyes came back down. "You will be a cloud reader. A trusted advisor to the Mother Confessor in the absence of a wizard." Richard frowned slightly at Zedd's grumble. "I'm sure you know how to play the part."

"Then you will hide your sword, your identity, from her as well?" Kahlan asked.

"No. The presence of the Seeker will give her pause, something else to worry about, something to keep her fangs in her mouth until we're away. The whole point is to give her something she's familiar with, a Confessor, so as not to raise an alarm. At the same time, give her something to keep her worried, a cloud reader and the Seeker, so she would rather be rid of us than find out what sort of trouble we might be able to cause. The way you two want to do it gets us in a fight, a fight where one or all of us could be hurt. My way puts us at minimum risk of a fight, and if it comes, at least it will be when we're on our way out with the box." He gave each of them a stern look. "You do remember the box, don't you? In case you've forgotten, that is what we're after, not Giller's head in a basket. Whose side he's on is not an issue. We must only get the box, no more."

Kahlan folded her arms with a frown; Zedd rubbed his chin while he looked into the fire. Richard let them mull it over for a while. He knew that the way they wanted to do it was sure to cause trouble, and that soon enough they would both realize it.

Zedd turned back to him. "Of course you are right. I agree." His thin face turned to Kahlan. "Mother Confessor?"

She studied Zedd's face a moment before looking up at Richard. "Agreed. But Richard, the two of you will have to play the part of courtiers to the Mother Confessor. Zedd knows the protocol, but you don't."

"I hope not to be there long. Just tell me what I need to know to get by for a short time."

Kahlan drew a deep breath. "Well, I guess the most important thing is to look like you are part of my escort, be . . . respectful." She cleared her throat, diverting her eyes. "Just pretend like I am the most important person you have ever been around, and treat me in that manner, and no one will question. Every Confessor allows her attendants different liberties, and as long as you are deferential, no one will think anything of it if you should happen to do something not quite proper. Even if you think my behavior . . . odd, just play along. All right?"

Richard watched her a moment while she studied the ground. He rose to his feet. "It would be my honor, Mother Confessor." He gave a bow.

Zedd cleared his throat. "A little deeper, my boy. You are not traveling with a mere Confessor. You are an escort to the Mother Confessor herself."

"All right," Richard sighed. "I'll do my best. Now, get some sleep. I'll take first watch." He started walking toward the trees.

"Richard," Zedd called after him. He stopped, turning back. "There are many in the Midlands who have magic. Many different, and dangerous, types of magic. There is no telling what manner of sycophants Queen Milena has surrounded herself with. You pay attention to what Kahlan and I tell you, and do your best not to cross anyone. You may not know who, or what, her attendants are."

Richard drew his cloak around himself. "In and out with minimum fuss. That's what I want too. If all goes well, tomorrow at this time we will have the box and our only worry will be to find a hole to hide in until winter."

"Good. You have it right, my boy. Good night."

In a spot thin of brush, Richard found a moss-covered log to sit on while he kept an eye toward the camp and the surrounding woods. He checked to make sure the moss was dry. He didn't want to sit in damp moss and then have wet pants to make him colder. The moss was dry, so he rearranged his sword, sat down, and wrapped his cloak tight. Clouds hid the moon. If it wasn't for the fire lending the little illumination it did to the surrounding woods, it would be the kind of dark that made you think you were blind.

Richard sat and brooded. He didn't like the idea of Kahlan having to put on the dress and put herself at risk. He liked it less that it was his own idea. He wondered, and worried, at what she meant about her acting "odd," and his playing along. He wondered, and worried even more at what she had said about pretending she was the most important person he had ever been around. He liked that not at all. He always pictured Kahlan in his mind as his friend, at the least. He didn't like to picture her as the Mother Confessor. It was Confessor's magic that made it impossible for them to be more than friends. He was afraid to see her as others saw her, as the Mother Confessor. Any reminder of what she was, her magic, only brought the hurt deeper into his heart.

It was the smallest of sounds that made him sit bolt upright.

The eyes were on him. They were close, and though he couldn't see them, he could feel them. The knowledge that something was close, watching him, sent a chill across his skin. It made him feel naked. Vulnerable.

His eyes were wide, his heart pounding, as he looked straight ahead to where he knew the thing was. The silence, except for his heart beating in his ears, was oppressive. Richard held his breath, trying to hear.

Again came the soft sound of a foot being lowered stealthily to the forest floor. It was coming toward him. Richard's wide eyes stared frantically into the blackness, trying to see a movement.

It was no more than ten paces away when the yellow eyes inched into view, hunkered low to the ground. The eyes were glowering right at him. The thing stopped. He held his breath.

With a howl, it sprang. Richard jumped to his feet, his hand going for the sword. When it bounded into the air, Richard saw that it was a wolf. The biggest wolf he had ever seen. It was to him before his hand even reached the hilt. The wolf's front paws hit his chest square. The powerful impact drove him backward over the log he had been sitting on.

As he fell backward, his breath knocked from him, he saw behind him something more frightening than the wolf.

A heart hound.

The huge jaws snapped at his chest just as the wolf reached the heart hound and went for its throat.

Richard's head hit something hard. He heard a yelp and the sound of teeth ripping tendon. Everything went black.

His eyes opened. Zedd was looking down at him, and had a middle finger to each side of Richard's forehead. Kahlan was holding a torch. He felt dizzy, but stood anyway on wobbly legs, until Kahlan made him sit on the log.

With a frown of concern, she stroked her fingers on his face. "Are you all right?"

"I think so," he managed. "My head . . . it hurts." He thought he might throw up.

Zedd took the torch from Kahlan and held it behind the log, casting light on the body of a heart hound, its throat ripped out. Zedd looked down at Richard's sword, still in its sheath.

"How is it the hound didn't have you?"

Richard felt the back of his head; it hurt like daggers twisting.

"I . . . don't know. It all happened so fast." Then he remembered, like a dream when waking. He stood up again. "A wolf! It was a wolf that has been following us."

Kahlan stepped closer and put an arm around his waist to steady him. "A wolf?" The odd tone of suspicion in her voice made him look to her narrowed eyes. "Are you sure?"

Richard nodded. "I was sitting here, and then all of a sudden I knew it was watching me. It came closer, and I saw its yellow eyes. Then it leapt at me. I thought it was attacking. It knocked me flat, right over the log. I never even had time to draw the sword, it was so fast. But it wasn't attacking me. It was going for the heart hound behind me, protecting me. I never even saw the heart hound until I was falling backward. It must have killed the hound. That wolf saved my life."

Kahlan straightened herself and put her fists on her hips. "Brophy!" she called into the darkness. "Brophy! I know you're out there. Come here this instant!"

The wolf trotted into the torchlight with its head down and its tail between its legs. Its thick fur was a charcoal color from the tip of its nose to the tip of its tail. Fierce yellow eyes glowed from its dark head. The wolf dropped to its belly and crawled to Kahlan's feet. Once there, it rolled onto its back with paws in the air, and whined.

"Brophy!" she admonished. "Have you been following us?"

"Only to protect you, Mistress."

Richard's jaw dropped. He wondered how hard he had been hit on the head. "He can talk! I heard him! That wolf can talk!"

Zedd and Kahlan both looked up at his wide eyes. Zedd glanced at her. "I thought you said you told him."

Kahlan winced a little. "Well, I guess I didn't remember to tell him everything." She frowned at Zedd. "It's hard to remember everything he doesn't know. We have lived it our whole lives. You just forget he hasn't."

"Come on," Zedd grumbled. "Let's go back to the camp. All of us."

The wizard led them with the torch, Kahlan following, the wolf slinking along at her side, ears lowered, tail dragging the ground.

When they sat around the fire, Richard addressed the wolf as it sat on its haunches next to Kahlan. "Wolf, I guess . . ."

"Brophy. The name's Brophy."

Richard sat back a little. "Brophy. Sorry. My name is Richard, and this is Zedd. Brophy, I would like to thank you for saving my life."

"Don't mention it," he growled.

"Brophy," Kahlan said in a disapproving voice, "what are you doing here?"

The wolf's ears flattened. "There is danger for you. I have been protecting you."

"You have been released," she scolded.

"Was that you, last night?" Richard asked.

Brophy regarded him with yellow eyes. "Yes. Whenever you camped, I cleared the area of heart hounds. And a few other nasty things. Last night, close to morning, one came near to your camp. I took care of it. This hound tonight was hunting you. He could hear your heart beating. I knew Mistress Kahlan would be unhappy if he ate you, so I kept him from doing it."

Richard swallowed hard. "Thank you," he said in a weak voice.

"Richard," Zedd asked, rubbing his chin, "the hounds are underworld beasts. They haven't bothered you up until now. What's changed?"

Richard almost choked. "Well, Adie gave Kahlan a bone to carry, to get us through the boundary, and to protect us from underworld beasts. I had an old bone, that my father gave me, and Adie said it would do the same thing. But I lost it a day or two ago."

Zedd's face was wrinkled up in thought. Richard looked to the wolf, hoping to change the subject. "How come you can talk?"

Brophy drew his long tongue around his lips. "Same reason you can talk. I can talk because . . ." He looked up at Kahlan. "You mean he doesn't know what I am?"

She gave him a look, and he sank to the ground, resting his head on his paws.

Kahlan locked her fingers around a knee, clicking her thumbnails together. "Richard, do you remember when I told you that sometimes, when we took a confession, the person turned out to

597

be innocent? And once in a great while, one who was to be executed would ask to give a confession so as to prove his innocence?" Richard nodded. She cast an eye to the wolf. "Brophy was to be executed for killing a little boy. . . ."

"I don't kill children," the wolf growled, coming to his feet.

"Do you wish to tell the story?"

The wolf sank back down. "No, Mistress."

"Brophy would have rather been touched by a Confessor's power than be thought a child killer. Not to mention what else was done to that little boy. He requested a Confessor. It's something done only rarely—most men choose the executioner—but it meant that much to him. I told you we have a wizard with us, when we take confessions. One reason is for protection, but there is another reason. In a case like this, where the person is unjustly accused, and found to be innocent, he is still left touched by our power, he cannot be returned to who he was. So, the wizard changes him to something else. The changing takes away some of the magic, of the Confessor, and gives him enough concern for himself to start over with a new life."

Richard was incredulous. "You were innocent? And yet you are to be left like this? For life?"

"Completely innocent," Brophy confirmed.

"Brophy." Kahlan spoke his name in a rising tone Richard was familiar with.

The wolf sank back down. "Of killing that boy." His cowering eyes looked up at Kahlan as she watched him. "That's all I meant. Innocent of killing that boy."

Richard frowned. "What does that mean?"

Kahlan looked over to him. "It means that when he gave his confession, he confessed to other things he was not accused of. You see, Brophy had been engaged in occupations of a dubious nature." She glanced down at the wolf. "At the gray edges of law."

"I was an honest businessman," the wolf protested.

Kahlan cast an eye toward Brophy while she spoke to Richard. "Brophy was a trader."

"My father was a trader," Richard said, his anger rising.

"I don't know what traders in Westland trade, but in the Midlands, some traders deal in things of magic."

Richard thought about the Book of Counted Shadows. "So what?"

Kahlan lifted an eyebrow to him. "Some of them happen to be alive at the time."

Brophy rose up on his front paws. "How am I to tell? You can't always tell. Sometimes, you think something is just an artifact, like a book, that a collector will pay handsomely for. Sometimes it's something more, a stone, a statue, or a staff, or perhaps a . . . Well, how am I to know if they are alive?"

Kahlan still had her eye on the wolf. "You traded things of magic other than books and statues," she scolded. "In this innocent business of his, he would also get himself into disagreements with people. Disagreements such as rights of ownership. When Brophy was a man, he was as big for a man as he is for a wolf. He sometimes used his size to 'persuade' people to do as he wished. Is this not true, Brophy?"

The wolf's ears wilted. "It's true, Mistress. I have a temper. A temper as big as my muscles. But it only came out when I was wronged. A lot of people think they can cheat traders; they think we are little more than thieves and will not stand up for ourselves. When I settled disagreements with my temper, they tended to stay settled."

Kahlan gave the wolf a little smile. "Brophy had a reputation that, although not unearned, was larger than the truth." She looked up at Richard. "The business he was in was dangerous, and therefore very profitable. Brophy made enough money at it to support his 'hobby.' Almost no one knew about it until after I touched him, and he made his confession."

The wolf put his paws over his head. "Oh, Mistress, please! Must we?"

Richard frowned. "What was this 'hobby'?"

Kahlan's smile widened. "Brophy had a weakness. Children. As he traveled around in search of things to trade, he would stop at orphanages and see to it they had what they needed to take care of the children. All the gold he made ended up in different orphanages, so the children could be cared for, and not go hungry. He twisted the arms of the people running the orphanages, to swear them to secrecy. He didn't want anyone knowing. Of course, he didn't have to twist very hard."

Brophy's paws were still over his head, and his eyes squeezed tightly shut. "Mistress, please," he whined, "I have a reputation." He opened his eyes and rose up on his front paws. "And a well-earned one at that! I've broken my share of arms and noses! I've done some pretty despicable deeds!"

Kahlan lifted an eyebrow to him. "Yes, you have. Some were reason enough to get you thrown in prison for a time. But none were reason enough to chop off your head." She looked back up at Richard. "You see, since Brophy had been seen around orphanages, and because of his reputation, no one was too surprised when he was accused of the murder of a little boy."

"Demmin Nass," Brophy growled. "Accused by Demmin Nass." His lips curled back, showing his long teeth as he growled.

"Why didn't the people at the orphanages stand up for you?"

"Demmin Nass," Brophy growled again. "He would have slit their throats."

"Who is this Demmin Nass?"

Kahlan exchanged a look with the wolf. "Remember when Darken Rahl came to the Mud People, and he took Siddin? Remember when he said Siddin was a gift for a friend? Demmin Nass is that friend." She gave Richard a meaningful look. "Demmin Nass has a very sick interest in little boys."

Richard felt a stab of fear, and pain, for Siddin, and for Savidlin and Weselan. He remembered his promise to try to find their boy. He had never felt so powerless.

"If I ever find him," Brophy growled fiercely, "I will settle a few scores. He's not fit to die. He must pay first for the things he's done."

"You just stay away from him," Kahlan warned. "He is a dangerous man. I don't want you hurt any more than you have been already."

The wolf's yellow eyes flared angrily at Kahlan for a moment before they cooled. "Yes, Mistress." He lay back down. "I would have faced the executioner with my head held high, the spirits know I may have earned it, but not for that. I would not let them kill me thinking I had done those things to children. So I demanded a Confessor."

"I didn't want to take his confession." Kahlan picked up a

stick and pushed at the dirt. "I knew he wouldn't have requested a Confessor unless he was innocent. I talked to the judge; he said that in view of the crime, he would not commute the sentence. It was death or a confession. Brophy insisted upon the confession." Richard could see the firelight reflecting in the wetness of her green eyes. "Afterward, I asked him to pick another creature he would choose to be, if he had a choice. He chose a wolf. Why a wolf, I don't know." She smiled a little. "I guess it fits his nature."

"Because wolves are honorable creatures." Richard smiled. "You haven't lived in the forest, you've lived among people. Wolves are very social creatures, have strong ties and relationships. They are fiercely protective of their young. The whole pack will fight to protect them. And all members of the pack care for the young."

"You understand," Brophy whispered.

"Really, Brophy?" she asked.

"Yes, Mistress. I have a good life, now." His tail swished back and forth. "I have a mate! She's a fine wolf. She smells divine, and her nips give me shivers, and she has the cutest little . . . well, never mind." He looked up at Kahlan. "She is the leader of our pack. With me at her side, of course. She is pleased with me. She says I'm the strongest wolf she has ever seen. We had a litter, this last spring. Six. They're fine pups, almost grown now. It's a fine life, hard, but fine. Thank you, Mistress, for releasing me."

"I'm so glad, Brophy. But why are you here? Why aren't you back with your family?"

"Well, when you were coming down out of the Rang'Shada, you passed near my den. I sensed your presence. I found I could smell you. The urge to protect you was too strong to overcome. I know you are in danger, and I can't be at peace in my pack until I know you're safe. I must protect you."

"Brophy," she protested, "we're fighting to stop Darken Rahl. It's too dangerous for you to be with us. I don't want you to lose your life. You have already sacrificed too much to Darken Rahl, through Demmin Nass."

"Mistress, when I was changed to the wolf, it removed most of my need for you, my need to please you. Yet I would still die for you. It is still extremely difficult for me to go against your wishes. But in this, I must. I will not leave you to danger. I must protect you, or I could never be at peace. Command me to leave if you will, but I will not go. I will shadow you until you are safe from Darken Rahl."

"Brophy," Richard said. The wolf looked over to him. "I too want Kahlan protected, so she can do her job and help stop Rahl. I would be honored to have you along. You have already proven your value and your heart. If you can help protect her, you just ignore what she says and go right on protecting her."

Brophy looked up at her. Kahlan smiled at him. "He is the Seeker. I'm sworn on my life to protect him, as is Zedd. If that is his word, then I must go along."

Brophy's muzzle opened in surprise. "He commands you? He commands the Mother Confessor?"

"He does."

The wolf shook his head. "Wonder of wonders." He licked his lips. "By the way, I would like to thank you for the food you have left me."

Kahlan frowned. "What are you talking about?"

"Whenever he trapped food, he always left some for me."

"You did?" she asked.

Richard shrugged. "Well, I knew he was out there, and I didn't know what he was, but I didn't think he meant us harm. So I left him food, to let him know we didn't mean him any harm either." He smiled at the wolf. "But when you came at me back there, I surely thought I had made a mistake. Thank you again."

Brophy seemed uncomfortable with the gratitude, and stood. "I have been here long enough. I have woods to patrol. There might be things about. The three of you need not stand watch with Brophy on the job."

Richard pushed a stick at the fire, watching the sparks swirl into the air. "Brophy, what was it like when Kahlan touched you? When she released her power into you."

No one spoke. Richard looked into the wolf's yellow eyes. Brophy's head turned to Kahlan.

"Tell him," she whispered in a broken voice.

Brophy lay back down, folding one paw over the other, his head held high. He was silent for a long time before he spoke.

602

"It's hard to remember everything of that time, but I will try to explain it the best I can." His head cocked a little to one side. "Pain. I remember the pain. It was exquisite, beyond anything you could imagine. The first thing I remember after the pain is fear. Overpowering fear I might be breathing wrong, and it would somehow displease her. I almost died from fear that I would displease her. And then when she told me what she wanted to know, it was a flush of the greatest joy I had ever known. Joy, because then I knew what I could do to please her. I was overjoyed that she had made a request of me, that there was something I could do to satisfy her. That's what I remember the most, the desperate, frantic need to do as she wanted, to satisfy her, and make her happy. Nothing else was in my mind, only to please her. To be in her presence was beyond bliss. The pleasure of being in her presence made me cry with elation.

"She told me to tell the truth, and I was so happy, because I knew I could do that. I was thrilled to have a task within my power. I started talking as fast as I could, to tell her all the truth I could. She had to tell me to slow down, because she couldn't understand me. If I had had a knife, I would have used it on myself for displeasing her. Then she told me it was all right, and I cried because she was not displeased with me. I told her what happened." His ears wilted a little. "After I told her I hadn't killed the boy, I remembered she put her hand on my arm—the touch nearly made me faint with pleasure—and she said she was sorry. I misunderstood. I thought she meant she was sorry I hadn't killed the boy. I begged her to let me go kill another boy for her." Tears ran from the corners of the wolf's eyes. "Then she explained that what she meant was that she was sorry for me, for me being accused wrongly of the murder. I remember crying uncontrollably, because she had shown me a kindness, she was sorry for me, she cared for me. I remember what it felt like to be near her, to be in her presence. I guess it was a feeling of love, but words are so hollow, next to the power of the wanting of her."

Richard stood. He could only make himself take the briefest of glances at Kahlan, at her tears. "Thank you, Brophy." He had to pause a moment to make sure his voice wouldn't fail him. "It's late. We better get some sleep; tomorrow is an important day. I'm going to take my watch. Good night."

Brophy stood. "You three sleep. I will stand watch tonight."

Richard swallowed the lump. "I appreciate that, but I will stand my watch. If you wish, you may guard my back."

He turned and started to leave.

"Richard," Zedd called out to him. Richard stopped without turning. "What bone is it, that your father gave you?"

Richard's mind raced in a panic. Please, Zedd, he said to himself, if you have ever believed a lie I have told you, believe this one. "You must remember it. It was that little round one. You've seen it before, I know you have."

"Oh. Yes, I guess I must have. Good night."

Wizard's First Rule. Thank you, my old friend, he thought to himself, for teaching me how to protect Kahlan's life.

He walked on into the night, his head pounding with pain, from without, and from within.

CHAPTER 39

THE CITY OF TAMARANG couldn't hold all the people who wanted in; there were simply too many. People coming from every direction, seeking protection and safety, had overflowed to the countryside around the established quarters. Tents and shacks had sprung up on the bare ground outside the city walls and out onto the hills. In the morning, people had flowed down from the hills into the impromptu market quarter outside the walls. People who had come from other towns, villages, and cities lined up in streets laid out in haphazard fashion at makeshift stands, selling whatever they had. Vendors sold everything from old clothes to fine jewelry. Fruits and vegetables were stacked at other stands.

There were barbers and healers and fortune-tellers, people who had paper and wanted to draw your face, and people who had leeches and wanted to draw your blood. Wine and spirits were for sale everywhere. Despite the circumstances of their presence, the people seemed in a festive mood. The imagined protection and ample supply of drink, Richard suspected. Talk floated freely of the wonders of Father Rahl. Speakers stood at the center of small knots of citizens, telling the latest news, the latest atrocities. The tattered folk moaned and wailed at the outrages done by the Westlanders. There were cries for vengeance.

Richard didn't see a single woman with hair past her jawline.

The castle proper sat at the top of a high hill, within its own walls, within the walls of the city. Red banners with a black wolf's head flew at evenly spaced intervals around the formidable castle walls. The huge wooden doors at the outer city walls stood closed. To keep the riffraff at bay, it appeared.

Patrols of soldiers prowled the streets on horseback, their armor glinting in the noonday sun, specks of light in an ocean of noisy people. Richard saw one detachment, red banners with black wolf's head flying over them, as they swept through the new streets. Some people cheered, some bowed, but all backed away as the horses passed. The soldiers ignored them, as if they didn't exist. People who didn't move out of the way quick enough got a boot to the head.

But none of the people moved out of the way of the soldiers the way they moved out of the way for Kahlan. People backed away from the Mother Confessor the way a pack of dogs backs away from a porcupine.

Her white dress shone in the bright sun. Back straight, head held high, she walked as if she owned the whole city. She kept her eyes straight ahead, and acknowledged no one. She had refused to wear her cloak, saying it wouldn't be proper, and that she wanted there to be no doubt as to who she was. There was no doubt.

People fell over each other getting out of her way. Everyone bowed in a wave in the wide circle around her as she passed. Hushed whispers carried Kahlan's title back through the throng. Kahlan didn't acknowledge the bows.

Zedd, wearing Kahlan's pack for her, walked at Richard's side, two paces behind her. Both his and Richard's eyes swept the crowds. In all the time he had known Zedd, Richard had never seen him wear a pack. To say it looked odd would be an understatement. Richard kept his cloak hooked back behind the Sword of Truth. It raised a few eyebrows, but nothing like the Mother Confessor did.

"Is it like this everywhere she goes?" Richard whispered to Zedd.

"I'm afraid so, my boy."

Without hesitation, Kahlan walked smoothly over the massive stone bridge to the city gates. Guards at the near end of the bridge fell back out of her way. She ignored them. Richard surveyed everything, in case he needed to find a fast way out.

The two dozen guards at the city gates were obviously under instruction to allow no one to enter. The guards, who had been standing at attention, looked nervously at each other; they hadn't expected a visit from the Mother Confessor. With a clank of metal against metal, some of them moved back, bumping into each other, and some didn't, not knowing what to do. Kahlan stopped; she stared ahead at the gates as if she expected them to evaporate out of her way. The guards in front of her pressed their backs against the gates as they looked sideways to their captain.

Zedd stepped around Kahlan, turned to her, bowed deeply, as if to excuse himself for stepping in front of her, then turned to the captain.

"What's the matter with you? Are you blind, man? Open the gates!"

The captain's dark eyes shifted between Kahlan and Zedd. "I'm sorry, but no one is to enter. And your name is ..."

Zedd's face turned bright red; Richard had to work at keeping his own face straight. The wizard's voice was a low hiss. "Are you telling me, Captain, that you were told 'If the Mother Confessor comes by, don't let her in'?"

The captain's eyes looked less sure. "Well ... I was ordered ... I'm not ..."

"Open the gates right now!" Zedd bellowed, fists at his side. "And get a proper escort here this instant!"

The captain almost jumped out of his armor. He yelled orders and men started running at his direction. The gates swung inward. Horses thundered up from behind and came around the little company, forming a rank in front of Kahlan with their banners at the lead. More horsemen formed up behind. Foot soldiers came at a run, falling in beside her, but not too close.

Richard was seeing her world for the first time, the loneliness of it. What had his heart gotten him into? With cold pain, he understood her need for a friend.

"You call this a proper escort?" Zedd roared. "Well, it will have to do." He turned to Kahlan and bowed deeply. "My apologies, Mother Confessor, for this man's insolence, and his feeble effort at an escort."

Her eyes went to Zedd and she gave a slight bow of the head.

Though he knew he had no right, the shape of her in that dress was making Richard sweat.

As best they could, the men in the ranks kept a wary eye to Kahlan, waiting, and when she started forward they stepped in with her. Dust rose around the horses as they started through the gates.

Zedd fell in next to Richard as the procession started moving, leaning toward the captain as he passed. "Count your blessings the Mother Confessor doesn't know your name, Captain!" he snapped.

Richard saw the captain sag with relief when they moved well past him. Richard smiled to himself. He had wanted to give them a worry, but he had no idea it would be so effective a worry.

There was as much order to the city inside the walls as there was disorder outside its gates. Shops with their wares displayed in windows lined the paved streets radiating out from the fortress castle. The streets lacked the dust and smells of those outside. There were inns that looked to be finer than any Richard had ever seen before, much less stayed in. Some had doormen standing at attention in red uniforms and white gloves. Elaborately carved signs hung above the doors: The Silver Garden Inn, The Collins Inn, The White Stallion, and The Carriage House.

Men in fine, richly colored coats, escorting ladies in elaborate dresses, went about their business with calm grace. One thing that wasn't different about the people inside the walls was that they, too, bowed deeply when they saw the Mother Confessor approaching. As the sound of the horses' hooves on the stone, and armor clanking, drew their attention, and they saw Kahlan, they backed away and bowed, although not as quickly. There was no snap in their deference, no sincerity in their submission. There was a wisp of contempt in their eyes. Kahlan ignored them. The people inside the walls also noticed the sword more than those outside had noticed it. Richard saw the men's eyes glide over it as he passed, saw the women's cheeks color with disdain.

Women's hair was still short, but occasionally there was some that touched the shoulders. None longer. That, too, made Kahlan stand out all the more, the way her hair cascaded off her shoulders and partway down her back. There was no woman with hair that even approached it. Richard was glad he hadn't cut it for her.

One of the horsemen was given orders, and he broke rank in a dead run toward the castle to announce the arrival of the Mother Confessor. As she proceeded, Kahlan wore the calm expression that showed nothing, an expression he was used to seeing on her. He now realized what it was. It was the expression worn by a Confessor.

Before they reached the castle gates, trumpets announced the arrival of the Mother Confessor. The tops of the walls were alive with soldiers: lancers, bowmen, and swordsmen. All stood in ranks, bowed as one when Kahlan was close enough, and stayed bowed until she passed through the iron gates that stood open for her. Inside the gates, soldiers standing at attention lined each side of the road, and bowed in unison as she passed.

Some of the terraces held stone urns that marched off to either side, some of them still holding greenery, or flowers that must have been brought out daily from greenhouses. Broad flat areas displayed hedges trimmed in intricate patterns, even mazes. Closer to the castle walls, hedges were larger, cut to mimic objects, or animals. They extended off to the sides as far as the eye could see.

The walls of the castle soared into the air above them. The complicated stonework left Richard awestruck. He had never been this close to anything man-made that was this huge. Shota's palace was big, but not this big, and he had never gotten close to it. Towers and turrets, walls and ramps, balconies and niches, all rose high into the air above them. He marveled at what Kahlan had told him, that this was an insignificant kingdom, and wondered at what the castles in the more important lands must be like.

The horsemen had left them at the rampart, and as they were swallowed into the castle the foot soldiers, six abreast with room for another six to each side, marched through the enormous pair of brass-clad doors and fanned out to the sides, leaving the three to walk on—Kahlan in the lead.

The room was immense. A gleaming sea of black and white marble tiles swept away ahead of them. Polished stone columns, so large it would take ten people holding hands to reach around each, and fluted with spiraling, carved roping, rose in a line to both sides of the room, supporting row upon row of arches at the edge of the ribbed, vaulted center ceiling. Richard felt as little as a bug.

Huge tapestries depicting heroic scenes of vast battles hung on the side walls. He had seen tapestries before; his brother had two. Richard rather favored them, and had always thought they were a grand extravagance. But Michael's tapestries were to these as a stick drawing in the dirt was to a fine oil painting. Richard hadn't even known such majestic things as these existed.

Zedd leaned a little closer to him and whispered. "Put your eyes back in your head, and shut your mouth."

Chagrined, Richard snapped his mouth closed and put his eyes to the front. He leaned close to Zedd, and asked in a low whisper, "Is this the kind of place she is used to?"

"No. The Mother Confessor is used to much better than this."

Overwhelmed, Richard straightened himself.

Ahead lay a grand stairway. By Richard's estimation, his entire house would fit, with room to spare, on its central landing. Carved marble railings swooped down each side. Between themselves and the stairs waited a knot of people.

At their front stood Queen Milena, an amply fed woman in layered silks of garish colors. She wore a cape trimmed in rare spotted fox. Her hair was as long as Kahlan's. At first, Richard couldn't figure out what she was holding, but when he heard the yapping, he realized it was a small dog.

As they approached, everyone but the Queen dropped to a knee in a deep bow. When they stopped, Richard stared openly; he had never seen a queen before. Zedd gave him a sideways kick. He dropped to one knee and, following Zedd's example, bowed his head. The only two who did not kneel or bow were Kahlan and the Queen. No sooner was he down than everyone was back up, with him coming to his feet last. Richard guessed that the two women must not have to bow to each other.

The Queen stared at Kahlan, who, with her head held high, didn't break her calm countenance and didn't even look at the Queen. No one spoke a word.

Kahlan lifted her hand a little, only about a foot away from her body, with her arm held unbending, her hand held limply in place. The Queen's expression turned darker. Kahlan's didn't change. Richard figured that if anyone had blinked, he would have heard it. The Queen turned slightly to the side and handed the little dog to a man in a bright green, sleeved doublet and black tights with red-and-yellow striped pantaloons. There was a whole gaggle of men behind the Queen dressed in similar fashion. The dog growled viciously and bit the man's hand; he did his best not to notice.

The Queen lowered herself to both knees in front of Kahlan.

A young man in plain black clothes immediately came to the Queen's side, holding a tray out in front of himself. He bowed, head bent impossibly low, holding the tray out to the Queen. She took a small towel from the tray, dipped it in a silver bowl of water, and used it to wipe her lips. She returned the towel to the tray.

The Queen took the Mother Confessor's hand lightly in her own, and kissed it with her freshly cleaned lips.

"Fidelity sworn to the Confessors, on my crown, on my land, on my life."

Richard had heard few people lie as smoothly.

Kahlan at last moved her eyes. She looked down at the Queen's bowed head. "Rise, my child."

More than a queen, indeed, Richard thought. He remembered teaching Kahlan to make a snare, to read tracks, to dig roots, and felt himself turning crimson.

Queen Milena laboriously pushed herself to her feet. Her lips smiled. Her eyes didn't. "We have not requested a Confessor."

"Nonetheless, I am here." Kahlan's voice could have frozen water.

"Yes, well, this is ... grand. Simply ... grand." Her face brightened. "We will have a banquet. Yes, a banquet. I will send out runners with invitations immediately. Everyone will come. I'm sure they will be most pleased to dine with the Mother Confessor. This is quite an honor." She turned, indicating the men in the red-and-yellow pantaloons. "These are my barristers." The men all bowed deeply again at the introduction. "I don't remember all their names." She held her hand out to two men in gold robes. "And this is Silas Tannic, and Brandin Gadding, the chief advisors to the crown." The two gave a nod. "And my minister of finance, Lord Rondel; my star guide, Lady Kyley." Richard didn't see a silver-robed wizard among the Queen's entourage. The Queen waved her hand at a shabbily dressed man in the back. "And James, my court artist."

From the corner of his eye, Richard saw Zedd stiffen. James kept his lecherous eyes on Kahlan as he gave a shallow bow. He was missing his right hand at the wrist. The oily smile he gave her made Richard reach for his sword instinctively before he realized what he was doing. Without looking over, Zedd's hand grabbed his wrist and took the hand away from the sword. Richard glanced around at the other people to see if anyone had noticed. No one had. They were all watching the Mother Confessor.

Kahlan turned to the two of them. "Zeddicus Zorander, cloud reader, trusted advisor to the Mother Confessor." Zedd bowed dramatically. "And Richard Cypher, the Seeker, protector to the Mother Confessor." Richard imitated Zedd's bow.

The Queen looked at him, lifting an eyebrow with a sour look. "Pretty pathetic protection for a Mother Confessor."

Richard made no change in his expression. Kahlan remained unruffled. "It is the sword that cuts; the man is unimportant. His brain may be small, but his arms are not. He tends to use the sword too often, though."

The Queen didn't seem to believe her. Behind the royal party, a small girl came gliding down the stairs. She wore a pink satin dress and jewelry that was too large for her. She strode up beside the Queen, flipping her long hair back over her shoulder. She did not bow.

"My daughter, the Princess Violet. Violet, dear, this is the Mother Confessor."

Princess Violet scowled up at Kahlan. "Your hair is too long. Perhaps we should cut it for you."

Richard detected the slightest smile of satisfaction on the Queen's face. He decided it was time to elevate her level of worry.

The Sword of Truth came out, sending its distinctive ring around the huge room, the stone amplifying the sound. With the sword point an inch from Princess Violet's nose, he let the anger of it rage through him, to make his words more dramatic.

"Bow to the Mother Confessor," he hissed, "or die."

Zedd acted bored. Kahlan waited calmly. No one else had eyes as wide as the Princess as she stared at the sword point. She dropped to her knees and bowed her head. Standing back up, her eyes went to him, as if asking if the bow was all right.

"Be careful how you use that tongue," Richard sneered. "The next time I will separate it from you."

She nodded and walked around her mother, standing on the far side of her. Richard sheathed his sword, turned, bowed deeply to Kahlan, who didn't look at him, and returned to his station behind her.

The demonstration had the desired effect on the Queen, her voice becoming a bright singsong. "Yes, well, as I was saying, it is grand having you here. We are all simply delighted. Let us show you to our finest room. You must be tired from your journey. Perhaps you would like to rest before dinner, and then after dinner we can all have a nice long . . ."

"I am not here to eat." Kahlan cut her off. "I am here to inspect your dungeon."

"Dungeon?" She made a face. "It's filthy down there. Are you sure you wouldn't rather . . ."

Kahlan started walking. "I know the way." Richard and Zedd fell in behind her. She stopped, and turned back to the Queen. "You will wait here"—her voice was like ice—"until I am finished." As the Queen began bowing her assent, Kahlan strode off with a swish of her dress as she turned on her heels.

If Richard hadn't known her as well as he did, the entire encounter would have scared the breath out of him. In fact, he wasn't sure it hadn't.

Kahlan led them downstairs and through rooms that became less and less grandiose the deeper they went into the castle. Richard was amazed at the size of the place.

"I was hoping Giller would have been there," Kahlan said. "Then we wouldn't need to do this."

"Me too," Zedd grumbled. "You just make a quick inspection,

613

ask if anyone wants to give a confession, and when they say no, we go back up and ask to see Giller." He gave her a smile. "You've handled it well so far, dear one." She returned the smile to the two of them. "And Richard," he cautioned, "you keep away from that artist, James."

"Why? He might draw a bad likeness of me?"

"Wipe that grin off your face. You stay away from him because he might draw a spell around you."

"A spell? Why would you need an artist to put a spell on someone?"

"Because there are many different languages in the Midlands, though the main one is the same as is spoken in Westland. To be spelled, you have to be able to understand it. If you can't speak their language, you can't put a spell on them. But everyone can understand a drawing. He can draw a spell on almost anyone, not Kahlan or me, but he can on you. Stay away from him."

Their footsteps echoed as the three quickly descended stone steps. The walls, far belowground, leaked water and were covered in places with slime.

Kahlan indicated a heavy door to the side. "Through here."

Richard pulled it open by the iron ring, the strap hinges creaking. Torchlight lit the way down a narrow stone corridor with a ceiling he had to stoop to avoid hitting with his head. Straw covered the wet floor, and smelled of decay. Near the end she slowed to a walk and approached an iron door with a grille in it. Eyes peered out at them when she stopped.

Zedd leaned around her. "The Mother Confessor, here to see the prisoners," he growled. "Open the door."

Richard could hear the echo of a key turning in the lock. A squat man in a filthy uniform pulled the door inward. An axe hung from his belt next to the keys. He bowed to Kahlan, but looked to be annoyed by it. Without a word, he led them through the little room just inside the door, where he had been sitting at a table, eating, and down another dark hall to another iron door. He pounded on it with his fist. The two guards inside bowed in surprise. The three guards took torches from iron stanchions and led them down a short hall and through a third iron door that they all had to duck through.

Flickering torchlight pierced the darkness. Behind cross-hatched, flat iron bars to each side, men pushed themselves back into the corners, shielding their eyes with their hands from the sudden light. Kahlan spoke Zedd's name quietly, indicating that she wanted something. He seemed to understand, and took a torch from one of the guards and held it up in front of Kahlan so all the men in the cells could see her.

There were gasps from the darkness when they recognized who she was.

Kahlan addressed one of the guards. "How many of these men are sentenced to die?"

He stroked his round, unshaven jaw. "Why, all of them."

"All of them," she repeated.

He nodded. "Crimes against the Crown."

She pulled her gaze away from him after a moment, turning to the prisoners. "Have all you men committed capital offenses?"

After a moment of silence, a hollow-faced man came and gripped the bars. He spat at her. Kahlan swept her hand back to stop Richard before he had a chance to move.

"Come to do the Queen's dirty work, Confessor? I spit on you and your filthy queen."

"I do not come here on behalf of the Queen. I come here on behalf of the truth."

"The truth! The truth is none of us has done a thing! Except maybe speaking up against the new laws. And since when is speaking up against your family starving, or freezing to death, a capital crime? The Queen's tax collectors came and took most of my crops, they barely left enough to feed my family. When I sold the precious little I could spare, they said I was overcharging people. The prices of everything are going wild. I'm doing nothing more than trying to survive. Yet I am to be beheaded for price gouging. These men in here with me are all innocent farmers, or tradesmen, or merchants. We are all to die for trying to earn a living from our work."

Kahlan looked to the men in the corner. "Do any of you wish to make a confession to prove your innocence?"

There were hushed whispers. A gaunt man in the darkness stood and came forward. His frightened eyes looked out at them from the gloom. "I do. I have done nothing, yet I am to be beheaded, my wife and children left to fend for themselves. I will give a confession." He pushed his arm through the bars, reaching for her. "Please, Mother Confessor, take my confession."

More men stood, coming forward, all asking to give a confession. Soon, they were all at the bars, begging to give a confession. Kahlan and Zedd exchanged a grim look.

"In my whole life I have seen only three men ask to give a confession," she whispered to the wizard.

"Kahlan?" The familiar voice came from the cell on the other side, from the darkness.

Kahlan gripped the bars with spread fingers. "Siddin? Siddin!" She spun to the guards. "These men have all given the Mother Confessor their confessions, I find them all to be innocent. Open the bars!"

"Now, hold on. I can't be letting all these men out."

Richard drew the sword in an arc as he spun. The sword crashed a swath through the iron bars, and shards of hot steel and sparks filled the air. He spun around and kicked the iron door shut behind the startled guards. He had the sword at their faces before a single one of them managed to clear an axe from his belt.

"Open the bars or I will slice you in half and take the keys from your belt that way!"

The shaking guard with the keys jumped to do as he was told. The door swung open and Kahlan rushed in, going back into the darkness. She came back holding a frightened Siddin in her arms, holding his head against her shoulder. She whispered in his ear, calming him. Siddin jabbered back in the Mud People language. She smiled and told him things he smiled back at. As she came out, the guard was opening the other cell door. She held Siddin in one arm, and with her free hand she grabbed the guard's shirt collar.

"The Mother Confessor finds all these men innocent." Her voice was as hard as the iron around her. "They are to be released upon my order. You three are to escort them to safety, outside the city." He was a head shorter than she; she pulled his face closer to hers. "If you fail in any way, you will answer to me."

He nodded vigorously. "Yes, Mother Confessor. I understand. It will be done as you say. On my word."

"On your life," she corrected.

She released him. The prisoners poured out of the cells, falling to their knees around her, crying, taking the hem of her dress in their hands, kissing it. She shooed them away.

"Enough of that. Be on your way, all of you. Just remember, Confessors serve no one. They serve only the truth."

They all swore they would remember, and followed the guards out. Richard saw that many of their shirts were shredded, or streaked with dried blood, their backs covered with welts.

Before they entered the room where the Queen waited, Kahlan stopped and put Siddin into Zedd's arms. With her hands she smoothed his hair, then her dress, and with a deep breath, her face.

"Just keep in mind what we are here for, Mother Confessor," the wizard said.

She gave him a nod, put her chin up, and strode into the room with the Queen. Queen Milena waited where they had left her, her entourage still with her. The Queen's eyes caught on Siddin.

"I trust you have found everything in order, Mother Confessor?"

Kahlan's face stayed calm, but her voice had a cold edge to it. "Why is this child in your dungeon?"

The Queen's hands spread wide. "Well, I'm not sure. I believe I remember he was found stealing, and was put there until his parents could be found, that's all. I can assure you, it was nothing more than that."

Kahlan regarded her coolly. "I have found all the prisoners innocent, and ordered them released. I trust you are pleased to find I have saved you from executing innocent men, and will see to it that their families are compensated for the trouble this 'error' has caused. If an 'error' such as this is repeated, the next time I return I will not only empty the prison, I will also empty the throne."

Richard knew he wasn't seeing Kahlan putting on a show to get the box; he was seeing her doing her job. This was why the wizards created the Confessors. This was who she was: the Mother Confessor.

The Queen's eyes opened wide. "Why ... yes. Of course. I have some overly ambitious army commanders, and they must have done this. I had no knowledge of it. Thank you ... for saving us from making a grave mistake. I will personally see to it that it is taken care of, just as you wish. Which, of course, is no less than I would have done myself had I ..."

Kahlan cut her off. "We will be leaving now."

The Queen's face brightened. "Leaving? Oh, what a shame. We were all so looking forward to the honor of your presence at dinner. I'm so sorry you must go."

"I have other pressing business. Before I go. I wish to speak with my wizard."

"Your wizard?"

"Giller," she hissed.

For the briefest of moments, the Queen's eyes flicked toward the ceiling. "Well ... that would not be ... possible."

Kahlan leaned closer to her. "Make it possible. Right now."

The color drained from the Queen's face. "Please believe me, Mother Confessor, you wouldn't want to see Giller in his present condition."

"Right now," Kahlan repeated.

Richard loosened the sword in its scabbard just enough to catch her attention.

"Very well. He is ... upstairs."

"You will wait here until I am finished with him."

The Queen looked at the floor. "Of course, Mother Confessor." She turned to one of the men in the pantaloons. "Show her the way."

The man led them up the grand stairway to the top floor, and down several halls, then up a spiral stone stairway to the top room in a tower, finally stopping with a weak look at a heavy wooden door on the landing. Kahlan dismissed him. He bowed, glad to leave. Richard opened the door, they entered, and he closed it behind them.

Kahlan gasped and hid her face against Richard's shoulder. Zedd pressed Siddin's face to his robes.

The room was destroyed. Completely. The roof was gone, as if it had been blasted away, letting in the sunlight and sky. Only a few of the exposed beams remained. A rope hung from one of the beams.

Giller's naked body swung slightly as it hung, upside down, from the end of the rope, a meat hook driven through the bone of his ankle. Were it not for the open roof, the stench would have driven them from the room.

Zedd handed Siddin to Kahlan and, ignoring the body, began walking slowly around the circular room, a thoughtful frown on his face. He stopped and touched splinters of furniture that had been driven into the walls, as if the stone were made of butter.

Richard stood, transfixed, staring at Giller's body.

"Richard, come look at this," Zedd called to him.

The wizard reached out and ran a finger through a gritty black area on the wall. There were two black areas, in fact. They stood next to each other. Two blackened spots, in the shapes of men standing at attention, as if the men had gone and left their shadows behind. Just above each elbow, instead of the black, was a band of gold-colored metal melted into the stone of the wall.

Zedd turned, raising an eyebrow to him. "Wizard's fire."

Richard was incredulous. "You mean these were men?"

Zedd nodded. "Burned them right into the wall." He tasted the black smudge on the end of his finger. He smiled to himself. "But this was more than just wizard's fire." Richard frowned. Zedd pointed at the black on the wall. "Taste it."

"Why?"

Zedd rapped Richard's head with his knuckles. "To learn something."

With a grimace, Richard ran his finger through the black grit, as Zedd had done. "It tastes sweet!"

Zedd smiled in satisfaction. "This is more than simple wizard's fire. Giller gave his life energy to it. He gave his life into the fire. This was a Wizard's Life Fire."

"He died, making this wizard's fire?"

"Yes. And it tastes sweet. That means he gave his life to save another. If he had done it only for himself, for instance to spare himself the torture, it would taste bitter. Giller has done this for another."

Zedd went and stood in front of Giller's body, swishing the flies away, twisting his own head around, trying to turn it upside down for a look. With a finger, he pushed a knotted cord of gut out of the way, so he could see Giller's face. He straightened.

"He has left a message."

"A message?" Kahlan asked. "What message?"

"There is a smile on his face. A smile, frozen in death, meant to tell anyone who knows of such things that he did not give up what was wanted." Richard stepped closer as Zedd pointed to the opening cut across the abdomen. "See here, the way this cut goes? This is done by one who practices the magic called anthropomancy, the divining of answers by the inspection of living entrails. Darken Rahl makes his cut very similar to the way his father did."

Richard remembered his own father, and how Rahl had done this very thing to him.

"You are sure it was Darken Rahl?" Kahlan asked.

Zedd shrugged. "Who else? Darken Rahl is the only one who would have been unharmed by a Wizard's Life Fire. Besides, this cut is his signature. Look here. See the end of the opening? See the way it starts to turn?"

Kahlan turned her face away. "What of it?"

"That's the hook. At least it should be. It should turn back in a hooked cut. While incantations are spoken, the hook is cut, binding the questioned to the questioner. The hook forces them to give up the answer to the question asked. But see here? The hook is begun, but it is not finished." Zedd gave a sad grin. "That is when Giller gave his life to the fire. He waited until Rahl was almost done, then, at the last instant, denied him what he sought. Probably the name of who has the box. Without life in them, his entrails could tell Rahl nothing."

"I never thought Giller capable of such a selfless act," Kahlan whispered.

"Zedd," Richard asked fearfully, "how could Giller have done it, taken the pain of having this done to him, and manage to leave a smile on his face?"

Zedd gave him a hard look that ran a chill up Richard's spine. "Wizards must know about pain. They must know it very well, indeed. It is to spare you that lesson that I would happily accept your choice not to be a wizard. It is a lesson few survive."

Richard wondered at the mysterious, secret things Zedd must know, but had never shared with him.

Tenderly, Zedd cupped a hand to the side of Giller's face. "You have done well, my student. Honor in the end."

"I bet Darken Rahl was livid," Richard said. "Zedd, I think we had better get out of here. This looks a little too much like bait on a hook to me."

Zedd nodded. "Wherever the box is, it is not here. At least Rahl does not have it—yet." He put his hands out. "Give me the boy. We need to leave as we came in. We don't want to tell them why we were really here."

Zedd whispered something in Siddin's ear, and the boy giggled, hugging the wizard's neck.

Queen Milena was still white, fumbling with the corner of her cape, as Kahlan strode purposefully but calmly up to her.

"Thank you for your hospitality," Kahlan said. "We will be leaving now."

The Queen bowed her head. "Always a pleasure to see the Mother Confessor." Her curiosity overcame her fear. "What of . . . Giller?"

Kahlan appraised her coolly. "I regret you have beaten me to him. I only wish I had had the pleasure of doing it myself, or at least witnessed it being done. But, the results are all that matter. Disagreement, was it?"

The color returned to the Queen's face. "He stole something that belonged to me."

"I see. Well, I hope you got it back. Good day." She started to move, then stopped. "And Queen Milena, I will be back to check, and make sure you have brought your overly ambitious commanders back in line, and that they are not mistakenly executing innocent people."

Richard and Zedd, holding Siddin, fell in behind Kahlan as she turned and left.

Richard's thoughts swirled desperately through his head as he walked woodenly next to Zedd, following Kahlan through all the bowing people and out of the city. What were they going to do now? Shota had warned him that the Queen wouldn't have the box for long. She had been right. Where could it be now? He certainly couldn't go back and ask Shota where it was. Who could Giller have given the box to? How were they going to find it? He felt desperately depressed. He felt like giving up. He could tell by the slump in Kahlan's shoulders that she felt the same way. Neither of them spoke. The only one talking was Siddin, and Richard couldn't understand him.

"What's he saying?" he asked Zedd.

"He says he has been being brave, just as Kahlan had told him, but he is glad that Richard With The Temper has come to take him home."

"I guess I know how he feels. Zedd, what are we going to do now?"

Zedd gave him a puzzled look. "How should I know? You're the Seeker."

Great. He had just done his best, and they still didn't have the box, but he was expected, somehow, to find it. He felt as if he had run square into a wall he hadn't known was there. They kept walking, but he didn't know where to go next.

The setting sun was golden among golden clouds. Richard thought he could see something ahead in the distance. He moved up and walked next to Kahlan. She was watching it, too. All the people had disappeared from the road for the night.

It wasn't long before he knew what it was. It was four horses galloping toward them. Only one had a rider.

CHAPTER 40

RICHARD TOUCHED THE HILT of the sword for reassurance as he watched the four horses raising a cloud of dust that turned golden in the setting sun. Soon the sound of thundering hooves reached him. The lone rider bent over his mount, urging him on. Richard lifted the sword a little in its scabbard, checking that it was clear, then let it drop back. As the darkly clad rider approached, Richard realized he looked familiar.

"Chase!"

The boundary warden brought the horses to a skidding halt in front of them. He looked down as the dust drifted away. "You all look to be well."

"Chase, is it ever good to see you!" Richard grinned. "How did you find us?"

He looked insulted. "I'm a boundary warden." He thought that was explanation enough. "Find what you were after?"

"No," Richard admitted with a sigh. He saw little arms clutching at Chase's sides. A little face peeked around the black cloak. "Rachel? Is that you?"

Her face came farther out, a grin spreading on it. "Richard!

I'm so happy to see you again. Isn't Chase wonderful? He fought a gar and saved me from being eaten."

"Didn't fight him," Chase grumbled. "Just put a bolt through his head, that's all."

"But you would have. You're the bravest man I ever saw."

With a pained frown, Chase rolled his eyes. "Isn't she just about the ugliest child you have ever seen?" He leaned around and looked at her. "I can't believe a gar would even want to eat you."

Rachel giggled and hugged her arms to his sides. "Look, Richard." She put a foot out toward him, showing off a shoe. "Chase brought down a buck. He said it was a mistake, because it was too big, so he traded it to a man, but all the man had to trade were these shoes, and this cloak. Aren't they wonderful? And Chase says I can keep them."

Richard grinned at her. "Yes, that is indeed wonderful." He noticed Rachel's doll and the bundle with the bread nestled between her and Chase. He also noticed her eyes going to Siddin, as if she had seen him before.

Kahlan put a hand on Rachel's leg. "Why did you run off? You scared us with worry for you."

Rachel flinched at Kahlan's touch. She hugged one arm to Chase and thrust a hand in her pocket. She didn't answer Kahlan's question, but looked instead toward Siddin. "Why do you have him?"

"Kahlan rescued him," Richard said. "The Queen had him locked up in the dungeon. That's no place for a child, so she took him out."

Rachel looked down at Kahlan. "Wasn't the Queen mad?"

"I don't allow anyone to hurt children," Kahlan said. "Not even a queen."

"Well, don't just stand there staring. I brought you all horses. Mount up. I figured I'd catch you today. I have a wild boar roasting back at the place you stayed last night, just this side of the Callisidrin."

With one hand on the saddle and the other arm holding Siddin, Zedd leapt to a horse. "Wild boar! What kind of fool are you? Leaving a wild boar roasting unprotected! Anyone could just come along and take it!"

"Why do you think I want you to hurry? The place is filthy with wolf tracks, though I doubt they'd come near a fire."

"Don't you dare hurt that wolf," Zedd warned. "He's a friend of the Mother Confessor."

Chase cast an eye to Kahlan, then to Richard, before turning his horse and leading them into the setting sun. Richard was heartened by having Chase back. It made him feel, once again, that anything was possible. After she had mounted, Kahlan took Siddin, the two of them talking and laughing as they rode.

At the camp, Zedd wasted no time before checking the roasting boar, and pronounced it fit to eat. He shifted his robes and sat down, waiting with a grin on his wrinkled face for someone with a knife to carve dinner. Siddin, with a grin frozen on his face, too, leaned against Kahlan after she sat down. Richard and Chase started carving up the boar. Rachel sat close to Chase's side, watching him, keeping an eye to Kahlan, her doll in her lap, and the loaf of bread, wrapped in the cloth, at her hip.

Richard cut a big piece and handed it to Zedd. "So, what happened? With my brother, I mean."

Chase grinned. "When I told him the things you told me to tell him, he said that if you were in trouble, he was going to help. He pulled together the army, and we sent most of them into defensive positions along the boundary, with the wardens commanding them. After the boundary came down he refused to wait behind. He led a thousand of his best men into the Midlands. They're all bivouacked up in the Rang'Shada right now, waiting to help you."

Richard had stopped carving, frozen in astonishment. "Really? My brother said that? He came to help? And with an army?"

Chase nodded. "He said if you're in this, then he is too."

Richard felt a pang of regret that he had doubted Michael, and elation that his brother would drop everything to come help. "He wasn't angry?"

"I thought sure he would be, and give me grief over this, but he only wanted to know about you, what risk you were at, and where you were. He said he knew you, and if you thought it was this important, then he did too. He offered to come along, but I wouldn't let him. He's with his men, probably waiting in his tent right now, pacing back and forth. I have to tell you, it surprised me too."

Richard's eyes were wide in wonder. "My brother and a thousand of his men, in the Midlands, come to help me." He looked at Kahlan. "Isn't that wonderful?" She only smiled at him.

Chase gave him a stern look while he carved. "For a while, I thought you were finished, when I saw your trail going into Agaden Reach."

Richard looked up. "You went into the Reach?"

"Do I look stupid? You don't become head of the boundary wardens by being stupid. I started thinking of how I was going to tell Michael you were dead. Then I found your trail coming out of the Reach." His brow wrinkled together. "How did you manage to come out of the Reach alive?"

Richard gave him a grin. "I think the good spirits . . ."

Rachel screamed.

Richard and Chase spun with their knives. Before Chase could use his knife, Richard stopped him.

It was Brophy. "Rachel? Is that you, Rachel?"

She took her doll's foot from her mouth. Her eyes were wide. "You sound like Brophy."

The wolf's tail swished back and forth. "That's because I am Brophy!" He trotted over to her.

"Brophy, how come you're a wolf?"

He sat on his haunches in front of her. "Because a kind wizard changed me into a wolf. That was what I wanted to be, and he changed me."

"Giller changed you into a wolf?"

The breath caught in Richard's throat.

"That's right. It's a wonderful new life I have."

She threw her arms around the wolf's neck. Brophy licked her face as she giggled.

"Rachel," Richard said, "you know Giller?"

Rachel hugged an arm around Brophy's neck. "Giller's a nice man. He gave me Sara." She gave a fearful look to Kahlan. "You want to hurt him. You're the Queen's friend. You're mean." She pushed against Brophy for protection.

Brophy gave her face a long lick. "You're wrong, Rachel. Kahlan is my friend. She is one of the nicest people in the world."

Kahlan smiled and held her hands out to Rachel. "Come here."

Rachel looked to Brophy, who gave her a nod that it was all right. She went with a pout on her face.

Kahlan took Rachel's hands in hers. "You heard me say something mean about Giller, didn't you?" Rachel nodded. "Rachel, the Queen is a bad person. I didn't know how bad until today. Giller used to be my friend. When he went to live with the Queen, I thought it was because he was bad too, and was on her side. I was wrong. I would never hurt Giller, now that I know he is still my friend."

Rachel turned her eyes up to Richard.

"She's telling you the truth. We're on the same side as Giller."

Rachel turned to Brophy. He nodded, too, that it was the truth.

"You and Richard aren't friends of the Queen?"

Kahlan laughed a little. "No. If I have my way, she will not be the queen much longer. And as for Richard, well, he drew his sword and threatened to kill the Princess. I don't think that makes him friends with the Queen."

Rachel's eyes got big. "Princess Violet? You did that to Princess Violet?"

Richard nodded to her. "She said some bad things to Kahlan, and I told her that if she did it again, I'd cut off her tongue."

Rachel's mouth dropped open. "And she didn't say to chop off your head?"

"We are not going to let them chop off any more heads," Kahlan said.

Rachel's eyes filled with tears as she looked to Kahlan. "I thought you were mean, and that you would hurt Giller. I'm so happy you're not mean." She put her arms around Kahlan's neck, hugging her tight. Kahlan hugged her back just as tight.

Chase leaned toward Richard. "You pulled a sword on a Princess? Do you know that's a capital offense?"

Richard gave him a cool look. "If I had had the time, I would have put her over my knee and spanked her too." Rachel giggled

627

at that. Richard smiled at her. "You know the Princess, don't you?"

The laughter left her. "I'm her playmate. I lived in a nice place with other children, but after my brother died, the Queen came and picked me out, to be the Princess's playmate."

Richard turned to Brophy. "He was the one?" The wolf nodded solemnly. "So you lived with the Princess. She's the one who cut your hair all crooked, isn't she? She hits you."

Rachel nodded with a pout. "She's mean to people. She's starting to say to chop off people's heads. I was afraid she would chop off my head too, so I ran away."

Richard eyed the loaf of bread she kept at her hip. He squatted down next to her. "Giller helped you run away, didn't he?"

She was near tears. "Giller gave me Sara. He wanted to run away with me. But then a mean man came. Father Rahl. He looked real mad at Giller. Giller told me to run, and to hide until winter, then to find a new family to live with." A tear ran down her cheek. "Sara told me he couldn't come with me anymore."

Richard glanced again at the loaf of bread. It was about the right size. He put his hands on her shoulders. "Rachel. Zedd, and Kahlan, and Chase, and I, are fighting against Darken Rahl, so that he won't be able to hurt people anymore."

She turned her head back to Chase.

Chase nodded. "He's telling you the truth, child. You tell him the truth too."

He tightened his grip on her shoulders. "Rachel, did Giller give you that loaf of bread?" She nodded. "Rachel, we were going to Giller to get a box, a box to help us stop Darken Rahl from hurting people. Will you give it to us? Will you help us stop Rahl?"

Her watery eyes looked at him; then with a brave smile, she picked up the bread and handed it to him. "It's in the loaf of bread. Giller hid it in there with magic."

Richard threw his arms around her, nearly hugging the breath out of her. He stood, hugging her to him, and spun in circles until she giggled. "Rachel, you are the bravest, smartest, prettiest girl I have ever known!" When he set her down, she ran to Chase and crawled into his lap. He mussed her hair and put his big arms around her as she smiled and hugged him.

Richard picked up the loaf of bread in both hands. He held it out to Kahlan. She smiled and shook her head. He held it to Zedd.

"The Seeker found it," Zedd smiled. "The Seeker should open it."

Richard broke the bread open, and there inside was the jeweled box of Orden. He wiped his hands on his pants, pulled the box out, and held it up to the firelight. He knew from the Book of Counted Shadows that the glittering box they saw was only a covering for the real box underneath. He even knew from the book how to remove the cover.

He put the box in Kahlan's lap. As she picked it up, she gave him the biggest smile he had ever seen. Before he even knew what he had done, he had leaned over and given Kahlan a quick kiss. Her eyes went wide, and she didn't kiss him back, but the feel of her lips shocked him into realizing what he had done.

"Oh. Sorry," he said.

She laughed. "Forgiven."

Richard hugged Zedd as they both laughed. Chase laughed watching him. Richard could hardly believe that just a short time ago, he had almost given up, had no idea what to do next, where to go, or how to stop Rahl. And now they had the box.

He set it on a rock where they could all see it in the firelight while they had the best dinner Richard could ever remember. Richard and Kahlan told Chase some of what they had been through. To Richard's delight, Chase was disturbed to learn that he owed his life to Bill, back at Southaven. Chase told them some of his own stories of bringing an army of a thousand men across the Rang'Shada. He enjoyed telling drawn-out tales of the foolishness of bureaucracy in the field.

Rachel cuddled in Chase's lap while she ate and he talked. Richard thought it was interesting that she chose the most fearsome among them for comfort. When at last he finished his story, she looked up and asked, "Chase, where should I go, to hide until winter?"

He regarded her with a glower. "You're too ugly to be left to wander about. A gar would eat you sure." That made her laugh. "I have other children, they're all ugly too. You'll fit right in. I guess I'll take you to live at my house."

"Really, Chase?" Richard asked.

"I've come home enough times and had my wife present me with a new child. I think it's about time I turned affairs about on her." He looked down at Rachel, who clung to him as if he might float away. "But I have rules, you know. You have to follow my rules."

"I'll do anything you say, Chase."

"Well, there you go, that's the first rule. I don't allow any of my children to call me Chase. If you want to be a member of my family, you have to call me Father. And about your hair, it's too short. My children all have long hair and I like it that way. You'll have to let your hair grow out some. And you'll have a mother. You'll have to mind her. And you'll have to play with your new brothers and sisters. Do you think you can do all that?"

She nodded against him, unable to talk as she hugged him, tears glistening in her eyes.

They all excitedly ate their fill. Even Zedd seemed to have had enough. Richard felt exhausted, and at the same time full of energy, to finally have the box in their hands. They had done the hard part, they had found the box before Rahl. Now they had only to keep it from him until winter.

"We have been weeks in this quest," Kahlan said. "The first day of winter is a month away. Earlier today, that seemed scarcely enough time to get the box. Now that we have it, it seems forever. What shall we do until it is finished?"

Chase spoke up first. "We have all of us to protect the box, and we have a thousand men to protect us. When we get back across the border, we will have many times that."

She looked at Zedd. "Do you think that's wise? We would be easy to find, a thousand men, I mean. Would it not be better to hide somewhere, by ourselves?"

Zedd leaned back and rubbed his full stomach. "We could hide better by ourselves, but we would also be more vulnerable, if discovered. Perhaps Chase is correct. There would be a lot of protection among a force that large, and if we had to, we could still leave them and go to cover."

"We better get an early start," Richard said.

It was barely light when they were off, the horses to the road, Brophy to woods, shadowing them, or at times scouting ahead. Chase, bristling with weapons, led them at a trot, Rachel holding him tight. Kahlan, back in her forest garb, and with Siddin sitting at her lap, rode next to Zedd. Richard had insisted that Zedd carry the box; it was wrapped in the cloth that held the bread before, and tied to the horn of his saddle. Richard followed behind, watching everything as they rode quickly into the cold morning air. Now that they had the box, he felt suddenly vulnerable, as if somehow everyone would know, just by looking at them.

Richard could hear the waters of the Callisidrin before they rounded the curve to the bridge. He was glad to see the road deserted. Chase spurred his horse to a gallop as he approached the big wooden bridge, the rest of them giving a heel to their horses to keep pace. Richard knew what Chase was doing. The boundary warden had always told him that bridges were the bane of the unwary. Richard watched in every direction as the other three galloped across in front of him. He saw nothing.

In the exact center of the bridge, at a full gallop, he ran solidly into something that wasn't there.

Stunned, Richard sat up, dumbfounded at finding himself on the ground, and seeing his big roan running with the other horses, then stopping with them as they halted and turned. The others looked back in confusion as Richard, still dazed and bewildered, rose painfully to his feet. He brushed himself off and started limping to retrieve his horse. Before he reached the center of the bridge, he smacked into it again. It felt like walking into a stone wall, but there was nothing there. He found himself sitting on the ground again. The others were around him this time as he got to his feet.

Zedd was off his horse, holding its reins in one hand, and helping Richard with the other. "What's the matter?"

"I don't know," Richard managed. "It felt like I ran into a

631

wall, right in the center of the bridge. I must have just fallen off, that's all. I think I'm all right now."

Zedd looked around and led him forward with a hand on his elbow. Before going far, he hit it again, but this time he had been moving slowly and wasn't knocked from his feet, only back a few steps. He took one slow step forward, and came in contact with it again. Zedd gave a serious frown. Richard put his hands out, feeling the solid form of the smooth wall that wouldn't let him pass but would let the rest of them through. The touch of it made him feel dizzy and sick. Zedd walked back and forth through the invisible barrier.

The wizard stood where the unseen wall stood. "Walk back to the end of the bridge, then walk to me."

Richard felt the lump on his forehead as he walked back to the end of the bridge. Kahlan jumped off her horse, next to Zedd. Brophy came up beside her, to see what the trouble was. This time, as he walked, Richard held his hands out in front of himself.

Before he was halfway back, he made solid contact, and could go no farther, having to back away from the sickening feeling at its touch.

Zedd rubbed his chin. "Bags!"

The rest of them came to Richard, since he couldn't come to them. Zedd led him forward again. When he made contact, he backed away a little.

Zedd took Richard's left hand. "Touch it, with your other hand."

Richard did as he was told until the sick feeling made him withdraw his hand. Zedd seemed to feel it, through Richard. By now, they were at the foot of the bridge. Every touch of the thing had made it move back the way they had come.

"Bags! And double bags!"

"What is it?" Richard demanded.

Zedd took a glance to Kahlan and Chase before he spoke. "It's a keeper spell."

"What's a keeper spell?"

"It's a spell drawn by that filthy artist, James. He's drawn it around you, and then when you touched it the first time, it activated the spell. Once you touch it, it pulls tighter, like a trap. If we don't get it off you, it will shrink until you are all that's in it, and then you won't be able to move."

"Then what?"

Zedd straightened. "The touch of it is poison. When it finishes closing around you, like a cocoon, it will crush you, or the poison of it will kill you."

Kahlan grabbed the sleeve of Zedd's robes, panic in her eyes. "We have to go back! We have to get it off him!"

Zedd pulled his arm free. "Well, of course we do. We'll find the drawing and erase it."

"I know where the sacred caves are," Kahlan offered as she grabbed hold of her saddle and put a foot in the stirrup.

The wizard turned to retrieve his horse. "We don't have any time to waste. Let's go."

"No," Richard said.

They all turned back to stare at him.

"Richard, we have to," Kahlan said.

"She's right, my boy. There's no other way."

"No." He looked at their startled faces. "That's what they want us to do. You said the artist couldn't spell you or Kahlan, so he did it to me, thinking that would get us all back. The box is too important. We can't take the risk." He looked to Kahlan. "You just tell me where these caves are, and Zedd, you tell me how to erase the spell."

Kahlan grabbed the reins of her horse and Richard's, pulling them forward. "Zedd and Chase can protect the box, I'm going with you."

"No, you're not! I'm going alone. I have the sword to protect me. The box is all that matters, it is our first responsibility. We must protect it above all else. Just tell me where the caves are, and how to fix the spell. When I'm finished, I'll catch up with you."

"Richard, I think . . ."

"No! This is about stopping Darken Rahl, not about any one of us. This is not a request, it's an order!"

They straightened, Zedd turning to Kahlan. "Tell him where the caves are."

Kahlan angrily handed the reins of her horse to Zedd and snatched up a stick. She drew a map in the dirt of the road, pulling the stick along one of the lines she had drawn. "This is the Callisidrin, and here, the bridge. This is the road, and here Tamarang and the castle." She drew the line of a road to the north of the city. "Here, in these hills northeast of the city, there is a stream that runs between twin hills. They're about a mile south of a small bridge that crosses the stream. The twin hills have cliffs on the sides toward the stream. The sacred caves are in the cliff on the northeast side of the stream. That is where the artist draws his spells."

Zedd took the stick from her and broke off two finger-length pieces. He rolled one between his palms. "Here. This will erase the curse. Without seeing it, I can't tell you what part you must erase, but you should be able to figure it out. It's a drawing and you will be able to make some sense of it. That is the whole purpose of a drawn spell; you must be able to make sense of it, or it won't work."

The stick Zedd had rolled in his palms no longer felt like wood. It felt soft and tacky. Richard put it in his pocket. Zedd rolled the other piece in his palms. He handed it to Richard, it too no longer a stick. This time it was black, almost like charcoal, but hard.

"With this," the wizard said, "you can draw on the spell, and change it if you have to."

"Change it how?"

"I can't tell you without seeing it. You'll have to use your own judgment. Now, hurry. But I still think we should . . ."

"No, Zedd. We all know what Darken Rahl is capable of. The box is all that is important, not any one of us." He shared a deep look with his old friend. "Take care of yourself. And Kahlan." He looked up to Chase. "Get them to Michael. Michael will be able to protect the box better than we can alone. And don't hold back, waiting for me. I'll catch up." Richard gave him a hard stare. "If I don't, I don't want any of you coming back for me. You just get the box away from here. Understand?"

Chase gave him a serious look. "On my life." He gave Richard brief instructions to find the Westland army, up in the Rang'Shada.

Richard looked to Kahlan. "Take care of Siddin. Don't worry, I'll be back with you soon enough. Now get going."

Zedd mounted his horse. Kahlan handed Siddin over to the wizard. She gave Chase and Zedd a nod. "Go on, get started. I will catch up in a few minutes."

Zedd started to protest, but she cut him off and told him again to start ahead. She watched the two horses and the wolf gallop across the bridge and down the road before she turned back to Richard.

Concern cut deeply into her features. "Richard, please, let me . . ."

"No."

She nodded and handed him the reins to his horse. Tears were filling her green eyes. "There are dangers in the Midlands you know nothing about. Be careful." A tear ran down her cheek.

"I'll be back with you before you have time to miss me."

"I'm afraid for you."

"I know. But I'll be all right."

She looked up at him with eyes he could lose himself in. "I shouldn't be doing this," she whispered.

Kahlan threw her arms around his neck and kissed him. Hard, fast, desperate.

For a moment as he reached his arms around her and pulled her tight against him, the touch of her lips on his, the little moan that came from her, and the feeling of her fingers through the back of his hair made him forget his own name.

He was in a daze as he watched her put a boot in the stirrup and throw her other leg over the saddle. She pulled the reins, bringing her horse around close to him.

"Don't you dare do anything stupid, Richard Cypher. Promise me."

"I promise." He didn't tell her that he thought letting harm reach her was what he considered stupid above all else. "Don't worry, I'll be back with you just as soon as I get rid of this spell. Protect the box. Rahl must not get it. That's what matters. Now, get going."

He stood holding the reins of his horse, watching her gallop across the bridge and disappear into the distance.

"I love you, Kahlan Amnell," he whispered.

With an encouraging pat to the splotch of gray on the roan's neck, Richard headed the big horse off the road after crossing the small bridge, and spurred it along the bank of the stream. The horse ran with ease, splashing its hooves in the shallow water when the brush blocked the way along the bank. Sunlit hills, mostly barren of trees, rose up around the stream. As the banks became steeper, he led the horse up along the higher ground where it could make easier progress. Richard kept a watch for anyone following, or observing, but saw no one. The hills seemed deserted.

Chalk white cliffs rose up to either side of the stream, cleft faces on identical hills straddling the water. Richard was off the horse before it stopped. Looking about, he tethered it to a sumac whose red fruit were already dried and shriveled. His boots slid on the loose ground as he descended the steep bank. There was a narrow foot trail through the slide of rock and dirt. Following it brought him to the tall mouth of a cave.

With a hand on the hilt of the sword, he peeked around the opening, checking for the artist, or anyone else. There was no one. Immediately inside the cave were drawings on the walls. They covered every surface, and continued back into the darkness.

Richard was overwhelmed. There were hundreds of drawings, maybe thousands. Some were little, no bigger than his hand; some were larger, tall as he. Each depicted a different scene. Most had only one person in them, but a few had many people. It was obvious that they had been drawn by different hands. Some were delicately rendered, rich in detail, with shading and highlights, depicting people with broken limbs, or drinking from cups with skulls and crossed bones on them, or standing next to fields of withered crops. Others were done by someone with little talent for the task: their figures were drawings of people made of simple lines. But the scenes in these were similarly gruesome. Richard guessed that the talent of the artist was of little importance; it was the message that counted.

Richard found drawings done by different hands but of the same subject. These people might have a map of some sort around them, but around each was a line drawn in a circle, the circle having a skull and crossed bones on it somewhere.

Keeper spells.

But how was he to find his? There were drawings everywhere. He didn't know what the drawing of his spell looked like. He searched the walls with growing panic, moving deeper into the darkness. He ran his hands over the pictures as he moved, trying to look at each, so as not to miss his. His eyes darted everywhere, overwhelmed by the number of spells, searching for something familiar, not knowing exactly what to look for, or where.

Richard worked his way back into the darkness, reasoning that maybe there was an end to the drawings, and maybe the latest were at the end. It was too dark to see. He went toward the mouth of the cave to retrieve reed cane torches he had seen there.

Before he had gone far, he ran smack into the invisible wall. With rising panic, he realized that he was trapped in the cave. He was running out of time. The torches were out of reach.

He ran back into the darkness, searching. He had trouble seeing the spells, and still there was no end to them. A thought he definitely didn't like came to him.

If there be need enough. The night stone.

With no time to lose, he pulled the leather pouch from his pack. He looked at it in his hand, trying to decide if this would be a help, or simply more trouble. Trouble he couldn't handle. He thought about the times he had seen the stone out of the pouch. Each time, it had taken a while for the shadow things to come. Maybe if he just pulled it out for a short time, had a look into the darkness, and then put the stone back, he would have the time he needed before the shadows found him. He didn't know if it was a good idea.

If there be need enough.

He dumped the stone into his hand. Light filled the cave. Richard wasted no time looking at individual drawings, but instead quickly went deeper, looking for where they ended. From

637

the corner of his eye, he saw the first shadow materialize. It was still a ways off. He kept going.

At last, he came to the end of the drawings. The shadows were almost upon him. He thrust the stone back in the leather pouch. In the darkness, he held his breath, eyes wide, expecting the painful touch of death. It didn't come. The only light was a dim glow with a bright spot in the center, the entrance, but it didn't provide enough light to see the drawings. He knew he would have to take out the stone again.

First, with his fingers, he searched through his pocket, and found the soft, tacky piece of stick Zedd had given him. With it firmly in hand, he pulled the stone out again. The light blinded him for a second. His head swiveled around, looking.

Then he saw it. The man in the drawing was as tall as he, but the rest of the drawing was larger still. It was crude, but he knew it was him. The sword held in the right hand had the word *Truth* written on it. There was a map around the figure, similar to the one Kahlan had drawn on the ground. On one side, the line around the outside edges went down the Callisidrin and across the center of the bridge. That was where he had run into it.

The shadows called his name. He looked up to see hands reaching for him. He thrust the stone into the pouch and pressed his back against the wall, over his drawing, listening to his heart pounding in his ears. In dismay, he realized that the drawing was too large for him to erase the entire circle around him. If he only erased part of it, he had no way of knowing where the gap would be, or how to make the gap where he was in the cave.

He backed away, to prepare himself to get a better look the next time he pulled the stone out. He bumped into the invisible wall. His heart felt as if it skipped a beat. The wall was almost around him. He had no time.

He pulled the stone out and immediately started erasing the sword, hoping that would take away his identity, take the spell off him. The lines erased only with great difficulty. He backed away a step, to look, and hit the wall. The shadows reached for him, calling his name seductively.

He dumped the stone back into the pouch and stood in the blackness, breathing hard, near panic at the feeling of being trapped. He knew he couldn't use the sword to fight the shadow things while he worked on the drawing; he had fought the shadows before and it took everything he had. His mind raced. He couldn't think of what to do. He had erased the sword, and that didn't work. The spell must still recognize him. He knew there wasn't enough time to erase the line all the way around him. His breath came in a desperate pant.

There was flickering light. He spun around. A man holding one of the reed torches came closer, an oily smile on his face. It was James, the artist.

"I thought I might find you here. I came to watch. Anything I can do to help?"

By his laugh, Richard knew James wasn't about to help him. James also knew that with the wall between them Richard couldn't use the sword on him. He laughed at Richard's helplessness.

Richard cast a quick glance sideways. The torch gave enough light for him to see the drawing. The invisible wall pushed at his shoulder, pushed him toward the wall. A wave of nausea and dizziness went through him at the touch. He was only a step away from the cave wall as it was. In moments, he would be encased, crushed, or poisoned.

Richard spun to the drawing. While he worked with one hand, he searched his pocket with the other. He pulled out the stick Zedd had told him he could use to alter the drawing.

James leaned forward with a chuckle, watching him work.

The chuckle stopped. "What are you doing there?"

Richard didn't answer as he erased the right hand on the figure.

"Stop that!" James yelled.

Richard ignored him and kept erasing. James threw the torch on the ground and pulled out a drawing stick of his own. The artist started drawing in fast slashing strokes, strands of his greasy hair whipping around as he worked. He was drawing a figure. He was drawing another spell. Richard knew that if James finished first, there would be no second chance.

"Stop that, you fool!" James yelled as he raced to complete his drawing.

The unseen wall pressed up against Richard's back, forcing him against the wall of the cave. He barely had room to move his arms. James was drawing a sword, starting to write the word *Truth*.

Richard took his drawing stick and, with a line, connected the sides of the wrist on the figure, making a stump. Just like the one James had.

As he finished it, the pressure on his back lifted, and the sick feeling left.

James screamed.

Richard turned to see him writhing on the floor of the cave, folding himself into a ball as he vomited. Richard shuddered and picked up the torch.

The artist's pleading eyes came up to him. "I . . . wasn't going to let it kill you . . . only trap you. . . ."

"Who had you do this spell on me?"

James gave a wicked little smile. "The Mord-Sith," he whispered. "You are going to die. . . ."

"What's a Mord-Sith?"

Richard heard the breath being squeezed from him, bones snapping. James was dead. Richard couldn't say he was sorry.

Richard didn't know what a Mord-Sith was, but he didn't want to wait around to find out. Suddenly he felt alone and vulnerable. Zedd and Kahlan both had warned him that there were many things in the Midlands, many creatures of magic, that were dangerous, that he knew nothing about. He hated the Midlands, the magic. He just wanted to get back to Kahlan.

Richard ran toward the cave entrance, dropping the torch along the way. Running out into the bright sunlight, shielding his eyes, he came to a halt. Squinting, he saw a ring of people around him. Soldiers. They wore uniforms of dark leather and mail, swords over their shoulders, battle axes at their wide belts.

At their lead, facing the cave, facing him, was someone different, a woman, with long auburn hair pulled back into a loose braid. She was sheathed in leather from neck to ground, cut to fit like a glove. Blood-red leather. The only deviation from the blood red of it was a yellow crescent and star across her stomach. Richard saw that the men wore the same crescent and star on their chests, only theirs was red. She watched him with no emotion except the slightest wisp of a smile.

Richard stood with his feet spread defensively, his hand on the hilt of the sword, not knowing what to do, without a clue to their intent. Her eyes gave a little flick, looking above and behind him. Richard heard two men drop from the cliff wall to the ground behind him. He could feel the anger of the sword racing urgently into him through his hand on the hilt. He held it at full rage as he gritted his teeth.

The woman snapped her fingers at the men behind him, then pointed at him. "Take him." He heard the sound of steel being drawn.

That was everything Richard needed to know. The commitment had been made.

Bringer of death.

His sword came out in an arc as he spun. He let the anger loose with a vengeance. It exploded through him. His eyes met those of the two men. Their jaws were set in a rage of their own as their swords cleared the scabbards over their shoulders.

Richard kept the Sword of Truth low. Waist height, with all his weight and strength behind it. Their swords came down defensively. He screamed with lethal rage. Lethal hate. Lethal need. He gave himself completely over to the lust to kill, knowing anything less would be the end of him. His sword tip whistled.

Bringer of death.

Shards of hot, shattered steel spiraled through the clear morning air.

Twin grunts. At impact, twin, wet thwacks, like ripe melons hitting the ground. Insides turned out in long red ropes. The top halves of their bodies tumbled as the legs collapsed.

The sword continued around, tracing its route with strings of blood. He refocused the rage, the hate, the need. She commanded them. Richard wanted her lifeblood. The magic surged through him unhindered. He was still screaming. She stood with a hand on her hip.

Richard met her eyes, made a slight alteration to the course of the sword so it too would meet them. Her widening smile only fed the violent fire of his wrath. Their eyes locked together. The sword tip whistled around toward her head. His need to kill was beyond retrieval.

Bringer of death.

The pain of the sword's magic hit him like a waterfall of icy

641

water on naked flesh. The blade never reached her. The sword clattered to the ground as the pain took him to his knees, ripping through him, doubling him over.

Hand still on her hip, smile still on her face, she stood over him, watching as he clutched his arms across his abdomen, vomiting blood, choking on it. Fire burned through every inch of him. The pain of the magic consumed him, took his breath from his lungs. Desperately, he tried to get a grip on the magic, tried to put away the pain as he had learned to do before. It did not respond to his will. With rising panic, he realized he no longer had control of it.

She did.

He collapsed to his face in the dirt, trying to scream, to breathe, but couldn't. He thought about Kahlan for an instant; then the pain took even that from him.

Not one of the men moved from the circle. The woman put a boot on the back of his neck and an elbow on her knee as she leaned over. With her other hand she grabbed a fistful of his hair and lifted his head. She leaned closer, the leather creaking.

"My, my," she hissed. "And here I thought I was going to have to torture you for days and days before I finally made you angry enough to use your magic against me. Well, not to worry, I have other reasons to torture you."

Through his pain, Richard realized he had made a fearful mistake. He had somehow given her the control of the sword's magic. He knew he was in more trouble than he had ever been in in his life. Kahlan was safe, he told himself; that was all that mattered.

"Do you want the pain to stop, my pet?"

The question enraged him. His anger at her, his want to kill her, twisted the pain tighter. "No," he managed with all of his strength.

She shrugged, dropping his head. "Fine by me. But when you decide you want the pain of the magic to stop, all you have to do is stop thinking those nasty thoughts about me. From now on, I control the magic of your sword. If you so much as think of lifting a finger against me, the pain of the magic will take you down." She smiled. "That is the only pain you will have any

642

control over. Just think something pleasant about me, and it will stop.

"Of course, I too will have control over the pain of the magic, and can bring it to you any time I choose, and I can bring you other pain too, as you will learn." She frowned. "Tell me, my pet, did you try to use the magic on me because you are a fool, or because you fancy yourself as brave?"

The pain let up the smallest bit. He gasped for air. She had relaxed it just enough to allow him to answer.

"Who ... are ... you?"

She took a fistful of his hair again, lifted his head, twisted it around to look into his eyes. As she leaned over, the boot on his neck sent a shard of pain through his shoulders. He couldn't move his arms. Her face was wrinkled in a frown of curiosity.

"You don't know who I am? Everyone in the Midlands knows me."

"I'm ... Westland."

Her eyebrows lifted in delight. "Westland! My, my. How delicious. This is going to be fun." Her smile widened. "I am Denna. Mistress Denna to you, my pet. I am a Mord-Sith."

"I'll not ... tell you ... where Kahlan is. You might as well ... kill me ... now."

"Who? Kahlan?"

"The ... Mother Confessor."

"Mother Confessor," she said with distaste. "Why in the world would I want a Confessor? It is you, Richard Cypher, that Master Rahl sent me for, no one else. One of your friends has betrayed you to him." She twisted his head up harder, pushed her boot down harder. "And now I have you. I had thought it might be difficult, but you hardly made it any fun at all. I'm to be in charge of your training. But then you wouldn't know about that, since you are from Westland. You see, a Mord-Sith always wears red when she's to train someone. That's so your blood won't show so much. I have a wonderful feeling I'm going to have a lot of your blood on me before I have you trained."

She dropped his head, and leaned her full weight on her boot, holding her hand out in front of his face. He could see that the back of her gloved hand was armored, even the fingers. A blood-red leather rod, about a foot long, hung loosely from her wrist by an elegant gold chain. It swung back and forth in front of his eyes. "This is the Agiel. This is part of what I will use to train you." She gave him a smooth smile, arching an eyebrow. "Curious? Want to see how it works?"

Denna pressed the Agiel against his side. The shock of the pain made him cry out, even though he had had no intention of giving her the satisfaction of seeing how much it hurt. Every muscle in his body locked rigid with the agony of the thing against his side. His mind was filled with the want of having it off him. Denna pushed the slightest bit harder, making him scream louder. He heard a pop, and felt a rib crack.

She took the Agiel away; warm blood oozed down his side. Richard was covered in sweat as he lay in the dirt, panting, tears running from his eyes. He felt as if the pain were pulling every muscle in his body apart. There was dirt in his mouth, and blood.

Denna gave him a cruel sneer. "Now, my pet, say 'Thank you, Mistress Denna, for teaching me.'" Her face came closer. "Say it."

With all his mental strength, Richard focused his hunger to kill her, and envisioned the sword exploding through her head. "Die, bitch."

Denna shuddered and half closed her eyes, running her tongue over her lip in ecstasy. "Oh, that was a deliciously naughty vision, my pet. Of course, you will learn to be seriously sorry you did it. Training you is going to be exquisite fun. Too bad you don't know what a Mord-Sith is. If you did, you would be very afraid. I would enjoy that." Her smile showed her perfect teeth. "But I think I'm going to delight in surprising you even more."

Richard maintained the vision of killing her until he was unconscious.

CHAPTER 41

RICHARD'S EYES CAME OPEN a little. His mind was in a fog. He was facedown on a cold stone floor, lit by flickering torchlight. The stone walls had no windows to tell him if it was day or night. There was a coppery taste in his mouth. Blood. He tried to think of where he could be, and why. A sharp pain in his side caught his breath when he tried to inhale too deeply. His whole body hurt. He throbbed everywhere. It felt as if someone had given him a beating with a club.

The memory of the nightmare seeped back into his mind. At the thought of Denna, his anger flashed. Instantly the pain of the magic made him inhale in a gasp. The unexpected shock of it made him draw his knees up and let out a moan of agony. He recoiled from the anger, put her from his mind. He thought of Kahlan, remembering the way she had kissed him. The pain melted away. Desperately, he tried to keep his mind on Kahlan; he couldn't take the pain again. He couldn't bear it; he already hurt too much.

He had to think of a way out of this. If he didn't get control of his anger, he had no chance. He remembered how his father had taught him that anger was wrong, how for most of his life he had been able to keep it choked off. Zedd had told him that there were times when bringing the anger out was more dangerous than keeping it in. This was one of those times. He had a whole lifetime of experience at keeping his anger under control; he must do it now. That thought gave him a sliver of hope.

Carefully, without moving too much, he took appraisal. His sword was back in its scabbard, his knife still in its sheath, the night stone still in his pocket. His pack lay against a far wall. The left side of his shirt was hard with dried blood. His head pounded with pain, but felt no worse than the rest of him.

Turning his head a little, he saw Denna. She was stretched out at an angle in a wooden chair with her ankles crossed. Her right elbow rested on a simple wooden table as she spooned something into her mouth from a bowl she held in her other hand. She was watching him.

He thought maybe he should say something. "Where are your men?"

Denna kept chewing for a time as she watched him. At last she set the bowl down and pointed to a spot on the floor next to her.

Her voice was calm, almost gentle. "Come and stand here."

With great difficulty, Richard rose to his feet and walked to stand where she had pointed. She watched him without emotion as he stood looking down at her. He waited in silence. She stood and with her boot pushed the chair back out of the way. She was almost as tall as he. She turned her back to him as she picked up a glove off the table and worked in into her right hand, pushing the fingers down tight.

Abruptly she spun around, backhanding him across the mouth. The armored back of the glove split his lip open on his teeth.

Immediately, before the anger could grip him, he thought about a beautiful place in the Hartland Woods. His eyes watered from the sting of the gash.

Denna gave him a warm smile. "You forgot the appellation, my pet. I told you before; you are to address me as Mistress, or as Mistress Denna. You are lucky to have me as your trainer; most Mord-Sith are not as lenient as I. They would have used the Agiel at the first offense. But I have a soft spot in my heart for good-looking men, and besides, even though the glove isn't a very effective punishment, I must admit I rather favor using it. I like to feel the contact. The Agiel is exhilarating, but there is no substitute for using your own hands to feel what you're doing." She gave a little frown, her voice hardening. "Take your hand away."

Richard took his hand off his mouth and held both at his sides. He could feel the blood dripping from his chin. Denna watched in satisfaction. Unexpectedly, she leaned forward and licked some of the blood off his chin, smiling at the taste. It seemed to excite her. She pressed herself against him, but this time she sucked his lip in her mouth and bit it, hard, on the cut. Richard squeezed his eyes shut, his hands in fists, and held his breath until she backed away, licking the blood from her lips with a smile. He shook with the pain, but held the vision of the Hartland Woods in his mind.

"That was just a gentle warning, as you will soon learn. Now, repeat the question properly."

Richard decided on the spot that he would call her Mistress Denna, and that it would, to him, be a term of disrespect, and that he would never, ever, call her simply Mistress. It would be his way of fighting her, of keeping his self-respect. In his own mind at least.

Richard took a deep breath to steady his voice. "Where are your men, Mistress Denna?"

"Much better," she cooed. "Most Mord-Sith don't allow those in training to talk, or to ask questions, but I think that becomes boring. I rather like to talk to my trainee. As I said, you are lucky to have me." She gave him a cool smile. "I've sent my men away. I no longer need them. They are only used for capture, and to hold the captive until he uses his magic against me; then they are no longer needed. There is nothing you can do to get away, or fight back. Nothing."

"And why do I still have my sword, and knife?"

Too late, he remembered. With an arm he blocked her fist to his face. The act of stopping her brought the pain of the magic. The Agiel came up into his stomach. He rolled over on the ground, crying out in agony.

"Stand up!"

Richard choked off the anger to shut away the pain of the magic. The pain of the Agiel didn't fade so quickly. He came to his feet with great difficulty.

"Now, get on your knees, and ask for my forgiveness."

When he didn't move quick enough for her, she laid the Agiel on his shoulder, pushing him down with it. His right arm went numb with hurt.

"Please, Mistress Denna, forgive me."

"That's better." She smiled at last. "Stand up." She watched him come to his feet. "You have your sword and knife because they are no danger to me, and perhaps someday you will use them to protect your Mistress. I prefer my pets to keep their weapons, so it can be a constant reminder that they are helpless against me."

She turned her back to him, removing her glove. Richard knew she was right about the sword: it had magic, and she controlled that. But he wondered if that was the only way. He had to know. His hands reached for her throat.

She continued to slowly remove the glove as he fell to his knees, crying out with the pain of the magic. Desperately, he brought his mind to the picture of the Hartland Woods. The pain eased, and he returned to his feet when she told him to do so.

Denna gave an impatient look. "You're going to make this hard, aren't you?" Her face softened, the smooth smile returning. "But then, I enjoy it when a man makes it hard. Now, you're doing it wrong. I told you that to make the pain stop, you should think something pleasant about me. That's not what you're doing. You're thinking about some boring trees. This is your last warning. Either think something pleasant about me, to stop the pain of the magic, or I will leave you in the agony of it all night. Do you understand?"

"Yes, Mistress Denna."

Her smile widened. "That was very good. See? You can be trained. Just remember, something pleasant about me." She took his hands and gazed into his eyes as she pressed his hands to her breasts. "I find most men seem to focus their pleasant thoughts here." She leaned closer, still holding his hands against her, her voice becoming airy. "But if there's anything you like better, please feel free to let your mind go there instead."

Richard decided that he thought her hair was pretty, and that that was the only place on her his mind was going to go to think anything pleasant. The pain unexpectedly took him to his knees, tightening its grip until he couldn't breathe. His mouth opened, but he could get no air. His eyes bulged.

"Now, show me you can do as you were told. Shut the pain off any time you wish, but do it in the way I told you."

He looked up at her, at her hair. His vision was blurring. With concentration, he thought about how attractive he thought her braid was. He forced himself to think of it as beautiful. The pain lifted, and he collapsed to his side, gasping for air.

"Stand up." He did as he was told, still struggling to breathe. "That was the proper way to do it. See to it that is the only way you dare to remove the pain in the future, or I will change the magic so you will be unable to remove it at all. Understand?"

"Yes, Mistress Denna." He was still catching his breath. "Mistress Denna, you said someone betrayed me. Who was it?"

"One of your own."

"None of my friends would do that. Mistress Denna."

She regarded him contemptuously. "Then I would guess they aren't really your friends, now, are they?"

He looked at the floor, a lump in his throat. "No, Mistress Denna, but who was it?"

She shrugged. "Master Rahl didn't think it important enough to tell me. The only thing that is important for you to know, now, is that no one is going to rescue you. You are never going to be free again. The sooner you learn that, the easier it will go for you; the easier your training will be."

"And what is the purpose of my training, Mistress Denna?"

The smile returned to her face. "To teach you the meaning of pain. To teach you that your life is no longer yours, that it is mine, and I can do anything I want with it. Anything. I can hurt you in any way I want, for as long as I want, and no one is going to help you but me. I'm going to teach you that every moment you have without pain is a moment only I can grant you. You are going to learn to do as I say without question, without hesitation, no matter what it is. You are going to learn to beg for anything you get.

"After a few days of training here, and I think you have made enough progress, then I will take you to another place, where there are other Mord-Sith, and I will continue training you there until I'm finished, no matter how long it takes. I will let some of the other Mord-Sith play with you, so you can see how lucky you are to have me. I rather like men. Some of the others hate them. I will let some of them have you for a while, so you can see how gentle I really am."

"And what is the purpose of this training, Mistress Denna? To what end? What is it you want?"

She seemed to genuinely enjoy telling him these things. "You are someone special. Master Rahl himself wants you trained." Her smiled widened. "He asked for me. I would guess he has something he wants to ask you. I will not let you embarrass me in his eyes. When I'm done with you, you will beg to tell him anything he wants to know. When he is finished with you, then you are to be mine, for life. However long that may be."

Richard had to concentrate on her hair, had to fight to keep the anger down. He knew what Darken Rahl wanted to know; he wanted to know about the Book of Counted Shadows. The box was safe. Kahlan was safe. Nothing else mattered. Denna could kill him, for all he cared. In fact, it would be doing him a favor.

Denna walked around him, looking him up and down. "If you prove to be a good pet, I may even choose you for my mate." She stopped in front of him, put her face close to his, gave him a coy smile. "Mord-Sith mate for life." Her smile showed her teeth. "I've had many mates. But don't get yourself too excited by the prospect, my pet," she breathed. "I doubt you will find it to be an experience you enjoy, if you live through it. None of the others have. They all died after a short time as my mate."

Richard didn't think that was anything he had to worry about. Darken Rahl wanted the book. If he didn't find a way to escape, Darken Rahl was going to kill him, in the same way he had killed Richard's father, and Giller. The most he would learn from reading Richard's entrails was where that place was—inside Richard's head—and there was no way any amount of the reading of his entrails was going to read the book out to him. Richard only hoped he could live long enough to see the look of surprise on Darken Rahl's face when he realized he had made a fatal mistake.

650

No book. No box. Darken Rahl was a dead man. That was all that mattered.

As for the question of him being betrayed, he decided that he didn't believe it. Darken Rahl knew the Wizard's Rules, and he was just using the first, trying to make him afraid of the possibility. The first step to believing. Richard decided that he was not going to be tricked by the Wizard's First Rule. He knew Zedd and Chase and Kahlan. He would not believe Darken Rahl over his friends.

"By the way, where did you get the Sword of Truth?"

He looked right into her eyes. "I bought it from the last man who had it. Mistress Denna."

"Is that so? What did you have to give for it?"

Richard held her eyes. "Everything I had. It would appear it is to also cost me my freedom, and probably my life."

Denna laughed. "You have spirit. I love breaking a man with spirit. Do you know why Master Rahl picked me?"

"No, Mistress Denna."

"Because I am relentless. I may not be as cruel as some of the others, but I enjoy breaking a man more than any of them. I love hurting my pets more than anything else in life. I live to do it." She arched an eyebrow and smiled. "I don't give up, I don't tire of it, and I don't ease up. Ever."

"I am honored, Mistress Denna, to be in the hands of the best."

She put the Agiel against the cut on his lip and held it there until he was on his knees and tears ran from his eyes. "That is the last flippant thing I ever want to hear from you." She took the Agiel away and kneed him in his mouth, knocking him sprawling on his back. She pressed the Agiel against his stomach. Before he passed out, she pulled it away. "What do you have to say?"

"Please, Mistress Denna," he managed with the greatest of effort, "forgive me."

"All right, get up. It's time to begin your training."

She went to the table and retrieved something. She pointed to a spot on the floor. "Stand there. Now!"

Richard moved as fast as he could. He couldn't straighten himself; the pain wouldn't allow it. He stood on the spot, breathing hard, sweating. She handed him something with a thin chain attached. It was a collar made of leather, the same color as she wore.

Her voice lost its pleasant quality. "Put it on."

Richard was in no condition to ask questions. He realized that he was starting to believe he would do anything to avoid the touch of the Agiel. He buckled the collar around his neck. Denna picked up the chain. The end of it had a loop of metal, which she slipped over the post on the back of the wooden chair.

"The magic will punish you for going against my wishes. When I place this chain somewhere, it is my wish for it to stay there until I remove it. I want you to learn that you are helpless to remove it." She pointed at the door, which stood open. "For the next hour, I want you to try your best to make it to that doorway. If you don't try your hardest, this is what I will do for the rest of the hour." She put the Agiel to the side of his neck until he was on his knees, screaming in agony, and begging for her to stop. She took it away and told him to begin, then went to lean, arms folded, against a wall.

The first thing he did was simply to try to walk to the door. The pain buckled his legs before he was able to put even a little tension on the chain, and stopped only when he scooted backward toward the chair.

Richard reached for the ring. The pain of the magic cramped his arms until he was shaking with the strain of reaching for it. Sweat ran off his face. He tried backing to the chair, then turning, but before his fingers could touch the chain, the pain took him to the ground again. He pushed against the pain, straining to reach the chair, but couldn't get there past the pain, the effort causing him to fall to the ground, vomiting blood. When it ended, he held himself up with one hand, tears dripping from his face as he held his stomach with his other hand and shook. From the corner of his eye, he saw Denna unfold her arms and stand up straight. He started moving again.

What he was doing was clearly not going to work. He had to think of something else. He drew the sword, thinking to lift the chain. For a brief instant, and with the greatest effort, he managed to touch the chain with the blade. The pain made him drop the sword. He was able to stop the hurt only by putting the sword back in its scabbard.

A thought came to him. He lay down on the ground, and in a quick movement, kicked the chair out from under the chain before the pain could paralyze him. The chair skidded across the floor, hit the table, and fell over. The chain fell from the post.

The victory lasted only the briefest of moments. With the chain off the chair, the pain elevated to a new height. He choked and gasped against the floor. With all his effort, he clawed his way across the stone. Each inch he moved only increased the pain until he was blinded by it. His eyes felt as if they would explode from his head. He had managed to move only about two feet. He didn't know what to do; the pain wouldn't let him move, and it was keeping him from thinking.

"Please, Mistress Denna," he whispered with all his strength, "help me. Please help me." He realized he was crying, but didn't care. He only wanted the chain back on the chair so the pain would stop.

He heard her boots walking toward him. She bent and picked up the chair, righted it, and replaced the loop. His pain lifted, but he couldn't stop crying as he rolled onto his back.

She stood over him with her hands on her hips. "That was only fifteen minutes, but since I had to come help you, the hour starts over. The next time I have to come help you, it will be two hours." She bent and pushed the Agiel against his stomach, making pain bloom inside him. "Understand?"

"Yes, Mistress Denna," he cried. He was afraid there was a way to escape, and afraid of what would happen to him if he found it, and afraid of not trying. If there was a way, by the end of the hour, he had not found it.

She came and stood over him as he rested on his hands and knees. "Do you think you understand now? Do you understand what will happen if you try to escape?"

"Yes, Mistress Denna." And he really did. There was no way for him to ever get away. Hopelessness closed around him, feeling as if it would suffocate him. He wanted to die. He thought about the knife at his belt.

"Stand up." As if reading his mind, she spoke softly. "If you should think you would end your service as my pet, think again.

653

The magic will prevent it, the same as it prevents you from moving the chain from where I put it." Richard blinked numbly at her. "There is no way for you to escape me, not even through death. You will be mine as long as I choose to let you live."

"That won't be long, Mistress Denna. Darken Rahl is going to kill me."

"Perhaps. But even if he does, it will only be after you tell him what he wants to know. What I want is for you to answer his questions, and you are going to do what I want without hesitation." Her brown eyes had the hardness of steel. "You may not believe that right now, but you have no idea how good I am at training people. I have never failed to break a man. You may think you will be the first, but you will soon be begging to please me."

The first day with her wasn't over, and already Richard knew he would do almost anything she said. She had weeks left to train him. If he could have willed himself to die on the spot, he would have done it. The worst thing was knowing she was right; there was nothing he could do to stop her. He was at her mercy, and he didn't think she had a shred of it.

"I understand, Mistress Denna. I believe you." Her pleasant smile made him need to think of how pretty her braid was.

"Good. Now, take off your shirt." Her smile widened at the puzzled look on his face, and the way he started unbuttoning his shirt nonetheless. She held the Agiel in front of his eyes. "It's time to teach you all the things the Agiel can do. If you leave your shirt on, it will be covered in blood, and I won't be able to find a fresh spot on you. You are going to see why the outfit I wear is this color."

He pulled his shirttail out. He was breathing hard, in a near panic. "But Mistress Denna, what have I done wrong?"

She cupped a hand to the side of his face with mock concern. "Why, don't you know?" He shook his head, swallowing back the lump in his throat. "You have let yourself be captured by a Mord-Sith. You should have killed all my men with your sword. I think you could have done it. You were very impressive, as far as you went. Then you should have used your knife or your bare hands to kill me, while I was vulnerable, before I had control of your magic. You should have never given me the chance to take control of the magic from you. You should have never tried to use it against me."

"But why must you use the Agiel on me, now."

She laughed. "Because I want you to learn. Learn that I can do whatever I want, and there is no way for you to stop me. You must learn that you are totally helpless, and that if you enjoy any time without pain, it is only because I choose it. Not you." The smile left her face. She went to the table, returned with manacles held with a length of chain. "Now. You have a problem that annoys me. You keep falling down. We are going to fix that. Put these on."

She threw them at him. He struggled to control his breathing as he latched each iron band to a shaking wrist. Denna dragged the chair over to a beam, made him stand under it. She stood on the chair to hook the chain to an iron peg.

"Stretch up. It doesn't reach yet." He had to stand on his toes and stretch before she could get it hooked. "There." She smiled. "Now we won't have any more problems with you falling down."

Richard hung from the chain, trying to control his terror, the iron bands digging into his wrists because of his own weight. He knew there was nothing he could do to stop her before, but this was different. It amplified his helplessness, made him all the more aware that there was no way for him to fight back. Denna pulled on her gloves, walked around him several times, tapping the Agiel against her hand, prolonging his anxiety.

If only he had been killed trying to stop Darken Rahl—that was a price he had been prepared to pay. This was different. This was death without dying. Living death. He was not even to be allowed the dignity of fighting back. He knew what the Agiel felt like; he didn't need her to show him anymore. She was only doing this to take away his pride, his self-respect. To break him.

Denna tapped the Agiel against his chest and back as she continued walking around him. Each touch of it was like a dagger knifing into him. Each touch made him cry out in pain and twist on the chain; and he knew she hadn't even really begun yet. The first day was still not over, and there would be many more to come. He cried at his helplessness.

Richard imagined his sense of self, his dignity, as a living thing, saw it in his mind. He imagined a room. A room that was impervious to anything, to any harm. He put his dignity, his self-respect, into that room, and locked the door. No one would have a key to that door. Not Denna, not Darken Rahl. Only him. He would endure what was to come, for as long as it was to come, without his dignity. He would do what he had to, and someday he would unlock the door, and be himself again, even it if was only in death. But for now, he would be her slave. For now. But not always. Someday, it would end.

Denna took his face in both her hands and kissed him, hard. Hard enough to make his cut lip throb and sting. She seemed to enjoy the kiss more when she was sure it hurt him. She took her face from his, her eyes wide with delight. "Shall we begin, my pet?" she whispered.

"Please, Mistress Denna," he whispered, "don't do this."

Her smile widened. "That's what I wanted to hear."

Denna began showing him what the Agiel would do, how if she dragged it lightly across his flesh, it raised fluid-filled welts, and how if she pressed a little harder, they filled with blood. When she bore down, he could feel warm wetness on his sweaty skin. She could also make the exact same pain without leaving a mark. His teeth hurt from gritting them so hard. Sometimes she would stand behind him, waiting until he was off guard before she touched it to him. When she tired of that she made him close his eyes and keep them closed while she walked around him, pressing it against him or dragging it around his chest.

She would laugh when she succeeded in making him think it was coming, and he would brace for it, and it didn't. One particularly sharp jab brought his eyes open wide, giving her an excuse to use the glove. She made him beg for forgiveness for opening his eyes without being told to do so. His wrists bled from the manacles cutting into them. It was impossible to keep his weight off them.

His anger only got away from him once, when she pressed the Agiel into his armpit. She stood with a smirk, watching, while he twisted, trying to think of her hair. Since putting the Agiel there caused him to lose control of the anger, she concentrated on that area for a long time, but he didn't make the same mistake twice. Since he didn't bring on the pain of the magic again, she did it for him, only when she did it he couldn't turn it off, no matter how hard he tried. He had to beg her to do it for him. Sometimes she would stand in front of him, watching him catch his breath. A few times, she pressed herself against him, hugging his chest, squeezing, the hardness of the leather making every wound it pressed against flare anew in pain.

Richard had no idea how long this torture lasted. Much of the time, he wasn't aware of anything but the pain, as if it were a living thing, there with him. He was only aware that at some point, he knew he would do anything she said, no matter what it was, if only she would stop hurting him. He looked away from the Agiel. The mere glimpse of it made tears well up in his eyes. Denna was right about herself; she never tired or became bored with what she did. It seemed to constantly fascinate her, keep her amused, satisfied. The only thing that seemed to make her happier than hurting him was when he begged her to stop. He would have begged more, to make her happy, but most of the time he was incapable of talking. Simply breathing was almost more than he could handle.

He no longer tried to keep the pressure off his wrists, and hung limp, delirious. He thought she stopped for a while, but he hurt so much from what she had already done that he wasn't sure. The sweat in his eyes was blinding him; the sweat running into the wounds caused them to burn.

When his head cleared somewhat, she returned, walking behind him. He braced for what he knew was coming. Instead, she grabbed a fistful of hair and jerked his head back.

"Now, my pet, I'm going to show you something new. I'm going to show you how kind a mistress I really am." She pulled his head back, hard, until the pain made him tense the muscles in his neck to resist the pressure. She put the Aigel against his throat. "Stop fighting me, or I won't take it away."

Blood was running into his mouth; he relaxed his neck muscles, allowing her to pull as hard as she wanted.

"Now, my pet, listen very carefully. I'm going to put the Agiel in your right ear." Richard almost choked with fear. She jerked his head back to make him stop it. "It's different from putting it anywhere else. It hurts a lot more. But you must do exactly as I say." Her mouth was right by his ear; she whispered to him like a lover. "In the past, when I have had a sister Mord-Sith with me, we would both put our Agiel in the man's ears at the same time. He would make a scream unlike any other. The sound of it is intoxicating. I get chills just thinking about it."

"But, it would also kill him. We were never successful at using two Agiel at the same time in that particular way without killing him. We kept trying, but they always died. Be thankful I am your mistress; there are others who still try."

"Thank you, Mistress Denna." He wasn't sure what he was thanking her for, but he didn't want her to do whatever it was she had planned.

"Pay attention," she whispered harshly. Her voice softened again. "When I do this, you must not move. If you move, it will damage things inside you. It won't kill you, but it will cause irrevocable disability. Some men who move go blind, some are no longer able to move anything on one side of their body, some can't talk anymore, or walk. But in all who move, something is spoiled. I want you fully functional. Mord-Sith who are more cruel than I don't tell their pets not to move, they just do it without warning them. So you see? I am not so cruel as you thought. Still, only a few of the men I do it to are able to hold still. Even though I warn them, they still jerk, and then they are left impaired."

Richard couldn't hold back from crying. "Please, Mistress Denna, please don't do it, please."

He could feel the breath of her smile. She ran her wet tongue into his ear, kissed it. "But I want to, my pet. Don't forget, hold still, don't move."

Richard clenched his teeth, but nothing could have prepared him for it. His head felt as it had been turned to glass and shattered into a thousand pieces. His fingernails cut into his palms. All sense of time shattered apart with everything else. He was in a wasteland of agony with no beginning, no end. Every nerve in his body seared with razor-sharp, burning misery. He had no idea how long she held the Agiel there, but when she took it away, his screams echoed from the stone walls.

When he finally went limp, she kissed his ear and whispered breathlessly in it. "That was a simply delightful scream, my pet. I've never heard one better. Except a scream in death, of course.

You did very well, my pet, you never moved an inch." She kissed his neck tenderly, then his ear again. "Shall we try the other side?"

Richard sagged in the shackles. He couldn't even cry. She pulled his head back harder as she moved to the other side of him.

When she was finally finished with him, and unhooked the chain, he collapsed to the floor. He didn't think himself capable of moving, but when she motioned him up with the Agiel, the mere sight of it made him do as she wanted.

"That's all for today, my pet." Richard thought he might die of joy. "I'm going to get some sleep. Today was only a part day; to-morrow we will get in a full day of training. You will find a full day more painful."

Richard was too exhausted to care about tomorrow. He wanted only to lie down. Even the stone floor would feel like the best bed he had ever slept in. He looked at it longingly.

Denna brought the chair over, took the chain that hung from his collar, and hooked it over the iron peg in the beam. He watched in confusion, too weary to try to figure out her intent. When finished, she walked toward the door. Richard realized there wasn't enough slack to allow him to lie down.

"Mistress Denna, how am I to sleep?"

She turned and gave him a condescending smile. "Sleep? I don't recall telling you that you were allowed to sleep. Sleep is a privilege you earn. You have not earned it. Don't you remember this morning, when you had that nasty vision of killing me with your sword? Don't you remember I told you that you would be sorry you did it? Good night, my pet."

She started to leave, but turned back. "And if you have any thoughts of simply pulling the chain off the peg and letting the pain make you pass out, I wouldn't try it if I were you. I changed the magic. It will not allow you to pass out anymore. If you pull the chain off, or fall down accidentally, and that pulls it off, I will not be here to help you. You will be all alone, for the night, with the pain. Think about that, if you get sleepy."

She turned on her heels and left, taking the torch with her.

Richard stood in the dark, crying. After a time, he forced himself to stop, and thought of Kahlan. That was something pleasant

Denna couldn't take away from him. At least not tonight. He made himself feel good by thinking of how she was safe, and had people to protect her. Zedd, and Chase, and soon Michael's army. He envisioned her where she must be, at a camp somewhere, right now, with Siddin and Rachel, taking care of them, telling them stories, making them laugh.

He smiled at the vision of her in his mind. He savored the memory of her kiss, the feel of her against him. Even if he wasn't with her, she could still make him smile, make him happy. What happened to him didn't matter. She was safe. That was all that counted. Kahlan, and Zedd, and Chase, were safe, and they had the last box. Darken Rahl was going to die, and Kahlan was going to live.

After it was over, what did it matter what happened to him? He might as well be dead. Denna, or Darken Rahl, would see to that. He had only to endure the pain until then. He could do that. What did it matter? Nothing Denna could do could match the pain of knowing that he couldn't be with Kahlan. The woman he loved. The woman he loved, who would choose another.

He was glad he was going to be dead before then. Maybe he could do something to hurry it along; it certainly didn't take much to make Denna angry. If he moved the next time she put the Agiel in his ear, he would be permanently impaired; then maybe he would be of no use to her. Maybe she would kill him then. He had never felt so alone in his life.

"I love you, Kahlan," he whispered into the dark.

As Denna had promised, the next day was worse. She seemed well rested, and anxious to work off some of her energy at the task of breaking him. He knew there was one thing he had control over, a choice in. He waited for her to use the Agiel in his ear again, so he could jerk his head with all his strength, and cause serious damage, but she never did, as if she sensed what he might do. That gave him a shred of hope; it was something he had made her do. He had made her not use the Agiel in that way. She didn't have all the control she thought she did; he still was able to force her to do something by his own choice. The thought heartened him. The thought of how he had locked his self-respect, his dignity, away in his secret room gave him the ability to do what was necessary. He let himself do as she wished, when she wished it.

The only time Denna paused was a few times to sit at the table to eat. She would watch him while she slowly ate fruit, smiling to herself when he moaned. He was given nothing to eat, only water from a cup she held for him after she was finished with her meal.

At the end of the day she hooked his chain to the beam again and made him stand for the night. He didn't bother to ask why; it didn't matter. She was going to do as she wished and there was nothing he could do to change it.

In the morning when she returned with the torch, he was still standing, but barely. She seemed in a good mood.

"I want a good-morning kiss." She smiled. "I expect you to return it. Show me how happy you are to see your mistress."

He did his best, but had to concentrate on how pretty her braid was. The embrace ignited the flames of pain in the wounds she pressed against. When she was finished, and the hurt left him shaking, she pulled the chain off the peg and tossed it on the floor.

"You are learning to be a good pet. You have earned two hours of sleep."

He collapsed to the floor, asleep before the sound of her footsteps faded.

He discovered that being awakened by the Agiel was a terror all its own. The brief sleep had done little to revive him. He needed much more than he had been allowed. He vowed to himself that he would struggle with all his might to get through the entire day without making a single mistake, to do exactly as she wished, and maybe she would grant him a whole night's sleep.

He put his effort into doing everything she wished, hoping he would please her. He was hoping, too, that he would be given something to eat. He hadn't eaten since she had captured him. He wondered which he wanted more—sleep, or food. He decided that what he wanted the most was for the pain to stop. Or for him to be allowed to die.

He was at the end of his strength, felt his life slipping away from him, and awaited the end with longing. Denna seemed to sense his waning endurance, and eased up, giving him more time to recover, taking longer breaks. He didn't care; he knew it was never going to end, he was lost. He surrendered his will to live, to go on, to hold out. She cooed to him soothingly, stroking his face, as he hung in the shackles, resting. She spoke encouragingly to him, told him not to give up, and promised that when he was broken, it would be better. He just listened, not even able to cry.

When at last she unhooked the shackles from the beam, he thought it must be night again; he had no sense of time anymore. He waited for her to hook up the chain, or throw it on the floor and tell him he could sleep. She did neither. She instead hooked it over the chair, told him to stand, and left. When she returned, she was carrying a bucket.

"On your knees, my pet." She sat in the chair next to him, took a brush from the hot soapy water, and started scrubbing him. The stiff bristles brought a pain all of their own as they worked into his wounds. "We have a dinner invitation. I have to get you cleaned up. I rather like the smell of your sweat, your fear, but I'm afraid it would offend the guests."

She worked with an odd sort of tenderness. It reminded him of the way a person would care for a dog. He fell against her, unable to hold himself up. He wouldn't lean against her for support if he had the strength not to, but he didn't. She let him stay where he was as she scrubbed. He wondered who the dinner invitation was from, but didn't ask.

Denna told him anyway. "Queen Milena herself has asked us to join her and her guests for dinner. Quite an honor, for someone as low as you, wouldn't you say?"

He only nodded, not having enough strength to speak.

Queen Milena. So they were in her castle. He guessed that didn't surprise him. Where else would she have had time to take him? When she was finished, she allowed him one hour of sleep, to rest for dinner. He slept at her feet.

She woke him with her boot instead of the Agiel. He almost cried at her mercy and heard himself thanking her profusely for her kindness to him. She gave him instructions as to his behavior. He would have his chain hooked to her belt, and was to keep his eyes to her, speak to no one unless they spoke to him first, and then only if he looked to her first for permission to answer. He would not be allowed to sit at the table, but would sit on the floor, and if he behaved himself, he would be given something to eat.

He promised to do as she wished. The idea of sitting on the floor sounded wonderful to him: to be able to rest, and not have to stand, or be hurt. And to be allowed something to eat, at last. He would make sure he did nothing to displease her, or to keep her from giving him food.

Richard's brain was in a fog as he followed behind Denna, attached to her by the chain on his collar, concentrating on keeping the proper amount of slack. The manacles were off his wrists, but the cuts from them were red and swollen, and throbbed painfully. He vaguely remembered some of the rooms they passed through.

In the room with other people, Denna stopped as she strode around, talking briefly with finely dressed people. Richard kept his eyes on her braid. The braid had obviously been done over for the dinner; the vigorous use of the Agiel caused it to loosen, and freed stray wisps of hair. She must have done it over while she had let him sleep.

He found himself thinking about how beautiful her hair really was, how much finer she looked than any of the other women at the dinner. He knew people were staring at him, at his sword, as he was led around the room by his collar and chain. He reminded himself that his pride was locked away for the time being. This was about getting a chance to rest, to eat, and about having her not hurt him for a while.

Richard bowed and stayed bowed while Denna spoke to the Queen. The Queen and the Mord-Sith gave only a bow of the head to each other. The Princess was at the Queen's side. Richard thought about how Princess Violet had treated Rachel, and had to return his thoughts to Denna's braid.

As she sat at the table, Denna snapped her fingers and pointed at the floor behind her chair. He knew what she wanted and sat on the floor, crossing his legs. Denna sat to the left of the Queen, to the right of Princess Violet, who eyed him coldly. Richard recognized some of the Queen's advisors. He smiled to himself. The court artist wasn't among them. The head table was higher than the others, but sitting on the floor, Richard couldn't see many of the gathered guests.

"Since you don't eat meat," the Queen said to Denna. "I had the cooks prepare a special dinner I know you will enjoy. Some wonderful soups and vegetables, and some rare fruits."

Denna smiled and thanked her. While she was eating, a server brought her a plain bowl on a tray.

"For my pet," she told him, interrupting her conversation only briefly.

The man took the bowl from the tray and handed it down to Richard. It was some sort of gruel, but to Richard, as he held the bowl in his trembling hands, preparing to drink it down, it looked like the best meal he had ever seen.

"If he's your pet," Princess Violet said, "why do you allow him to eat like that?"

Denna looked over to the Princess. "What do you mean?"

"Well, if he's your pet"—the Princess smiled—"he should eat off the floor, without his hands."

Denna grinned, a glint in her eye. "Do as she says."

"Put it on the floor," Princess Violet said, "and eat it like a dog, for us all to see. Let everyone see that the Seeker is no better than a dog."

Richard was too hungry to do anything to lose his meal. He concentrated on a mental image of Denna's braid and set the bowl carefully on the floor as he glanced into Princess Violet's eyes, to her smirk, and ate the gruel to the sound of laughter. He licked the bowl clean, telling himself it was because he needed the strength, in case he ever got the chance to use it.

After the Queen and her guests had finished eating, a man in chains was brought in and made to stand in the center of the room. Richard recognized him. He was one of the men Kahlan had freed from the dungeon. They exchanged a brief look of understanding, despair.

There was talk of crimes and foul deeds done. Richard did his best to ignore it; he knew it was merely a pretext. The Queen gave a short lecture on the man's crimes, then turned to the Princess.

"Perhaps the Princess would like to pronounce this man's punishment?"

Princess Violet stood, beaming. "For his crimes against the Crown, one hundred lashes. Then, for his crimes against the people, his head."

A murmur of agreement swept the room. Richard felt sick, but at the same time he wished he could exchange places with the man. The one hundred lashes would be easy, and there would be an axe at the end of it.

Princess Violet turned to Denna as she sat back down. "Sometime I would enjoy seeing how you handle your punishments."

"Stop down anytime you wish." Denna glanced over her shoulder. "I'll let you watch."

When they were back in the stone room, Denna wasted no time in getting his shirt off, and he was soon hanging from the beam again. She coolly informed him that his eyes had strayed too much at dinner. Richard's heart sank. The shackles around his wrists burned into his flesh once more. Denna's talents had him covered in sweat in no time, gasping for air, crying out in agony. She told him it was still early and she wanted to get in a lot of training before the evening ended.

Richard's muscles flexed and tightened, lifting him off the floor as Denna twisted the Agiel into his back. He begged her to stop, but she didn't. When he sagged once more in the shackles, he saw a silhouette in the doorway.

"I like the way you can make him beg," Princess Violet said.

The Mord-Sith smiled to her. "Come closer, my dear, and I'll show you more."

Denna hugged him with one arm, pressing herself into his wounds. She kissed his ear and whispered to him. "Let's show the Princess how well you can beg, shall we?"

Richard vowed to himself he wouldn't, but it wasn't long before he broke his vow. Denna put on a demonstration for Princess Violet, showing her the different ways she could hurt him. She seemed proud to show off her talents.

"Can I try?" the Princess asked.

Denna looked down at her a moment. "Why, of course, my dear. I'm sure my pet wouldn't mind." She smiled at him. "Now would you?"

"Please, Mistress Denna, don't let her. Please. She's just a little girl. I'll do anything you say, but don't let her. Please."

"There, you see, my dear, he doesn't mind at all."

Denna handed her the Agiel.

Princess Violet stood grinning up at him while she fingered the Agiel. Experimentally, she poked it at his thigh muscle, happy at the way it made him flinch in pain. Pleased with the results, she walked around him, poking it into his flesh.

"It's easy!" she said. "I never thought it would be this easy to make someone bleed."

Denna stood with her arms folded across her breasts, watching him with a smile while the Princess became bolder. It wasn't long before her cruelty came fully to the surface. She delighted in her new game.

"Remember what you did to me?" she asked him. She jabbed the Agiel into his side. "Remember how you embarrassed me? I guess you're getting what you deserve, don't you think?" Richard kept his teeth clenched tightly together. "Answer me! Don't you think this is what you deserve?"

Richard kept his eyes closed as he tried to control his grip on the pain.

"Answer me! And then beg me to stop. I want to do it while you beg."

"You better answer her," Denna said. "She seems to learn fast."

"Please, Mistress Denna, don't teach her this. What you are doing to her is worse than what you are doing to me. She's only a little girl. Please don't do this to her. Don't let her learn these things."

"I'll learn what I please. You better start begging. Right now!"

Even though he knew he was only making it worse for himself, Richard waited until he could absolutely bear it no longer before he let himself answer. "I'm sorry, Princess Violet," he gasped. "Please forgive me. I was wrong."

Richard found that answering her was a mistake; it only seemed to excite her. It didn't take her long, though, before she learned to make him beg, and cry, even though he tried not to. Richard couldn't believe the absurdity of a little girl doing this. Much less enjoying it. This was madness.

She held the Agiel against his stomach while she leered up at him. "But this is less than that Confessor deserves. She will get more than this someday. And I'm going to be the one to do it. My mother said I get to be the one when she comes back. I want you to beg me to hurt her. Let's hear you beg me to chop off the Mother Confessor's head."

Richard had no idea what it was, but something inside him came awake.

Princess Violet gritted her teeth and jammed the Agiel into his gut hard as she could, twisting it. "Beg me! Beg me to kill that ugly Kahlan!"

The pain made Richard scream at the top of his lungs.

Denna stepped between them, snatching the Agiel from Princess Violet's hand. "Enough! You will kill him if you use the Agiel in that way."

"Thank you, Mistress Denna," he panted. He felt a peculiar affection for her, at the way she stepped to his defense.

Princess Violet took a step back, her face a picture of bad temper. "I don't care if I kill him!"

Denna's voice was cool and authoritative. "Well, I do. He is too valuable to waste in this manner." Denna was clearly the one in charge around here. Not the Princess, not even the Queen. Denna was an agent of Darken Rahl.

Princess Violet glared at him. "My mother says that Confessor Kahlan will come back and that we'll have a surprise for her the next time she comes here. I just want you to know because my mother said you'll be dead by then. My mother says I get to decide what to do to her. First, I'm going to cut off her hair." Her hands were in fists, her face red. "Then I'm going to let all the guards rape her, every one! Then I'm going to put her in the dungeon for a few years so they'll have someone to play with! Then when I get tired of hurting her, I'll have her head chopped off and put it on a pole where I can watch it rot!"

Richard actually felt sorry for the little Princess. The sadness for her came over him in a wave. At that feeling, he was surprised to feel the thing in him that had come awake rise up.

Princess Violet squeezed her eyes shut and stuck her tongue out far as she could.

It was like a red flag.

The strength of the awakened power exploded through him.

When his boot came up under her jaw he could feel it shatter like a crystal goblet on a stone floor. The impact of the blow lifted the Princess into the air. Her own teeth severed her tongue before they, too, shattered. She landed on her back, a good distance away, trying to scream through the gushing blood.

Denna's eyes snapped to him. For an instant, he saw fear pass across them. Richard had no idea how he was able to what he had done, why the magic hadn't stopped him, and from the look on Denna's face, he knew he shouldn't have been able to do it.

"I warned her before," Richard said, holding Denna's glare. "Promise made. Promise kept." He smiled. "Thank you, Mistress Denna, for saving my life. I owe you."

She stared at him a moment before her expression turned dark. She stalked out of the room. He watched the Princess writhing on the floor as he hung in the shackles.

"Turn over, Violet, or you'll drown in your own blood. Turn over!"

The Princess managed to flip herself over, a red pool spreading under her. Men appeared in a rush, tending to her. Denna watched. They lifted her carefully, carrying her away. He could hear their urgent voices fading, disappearing down the hall.

And then he was alone with Denna.

The strap hinges creaked as she pushed the door closed with one long-nailed finger. Richard had learned over the last few days that Denna truly did have a perverse kindness to her. He had learned to interpret the way she used the Agiel, to interpret her mood through it. Sometimes when she was hurting him he could tell she was holding back out of a twisted caring for him. He knew it was insane, but he understood that there were times she felt she was sharing her feelings for him by doing her worst. He knew, too, that tonight she was going to do her worst.

She stood by the door, watching him. Her voice was soft. "You are a very rare person, Richard Cypher. Master Rahl warned me about you. Warned me to take care; that the prophecies speak of you." She walked slowly, her boots echoing her steps on the stone, to stand in front of him, close. She looked into his eyes, a slight wrinkle to her brow. Her breath on his face was quicker than normal. "That was quite extraordinary," she whispered. "Thoroughly exciting." Her eyes searched his face hungrily. "I have decided," she said breathlessly, "to have you as my mate."

Richard hung from the chains, helpless against this madness. He didn't know what the power was that had risen up in him, or how to call it back. He tried. It did not come.

Denna seemed to be in the grip of something he didn't understand, as if she were trying to summon the courage to do something, fearing it, yet anxiously wanting it. Her breathing was quickening, her chest heaving, as she looked into his eyes. Incredulous, he saw something the ugliness of her cruelty had never let him see before: she was attractive. Breathtakingly, stunningly, attractive. He thought he must be losing his mind.

Shocked, and strangely worried, Richard watched as she slowly put the Agiel between her teeth. He could tell by the way her pupils suddenly expanded that it was hurting her. Her skin paled. She inhaled sharply, trembling the slightest bit. Denna put her fingers into the back of his hair and held his head. Slowly she brought her lips to his. She kissed him deeply, passionately, sharing the shattering pain of the Agiel with him. With her tongue, she held it between their lips. Her kiss was savage, bestial, as she twisted against him.

Every fiber of his being burned with the torture. His gasp sucked the air from her lungs, hers did the same to him. He could get no breath but hers, she none but his. The pain made him forget everything but her. It marauded through his mind. He knew by the sounds she was making that she was feeling the same agony as he. Her fingers in his hair tightened into fists from the pain. She moaned in suffering. Her muscles tightened with it. It raged through the both of them.

Without comprehending why, he found himself kissing her back just as passionately, just as savagely. The pain was altering his perception of everything. He had never kissed anyone with this kind of lust. Desperately, he wanted her to stop. Desperately, he didn't.

The strange power awakened again. He tried to reach for it, grasp for it, hold on to it. But it slipped from him and was gone.

The pain was overwhelming him as Denna crushed her lips to his, the Agiel between them, their teeth grating together. She pressed her body to his, hooked a leg around his, clung to him. Her cries of anguish were growing more desperate. He ached to hold her.

As he was about to lose consciousness, she pulled away from him, still gripping his hair in her fists. Tears ran from her eyes as she looked into his, not two inches away. She rolled the Agiel into her mouth with her tongue and held it there with her teeth as she shook with the pain, as if to show him she was stronger than he. Her hand came slowly and took away the Agiel as her eyes rolled back in her head. She gasped for air.

Her brow wrinkled together. Tears from the pain, and from something else, flooded from her eyes. She gave him a kiss. The tenderness, the gentleness, of it, shocked him.

"We are bonded," she whispered intimately. "Bonded in the pain of the Agiel. I am sorry, Richard." She brushed his cheek with trembling fingers, the glaze of pain still in her eyes. "Sorry for what I will do to you. You are my mate for life."

Richard was stunned by the compassion in her voice. "Please, Mistress Denna. Please let me go. Or at least help me stop Darken Rahl. I promise you, I will willingly be your mate for life, if you help me stop him. I swear on my life, if you help me, I will stay without the magic holding me. Forever."

She put a hand to his chest, to steady herself as she recovered. "Do you think I do not understand what I am doing to you?" Her eyes had an empty gloss to them. "Your training and service will last for mere weeks, before you die. The training of a Mord-Sith lasts for years. Everything I do to you, and more, has been done to me, a thousand times over. A Mord-Sith must know her Agiel better than she knows herself. My first trainer took me for his mate when I was fifteen, after he had trained me since I was twelve. There is no way I could ever live up to his cruelty, or his ability to keep a person on the cusp between life and death. He trained me until I was eighteen, when I killed him. For that, I was punished with the Agiel every day for the next two years. This Agiel. The very same one I use on you was the one used to train me. It was presented to me when I was proclaimed Mord-Sith. I live for nothing else but to use it."

"Mistress Denna," he whispered. "I'm sorry."

The steel returned to her eyes. She nodded. "You will be.

670

There is no one who will help you. That includes me. You will find that being the mate to a Mord-Sith brings you no added privileges, only a great deal of added pain."

Richard hung helpless in the shackles, overwhelmed by the enormity of it all. Understanding her a little only increased his hopelessness. There was no escape for him. He was the mate of a madwoman.

The frown and the smile returned. "Why would you be so foolish as to do what you did? Surely, you must know I will hurt you for doing it."

He looked at her puzzlement for a moment. "Mistress Denna, what difference does it make? You are going to hurt me anyway. I can't imagine what more you could do to me."

Her lip curled in a sneer. "Oh, my love, you have a very limited imagination."

He felt her grab the tongue of his belt and yank the buckle open.

She gritted her teeth. "It is time we found some new places on you to hurt. It is time to see what you are really made of." The look in her eyes made him go cold. "Thank you, my love, for giving me the excuse to do this to you. I have never before done it to another, but it has been done to me enough times. It is what broke me when I was fourteen. Tonight," she whispered, "neither of us is going to get any sleep."

671

CHAPTER 42

THE BUCKETFUL OF COLD water on his naked flesh barely revived him. He only dimly saw the little rivers of water that were stained bright red as they ran away from him in the cracks of the stone floor his face lay against. Each shallow breath he took was a mighty effort. He wondered idly how many of his ribs she had broken.

"Put your clothes on. We're leaving," she called down to him.

"Yes, Mistress Denna," he whispered, his voice so hoarse from screaming he knew she couldn't hear him, and knew she would hurt him for not answering, and yet he could do no more.

When the Agiel didn't come, he moved a little, saw his boot and reached out to it, pulling it to him. He sat up, but couldn't raise his head above his shoulders. It hung limply. With great difficulty, he started putting on his boot. Gashes on his feet brought tears to his eyes when he pulled.

Her knee to his jaw knocked him flat on his back. She fell on him, sitting on his chest, hitting his face with her fists.

"What's the matter with you! Are you stupid? Your pants go on before your boots! Do I have to tell you everything!"

"Yes Mistress Denna, no Mistress Denna, forgive me Mistress Denna, thank you Mistress Denna for hurting me, thank you Mistress Denna for teaching me," he mumbled.

She sat on his chest, panting in rage. Her breathing slowed after a time.

"Come on. I will help you." She leaned over and kissed him. "Come on, my love. You'll be able to rest while we travel."

"Yes, Mistress Denna." The sound of his voice was hardly more than a breath.

She kissed him again. "Come on, my love. It will be better, now that I have broken you. You will see."

A closed carriage stood waiting for them in the dark. Clouds from the horses' breath rose and drifted slowly in the cold, still air. Richard stumbled a few times as he walked behind her, trying to keep the proper slack to the chain. He had absolutely no idea how long it had been since she had decided he was to be her mate, nor did it matter to him. A guard opened the carriage door.

Denna tossed the end of his chain on the floor. "Get in."

Richard grabbed the sides of the door. He dimly heard someone approach in a huff. Denna gave a little tug to the chain, indicating she wanted him to wait where he was.

"Denna!" It was the Queen, at the head of her advisors.

"Mistress Denna," she corrected.

The Queen looked to be in a foul mood. "Where do you think you are going with him?"

"That is none of your concern. It is time we were on our way. How is the Princess?"

The Queen glowered. "We don't know if she will live. I will be taking the Seeker. He is to pay."

"The Seeker is the property of myself and of Master Rahl. He is being punished, and will continue to be punished until either Master Rahl, or myself, kills him. There is nothing you could do to him that could equal what is already being done."

"He is to be executed. Right now."

Denna's voice was as cold as the night air. "Go back to your castle, Queen Milena, while you still have a castle."

Richard saw a knife in the Queen's hand. The guard standing next to him unhooked his battle-axe, gripping it tightly in his fist. There was a crystal clear moment of silence.

The Queen backhanded Denna and lunged with the knife for Richard. Denna effortlessly caught her with the Agiel against her large chest.

As the guard went past him, raising the axe to Denna, the strange power roared awake. Richard summoned all his strength, became one with the power. He hooked his left arm around the guard's throat and drove his knife home. Denna gave a casual glance back as the man let out a death scream. She smiled, and her eyes glided back to the Queen, who stood shaking, paralyzed in place, the Agiel between her breasts. Denna gave a twist to the Agiel. The Queen dropped straight down in a heap.

Denna turned her glare to the Queen's advisors. "The Queen's heart has given out." She arched an eyebrow. "Unexpectedly. Please express my condolence to the people of Tamarang on the death of their ruler. I would suggest you find a new ruler who is more attentive to the wishes of Master Rahl."

They all gave a quick bow. The awakened power flickered and was gone. The effort of stopping the guard had taken all the strength Richard had left. His shaking legs would no longer hold him. The ground tilted and came up to meet him.

Denna grabbed his chair near the collar, raising his head off the ground. "I didn't tell you to lie down! You were not given permission! On your feet!"

He couldn't move. She drove the Agiel into his stomach, dragged it up his chest, to his throat. Richard convulsed in pain, but could not make his body respond to her wishes.

"Sorry . . ." he breathed.

She let his head drop to the ground when she realized he wasn't able to move and turned to the guards. "Put him inside."

She climbed in after him, yelling up to the driver to be off, and pulled the door shut. Richard slumped back as the carriage jerked ahead.

"Please, Mistress Denna," he said in a slur, "forgive me for letting you down, for failing to stand as you wished. I'm sorry. I will do better in the future. Please punish me to teach me to be better."

She gripped the chain, close to the collar, her knuckles white, lifting him from the seat back. Her lips curled a sneer over gritted teeth. "Don't you dare die on me now, not yet; you have things to do first."

His eyes were closed. "As you command . . . Mistress Denna."

She let go of the chain, took his shoulders, laid him across the seat, and gave him a kiss on his forehead. "You have my permission to rest now, my love. It's a long way. You will have a long time to rest, before it starts again."

Richard felt her fingers smoothing his hair back and the bouncing of the carriage as it sped along the road, and fell asleep.

From time to time, he came partly awake, never fully conscious. Sometimes Denna sat next to him, letting him lean against her as she spooned food into his mouth. Swallowing was painful, almost more effort than he could bring forth. He winced with each spoonful, his hunger not sufficient to overcome the pain in his throat, and he turned his head from the spoon. Denna murmured encouragement to him, urging him to eat for her. Doing it for her was the only thing he responded to.

Whenever a bump in the road brought him awake suddenly, he would clutch at her for protection, safety, until she told him it was nothing, and to go back to sleep. He knew that sometimes he slept on the ground, sometimes in the carriage. He saw nothing of the countryside they traveled through, nor did he care. As long as she was near him, that was all that mattered; nothing else was important, except being ready to do as she commanded. A few times, he slowly came awake to find her wedged into the corner with him stretched out, his cloak tucked around him, his head on her breast, as she stroked his hair. When it happened, he tried not to let her know he was awake, so she wouldn't stop.

When this happened, and he felt the warm comfort of her, he also felt the power in him come awake. He didn't try to reach it, to hold it; he only noted it. One time when it happened, he recognized it, knew what it was. It was the magic of the sword.

As he lay against her, feeling the need of her, the magic stood within him. He touched it, fondled it, felt its power. It was like the power he had called forth when he was going to kill with the sword, but different in a way he couldn't understand. The power he had known before, he could no longer feel. Denna had that power now, but this she didn't. When he tried to grasp the magic, it vanished, like vapor. A dim part of his mind wanted its help, but since he couldn't control it, call it forth to aid him, he lost interest in it.

As the time passed, his wounds began healing over. Each time he came awake he was a little more alert. By the time Denna announced that they had arrived at their destination, he was able to stand by himself, although he was still not completely clear-headed.

In the darkness, she led him from the carriage. He watched her feet as she walked, keeping the proper slack in the chain attached to her belt. Even though he kept his eyes on her, he still noticed the place they were entering. It was immense, dwarfing the castle at Tamarang. Walls stretched off into the nothingness of the distance, towers and roofs rose to dizzying heights. He was aware enough to note that the design of the vast structure was elegant and graceful. It was imposing, but not harsh, not forbidding.

Denna led him through halls of polished marble and granite. Columns held majestic arches to the sides. As they walked on and on, he noticed how his strength had grown. He wouldn't have been able to stand for this long even a few days ago.

They saw no other people. Richard looked up at her braid, and thought about how pretty her hair was, how lucky he was to have such a fine mate. At the thought of his caring for her, the power rose up. Before it had a chance to fade, the dim, locked-away part of his mind grabbed it, held it, while the rest of his mind thought about his affection for her. The realization that he had control of it made him stop thinking about her, and grab the hope of escape. The power evaporated.

His heart sank. What did it matter, he thought; he was never going to escape, and why would he want to anyway? He was Denna's mate. Where would he go? What would he do without her to tell him what to do?

Denna went through a door, closing it behind him. A window with a pointed top was trimmed with simple drapes and open to the darkness outside. There was a bed with a thick blanket and fat pillows. The floor was polished wood. Lamps stood lit on the table next to the bed, and on the table with a chair on the other side of the room. There were cabinets of dark wood built into one wall next to another door. A stand held a basin and pitcher.

Denna unhooked his chain. "These are my quarters. Since you are my mate, you will be permitted to sleep here if you please me." She hooked the loop over the post of the footboard, snapped her fingers, and pointed at the floor at the foot of the bed. "You may sleep there tonight. On the floor."

He looked at the floor. The Agiel laid on the top of his shoulder took him to his knees.

"I said on the floor. Now."

"Yes Mistress Denna. I'm sorry Mistress Denna."

"I'm exhausted. I don't want to hear another sound out of you tonight. Understand?"

He nodded, afraid to voice his agreement.

"Good." She flopped facedown in the bed and was asleep in moments.

Richard rubbed the hurt in his shoulder. It had been a while since she had used the Agiel on him. At least she hadn't chosen to draw blood. Maybe, he reasoned, she didn't want blood in her quarters. No, Denna liked his blood. He lay down on the floor. He knew that tomorrow she was going to hurt him some more. He tried not to think about it; he was just getting healed from before.

He was awake before her; the shock of being awakened by the Agiel was something he wanted to avoid. A bell rang with a long peal. Denna woke, lay on her back awhile, saying nothing, then sat up, checking that he was awake.

"Morning devotions," she announced. "That was the bell, the call. After devotions, you will be trained."

"Yes, Mistress Denna."

She hooked his chain to her belt and led him once more through the halls to a square, open to the sky, with pillars supporting arches on all four sides. The center of the square, under the open sky, was white sand, raked in concentric lines around a dark, pitted rock. On the top of the rock was a bell—the one he had heard before. On the tile floor among the columns were people on their knees, bent forward, with their foreheads touching the tile.

The people chanted in unison. "Master Rahl guide us. Master Rahl teach us. Master Rahl protect us. In your light we thrive. In

677

your mercy we are sheltered. In your wisdom we are humbled. We live only to serve. Our lives are yours."

Over and over they chanted the same thing. Denna snapped her fingers, pointing at the floor. Richard kneeled down, imitating the others. Denna kneeled next to him, putting her forehead to the tiles. She started chanting in unison with the others, but stopped when she heard he wasn't.

"That's two hours." She frowned darkly at him. "If I have to remind you again, it's six."

"Yes, Mistress Denna."

He began chanting along. He had to concentrate on a vision of Denna's braid to be able to say the words without bringing on the pain of the magic. He wasn't sure how long the chanting lasted, but he thought it was about two hours. His back hurt from bending with his head to the floor. The words never varied. After a time they melted into the sound of gibberish, feeling like mush in his mouth.

The bell rang twice, and the people rose to their feet, going off in different directions. Denna rose. Richard stayed where he was, unsure of what to do. He knew he might get in trouble for staying where he was, but knew if he got up and wasn't supposed to, the punishment would be much worse. He heard footsteps coming toward them, but didn't look up.

A woman's husky voice spoke. "Sister Denna, how good to see you've returned. D'Hara has been lonely without you."

D'Hara! Through the fog of his training, the word ignited his thoughts. Instantly, he brought to mind the vision of Denna's braid, protecting him.

"Sister Constance. It's good to be home, and see your face again."

Richard recognized the ring of sincerity in Denna's voice. The Agiel touched the back of his neck, taking his breath away. It felt as if a rope were tightening around his throat. By the way it was held, he knew it wasn't Denna's.

"And what have we here?" Constance asked.

She took the Agiel away. Coughing in pain, Richard gasped for air. He came to his feet when Denna told him to do so, wishing he could hide behind her. Constance was a good head shorter than Denna, her stout figure dressed in a leather outfit like

678

Denna's, only brown. Her dull brown hair was done in a braid, too, but didn't have the fullness of Denna's. The look on her face made it seem she had just eaten something she didn't like.

Denna gave his stomach an easy slap with the back of her hand. "My new mate."

"Mate." Constance spat the word out as if it tasted bitter. "I swear, Denna, I'll never understand how you can bear to take a mate. The thought of it gives me a stomach ache. So, the Seeker, I see by his sword. Quite a catch, anyway. It must have been difficult."

Denna smiled smugly. "He only killed two of my men, before he turned his magic on me." The look of shock on Constance's face made Denna laugh. "He's from Westland."

Constance's eyebrows went up. "No!" She peered into Richard's eyes. "Is he broken?"

"Yes," Denna said, sighing. "But he still gives me reason to smile. It's only the morning devotion, and already he's earned two hours."

A grin spread on Constance's face. "Mind if I come along?"

Denna gave her a warm smile. "You know that anything that is mine, is yours also, Constance. In fact, you will be my second."

Constance seem pleased, and proud. Richard had to furiously think of Denna's braid as the edges of the anger burned to get away from him.

Denna leaned closer to her friend. "In fact, for you only, if you wish to borrow him for a night, I would not object." Constance stiffened with displeasure. Denna laughed. "Never try, never know."

Constance scowled. "I will have my pleasure from his flesh in other ways. I'll go change into the red, and meet you there."

"No ... the brown is fine, for now."

Constance studied her face. "That's not like you, Denna."

"I have my reasons. Besides, Master Rahl himself sent me for this one."

"Master Rahl himself. As you wish, then. After all, he is yours to do with as you will."

The training room was a simple square with walls and floor of gray granite and a beamed ceiling. On the way in, Constance tripped him. He landed on his face. Before he could stop it, the anger gripped him. She stood over him, pleased with herself, watching him struggle to regain control.

Denna attached a device to him that held his wrists and elbows tightly together behind his back. It was hooked to a rope that ran through a pulley in the ceiling, and was tied off at the wall. She hoisted him up until he had to stand on his toes before she tied the rope off at the wall. The pain in his shoulders was excruciating, making it hard to breathe, and she hadn't even touched the Agiel to him yet. He was helpless, off balance, and in agony before she even started. His mood sank.

Denna sat in a chair against the wall, telling Constance to enjoy herself. When Denna had trained him, she often had a smile on her face. Constance never smiled once. She went about her work like an ox at a plow, strands of hair coming loose, and in no time her face was covered with a sheen of sweat. She never varied the touch of her Agiel. It was always the same, always hard, harsh, angry. Richard didn't have to anticipate; there was no pause. She worked with rhythmic timing, never giving him a rest. But she didn't draw blood. Denna had a constant smile on her face as she sat with the chair leaned against the wall. At last Constance stopped, Richard panting, groaning.

"He can take it well. I haven't had a workout like this in quite a time. All the pets I've gotten lately fold at the first touch."

The chair came down on its front legs with a clunk. "Maybe I can help, Sister Constance. Let me show you where he doesn't like it."

Denna came up behind him and paused, making him flinch in expectation of what didn't come. Just as he breathed out, the Agiel drove into a tender spot on the right side. He cried out as she held the pressure against him. He couldn't hold his weight, and the rope pulled his shoulders so hard he thought his arms would come out of their sockets. With a sneer, Denna held the Agiel to him until he started crying.

"Please, Mistress Denna," he sobbed. "Please."

She withdrew the Agiel. "See?"

Constance shook her head. "I wish I had your talent, Denna."

"Here is another place." She made him scream. "And here,

and here too." She came around and smiled to him. "You don't mind if I show Constance all your special little places, do you?"

"Please, Mistress Denna, don't. It hurts too much."

"There, you see? He doesn't mind at all."

She went back to her chair as tears ran down his face. Constance never smiled; she simply went to work, and also had him begging breathlessly. But the way she never varied the pressure, never letting up, was worse than Denna. She never gave him a moment to rest. Richard learned to fear her touch more than he feared Denna's. Denna had an odd compassion at times. Constance never did. When it was beyond a certain point, Denna would tell her to stop, wait a moment, and guide her so as not to cripple him. Constance complied with her wishes and let Denna direct the way she wanted him hurt.

"You don't have to stay, Denna, if you have things to do. I won't mind."

Fear and panic raced through his mind. He didn't want to be left alone with Constance. He knew that Constance wanted to do things to him that Denna didn't want done. He didn't know what they were, but he feared them.

"Another time, I will leave you alone with him ... to do things your way, but today, I will stay."

Richard made sure he showed no sign that he was relieved. Constance went back to work.

After a while longer, when she was behind him, Constance grabbed a fistful of his hair and yanked his head back, hard. Richard knew very well what it meant to have his head pulled back in this manner. He remembered the pain of what she was about to do. The pain of having the Agiel in his ear. He shook uncontrollably, couldn't breathe with the fear of it.

Denna came out of her chair. "Don't do that, Constance."

Constance gritted her teeth as she looked at him, pulling his head back harder. "Why not? Surely you've done it?"

"Yes, I just don't want you to, that's all. Master Rahl hasn't talked to him yet. I don't want to take any chances."

A grin came to Constance's face. "Denna, let's do it together, at the same time. You and me. Like we used to."

"I told you, Master Rahl wants to talk to him."

"After that?"

Denna smiled. "It has been a long time since I've heard that scream." She looked to Richard's eyes. "If Master Rahl doesn't kill him, and he doesn't die first from ... from other things, then, yes, we will do it to him. All right? But not now. And Constance, please respect my wishes, about using the Agiel in his ear?"

Constance nodded and released his hair. "Don't you think you have gotten off easy." She scowled at him. "Sooner or later, you and I will be alone, and then I will take my pleasure from you."

"Yes, Mistress Constance," he whispered hoarsely.

After they were finished training him, they went to lunch. Richard followed behind, the chain hooked to Denna's belt. The dining hall was tasteful in its simple style of frame and panel oak over a white marble floor. There was the soft murmur of conversation at the various tables as people ate. Denna snapped her fingers as she sat, pointing at the floor behind her chair. Servers brought food to the two Mord-Sith, but none for Richard. Lunch was a hearty-looking soup, cheese, brown bread, and fruit. The good smells drove Richard to distraction. There was no meat served. Halfway through her meal, Denna turned and told him that he would get no lunch, for having earned two hours that morning. She said that if he behaved himself, he would get dinner.

The afternoon was spent at devotions, and after that, several hours of training. Denna and Constance shared the task. Richard did his best to do nothing wrong, and at dinner was rewarded with a bowl of rice with vegetables over it. After dinner were more devotions and more training, until at last they left Constance and returned to Denna's quarters, Richard dead tired and stooping because of pain as he walked.

"I wish a bath," she said. She showed him the room adjoining hers. It was small, empty of everything except a rope holding the binding device from the ceiling, and a bathing tub in the corner. She told him the room was for training if he needed it on the spot and she didn't want blood in her room, and for when she wanted to leave him hanging all night. She promised him he would be spending a great deal of time in the little room.

She had him drag the tub to the foot of her bed. He took the bucket from the tub and was instructed where to go for hot wa-

682

ter. He was to speak to no one, even if spoken to, and he was to run, there and back, so her bathwater wouldn't get cold before the tub was filled. She told him that if he didn't follow her instructions exactly while out of her sight, the pain of the magic would take him down, and if she had to come looking for him, he would be very sorry he had disappointed her. He swore his solemn oath to do as she commanded. The place where the hot water came from, a hot spring in a pool surrounded by white marble seats, was a goodly distance. He was sweating and exhausted by the time he had the tub filled.

While she sat soaking in the tub Richard scrubbed her back, brushed her hair out, and helped her wash it.

Denna draped her arms over the sides of the tub, put her head back, and closed her eyes, relaxing, while he knelt next to her, in case she wanted anything. "You don't like Constance, do you?"

Richard didn't know how to answer. He didn't want to say anything bad about her friend, but lying would get him punished, too. "I am ... afraid of her, Mistress Denna."

Denna smiled with her eyes still closed. "Clever answer, my love. You aren't trying to be flip, are you?"

"No, Mistress Denna. I told you the truth."

"Good. You should be afraid of her. She hates men. Every time she kills one, she cries out the name of the man who first broke her, Rastin. Remember I told you about the man who broke me, took me for his mate, and that later I killed him? Before he broke me, he was Constance's trainer. His name was Rastin. It was he who broke her. Constance is the one who told me how I could kill him. I would do anything for her. And because I killed the man she hated so, she would do anything for me."

"Yes, Mistress Denna. But Mistress Denna, please don't leave me alone with her?"

"I suggest you be very attentive to your duties. If you are, and you do not earn too much time, I will remain when she is training you. You see? You see how lucky you are to have a kind mistress?"

"Yes, Mistress Denna, thank you for teaching me. You are a gifted teacher."

She opened one eye, as if to check his face for a trace of a smirk. There was none.

"Get me a towel, and lay my nightclothes on the table by the bed."

Richard helped towel her hair dry. Denna didn't put on her nightclothes, but lay back on the bed with her damp hair spread out on the pillow.

"Go blow out the lamp on the table over there." He went immediately and blew out the flame. "Bring me the Agiel, my love."

Richard flinched. He hated it when she had him fetch the Agiel; touching it hurt. Fearing the result of hesitation more, he gritted his teeth and snatched it up, holding it in the open palms of his hands. The pain of it vibrated in his elbows and shoulders. He could hardly wait for her to take it. She had propped up the pillows against the headboard and was sitting up a little, watching him. He let out a deep breath when she picked it out of his hand.

"Mistress Denna, why doesn't it hurt you to touch it?"

"It does, same as you. It hurts me to touch it because it is the one used to train me."

His eyes opened wide. "You mean, the whole time you hold it, it hurts you? The whole time you are training me?"

She nodded, rolling it in her fingers, looking away from his eyes for a second. She gave him a little frown and smile. "There is rarely a time I am without pain, of one kind or another. That is one reason the training of a Mord-Sith takes years—to learn to handle the pain. I guess it's also why only women are Mord-Sith; men are too weak. The chain around my wrist allows me to let it hang; it doesn't hurt when it hangs by the chain. But while I use it on someone, it causes constant pain."

"I never knew." Richard's insides knotted in anguish. "I'm sorry, Mistress Denna. I'm sorry it hurts you, that you must suffer to teach me."

"Pain can bring pleasure all its own, my love. That's one of the things I'm teaching you. And it's time for another lesson." Her eyes glided up and down him. "Enough talk."

Richard recognized the look in her eyes, the quickening of her breathing. "But, Mistress Denna, you've just bathed, and I'm all sweaty."

A small smile came to one side of her mouth. "I like your sweat."

With her eyes locked on his, she put the Agiel between her teeth.

The days passed with a numbing sameness. Richard didn't mind the devotions, because he wasn't being trained, hurt. But he hated saying the words, and had to concentrate on Denna's braid the whole of the time he chanted. Chanting the same thing, hour after hour, on his knees with his head against the floor tiles, was hardly less onerous than the training. Richard found himself waking at night, or in the morning, chanting the words. *Master Rahl guide us. Master Rahl teach us. Master Rahl protect us. In your light we thrive. In your mercy we are sheltered. In your wisdom we are humbled. We live only to serve. Our lives are yours.*

Denna didn't wear the red anymore; instead, she wore white leather. She told him it was a gesture that said he was broken, had been taken for a mate, and that to show her power over him she chose not to make him bleed. Constance didn't like it. It didn't make much difference to Richard; the Agiel felt the same whether it drew blood or not. Constance was with Denna about half the time, occasionally going off to train a new pet. Constance became more and more insistent about being left alone with Richard, but Denna wouldn't permit it. Constance threw her all into his training. The more Richard saw of her, the more terrified he became of her. Denna smiled at him whenever she told Constance to take over.

One day, after the afternoon devotion, when Constance had gone off to train someone else, Denna took him back to the little room adjacent to her quarters for his afternoon training. She hoisted him up by the rope until he was hardly able to touch the floor.

"Mistress Denna, with your permission, would you allow Mistress Constance to do all my training from now on?"

His question had an effect he hadn't expected. It enraged her. She stared at him, her face turning a deep red; then she started hitting him with the Agiel, driving it into him, screaming at him, telling him how worthless he was, how insignificant, how she was sick of his talking. Denna was strong, and she beat him with the Agiel as hard as she could. It went on and on.

Richard couldn't remember her being so angry, so severe, so cruel. Soon he couldn't remember anything, even where he was. He convulsed in pain. He couldn't say anything or beg her to stop, or even breathe most of the time. She never slowed or let up. She just seemed to get angrier as she hurt him. He saw blood on the floor, a lot of blood. It splattered all over her white leather. Her chest heaved with her effort, her rage. Her braid came loose.

Denna grabbed his hair and yanked his head back. She gave him no warning. She drove the Agiel in his ear harder than she ever had. She did it again and again. Time distorted into eternity. He no longer knew who he was, or what was happening. He no longer tried to beg, to cry, to hold on.

She stopped, standing next to him, panting in ire. "I'm going to dinner." He felt the agony of the magic come on in him. He gasped, his eyes going wide. "While I'm gone, and I'm going to take my time, I've leaving the pain of the magic on you. You will not be able to pass out, or to stop it. If you let the anger get away from you, it will make the pain worse. And it will get away from you. I promise."

She went to the wall and hoisted the rope up until his feet were off the floor. Richard cried out. His arms felt as if they would be torn out.

"Enjoy yourself." She turned on her heels and left.

Richard balanced on the edge of sanity and madness, the suffering twisting in him, making him unable to control the anger, as she had promised. The flames of his hurt consumed him. It was somehow worse that she wasn't there. He had never felt so alone, so helpless, and the pain wouldn't even let him cry; he could only gasp in agony.

He had no idea how long he was left alone. He was aware only of suddenly dropping to the floor, then Denna's boots to either side of his head as she stood over him. She turned off the pain of the magic, but his arms were still clamped helplessly behind his back, and the burning inferno of pain in his shoulders didn't extinguish. He cried against the blood on the floor as she stood over him.

"I told you before," she hissed through gritted teeth, "you are my mate for life." He could hear her heavy breathing, the rage in her. "Before I begin doing worse to you, and you are no longer able to speak, I want you to tell me why you asked to have Constance train you instead of me."

He coughed up blood, trying to speak.

"That is not the way you talk to me! On your knees! Now!"

He tried to get to his knees, but with his arms behind his back, he was unable to. Denna took a fistful of his hair and pulled him up. Dizzy, he fell against her, his face against the wet blood on her belly. His blood.

She pushed him away from her with the tip of the Agiel against his forehead. That brought his eyes open. He looked up at her, to answer.

Denna backhanded him across the mouth. "Look at the ground when you speak to me! No one gave you permission to look at me!" Richard looked down at her boots. "You're running out of time! Answer the question!"

Richard coughed up more blood; it ran down his chin, and he had to struggle to keep from vomiting. "Because, Mistress Denna," he said hoarsely, "I know it hurts you to hold the Agiel. I know it hurts you to train me. I wanted Mistress Constance to do it, to spare you the pain. I don't want you to hurt. I know what it feels like to hurt; you have taught me. You have already been hurt enough; I don't want you to hurt any more. I would rather have Mistress Constance punish me than have you be in pain."

He strove to balance himself on his knees. There was a long silence. Richard stared at her boots, and coughed a little, struggling to breathe with the pain in his shoulders. The silence seemed as if it would never end. He didn't know what she was going to do to him next.

"I don't understand you, Richard Cypher," she said softly, at last, the anger gone from her voice. "The spirits take me, I don't understand you."

She walked behind him, unhooked the device that held his arms, and walked out of the room without another word. He couldn't straighten out his arms properly, and fell on his face. He didn't try to get up, he only cried against the bloody floor.

After a time, he heard the bell, calling them to the evening devotion. Denna came back in, squatted down next to him, put her arm gently around him, and helped him to his feet.

"We are not allowed to miss a devotion," she explained in a quiet voice, hooking the chain to her belt.

The sight of his blood all over the white leather was shocking. There were strings of it across her face and in her hair. As they walked to the devotion, people who usually spoke to her averted their eyes and gave her wide passage. Kneeling with his head to the floor hurt his ribs, making it hard to breathe, much less chant. He didn't know if he was getting the words right, but Denna didn't correct him, so he just went on. How he stayed upright the whole time, without tipping over, he didn't know.

When the bell rang twice, Denna rose, but didn't help him. Constance appeared, a rare grin on her face.

"My, my, Denna, looks like you've been having fun." Constance backhanded him, but he managed to stay on his feet. "Been a bad boy, have you?"

"Yes, Mistress Constance."

"Very bad, it would appear. How delightful." Her hungry eyes turned to Denna. "I'm free. Let's go teach him what two Mord-Sith can really do."

"No, not tonight, Constance."

"No? What do you mean, no?"

Denna exploded. "I mean no! He is my mate, and I'm taking him back to train him as such! Do you wish to come and watch when I lie with my mate! Do you want to watch, too, what I do when I have the Agiel between my teeth!"

Richard shrank back. So that was what she had planned. If she did that to him tonight, as badly as he was already hurt . . .

People in white robes—missionaries, Denna had called them—were staring. Constance glared back and they hurried off. Both women's faces were red—Denna's from anger, Constance's from embarrassment.

"Of course not, Denna," she said in a low voice. "I'm sorry.

I didn't know. I will leave you to it." She gave Richard a smirk. "You look to be in enough trouble already, my boy. I hope you are up to your duties."

She gave him a jab in the stomach with her Agiel, and walked off. Dizzy, Richard put his hand across himself with a moan. Denna's hand come up under his arm, holding him up. Denna glared after Constance, then started off, expecting him to follow. He did.

When they were back in Denna's quarters, she gave him the bucket. He almost collapsed at the thought of filling her tub.

Her voice was quiet. "Go and get one bucket of hot water."

Richard could have died with relief, knowing that he didn't have to fill a tub. He retrieved the water, a little confused. She seemed to be angry, but wasn't directing her anger at him. After he set the bucket on the floor, he waited with his eyes cast downward. Denna brought the chair over. He was surprised she didn't have him do it.

"Sit down." She went to the table by her bed and came back with a pear. She looked at it in her hand a moment, turning it around and around, rubbing it a little with her thumb, then held it out to him. "I brought this back from dinner. I find I am no longer hungry. You had no dinner; you eat it."

Richard looked at the pear in her hand as she held it toward him. "No, Mistress Denna. It's yours. Not mine."

"I know whose it is, Richard." Her voice was still quiet, "Do as I say."

He took the pear, eating it all, even the seeds. Denna knelt down and started washing him. He had no idea what was going on, but the washing hurt, although it was nothing to compare with the Agiel. He wondered why she was doing this, when it was time to train him again.

Denna seemed to sense his apprehension. "I have a backache."

"I'm sorry, Mistress Denna, I've caused it by my behavior."

"Be quiet," she said gently. "I want to sleep on something hard, for my back. I will sleep on the floor. Since I will sleep on the floor, you will have to sleep in my bed, and I don't want your blood in it."

Richard was a little perplexed. The floor was certainly big enough for the two of them, and she had certainly gotten his blood in her bed before. It had never bothered her in the past. He decided it was not his place to question, and so didn't.

"All right," she said when she had finished, "get in the bed."

He lay down while she watched him. With resignation, he picked up the Agiel from the side table and held it out to her, the pain from it hurting his arm. He wished she weren't going to do this to him tonight.

Denna took the Agiel from him and returned it to the table. "Not tonight. I told you, I have a backache." She blew out the lamp. "Go to sleep."

He heard her lie on the floor, whispering a curse to herself. He was too exhausted to think, and was asleep in a short time.

When the peal of the bell woke him, Denna was already up. She had cleaned the blood from her white outfit, and had fixed her braid. She said nothing to him as they walked to the devotion. It was painful for him to kneel, and he was glad when it was finished. He didn't see Constance. Walking behind Denna, he began to turn toward the training room, but she didn't, and the chain pulled taut. The pain brought him up short.

"We're not going that way," she said.

"Yes, Mistress Denna."

She walked awhile, down halls that stretched forever, then gave him an impatient look. "Walk next to me. We're going for a walk. It's something I enjoy doing occasionally. When my back hurts. It helps me."

"I'm sorry, Mistress Denna. I was hoping it would be better by this morning."

She glanced at him, then looked back to where she was going. "Well, it's not. So we will go for a walk."

Richard had never been this far from Denna's quarters before. His eyes took little journeys to the new sights. At intervals, there were places just like the one where they went for their devotions, opened to the sky and the sun, each with a rock in the center, and a bell. Some had grass instead of sand, and some even a pool of water that the rock sat in. Fish glided in groups through the clear water. The halls were sometimes wide as rooms, with patterned tiles on the floor, arches and columns all about and ceilings soaring high above. Windows let light stream into these places, making them bright and airy.

People were everywhere, most in robes of white or some other pale color. No one ever seemed in a hurry, but most seemed as if they had a place to go, although a few sat on marble benches. Richard saw few soldiers. Most people walked past Denna and him as if they were invisible, but a few smiled and exchanged a greeting with her.

The size of the place was astounding; the halls and passages stretched out of sight. Wide stairs led up or down to unknown parts of the great edifice. One hall had statues of naked people in proud poses. The statues were made of carved and polished stone, mostly white, some with gold veining through it, and each was twice as tall as he. Richard never saw one place that was dark, or ugly, or dirty; everything he saw was beautiful. The sound of people's footsteps echoed through the halls like reverent whispers. Richard wondered how a place as large as this could even be conceived of, much less built. It must have taken lifetimes.

Denna led them to a sprawling square that was open to the sky. Full-grown trees covered the mossy ground, and a path of brown clay tiles meandered through the center of the indoor forest. They strolled along the path, Richard looking up at the trees. They were beautiful, even if they were bare of leaves.

Denna watched him. "You like the trees, don't you."

He nodded, looking about. "Very much, Mistress Denna," he whispered.

"Why do you like them?"

Richard thought a moment. "It seems they are part of my past. I can dimly recall that I was a guide. A woods guide, I think. But I don't remember much about it, Mistress Denna. Except I liked the woods."

"Being broken makes you forget things from before," she said quietly. "The more I train you, the more you will forget the past, except specific questions I ask you. Soon, you will remember none of it."

"Yes, Mistress Denna. Mistress Denna, what is this place?"

"It's called the People's Palace. It's the seat of power in D'Hara. It is the home of Master Rahl."

They had lunch in a different place than they usually ate. She had him sit in a chair; he didn't know why. They went to the afternoon devotion at one of the places with water instead of sand, and after devotion, they walked some more through the vast halls, to find themselves back in familiar territory for dinner. The walking made him feel better. His muscles had needed to be stretched.

After the evening devotion, in the little room in her quarters, Denna locked his arms behind his back in the binding device, and hoisted it up, but not enough to take the weight off his feet. It still brought the pain back to his sore shoulders, but it made him wince only a little.

"Is your back better, Mistress Denna? Did the walking help?"

"It's nothing I can't tolerate."

She walked slowly around him, watching the floor. She stopped at last in front of him, rolling the Agiel in her fingers for a time, scrutinizing it.

Her eyes didn't come up. Her voice was hardly more than a whisper. "Tell me you think I'm ugly."

He looked at her until her eyes finally came up. "No. That would be a lie."

A sad smile spread on her lips. "That was a mistake, my love. You have disobeyed my direct order, and you have forgotten the appellation."

"I know, Mistress Denna."

Her eyes closed, but a little of the strength came back to her voice. "You are nothing but trouble. I don't know why Master Rahl burdened me with your training. You have earned yourself two hours."

She gave him his two hours, not as hard as she usually did, but hard enough to make him cry in pain. After the training, she told him that her back still hurt, and slept on the floor again, having him sleep in the bed.

The next few days went back to the regular routine, the training not being as long or as strenuous as before, except when Constance was there. Denna kept a close watch on her, guiding more than she had in the past. Constance didn't like it, sometimes glaring at Denna. When Constance was rougher than Denna wished, she wasn't invited for the next session.

With the lighter training sessions, his head started to clear, and he began remembering things, things about his past. A few times, when Denna's back hurt, they went for long walks, looking at the various, astonishingly beautiful places.

After an afternoon devotion one day, Constance asked if she could come along. Denna smiled and said yes. Constance asked to do the training, and was given permission. She was rougher than usual, and had Richard in prolonged agony, tears of pain streaming down his cheeks. Richard was hoping Denna would put a stop to it, as he was on his last strings of tolerance. As Denna came out of her chair, a man came into the room.

"Mistress Denna, Master Rahl has requested you."

"When?"

"Right now."

Denna gave a sigh. "Constance, would you finish the session?"

Constance looked into Richard's eyes and smiled. "Why, of course, Denna."

Richard was terrified, but didn't dare say a word.

"His time is nearly up, just take him back to my quarters and leave him there. I'm sure I won't be long."

"My pleasure, Denna. You can count on me."

Denna started to leave. Constance grinned at him wickedly, her face close to his. She grabbed his belt and yanked it open. Richard couldn't breathe.

"Constance"—Denna had come back in—"I don't want you doing that."

Constance was caught off guard. "In your absence, I'm in charge of him, and I'll do as I wish."

Denna came and put her face close to the other's. "He is my mate, and I said I don't want you to do that. And I don't want you to put the Agiel in his ear either."

"I'll do as I . . ."

"You will not." Denna gritted her teeth as she looked down to the shorter woman. "I am the one who took the punishment when we killed Rastin. Me. Not you and me, only me. I have never made a point of it before, but I do now. You know what they did to me, and I never told them you had a part in it. He is my mate, and I am his Mord-Sith. Not you. Me. You will respect my wishes or there is going to be trouble between us."

"All right, Denna," she huffed. "All right. I'll mind your wishes."

Denna still glared at her. "See that you do, Sister Constance."

Constance finished the session with all the effort she could bring forth, although she kept the Agiel mostly where Denna wanted it. Richard knew it went on for longer than it should have. When she took him back to Denna's quarters, she spent a good hour slapping him around, then hooked the chain over the footboard of the bed and told him he was to stand until Denna came back.

Constance put her face close to his, as best she could, considering her height, and grabbed him between the legs.

"Take good care of this for me," she sneered. "You aren't going to have it much longer. I have reason to believe Master Rahl will shortly be reassigning you to me, and when he does, I'm going to alter your anatomy." A grin spread on her face. "And I don't think you're going to like it."

His anger flashed, bringing on the pain of the magic. It took him to his knees. Constance laughed as she left the room. He managed to get the anger under control, but the pain wouldn't stop until he stood.

Warm sunlight was streaming in the window. He hoped Denna would be returning soon. The sun set. Dinnertime came and went. Still Denna did not return. Richard began to worry. He had a feeling that something was wrong. He heard the peal of the bell for the evening devotion, but couldn't go to it, being chained to the bed. He wondered if he was supposed to kneel where he was, but realized he couldn't do that either; he had been told to stand. He thought maybe he should still chant the devotion, but decided there was no one to hear him, and it wouldn't matter.

It was long since dark out the window, but thankfully the lamps were lit and at least he didn't have to stand in the dark. The two bells announced the end of evening devotion. Still Denna was not back. His training time came and went. Still no Denna. Richard was fraught with worry.

At last, he heard the door push open. Denna's head was bowed, her posture stiff. The braid was undone and her hair disheveled. She laboriously pushed the door closed. He saw that her skin was ashen, her eyes wet. She didn't look at him.

"Richard," she said in a small voice, "fill my bath for me. Please? I need a bath, I feel very dirty right now."

"Of course, Mistress Denna."

He dragged the tub in and ran as fast as he could to fill it. He didn't think he had ever done it more quickly. She stood and watched as he brought in bucket after bucket. When he was finished, he stood panting, waiting.

Her trembling fingers started unbuttoning the leather. "Help me with this? I don't think I can do it by myself."

He unbuttoned it for her as she shivered. Wincing, he had to peel it off her back; some of her skin came with it. His heart was pounding. Denna was covered with welts from the back of her neck to the back of her ankles. Richard was frightened, and he ached with hurt for her, for the pain she was in. Tears came to his eyes. The power roared up in him. He ignored it.

"Mistress Denna, who did this to you?" he demanded.

"Master Rahl. It is nothing I did not deserve."

He held her hands and helped her into the tub. She let out a little sound as she sank slowly into the hot water, sitting stiffly.

"Mistress Denna, why would he do this to you?"

She winced when he put the soapy cloth to her back. "Constance told him I was being too easy on you. I deserve what was done to me. I have been lax in your training. I am Mord-Sith. I should have done better. I received only that which I deserve."

"You do not deserve this, Mistress Denna, it is me who should have taken the punishment. Not you."

Her hands trembled as she held the sides of the tub and he carefully washed her. He gently wiped the sweat off the white skin of her face. She stared ahead the whole time he worked, a few tears rolling down her cheeks.

Her lip quivered. "Tomorrow, Master Rahl will see you." His hand stopped washing for a second. "I'm sorry, Richard. You will answer his questions."

He glanced up at her face, but she didn't look back. "Yes, Mistress Denna." He rinsed her off with water cupped in his hands. "Let me dry you off." He did it as gently as he could. "Do you wish to sit, Mistress Denna?"

She gave an embarrassed smile. "I don't think I would like that, just now." She turned her head stiffly. "Over there. I will lie

695

on the bed." She took his hand when he put it out for her. "I can't seem to stop shaking. Why can't I stop shaking?"

"Because it hurts, Mistress Denna."

"I've had much worse than this done to me. This was only a small reminder of who I am. But still, I can't stop shaking."

She lay facedown on the bed, her eyes on him. Richard's worry made his mind start working again.

"Mistress Denna, is my pack still here?"

"In the cabinet. Why?"

"Just lie still. Mistress Denna, let me do something, if I can remember how."

He pulled his pack from a high shelf in the cabinet, laid it on the table, and started rummaging through it. Denna watched him, the side of her face resting on the backs of her hands. Beneath a carved bone whistle on a leather thong, he found the package he was searching for, and laid it open on the table. He pulled out a tin bowl, took his knife from his belt, and laid it, too, on the table. He stood and took a jar of cream from the cabinet. He had seen her spread it on her skin. It was just what he needed.

"Mistress Denna, may I use this?"

"Why?"

"Please?"

"Go ahead."

Richard took the entire pile of neatly stacked, dried aum leaves and put them in the tin bowl, then selected a few other herbs he remembered by smell, but not by name, and dumped them in with the aum leaves. With the knife handle, he ground it all into a powder. Picking up the jar of cream, he scooped it all out and plopped it into the bowl, mixing it with two fingers. He took the bowl and sat on the bed next to her.

"Just lie still," he told her.

"The appellation, Richard, the appellation. Will you never learn?"

"Sorry, Mistress Denna," he smiled. "You may punish me later. For now, lie still. When I'm finished you will feel well enough to punish me all night. I promise."

He spread the paste gently on the welts, smoothing it out as he went. Denna moaned. Her eyes closed while he worked. By the time he reached the back of her ankles, she was almost asleep. He stroked her hair while the aum cream soaked in.

"How does that feel, Mistress Denna?" he whispered.

She rolled onto her side, her eyes opening wide. "The pain is gone! How did you do that? How did you make the pain leave?"

Richard smiled in satisfaction. "I learned it from an old friend named . . ." He frowned. "I can't remember his name. But he's an old friend, and he taught me. I'm so relieved, Mistress Denna. I don't like to see you in pain."

She gently touched her fingers to the side of his face. "You are a very rare person, Richard Cypher. I have never had a mate like you before. The spirits take me, I have never even seen a person like you before. I killed the one who did the things to me that I have done to you, and you instead help me."

"We all can be only who we are, no more, and no less, Mistress Denna." He looked down at his hands. "I don't like what Master Rahl has done to you."

"You don't understand about the Mord-Sith, my love. We are carefully selected, as young girls. Those chosen to be Mord-Sith are the most gentle, the most kindhearted, that can be found. It is said that the deepest cruelty comes from the deepest caring. All of D'Hara is searched, and each year only about a half dozen are chosen. A Mord-Sith is broken three times."

His eyes were wide. "Three times?" he whispered.

Denna nodded. "The first is the way in which I broke you, to break the spirit. The second is to break our empathy. To do it, we must watch our trainer break our mother, and make her his pet, and watch him hurt her until she dies. The third is to break us of our fear of hurting another, to make us enjoy giving pain. To do it, we must break our fathers, under the guidance of our trainer, and make him our pet, and keep hurting him until we kill him."

Tears trickled down Richard's cheeks. "They did all this to you?"

"What I did to you, to break you, is nothing compared to what must be done to us to break us the second and third time. The more kindhearted a girl is, the better Mord-Sith she makes, but it makes it harder to break her the second and third time. Master Rahl thinks me special because they had a very difficult time with the second breaking of me. My mother lived a long time, to try to keep me from giving up hope, but that only made it harder. On both of us. They failed at the third breaking, had given up, and were going to kill me, but Master Rahl said that if I could be broken, I would be someone special, and so took over my training himself. He is the one who broke me the third time. On the day I killed my father, he took me to his bed, as a reward. His reward left me barren."

Richard could hardly speak past the lump in his throat. With shaking fingers, he brushed some of her hair back off her face. "I don't want anyone hurting you. Not ever again, Mistress Denna."

"It is an honor," Denna whispered through tears, "that Master Rahl would spare the time to punish one as low as me with my own Agiel."

Richard sat numb. "I hope he kills me tomorrow, so I don't have to learn anything else that gives me this much pain, Mistress Denna."

Her wet eyes shone in the lamplight. "I have done things to hurt you that I have done to no other, yet you are the first person since I was chosen who has done anything to stop my pain." She sat up and picked up the tin bowl. "There is some left. Let me put it on you where Constance did what I told her not to."

Denna spread the aum cream on the welts on his shoulders, then on his stomach and chest, working up to his neck. Her eyes met his. Her hand stopped. The room was dead quiet. Denna leaned forward and gently kissed him. She put her hand with the cream on the back of his neck and kissed him again.

She lay back on the bed, holding his hand against her belly with both of hers. "Come to me, my love. I want you very badly right now."

He nodded and started to reach for the Agiel on the side table. Denna touched his wrist.

"Tonight, I want you without the Agiel. Please? Teach me what it's like without the pain?"

She put a hand behind his neck and gently pulled him on top of her.

CHAPTER 43

DENNA DIDN'T TRAIN HIM the next morning, but instead took him for a walk. Master Rahl had said he wanted to see Richard after the second devotion. After it was over and they were starting to leave, Constance stopped them.

"You look surprisingly well today, Sister Denna."

Denna looked at her without emotion. Richard was furious at Constance for talking to Master Rahl about Denna, for getting her punished, and had to concentrate on Denna's braid.

Constance turned to Richard. "Well. I hear you are to be granted an audience with Master Rahl today. If you are still alive afterward, you will be seeing more of me. Alone. I want a piece of you, as it were, when he's finished with you."

He spoke before he thought. "The year they chose you, Mistress Constance, must have been a year of desperate need; otherwise, one of such limited intelligence would never have been selected to be Mord-Sith. Only the most ignorant would put their own petty ambitions above the value of a friend. Especially a friend who has sacrificed much for you. You are not worthy to kiss Mistress Denna's Agiel." Richard smiled smoothly, confidently, as she stood startled. "You had better hope Master Rahl kills me, Mistress Constance, because if he doesn't, then the next time I see you, I'm going to kill you for what you've done to Mistress Denna."

Constance stared in shock, then suddenly drove her Agiel toward him. Denna's longer arm came up. She slammed her own Agiel against Constance's throat, holding her back. Constance's eyes bulged in surprise. She coughed blood, and dropped to her knees, clutching her hands to her throat.

Denna stared down at her a moment before starting off without a word. Richard followed, attached by the chain. He sped up to walk beside her.

Denna kept her eyes ahead, showing no emotion. "Just try and guess how many hours that has earned you."

Richard smiled. "Mistress Denna, if there is a Mord-Sith who could raise a scream from a dead man, it would be you."

"And if Master Rahl doesn't kill you, how many hours?"

"Mistress Denna, there are not enough hours in a lifetime to dim my pleasure at what I have done."

She smiled a little, but didn't look over. "I'm glad, then, that it was worth it for you." She gave him a sidelong glance. "I still don't understand you. As you said, we can be no more, no less, than who we are. I regret I can be no more than I am, and I fear you can be no less. Were we not warriors fighting on opposite sides in this war, I would keep you as a mate for life, and work to see you die of old age."

Richard was warmed by her gentle tone. "I would try my best to live a long life for you, Mistress Denna."

They walked on through the halls, past the devotion squares, past the statues, past the people. She took him upstairs, through vast rooms of exquisite decorations. She stopped in front of a pair of doors covered in carvings of rolling hills and forests, all sheathed in gold.

Denna turned to him. "Are you prepared to die this day, my love?"

"The day is not over yet, Mistress Denna."

She slipped her arms around his neck, kissing him tenderly. She pulled her face away a few inches, stroked the back of his head. "I'm sorry, Richard, that I do these things to you, but I have been trained to do them, and can do nothing less; I live only to hurt you. Know that it is not by choice, but by training. I can be no more than what I am: Mord-Sith. If you are to die this day, my love, then make me proud, and die well."

He was mate to a madwoman, he thought sadly. And one not of her own making.

She pushed the doors open and entered a grand garden. Richard would have been impressed, had his mind not been on other things. They went down a path between flowers and shrubs, past short, vine-covered stone walls, and small trees, to an expanse of lawn. A glass roof let in the light, keeping the plants healthy and in flower.

In the distance were two identically huge men. Their folded arms had metal bands with sharp projections just above their elbows. Guards of some sort, Richard thought. To their side stood another man. Imposing muscles flexed on his smooth chest. His short-cropped blond hair stood up in spikes, with a single black streak running through it.

Near the center of the lawn, near a circle of white sand, in a warm shaft of late-afternoon sunlight, stood a man with his back to them. The sunlight made his white robes and shoulder-length blond hair glow. Sparks of the sunlight glinted off the gold belt and curved dagger at his waist.

As Richard and Denna approached him, Denna dropped to her knees, putting her forehead to the ground. Richard had been instructed and did the same as he pushed his sword out of the way.

Together, they chanted. "Master Rahl guide us. Master Rahl teach us. Master Rahl protect us. In your light we thrive. In your mercy we are sheltered. In your wisdom we are humbled. We live only to serve. Our lives are yours."

They chanted only once, then waited, Richard trembling slightly. He remembered that he was never to get near Master Rahl, to stay away from him, but couldn't remember who told him so, only that it was important. He had to concentrate on Denna's braid, to control the anger at what Master Rahl had done to her.

"Rise, my children."

Richard stood with his shoulder close against Mistress Denna while intense blue eyes studied him. That the Master's face

701

looked kind, intelligent, pleasant, did not calm Richard's churning fears, and the thoughts that boiled just below the surface of his mind. The blue eyes glided to Denna.

"You look surprisingly well this morning, my pet."

"Mistress Denna is as good at taking pain as giving it, Master Rahl," Richard heard himself say.

The blue eyes returned to his. The calmness, the peace, in Rahl's face made Richard quiver. "My pet has told me you are nothing but trouble. I am pleased to see she has not lied to me. But not pleased to find it true." He clasped his hands in a relaxed manner. "Well, no matter. How good to meet you at last, Richard Cypher."

Denna drove the Agiel into his back with a sharp jab to remind him of what it was he was supposed to say. "It is my honor to be here, Master Rahl. I live only to serve. I am humbled in your presence."

A small smile came to Rahl's lips. "Yes, I am sure you are." He studied Richard's face for an uncomfortable moment. "I have some questions. You are going to give me the answers."

Richard felt himself shaking slightly. "Yes, Master Rahl."

"Kneel," he said softly.

Richard went to his knees with the aid of the Agiel on his shoulder. Denna stepped behind and put a boot to each side of him. She pressed her thighs against his shoulders, bracing against them for leverage as she held his hair in her fist. She pulled his head back a little, making him look up into the Master's blue eyes. Richard swallowed in terror.

Darken Rahl looked down without emotion. "You have seen the Book of Counted Shadows before?"

Something powerful in the back of his mind told Richard he shouldn't answer. When he said nothing, Denna tightened her grip on his hair, and pushed the Agiel against the base of his skull.

There was a stunning explosion of pain in his head. Denna's grip on his hair was all that kept him upright. It was as if she had compressed the pain of an entire training session into that one touch. He couldn't move, breathe, or even cry out. He was beyond being in pain; the shock took everything from him, and in its place left an all-consuming agony of fire and ice. She took

702

away the Agiel. He didn't know where he was, who he was, or who was holding him, only that this was more pain than he had ever known before, and that there was a man in front of him, dressed in a white robe.

Blue eyes looked down at him. "You have seen the Book of Counted Shadows before?"

"Yes," he heard himself say.

"Where is it now?"

Richard hesitated. He didn't know how to answer; he didn't know what the voice wanted. The pain exploded in his head again. When it stopped, he felt tears running down his cheeks.

"Where is it now?" the voice repeated.

"Please, don't hurt me anymore," he cried. "I don't understand the question."

"What is there not to understand? Simply tell me where the book is now."

"The book, or the knowledge of the book?" Richard asked fearfully.

The blue eyes frowned. "The book."

"I burned it in a fire. Years ago."

Richard thought the eyes were going to tear him apart. "And where is the knowledge?"

Richard hesitated too long. When he was aware again, Denna yanked his head up to look into the blue eyes again. Richard had never felt so alone, so helpless, so afraid.

"Where is the knowledge that was in the book?"

"In my head. Before I burned the book, I learned the words, the knowledge."

The man stood staring, unmoving. Richard cried softly.

"Recite the words of the book."

Richard desperately didn't want the Agiel in the back of his head again. He shook with the fear of it. *Verification of the truth of the words of the Book of Counted Shadows, if spoken by another, rather than read by the one who commands the boxes, can only be insured by the use of a Confessor. . . ."*

Confessor.

Kahlan.

The name Kahlan went through Richard's mind like a bolt of lightning. The power roared to life, blasting away the fog with the burning, white-hot glare of his memories. The door to the locked room in his mind was flung open. It all came back to him, brought back by the power as it rose in him. Richard was one with the power, at the thought of Darken Rahl having Kahlan; hurting her.

Darken Rahl turned to the other men. The one with the black stripe came forward.

"You see, my friend? The fates work for me. She is already on her way here with the Old One. Find her. See to it she is brought to me. Take two quads, but I want her alive, do you understand?" The man gave a nod. "You and your men will have the protection of my spell. The Old One is with her, but he will have no weapon against an underworld spell, if he is even alive by then." Rahl's voice became harder. "And Demmin, I don't care what your men do to her, but she had better be alive when she gets here, and able to use her power."

A little of the color left the man's face. "I understand. It will be done as you wish, Lord Rahl." He bowed deep.

He turned and left after meeting Richard's eyes and giving a knowing smile.

Darken Rahl returned his blue eyes to Richard. "Continue."

Richard had gone as far as he was going to go. He remembered everything.

It was time to die.

"I will not. There is nothing you can do to make me tell you. I welcome the pain. I welcome death."

Before the Agiel could come, Rahl's eyes snapped up to Denna. Richard felt her fist loosen on his hair. One of the guards marched forward, grabbed her by the throat with his big hand, squeezing, until Richard could hear her struggling to breathe.

Rahl glared at her. "You told me he was broken."

"He was, Master Rahl." She struggled to speak as she was being choked. "I swear."

"I am very disappointed in you, Denna."

As the man lifted her feet off the ground, Richard could hear her sounds of pain. Again, the power turned white-hot in him. Denna was being hurt. Before anyone knew what was happening, he was on his feet, the power of the magic raging through him.

Richard threw one arm around the man's thick neck, grasping

his opposite shoulder. He grabbed the man's head with his other arm and in a blink gave a powerful twist. The man's neck snapped. He went down in a heap.

Richard spun. The other guard was almost on him, his hand reaching out. Richard seized the man's wrist and used his advancing weight to pull his adversary into the knife. He drove it in up to his fist and gave a mighty pull, cutting all the way up to the man's heart as his blue eyes went wide in surprise. His insides spilled across the ground when he hit.

Richard stood panting with the power. Everything in his peripheral vision was white. White from the heat of the magic. Denna had her hands to her throat, clutching at the pain.

Darken Rahl stood calmly, licking the tips of his fingers as he watched Richard.

Denna brought on the pain of the magic enough to take Richard to his knees. He folded his arms across his gut.

"Master Rahl," Denna gasped, "let me take him back for the night. I swear that in the morning, he will answer anything you ask. If he's still alive. Allow me to redeem myself."

"No," Rahl said, deep in thought, waving his hand a little. "I apologize, my pet. This is not your failing. I had no idea what we were dealing with. Turn off the pain in him."

Richard recovered and returned to his feet. The fog had cleared from his head. He felt as if he were waking from a dream only to find himself in a nightmare. The rest of him was out of the little locked room in his mind, and he wasn't putting it away again. He would die with all of his mind, his dignity, intact. He kept the anger choked off, but there was fire in his eyes. Fire in his heart.

"Did the Old One teach you that?" Rahl asked, a curious frown on his face.

"Teach me what?"

"To partition your mind. That was how you kept from being broken."

"I don't know what you're talking about."

"You put up a partition, to protect the core, sacrificed the rest to what would be done. A Mord-Sith cannot break a partitioned mind. Punish, yes. Break, no." He turned to Denna. "Once again, I am sorry, my pet. I thought you had failed me. You have not.

None but the most talented could have taken him this far. You have done well, but this makes matters altogether different."

He smiled, licked his fingertips, smoothed them over his eyebrows. "Richard and I are going to have a private conversation now. While he is in this room with me, I wish you to let him speak without the pain of the magic. It interferes with what I may need to do. While he is here, he is to be free of your control. You may return to your quarters. When I am done with him, and if he is still alive, I will send him back to you, as promised."

Denna bowed deeply. "I live to serve, Master Rahl."

She turned to Richard, her face crimson, and put a finger under his chin, lifting it a little. "Don't disappoint me, my love."

The Seeker smiled. "Never, Mistress Denna."

He let the anger rage, just to feel it again, as he watched her walk away. Rage at her, and at what had been done to her. Don't think of the problem, he told himself, think of the solution. Richard turned to face Darken Rahl. The other's face was calm, and showed nothing. Richard made his do the same.

"You know I want to know what the rest of the book says."

"Kill me."

Rahl smiled. "So eager to die, are we?"

"Yes. Kill me. Just like you killed my father."

Darken Rahl frowned, the smile still on his lips. "Your father? I have not killed your father, Richard."

"George Cypher! You killed him! Don't try to deny it! You killed him with that knife at your belt!"

Rahl spread his hands in mock innocence. "Oh, I don't deny killing George Cypher. But I have not killed your father."

Richard stood caught off guard. "What are you talking about?"

Darken Rahl strolled around him, watching his eyes as Richard tried to follow him by turning his head. "It's quite good. It really is. The best I have ever seen. Done by the great one himself."

"What?"

Darken Rahl licked his fingers and stopped in front of him. "The wizard's web around you. I've never seen one like it. It's wound around you tight as a cocoon. Been there a good long time. It's quite intricate; I don't think even I could untangle it."

"If you are trying to convince me George Cypher is not my father, you have failed. If you are trying to convince me you are mad, you needn't bother. That much I already know."

"My dear boy," Rahl laughed, "I couldn't care less who you believe your father to be. Nonetheless, there is a wizard's web hiding the truth from you."

"Really? I'll play along. Who's my father, if it's not George Cypher?"

"I wouldn't know," Rahl shrugged. "The web hides it. But from what I've seen, I have my suspicions." The smile left. "What does the Book of Counted Shadows say?"

Richard shrugged. "That's your question? You disappoint me."

"How so?"

"Well, after what was done to your bastard father, I thought sure you'd want to know the old wizard's name."

Darken Rahl glared as he slowly licked his fingertips. "What is the old wizard's name?"

It was Richard's turn to smile. He spread his arms wide. "Cut me open. It's written on my guts. You will have to find it there."

Richard kept the smirk on his face; he knew he was defenseless and was hoping Rahl would be driven to kill him. If he was dead, the book died with him. No box, no book. Rahl was going to die; Kahlan would be safe then. That was all that mattered.

"In one week, it will be the first day of winter, and I will know the name of the wizard, and have the power to snatch him from wherever he is, and bring his hide to me."

"In one week, you will be dead. You have only two boxes."

Darken Rahl licked his fingers again and smoothed them over his lips. "I have two right now, and the third is on its way here, as we speak."

Richard tried not to believe him. He let his face show nothing. "A brave boast. But a lie, nonetheless. In one week, you are going to die."

Rahl raised his eyebrows. "I speak the truth. You have been betrayed. The same one who has betrayed you to me has also betrayed the box to me. It will be here in a few days."

"I don't believe you," Richard said flatly.

Darken Rahl licked his fingertips and turned, walking around the circle of white sand. "No? Let me show you something."

Richard followed him to a wedge of white stone upon which

sat a flat slab of granite held up by two short fluted pedestals. In the center of the slab sat two of the boxes of Orden. One was ornately jeweled like the one Richard had seen before. The other was as black as the night stone, its surface a void in the light of the room: the box itself, its protective covering removed.

"Two of the boxes of Orden," Rahl announced, holding his hand out to them. "Why would I want the book? The book would be useless to me without the third box. You had the third box. The one who betrayed you told me so. If the box were not on its way, why would I need the book? I would instead cut you open to get the location of the box."

Richard shook with anger. "Who betrayed me and the box? Tell me the name."

"Or what? Or you will cut me open and read the name on my guts? I will not betray the name of one who has helped me. You are not the only one with honor."

Richard didn't know what to believe. Rahl was right about one thing. He wouldn't need the book if he didn't have all three boxes. Someone really had betrayed him. It was impossible, but it must be true.

"Just kill me," Richard said in a weak voice, turning away. "I'm not going to tell you. You might as well cut me open."

"First you must convince me you are telling the truth. You could be deceiving me that you really know the whole book. You may have read just the first page, and burned the rest, or simply be inventing what you have told me of it."

Richard folded his arms and looked back over his shoulder. "And what possible reason could I have for wanting you to believe me?"

Rahl shrugged. "I thought you cared about this Confessor. Kahlan. I had thought you cared what happened to her. You see, if you can't convince me that you are telling the truth, then I will have to cut her open, and have a look at her entrails, see if they have anything to say about this."

Richard glared. "That would be the biggest mistake you could make. You need her to confirm the truth of the book. If you harm her, you destroy your chance."

Rahl shrugged. "So you say. How would I know you really do

know what the book says? It could even be that this is the manner in which she will confirm the truth."

Richard said nothing, his mind racing in a thousand directions at once. Think of the solution, he told himself, not the problem.

"How did you get the covering off that box, without the book?"

"The Book of Counted Shadows is not the only source of information about the boxes. There are other places that are of aid to me." He looked down at the dark box. "It took a full day, and every talent I have, to get the covering off." He looked back up, lifting an eyebrow. "It's held on with magic, you know. But I did it, and I will be able to do it to the other two."

It was discouraging that Rahl had managed to get the covering off. To open a box, the covering had to be removed. Richard had hoped that without the book, Rahl wouldn't be able to figure out how to remove the covers, and not be able to open a box. That hope was now lost.

Richard stared blankly at the jeweled box. "Page twelve of the Book of Counted Shadows. Under the heading *Shedding the Covers*, it says: *The covering on the boxes may be removed by anyone with the knowledge, not only the one who has put them in play.*" Richard reached out and lifted the jeweled box off the granite. "Page seventeen, third paragraph down on the page. *If not, however, in the hours of darkness, but in the hours of the sun, the covering may be removed from the second box in the following manner. Hold the box where the sun may touch it, and face north. If there be clouds, hold the box where the sun would touch it if they were not present, but face the west.*" Richard held the box up in the late-day sunlight. "*Turn the box that the small end with the blue stone may face the quadrant with the sun. The yellow stone is to face up.*" Richard turned the box. "*With the second finger of the right hand on the yellow stone in the center of the top, place the thumb of the right hand on the clear stone in the corner of the bottom.*" Richard grasped the box as directed. "*Place the first finger of the left hand on the blue stone on the side facing away, the thumb of the left hand on the ruby stone of the side closest.*" Richard placed his fingers so. "*Clear your mind of all thought, and in its place, put nothing but the im-*

709

age of white with a square of black in its center. Pull the two hands apart, taking the covering away with them."

As Rahl watched, Richard cleared his mind, pictured white with black in the center, and pulled. The cover made a clicking sound, and came apart. He held the box just over the granite and pulled the cover away as if he were putting an egg in a frying pan. Two equally black boxes sat side by side, seeming as if they would suck the light from the room.

"Remarkable." Rahl breathed. "And you know every part of the book this well?"

"Every word." Richard glared. "What I have told you will be of no aid in removing the third cover, however. They each come off differently."

Rahl gave a little wave of his hand. "No matter. I will get it off." He held an elbow in one hand and touched a finger of the other to his chin, absorbed in thought. "You are free to go."

Richard frowned. "What do you mean, I am free to go? Aren't you going to try to get the book out of me? Kill me?"

Rahl shrugged. "It would do me no good. The ways I have of getting information from you would damage your brain. The information would be disjointed. If it were anything else, I would be able to put the pieces together, and figure it out, but I can see the book is too specific for that. The information would only end up being spoiled, and of no use to me. You, therefore, are of no use to me right now, so you may go."

Richard was worried. There was something more to this. "Just like that? I may go? You must know I will try to stop you."

Rahl licked his fingers. His eyes came up. "I'm not worried about anything you could do. But you must be back here in one week, when I open the boxes, if you care at all what happens to everyone."

Richard narrowed his eyes. "What do you mean, if I care what happens to everyone?"

"In one week, on the first day of winter, I'm going to open one of the boxes. I have been able to learn, from sources other than the Book of Counted Shadows, the same sources that told me how I might remove the cover, how to tell which box it is that would kill me. Beyond that, I will have to guess. If I open the right one, I will rule unchallenged. If I open the other, the world will be destroyed."

"You would let that happen?"

Darken Rahl's eyebrows lifted as he leaned toward Richard. "One world, or no world. That is the way it shall be."

"I don't believe you. You don't know which box will destroy you."

"Even if I were lying, I would still have two chances in three of having my way. You would have only one in three of it working out in your favor. Not good odds, for you. But, I'm not lying. Either the world is destroyed, or I rule it. You must decide which you would rather have happen. If you don't help me, and I open the wrong box, I will be destroyed, along with everyone else, including those you care for. If you don't help me, and I open the one I want, then I will turn Kahlan over to Constance, for training. A good long training. You will watch the whole thing before I kill you. Then Kahlan will bear me a son, an heir. A son who will be a Confessor."

Richard went cold with pain worse than any Denna had given him. "You are trying to make me an offer of some sort?"

Rahl nodded. "If you come back in time, and help me, you will be permitted to go about your life. I will let you be."

"What about Kahlan?"

"She will live here, in the People's Palace, and be treated like a queen. She will have every comfort any woman could have; the kind of life a Confessor is used to. Something you could never provide her. She will live a life of peace and safety, and she will bear me the Confessor son I wish. Either way, she will bear me a son. That is my choice. Your choice is how: as Constance's pet, or as a queen. So you see? I think you will be back. And if I am wrong . . ." He shrugged. "One world, or no world."

Richard could hardly breathe. "I don't think you know which box will destroy you."

"You will have to decide what you will believe. I feel no need to convince you." His expression darkened. "Choose wisely, my young friend. You may not like the choices I have given you, but you will like the results of not helping me even less. Not all choices in life are ones you would like, but those are all that are presented to you. Sometimes you must choose what is better for the ones you love than yourself."

"I still don't think you know which box will kill you," Richard whispered.

"Think what you will, but ask yourself if you are willing to bet Kahlan's future with Constance on what you think. Even if you were right, it still gives you only one chance in three."

Richard felt empty, devastated. "Am I free to go now?"

"Well, there are a few other matters you may want to know about."

Richard felt himself abruptly paralyzed, as if invisible hands were gripping him. He couldn't move a muscle. Darken Rahl reached into Richard's pocket and took out the leather pouch with the night stone. Richard fought against the force that held him, but could not move. Rahl dumped the night stone in his hand. He held it up in his palm, smiling.

Shadow things began to materialize. They gathered around Rahl, their numbers growing. Richard wished he could back away, but he couldn't move.

"Time to go home, my friends."

The shadows began swirling around Rahl, faster and faster, until they were a blur of gray. A howl rose as they were sucked into the night stone in a whirl of shadows and shapes. Silence. They were gone. The night stone turned to ash in Rahl's palm. He blew on it and the ash puffed into the air.

"The Old One has been checking on you, using the night stone to find where you are. The next time he searches, he is going to have a very unpleasant experience. He is going to find himself in the underworld."

Richard was furious at what Darken Rahl was doing to Zedd, and he was furious that he couldn't move, that he was helpless and could only watch.

Richard relaxed his mind, shed the effort of trying to move, and replaced it with calm. He let his mind be empty, let himself be soft, limp. The force melted away. He took a step forward, free of the grip that had held him.

Rahl smiled warmly. "Very good, my boy. You know how to break a wizard's web, at least a little one. But very good nonetheless. The Old One chooses his Seekers well." He nodded.

"But you are more than a Seeker. You have the gift. I look forward to the day we will be on the same side. I will enjoy having you around. The ones I have to deal with are very limited. After the world is joined, I will teach you more, if you wish."

"We will never be on the same side. Never."

"That is your choice, Richard. I bear no ill will toward you. I hope we will become friends." Rahl studied Richard's face. "There is one more thing. You may stay in the People's Palace, or you may leave if you wish. My guards will accommodate you. You will, however, have a wizard's web around you. Unlike the one you just broke, it will not affect you, but those who see you, and therefore you will not be able to break it. It's called an enemy web. All will see you as their enemy. That means that when your allies see you, they will see an enemy. Those who honor me will see you as yourself, since you are my enemy, for the time being, and therefore already their enemy. At least for now. But those who are your friends will see you as the person they fear most, their worst enemy. I would like you to see the way people think of me, see the world through my eyes, see how unjustly I am regarded."

Richard didn't have to try to hold back the anger; there was none. He felt an odd sort of peace. "Am I free to go now?"

"Of course, my boy."

"What about Mistress Denna?"

"Once you leave this room, you will be back under her power. She still controls the magic of your sword. Once a Mord-Sith has your magic, it is hers to keep. I cannot take it from her to give it back to you. You must get it back yourself."

"Then how am I free to leave?"

"Isn't it obvious? If you want to leave, you must kill her."

"Kill her!" Richard was stunned. "Don't you think if I could kill her, I would have done so by now? Do you think I would have endured what she has done to me if I could have killed her?"

Darken Rahl smiled a little smile. "You have always been able to kill her."

"How?"

"There is nothing that exists that has only one side. Even a piece of paper, thin as it is, has two sides. Magic is not one-dimensional either. You have been looking at only one side of it; most people do. Look at the whole." He pointed at the bodies of his two guards. The guards Richard had killed. "She controls your magic, yet you did this."

"But that's different, it won't work against her."

Rahl nodded. "Yes, it will. But you must be its master; half measures will get you in a lot of trouble. She controls you with one dimension of your magic, the side you offered her. You must use the other side. It is something all Seekers have been capable of, but none has ever succeeded in mastering. Perhaps you will be the first."

"And if I'm not? If I don't succeed at it?" Darken Rahl was sounding altogether too much like Zedd for Richard's comfort. This was the way Zedd had always taught him—by making him think for himself, find the answers in his own way, with his own mind.

"Then, my young friend, you are going to be in for a very rough week. Denna is not pleased at how you embarrassed her. At the end of the week, she will bring you to me, and you will tell me your decision; to help, or to let all your friends suffer and die."

"Just tell me how to use the magic of the sword, how to master it."

"Of course. Right after you tell me the knowledge in the Book of Counted Shadows." Rahl smiled. "I didn't think so. Good night, Richard. Don't forget, one week."

The sun was fading as Richard left the garden and Darken Rahl. His mind was spinning with all the things he had learned. That Darken Rahl knew which box would kill him was troublesome, but he reasoned that Rahl might be using the Wizard's First Rule on him. Worse was that one of his own had betrayed him. He liked that not one bit. What he liked less was that he knew who it had to be. Shota had told him that Zedd and Kahlan would use their power against him. It had to be Zedd or Kahlan. He couldn't make that fit, no matter how he tried, no matter how he reasoned it out. It couldn't be either, yet it had to be one. He loved them both more than his need to live. Zedd had told him he had to be prepared to kill any of them if they jeopardized winning, even if he thought there was only a chance that they did. He forced the thought out of his mind.

He had to think of a way to get away from Denna. He could be of no help, and none of the rest of it mattered if he couldn't get away from Denna. It would do him no good to think of the other problems if he couldn't get away, and if he didn't figure it out soon, then Denna was going to hurt him, and he wouldn't be able to think anymore. The things she did to him made it too hard to think, made him forget things. He had to concentrate on that problem first, and worry about the others later.

The sword, he thought—Denna controlled the magic of the sword. He didn't need the sword; maybe he could just get rid of it, get rid of the magic she controlled. He reached for the hilt, but the pain of the magic stopped him before he could even touch it.

He walked on through the halls, toward Denna's quarters. It was still a long way. Maybe he could simply go another way, leave the People's Palace. Darken Rahl had told him none of the guards would stop him. When the next intersection of halls came, he started to turn down one. The pain dropped him to his knees. With great effort, he managed to get back to the hall he was supposed to be in. He had to stop and rest, the pain having taken his breath away.

Close, just ahead, the way he was going, the bell for the evening devotion rang. He would go to the devotion; that would give him time to think. He knelt, relieved that the pain of the magic didn't come on. It was one of the squares with water. He liked them best; they were the most peaceful. Close to the edge of the water, with people all about, Richard put his head to the tile floor and began chanting, clearing his mind, letting himself go empty. He used the chanting to melt his worries, his fears, his concerns. He put his thoughts of all the problems away, let his mind seek peace, let it wander where it would. The devotion was over, it seemed, in no time. He stood, refreshed, renewed, and started off again toward Denna's quarters.

The halls he passed through, the rooms and stairways, were breathtakingly beautiful, and Richard again marveled at them as he passed. He wondered at how someone as vile as Darken Rahl would care to surround himself with such loveliness.

Nothing was one-dimensional. Two sides to the magic.

715

Richard thought about the times the strange power had come awake in him. When he had felt sorry for Princess Violet, when the Queen's guard had tried to harm Denna, when he had felt the pain of what had been done to Denna, when he thought of Rahl hurting Kahlan, when Rahl's guards had tried to hurt Denna. He remembered that each time it had made part of his vision turn white.

Each time, he knew, it was the magic of the sword. But in the past the magic of the sword had been rage, too. Yet this was a different kind of rage. He thought of how he used to feel when he drew the sword in anger. The wrath, the fury, the want to kill.

The hate.

Richard stopped dead still in the center of the quiet hall. It was late and there were no people around. He was alone. He felt a wave of cold wash through him, prickling his skin.

Two sides. He understood.

The spirits help him, he understood.

He brought it forth, let it cast everything in a white sheen.

Cradled numbly in the white haze of the magic, nearly in a trance, Richard pushed the door to Denna's quarters closed behind himself. He calmly held the power, held the whiteness of it, held the joy and the sorrow of it. The quiet room was lit by one lamp on the bedside table, giving the softly scented air a warm, flickering glow. Denna sat completely naked in the center of the bed. Her legs were crossed, her braid undone, and her hair brushed out. The Agiel was on a gold chain around her neck, hanging between her breasts. Her hands lay nested in her lap. She watched him with big, wistful eyes.

"You have come to kill me, my love?" she whispered.

He nodded slowly, watching her. "Yes, Mistress."

She smiled a little. "That is the first time you have ever called me simply 'Mistress.' You have always called me Mistress Denna, in the past. It means something?"

"Yes. It means everything, my mate. It means I forgive you everything."

"I have made myself ready."

"Why are you naked?"

The lamplight reflected in the wetness of her eyes. "Because everything I have to wear is Mord-Sith. I have nothing else. I did not wish to die in the clothes of a Mord-Sith. I wish to die as I was born. Denna. Nothing more."

"I understand," he whispered. "How did you know I was coming to kill you?"

"When Master Rahl chose me to go after you, he said he wouldn't order me to go, but that I must volunteer. He said the prophecies foretold of a Seeker who would be the first to master the magic of the sword: the white magic. That this one would cause the blade of the sword to turn white. He said that if you turned out to be the one of whom the prophecies spoke, it would mean that I was to die by your hand, if you so chose. I asked to be sent, to be your Mord-Sith. Some of the things I have done to you, I have done to no other, in the hope you would be the one and kill me for it. When you did what you did to the Princess, I suspected. When you killed the two guards today, I knew. You should not have been able to. I was holding you by the sword's magic at the time."

Everything was white around the childlike beauty of her face. "I'm so sorry, Denna," he whispered.

"You will remember me?"

"I will have nightmares the rest of my life."

Her smile widened. "I'm glad." She seemed genuinely proud. "You love this woman, Kahlan?"

He frowned a little. "How do you know that?"

"Sometimes, when I hurt men enough, and they don't know what they're saying, they cry for their mothers, or their wives. You cried for one named Kahlan. You will choose her for your mate?"

"I cannot," he said past the lump in his throat. "She is a Confessor. Her power would destroy me."

"I'm sorry. This hurts you?"

He nodded slowly. "More than anything you have done to me."

"Good." Denna smiled sadly. "I'm glad the one you love is able to give you more pain than was I."

Richard knew that in her twisted way, Denna meant this as a comfort to him; that for her to be happy that he would get more pain from another was a giving of her love. He knew that Denna sometimes gave him pain to show that she cared for him. In her eyes, at least, if this other woman could give him more pain, that was a demonstration of love.

A tear ran down his face. What had they done to this poor child?

"It is a different kind of pain. None could be your equal in the things you have done."

A tear of pride rolled down her cheek. "Thank you, my love," she breathed. She took the Agiel from her neck and held it up hopefully. "Would you wear this, to remember me by? It will not hurt you around your neck, or if you hold the chain, only if you hold the Agiel itself in your hand."

Richard held her face in the white glow. "It would be my honor, my mate." He bent, letting her put it over his head, letting her give his cheek a kiss.

"How will you do it?" she asked.

He knew what she meant. He swallowed back the lump in his throat. His hand went smoothly to the hilt of the sword.

Slowly, he drew the Sword of Truth. It didn't ring, the way it always had in the past.

It hissed. A white-hot hiss.

Richard didn't look, but he knew, knew the blade had turned white. He held her wet eyes. The power flooded through him. He was at peace. All anger, all hate, all malice, was gone. Where he had felt these things from the sword before, he now felt only love for this child, this vessel into whom others had poured pain, this receptacle of cruelty, this innocent, tortured soul, who had been trained to do the things she hated above all else: hurting others. His empathy with her made him ache with sorrow for her; with love for her.

"Denna," he whispered. "You could just let me go; there is no need to do this. Please. Let me go. Don't make me have to do this."

She held her chin up. "If you try to leave, I will stop you with the pain of the magic, and make you sorry you have been trouble to me. I am Mord-Sith. I am your mistress. I can be no more than who I am. You can be no less, my mate."

He nodded sadly, and put the tip of the sword between her breasts, the tears in his eyes and the white glow making it difficult to see.

Denna gently took the tip of the sword and moved it up a few inches. "My heart is here, my love."

Holding the sword against her, he bent and put his left arm tenderly around her soft shoulders. He held the power with all his strength as he kissed her cheek.

"Richard," she whispered, "I have never had a mate like you before. I'm glad I will have no other. You are a very rare person. You are the only person since I was chosen who has cared that I was in pain, or done anything to stop it. Thank you for last night, for teaching me what it could be like."

Tears dripped from his face. He held her close. "Forgive me, my love."

She smiled. "Everything. Thank you for calling me 'my love.' It is good to hear it once in truth before I die. Twist the sword, to be sure it is finished. And Richard, please, take my last breath? As I have taught you? I wish you to have my last breath of life."

In a daze, he put his mouth over hers, kissing her, and didn't even feel his right hand moving. There was no resistance. The sword went through her as if she were gossamer. He felt his hand twist the sword, and he took her last breath of life.

He laid her gently back on the bed, lay down next to her, and cried uncontrollably as he stroked her ashen face.

He grieved to undo what he had done.

CHAPTER 44

IT WAS DEEP IN the night when he left Denna's quarters. The halls were empty except for flickering shadows. Richard's footsteps echoed from the polished stone floors and walls as he walked in a mournful daze, watching his shadow rotate around himself as he passed torches, feeling comfort only at having his pack on his back once more, and to be leaving the People's Palace. He didn't know where he was going, only that he was going to go away from here.

The pain of an Agiel in the small of his back slammed him to a halt, and brought sweat instantly to his face as he tried to take a breath, but couldn't. Fire seared through his hips and legs.

"Going somewhere?" came a ruthless whisper.

Constance.

His shaking hand struggled to reach his sword. She laughed as she watched him. A vision of giving her control of the magic, of the whole nightmare starting over again, flashed through his mind. His hand backed away from the sword and kept the anger of the magic in check. She came around to stand before him, her arm around him, holding the Agiel against his back, keeping his legs paralyzed. She was wearing her red leather.

"No? Not ready to try to use the magic on me yet? You will. You will try before long; you will try to save yourself with it," She smiled. "Save yourself the extra pain, use it now. Maybe I will have mercy on you if you try it now."

Richard thought about all the ways Denna had given him pain, and how she had taught him to tolerate it, so she could give him more. He brought to bear everything he had learned. He controlled the pain, blocking it enough to draw a deep breath.

He swept his left arm around Constance, forcing her body tight against himself. He grabbed the Agiel in his fist, Denna's Agiel, hanging from his neck. Pain shot up his arm. He endured it, dismissed it. Constance gave a grunt as he lifted her off her feet, pulling her up his body. She tried to press her Agiel harder into his back, but she didn't have the leverage, and he had her arm pinned, so she couldn't move it.

When he had her lifted high enough, her contorted face in front of his, he pressed Denna's Agiel to her chest. Her eyes widened. Her expression slackened. Richard remembered Denna holding her Agiel against Queen Milena in this manner. It had the same effect on Constance. She shook, easing the pressure against his back. Still, it was hurting him, as was the Agiel in his hand.

Richard gritted his teeth against the pain. "I'm not going to kill you with the sword. To do that, I would have to forgive you everything. I could never bring myself to forgive you for betraying a friend. I could forgive your deeds against me, but not those against your friend, Denna. That is the one thing I could never forgive."

Constance gasped with the agony. "Please . . ."

"Promise made . . ." he sneered.

"No . . . please . . . don't."

Richard twisted the Agiel as he had seen Denna do to the Queen. Constance flinched, and went limp in his grip. Blood ran from her ears. He let her lifeless body slip to the ground.

"Promise kept."

Richard stared a long time at the Agiel held tightly in his fist, before he realized it was causing pain, and released it at last to hang from its chain around his neck.

He looked down at the dead Mord-Sith as he caught his breath. Thank you, Denna, he thought, for teaching me to endure the pain. You have saved my life.

It took him the better part of an hour to find his way out of the labyrinth of halls, out into the frigid night, to the expanse of grounds. He kept a tight grip on the hilt of the sword as he went past two big guards at the open gate through the outer wall, but they only gave a polite nod of their heads, as if he were an invited guest departing after a royal dinner.

He stopped, gazing out at the starlit country before him. He had never been so happy to see stars. He turned about, looking at everything. The People's Palace, surrounded by imposing sheer walls, sat atop an immense plateau that dropped off before him to a plain. The plateau stood hundreds of feet above the barren land, but there was a road cut into the cliffs, switching back and forth, descending to the flat land.

"Horse, sir?"

Richard spun around. One of the guards had spoken to him. "What?"

"I asked if you would like a horse brought up, sir. You look to be leaving. It's a long walk."

"What's a long walk?"

The guard gave a nod at the drop. "The Azrith Plains. You're looking to the west, across the Azrith Plains. It's a long walk across. Would you like a horse?"

It unnerved him that Darken Rahl had so little concern for what he might do that he would let him have a horse. "Yes, I would like a horse."

The guard blew a small whistle in a series of short and long bursts to anther man on the wall. Richard heard the short tune repeated into the distance.

The guard resumed his post. "Won't be long, sir."

"How far to the Rang'Shada Mountains?"

The man frowned a little. "Where in the Rang'Shada? They run a long way."

"Northwest of Tamarang. As close as they come to Tamarang."

722

He rubbed his chin in thought. "Four, maybe five days." He considered the other guard. "Wouldn't you say?"

The other shrugged. "If he rides hard, day and night, and changes horses often, maybe five, but I doubt it could be done in four."

Richard's heart sank. Of course Rahl didn't care if he had a horse. Where was he going to go? Michael and the Westland army were four or five days away, in the Rang'Shada. He couldn't get to them, and back, before the week was out, before the first day of winter.

But Kahlan had to be closer. Rahl had sent that man with the black stripe in his hair, and two quads, to get her. What was she doing this close? He had told them not to come after him. His anger flashed at Chase for not following his instructions, for not keeping them all away. Then his anger wilted. If it were him, he wouldn't have been able to sit back and not know what had happened to a friend. Maybe they weren't in the mountains, but all on their way. But what good was an army going to do? Ten good men in a place like this could hold off an army for a month.

Two soldiers in full battle armor came riding through the gate, bringing a third horse with them.

"Would you like an escort, sir?" the guard asked. "They're good men."

"No." Richard glared. "I will be going alone."

The guard waved the soldiers off.

"You'll be going west-southwest, then?" Richard didn't answer, so he went on. "Tamarang. The place in the Rang'Shada you asked about. It's to the west-southwest. Piece of advice, if I may, sir?"

"Go on," Richard said cautiously.

"If you go that way, across the Azrith Plains, then near morning, you'll come to a boulder field among sharp hills. There'll be a split in the road in a deep canyon. Take to the left."

Richard's eyes narrowed. "Why?"

"Because to the right, there be a dragon. A red dragon. A red dragon of a bad temper. Master Rahl's dragon."

Richard mounted the horse and stared down at the guard. "Thanks for the advice. I'll remember."

He put heel to the horse and took to the steep road, down the side of the plateau, down the switchbacks. Beyond one, he saw a drawbridge being lowered as he approached. By the time he reached it, it was down and he never slowed, galloping the horse across the heavy wooden planks. He could see that the road was the only practical way up the cliffs of the plateau, and the yawning gap spanned by the bridge would prove an impasse to any advancing army. Even without the formidable force of defenders he knew was behind him, even without Darken Rahl's magic, the simple inaccessibility of the People's Palace was defense enough.

As he rode, Richard unbuckled the hated collar and flung it into the night. He vowed that he would never again wear a collar. Not for anyone. Not for any reason.

Running the horse across the plain, Richard looked over his shoulder at the black shape of the People's Palace atop the plateau, looming up, blotting out an entire quadrant of stars. The cold air against his face made his eyes water. Or else it was his thoughts about Denna. Try as he might, he couldn't get her out of his mind. If it weren't for Kahlan, and Zedd, he would have killed himself back there; he was hurting that much.

Killing with the sword in anger, out of rage and hate, was horrible. Killing with the sword's white magic, out of love, was beyond horror. The blade had returned to its polished silver gloss, but he knew how to make it white again. He hoped he would die before that was ever required. He didn't know if he could ever bring himself to do it again.

And yet, here he was, racing across the night, on his way to find Zedd and Kahlan, to find which of them had betrayed the box to Darken Rahl, had betrayed everyone to Darken Rahl.

The whole thing didn't make any sense. Why would Rahl use the night stone to trap Zedd, if Zedd was the traitor? And why would he send men after Kahlan, if she was the one? Yet Shota had said each would try to kill him. It had to be one of them. What was he to do? Turn the sword white, and kill both? He knew that was foolish. He would rather die himself first than harm either. But what if Zedd was betraying them, and the only way to save Kahlan would be to kill his old friend? Or what if it was the other way around? Would he still rather die first, then?

The important thing was to stop Rahl. He had to recover the

last box. He had to stop wasting his energy thinking about things he couldn't know. All that mattered was stopping Rahl; then everything else would fall into place. He had found the box once; he would have to find it again.

But how? There was no time. How was he going to find Zedd and Kahlan? He was one man on a horse, and there was a whole country to search. They wouldn't be traveling by road, not if Chase was with them. Chase would keep them off the roads, well hidden. Richard didn't know the roads, much less the trails.

This was a fool's task. There was too much country to search. Darken Rahl had planted too many doubts in him. Swirling thoughts twisted on themselves, became more and more confusing, hopeless. He felt that his own mind was his worst enemy right now. Richard cleared his mind and chanted the devotion to keep himself from thinking. He smiled at the stupidity of chanting a devotion to a man he wanted to kill, but he chanted anyway as he rode on into the night. *Master Rahl guide us. Master Rahl teach us. Master Rahl protect us. In your light we thrive. In your mercy we are sheltered. In your wisdom we are humbled. We live only to serve. Our lives are yours.*

Twice, he walked the horse to rest it, but pushed on hard the rest of the time. The Azrith Plains seemed endless. The flat country, devoid of almost all vegetation, stretched on forever. The chanting helped him keep his mind clear of all thoughts, except one: the horror of killing Denna. That memory he couldn't shake. Those tears he couldn't keep back.

Dawn brought him his own shadow to chase. Boulders appeared, looking out of place on the flat ground, casting long shadows of their own. They gathered in numbers as he rode. The terrain began undulating, opening up in gullies, rising in ridges. He rode through narrow passes and rifts, down a canyon with walls of crumbling rock. The road took a bend to the left, with a narrower road to the right. Richard took the horse to the left, remembering what the guard had told him.

Out of the clearness of his mind, a thought came to him. Richard brought the horse to a skidding halt. He looked off down the right road. He thought about it a minute, then pulled the reins to the right, urging the animal on, down the right-hand road.

Darken Rahl had told him he was free to go where he pleased.

He had even let him have a horse so he might go where he wished. Maybe Darken Rahl wouldn't mind if Richard borrowed his dragon.

Letting the horse pick its own way, he watched carefully all about, resting his hand on the hilt of the sword. Surely a red dragon wouldn't be hard to spot. There was no sound but the horse's hooves on the hard ground. Richard didn't know how far it was, and rode for a long time among the rubble of boulders on the canyon floor. He began to worry that the dragon was gone, that maybe Rahl himself was riding it somewhere. Maybe to get the box. He didn't know if his present course was a good idea, but it was the only idea he could think of.

A blinding burst of fire erupted with a deafening roar. The horse reared. Richard leapt off, landed on his feet, and scrambled behind a boulder as the air was filled with flying stones and fire. Shards of rock ricocheted past his head. He heard the horse thud to the ground and smelled burnt hair. It screamed a terrible neigh until there was a snapping of bones. Richard crouched tighter against the rock, afraid to look.

As he listened to the periodic roar of fire, the breaking of bones, the ripping of flesh, Richard decided that this had been a very stupid idea. He could hardly believe the dragon was so well hidden that he hadn't even seen it. He wondered if it had seen him dive behind the boulder. At least for the moment, it didn't seem so. He searched about for a way to escape, but the terrain was too open to run without being seen. The sound of the horse being eaten made his stomach turn. At last it ended. He wondered if dragons took naps after they ate. There were a few snorts. The snorts came closer. Richard tried to make himself smaller.

Talons rasped over the boulder he was hiding behind and lifted it right off the ground, tossing it aside. Richard looked up into piercing yellow eyes. Almost everything else was an intense red. The head, with flexible black-tipped spikes around the base of the jaw and on the back of its skull behind the ears, was at the end of a long, thick neck rising from an immense body. The sinewy tail terminated in black-tipped spikes, like the ones on the head, only stiff and hard. The tail swished idly, pushing rocks aside. As it flexed its wings, powerful muscles rippled beneath the glossy, red interlocking scales on its shoulders. Razor-sharp teeth, stained red from its recent meal, sprouted just inside the snarling lips and lined the long muzzle. The beast snorted. Smoke rose from nostrils at the end of the tapered snout.

"What have we here?" came a decidedly female voice. "A tasty treat?"

Richard sprang to his feet and drew the sword, sending its ring into the air.

"I need your help."

"Only too glad to help you, little man. But not until after I eat you."

"I'm warning you, stay back! This sword has magic."

"Magic!" the dragon gasped in mock fright. It put a claw to its breast. "Oh, please, brave man, don't slay me with your magic sword!" It made a smoky rumble that Richard took for laughter.

Richard kept the sword out, but felt suddenly foolish. "You intend to eat me, than?"

"Well, I must admit, more for the amusement than the taste."

"I had heard red dragons were an independent sort, but that you are little more than a lapdog to Darken Rahl." A ball of flame boiled from the mouth, rising into the air. "I thought you might like to be free of your bonds, and be independent once more."

The head, bigger than he, Richard was frightened to note, came closer, to within a few yards. Its ears swiveled forward. A glossy red tongue, split at the end like a snake's, slithered out toward him, making a curious investigation. Richard held the sword out of the way as the tongue raked up his body from his crotch to his throat. It was a gentle touch, for a dragon, yet it knocked him back a few steps.

"And how would a little man like you be able to do that?"

"I'm trying to stop Darken Rahl, kill him. If you helped me, then you would be free."

The dragon threw its head up, smoke puffing from its nostrils as it rumbled in laughter. The ground shook. It looked down at him, blinked, then threw its head back again, rumbling in laughter once more.

The rumbling died out and the head returned, the eyebrows bunching up in an angry frown. "I don't think so. I don't think

I would like to put my fate in a little man like you. I would rather put my future in continuing to serve Master Rahl." It made a grunt, blowing small clouds of dust away to the sides at Richard's feet. "The entertainment is over. Time for my tasty treat."

"All right. I'm prepared to die." Richard had to think of a stall, to give himself time to think. Why would a red dragon be at the service of Darken Rahl? "But before you eat me, may I tell you something first?"

"Speak," the dragon snorted. "But make it short."

"I'm from Westland. I've never seen a dragon before. I always thought they would be fearsome creatures, and I must admit, you certainly are fearsome, but there is one thing I wasn't prepared for."

"And what would that be?"

"You are, without a doubt, the most stunningly beautiful creature I have ever seen."

It was the truth. Despite the deadly nature of it, it was strikingly beautiful. The neck of the dragon made itself into an S shape as it pulled its head back, blinking in surprise. The eyes frowned a little, doubting.

"It's true," Richard said. "I'm to be eaten. I have no reason to lie. You are beautiful. I never thought I would see anything as magnificent as you. Do you have a name?"

"Scarlet."

"Scarlet. What a lovely name. Are all red dragons as stunning as you, or are you special?"

Scarlet put a claw to her breast. "That would not be for me to say." The head snaked its way toward him again. "I have never had a man I was about to eat tell me such a thing."

An idea began forming in Richard's mind. He put the sword back in its scabbard. "Scarlet, I know a creature as proud as you would not be at the beck of anyone, much less one as demanding as Darken Rahl, unless there was terrible need. You are too beautiful and noble a creature for that."

Scarlet's head floated closer. "Why would you say such things to me?"

"Because I believe in the truth. I think you do too."

"What is your name?"

"Richard Cypher. I am the Seeker."

Scarlet put a black-tipped talon to her teeth. "Seeker." She frowned. "I don't believe I've ever eaten a Seeker before." A strange, dragon's smile crossed her lips. "It will be a treat. Our talk is over, Richard Cypher. Thank you for the compliment." The head floated closer, the lips pulling back in a snarl.

"Darken Rahl stole your egg, didn't he?"

Scarlet pulled back. She blinked at him, then threw her head back, jaws wide. An earsplitting roar made the scales on her throat vibrate. Fire shot skyward in a booming blast. The sound echoed off the cliff walls, causing little rock slides.

Scarlet's head whipped back to him, smoke rising from the nostrils. "What do you know about that!"

"I know that a proud creature such as you would not subject herself to such demeaning duties, except for one reason. To protect something important. Like her young."

"So you know. That will not save you," she snarled.

"I also know where Darken Rahl is keeping your egg."

"Where!" Richard had to dive to the side to avoid the flames. "Tell me where it is!"

"I thought you wanted to eat me now."

One eye came close. "Someone should teach you not to be flippant," she rumbled.

"Sorry, Scarlet. It's a bad habit that has brought me to grief in the past. Look, if I help you get your egg back, then Rahl would have no hold on you. If I could do that, would it be worth helping me?"

"Helping you how?"

"Well, you fly Rahl around. That's what I need. I need you to fly me around for a few days, help me look for some friends of mine, so I can protect them from Rahl. I need to be able to cover a lot of ground, search a lot of area. I think if I could do it from the sky, like a bird, I could find them, and have enough time to stop Rahl."

"I don't like flying men about. It's humiliating."

"Six days from now, it will all be over, one way or another. If you help me, that's all I would need. After that, it won't matter, one way or the other. How long will you have to serve Rahl if you don't help me?"

"All right. Tell me where my egg is, and I will let you go. Let you live."

"How would you know I was telling the truth? I could just invent a place, to save myself."

"Like dragons, real Seekers have honor. That much I know. So, if you really know, tell me and I will free you."

"No."

"No!" Scarlet roared. "What do you mean 'No'?"

"I don't care about my life. Just as you, I care about things more important. If you want me to help you get your egg back, then you will have to agree to help me save the ones I care about. We will get the egg first, then you help me. I think it more than a fair trade. The life of your offspring, in exchange for flying me about for a few days."

Scarlet's piercing yellow eye came close to his face; her ears swiveled forward. "And how do you know that once I have my egg, I will keep my end of the bargain?"

"Because," Richard whispered, "you know what it is like to fear for the safety of another, and you have honor. I have no choice. I don't know any other way to save my friends from living the rest of their lives as you are living now—under the heel of Darken Rahl. I will be putting my life at great risk to save your egg. I believe you to be a creature of honor. I will trust your word, with my life."

Scarlet gave a snort, backing away a little, peering at him. She folded her huge wings against herself. Her tail swished about, knocking stones and a few small boulders skidding across the ground. Richard waited. One arm came forward; a single black-tipped talon, thick as his leg, sharp as his sword point, hooked through the sword's baldric, and gave a snug pull. Her head came close.

"Bargain struck. On your honor, on mine," Scarlet hissed. "But I have not given my word I will not eat you at the end of the six days."

"If you help me save my friends, and stop Rahl, I don't care what you do to me after that." Scarlet snorted. "Are short-tailed gars a threat to dragons?"

The dragon unhooked her talon from him, "Gars." She spat the name. "I have eaten enough of them. They are no match for me, not unless there were eight of ten together, but gars don't like to gather together in numbers, so that's not a problem."

"It's a problem now. When I saw your egg, there were dozens of gars around it."

Scarlet gave a grunt, and tongues of flame licked out between her teeth. "Dozens. That many could pull me from the sky. Especially if I were carrying my egg."

Richard smiled. "That's why you need me. I will think of a plan."

Zedd screamed. Kahlan and Chase both jerked back. Kahlan's brow wrinkled. He had never done this before when he had sought out the night stone. The sun was already down, but in the fading light she could see his skin was nearly as white as his hair.

She grasped him by the shoulders. "Zedd! What is it?"

He didn't answer. His head fell to the side as his eyes rolled back. He still wasn't breathing, but that much was normal; he hadn't breathed in the past when he sought the night stone. She exchanged a worried glance with Chase. Kahlan could feel Zedd shivering under her hands. She shook him again.

"Zedd! Stop it! Come back!"

He gave a gasp, then whispered something. Kahlan put her ear by his mouth. He whispered again.

Kahlan was horrified. "Zedd, I can't do that to you."

"What did he say?" Chase demanded.

She looked up at the boundary warden, her eyes wide in fear. "He said to touch him with my power."

"Underworld!" Zedd gasped. "Only way."

"Zedd, what's happening?"

"I'm trapped," he whispered. "Touch me or I'm lost. Hurry."

"You better do as he says," Chase warned.

Kahlan didn't like that idea one bit. "Zedd, I can't do that to you!"

"It's the only way to break the hold. Hurry."

"Do it!" Chase bellowed. "There's no time to argue!"

"May the good spirits forgive me," she whispered as she closed her eyes.

She felt trapped by panic; she had no choice. Dreading what she was going to do, her mind fell silent, calm. In the calm, she relaxed her restraint. She felt her power build, taking her breath away. Released, the power slammed into the wizard. There was a hard impact to the air all about. Thunder with no sound. Pine needles rained down all about. Leaning over them, Chase gave a little grunt of pain; he was closer than he should have been. Silence fell over the woods. Still the wizard did not breathe.

Zedd stopped shaking, his eyes came down, he blinked a few times, his hands came up and he gripped Kahlan's arms. With a gasp, he took a breath.

"Thank you, dear one," he managed through the deep breaths.

Kahlan was surprised that the power, the magic, didn't seem to have taken him. It should have. She was relieved it hadn't, but astonished.

"Zedd, are you all right?"

The wizard gave a nod. "Thanks to you. But if you hadn't been here, or had waited any longer, I would have been trapped in the underworld. Your power has brought me back."

"Why didn't it change you?"

Zedd straightened his robes, seeming a little embarrassed at his helpless predicament. "Because of where I was." He held his chin up. "And because I'm a wizard of the First Order. I used your Confessor's power as a lifeline, to find my way back. It was like a beacon of light in the darkness. I followed it back without letting it touch me."

"What were you doing in the underworld?" Chase asked before she had a chance.

Zedd gave a cross look to the boundary warden, and didn't answer.

Kahlan's worry surged. "Zedd, answer the question. This never happened before. Why were you pulled into the underworld?"

"When I seek the night stone, part of me goes to it. That's how I find it, and can tell where it is."

Kahlan tried not to think of what he was saying. "But the

night stone is still in D'Hara. Richard is still in D'Hara." She grabbed fists full of his robes. "Zedd . . ."

Zedd's eyes went to the ground. "The night stone is no longer in D'Hara. It's in the underworld." His angry eyes came up to her. "But that doesn't mean Richard is not still in D'Hara! It doesn't mean anything has happened to him! Only the night stone."

With a strained expression, Chase turned to setting up the camp before darkness fell. Kahlan still held Zedd's robes, frozen in terror.

"Zedd . . . please. Could you be wrong?"

He shook his head slowly. "The night stone is in the underworld. But dear one, that doesn't mean Richard is. Don't let your fear run away with you."

Kahlan nodded as she felt tears run down her cheeks. "Zedd, he has to be all right. He has to. If Rahl has kept him there this long, he wouldn't kill him now."

"We don't even know that Rahl has him."

She knew he just didn't want to admit it out loud. Why else would he be at the People's Palace, if Darken Rahl didn't have him?

"Zedd, when you sought the night stone before, you said you could feel him, that he was alive." She almost couldn't bring herself to ask, could hardly get the words out, afraid of what he might say. "Did you sense him in the underworld?"

He looked into her eyes a long time. "I didn't sense him. But I don't know if I would, if he were in the underworld. If he were dead." When she started crying, he pulled her against him, hugging her head to his shoulder. "But I think it was only the night stone there. I think Rahl was trying to trap me there. He must have gotten the night stone from Richard, and then sent it to the underworld to snare me."

"We're still going after him," she cried. "I'm not turning back."

"Well, of course we are."

Kahlan felt a warm tongue on the back of her hand. She stroked the wolf's fur as she smiled over at him.

"We'll find him, Mistress Kahlan. Don't you worry, we'll find him."

"Brophy's right," Chase called over his shoulder. "I'm even looking forward to the lecture we'll be getting about coming after him."

"The box is safe," the wizard said, "that's what matters. Five days from tomorrow is the first day of winter, and then Darken Rahl will be dead. We will have Richard back after that, if not before."

"I'll get us there before then, if that's what you're getting at," Chase grumbled.

CHAPTER 45

RICHARD HELD THE THICK spines of Scarlet's shoulders in a death grip as she made a banking turn to the left. He had learned, much to his amazement, that when she leaned into a turn, it didn't make him slide off the side, but pressed him harder against her. Richard found the experience of flying at once exhilarating and frightening, like standing on the edge of an impossibly high cliff—that moved. The feel of her body lifting him into the air made him grin. Muscles flexed beneath him as she stroked the air with her powerful wings, each beat giving a lift. When she folded her wings back and dove toward the ground, the wind made his eyes water, and the feeling of falling took his breath away and made him feel as though his stomach would rise inside him. He marveled at the very idea of riding a dragon.

"Do you see them?" he called out over the sound of the wind.

Scarlet gave a grunt to indicate that she did. In the fading light, the gars looked like black dots moving about on the rocky ground below. Steam trailed up from Fire Spring, and even this high up Richard could smell the acrid fumes. Scarlet rose steeply into the air, making his legs press against her as she lifted them higher; then she rolled into a sharp bank to the right.

"There are far too many," she called back.

Her head tilted behind, one yellow eye peering at him. Richard pointed.

"Go down there, behind those hills, and don't let them see us."

Scarlet climbed with strong strokes. When they were higher than they had been so far, she glided away from Fire Spring. She swooped down, between the rocky slopes, threading her way back toward where Richard had told her to land. With a silent flutter of wings, she gently settled on the ground near the mouth of a cave, and lowered her neck so he could climb down. Richard knew she didn't want him on her back any longer than necessary.

Her head swung around toward him, her eyes angry, impatient. "There are too many gars. Darken Rahl knows I can't fight that many; that's why there are so many there—in case I ever found my egg. You said you would think of a plan. What is it?"

Richard glanced over at the mouth of the cave. The Shadrin's cave, Kahlan had told him. "We need a diversion, something to distract them while we get the egg."

"While you get the egg," Scarlet corrected, with a little flame to make her point.

He looked over at the cave again. "One of my friends told me the cave goes all the way through, to where the egg is. Maybe I could go through, snatch the egg, and bring it back."

"Get going."

"Shouldn't we discuss if it's a good idea? Maybe we could think of something better. I've also heard there might be something in the cave."

Scarlet brought her angry eye closer to him. "Something in the cave?" She snaked her head around to the opening and sent a horrific blast of fire into the darkness. Her head came back. "Now there's nothing in the cave. Go get my egg."

The cave was miles long. Richard knew the fire wouldn't have harmed anything farther back. He also knew he had given his word. Collecting cane reeds growing nearby, he bound them together with a sinewy vine into several bundles. He held one bundle up to Scarlet as she watched him.

736

"Light the end of this for me?"

The dragon pursed her lips and blew a thin stream of flame across the end of the cane reeds.

"You wait here," he told her. "Sometimes it's better to be small than big. I won't be spotted so easily. I'll think of something, and get the egg, and bring it back through the cave. It's a long way. It may take until morning before I'm back. I don't know how close the gars will be behind me, so we might need to leave in a hurry. Stay sharp, all right?" He hooked his pack over a spine on her back. "Keep this for me. I don't want to carry more than I have to."

Richard didn't know if a dragon could look worried, but he thought she did.

"Be careful with the egg? It will hatch soon, but if the shell is broken now, before it is time . . ."

Richard gave her a reassuring smile. "Don't worry, Scarlet. We're going to get it back."

She waddled to the cave entrance behind him, poking her head in, watching him disappear inside.

"Richard Cypher," she called after him, her voice echoing, "if you try to run away, I'll find you, and if you come back without the egg, you will wish the gars had killed you, because I will cook you slow, starting at your feet."

Richard stared back at the hulk filling the cave entrance. "I have given my word. If the gars get me, I'll try to kill enough of them so you can get the egg and escape."

Scarlet grunted. "Try not to let that happen. I still want to eat you when this is done."

Richard smiled and went into the darkness. The blackness swallowed up the light of the torch, making him feel as if he were walking into nothingness. Only a small spot of ground before him was lit. As he went on, the floor of the cave sloped downward, descending into cold, still air. A ceiling of rock appeared, and walls, as the way narrowed into a tunnel that snaked deeper. The tunnel opened into a huge room. The path led along a narrow ledge at the edge of a still, green lake. Flickering torchlight showed a jagged ceiling and walls of smooth stone. The ceiling sloped downward as he went into a wide, low passage. He had to bend over to pass through. For a good hour, he walked, hunched over, his neck starting to hurt from holding it sideways. Occasionally he pressed the torch to the rock ceiling to shed its ash and keep it burning brightly.

The darkness was oppressive; it surrounded him, followed him, sucked him deeper, calling him onward with unseen sights. Delicate, colorful formations of rock grew like vegetation, flowering and blossoming from solid rock. Sparkling crystals flashed at him as he passed with the torch, its flame the only sound, echoing back to him from the blackness.

Richard went through rooms of astounding beauty. Into the darkness rose immense columns of rippled stone, some ending before they reached their destination, with mates hanging down trying to meet them halfway. Crystalline sheets flowed over the walls in places, like melted jewels.

Some passages were clefts in the rock he had to squeeze through, others holes he had to traverse on hands and knees. The air had an odd lack of smell. This was a place of perpetual night; no light, nothing alive, ever touched it. As he walked on and on, warm from the effort, the chill of the air made steam rise from his skin. When he held the torch near his other hand, he could see vapor rise from each finger, like life's energy draining away. Although it wasn't frigid, the way winter was frigid, it was the kind of cold that would bleed a person of all their heat if they stayed here long enough. A slow sucking death. Without the light he would be lost in a matter of minutes. This was a place that could kill the unwary, or the unlucky. Richard checked the torch and extra cane reeds often.

Eternal night wore on slowly. Richard's legs were tired from the constant climbing and descending. In fact, all of him was tired. He hoped the cave would end soon; it seemed he had walked the whole night. He had no idea of time.

The rock closed around him. The flat shelf of the roof lowered until he was walking hunched over again, and lowered more until he was on his hands and knees, the ground cold and wet with slimy mud that smelled of rot. It was the first thing he had smelled in a long time. His hands were cold with the wet, stinking mud.

The way diminished to a single small opening, a black hole in the torchlight. Richard didn't like how small it looked. Air

738

moaned through the passage, making the flame flap and whip. He held the torch into the hole, but could see nothing but blackness beyond. He pulled back the torch, wondering what he should do. It was an awfully small hole, flat on the top and bottom, and he had no idea how long it was, or what was through on the other side. Air was coming through, so it must lead to the other end of the cave, to the gars, the egg, but he didn't like how small it was.

Richard backed away. There might be other routes from farther back, in one of the other rooms, but how much time could he waste searching, only to fail? He came back to the hole, staring at it with rising dread.

Trying not to think about his fear, he took off the sword, held it with the spare reeds and torch out ahead of himself, and pushed into the hole. He was immediately frightened of the way the rock pressed against him, top and bottom. Arms straight out, head turned sideways, he wriggled his way in deeper. The closeness increased, making him wiggle and snake his way, inches at a time. Cold stone pressed against his back and chest. He couldn't take a deep breath. The smoke from the torch burned his eyes.

He squeezed deeper, tighter. He rocked his shoulders forward and back, pulling one leg a few inches, then the other, feeling like a snake trying to shed its skin. The torch showed only blackness ahead. Anxiety gripped him. Just get through, he told himself, just push ahead and get through.

With the toes of his boots braced against rock, Richard gave himself a push as he wiggled. The push wedged him tight. He tried to push again. He didn't move. Angry, he pushed harder. Still he didn't move. Panic ignited in him. He was stuck. Rock was pressing his chest and back together, and he could hardly get a breath. He envisioned the mountain of rock that was pressing on his back, unimaginable weight towering above him. Fearful, he wiggled and squirmed, trying to back up, but couldn't. He tried to grasp something with his hands to get leverage to push back against. It didn't help. He was stuck. Panting, he couldn't get enough breath. He felt as if he were suffocating, his lungs burning for air, as if he were drowning, unable to breathe.

Tears filled his eyes, and fear gripped his throat. His toes scraped at the rock, trying to move him one way or the other. He didn't budge. The way his arms were pinned ahead of him reminded him of the way Denna had kept him in the shackles. Helpless. Not being able to move his arms made it worse. Cold sweat covered his face. He started gasping in panic, feeling as if the rock were moving, pressing harder. Hopeless, he wanted someone to help him. There was no one who could.

With a grunt of desperate effort, he moved ahead a few inches. That only made it worse, tighter. He heard himself crying in hysteria. Gasping for air. Felt the rock crushing him.

Master Rahl guide us. Master Rahl teach us. Master Rahl protect us. In your light we thrive. In your mercy we are sheltered. In your wisdom we are humbled. We live only to serve. Our lives are yours.

He chanted the devotion over and over, focusing his mind on it, until his breathing slowed, until he was calm once more. He was still stuck, but at least his mind was working again.

Something touched his leg. His eyes went wide.

It was a tentative, timid touch. Richard kicked his leg. At least he kicked it as best he could in the confines of the hole. It was more of a jerk. The touch left.

It came back. Richard froze. This time, it went up inside his pant leg. Cold, wet, slimy. Slithering, the hard-tipped thing worked up his leg, caressing his skin, to the inside of his thigh. Richard kicked and jerked his leg again. This time, it didn't leave. The tip moved in probing touches. Something along the length of it pinched his skin. Panic threatened to take him again, but he fought it back.

Now he had no choice. Richard expelled the air from his lungs, having had the thought before, but having been afraid to try it. When his lungs were empty, and he was as small as he could make himself, he pushed with his toes, pulled with his fingers, and wriggled with his body. He moved ahead about a foot.

It was tighter yet. He couldn't inhale. It hurt. He fought to keep the panic down. His fingers felt something. An edge of the opening, maybe. Maybe the opening to the hole he was in. He squeezed even more air out of his lungs. The thing gripped his leg painfully, urgently. He heard an angry, clicking growl. He pulled with his fingers, seizing the edge, and pushed with his toes. He moved ahead. His elbows were up to the edge. Something sharp along the length of the thing on his leg, sharp like little cat's claws, sank into his flesh. Richard couldn't cry out. He squeezed ahead. Fire burned into the flesh of his leg.

The torch, cane reeds, and his sword fell away. Clattering, the sword slid down the rock. Using his elbows for leverage, he squeezed the upper half of his body through the opening, gasping for air in deep draughts. The hooks pulled his leg. Richard wriggled the rest of the way out of the hole, sliding, falling headfirst down steep, smooth rock.

The torch burned on the curving bottom of the egg-shaped chamber. His sword was just beyond it. As he slid headfirst, his hands out in front, he stretched for his sword. The hooked claws in the flesh of his leg brought him up short, holding him upside down. Richard screamed out in pain, the sound echoing around the chamber. He couldn't reach the sword.

Painfully, slowly, he was dragged back up by claws in his leg. They tore the flesh. He screamed again. Another appendage slipped up the other pant leg, feeling his calf muscle with its hard tip.

Richard pulled his knife and twisted himself in half to reach the thing that held him. Over and over he drove the blade into it. From deep in the hole came a high-pitched squeal. The claws retracted. Richard fell, sliding along the rock, coming to a stop next to the torch. Grasping the scabbard in one hand, he drew the sword as snakelike appendages came out of the hole, wriggling about in the air, searching. They probed their way down the rock toward him. Richard swung the sword, lopping off several of the arms. With a howl, they all whipped back into the hole. There was a low growl from the depths of the blackness.

In the flickering light of the torch that lay on the stone floor, he could see a bulk squeezing out of the opening, expanding as it exited. He couldn't reach it with the sword, but he knew he didn't want to let it into the chamber with him.

An arm whipped around his waist, lifting him. He let it. An eye peered down, glistening in the torchlight. He saw wet teeth. As the arm pulled him toward the teeth, he drove the sword through the eye. There was a howl, and the arm released him. He slid to the bottom once more. The whole creature pulled back into the hole, and the arms whipped about, yanking in after it. The howls faded back into the distant darkness, and were gone.

Richard sat on the floor, shaking, running his fingers through his hair. At last his breathing slowed and his fear settled. He felt his leg. Blood soaked his pants. He decided there was nothing he could do about it right now; he had to get the egg first. Dim light came from across the chamber. Following the large tunnel on the other side, he came at last to the opening of the cave.

Faint light of dawn and the chirping of birds greeted him. Below, he could see dozens of gars prowling about. Richard settled behind a rock to rest. He could see the egg below, with steam rising around it. He could also see that the egg was far too big to carry back through the cave. Besides, he didn't ever want to go into a cave again. What was he going to do if he couldn't carry it back through the cave? It would be light soon. He had to think of an answer.

Something bit his leg. He smacked it. It was a blood fly.

He groaned to himself. Now the gars would find him. They were being drawn by the blood. He had to think of something.

A second fly bit him, and he had a thought. Quickly, he took the knife and cut off strips of the wet, blood-soaked pant leg. He used them to wipe the blood off his leg, then tied a rock on the end of each.

Richard put the Bird Man's whistle between his lips and blew hard as he could. He blew over and over. Picking up a strip of cloth tied to a rock, he swung it in a circle over his head, letting go, letting it sail out and down. Among the gars. He threw the blood-soaked strips farther and farther to his right, into the trees. He couldn't hear them, but he knew the blood flies were roused. That much fresh blood would have them in a feeding frenzy.

Birds, hungry birds, a few at first, then hundreds, then thousands, swooped and dived down on Fire Spring, eating flies as they went. There was mass confusion. Gars howled as the birds swooped up and pecked flies off their bellies, or snatched them from the air. Gars were running everywhere; some took to the air. For every bird a gar caught out of the air, a hundred took its place.

Richard ran down the hill in a crouch, from rock to rock. There was no worry of being heard; the birds were making far too much noise for that. The gars were frantic, swinging at the birds, chasing them, howling and screaming. The air was thick with feathers. If only the Bird Man could see this, he thought, smiling.

Richard broke from the rock and ran toward the egg. In the chaos, gars began falling on one another, ripping and tearing. One saw him. He ran it through with the sword. The next he only cut off at the knees. It fell to the ground howling. Another came and he took off a wing, and yet another, both arms. He deliberately didn't kill them, but let them flap around on the ground, howling and screaming, to add to the mayhem. In the disorder, gars that saw him didn't even attack. But he did.

He killed two by the egg. With his forearms, he lifted the egg from its resting place. It was hot, but not hot enough to burn. The egg was heavier than he expected, and it took both arms to carry it. Wasting no time, he ran to the left, toward the gully between the hills. Birds flew in every direction, some crashing into him. It was chaos. Two gars came for him. He set down the egg, killed the first, and took the legs off the second. He ran with the egg as fast as he could without risking a fall. Another gar came. He missed with the first swing, but ran it through when it leapt for him.

Breathing hard with the effort, Richard ran between the hills. His arms were painfully weary from the weight of the egg. Gars landed about him, their green eyes enraged. He set down the egg and swung at the first gar to come, taking off part of a wing and its head. With howls, the others rushed him.

Trees and rocks all about lit with bright light as flame incinerated several of the beasts. Richard looked up and saw Scarlet hovering over his head, beating her giant wings and raking everything around him with flame. She reached down with one claw, snatched up the egg, reached down with the other, gripped his middle, and lifted him away. They took to the air as two gars came for him. One he caught with the sword, the other burst into flame and fell away.

Scarlet roared in anger at the gars as she lifted into the sky with Richard hanging from her claw. He decided that this wasn't his favorite way to fly, but it was still better than being back with the gars. Another gar came up from underneath, reaching for the egg. Richard whacked off a wing. It spun, howling, toward the ground. No more came.

Scarlet carried him high into the air, up and away from Fire Spring. Hanging in her claw, he felt like a meal being taken back to the young. Her grip was hurting his ribs a little, but he didn't complain. He didn't want her to loosen her hold on him; it was a long way down.

They flew for hours. Richard managed to rearrange himself and get a little more comfortable in her talons as he watched the hills and trees pass below. He saw streams and fields, even a few small towns. The hills grew, becoming rocky, as if the stone were sprouting from the landscape. Jagged rock cliffs and peaks rose up before them. Stroking the air smoothly, Scarlet lifted them higher, over rock Richard thought would scrape his feet. She took them into a desolate land, barren of life. Brown and gray stone looked to have been haphazardly stacked up by a giant, like coins on a table, into thin columns, some singular, others clumped in bunches, still more having toppled.

Beyond and above the columns of rock stood massive, craggy stone cliffs, riddled with splits and cracks, shelves and projections. A few clouds drifted past the face of the cliffs. Scarlet banked toward a wall of rock. It seemed to Richard that they would run smack into it, but before they did, she brought them up short with a fluttering of her huge wings, setting him on a ledge before landing herself.

At the back of the ledge was an opening into the rock. Scarlet squeezed her bulk through. In the back, in the cool darkness, was a nest of rock, where she placed the egg, then breathed fire over it. Richard watched as she stroked the egg with a claw, turning it gently, inspecting it, cooing to it. She played fire gently over the egg, turning her head, listening, watching.

"Is it all right?" Richard asked quietly.

Her head turned to him, a dreamy look in her yellow eyes. "Yes. It is well."

Richard nodded. "I'm glad, Scarlet. I really am."

He started toward her as she lay down next to the egg. Her head came up in warning.

He halted. "I just want my pack. It's hanging on a spike, on your shoulder."

"Sorry. Go ahead."

Richard retrieved the pack and went to the side, against the wall, a little closer to the light. He glanced over the ledge. It looked to be thousands of feet down. Richard fervently hoped Scarlet was a dragon of her word. He sat down and pulled out a fresh pair of pants.

He found something else, too: the jar from Denna's room. Inside was some of the aum cream he had made when Rahl had hurt her. She must have taken what was left over and put it in his pack. Looking down at the Agiel, he smiled sadly at the memory of her. How could he care about someone who had done those things to him? He had forgiven her, that was how, forgiven her with the white magic.

The aum cream felt wonderful. He let out a little moan. It cooled the burning of his wounds, soothed the pain. Richard said a silent thank-you to Denna for putting it in his pack. He took off the shredded remnants of his pants.

"You look funny without your pants."

Richard spun around. Scarlet was watching him.

"Those are not reassuring words for a man to hear from a female, even if the female is a dragon." Turning his back to her, he pulled on his fresh pants.

"You are injured. From the gars?"

Richard shook his head. "In the cave." His voice was quiet with the haunting fear of the memory. He sat down, leaning against the wall, watching his boots. "I had to go through a small hole in the rock. It was the only way. I became stuck." He looked up at the big yellow eyes. "Since I left my home to stop Darken Rahl, I've been frightened often. But when I was stuck in that hole, in the dark, the rock pressing against me so tight I couldn't breathe . . . well, that was one of the worst times. While I was stuck there, something grabbed my leg, dug into the flesh with sharp little claws. It did this to me as I tried to get away."

Scarlet watched him in silence a long time, one claw over the egg. "Thank you, Richard Cypher, for doing as you said you would. For getting my egg back. You are brave, even if you are not a dragon. I never believed a man would risk himself so, for a dragon."

"I did it for more than your egg. I did it because I had to, to get help finding my friends."

Scarlet shook her head. "Honest, too. I think maybe you would have done it anyway. I am sorry you were injured, and that you had to be frightened so, to help me. Men try to kill dragons. You may be the first who has ever helped one. For any reason. I had my doubts."

"Well, it's a good thing you showed up when you did. Those gars almost had me. By the way, I thought I told you to stay put. What were you doing coming after me?"

"I'm embarrassed to admit, I thought you were trying to escape. I was coming for a closer look, when I heard the uproar. I will make it up to you. I will help you find your friends, as I promised."

Richard grinned. "Thanks, Scarlet. But what about the egg? Can you leave it alone? Maybe Rahl will steal it again."

"Not from here, he won't. I searched a long time for this place after he stole my egg, so if I ever got it back, I would have a safe place for it. He will not be able to reach it here. As for leaving it, that is not a problem. When dragons hunt for food, they simply heat the rock with their flame, to keep the egg warm in their absence."

"Scarlet, time is short. When can we start?"

"Right now."

CHAPTER 46

IT WAS A FRUSTRATING day. Scarlet flew low over thick woods as they both scanned the roads and trails. Richard was discouraged that they had seen no sign of his friends. He was so exhausted that he could hardly hold on to Scarlet's spikes as she flew him over the land, searching, but he didn't want to rest; he had to find Zedd and Kahlan. On top of being tired, he had a terrific headache from concentrating his eyesight so. He forgot his fatigue, his lack of sleep, every time they spotted people on the ground, only to have to tell Scarlet each time that it wasn't his friends.

The dragon went low, skimming the tops of pine trees at the edge of a field. She let out a piercing scream that made Richard jump and banked into a steep turn that made him dizzy. A buck broke into a run across the field, flushed from cover by the dragon's roar. Building speed in a quick dive, she swooped into the field. Without effort, Scarlet snatched the deer from the tall brown grass, snapping its neck in the process. Richard felt intimidated by how easy it was for her to take the prey.

Scarlet pulled higher into the air, into the golden light of the setting sun, among the puffy clouds. Richard felt as if his heart were sinking with the sun. He knew Scarlet was heading back to her egg. He wanted to tell her to search some more, while there was still light, but he knew she had to get back to her nest, her egg.

In near darkness, Scarlet landed on the ledge of rock, waiting for him to climb down over her red scales before she hurried to her egg. Richard went to one side and curled up in his cloak, shivering with the cold.

After she checked her egg, cooed to it, and warmed it with fire, she turned to see about the buck. She paused to say to Richard. "You don't look like you could eat much. I guess I could let you have some."

"Will you cook it for me? I don't eat raw meat."

She said she would, so he cut himself a chunk, stuck it on the end of his sword, and, holding it up, turned his head from the heat while she blew a thin stream of flame over it. Richard returned to the side, eating his meal, trying not to watch as the dragon tore the buck apart with fang and claw, tossing great chunks in the air and swallowing with hardly a chew.

"If we don't find your friends, what will you do?"

Richard swallowed. "We had better find them, that's all."

"The first day of winter is four days from tomorrow."

With a finger and thumb, he pulled off a small strip of meat. "I know."

"For a dragon, it is better to die than be ruled."

Richard looked up at her as she swished her tail. "If choosing for yourself, maybe, but what of others? You chose to be ruled, to save your egg, to give it a chance at life."

Scarlet grunted without answering and turned once more to her egg, stroking her talons over it.

Richard knew that if he couldn't find the last box and stop Rahl, he would have to save everyone else's life, he would have to spare Kahlan the torture of a Mord-Sith—he would have to agree to help Darken Rahl open the right box. Then Kahlan could live the kind of life a Confessor was used to.

It was a desperately depressing thought—that he could help Darken Rahl gain unchallenged power over everyone. But what choice did he have? Maybe what Shota said was right. Maybe

Zedd and Kahlan would try to kill him. Maybe he should be killed for even thinking of helping Darken Rahl. If he had to choose, though, he would not let Kahlan be hurt by a Mord-Sith. He would have to help Rahl.

Richard lay back down, too sick at his choices to finish his meal. He put his head against his pack, pulling the cloak around himself, and thought about Kahlan. He was asleep in moments.

The next day, Scarlet took him into D'Hara, over where she said the boundary used to be, searching the roads and trails. Thin, high clouds filtered the sunlight. Richard hoped his friends wouldn't be this close to Darken Rahl, but if Zedd had sought the night stone before Rahl had destroyed it, and knew he had been at the People's Palace, they would be heading there. The dragon swept low over people they saw, giving them a fright, but they weren't the ones he sought.

Near midday, Richard saw them. Zedd, Chase, and Kahlan were riding horses on a trail near the main road. He yelled at Scarlet to take them down. The dragon rolled into a banking turn, diving toward the ground, a streak of red. The three riders saw them coming, stopped, and dismounted.

Scarlet spread her crimson wings, stopping their descent, and set them in a clearing next to the trail. Richard jumped off, running as he hit the ground. The three stood holding the reins to their horses. Chase held a mace in his other hand. Seeing Kahlan overwhelmed Richard with elation. Every memory of her was suddenly true to life in front of him. They stood still as he ran toward them, down a short, steep decline in the trail. Richard watched the ground so he wouldn't trip over roots.

When he looked up, wizard's fire was wailing toward him. He froze in surprise. What was Zedd doing? The ball of liquid fire was bigger than any he had seen before. It illuminated the trees all around with its blue and yellow flame, shrieking as it advanced. Richard watched, wide-eyed, as it came, tumbling, twisting, expanding.

With the fright of what was about to happen, Richard's hand went to the hilt, feeling the word *Truth* press into the flesh of his palm. With a strong pull, he drew the sword, sending metallic ringing into the air. Released, the magic raced instantly through him. The fire was almost there. As he had done when he had been with Shota, he held the sword up, gripping the hilt in one hand, the point in the other, arms locked, holding it before him as a shield. Wrath took him, at the thought of Zedd betraying them. It couldn't be Zedd.

The impact drove him back a step. Heat and fire was all around him. The anger of the wizard's fire exploded, scattering back into the air from where it came, and then it was gone.

"Zedd! What are you doing? Are you crazy! It's me, Richard!" He advanced, angry. Angry that Zedd would do this, angry from the magic of the sword. The heat of his rage pounded through his veins.

Zedd, in his simple robes, looking as thin and frail as ever, stood his ground. Chase, bristling weapons, looking as dangerous as ever, stood his. Zedd took Kahlan's arm in his sticklike hand and pulled her protectively behind himself. Chase started forward, the look in his eyes as dark as his clothes.

"Chase," Zedd cautioned in a low voice, "don't be a fool. Stay where you are."

Richard looked from one grim face to another. "What's the matter with you three? What are you doing here? I told you not to come after me! Darken Rahl has sent men to capture you. You must turn back!"

Zedd, his white hair in its usual disarray, turned a little to Kahlan, but kept his eyes on Richard. "Do you know what he's saying?"

Kahlan shook her head, pulling some of her long hair back. "No. I think it's high D'Haran; I don't speak high D'Haran."

"High D'Haran? What are you talking about? What are . . ."

With a cold wave of understanding, he remembered. It was the enemy web Darken Rahl had put on him. They didn't recognize him. They thought he was their worst enemy. They thought he was Darken Rahl.

Another thought came to him. Bumps ran up his arms to the back of his neck. Zedd, at least, thought he was Darken Rahl, and had used wizard's fire against him. Zedd wasn't the traitor. That left only Kahlan. Could it be she saw him for who he really was?

Choked with fear at the thought, he advanced toward her as his stare locked on her green eyes, Kahlan's back stiffened, her hands at her sides, her head held up. Richard recognized the stance; it was one of warning. Serious warning. He knew what her touch would do to him. He remembered Shota's warning that he might beat Zedd, but that Kahlan would not fail.

Zedd tried to stay between them. Richard hardly noticed him as he pushed the old man out of the way. Zedd came up behind him and put his thin fingers on the back of Richard's neck. They gave a pain something like the Agiel had given. Fire burned through the nerves of his arms, and all the way down his legs. Before all the time spent at the mercy of Denna, the wizard's fingers would have paralyzed him with pain. But Denna had spent a long time training him, forcing him to tolerate pain, to deal with this much and more. Zedd was a match for what Denna had been able to do, but Richard pulled resolve from deep within himself, and put the pain from his mind, letting the anger of the sword take its place. He gave Zedd a look of warning. The wizard didn't back off. Richard gave him another shove. He pushed harder than he intended to, and Zedd tumbled to the ground. Kahlan stood frozen in front of him.

"Who do you see me as?" the Seeker whispered. "Darken Rahl, or Richard?"

She trembled slightly, seemingly unable to move. Richard's eye was caught by something, his view flicked down for an instant, and he saw that he had the sword point at her throat, at the hollow of her neck. He hadn't been aware of putting it there; it was as if the magic had taken it there of its own accord. But he knew that wasn't true. He had put it there. That was why she was trembling. A drop of blood grew against her skin, under the sword's point. If she was the traitor, he had to kill her.

The blade had turned white. So had Kahlan's face.

"Who do you see?" he whispered again.

"What have you done to Richard?" Her whisper was ragged with rage. "If you have harmed him, I swear I will kill you."

He remembered the way she had kissed him. It was not the kiss of a traitor, it was a kiss of love. He realized there was no way he could kill her, even if his fear was true. But he knew now it wasn't. With tears in his eyes, he slid the sword into its scabbard.

"I'm sorry, Kahlan. May the good spirits forgive me for what

I almost did. I know you can't understand me, but I'm sorry. Darken Rahl is using the Wizard's First Rule on me, trying to turn us against one another. He is trying to make me believe a lie, and I almost did. I know you and Zedd would never betray me. Forgive me for thinking it."

"What do you want?" Zedd asked. "We can't understand you."

"Zedd . . ." He ran his fingers through his hair in frustration. "How can I make you understand?" He grabbed the wizard's robes in his fists. "Zedd, where's the box? I have to have the box before Rahl finds it! We can't let him get it!"

Zedd frowned. Richard knew this was doing no good; none of them could understand him. He went to the horses and started searching through the packs.

"Look all you want, you'll never find it," the wizard smiled. "We don't have the box. You are going to die in four days."

Richard sensed something move behind him. He spun around; Chase had the mace raised. A stream of fire shot past, between them. Scarlet kept the fire up until Chase stepped back.

"Some friends you have," the dragon grumbled.

"Darken Rahl put a wizard's web on me. They don't recognize me."

"Well, if you stay with them much longer, they are going to kill you."

Richard realized that they wouldn't have the box. Not if they were coming to D'Hara to save him. They wouldn't have risked taking the box to Rahl. The three of them silently watched him and the dragon.

"Scarlet, say something to them, see if they can understand you."

The dragon's head swept closer to the three. "This is not Darken Rahl, but your friend, hidden by a wizard's web. Can any of you understand me?"

The three stood mute. Aggravated, Richard stepped closer to Zedd.

"Zedd, please try to understand me. Don't seek the night stone. If you do, Rahl will trap you in the underworld. Try to understand!"

None of the three grasped a word he was saying. He had to get the box first; then he would come back and protect them from the men Rahl had sent. Reluctantly, he climbed back up onto Scarlet. She kept a wary eye to the three, puffing a little smoke and flame in warning. Richard wanted desperately to stay with Kahlan, but he couldn't—he had to get the box first.

"Let's get out of here. We have to go find my brother."

With a roar of flame, warning the three to stay back, Scarlet took to the air. Richard held her spikes tight. Her red, scaled neck stretched out as she climbed into the sky among the drifting white clouds, weaving between them. He watched his three friends watching back until he could see them no more. He felt desperately helpless. He wished he could have seen Kahlan's smile, just once.

"Now what?" Scarlet asked over her shoulder.

"We have to find my brother. He should be with an army of about a thousand men, somewhere between here and the Rang'Shada. They shouldn't be as hard to find."

"They couldn't understand my words; the web must affect me too, since I'm with you. But it must be a web for people, not dragons, for I see the truth. If these three wanted to kill you because of a wizard's web, surely the others will too. I can't protect you against a thousand men."

"I have to try. I'll think of something. Michael is my brother, I'll think of a way to make him see the truth. He's on his way with the army to help me. I need his help very badly."

Since an army would be easier to spot, they flew high, to see more ground. Scarlet made gentle sweeping turns among the immense, cottony clouds. Richard hadn't realized how big clouds really were, when viewed this close. As some of them gathered, it was like being in a wonderland of white mountains, and valleys. The dragon skimmed under their dark bases, sometimes passing through a damp wisp that hung down, her head disappearing in the whiteness at the end of her neck, the tips of her wings vanishing, too. The size of the clouds made even Scarlet seem small and insignificant.

They searched for hours without seeing any sign of an army. Richard was getting so used to flying, he didn't have to hold on to Scarlet's spikes all the time. He leaned back against two of them, letting his body relax while he looked at the landscape below.

As they flew, Richard thought about what he could do to convince Michael of who he was. Michael would have the box; that had to be where Zedd had left it. Zedd would have hidden it from Rahl with magic, and let the army protect it. He had to think of a way to show Michael who he was. Once he had the box, he would have Scarlet fly it up to her cave with her egg. There it would be safe from Rahl.

Then he could go back to Kahlan and protect her from Rahl's men. Maybe he could have Scarlet fly her to the cave, too. There she would be safe from the men.

Three and a half days, and then Darken Rahl would die. Then Kahlan would be safe for sure. Forever. Then he would go back to Westland, and be finished with the magic. Be finished with Kahlan. The thought of never seeing her again made him weak with pain.

Late in the afternoon, Scarlet spotted the army. She was better at seeing things from this height than he. They were still a long way off and Richard had to stare awhile. At first he saw only a wispy column of dust; then he saw the ranks, moving along a road.

"Well, what's your plan? What do you want to do?" she called back to him.

"Do you think you could land us ahead of them, without letting them see us?"

A big yellow eye frowned back at him. "I'm a red dragon. I could land us in the middle of them, and they wouldn't see me, if I didn't want them to. How close do you want to be to them?"

"I don't want them to see me. I have to get to Michael without his men seeing me. I need to avoid trouble." Richard thought a moment. "Set us down a few hours' march ahead of them. Let them come to us. It'll be dark soon; then I can get to Michael."

Scarlet held her wings spread, gliding in a spiral toward hills ahead of the advancing army. She came down behind some of the higher ground, flew up the valleys, keeping out of sight of the road, and landed in a small clearing of long brown grass. Her bright red scales, glossy and lustrous, stood out in the late-afternoon light. Richard slid off her shoulder.

Her head came around. "What now?"

"I want to wait until dark, until they set up camp for the night.

After they eat, I'll be able to sneak into Michael's tent, and talk to him alone. I'll think of a way to convince him of who I really am."

The dragon grumbled, looking up at the sky, and toward the road. Her head swung back around, tilting, a big yellow eye peering at him.

"It will be dark soon. I must return to my egg. It needs to be warmed."

"I understand, Scarlet." Richard let out a deep breath, thinking. "Come back for me in the morning. I'll wait for you in this field at sunrise."

Scarlet looked up at the sky. "Clouds are gathering." Her head came back down. "If there are clouds, I can't fly in them."

"Why?"

She grunted, a puff of smoke rising from her nostrils. "Because clouds have rocks in them."

Richard frowned. "Rocks?"

Her tail swished impatiently. "The clouds hide things; it's like fog, you can't see. When you can't see, you run into things, like hills and mountains. I may be strong, but running into rock when I'm flying would break my neck. If the cloud bottoms are high enough, I can fly under them. If the tops are low enough, I can fly over them, but then I won't be able to see the ground. I won't be able to find you. What if there are clouds and I can't find you, or what if something else goes wrong?"

Richard rested his hand on the hilt of his sword, looking off toward the road. "If anything goes wrong, I'll have to go back to my other three friends. I'll try to stick to the main road, so you will be able to see me." Richard swallowed hard. "If all else fails, I will have to go back to the People's Palace. Please, Scarlet, if I can't stop Rahl with what I do here, I must be in the People's Palace three days from tomorrow."

"Not much time."

"I know."

"Three days from tomorrow, and then I'm done with you."

Richard smiled. "That's our bargain."

Scarlet peered up once more. "I don't like the look of the sky. Good luck, Richard Cypher. I will return in the morning."

She took a little run and lifted into the air. Richard watched her circle around him once, low, then fly off, getting smaller, disappearing between hills. A memory struck him: the memory of having seen her before. It had been the day he had first met Kahlan, right after the snake vine had bit him. He had seen her fly overhead just as she had done now, and disappear behind hills. He wondered what she had been doing in Westland that day.

Making his way through the tall, dry grass, Richard hiked to a nearby hill, climbing to the top of its sparsely wooded slope, where he could watch the approaches to the west. He found a well-hidden nook in the brush, made himself comfortable, and took out some dried meat and fruit. He found he even had a few apples left. He ate without enjoyment while he watched for the Westland army and his brother, wondering all the while what he could do to convince Michael of who he was.

He thought of trying to write it out, or maybe even drawing a picture, or a map, but he had doubts that would work. If the enemy web around him changed his spoken words, it would probably change the written ones as well. He tried to think of games they had played when they were young, but none stood out in his mind. Michael hadn't played all that much with him when they were young. Richard remembered that Michael only really liked fighting with play swords. He didn't think pulling his sword on his brother would have the desired effect.

But there was one thing, he remembered. When they had played at swords, Michael had liked Richard to salute him, while on one knee. Would Michael remember that? He had liked it done often; it made him smile more than anything else. Michael called it the loser's salute. When Richard had won, Michael wouldn't give him the salute, and Richard wasn't his match in size at the time, and hadn't ever been able to make Michael give the salute. But Michael had made Richard give it often enough. He smiled at the memory, though at the time it had hurt. Maybe Michael would remember. It was worth a try.

Before dark came, Richard heard the sound of the horses coming, the sound of gear clattering, leather creaking, metal rattling, the sound of a lot of men on the move. About fifty well-armed horsemen rode past at a quick pace, raising dust and kicking up dirt. He saw Michael, dressed in white, at their lead. Richard recognized the uniforms, the Hartland crest on each shoulder, the yellow banner with a blue silhouette of a pine tree and crossed swords under it. Each man wore a short sword over his shoulder, had a battle-axe hooked to a wide belt, and carried a short spear. Their mail armor, called battle nets, sent sparks of light through the dust. These were not regular Westland soldiers; these were Michael's personal guards.

Where was the the army? From the air, he had seen all of them together, horsemen and foot soldiers. These horses were moving too fast for foot soldiers at a march to keep up. Richard stood after they passed, looking back up the road to see if the others were to follow. No one else came.

At first worried about what this could mean, he relaxed, when it came to him. Zedd, Chase, and Kahlan had left the box with Michael, and told him they were going to D'Hara, going after Richard. Michael probably couldn't wait any longer, and was going himself to help. The foot soldiers couldn't keep up the pace needed to reach the People's Palace in time, so Michael had taken his personal guard and ridden on ahead, leaving the rest to catch up when they could.

Fifty men, even Michael's personal guard, tough as they were, were still not many if they ran into a good-size force of Rahl's men. Richard guessed that Michael was putting his heart above his head.

Richard didn't catch them until well after dark. They had ridden hard, and stopped late. They had gotten farther ahead of him than he had expected, and it was well past dinner when he finally reached their camp. The horses had been tended to and picketed for the night. Some men were already in their bedrolls. Guards were posted, and hard to spot in the dark, but Richard knew where to expect them, as he looked down from a hilltop, watching the camp's small fires.

It was a dark night. Clouds hid the moon. He worked his way carefully down the hill, creeping silently between the guards. Richard was in his element. It was easy for him; he knew where they were, and they weren't expecting him to be gliding through their midst. He watched them watching, and ducked down when they looked his way. Once inside the ring of guards, he made his way to the camp. Michael had made it easy for him; his tent was set off, away from the men. If he had put his tent among his men, it would have been more difficult. Still, there were guards around the tent. Richard studied them for a while, analyzing the weak points, until he found the place where he would pass between them: in the shadow of the tent, the shadow cast by the fires. The guards stayed to the light because they couldn't see anything in the shadow.

Richard stalked through the blackness, to the tent, and squatted down, making himself still, silent, low to the ground. He listened for a long time to determine if anyone was in the tent with Michael. He heard papers being shuffled, and there was a lamp burning, but he heard no one else inside. Carefully, he made a tiny cut with his knife, just enough to see through. He saw Michael's left side to him as he sat at a small, collapsible field table, looking over papers. His head of unruly hair was cradled in one hand. The papers didn't seem to have lines of words on them, and from what Richard could see, they were large. Probably maps.

He had to get inside, stand tall, drop to one knee, and do his salute, before Michael had a chance to raise an alarm. Just inside, below him, was a cot. That was what he needed to hide his entry. Holding the rope taut so the canvas wouldn't jerk back suddenly, Richard cut the tie down in about the center of where the cot sat, then lifted the edge of the canvas a little and rolled carefully underneath it, behind the cot.

When Michael turned to a sound, Richard rose up in front of the little table, in front of his brother. Richard had a smile on his face at seeing his older brother again. Michael's head snapped to him. The color left his soft cheeks. He leapt to his feet. Richard was just about to do his salute when Michael spoke.

"Richard . . . how did you . . . What are you doing here? It's . . . so . . . good to see you again. We have all been so . . . worried."

Richard's smile withered.

When the enemy web was put on him, Rahl had said those who honored Rahl would see Richard for who he was.

Michael saw him for who he was.

Michael was the one who had betrayed him. Michael was the one who allowed him to be captured and tortured by a Mord-Sith. Michael was the one who would give Kahlan and Zedd

758

over to Darken Rahl. Michael was the one who would give everyone over to Darken Rahl. His insides turned to ice.

Richard could manage no more than a whisper. "Where is the box?"

"Ah ... you look hungry, Richard. Let me have some dinner brought in for you. We'll have a talk. It's been so long."

Richard kept his hand away from the sword, for fear he would use it. He sternly reminded himself that he was the Seeker, and that was all that mattered right now. He was not Richard; he was the Seeker. He had a job to do. He could not allow himself to be Richard. He could not allow himself to be Michael's brother. There were more important things right now. Much more important.

"Where is the box?"

Michael's eyes darted about. "The box ... well ... Zedd told me about it. . . . He was going to give it to me ... but then he said something about finding you in D'Hara by a stone of some sort, and the three of them went off after you. I told them I wanted to come too, to save my brother, but I had to get the men together, and prepare, so they started ahead of me. Zedd kept the box. He has it."

Richard now knew; Darken Rahl had the third box. Darken Rahl had spoken the truth.

The Seeker suppressed his emotions and made a quick assessment of the situation. The only thing that mattered now was getting to Kahlan. If he lost his head now, she would be the one to suffer; she would be the one at the end of an Agiel. He found himself concentrating on a mental image of Denna's braid. He let himself do it. Whatever worked, he told himself. He couldn't kill Michael, couldn't risk being captured by all those men outside. He couldn't even let Michael know what he knew; that would accomplish nothing, and risk others.

He took a deep breath and forced a smile. "Well, as long as the box is safe. That's what counts."

Some of the color returned to Michael's face, bringing with it a smile. "Richard are you all right? You look ... different. You look like you have been through ... a lot."

"More than you could ever know, Michael." He sat down on the cot. Michael returned cautiously to his chair. Dressed in his

759

baggy white trousers and shirt, a gold belt at his waist, he looked like a disciple of Darken Rahl. Richard noticed the maps his brother had been looking at. Maps of Westland. Maps of Westland, for Darken Rahl. "I was in D'Hara, just as Zedd told you, but I escaped. We have to get away from D'Hara. As far away as possible. I must go get the others, before they go there looking for me. You can take your men back now, take the army back and protect Westland. Thank you, Michael, for coming to help me."

His brother's smile widened. "You're my brother. What else was I going to do?"

With the pain of betrayal burning hotly in him, Richard forced a warm smile. In some ways, this was worse than if the traitor had been Kahlan. He had grown up with Michael; they were brothers, and had shared a good portion of their lives. He had always admired Michael, always supported him, given him his unconditional love. He remembered bragging to other boys about his older brother.

"Michael, I need a horse. I must be on my way. Right now."

"We'll all go with you. Me and my men." His grin widened. "Now that we're back together, I don't want to lose sight of you again."

Richard jumped to his feet. "No!" He calmed his voice. "You know me, I'm used to being alone in the woods. It's what I do best. You would only slow me down. I don't have the time now."

Michael stood, his eyes shifting to the tent's opening. "I'll not hear of it. We are . . ."

"No. You are First Councilor of Westland. That is your first responsibility, not watching after your little brother. Please, Michael, take the army back to Westland. I'll be fine."

Michael rubbed his chin. "Well, I guess you're right. We were only going to D'Hara to help you, of course, and now that you're safe . . ."

"Thank you for coming to help me, Michael. I'll get my own horse. You go back to your work."

Richard felt like the biggest fool that had ever lived. He should have known. He should have figured it out a long time ago. He remembered the speech Michael had given about fire being the enemy of the people. He should have known from that, if nothing else. Kahlan had tried to warn him that first night. Her suspicions that Michael was on Rahl's side were correct. If only he had listened to his head instead of his heart.

Wizard's First Rule: people are stupid, they believe what they want to believe. He had been the stupidest of them all. He was too angry with himself to be angry with Michael.

His refusal to see the truth was going to cost him everything. He had no choices left him now. He deserved to die.

With wet eyes held on Michael, Richard slowly dropped to one knee, and gave the loser's salute.

Michael put his hands on his hips and smiled down. "You remember. That was a long time ago, little brother."

Richard rose. "Not so long ago. Some things never change; I always loved you. Good-bye, Michael."

Richard gave momentary thought, again, to killing his brother. He knew he would have to do it with the anger of the sword; he would never be able to bring himself to forgive Michael and make the blade white. For himself, maybe, but for what he had done to Kahlan, and Zedd, never. Killing Michael wasn't as important as helping Kahlan; he couldn't take the risk just to soothe his own stupidity. He went through the tent's opening. Michael followed.

"At least stay and have something to eat. There are other things to discuss. I'm still not sure . . ."

Richard turned back, looking at his brother standing in front of the tent. A light mist had begun to fall. He realized by the look on Michael's face that he didn't have any intention of letting him go; he was only waiting until he could get to his men for support.

"Do it my way, Michael, please. I have to go."

"You men," he called to the guards, "I want my brother to stay with us, for his own protection."

Three guards started for him. Richard leapt over the brush and into the blackness of the night. They followed, clumsily. These were not woodsmen, they were soldiers. Richard didn't want to have to kill them; they were Westlanders. He slipped through the darkness while the camp came to life with the sound of orders being yelled. He heard Michael yelling for them to stop him, but not to kill him. Of course not; he wanted to hand Richard over to Darken Rahl personally.

Richard made his way around the camp to the horses, slipping between the guards. He cut all the lead lines, then mounted one, bareback. He yelled and kicked and slapped at the others. They bolted in panic. Men and horses ran in every direction. He put his heels to his horse.

The sound of frantic voices faded behind him. His face was wet with mist and tears as he ran his horse into the blackness.

CHAPTER 47

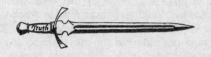

ZEDD LAY AWAKE IN the early dawn light, his mind filled with troubling thoughts. Clouds had gathered during the night, and it looked to be a wet journey ahead. Kahlan lay on her side, facing toward him, close to him, breathing slowly in a deep sleep. Chase was off somewhere on watch.

The world was coming apart, and he felt helpless. A leaf in the wind. He thought that somehow, being a wizard, after all these years, he should have some control of events. Yet he was hardly more than a bystander, watching others being hurt, killed, while he tried to guide those who could make a difference, to do what needed to be done.

As a Wizard of the First Order, he knew better than to go to D'Hara, and yet what else could he do? He had to go if there was any chance of rescuing Richard. In three days, it would be the first day of winter. Darken Rahl had only two boxes; he was going to die. If they didn't get Richard out of there, Darken Rahl would kill him first.

He thought again of the encounter with Darken Rahl the day before. Try as he might, he couldn't understand it. It was bizarre in the extreme. Rahl had obviously been frantic to find the box, so frantic that he didn't kill him when he had the chance. The wizard who had killed his father, the one he had been searching for, and when he found him, he did nothing. But his other behavior defied sense.

The sight of him wearing Richard's sword gave Zedd chills. Why would Darken Rahl, master of the magic of both worlds, be wearing the Sword of Truth? More to the point, what had he done to Richard to get the sword from him?

The most disturbing behavior had been when he held the sword to Kahlan. Zedd had never felt more helpless in his life. It was stupid to try to use wizard's pain on him. Those with the gift, and who had survived the test of pain, could survive the touch. But what was he to do? To see Darken Rahl holding the Sword of Truth at her throat gave him pain, the worst kind of pain. For a moment, he had been sure Rahl was going to kill her, and then the next moment, before Zedd had a chance to do anything, futile as it would have been, Rahl got tears in his eyes, and put the sword away. Why would Darken Rahl bother to use the sword, if he wanted to kill her, or any of them for that matter? He could kill any of them with a snap of his fingers. Why would he want to use the sword? And why then stop?

Worse, though, was that he had made the blade turn white. When Zedd had seen that, he had almost parted company with his skin. The prophecies spoke of the one who would turn the Sword of Truth white. Spoke with great caution. That it would be Darken Rahl gave him a fright to his very core. That it might have been Richard who would turn the sword white had caused him a dread all its own, but for it to be Rahl . . .

The veil, the prophecies called it, the veil between the world of life and the underworld. If the veil was torn by the magic of Orden, through an agent, the prophecies foretold, only the one who had turned the Sword of Truth white could restore it. Unless he was able to, the underworld would be loosed on the world of the living.

The word *agent* had terrible significance that worried Zedd greatly. It could mean that Darken Rahl was not acting on his own, but was an agent. An agent of the underworld. That he had gained mastery of the subtractive magic, the underworld magic,

764

implied that he was. It also implied that even if Rahl failed, and was killed, the magic of Orden would still tear the veil. Zedd tried not to think of what these prophecies meant. The idea of the underworld being loosed made his throat clench shut. Better for him to be dead first. Better for everyone to be dead first.

Zedd rolled his head to the side, watching Kahlan sleep. The Mother Confessor. The last of the ones created by the old wizards. His heart ached for her pain, ached because he hadn't been able to help her when Rahl held the sword at her throat; ached for what she felt for Richard, and for what he couldn't tell her.

If only it had not been Richard. Anyone but Richard. Nothing was ever easy.

Zedd sat up in a rush. Something was wrong. It was too light out for Chase not to be back. With a finger to Kahlan's forehead, Zedd brought her wide awake.

Kahlan reflected his worry in her face. "What is it?" she whispered.

Zedd sat still, feeling for life around him. "Chase isn't back, and he should be."

She looked about. "Maybe he fell asleep." Zedd lifted an eyebrow. "Well, maybe there is a good reason. Maybe it's nothing."

"Our horses are gone."

Kahlan came to her feet, checking her knife. "Can you sense where he is?"

Zedd flinched. "There are others about. Others touched by the underworld."

He jumped to his feet. As he did, Chase, having been pushed, stumbled and fell face first into the camp. His arms were tied securely behind his back, and there was blood on him. A lot of blood. He groaned in the dirt. Zedd felt the presence of men around them. Four men. He recoiled at what he felt of them.

The big man who had pushed Chase stepped forward. His short blond hair stood up in spikes, and a black streak ran back through it. His cold eyes, his smile, sent a chill through the wizard.

Kahlan was in a half crouch. "Demmin Nass," she hissed.

He hooked his thumbs in his belt. "Ah. You've heard of me, Mother Confessor." His wicked smile widened. "I've certainly heard of you. Your friend here has killed five of my best men.

765

I'll execute him later, after the festivities. I'd like him to the have the enjoyment of watching what we do to you."

Kahlan looked about as three other men, not as big as Demmin Nass, but bigger than Chase, stepped out of the woods. They were surrounded, but that was not a problem for a wizard. Each of the men was blond-haired, heavily muscled, and covered in sweat despite the chill to the air. Chase had obviously given them trouble. For now, their weapons were put away; they had no fear of their control of the situation.

Their confidence irritated Zedd. Their grins made him furious. The early light made the four pairs of blue eyes all the more penetrating.

Zedd knew very well that this was a quad, and he knew very well what it was that quads did to Confessors. Very well. His blood boiled at the knowing. There was no way he was going to let that happen to Kahlan. Not as long as he was alive.

Demmin Nass and Kahlan stared at one another.

"Where is Richard? What has Rahl done with him?" she demanded.

"Who?"

She gritted her teeth. "The Seeker."

Demmin smiled. "Well now, that is Master Rahl's and my business. Not yours."

"Tell me," she glared.

His smiled widened. "You have more important things to worry about right now, Confessor. You are about to give my men a very good time. I want you to keep your mind on that, and make sure they enjoy themselves. The Seeker does not concern you."

Zedd decided that it was time to stop this, before something more happened. He brought his hands up, and released the most powerful paralysis web he could marshal. The camp lit with a loud crack of green light as it flashed in four directions at once, toward each of the blue-eyed men. The green light hit each man with a hard thud.

Before the wizard had time to react, things went terribly wrong.

As fast as the green light hit them, it reflected back from each. Too late, Zedd realized that they were protected by a spell of some sort—an underworld spell that he hadn't been able to see. From four directions at once, the green light hit him. His own web paralyzed him in place. He was frozen tight as stone. Helpless. Try as he might, he could not move.

Demmin Nass took his thumb out of his belt. "Problem, old man?"

Kahlan, a look of rage on her face, stretched her arm out and planted her hand against his smooth chest. Zedd braced for the release of her power, for the thunder with no sound.

It didn't come.

By the look of surprise on Kahlan's face, he knew it should have.

Demmin Nass brought his fist down and broke her arm.

Kahlan fell to her knees with a cry of pain. She came back up with her knife in her other hand, slashing at the man before her. He grabbed her hair with his fist, holding her away. She drove the knife up into the arm that held her. He pulled the knife out and twisted it from her hand. With a toss, he stuck it in a tree. Holding her by the hair, he backhanded her across the face a few times. She kicked and clawed and screamed at him while he chuckled. The other three closed in.

"Sorry, Mother Confessor, I'm afraid you're not my type. But not to worry, these fellows here will be only too happy to do the honors. Try to wiggle your bottom, though," he sneered. "I'll enjoy that much of it."

Demmin tossed her by her hair to the other three. They shoved her back and forth among them, slapping her, hitting her, spinning her around roughly until she was too dizzy to stand and fell from one pair of arms to another. She was as helpless as a mouse held by three cats. Her hair fell across her face. Kahlan swung her fist at them, too disoriented to make contact. They laughed all the more.

One of them slammed his fist into her stomach. Kahlan doubled over, dropping to her knees, convulsed in pain. Another lifted her by her hair. The third ripped the buttons off the front of her shirt. They threw her violently back and forth, tearing her shirt, yanking it off with each throw. When it pulled over her broken arm, she screamed in pain.

Zedd couldn't even shake with the rage storming through him.

He couldn't even close his eyes against the sight of it, close his hearing against the the sound of it. Painful memories of having seen this before overlaid themselves on the reality of what was happening now. He couldn't breathe with the pain of those memories. He couldn't breathe with the pain of what was happening now. He would have given his life to free himself. He wished she wouldn't fight them; it was only going to make it worse. But he knew Confessors always fought it. Fought it with everything they had. And what she had, he knew, was not going to be enough.

From the prison of his body, as if frozen into stone, Zedd railed against his helplessness with everything he had, every spell, every trick, every power he possessed. It was not enough. He felt tears running down his cheeks.

Kahlan screamed when one of the men tossed her by her broken arm into the powerful arms of the other two. With her lips pulled back over gritted teeth, she twisted and kicked against them while they held her tight by her arms and hair. The third man unbuckled her belt and tore open the buttons. She spat at him, screamed curses at him. He laughed as he yanked and pulled her pants down her legs, stripping them inside out over her feet. The other two had their arms full holding her; she was almost more than they could handle. Had her arm not been broken, they might not have been able to hold her. One of them twisted it brutally, making her scream.

The two holding her jerked her head back by her hair while the third put his lips and teeth to her neck, biting her. Pawing her with one hand, he undid his belt and unfastened his pants with the other. He put his mouth over hers, suffocating her screams while his thick fingers moved from her breasts to the darkness between her legs.

His pants dropped, his leg forced her thighs open. She grunted against his mouth with the effort of trying to prevent what he was doing, but she could not. His thick fingers groped and wormed into her. Her eyes opened wide. Her face was red with rage, her breast heaved with ire.

"Put her on the ground and hold her down," he growled.

Kahlan's knee came up into his groin. He doubled over with a groan while the other two laughed. There was fire in his eyes as he straighted. His fist cut her lip open. Blood gushed over her chin.

Chase, his arms still tired securely behind him, crashed head-first into the man's middle. They both fell to the ground, the pants around the man's ankles tripping him up, and before he could react, Chase clamped his thighs around the man's thick neck. His blue eyes bulged. The boundary warden rolled onto his side, pulling the head back sharply. There was a loud pop, and the man went limp.

Demmin Nass kicked Chase in the ribs and head, until he didn't move anymore.

Seemingly from midair, fur and fangs landed on Nass. The wolf growled savagely as he tore at the big man. They tumbled to the ground, rolling over in the dirt, through the fire. A knife flashed through the air.

"No!" Kahlan screamed. "Brophy! No! Get away!"

It was too late. The knife slashed into the wolf with a sickening thud as the fist holding it slammed against the ribs. Over and over, Nass tore the wolf open. In moments, it was over. Brophy lay sprawled on the ground, his fur matted with blood. His legs jerked a little, then were still.

Kahlan hung by her arms and hair, crying and sobbing the wolf's name.

Nass came to his feet, panting from the effort of the short but fierce fight. Blood ran from wounds on his chest and arm. Anger flared in his eyes.

"Make her pay," he hissed to the two men holding her. "Do her good."

Kahlan struggled and twisted against them. "What's the matter, Demmin?" she screamed. "Not man enough to do it yourself? Have to have real men do it for you?"

Please, Kahlan, Zedd begged silently in his mind, please, keep your mouth shut. Please, don't say anything else.

Nass's face heated to red. His chest heaved. He glared at her.

"At least these are real men! At least they have what it takes to handle a woman! You probably don't! You only have enough for little boys! What's the matter, little boy? Afraid to show a real woman what you have? I'll be laughing at you while real men do what you can't!"

Nass took a step closer, his teeth gritted. "Shut up, bitch."

She spat in his face. "That's what your father would do if he knew you couldn't handle a woman. You're a disgrace to your father's name!"

Zedd wondered if Kahlan had lost her mind. He had absolutely no idea why she was doing this. If she wanted to provoke Nass to do worse, this would do it.

Nass looked as if he might explode, but then his face relaxed, his smiled returned. He looked around and saw what he wanted.

"Over there," he pointed. "Hold her face down over that log." He put his face close to hers. "You want it from me? All right, bitch, you'll get it from me. But you'll get it my way. Now we'll see how good you can squirm."

Kahlan's face was crimson with fury. "I think your talk is all that's big! I think you're going to embarrass yourself. Your men and I will have a good laugh. Once again, they will have to do the job for you." Her mouth spread into a defiant smile. "I'm waiting, little boy. Do it to me like your father did it to you, so we can all have a good laugh, thinking about you on your knees under him. Show me how he did it to you."

The veins on his forehead threatened to burst; his eyeballs bulged. Nass's hand sprang to her throat, tightening, lifting her. He shook with rage. His grip tightened, choking her.

"Commander Nass," one of the men cautioned in a low voice, "you're going to kill her."

Demmin looked up, glaring at the man, but then relaxed his grip. He looked back to Kahlan. "What does a bitch like you know of anything?"

"I know you're a liar. I know your master wouldn't let a little boy like you know what had been done with the Seeker. You know nothing. You couldn't tell me because you don't know, and you're so worthless you couldn't even admit it."

So that was it. Zedd understood. Kahlan knew she was going to die, and was willing to trade whatever worse Nass could do to her for knowing if Richard was all right. She didn't want to die without knowing if he was safe. The enormity of what was happening made tears roll down Zedd's face. He heard Chase stir at his feet.

Nass released her throat and motioned to the two men to let go

770

of her. In a sudden burst he struck her with his fist. She landed flat on her back. He leaned over, lifting her by her hair as if she weighed nothing.

"You know nothing! Your fist says it all. Your master might tell your father," she sneered, "but he wouldn't tell your father's little girl anything."

"All right. All right, I'll tell you. It will make it more fun when I'm on you, to have you know what we do to little pests like the Seeker. Then maybe you'll understand you waste your time fighting us."

Kahlan stood naked in front of him, her face red with anger. She was not a small woman, but she looked small in front of Demmin Nass. She breathed hard as she waited, one fist at her side, the other arm hanging limp, blood down the front of her.

"Almost a month ago, an artist drew a spell, so the Seeker could be captured. He killed the artist, but he was captured anyway. Captured by a Mord-Sith."

The color drained from Kahlan's face. She turned white as a lily.

Zedd felt as if he had been stabbed through the heart. If it had been possible, he would have collapsed to the ground in agony.

"No," she whispered, her eyes wide.

"Yes," he mocked. "And a particularly nasty Mord-Sith at that. One by the name of Denna. Even I give this one a wide berth. She is the favorite of Master Rahl, because of her ..." He grinned. "... talents. From what I have heard, she outdid herself on the Seeker. I even saw her myself one day, at dinner, covered from head to foot with his blood."

Kahlan shook slightly, her eyes wet, and Zedd was sure she turned even whiter.

"But he is still alive," she whispered in a broken voice.

Demmin gave a self-satisfied smile, happy with the telling, at seeing her reaction. "As a matter of fact, Mother Confessor, the last I saw of the Seeker, he was on his knees in front of Master Rahl, with Denna's Agiel at the back of his head. I don't think he even knew his own name. Master Rahl wasn't happy at the time. When Master Rahl is unhappy people always die. From what Master Rahl said to me when I left, I'm sure the Seeker never rose from his knees. His corpse is rotten by now."

Zedd wept that he couldn't comfort her, that she couldn't comfort him.

Kahlan went dead calm.

Her arms rose slowly into the air, her fists to the sky. Her head rolled back.

She let out an unearthly scream. It went through Zedd like a thousand needles of ice, it echoed against the hills, through the valleys, against the trees all around, making them vibrate. Zedd's breath was taken away. Nass and the other two men stumbled back a few paces.

If he had not already been frozen to stone, he would be now, at the fear of what she was doing. Kahlan should not be able to do this.

She took a deep breath, her fists getting tighter, tears streaming from her face.

Kahlan screamed again. Long, piercing, otherworldly. The sound avalanched through the air. Pebbles danced on the ground. Water danced in the lakes around. The very air danced, and began to move. The men covered their ears. Zedd would have, too, had he been able to move.

She took another deep breath. Her back arched as she stretched to the sky.

The third scream was worse. The magic of it tore through the fabric of the air. Zedd felt as if it would pull his body apart. The air began to turn about her, dust rising at its passing.

Darkness began to gather, the magic of the scream taking the very light away, pulling the darkness as it was pulling the wind. Light and dark moved around the Mother Confessor as she released ancient magic into the scream.

Zedd nearly choked with the fear of what she was doing. He had seen this being done only once before, and it came to no good end. She was joining the Confessor's magic, the additive, the love, with its counterpart from the underworld, the subtractive, the hate.

Kahlan stood screaming in the center of a maelstrom. The light was sucked to her. Darkness fell all about. Where Zedd stood, it was black as night. The only light was around Kahlan. Night around day.

Lightning tore violently across the blackness of the sky, flashing rapidly in every direction, forking, doubling, over and over until the sky burned. Thunder rolled through the countryside, coalescing into a continuous fury, mixing with the scream, becoming part of it.

The ground shook. The scream went beyond sound, to something else entirely. All about, the ground cracked open in jagged, ferocious tears. Shafts of violet light shot upward from the cracks. The bluish purple curtains of light vibrated, danced, and with gathering speed were pulled into the vortex, sucked to Kahlan. She was a glowing form of light in a sea of darkness. She was the only thing in existence; all else was nothingness, devoid even of light. Zedd could see nothing but Kahlan.

There was a horrific impact to the air all about. In a brief, tremendous flash of light, Zedd saw the trees around them suddenly stripped of pine needles, as every one of them was blown back in a cloud of green. A wall of dust and sand hit his face, feeling as if it would take the skin from his bones in its explosive passing.

The ferocity of the concussion tore the darkness away. The light was returned.

The joining was complete.

Zedd saw Chase standing next to him, watching, his arms still tied behind his back. Boundary wardens, Zedd thought, were tougher than they had a right to be.

Pale blue light coalesced into a jagged egg shape around her, gathered in intensity, purpose, and somehow, violence. Kahlan turned. One arm, the broken one, came down to her side. The other arm stopped halfway down, her fist reaching toward the wizard. The blue light bled from the ring that surrounded her into one spot, where her fist was. It seemed to fuse and in a sudden release, blasted in a line of light through the space between them.

With a solid strike, it hit him, lighting him at contact, as if he were connected to Kahlan by a thread of living light. It bathed him in the pale blue glow. The wizard felt the familiar touch of additive magic and the unfamiliar tingle of the subtractive, underworld magic. He was thrown back a step; the web that held him shattered. He was free. The line of light extinguished itself.

Zedd turned to Chase and parted the ropes with a quick spell. Chase gave a grunt of pain at having his arms free.

"Zedd," he whispered, "what in the name of the prophets is going on? What has she done?"

Kahlan ran her fingers through the pale blue light that vibrated around her, stroking it, caressing it, bathing in it. Demmin Nass and one of his men watched her, but held their ground, waiting. Her eyes gazed at things they couldn't see. Her eyes were in another world. Her eyes, Zedd knew, were seeing the memory of Richard.

"It's called the Con Dar. The Blood Rage." Zedd looked slowly from Kahlan to the boundary warden. "It's something only a few of the strongest Confessors can do. And she should not be able to do it at all."

Chase frowned. "Why not?"

"Because it must be taught by her real mother; only the mother can teach how to bring it on, if there be call enough. It's an ancient magic, ancient as the Confessor's magic, part of it, but rarely used. It can only be taught after the daughter reaches a certain age. Kahlan's mother died before she could teach her. Adie told me. Kahlan should not be able to do this. Yet she has. That she could do it without having been taught, by instinct and desire alone, speaks to very dangerous things in the prophecies."

"Well, why didn't she do it before? Why didn't she put a stop to what was happening before now?"

"A Confessor can't invoke it for herself, only on behalf of another. She has invoked it on behalf of Richard. On the rage at his murder. We are in a great deal of trouble."

"Why?"

"The Con Dar is invoked for vengeance. Confessors who invoke it rarely survive; they give their lives over to the goal, give their lives to carry out the vengeance. Kahlan is going to use her power on Darken Rahl."

Chase stared in shock. "You told me her power can't touch him, can't take him."

"It couldn't before. I don't know if it can now, but I doubt it. Nonetheless, she is going to try. She is in the grip of the Con Dar, the Blood Rage. She doesn't care if she dies. She is going to try, she is going to touch Darken Rahl even if it's futile, even if it kills her. If anyone gets in her way, she will kill them. Without a second thought." He put his face closer to Chase to make his point. "That includes us."

Kahlan was curled almost into a ball against the ground, her head bowed, her hands on opposite shoulders, the pale blue light tight around her. She stretched slowly to her feet, pushing through the light, as if she were emerging from an egg. She stood naked, blood still throbbing from her wounds. Blood, still wet and fresh, dripped from her chin.

But her face showed the pain of wounds other than the ones on her body. And then even that expression was gone, and she showed nothing but a Confessor's face.

Kahlan turned a little, to one of the two men who had held her. The other one was nowhere to be seen. She calmly lifted a hand toward him. He was a dozen feet away.

There was an impact to the air, thunder with no sound. Zedd felt the pain in his bones.

"Mistress!" the man called out as he fell to his knees. "What do you command of me? What do you wish of me?"

She regarded him coolly. "I wish for you to die for me. Right now."

He convulsed and fell over, face first, into the dirt, dead. Kahlan turned and stepped to Demmin Nass. He had a smile on his face; his arms were folded. Kahlan's broken arm hung at her side. She put her other hand against his chest with a sharp slap. The hand stayed there as their eyes locked together. He towered over her.

"Very impressive, bitch. But not only have you used your power, I am also protected by Master Rahl's spell. You cannot touch me with your power. You still have a lesson to learn, and I'm going to teach you as I have never taught anyone before." His hand came up and grabbed her tangled, matted hair. "Bend over."

Kahlan's face showed no emotion. She said nothing.

There was an impact to the air, thunder with no sound. Again, Zedd felt the ache of it in his bones. Demmin Nass's eyes went wide. His mouth fell open.

"Mistress!" he whispered.

Chase leaned over. "How did she do that! She wasn't even

touching the first one, and Confessors can only use their power once, and then must rest and recover it!"

"Not anymore. She is in the Con Dar."

"Stand there and wait," she said to Nass.

With graceful smoothness, Kahlan walked to the wizard. She stopped, and lifted her broken arm to him.

Her eyes had a glaze to them. "Fix this for me, please. I need it."

Zedd took his eyes from hers and looked down at the arm. He reached out and took it gently, speaking softly to distract her mind from the pain while he gripped above and below the break, pulling, setting the bone. She didn't cry out, or even flinch. He wondered if she even felt it. Tenderly, his fingers surrounded the damage, letting the warmth of the magic flow into her, taking the cold pain into himself, feeling it, suffering with it, tolerating it with resolve.

His breathing stopped momentarily with the sharpness of the hurt. He felt all of her hurt; it mixed with his own pain, threatening to overwhelm him, until he was able to put it down at last. He felt the bone knit together, and added more magic to protect and strengthen it until it could heal the rest of the way on its own. He removed his hands from her at last, finished. Her green eyes came up to his, and the cold anger in them was frightening.

"Thank you," she said softly. "Wait here."

She returned to Demmin Nass, who stood where he had been told to wait.

There were tears in his eyes. "Please, Mistress, command me."

Kahlan pulled a knife from his belt, ignoring his request. With her other hand she unfastened the flanged battle mace from its hook. "Take off your pants." She waited until he had pulled them off and stood once more before her. "Kneel."

The coldness of her voice sent a shiver through Zedd as he watched the big man kneel before her.

Chase grabbed a fistful of his robes. "Zedd, we have to stop her! She's going to kill him! We need information. Once he tells us what we need to know, then she can do whatever she wants, but not until we question him first!"

Zedd gave him a stern look. "As much as I agree with you, there is nothing we can do. If we interfere, she will kill us. If you

776

take two steps toward her, she will kill you before you can take the third. A Confessor in the Blood Rage cannot be reasoned with. It's like trying to reason with a thunderstorm; it will only get you hit by lightning."

Chase released the wizard's robes with a frustrated huff and folded his arms in resignation. Kahlan turned the mace around, holding the handle down to Nass.

"Hold this for me."

He took it and held it at his side. Kahlan kneeled down in front of him, close.

"Spread your legs," she ordered in an icy voice. She reached down between his legs, gripping him in one hand. He flinched, grimaced. "Don't move," she warned. He became still. "How many of the little boys you've molested have you killed?"

"I don't know, Mistress. I don't keep count. I've done it for many years, since I was young. I don't always kill them. Most live."

"Make a good guess."

He thought a moment. "More than eighty. Less than one hundred twenty."

Zedd could see a glint off the knife as she put it under him. Chase unfolded his arms and stood up straighter, his jaw muscles tightening when he heard what Demmin Nass had done.

"I'm going to cut these off. When I do, I don't want you to make a sound," she whispered. "Not one sound. Don't even flinch."

"Yes, Mistress."

"Look into my eyes. I wish to see it in your eyes."

Her arm with the knife strained, and jerked up. The blade came up red.

Demmin's knuckles around the mace were white.

The Mother Confessor rose to her feet in front of him. "Hold out your hand."

Demmin held a shaking hand before her. She put the bloody sack in his palm.

"Eat them."

Chase smiled as he watched. "Good for her," he whispered to no one in particular. "A woman who knows the meaning of justice."

She stood before him, watching, until he finished. She tossed the knife aside. "Give me the mace."

He handed it up. "Mistress, I am losing a lot of blood. I don't know if I can remain upright."

"It will displease me greatly if you don't. Just hold on. It won't be long."

"Yes, Mistress."

"Was what you told me about Richard, the Seeker, true?"

"Yes, Mistress."

Kahlan's voice was deadly calm. "All of it?"

Demmin thought a moment, to be sure. "All that I told you, Mistress."

"There is some you did not tell me?"

"Yes, Mistress. I did not tell you that Mord-Sith Denna also took him as her mate. I presume so that she might hurt him more."

There was an eternity of silence. Kahlan stood motionless over Demmin. Zedd could hardly breathe with the pain, could hardly breath past the lump in his throat. His knees shook.

Kahlan's voice came so soft, Zedd could hardly hear it. "And you are sure he is dead?"

"I did not see him killed, Mistress. But I am sure."

"Why is that?"

"It looked to me as if Master Rahl was in the mood to kill him, and even if he didn't, Denna would have. That is what Mord-Sith do. Mates of Mord-Sith do not live this long. I was surprised he was still alive when I left him. He looked to be in bad shape. I have not seen a man have the Agiel put to the base of his skull that many times and still be alive.

"He cried your name. The only reason Denna hadn't allowed him to die before that day was because Master Rahl wanted to talk to him first. While I did not see it with my own eyes, Mistress, I am sure. Denna held him with the magic of his sword, there could be no escape for him. She had him for a lot longer than is usual, she hurt him more than is usual, she held him on the cusp between life and death longer than is usual. I have never seen a man last as long as he had. For some reason, Master Rahl wanted the Seeker to suffer a long time, which is why he chose Denna; none enjoy it more than her, none have her talent

778

for prolonging the pain, the others don't know how to keep their pets alive that long. If nothing else, he would be dead now from being the mate of a Mord-Sith. He could not have survived until now."

Zedd sank to his knees, his heart breaking with agony. He cried with the pain. He felt as if his world had ended. He didn't want to go on. He wanted to die. What had he done? How could he have allowed Richard to be pulled into this? Richard, of all people. Now he knew why Rahl hadn't killed him when he had had the chance; he wanted Zedd to suffer first. That was the way of a Rahl.

Chase squatted down next to him and put his arm around him. "I'm sorry, Zedd," he whispered. "Richard was my friend, too. I'm so sorry."

"Look at me," Kahlan said, the mace held high in both her hands.

Nass's eyes came up to hers. She brought the mace down with all her strength. With a sickening sound, it buried in his forehead, stuck solid, tearing from her hands as he went down, limp and fluid, as if he had no bones.

Zedd forced himself to stop crying and come to his feet as she walked toward them, picking up a tin bowl from a pack along the way.

She handed the bowl to Chase. "Fill this half full with poison berries from a bloodthroat bush."

Chase looked at the bowl, a little confused. "Now?"

"Yes."

He noticed the warning in Zedd's eyes, and stiffened. "All right." He turned starting to leave, but turned back, taking his heavy black cloak off, putting it around her shoulders, covering her nakedness. "Kahlan . . ." He stared at her, finally unable to bring forth the words, and went off to his task.

Kahlan gazed fixedly, vacantly, at nothing. Zedd put his arm around her and sat her down on a bedroll. He retrieved what was left of her shirt, ripping it into strips, which he wet with water from a skin. As she sat without protest, he cleaned the blood off her, applied salve to some of her wounds and magic to others. She endured it without comment. When he finished, he put his fingers under her chin, lifting her eyes to his.

779

Zedd spoke softly. "He did not die for nothing, dear one. He found the box, he has saved everyone. Remember him for doing what no other could have."

Light mist from the thick clouds that hugged the ground began to dampen their faces.

"I will remember only that I love him, and that I could never tell him."

Zedd closed his eyes against the pain, the burden, of being a wizard.

Chase returned, offering her the bowl of poison berries. She asked for something to crush them with. With a few quick strokes, Chase whittled a stout stick into a shape that satisfied her and she went to work.

She stopped as if she thought of something and looked up at the wizard, her green eyes ablaze. "Darken Rahl is mine." It was a warning. A threat.

He nodded to her. "I know, dear one."

She went back to crushing, a few tears running down her face.

"I'm going to bury Brophy," Chase said softly to Zedd. "The others can rot."

Kahlan crushed the red berries into a paste, adding a little ash from the fire. When she was finished, she had Zedd hold a little mirror for her while she applied it in the pattern of the Con Dar, twin lightning bolts, the magic guiding her hand. Starting from the temple on each side, in a mirror image of each other, the top part of each bolt zigzagged over the eyebrow, the center lobe of each passed over an eyelid, with the bottom zigzag over the cheekbones, finally terminating in a point at the hollow of each cheek.

The effect was frightening—and meant to be. It was a warning to the innocent. A vow to the guilty.

After she had brushed the tangles from her hair, she pulled her Confessor's dress from her pack, took the cloak off, and slipped on the dress. Chase returned. Kahlan handed him his cloak, thanking him.

"Wear it," Chase said, "it's warmer than yours,"

"I am the Mother Confessor. I will wear no cloak."

The boundary warden didn't argue. "The horses are gone. All of them."

She gave him an indifferent look. "Then we will walk. We will not stop at night, we will keep going. You may come if you wish, if you do not slow me down."

Chase raised an eyebrow at the unwitting insult, but let it drop. Kahlan turned and started off without picking up any of her things. Chase looked over at Zedd, letting out a noisy breath.

He bent to collect his things. "I'm not leaving without my weapons."

"We better hurry before she gets too far ahead. She won't wait for us." The wizard picked up Kahlan's pack, stuffing gear into it. "We better at least grab some of our supplies." He smoothed a wrinkle on the pack. "Chase, I don't think we are going to return from this; the Con Dar is a suicide venture. You have a family. There is no need for you to go."

Chase didn't look up. "What's a Mord-Sith?" he asked quietly.

The wizard swallowed hard, his hands gripping the pack so firmly they shook. "Mord-Sith are trained from a young age in the art of torture, and the use of a merciless weapon of pain, called an Agiel. That was the red thing hanging from Darken Rahl's neck. Mord-Sith are used against those with magic. They have the power to take a person's magic, and use it against them." Zedd's voice broke, "Richard would not have known that. He had no chance. The only purpose in life for a Mord-Sith, the only thing they live for, is to torture to death those with magic."

Chase rammed a fistful of blanket into the pack. "I'm going."

Zedd nodded his understanding. "I will be glad for your company."

"Are these Mord-Sith a danger to us?"

"Not to you, you have no magic, and not to wizards, I have protection."

"What about to Kahlan."

Zedd shook his head. "A Confessor's magic is different from any other. The touch of a Confessor's magic is death to a Mord-Sith. A very bad death. I saw it once. I don't want to ever see it again." Zedd's eyes glided over the bloody mess, thinking of what they had done to Kahlan, and what they almost did. "I guess," he whispered, "I have seen a lot of things I wish to never see again."

As Zedd hoisted Kahlan's pack to his shoulder, there was an

impact to the air, thunder with no sound. They both ran to the trail, ran for Kahlan. They had only gone a short distance when they found the last man, sprawled across the way where he had lain in wait. His own sword jutted from his chest. Both his hands held the hilt in a death grip.

They both kept running until they caught up with her. She strode purposefully along, eyes ahead, disinterested in what was about her. Her Confessor's dress flowed and flapped behind her like a flame in wind. Zedd had always thought Confessors looked beautiful in their dresses, especially the white of the Mother Confessor.

But he saw it now for what it really was. Battle armor.

CHAPTER 48

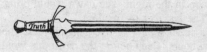

WATER FROM THE DRIZZLE collecting on Richard's face ran down his nose, hanging in a drip at the end, tickling. He angrily wiped it off. He was so tired that he hardly knew what he was doing anymore. The only thing he knew for sure was that he couldn't find Kahlan, and Zedd, and Chase. He had searched relentlessly, going down endless trails and roads, back and forth, crisscrossing his way toward the People's Palace, and had not seen a sign of them. There were trails and paths everywhere, and he knew he had searched only a fraction of them. He had stopped only for a few hours at night, mostly to rest the horse, and then he had sometimes searched on foot. Since he had left his brother, the clouds had hung low and thick, limiting visibility. He was furious that they had to come now, when he needed Scarlet more than ever.

He felt that everything was conspiring against him, that the fates did indeed work for Darken Rahl. Rahl would have Kahlan by now. It was too late; she must be in the People's Palace by now.

He urged the horse up the mountain trail, through stands of

big spruce that grew on the steep ground. Spongy moss muffled the passing of the horse's hooves. Darkness hid nearly everything. As he rode higher, through the mist and darkness, the trees thinned, exposing him to the cold wind coming up the slope. It flapped his cloak and moaned in his ears. Black patches of cloud and mist blew across the trail. Richard pulled his hood up against the elements. Although he couldn't see anything, he knew he had reached the top of the mountain pass and was starting down the opposite side.

It was deep in the night. The dawn would bring the first day of winter. The last day of freedom.

Finding a small shelter of overhanging rock, Richard decided to get a few hours' sleep before the dawn that would be his last. He warily slid off the horse's wet back and tethered it to a nearby scrub pine that hunched among long grass. He didn't even take his pack off, but simply rolled himself in his cloak under the rock and tried to sleep, thinking of Kahlan, thinking of what he would have to do to keep her out of the hands of a Mord-Sith. After he finished helping Darken Rahl open the box that would give him the power he sought, Rahl would kill him. Despite Darken Rahl's assurance that Richard would be free to go about his life, what life could he have after he was touched by Kahlan's power?

Besides, he knew Rahl was lying. Rahl intended to kill him. He hoped only that his death would be quick. He knew his decision to help Darken Rahl meant that Zedd would die, too, but it meant that many more would live. Live under the brutal rule of Darken Rahl, but live nonetheless. Richard couldn't bear the thought of being responsible for everyone and everything dying. Rahl had told the truth about Richard being betrayed, and he probably was telling the truth about knowing which box would kill him. Even if he was lying, Richard couldn't risk everyone on that one chance. Richard had run out of options; he had no choice but to help Darken Rahl.

His ribs still hurt from what Denna had done to him. It was still hard to lie down, and still hurt to breathe. His sleep brought the nightmares he had had every night since leaving the People's Palace, the nightmares of the things Denna had done to him, the nightmares he had promised her he would have. He dreamed of hanging helpless while Denna hurt him, of being powerless to stop her, of never being able to escape. He dreamed of Michael standing there, watching. He dreamed of seeing Kahlan being tortured, and Michael watching that, too.

He came awake drenched in sweat, shaking with fear, heard himself whimpering with the terror of the dreams. Sunlight was slanting sideways under the overhang of the rock. The orange sun was just breaking above the horizon to the east.

Richard stood and stretched the cramps from his muscles, surveying the dawn of the first day of winter. He was high on a mountain. The surrounding peaks thrust themselves above a blanket of clouds below that stretched off before him, to the eastern horizon, like a sea of gray tinged in orange.

The sea of clouds was unbroken except for one thing—the People's Palace. Touched by the sunlight, in the far distance, it rose proud on its plateau, standing above the clouds, waiting for him. A cold feeling ran through his gut; it was a long way off. He had misjudged how far he was from it; it was a lot farther than he had thought. He had no time to waste. When the sun was at its zenith, the boxes could be opened.

As he turned, movement caught his eye. The horse let out a terrified neigh. Howls split the morning silence. Heart hounds.

Richard drew his sword as they poured over the rock. Before he could start for the horse, the hounds took it down. In a dead run, more came for him. Frozen in shock for only an instant, he leapt up onto the rock he had slept under. The hounds, teeth snapping, bounded up the rock toward him. He cut down the first wave, then retreated farther up the rock as more hounds came for him. Richard swung the sword, cutting through them as they advanced, snarling and howling.

It was like a sea of tan fur, coming for him in waves. Frantically, he slashed and stabbed at them, trying to back away at the same time. Hounds came over the rock behind. He jumped to the side as the two groups crashed together, tearing at each other for the chance to be the first to get at his heart.

Richard climbed higher, fighting the beasts back, killing any that got close enough. It was a futile effort, he knew; there were more than he would be able to hold back. He released himself into the anger of the sword's magic, fighting with fury as he advanced into their ranks. He couldn't fail Kahlan, not now. The air seemed filled with yellow teeth, all coming for him. Blood from the killing was everywhere. The world turned to red.

And then it turned to flame.

Fire erupted all about. Hounds howled in mortal pain. The dragon roared in anger. Scarlet's shadow swept over him. Richard's sword cut through the hounds that came close enough. The air smelled of blood and burning fur.

Scarlet's claw gripped him around the middle, lifting him away from the leaping, snapping beasts. Richard panted in exhaustion from the fierce fight as the dragon flew to a clearing on another mountain. She set him gently on the ground and landed.

Richard, nearly in tears, threw his arms against her red scales, stroking them, and laid his head against her. "Thank you, my friend. You have saved my life. You have saved many lives. You are a dragon of honor."

"I made a bargain, that is all." She snorted a puff of smoke. "Besides, someone has to help you; you can't seem to stay out of trouble on your own."

Richard smiled. "You are the most beautiful beast I have ever seen." Still panting as he tried to catch his breath, he pointed to the plateau. "Scarlet, I need to get to the People's Palace. Will you take me? Please?"

"You didn't find your friends? Your brother?"

He swallowed the lump in his throat. "My brother has betrayed me. Betrayed me, and everyone, to Darken Rahl. I wish people had half the honor of dragons."

Scarlet gave a grumble, vibrating the scales on her throat. "I'm sorry, Richard Cypher. Climb on. I will take you."

The dragon made slow, steady strokes of her wings, lifting him above the sea of clouds that covered the Azrith Plains, carrying him to the last place in the world he would wish to go, had he a choice. The journey, which would have taken him a good part of the day on a horse, took less than an hour on the dragon. She folded her wings back, diving toward the plateau. The wind tore at his clothes as she plunged downward. From the air, Richard could see how big the People's Palace really was. It was hard to believe it had been made by men; it seemed beyond even a dream. It was like the biggest of cities, all melted together into one complex.

Scarlet flew once around the plateau, past towers, walls, and roofs. They flashed past in endless variety, making him dizzy. She lifted over the outer wall, and swooped down into a vast courtyard, fluttering her wings to stop their descent. There were no guards, no people, to be seen.

Richard slid down her red scales, landing on his feet with a thump. She swept her head about, then tilted it down, gazing at him. Her ears swiveled forward.

"Are you sure you want me to leave you here?" Richard nodded, casting his eyes to the ground. Scarlet snorted. "Then the six days are at an end. Our bargain is at an end. The next time I see you, you will be fair game."

Richard smiled up at her. "Fair enough, my friend. But you'll not get the chance. Today, I am going to die."

Scarlet watched him with one yellow eye. "Try not to let that happen, Richard Cypher. I would still like to eat you."

Richard's smile widened as he rubbed a glossy scale. "Take care of your little dragon, when it hatches. I wish I had had a chance to see it. It will be beautiful too, I know. I realize you hate flying men about, because it's against your will, but thanks for letting me know the joy of flying. I considered it a privilege."

She nodded. "I like flying too." She let out a puff of smoke. "You are a rare man, Richard Cypher. I have never seen one the match of you."

"I am the Seeker. The last Seeker."

She gave another nod of her big head. "Take care, Seeker. You have the gift. Use it. Use everything you have to fight. Don't give in. Don't let him rule you. If you are to die, die fighting with everything you have, everything you know. That is the way of a dragon."

"If it were only that easy." Richard looked up at the red dragon. "Scarlet, before the boundary came down, did you carry Darken Rahl into Westland?"

She gave a nod. "A number of times."

"Where did you take him?"

"To a house, bigger than the other houses. It was made of white stone, with slate roofs. One time, I took him to another. A simple house. He killed a man there. I heard the screams. And once to another simple house."

Michael's house. And his father's. And his own.

With the pain of hearing it, Richard looked down at his feet, nodding. "Thanks, Scarlet." He fought back the lump in his throat, and looked back up. "If Darken Rahl ever tries to rule you again, I hope your little dragon will be safe, and you will be able to fight to the death. You are too noble to be ruled."

Scarlet gave a dragon's grin and lifted into the air. Richard watched as she circled overhead, looking down at him. Her head turned to the west and the rest of her followed. Richard watched a few minutes as she became smaller in the distance. He turned to the palace.

Richard eyed the guards at an entrance, prepared for a fight, but they only gave a polite nod. A guest returning. The vast halls swallowed him.

He knew the general direction of the garden room where Rahl kept the boxes, and headed that way. For a long time, he didn't recognize the halls, but after a time, some of them started looking familiar. He recognized the arches and columns, the devotion squares. He passed the hall where Denna's quarters were. He didn't look down it as he walked past the intersection.

His mind was in a daze, overpowered by the decision he had made. He was overwhelmed by the very idea of being the one who would deliver the power of Orden to Darken Rahl. He knew he would be saving Kahlan from a worse fate, and many others from death, but he still felt like a traitor. He wished it could be anyone but him who would help Rahl. But no one else could. Only he had the answers Rahl needed.

He stopped at a devotion square with a pool and watched the fish gliding through the water as he stared at the ripples. Fight with everything he knew, Scarlet had said. What would that gain him? What would that gain anyone? The same in the end, or worse. He could gamble with his own life, but not with everyone else's. Not with Kahlan's. He was here to help Darken Rahl, and that was what he had to do. His mind was made up.

The bell for devotion tolled. Richard watched people gather around and bow down as they began chanting. Two Mord-Sith dressed in red leather approached and eyed him standing there.

This was no time for trouble. He went to his knees, touched his forehead to the tile, and began chanting the devotion. Since he had already decided, there was no reason to think, and he let his mind go empty.

"Master Rahl guide us. Master Rahl teach us. Master Rahl protect us. In your light we thrive. In your mercy we are sheltered. In your wisdom we are humbled. We live only to serve. Our lives are yours."

He chanted over and over, letting himself go, letting his worry go. His mind calmed as he sought the peace within and joined with it.

A thought caught the words in his throat.

If he was going to give a devotion, it was going to be one that meant something to him. He changed the words.

"Kahlan guide me. Kahlan teach me. Kahlan protect me. In your light I thrive. In your mercy I am sheltered. In your wisdom I am humbled. I live only to love you. My life is yours."

The shock of realization made sit bolt upright on his heels, his eyes wide.

He knew what he must do.

Zedd had told him, told him that most of the things people believed were wrong. Wizard's First Rule. He had been the fool long enough, listened to others enough. He avoided the truth no longer. A smile spread on his face.

He stood. He believed with all his heart. Excited, he turned, stepping among the people chanting the devotion on their knees.

The two Mord-Sith rose. They stood grim-faced, shoulder to shoulder, blocking his way. He jerked to a halt. The one with blond hair and blue eyes brought her Agiel up to a menacing posture, waving it in front of him.

"No one is allowed to miss a devotion. No one."

Richard returned the threatening glare. "I am the Seeker." He lifted Denna's Agiel in his fist. "Mate to Denna. I am the one who killed her. Killed her with the magic by which she held me. I have said my last devotion to Father Rahl. The next move you make will determine if you live or die. Choose."

An eyebrow lifted over a cold blue eye. The two Mord-Sith glanced at each other, then stepped aside. Richard marched off to the Garden of Life, to Darken Rahl.

Zedd warily scanned the edges as they ascended the road up the side of the plateau, the surroundings brightening the higher they went. The three of them emerged from the fog into mid-morning sunlight. Ahead, a drawbridge began lowering, the catch on the gears clattering as the span lowered across a chasm. Chase loosened the short sword in the scabbard over his shoulder when the lowering bridge revealed a couple of dozen soldiers waiting on the other side. Not one of the soldiers brought a weapon to hand, nor did they move to block the way, but stood at ease to the side, seemingly disinterested in the three.

Kahlan gave them no notice as she strode past. Chase did. He looked like a man about to preside over a slaughter. The guards nodded and smiled politely.

The boundary warden leaned a little closer to Zedd, but kept his eyes on the well-armed soldiers. "I don't like this. It's too easy."

Zedd smiled. "If Darken Rahl is to kill us, he must first let us get to where we are to be killed."

Chase frowned over at the wizard. "That doesn't make me feel any better."

Zedd put his hand on Chase's shoulder. "No loss of honor, my friend. Go home, before the door closes behind us forever."

Chase stiffened. "Not until it is done."

Zedd nodded and walked a little faster to stay close to Kahlan. When they gained the top of the plateau, they were confronted by a huge wall stretching off to either side. The battlements at the top were alive with men. Kahlan didn't pause, but marched toward the gate. Straining with the weight, two guards pushed the immense doors back as she approached. She didn't lose a step as she went through the opening in the wall.

Chase glared at the captain of the guards. "You let anyone in?"

The captain gave a surprised stare. "She is expected. By Master Rahl."

790

Chase grunted and followed after. "So much for our sneaking up on him."

"One does not sneak up on a wizard of Rahl's talents."

Chase grabbed Zedd's arm. "Wizard! Rahl is a wizard?"

Zedd frowned at him. "Of course. How do you suppose he is able to command magic the way he does? He is descended from a long line of wizards."

Chase seemed annoyed. "I thought wizards were only supposed to help people, not rule them."

Zedd let out a deep breath. "Before some of us decided to no longer interfere with the affairs of man, wizards used to rule. There was a rift—the wizard wars, as they were known. A few on their side survived, and continued to follow the old ways, continued to take power for themselves, continued to rule people. Darken Rahl is a direct descendant of that line—the house of Rahl. He was born with the gift; not all are. But he uses it only for himself; he is a person who does not bear the burden of conscience."

Chase fell silent as they ascended a hillside of steps, passing into the shade between fluted columns, and through an opening surrounded by carved stone vines and leaves. They entered the halls. Chase's head swiveled about, astonished by the size, the beauty, the sheer overwhelming volume of polished stone about them. Kahlan walked down the center of the vast hall, seeing none of it, the folds of her dress flowing fluidly behind her, the soft sound of her boots on the stone whispering into the cavernous distance.

People dressed in white robes strolled the halls. A few sat on marble benches, and others knelt at squares with a stone and bell, meditating. All wore the same perpetual smile of the divinely deluded, the peaceful countenance of those self-assured in their fantasy of certainty and understanding. Truth was only a shifting fog to them, to be burned off by the light of their convoluted reasoning. Followers, disciples, of Darken Rahl, one and all. Most paid the three no attention, giving them no more than a vacant nod.

Zedd caught a glimpse of two Mord-Sith, proud in their red leather, sauntering up a side hall toward them. When they saw Kahlan, saw the twin red lightning bolts of the Con Dar painted

791

across her face, the two blanched, reversed course, and quickly vanished.

The route they followed took them to an intersection of enormous halls, built in the pattern of a wheel. Stained-glass windows that formed the hub high overhead let in sunlight that streamed in colored shafts through the cavernous central area.

Kahlan stopped and turned her green eyes to the wizard. "Which way?"

Zedd pointed down a hall to the right. Kahlan started off without hesitation.

"How do you know where we're going?" Chase asked.

"Two ways. First, the People's Palace is built on a pattern I recognize, the pattern of a magic spell. The entire palace is one giant spell drawn on the face of the ground. It's a power spell, meant to protect Darken Rahl, keep him safe here, amplify his power. It's a spell drawn to protect him from other wizards. I have very little power here. I am next to helpless. The core of it is a place called the Garden of Life. Darken Rahl will be there."

Chase gave a troubled look. "What's the second."

Zedd hesitated. "The boxes. Their covers are removed. I can sense them. They, too, are in the Garden of Life." Something was wrong. He knew what it was to sense one of the boxes, and two should be twice as strong. But the feeling wasn't; it was three times as strong.

The wizard directed the Mother Confessor down the proper halls as they came to them, and up the proper stairways as they appeared. Each hall, each different level, had stone of unique color or type. In some places the columns stood several levels high. Balconies between them looked down on the hall. Stairways were all marble, each of a different color. They passed huge statues, standing like stone sentinels at the walls to each side. The three walked for several hours, working their way higher into the center of the People's Palace. It was impossible to go in a straight course; there was none.

At last they came to closed doors, carved in a country scene, clad in gold. Kahlan stopped and looked to the wizard.

"This is the place, dear one. The Garden of Life. The boxes are in here. Darken Rahl will be, too."

She gave him a deep stare. "Thank you, Zedd, and you, too, Chase."

Kahlan turned to the door, but Zedd put his hand gently on her shoulder and turned her back around. "Darken Rahl has only two boxes. He will be dead soon. Without your help."

Her eyes were cold fire in the heart of the sharp, red lightning bolts drawn on her resolute face. "Then I have no time to waste."

She pushed the doors open, and strode into the Garden of Life.

CHAPTER 49

THE FRAGRANCE OF FLOWERS engulfed them as they stepped into the Garden of Life. Zedd knew immediately that something was wrong. There was no doubt; all three boxes were in the room. He had been wrong. Rahl did have all three. He sensed something else, too, something out of place, but with his power diminished, he couldn't put his trust in the feeling. With Chase at his heels, Zedd stayed close behind Kahlan as she walked along the path, among the trees, past the vine-covered walls and colorful flowers. They came to grass. Kahlan stopped.

Across the lawn was a circle of white sand. Sorcerer's sand. In his whole life, Zedd had never seen so much of it in one place, never seen more than a pouchful. This much was worth ten kingdoms. Tiny flecks of prismatic light reflected up at him. With rising trepidation, Zedd wondered what Rahl needed with that much sorcerer's sand, what he did with it. He found it hard to take his eyes from the lure of it.

Beyond the sorcerer's sand sat a sacrificial altar. There, on the stone altar, were the three boxes of Orden. Zedd's heart felt as if it skipped a beat, to see, for sure, that all three were there together. Each had its cover removed. Each was black as midnight.

In front of the boxes, with his back to them, stood Darken Rahl. Zedd raged at seeing the one who had harmed Richard. The sunlight coming straight down from the glass roof lit the white robes and long blond hair, making them glow. Rahl stood gazing at the boxes, his prizes.

Zedd felt his face heat. How had Rahl found the last box? How had he gotten it? He dismissed the questions; they were irrelevant. The question was what to do now. With all three, Rahl could open one. Zedd watched Kahlan as she stared across at Darken Rahl. If she could in fact touch Rahl with her power, they would be saved, but he doubted that she had the necessary power. In this palace, especially in this room, Zedd could feel that his own power was virtually useless. The whole place was one giant spell against any wizard but a Rahl. If Darken Rahl was to be stopped, only Kahlan could do it. He felt the Blood Rage emanating from her, the seething fury.

Kahlan started across the grass. Zedd and Chase followed, but when they had almost reached the sand opposite Rahl, she turned and placed a hand on the wizard's chest.

"Both of you will wait here."

Zedd felt the wrath in her eyes, and understood it because he shared it. He, too, felt the pain of losing Richard.

When Zedd's head came up, he was staring into the blue eyes of Darken Rahl. They held each other's gaze a moment. Rahl's eyes shifted to Kahlan as she walked around the circle of sand, her countenance dead calm.

Chase leaned closer and whispered, "What are we going to do if this 'oesn't work?"

"We are going to die."

Zedd's hopes lifted when he saw the look of alarm on Darken Rahl's face. Alarm, and fear, at seeing Kahlan painted with the twin lightning bolts of the Con Dar. Zedd smiled. Darken Rahl hadn't counted on that, and appeared to be frightened by it.

The alarm turned to action. As Kahlan approached, Darken Rahl suddenly drew the Sword of Truth. It hissed coming out, and it came out white. He held it out, stopping Kahlan at its point.

They were too close to be stopped now. Zedd had to help her, help her use the only thing that could save them. The wizard used every bit of strength he had, which wasn't as much as he wished, and threw a bolt of lightning across the white sorcerer's sand. He drained all his power into it. The blue lightning hit the sword, knocking it from Rahl's hands. It flew through the air, landing a good distance away. Darken Rahl screamed something to Zedd, then turned to Kahlan, speaking to her, but neither could understand him.

Darken Rahl backed away as Kahlan advanced. He bumped into the altar, able to back away no farther. He ran his fingers through his hair as Kahlan stopped in front of him.

Zedd's smile faded. Something was wrong. The way Rahl ran his fingers through his hair sparked his memory.

The Mother Confessor reached out and seized Darken Rahl by the throat. "This is for Richard."

Zedd's eyes went wide. Ice flashed through him. He understood what was wrong. He gasped in recognition.

That wasn't Darken Rahl.

Zedd screamed. "Kahlan, no! Stop! That's . . ."

There was an impact to the air, thunder with no sound. The leaves on the trees about shuddered. The grass shook in a wave, radiating outward.

". . . Richard!" Too late, the wizard realized the truth. Pain gripped him.

"Mistress," he whispered, falling to his knees before her.

Zedd stood frozen. Despair crushed the elation of Richard being alive. A vine-covered door in a wall to the side opened. The real Darken Rahl emerged, followed by Michael and two big guards. Kahlan blinked in confusion.

The enemy web wavered, and in a shimmer of light the one who had been Darken Rahl was returned to who he really was. Richard.

Kahlan's eyes went wide in horror as she backed away. The power of the Con Dar faltered, and extinguished. She screamed in anguish at what she had done.

The two guards stepped behind her. Chase reached up for his sword. He was frozen in place before his hand reached it. Zedd brought his hands up, but there was no power left. Nothing happened. He ran for them, but before he could take two steps, he hit an invisible wall. He was encased in it, held like a prisoner in a stone cell. He railed in rage at his own stupidity.

At seeing what she had done, Kahlan yanked a knife from the belt of a guard. With a cry of anguish, she held it up in both hands to plunge it into herself.

Michael grabbed her from behind, twisted the knife from her hands, and held it to her throat. Richard launched himself in a fury at his brother but crashed into an invisible wall and was knocked back. Kahlan had expended all her energy in the Con Dar, and was too weak to fight back; she collapsed in tears. One of the guards tied a gag to her mouth, preventing her from even mumbling Richard's name.

Richard, on his knees, fell against Darken Rahl, gripping his robes, pleading up to him. "Don't hurt her! Please. Don't hurt her."

Darken Rahl put a hand on Richard's shoulder. "So glad to see you have come back, Richard. I thought you might. I'm glad you've decided to help me. I admire your devotion to your friends."

Zedd was bewildered. What help could Darken Rahl possibly need from Richard?

"Please," Richard begged in tears, "don't hurt her."

"Well now, that's entirely up to you." He pulled Richard's hands from his robes.

"Anything! I'll do anything. Just don't hurt her."

A smile spread on Darken Rahl's lips. He licked the tips of his fingers. He ran his other hand through Richard's hair. "I'm sorry it had to be this way, Richard. I really am. It would have been a pleasure having you around as you were. Although you don't realize it, you and I are very much alike. But I'm afraid you have fallen victim to the Wizard's First Rule."

"Don't hurt Mistress Kahlan," Richard cried. "Please."

"If you do as I say, I will do as I promised, and she will be treated well. I may even turn you into something pleasant, something you would like to be, maybe a lapdog. I may even let you sleep in our bedchamber so you might see that I keep my word. Maybe I will even name my son in honor of you, for helping me.

Would you like that? Richard Rahl. Sort of ironic, don't you think."

"Do whatever you want with me, but please don't hurt Mistress Kahlan. Tell me what you want me to do, please."

Darken Rahl patted Richard's head. "Soon, my son, soon. Wait here."

Darken Rahl left Richard on his knees, and glided around the circle of white sand to Zedd. The blue eyes locked on the old man as he came. Zedd felt hollow, empty.

Rahl stopped in front of him and licked his fingers, stroking them over his eyebrows.

"What is your name, Old One?"

Zedd stared back, his hopes destroyed. "Zeddicus Zu'l Zorander." He held his chin up. "I am the one who killed your father."

Darken Rahl nodded. "And do you know that your wizard's fire also burned me? Do you know it almost killed me when I was but a child? And that I spent months in agony? And that to this day I carry the scars of what you did, both those on the outside, and others on the inside?"

"I'm sorry I hurt a child, regardless of who the child was. But in this case, I would call it premature punishment."

Rahl's face remained pleasant, the hint of a smile still on his lips. "We are going to have a long time together, you and I. I am going to teach you of the pain I endured, and more. You will know what it was like."

Zedd gave a bitter look. "Nothing could match the pain you have already given me."

Darken Rahl licked his fingertips as he turned away. "We will see."

Zedd watched in hopeless frustration as Rahl returned to stand once more in front of Richard. "Richard!" Zedd screamed. "Don't help him! Kahlan would rather die than have you help him!"

Richard looked blankly to the wizard before he gazed up at Darken Rahl. "I'll do anything if you don't hurt her."

Darken Rahl motioned him to his feet. "You have my word, my son. If you do as I ask." Richard nodded. "Recite the Book of Counted Shadows."

Zedd reeled in shock. Richard turned to Kahlan.

"What should I do, Mistress?"

Kahlan struggled against Michael, against the knife at her throat, screamed muffled words against the gag.

Rahl's voice was calm, gentle. "Recite the Book of Counted Shadows, Richard, or I will have Michael start by cutting off her fingers one at a time. The longer you remain silent, the more he will cut her."

Richard spun back to Rahl, panic in his eyes. *"Verification of the truth of the words of the Book of Counted Shadows, if spoken by another, rather than read by the one who commands the boxes, can only be insured by the use of a Confessor. . . ."*

Zedd sank to the ground. He couldn't believe what he was hearing. As he listened to Richard reading out the book, he knew it was true; he recognized the unique syntax of a book of magic. Richard couldn't be making it up. It was the Book of Counted Shadows. Zedd didn't have the strength to wonder at how Richard had learned it.

The world as they knew it was ending. This was the first day of the rule of Rahl. All was lost. Darken Rahl had won. The world was his.

Zedd sat numbly, listening. Some of the words themselves were magic, and none but one with the gift could keep the words in his head; the magic would erase the whole of it at certain magic trigger words. Protection against unseen circumstances. Protection against just anyone getting hold of the magic within. That Richard could recite them was proof he was born to it. Born of and to the magic. As much as Richard hated the magic, he was magic, as the prophecies foretold.

Zedd mourned the things he had done. Mourned that he had tried to protect Richard from the forces that would have sought to use him, had they known what he was. Those born with the gift were always vulnerable when they were young. Darken Rahl was proof of that. Zedd had deliberately chosen not to teach Richard, as a way of protecting him from those forces learning of him. Zedd had always feared, and hoped, that Richard had the gift, but had hoped he would grow before it manifested itself, and then Zedd might have the time to teach him when he was strong enough, when he was old enough. And before it could kill him. It had been a futile effort. It had come to no good end. Zedd guessed that he had always known Richard had the gift, was someone special. Everyone who knew Richard knew he was someone special. Rare. The mark of magic.

Zedd wept as he recalled the time he had enjoyed with Richard. They had been good years. None had been better in his life. The years away from the magic. To have someone love him without fear, and only for himself. To be a friend.

Richard read out the book without hesitation or a single falter. Zedd marveled that he knew it so perfectly, and caught himself being proud, but then wished Richard weren't so talented. Much of what he recited was about things already finished with, such as removing the covers from the boxes, but Darken Rahl didn't stop him or hurry him over those sections for fear that he might miss something. He let Richard recite it at his own pace, and stood mute, listening carefully. Occasionally, Rahl had him repeat a section, to be sure he had it right, and stood absorbed in thought as Richard told of sun angles, of clouds, of wind patterns.

The afternoon wore on, Richard reciting, Rahl standing before him listening, Michael with a knife at Kahlan's throat, the two guards holding her arms, Chase frozen in place, his hand halfway to his sword, and Zedd sitting on the ground, doomed, locked in his invisible prison. Zedd realized that the procedure for opening the boxes was going to take longer than he would have thought. It would take all night. There were enchantments to be drawn. That was the reason Darken Rahl needed so much sorcerer's sand. The boxes had to be placed just so, the winter's first sun touching them, dictating their position once they each cast a shadow.

Each box, although they looked identical, cast a different shadow. As the sun sank lower in the sky, the fingers of shadows grew away from each box. One of the boxes cast a single finger of shadow, another cast two fingers of shadow, and the third cast three. Now he knew why it was called the Book of Counted Shadows.

At the proper places in the book, Darken Rahl had Richard stop while the enchantments were drawn in the sorcerer's sand. Some of the spells were called by names Zedd had never heard before. But Rahl had. He drew without hesitation. When darkness fell, he lit torches in a ring around the sand. Under the light of the torches, he drew the enchantments as they were called for. Everyone stood in silence, watching as he carefully drew in the sand. Zedd was impressed by his level of skill at drawing the charms, and was more than a little uneasy at seeing underworld runes.

The geometric patterns were complex, and Zedd knew they must be done without error, and in the proper order, each line drawn at the proper time, in the proper sequence. They could not be corrected or erased and started over if there was a mistake. A mistake was death.

Zedd had known wizards who had spent years studying a spell before they would dare to attempt drawing it in sorcerer's sand, for fear of making a fatal mistake. Darken Rahl didn't look to be having the slightest trouble. His steady hand moved with precision. Zedd had never seen a wizard of his talents. At least, he thought bitterly, they would be killed by the best. He couldn't help admiring the level of mastery. It was a magnitude of proficiency he had never witnessed before.

All of this endeavor was simply to tell which box was the one Rahl wanted; he could open one at any time, the book stated. Zedd knew from other books of instruction that all this effort was a precaution against the magic being used easily. No one was simply going to decide to be the master of the world and read how in a book of magic. Zedd, as much as he knew, didn't have the required knowledge to carry out the instructions. Darken Rahl had been studying for this moment almost his whole life. His father had probably begun the instruction when he was young. Zedd wished the wizard's fire that had killed his father had killed Darken Rahl, too. He considered that thought a moment, and then took it back.

At dawn, after all the enchantments were drawn, the boxes were placed on them; each box, distinguished by the number of shadows it threw, was placed on a specific drawing. Spells were cast. As the rays of sun from the second day of winter lit the stone, the boxes were placed on the altar once more. Zedd was amazed to see that the boxes that had thrown a particular number of shadows the day before now threw a different number—

another precaution. As directed, the boxes were rearranged so the one throwing a single shadow was to the left, the one that threw two was in the center, and the one that threw three was to the right.

Darken Rahl stared at the black boxes. "Continue."

Without hesitation, Richard went on. *"Once so arranged, Orden is at the ready to be commanded. Where one shadow is insufficient to gain the power to sustain the life of the player, and three more than can be tolerated by all life, the balance is struck by opening the box with two shadows; one shadow for yourself, and one for the world that would be yours to command by the power of Orden. One world under one command is marked by the box with two shadows. Open it to gain your reward."*

Darken Rahl's face turned slowly to Richard. "Go on."

Richard blinked. *"Rule as you have chosen.* That is the end."

"There must be more."

"No, Master Rahl. *Rule as you have chosen.* That's the end, the last words."

Rahl grabbed Richard's throat. "Did you learn it all? The entire book?"

"Yes, Master Rahl."

Rahl's face reddened. "That can't be right! That isn't the right box! The box with two shadows is the one that will kill me! I told you, I learned that much! I learned which one will kill me!"

"I have told you every word true. Every single word."

Darken Rahl released his throat. "I don't believe you." He looked to Michael. "Cut her throat."

Richard fell to his knees with a scream. "Please! You gave me your word! You said if I told you, you wouldn't harm her! Please! I have told you the truth!"

Rahl held his hand up to Michael, but kept his eyes on Richard. "I don't believe you. Unless you tell me the truth, right now, I will cut her open. I will kill your mistress."

"No!" Richard screamed. "I have told you the truth! I can't tell you anything different, it would be a lie!"

"Last chance, Richard. Tell me the truth, or she dies."

"I can't tell you anything differently," Richard cried. "Anything different would be a lie. I have told you every word true."

Zedd came to his feet. He watched the knife at Kahlan's

throat; her green eyes were wide; he watched Darken Rahl. Rahl had obviously found some of the information from a source other than the Book of Counted Shadows, and that information was in conflict with the information in the book. This was not uncommon; surely Darken Rahl must know that. When there was a conflict, the information in the instruction book for that specific magic must always take precedence. To do otherwise was always fatal—it was a safeguard to protect the magic. Zedd hoped against hope that Rahl's arrogance would make him go against the book.

The smile came back to Darken Rahl's face. He licked his fingertips, and wiped them on his eyebrows. "All right, Richard. I just had to be sure you were telling me the truth."

"I am, I swear on Mistress Kahlan's life. Every word I told you is true."

Rahl nodded. He gave a wave of his hand to Michael. Michael relaxed the knife. Kahlan closed her eyes as tears ran down her cheeks. Rahl turned to the boxes, letting out a deep breath.

"At last," he whispered. "The magic of Orden is mine."

Zedd couldn't see it, but he knew that Darken Rahl lifted the lid on the middle box, the one with two shadows; he could tell by the light expanding from it. Golden light lifted and as if it were a great weight, it settled over Master Rahl, lighting him in a golden glow. He turned, smiling. The light about him moved with him as he moved. He lifted slightly into the air, enough to take the weight from his feet, and floated to the center of the sorcerer's sand, his arms extended, the light beginning to swirl slowly around him. He faced toward Richard.

"Thank you, my son, for coming back, for helping Father Rahl. You will be rewarded for helping me, as I promised. You have delivered to me that which is mine. I can feel it. It's marvelous. I can feel the power."

Richard stood without emotion, watching. Zedd sank to the ground again. What had Richard done? How could he? How could he give Rahl the magic of Orden? Allow him to rule the world? He had been touched by a Confessor, that was how; it wasn't his fault, he had no control. It was over. Zedd forgave him.

Had he the power, Zedd would have made Wizard's Life Fire,

and put his life into it. But he had no power here, no power in the face of Master Rahl. He felt very tired, very old. He knew he would not get the chance to get much older. Darken Rahl would see to that. But it was not himself he grieved for—it was everyone else.

Bathed in the golden light, Darken Rahl slowly rose a few feet off the ground, above the white sorcerer's sand, a satisfied grin on his face, his blue eyes sparkling. His head rolled back in rapture, his eyes closing, his blond hair hanging away. Sparkles of light rotated about him.

The white sand turned a golden color, continued turning darker, to a burnt brown. The light around Rahl darkened to amber. His head came down, his eyes coming open, his smile fading.

The sorcerer's sand crisped to black. The ground trembled.

A smile spread on Richard's face. He went and retrieved the Sword of Truth, the anger of the sword's magic flooding into his gray eyes. Zedd came to his feet. The light around Darken Rahl turned an ugly brown. His blue eyes went wide.

A wailing roar came from the ground. The black sand under Rahl's feet split open. Violet light shot up, engulfing him. He twisted in it, screaming out.

Richard, his chest heaving, stood transfixed, watching.

The invisible prison around Zedd shattered. Chase's hand abruptly completed its journey to his sword, yanking it free as he flew toward Kahlan. The two guards released her arms and met him halfway.

Michale's face paled. He stared in shock as Chase cut down one of the men. Kahlan drove her elbow into Michael's gut and grabbed the knife, twisting it from his hand. Disarmed, Michael scanned about with quick jerks of his head, his eyes wild, and raced off down a path between the trees.

Chase and the second guard tumbled to the ground, both grunting with lethal intent as they rolled over each other trying to gain advantage. The guard cried out. Chase came to his feet. The other didn't. He gave a glance at Darken Rahl, and ran off down the path Michael had taken. Zedd saw a glimpse of Kahlan's dress as she disappeared in another direction.

Zedd stood as Richard did, spellbound, their stares riveted to

Darken Rahl as he struggled, trapped in the grip of the magic of Orden. Violet light and dark shadows held him tight in the air above the black hole.

"Richard!" Rahl shrieked. "What have you done!"

The Seeker stepped closer to the circle of black sand. "Why, only what you wanted, Master Rahl," he said innocently. "I have told you what you wanted to hear."

"But it was the truth! You told the words true!"

Richard nodded. "Yes, I did. I just didn't tell you all of them. I left out most of the paragraph at the end. *Be cautioned. The effect of the boxes is fluid. It shifts with the intent. To be Master of all, so you may help others, shift one box to the right. To be Master of all, so all will do your bidding, shift one box to the left. Rule as you have chosen.* Your information was correct; the box with two shadows was the one that would kill you."

"But you had to do as I said! You were touched by a Confessor's power!"

Richard smiled. "Was I? Wizard's First Rule. It's the first rule because it's the most important. You should have guarded better against it. That's the price of arrogance. I accept my vulnerability, you don't.

"I didn't like the choices you gave me. I couldn't win by your rules, so I made some new ones. The book said you had to confirm the truth with the use of a Confessor. You only thought you had done that. Wizard's First Rule. You believed because you wanted to. I have beaten you."

"It can't be! It's not possible! How could you have known how to do this!"

"You taught me: nothing, including magic, is one-dimensional. Look at the whole, you said; nothing that exists has only one side. Look at the whole." Richard shook his head slowly. "You should never have taught me something you didn't want me to know. Once you teach me something, it's mine to use. Thank you, Father Rahl, for teaching me the most important thing I will ever learn—how to love Kahlan."

Darken Rahl's face distorted in pain. He laughed and screamed.

Richard looked around. "Where's Kahlan?"

Zedd pointed a long finger. "I saw her leave that way."

Richard slid the sword back into its scabbard as he turned his eyes to the figure held in the shadows and light. "Good-bye, Father Rahl. I trust you will die without my watching it."

"Richard!" Rahl shrieked as he watched the Seeker stride away. "Richard!"

Zedd stood alone with Darken Rahl. He watched as transparent fingers of smoke entwined around the white robes, pinning Rahl's arms to his sides. Zedd stepped closer, the blue eyes coming to the old wizard.

"Zeddicus Zu'l Zorander, you have won this much of it, but maybe not all of it."

"Arrogant to the end?"

Rahl smiled. "Tell me who he is."

Zedd shrugged. "The Seeker."

Rahl laughed, struggling in pain. The blue-eyed gaze came back to Zedd. "He is your son, isn't he? I have at least been defeated by wizard blood. You are his father."

Zedd shook his head slowly, a wistful smile coming to his lips. "He is my grandson."

"You lie! Why put a web around him, hide his father's identity, if it is not you!"

"I put a web around him because I did not want him to know who the blue-eyed bastard was who raped his mother and gave him life."

Darken Rahl's eyes widened. "Your daughter was killed. My father told me so."

"A little trick, to keep her safe." Zedd's expression darkened. "Though you didn't know who she was, you hurt her. Without intending it, you also gave her happiness. You gave her Richard."

"I am his father?" Rahl whispered.

"When you raped my daughter, I knew I couldn't harm you, and my first thought was to comfort her, protect her, so I took her to Westland. She met a young man, a man widowed with a baby son. George Cypher was a good, kind man; I was proud to have him as my daughter's husband. George loved Richard as his own, but he knew the truth, except about me, who I was; that was hidden by the web.

"I could have hated Richard for his father's crimes, but chose

806

instead to love him for himself. He turned out to be quite a man, don't you think? You have been defeated by the heir you wanted. An heir born with the gift. That is rare. Richard is the true Seeker. From the Rahl blood, he has the rage of the anger, the capacity for violence. But it's balanced with Zorander blood, the capacity for love, understanding, and forgiveness."

Darken Rahl shimmered in the shadows of the magic or Orden. He twisted in pain as he became transparent as smoke. "To think, the Zorander and Rahl bloodlines, joined in one. Yet he is still my heir. In a way," he managed, "I have won."

Zedd shook his head. "You have lost, in more ways than one."

Vapor, smoke, shadows, and light spun in a roar. The ground shook violently. The sorcerer's sand, now black as pitch, was sucked into the vortex. The whole of it rotated over the abyss, the sounds of the world of life and the underworld mixing in a terrible howl.

Darken Rahl's voice came hollow, empty, dead. "Read the prophecies, old man. Things may not yet be as final as you think. I am an agent."

A point of blinding light ignited in the center of the spinning mass. Zedd shielded his eyes. Beams of white-hot light shot upward, through the windows overhead, into the sky, and downward, into the blackness of the abyss. There was a piercing shriek. The air shimmered with the heat, light, and sound. A flash lit everything around to white, and then there was silence.

Cautiously, Zedd took his hands from his eyes. It was gone. The whole of it was gone. Winter sunlight warmed the ground where only moments before the black abyss had been. The sorcerer's sand was gone. The bare circle of earth it had covered was whole. The rupture between worlds healed. At least Zedd hoped it was.

The wizard felt his power seeping back into his bones. The ones who had drawn the spell against him were gone. The effect of the spell was gone.

He stood before the altar, spread his arms into the sunlight, and closed his eyes.

"I recall the webs. I am who I was before: Zeddicus Zu'l Zorander, Wizard of the First Order. Let all know it once more. And the rest, too."

The people of D'Hara were linked to the House of Rahl, a link forged in magic long ago by those who would rule; a link that chained the people of D'Hara to the House of Rahl, and House of Rahl to them. With the webs removed, that link to the gift would be felt by many, and let them know that Richard was now Master Rahl.

Zedd would have to tell Richard that Darken Rahl was his father, but not this day. He would have to find the words first. There were many things to tell him, but not this day.

Richard found her, kneeling before one of the deserted devotion pools. The gag was still tied around her neck, left there when she had pulled it from her mouth. Kahlan hunched over in tears, her long hair cascading off her shoulders as she leaned forward, the knife gripped in both fists, the point held to her chest. Her shoulders shook with her sobs. Richard came to a stop next to the folds of her white dress.

"Don't do that," he whispered.

"I must. I love you," Kahlan gave a little moan. "I have touched you with my power. I would rather die than be your mistress. It is the only way to release you." She gave a tearful shudder. "I would like you to give me a kiss, and then leave me. I don't want you to see it."

"No."

Her eyes snapped up to his. "What did you say?" she whispered.

Richard put his fists on his hips. "I said 'no.' I'm not going to kiss you with those silly things painted on your face. They nearly scared the life out of me."

Her green eyes stared in disbelief. "You can deny me nothing, once I have touched you with my power."

Richard squatted down close to her. He untied the gag from her neck. "Well, then, you have ordered me to kiss you"—he dunked the cloth in the water—"and I told you I won't do it with this thing painted on your face." He began wiping the lightning bolts from her skin. "So, I guess the only solution is to get rid of it."

She knelt, frozen, while he cleaned the red off her face. Richard looked into her wide eyes when he finished. He tossed the rag aside, and knelt in front of her, slipping his arms around her waist.

"Richard, I touched you with the magic. I felt it. I heard it. I saw it. How could the power not have taken you?"

"Because I was protected."

"Protected? How?"

"By my love for you. I realized I loved you more than life itself, and I would rather give myself into your power than live without you. Nothing the magic could do to me could be worse than living without you. I was willing to give it all over to you. I offered the power everything I have. All of my love for you. Once I realized how much I loved you, was willing to be yours on any terms, I understood that there could be nothing for the magic to harm. I'm already devoted to you; it didn't need to change me. I was protected, because I have already been touched by your love. I had utter faith that you felt the same, and had no fear of what would happen. Had I had any doubt, the magic would have latched on to that crack and taken me, but I had no doubt. My love for you is smooth and seamless. My love for you protected me from the magic."

She gave him her special smile. "You felt that way? You had no doubt?"

Richard smiled back. "Well, for a moment, when I saw those lightning bolts on your face, I have to admit, I was worried. I didn't know what they were, what they meant. I pulled the sword, trying to gain time to think. But then I realized it didn't matter; you were still Kahlan, and I still loved you, no matter what. I wanted you to touch me more than anything, to prove my love and devotion for you, but I had to put on an act for Darken Rahl's benefit."

"These symbols mean that I, too, gave everything over to you," she whispered.

Kahlan circled her arms around his neck, kissing him. They knelt on the tiles in front of the devotion pool, pressed against one another. Richard kissed her soft lips the way he had dreamed a thousand times of kissing her. He kissed her until he was dizzy, and then kissed her some more, not caring that bewildered people who passed watched them.

Richard had no idea how long they knelt there embracing, but decided at last that they had better go find Zedd. With her arm around his waist and her head leaning against him, they walked back to the Garden of Life, kissing once more before they went through the doors.

Zedd stood with one hand on a bony hip, the other stroking his chin, as he inspected the altar and other things behind it. Kahlan fell to her knees before him, taking his hands in hers, kissing them.

"Zedd, he loves me! He figured out how to make it work, with the magic. There was a way, and he found it."

Zedd frowned down at her. "Well, it took him long enough."

Kahlan came to her feet. "You knew how to do it?"

Zedd looked indignant at the question. "I'm a wizard of the First Order. Of course I knew."

"And you never told us?"

Zedd smiled. "Had I told you, dear one, it wouldn't have worked. The foreknowledge would have interjected a grain of doubt. That single grain would have caused failure. To be the true love of a Confessor, there must be total commitment, to get past the magic. Without the willingness to give himself over to you, selflessly, despite the knowledge of the consequence, it wouldn't work."

"You seem to know a lot about it," Kahlan frowned. "I have never heard of it before. How often does this happen?"

Zedd rubbed his chin in thought, looking up at the windows. "Well, only once before that I know of." His eyes rested on the two of them. "But you can tell no one, just as I wasn't able to tell you. No matter how much pain it may cause, no matter the consequences, you can never tell. If even one other knows, it could be passed on, destroying forever the chance for others. It's one of the ironies of magic; you have to accept failure before you can have success. It is also one of the burdens of magic; you must accept the results, even the death, of others, to protect the hope for the future. Selfishness costs the lives, the chances, of those yet unborn."

Kahlan nodded. "I promise."

"Me too," Richard said. "Zedd, is it over? With Darken Rahl, I mean. Is he dead?"

Zedd gave Richard a look he found unexpectedly uncomfortable. "Darken Rahl is dead." Zedd put a thin hand on Richard's shoulder, his bony fingers gripping tightly. "You have gotten it right, Richard, all of it. You scared the wits out of me. I have never seen a performance to match it."

Richard grinned in pride. "Just a little trick."

Zedd nodded, his white hair sticking out in every direction, looking wild. "More than a trick, my boy. More than little."

They all turned when they heard the sound of someone approaching. Chase came dragging Michael in by the scruff of his neck. His dirty white trousers and shirt spoke that he had not come willingly. Chase gave him a shove, forcing him in front of Richard.

Richard's mood darkened at seeing his brother. Michael's defiant eyes came up to meet Richard's gaze.

"I'll not be treated in this manner, little brother." His voice was as condescending as it had ever been. "You don't know what you've interfered with, what I was trying to do, how I would have helped everyone by uniting Westland and D'Hara. You have doomed the people to needless suffering that Darken Rahl could have spared. You are a fool."

Richard thought about all he had been though, about all that Zedd, and Chase, and Kahlan had been through. He thought about all those he knew who had died at Rahl's hands, and the countless number of dead he would never know of. The suffering, the cruelty, the brutality. He thought of all the tyrants allowed to flourish under Darken Rahl, all the way from Darken Rahl himself down to Princess Violet. He thought of those he had killed. He felt pain and grief at the things he had had to do.

The metallic ring of the Sword of Truth filled the air. Michael's eyes went wide at seeing its point at his throat.

Richard leaned a little closer to his brother. "Give me the loser's salute, Michael."

Michael's face turned crimson. "I would rather die first."

Richard nodded as he straightened. He looked deep into his brother's eyes as he took the sword away. Richard pulled the an-

811

ger back, tried to make the sword turn white. It would not. He slid the blade home into its scabbard.

"I'm glad to see we have one thing in common, Michael. We would both die for what we believe in." He took his gaze from Michael, to the big, crescent battleaxe hanging at Chase's belt. His eyes came up to the boundary warden's grim face. "Execute him," he whispered. "Take his head to his personal guard. Tell them he was executed by my order, for treason against Westland. Westland will have to find a new First Councilor."

Chase's big fist grabbed Michael by the hair. Michael screamed out, falling to his knees, giving the loser's salute.

"Richard! Please, I'm your brother! Don't do this! Don't let him kill me! I'm sorry, forgive me. I was wrong. Please, Richard, forgive me."

Richard stared down at his brother, who was on his knees before him, his hands together, imploring. Richard held out the Agiel in his fist, feeling the pain it gave him, tolerating it, remembering it, the visions flashing through his mind. "Darken Rahl told you what he was going to do to me. You knew. You knew what was going to happen to me, and you were indifferent because it brought you personal gain. Michael, I forgive everything you have done against me."

Michael sagged in relief. The Seeker stiffened. "But I cannot forgive what you have done against others. Others have forfeited their lives because of the things you have done. It is for those crimes that you are to be executed, not the ones against me."

Michael screamed and cried as Chase dragged him away. Richard watched in pain, shaking, as his brother was taken to his execution.

Zedd placed his hand over Richard's on the Agiel. "Let it go, Richard."

Richard's thoughts masked the pain it was giving him. He looked to Zedd, standing before him with his bony, leathery hand over his, saw things in his friend's eyes he had never seen before, a shared understanding of the pain. He released the Agiel.

Kahlan's eyes went to it as it fell against his chest. "Richard, do you have to keep that?"

"For now, I do. It was a promise I made to one who I killed. One who helped teach me how much I love you. Darken Rahl thought this would defeat me. Instead, it taught me how to defeat him. If I discard it now, I would be denying what is inside me, what I am."

Kahlan put her hand on his arm. "Right now, I don't understand, but someday, I hope I will."

Richard looked around the Garden of Life, thinking about Darken Rahl's death, and about his father's death. He had seen justice done. He grieved a moment when his memories touched his father. But then the pain lifted as he realized that he had completed the task his father had given him. Richard had remembered every word of the secret book perfectly. His duty was done. His father could rest in peace.

Zedd straightened his robes with a huff. "Bags! A place this big must have something to eat, don't you suppose?"

Richard grinned, putting an arm around each of them as he led them out of the Garden of Life. He took them to a dining hall he remembered. People sat at tables as if nothing had changed. The three of them found a table in the corner. Servers brought plates of rice, vegetables, brown bread, cheese and bowls of steaming spice soup. The surprised but smiling servers kept bringing more as Zedd resolutely emptied the plates of food.

Richard tried the cheese, and to his surprise found it had a sickening flavor. He threw it back on the table as he made a sour face.

"What's the matter?" Zedd asked.

"That has to be the worst-tasting cheese I've ever eaten!"

Zedd sniffed it and took a bite. "Nothing wrong with the cheese, my boy."

"Fine, then you eat it."

Zedd was only too happy to comply. Richard and Kahlan ate spice soup and brown bread, and smiled as they watched their old friend eat. Zedd had his fill at last, and they resumed their journey out of the People's Palace.

As they strode through the halls, the bells tolled in a single, long peal, calling people to the devotion. Kahlan watched with a frown as everyone gathered at the squares, bowing to the center, chanting. Since Richard had changed the words in his devotion, he no longer felt the pull, the nervous need to join the people. They passed a number of squares as they continued on, each filled with people chanting. Richard wondered if he should do something about it, stop them somehow, but decided at last he had already done the most important part.

The three emerged from the cavernous halls out into the winter sunlight. The hillside of steps cascaded down before them, to the huge expanse of courtyard. The three paused at the brink. Richard gasped when he saw the numbers gathered there.

Spread out before them were thousands of men, standing tall in rank upon rank. At the head, at the base of the steps, stood Michael's personal guard, formerly known as the Home Guard, before Michael took that name from them. Their mail, shields, and yellow banners shone brightly in the sun. Behind them, nearly a thousand men of the Westland army. Behind them, many more of the D'Haran forces. Chase stood before them all, his arms folded, looking up the steps. Next to him, planted in the ground, was a pole with Michael's head atop it. Richard stood, stunned by the silence. If a man in the back, a half mile away, had coughed, he would have heard it.

Zedd's hand on his back started him down the steps. It felt a little too much like a push. Kahlan took his arm, giving it a squeeze, and held herself tall as they descended the series of steps and expansive landings. Chase watched Richard's eyes as he came. Richard saw Rachel beside him, clutching one arm around his leg, holding Sara in the other hand. Sharing the grip with the doll was Siddin's hand. Siddin saw Kahlan and broke from the hand, running to meet her. Kahlan laughed and scooped him up in her arms. He grinned at Richard and jabbered something Richard didn't understand, before throwing his arms around Kahlan's neck. After she hugged him and whispered to him, she put him down, holding his hand tightly.

The captain of the Home Guard stepped forward. "The Home Guard stands ready to swear loyalty to you, Richard."

The commander of the Westland army stepped up next to the captain. "As does the Westland army."

A D'Haran officer came forward. "As do the D'Haran forces."

Richard stared numbly at them, blinking. He felt the anger heat in him.

"No one's swearing loyalty to anyone, least of all me! I'm a woods guide. Nothing more. Get that through your heads right now. A woods guide!"

Richard gazed out over the sea of heads. All eyes were on him. He glanced over to Michael's gory head stuck on the pole. He closed his eyes a moment, then turned to some men of the Home Guard, and pointed to the head.

"Bury that thing with the rest of him." No one moved. "Right now!"

They jumped and made for the head. Richard returned his gaze to the D'haran officer standing before him. Everyone waited.

"Send word: all hostilities are ended. The war is ended. See to it that all forces are recalled to their homelands, all armies of occupation are withdrawn. I expect every man who has committed crimes against defenseless people, whether he be foot soldier or general, to be put on trial, and if found guilty, punished according to the law. The D'Haran forces are to help get food to the people who would otherwise starve over the winter. Fire is no longer outlawed. If any forces you encounter don't follow these orders, you will have to deal with them." Richard pointed to the commander of the Westland army. "Take your forces and help him. Together, you will be too strong to ignore." The two officers stared. Richard leaned closer. "It won't get done if you don't get to it."

Both men put a fist over their hearts in salute, giving a bow.

The D'Haran officer's eyes came up to Richard's. His fist was still over his heart. "By your command, Master Rahl."

Richard stared in surprise, then dismissed it. The man, he decided, must just be used to saying "Master Rahl."

Richard noticed a guard to the side. He recognized the man. He was the captain of the guards at the gate when Richard had left the People's Palace before. The one who had offered him a horse and warned him about the dragon. Richard motioned him to come forward. The man came and stood stiffly at attention, looking a little worried.

"I have a job for you." The man waited in silence. "I think you would be good at getting it done. I want you to collect all the Mord-Sith. Every last one."

"Yes, sir." He looked a little pale. "They will all be executed before sunset."

"No! I don't want them executed!"

The man blinked in confusion. "What am I to do with them?"

"You are to destroy their Agiels. Every last one. I don't ever want to see an Agiel again." He held up the one at his neck. "Except this one. Then you are to find them new clothes. Burn every stitch of Mord-Sith clothes. They are to be treated with kindness, and respect."

The man's eyes went wide. "Kindness," he whispered, "and respect?"

"That's what I said. They are to be given jobs helping people, they are to be taught to treat people in the same way they are treated: with kindness and respect. I don't know how you are to do that, you'll just have to figure it out yourself. You look like a bright fellow. All right?"

He frowned. "And what if they refuse to change?"

Richard glared at the man. "Tell them that if they choose to stay on the same path, instead of taking another, then they will find the Seeker with the white sword at the end of the road."

The guard smiled, put his fist to his heart in salute, and gave a smart bow.

Zedd leaned forward. "Richard, the Agiel are magic, they can't simply be destroyed."

"Then help him, Zedd. Help him destroy them, or lock them away, or something. All right? I don't want anyone to ever be hurt by an Agiel again."

Zedd gave a little smile and nod. "I'd be glad to help with that, my boy." Zedd hesitated, stroking his chin with a long finger, and then spoke softly. "Richard, do you really think this is going to work, calling the forces home, having the Westland army help them?"

"Probably not. But you can never tell about your First Rule, and it should gain time until we can get everyone home again, and you can put the boundary back up. Then we'll be safe once more. Then we'll be finished with the magic."

A roar came from the sky. Richard looked up to see Scarlet circling. The red dragon spiraled down through the crisp air. Men fell back, yelling and scattering as they saw that she was going

816

to land at the base of the steps. Scarlet fluttered to a landing in front of Richard, Kahlan, Zedd, Chase, and the two children.

"Richard! Richard!" Scarlet called out, hopping from one foot to another, her wings held out, quivering in excitement. Her huge, red head swept down to him. "My egg hatched! It's a beautiful little dragon, just as you said it would be! I want you to come see it! It's so strong. I bet it flies within a month." Scarlet seemed suddenly to notice all the men. Her head scanned about, surveying them. Her big yellow eyes blinked, her head swept down to Richard. "Are we having trouble here? Do we need some dragon fire?"

Richard grinned. "No. Everything is fine."

"Well, then, climb up and I'll take you to see the little one."

Richard put his arm around Kahlan's waist. "If you'll take Kahlan, too, I would love to come."

Scarlet eyed Kahlan up and down. "If she is with you, she is welcome."

"Richard," Kahlan said, "what about Siddin? Weselan and Savidlin will be worried sick over him." Her green eyes gazed deep into his. She leaned closer, and whispered, "And we have unfinished business in the spirit house. I believe there is still an apple there we have yet to finish." Her arm tightened around his waist, and a little twist of a smile came to her lips. The shape of the smile caught his breath in his throat.

With difficulty, Richard tore his eyes from her and looked up at Scarlet. "This little one was stolen from the Mud People when you took Darken Rahl there. His mother will be as anxious to have him back as you were to have your young one returned. After we see your little dragon, could you take us there?"

Scarlet's big eye peered down at Siddin. "Well, I guess I can understand his mother's worry. Done. Climb up."

Zedd stepped forward, his hands on his hips, his voice incredulous. "You would let a man fly upon you? A red dragon? You would take him where he wishes to go?"

Scarlet puffed smoke at the wizard, forcing him to take a step back. "A man, no. This is the Seeker. He commands me. I would fly this one to the underworld and back."

Richard gripped the spines and climbed onto Scarlet's shoulders as she lowered herself for him. Kahlan handed Siddin up.

Richard put him in his lap and took Kahlan's hand as she swung her leg over Scarlet behind him. She put her arms around his waist, her hands against his chest, and her head against his shoulder squeezing tightly.

Richard leaned a little toward Zedd. "Take care, my friend." He gave his old friend a big smile. "The Bird Man will be happy to learn I have finally decided to take a Mud Woman as my wife. Where will I find you?"

Zedd reached up with a thin arm and put a hand on Richard's ankle, giving it a pat. "I will be in Aydindril. Come to me when you are ready.'"

Richard gave the wizard his sternest frown, leaning down even more. "And then we are going to have a talk. A long talk."

Zedd nodded with a smile. "Yes, I expect we will."

Richard smiled at Rachel, gave her and Chase a wave, then gave a pat to one of Scarlet's scales. "To the sky, my red friend!"

Scarlet gave a roar of flame as she took to the air, Richard's dreams and joy lifting with her.

Zedd stood watching the dragon shrinking in the sky, keeping his worries to himself. Chase stroked Rachel's hair, and then folded his arms as he lifted an eyebrow to the wizard.

"Gives a lot of orders for a woods guide."

Zedd laughed. "That he does."

A little, bald-headed man came running down the hill of steps, a hand held up, beckoning. "Wizard Zorander! Wizard Zorander!" He finally came to a panting halt in front of them. "Wizard Zorander."

"What is it?" Zedd asked with a frown.

He struggled to catch his breath. "Wizard Zorander, there is trouble."

"What sort of trouble? And who are you?"

He leaned closer, conspiratorially, lowering his voice. "I am the head master of the crypt staff. There's trouble." His beady eyes darted about. "Trouble in the crypt."

"What crypt?"

The man's eyes looked surprised at the question. "Why, the crypt of Panis Rahl, Master Rahl's grandfather, of course."

Zedd's brow wrinkled. "And what's the trouble?"

The head master put his fingers nervously to his lips. "I didn't see it myself, Wizard Zorander, but my people would never lie. Never. They told me, and they wouldn't lie."

"What is it!" Zedd bellowed. "What's the trouble!"

His eyes darted about again, his voice lowered to a whisper. "The walls, Wizard Zorander. The walls."

Zedd gritted his teeth. "What about the walls?"

He looked up at the wizard, his eyes wide. "They are melting, Wizard Zorander. The walls in the crypt are melting."

Zedd straightened and glared at the man. "Bags! You have white stone on hand, white stone from the quarry of the prophets?"

The man nodded vigorously. "Of course."

Zedd reached into his robes, pulling out a small pouch. "Seal the opening to the tomb with white stone from the quarry of the prophets."

"Seal it shut?" he gasped.

"Yes. Seal it shut. Or the entire palace will melt." He handed the man the pouch. "Mix this magic dust with the mortar. It must be done before the sun sets, understand? Sealed shut before the sun sets."

The man nodded, snatched the pouch from Zedd's hand, and ran back up the steps as fast as his short legs would take him. Another man, taller, with his hands in the opposite sleeves of his gold-trimmed white robes, passed him as he came down. Chase glared at Zedd, poking a big finger at the wizard's chest.

"Panis Rahl, Master Rahl's grandfather?"

Zedd cleared his throat. "Yes, well, we will have to have a talk."

The man in the white robes approached. "Wizard Zorander, is Master Rahl about? There are matters to be discussed."

Zedd peered up at the dragon disappearing in the sky. "Master Rahl will be away for a time."

"But he will return?"

"Yes." Zedd looked back to the man's waiting face. "Yes, he will return. You will just have to carry on until then."

The man shrugged. "We are used to that, here at the People's Palace—waiting for the Master to return." He turned and started off, but stopped when Zedd called him back.

"I'm hungry. Is there anywhere to get something to eat around here?"

The man smiled and held his arm out to the palace entrance. "Of course, Wizard Zorander. Allow me show you to a dining hall."

"How about it, Chase? Care for some lunch before I'm on my way?"

The boundary warden looked down at Rachel. "Lunch?" She grinned and nodded in earnest. "All right, Zedd. And where is it you're going?"

Zedd shifted his robes. "To see Adie."

Chase lifted an eyebrow. "A little rest and relaxation?" He grinned.

Zedd couldn't help smiling a little. "That, and I must take her to Aydindril, to the Wizard's Keep. We have a lot of reading to do."

"Why would you want to take Adie to Aydindril, to the Wizard's Keep, to read?"

Zedd gave the boundary warden a sidelong glance. "Because she knows more about the underworld than anyone alive."

SPECIAL SNEAK PREVIEW

On the following pages you will find a brief excerpt from

Stone
of
Tears

the sequel to *Wizard's First Rule* and the second book in
Terry Goodkind's *Sword of Truth* series.

As Sister Margaret turned the corner at the top of the stone steps, an old maidservant carrying a mop and bucket saw her and fell to her knees. The Sister paused momentarily to touch the top of the old woman's bowed head.

"The Creator's blessing on His child."

The woman looked up, her face wrinkling into a warm, toothless smile. "Thanks be to you, Sister, and blessings to you in His work."

Margaret smiled back and watched as the old woman lugged her heavy bucket on down the hall. Poor woman, she thought, having to work in the middle of the night. But then, here she was herself, up and about in the middle of the night.

The shoulder of her dress pulled uncomfortably. She looked down and saw that in her haste she had misaligned the top three buttons. She redid them before pushing open the heavy oak door out into the darkness.

A pacing guard saw her and came at a run. She held the book over her mouth to hide her yawn. He lurched to a halt.

"Sister! Where's the Prelate? He's been yelling for her. Runs shivers up my spine, it does. Where is she?"

Sister Margaret scowled at the guard until he remembered his manners and dropped a quick bow. When he came back up she started off down the rampart with the man at her heels.

"The Prelate does not come simply because the Prophet roars."

"But he called out for her specifically."

She stopped and clasped her hand over the one holding the book. "And would you like to be the one to bang on the Prelate's bedchamber door in the middle of the night and wake her, simply because the Prophet shouts for it?"

His face paled in the moonlight. "No, Sister."

"It is enough that a Sister must be dragged out of bed for his nonsense."

"But you don't know what he's been saying, Sister. He's been yelling that—"

"Enough," she cautioned in a low tone. "Need I remind you that if a word he says ever touches your tongue, you will lose your head?"

His hand went to his throat. "No, Sister. I would never speak a word of it. Except to a Sister."

"Not even to a Sister. It must never touch your tongue."

"Forgive me, Sister." His tone turned apologetic. "It's just that I've never heard him cry out so before. I've never heard his voice except to call for a Sister. The things he said alarmed me. I have never heard him speak such things."

"He has contrived to get his voice through our shields. It has happened before. He manages it sometimes. That is why his guards are sworn on an oath never to repeat anything they should happen to hear. Whatever you heard, you had best forget it before this conversation is over, unless you want us to help you forget."

He shook his head, too terrified to speak. She didn't like frightening the man, but they couldn't have him wagging his tongue over a mug of ale with his fellows. Prophecies were not for the common mind to know. She laid a gentle hand on his shoulder.

"What is your name?"

"I am Swordsman Kevin Andellmere, Sister."

"If you will give me your word, Swordsman Andellmere, that

you can hold your tongue about whatever you heard, to your grave, I will see about having you reassigned. You are obviously not cut out for this duty."

He dropped to a knee. "Praise be to you, Sister. I'd rather face a hundred heathens from the wilds than have to hear the voice of the Prophet. You have my oath, on my life."

"So be it, then. Go back to your post. At the end of your duty, tell the captain of the guards that Sister Margaret ordered you reassigned." She touched his head. "The Creator's blessing on His child."

"Thank you for your kindness, Sister."

She walked on, across the rampart, to the small colonnade at the end, down the winding stairs, and into the torchlit hall before the door to the Prophet's apartments. Two guards with spears flanked the door. They bowed together.

"I hear the Prophet has been speaking out, through the shield."

Cold, dark eyes looked back at her. "Really? I haven't heard a thing." He spoke to the other guard while holding the sister's gaze. "You hear anything?"

The other guard leaned his weight on his spear and turned his head as he spat. He wiped his chin with the back of his hand. "Not a thing. Been quiet as grave."

"That boy upstairs been waggin' his tongue?" the first asked.

"It has been a long time since the Prophet found a way to get anything other than a call for a Sister through our shields. He has never heard the Prophet speak before, that's all."

"You want we should make it so's he don't hear nothin' again? Or speak it?"

"That won't be necessary. I have his oath, and have ordered him reassigned."

"Oath." The man made a sour face at the word. "An oath is nothin' more than babbled words. A blade's oath is truer."

"Really? Am I to assume that your oath of silence is nothing more than 'babbled words,' too? Should we see to your silence, then, in a 'truer' way?" Sister Margaret held his dark gaze until it at last broke with a downward glance.

"No, Sister. My oath is true enough."

She nodded. "Has anyone else been about to hear him yelling?"

825

"No, Sister. As soon as he started in calling for the Prelate, we checked the area, to be sure there were none of the staff, or anyone else, about. When we found everything was clear, I posted guards at all the far entrances and sent for a Sister. He's never called for the Prelate before, only a Sister. I thought it should be up to a Sister, not me, to decide if the Prelate was to be awakened in the middle of the night."

"Good thinking."

"Now that you're here, Sister, we should be off to check the others." His expression darkened again. "To make sure no one heard anything."

She nodded. "And you had better hope Swordsman Andellmere is careful and doesn't fall off a wall and break his neck, or I will come looking for you." He gave an annoyed grunt. "But if you hear him repeat so much as a single word of what he heard tonight, you find a Sister before you take another breath."

Through the door and halfway down the inner hall, she stopped and felt the shields. She held the book to her breast in both arms as she concentrated, searching for the breach. She smiled when she found it: a tiny twist in the weave. He had probably been picking at it for years. She closed her eyes and wove the breach together, binding it with a barb of power that would thwart him if he tried the same thing again. She was ruefully impressed by his ingenuity, and his persistence. Well, she sighed to herself, what else had he to do?

Inside his spacious apartments the lamps were lit. Tapestries hung on one of the walls, and the floors were generously covered with the local colorful, blue and yellow carpets. The bookshelves were half empty. Books that belonged on them lay open everywhere; some on the chairs and couches, some facedown on pillows on the floor, and some stacked in disheveled piles next to his favorite chair beside the cold hearth.

Sister Margaret went to the elegant, polished rosewood writing table to the side of the room. She sat at the padded chair and, opening the book on the desktop, flipped through it until she came to a clean page at the end of the writing. She didn't see the Prophet anywhere. He was probably in the garden. The double doors to the small garden were open, letting in a gentle breath of warm air. From a drawer in the desk she took an ink bottle, pen,

826

and a small sprinkle box of fine sand, setting them beside the open book of prophecies.

When she looked up, he was standing in the half light in the doorway to the garden, watching her. He was in black robes with the hood drawn up. He stood motionless, his hands in the sleeves of the opposite arms. He filled the doorway not just with his size, but with his presence.

She wiggled the stopper from the ink bottle. "Good evening, Nathan."

He took three strong, slow strides out of the shadows and into the lamplight, pushing back the black hood to uncover his full head of long, straight, white hair that touched his broad shoulders. The top of the metal collar just barely showed at the neck of his robes. The muscles in his strong, clean-shaven jaw tightened. White eyebrows hooded his deep, dark, azure eyes. He was a ruggedly handsome man, despite being the oldest man she had ever known.

And, he was quite mad. Or he was quite clever, and wanted everyone to think he was mad. She wasn't sure which was true. No one was.

Either way, he was probably the most dangerous man alive.

"Where is the Prelate?" he asked in a deep, menacing voice.

She picked up the pen. "It is the middle of the night, Nathan. We are not going to wake the Prelate simply because you throw a fit, demanding she come. Any Sister can write down a prophecy. Why don't you sit down and we can begin."

He came to the desk, opposite her, towering over her. "Don't test me, Sister Margaret. This is important."

She glowered up at him. "And don't you test me, Nathan. Need I remind you that you will lose? Now that you have gotten me out of my bed in the middle of the night, let's get this over so I may return to it and try to salvage a part of a night's sleep."

"I asked for the Prelate. This is important."

"Nathan, we have yet to decipher prophecies you gave us years ago. It could not possibly make any difference if you give this one to me and she reads it in the morning, or next week, or next year for that matter."

"I have no prophecy to give."

827

Her anger rose. "You have called me from my bed for company?"

A broad smile spread on his lips. "Would you object? It's a beautiful night. You are a handsome enough woman, if a little tightly wound." He cocked his head to the side. "No? Well, since you have come, and must have a prophecy, would you like me to tell you of your death?"

"The Creator will take me when He chooses. I will leave it to Him."

He nodded, staring off over her head. "Sister Margaret, would you have a woman sent to visit me? I find I am lonely of late."

"It is not the task of the Sisters to procure harlots for you."

"But they have seen to a courtesan for me in the past, when I have given prophecies."

With deliberate care, she set the pen on the desk. "And the last one left before we could talk to her. She ran back half naked and half mad. How she got through the guards, we still don't know.

"You promised not to speak prophecies to her. You promised, Nathan. Before we could find her she had repeated what you had told her. It spread like a wild fire. It started a civil war. Nearly six thousand people died because of what you told that young woman."

His worried, white eyebrows went up. "Really? I never knew."

She took a deep breath and spoke in a soft voice to control her anger. "Nathan, I myself have told you this three times now."

He looked down with sad eyes. "I'm sorry, Margaret."

"*Sister* Margaret."

"Sister? You? You are far too young and attractive to be a Sister. Surely you are but a novice."

She stood. "Good night, Nathan." She closed the cover on the book and started to pick it up.

"Sit down, Sister Margaret," came his voice, again full of power and menace.

"You have nothing to tell me. I am returning to my bed."

"I did not say I had nothing to tell you. I said I had no prophecy to give."

"If you have had no vision and have no prophecy, what could you possibly have to tell me?"

He withdrew his hands from his sleeves and placed his knuckles on the desk, leaning close to her face. "Sit down, or I won't tell you."

Margaret contemplated using her power, but decided that it was easier, and quicker, to simply make him happy and sit down. "All right, I'm sitting. What is it?"

He leaned over even more, his eyes going wide. "There has been a fork in the prophecies," he whispered.

She felt herself rising out of the chair. "When?"

"Just today. This very day."

"Then why have you called me in the middle of the night?"

"I called out as soon as it came to me."

"And why have you not waited until the morning to tell us this? There have been forks before."

He slowly shook his head as he smiled. "Not like this one."

She didn't relish telling the others. No one was going to be happy about this. No one but Warren, that is. He would be in a state of glee to have a piece to fit into the puzzle of the prophecies. The others, though, would not be pleased. This meant years of work.

Some prophecies were "if" and "then" prophecies, bifurcating into several possibilities. There were prophecies that followed each branch, prophecies to foretell events of each fork, since not even the prophecies always knew which events would come to pass.

Once one of these kind of prophecies came to pass and resolved which fork was to be true, and one of the alternatives took place, a prophecy had forked, as it was called. All the prophecies that followed down the path that had been voided now became false prophecies. These themselves multiplied, like the branches of a tree, clogging the sacred prophecies with confusing, contradicting, and false information. Once a fork had occurred, the prophecies they now knew to be false had to be followed as far as could be traced, and pulled out.

It was a formidable task. The further the event in question was from the fork, the more difficult it was to know if it was of the false fork, or of the true. Worse, it was difficult to tell if two prophecies, one following another, belonged together, or if they were to happen a thousand years apart. Sometimes the events themselves helped them to decipher where it was to be placed chronologically, but only sometimes. The further in time from the fork, the more difficult was the task of relating them.

The effort would take years, and even then, they could be sure only of accomplishing part of it. To this day, they could not know with confidence if they were reading a true prophecy, or the descendant of a false fork in the past. For this reason, some considered the prophecies unreliable at best, useless at worst. But if they now knew of a fork, and more importantly, knew the true and the false branches, they would have a valuable guide.

She sank back into the chair. "How important is the prophecy that forked?"

"It is a core prophecy. There could be none more important."

Decades. It wouldn't take years, it would take decades. A core prophecy touched almost everything. Her insides fluttered. This was like going blind. Until the tainted fruit of the false fork could be culled, they couldn't trust anything.

She looked up into his eyes. "You do know which it was that forked?"

He smiled proudly. "I know the false fork, and the true. I know what has come to pass."

Well, at least there was that. She felt a ripple of excitement. If Nathan could tell her which fork was true, and which was false, and the nature of each branch, it would be valuable information indeed. Since the Prophecies were not in chronological order, there was no way to simply follow a branch, but this would be a very good start: they would know right where to begin. Better yet, they had learned of it as it happened, and not years later.

"You have done well, Nathan." He grinned like a child who had pleased his mother. "Bring a chair close, and tell me of the fork."

Nathan seemed drawn up in the excitement as he pulled a chair to the side of the desk. He flounced down in it, squirming like a puppy with a stick. She hoped she wouldn't have to hurt him to get this stick out of his mouth.

"Nathan, can you tell me the prophecy that has forked?"

His eyes twinkled with mischief. "Are you sure you want to know, Sister Margaret? Prophecies are dangerous. The last time I told one to a pretty lady, thousands died. You said so yourself."

"Nathan, please. It's late. This is very important."

The mirth left his face. "I don't remember the words, exactly."

She doubted the truth of that; when it came to prophecies, Nathan's mind saw the words as if they were written on a stone tablet. She put a reassuring hand on his arm. "That is to be understood. I know it is difficult to remember every word. Tell it as best you can."

"Well, let's see." He looked at the ceiling as he stroked his chin with his thumb and fingertips. "It is the one that says something about the one from D'Hara who would shadow the world by counting shadows."

"That's very good, Nathan. Can you remember more?" She knew he probably remembered it word for word, but he liked to be coaxed. "It would be a tremendous help to me."

He eyed her a moment and then nodded. *"By winter's breath, the counted shadows shall bloom. If the heir to D'Hara's vengeance counts the shadows true, his umbra will darken the world. If he counts false, then his life is forfeit."*

A forked prophecy indeed. This had been the first full day of winter's season. She didn't know what the prophecy meant, but she knew of it. This one was the matter of much study and debate down in the vaults, and worry over which year this Prophecy might come to pass. "And which fork has the prophecy taken?"

His face turned grim. "The worst one."

Her fingers fumbled with a button. "We are to fall under the shadow of this one from D'Hara?"

"You should study the prophecies closer, Sister. The following prophecy goes on to say: *Should the forces of forfeit be loosed, the world will be shadowed yet by darker lust through what has been rent. Salvation's hope, then, will be as slim as the white blade of the one born True."* He leaned closer and whispered. "The only one of darker lust, Sister Margaret, would be the Lord of Anarchy."

She whispered a prayer. "May the Creator shelter us in his light."

His smile was mocking. "The prophecy says nothing about the Creator coming to our aid, Sister. If it is protection you seek, you had better follow the true fork. It is in that way He has offered you a glimmer of hope for defense from what will be."

She smoothed the folds of her dress on her lap. "Nathan, I don't know what this prophecy means. We can't follow the true and false forks if we don't know what it means. You said you know these forks. Can you tell me? Can you tell me a prophecy on each fork, one that leads each way, so we may follow their path?"

"*Vengeance under the Master will extinguish every adversary. Terror, hopelessness, and despair will reign free.*" He peered at her intently with one eye. "This one leads down the false fork."

She wondered how it was possible for the true prophecy to be worse. "And one of the true fork?"

"A close prophecy after the true fork says: *Of all there were, but a single one born of the magic to bring forth truth will remain alive when the shadow's threat is lifted. Therefore comes the greater darkness of the dead. For there to be a chance at life's bond, this one in white must be offered to her people, to bring their joy and good cheer.*"

Margaret pondered these two prophecies. She didn't recall either. The first seemed simple enough to understand. They could follow the false branch, for a ways, anyway, from this one. The second was more oblique, but seemed as if it could be deciphered with a little study. She recognized it as a prophecy about a Confessor. The reference to "one in white" meant the Mother Confessor.

"Thank you Nathan. This will make the false fork easier to follow. The other, the true fork, will be a little harder, but with this prophecy to lead the way, we should be able to reason it out. We will just have to look for prophecies leading away from this event. Somehow she is to bring happiness to her people." That brought a small smile to her lips. "It sounds as if maybe she is to be wed, or something of that nature."

The Prophet blinked at her, then threw his head back and howled. He rose to his feet, roaring in laughter until he coughed and choked. He turned back to her, his face red.

"You pompous fools! The way you Sisters strut around as if what you do is meaningful, as if you even knew what you were doing! You remind me of a yard of chickens, cackling to one another as if they thought they understood higher mathematics! I

832

cast the grain of prophecy at your feet, and you cluck and scratch at the dirt, and then peck at gravel!"

For the first time since she became a Sister, she felt small and ignorant. "Nathan, that will be quite enough."

"Idiots," he hissed.

He lurched toward her so quickly it frightened her. Before she knew it, she had released a bolt of power. It dropped him to his knees. He clutched at his chest as he gasped. Margaret recalled her power almost instantly, sorry she had reacted in this manner: out of fear.

"I apologize, Nathan. You frightened me. Are you all right?"

He grasped the chair back, drawing himself up into it as he gasped. He nodded. She sat still, ill at ease, waiting for him to recover.

A grim smile spread on his lips. "Frightened you, did I? Would you like to be really frightened? Would you like me to *show* you a prophecy? Not tell you the words, but show it to you? Show it to you the way it was meant to be passed on? I have never shown a Sister before. You all study them and think you can decipher their meaning from the words, but you don't understand. That is not the true way they work."

She leaned forward. "What do you mean that is not the way they work? They are meant to foretell, and that is what they do."

He shook his head. "Only partly. They are passed on by ones with the gift, ones like me: prophets. They are intended to be read and understood through the gift, by ones with the gift, ones like me, not to be picked over by the likes of your power."

As he straightened himself, pulling the aura of authority around himself again, she studied his face. She had never heard of such a thing. She wasn't sure if he was telling the truth, or just talking out of anger. But if it was the truth . . .

"Nathan, anything you could tell me, or show me, would be a great help. We are all struggling on the side of the Creator. His cause must prevail. The forces of the Nameless One struggle always to silence us. Yes, I would like you to show me a prophecy the way it is meant to be passed on, if you can."

He drew himself up, peering at her with burning intensity. At last he spoke softly. "Very well, Sister Margaret." He leaned toward her, his expression so grave it nearly took her breath away.

833

"Look into my eyes," he whispered. "Lose yourself in my eyes."

His gaze drew her in, the deep, azure color spreading in her vision until it seemed she was looking up into the clear sky. She felt as if he were drawing every breath for her.

"I will tell you the prophecy of the true fork again, but this time, I will show it to you as it is meant to be." She floated as she listened. *"Of all there were, but a single one born of the magic to bring forth truth will remain alive ..."*

The words melted away, and instead, she saw the prophecy as if seeing a vision. She was pulled into it. She was no longer in the palace, but in the vision itself.

She saw a beautiful woman with long hair, dressed in a satiny white dress: the Mother Confessor. Margaret saw the other Confessors being killed by quads sent from D'Hara, and she felt the blinding horror of it. She saw the woman's best friend and sister Confessor die in her arms, felt the grief of the Mother Confessor.

Then, Margaret saw the Mother Confessor before the one from D'Hara who had sent the quads to kill the other Confessors. The handsome man in white stood before three boxes. To Margaret's surprise, each box cast a different number of shadows. The man in white robes performed rituals, cast evil spells, underworld spells, late into the night, through the night, until the sun rose. As the day brightened, somehow Margaret knew that it was this day. She was seeing what had happened this very day.

The man in white had finished with the preparations. He stood before the boxes. Smiling, he reached out and opened the one in the center, the one that cast two shadows. Light from within the box bathed him in its brilliance at first, but then in a flash of power, the magic of the box swirled about him and snuffed out his life. He had chosen wrong; he forfeited his life to the magic he sought to claim.

She saw the Mother Confessor with a man. A man she loved. She felt her happiness. It was a joy the woman had never experienced before. Margaret's heart swelled with the bliss the Mother Confessor felt at the side of this man. It was a vision of what was happening at this very moment.

And then Margaret's mind swept forward in a swirl. She saw war and death sweep across the land. She saw death brought by the Keeper of the underworld, to the world of the living with a wicked lust that choked her with terror.

Again the prophecy swept her forward to a great crowd. At the center was the Mother Confessor, standing on a heavy platform. The people were excited and in a celebratory mood.

This was the joyous event that would bring the fork of the prophecy, one of the forks that must be passed correctly to save the world from the darkness snatching at it. She was caught up in the festive mood of the crowd. She felt a tingle of expectant hope, wondering if the man the Mother Confessor loved was to be the one she was to wed, and if that was the happy event the prophecy spoke of that would bring joy to the people. Her heart ached for it to be so.

But something wasn't right. Margaret's warm delight cooled until her flesh prickled with icy bumps.

With a wave of worry, Margaret saw that the Mother Confessor's hands were bound, and next to her stood a man, not the man she loved, but a man in a black hood. He held a great axe. Margaret's worry turned to horror.

A hand forced the Mother Confessor to kneel, siezed her hair and laid her face to the block. Her hair was short now, not long as it had been before, but it was the same woman. Tears seeped from the Mother Confessor's closed eyes. Her white dress shimmered in the bright sunlight. Margaret couldn't breathe.

The great crescent axe rose into the air. It flashed through the sunlight, thunking solidly into the block. Margaret gasped. The Mother Confessor's head dropped into the basket. The crowd cheered.

Blood gushed and spread down the dress as the headless, lifeless corpse collapsed to the wooden floor. A pool of bright blood spread under the body, turning the white dress red. So much blood. The crowd roared with elation.

A wail of horror escaped Margaret's throat. She thought she might vomit. Nathan caught her as she fell forward, crying and sobbing. He held her to him as a father would a frightened child.

"Ah, Nathan, is that the event that will bring joy to the people? Is this what must happen if the world of the living is to be saved?"

"It is," he said softly. "Almost every prophecy down this true branch is a fork. If the world of the living is to be saved from the Keeper of the underworld, then every event must take the correct branch. In this prophecy, the people must rejoice at seeing the Mother Confessor die, for down the other fork lies the eternal darkness of the underworld. I don't know why it is so."

Margaret sobbed into his robes as his strong arms held her tight against him. "Oh dear Creator," she cried, "take mercy on your poor child. Give her strength."

"There is no mercy when fighting the Keeper."